GLOUCESTERTIDE

GLOUCESTERTIDE

JONATHAN BAYLISS

PROTEAN PRESS
Rockport, Massachusetts

Gloucesterbook (ISBN 0-9625780-1-0), the first novel in this GLOUCESTERMAN series, was published by Protean Press in 1992.

Copyright © 1996 by Jonathan Bayliss.

All rights reserved. No part of this book may be reproduced or transmitted in any form or by any means, electronic or mechanical, including photocopying and recording, or by any information storage and retrieval system, without the permission of the author. Requests for permission should be made in writing to Jonathan Bayliss, 2 Graystone Road, Gloucester, MA 01930.

Library of Congress Catalog Card Number: 95-72786

ISBN: 0-9625780-2-9

Manufactured in the United States of America.

Text and cover design by Judy Arisman, Arisman Design, Essex, Massachusetts.

This book was typeset in Adobe Garamond 3 by Cathleen Collins, Blue Mountain Lake, New York. Printing and binding were done by Hamilton Printing Company in Castleton, New York.

Edited by Eugene R. Bailey and produced by Bailey Publishing Services, Westborough, Massachusetts.

To my brother Peter

CONTENTS

INTERPOLATION   *1*

PARABASIS   *5*

THIRD MOVEMENT

1	Caleb Karcist	*11*
2	Mooncloud	*29*
3	IRTH	*37*
4	Voice	*41*
5	Stormcloud	*51*
6	Tablet One	*65*
7	Languedoc	*77*
8	Moonstop	*91*
9	Tablet Two	*101*
10	Confession	*109*
11	The Princess Tower	*127*
12	Tablet Three	*151*
13	Mummery	*159*
14	Moontime Blues	*175*
15	Tablet Four	*197*
16	Ion	*205*
17	Ort-an-sich	*213*
18	Tablet Five	*225*
19	Westerly Sunrise	*237*
20	Rock Dance	*251*
21	Tablet Six	*275*
22	Troubadour	*289*
23	Sirens	*301*
24	Tablet Seven	*321*
25	The Keith Family	*337*
26	Symposium	*349*
27	Peripeteia	*367*

FOURTH MOVEMENT

1	Norman Marooned	*385*
2	Mundane Dinner	*403*
3	Robin Redbreast	*425*
4	Extracts from the Secret Diary of Tessa Barebones	*437*
5	Argo Cove	*465*
6	The Laboratory of Melchizedec and the Mesocosm	*489*
7	The Main-Top Bar	*523*
8	Chremetistics	*563*
9	Exisle	*603*
10	Chapter	*629*

INTERPOLATION

*A*ccording to my father's *Gloucesterbook* the place now called Dogtown was first begun by the Atlindu tribe that called itself "The People of the Dawn". Its name Nama-auche meant "the sound of juice being tasted"—whether that of grapes or of rosehips no one now can say. But the popular lawlessness that governs it as Dogtown goes back only to the time just before its permanent English settlement when somebody stole 171 hogsheads of the Casterbridge Company's salt—a more valuable ingredient in the cost of goods sold than the codfish it was used to preserve. In salt imported from Europe was the adventurers' largest investment. Their own lives were hardly reckoned as much.

Dogtown still doesn't seem much more orderly than Jamestown. It's always been a place found by some and lost by others, a port of entry and departure. As a beachhead of Europeans, left to its own devices, it has spawned many another colony without keeping a majority of its own children. Some of its expatriates are of more renown than the place itself. To the world it has seemed chiefly a refuge for all sorts of malcontents, where certain homeborn and foreign individuals intersect who are alien to mainland civilization, or at least converge.

Yet this perduring locus of marooners and sojourners is no mere relay station, ford, crossroads, campground, or whistlestop. For centuries of labile equilibrium the gulls have been scolding the dogs, the dogs have been annoying the people, and the place, stinking also from carelessly handled fish captured further and further off in the waters that nearly surround it, has been soiled by them all.

Anger is the wisdom of old age, when the personal struggle is given over, and I suppose that I shall come to it too. As a working newcomer, though with Dogtown in my genes, I too believe that "this foul island of dogs and gulls" should be better than its nation—uniquely worth a long fight. My father's brooding transcontinental rage (by virtue of origin) was anchored to experience of the real Cape in childhood only, which was not much less inchoative than his knowledge of mathematics. I'm sure that the native son's protracted vision which I have transcribed on my latterday word-computer from his manuscripts was an Apolline anodyne for the pain of savage indignation.

At the epoch of these Movements he was toiling three thousand miles away as Controller of the Tubalcain Manufacturing Company, in the Cornucopian "exisle" that I was born into. I'm glad he was spared the pain of being forced as an eye-witness to take in the cultural devolution of Dogtown following local extinction of the vestigial Resistance, even though he was well enough aware that it exceeded the degradation he had hoped was limited. True annals of Cape Gloucester (which chiefly comprises the quasi-peninsular island politized as Dogtown) have been lost to dispassionate scholarship because the literate progeny of its defenders and critics alike have continually dispersed to seek a better fortune.

Thus my old man, the passionate Controller of diasporic imagination, initially stimulated by casual travel reports of Raphael Opsimath his employer (who thereupon in 1960 unwittingly became his virtual agent), and nourished only by his subscription to rather dilatory mail-deliveries of *The Dogtown Daily Nous & Weekly Pantograph*, would never have claimed to know much more of what was actually going on here—two decades after he and his siblings had been removed from the place by an out-of-town opportunity for my grandfather in one of the Federal Theater companies of the

Great Depression—than do I (in residence three decades later yet), having but lately come to settle in my ancestral city as a comparatively objective stranger.

The Controller himself was broadly nescient or insensitive even in his own factitious reconstruction. (I say nothing in particular of his anachronistic attitude toward women.) But how much more so the night-prowling Ipsissimus Charlemagne, who subsumed immensely beyond the universe he occupied! Not to mention the affable Rafe himself, less overweening, who began as an adventurous observer. Even the aboriginal "Commodore" Wat Cibber, a fountain of Dogtown wit and matter, by whom I came upon the scene in time to be befriended before his death, had little inkling of such Dogtown lives as most of those that interested his young friend Caleb Karcist. (In characteristic contrast to a successful performer, my father flattered himself on transparency in his all-too-opaque *Gloucesterbook*; yet Wat Cibber it was who perspicaciously called him "the Interminable Slowman, dying of authorwritus".)

Perhaps I'm a chip off the old block, as the medium of these virtual biographies. But thanks simply to a woman's intuition conditioned for the expectation of flaws almost as readily in history as in prophecy, I've always been too critical to suffer greatly from disillusionment about society or my own family. I make no attempt to excuse my father's prose or to render his catholic English—so devoid of vivid metaphor—into the promiscuous dialect of our day (which is so continuously debased by contempt for apical culture), lest I simplify and thus falsify the function as well as the form of his "verifiction". His axiological sensibility, like a cathedral-builder's, demanded "an ancient living language" which might be intelligible to some trace-element of common readers backward-looking enough to care for etymological precision in workmanship that's unappreciated if not unnoticed by pleasureseeking tourists.

But if this unmarketable text is ever transferred from my computer to the printed page I will offer myself as its partial exegete. By heritage, and then by public service, I've become a practical patriot and an unintended student of our chorography. Dogtown's uncertain amalgam of religions, nationalities, clans, and phratries has prevented the cruel unity of tribalism. Our solidarity and our divisions are not tribal but local, as with the resident company of a repertory theater. Throughout most of its life the colony—the township, the city—has governed itself as a mixture of contentions; but the place herself is the locus of all argument.

The more famous southern cape of Vinland is a fragile spit of sand lying upon rock that's more than a hundred feet below the water line; it gives way to waves, and can no more definitely keep its banks without the Corps of Engineers than a spinal conduit like the Mississippi: but our northern granite seamark (as my father said) holds her aeonian shape at the eoan steep of the continent.

But unlike the assaults of Oceanus, those that our promontory lately most suffers are cumulative—more pernicious than any the French or British ever threatened, less resistible than the nation's political landslides. Kilroys, especially "infernal consumption angel-makers", as my father cursed all trucks and cars, have long since infested our paved and unpaved paths too narrow and tortuous to contain their hardly regulated flood. And now our overpopulating nest-builders, as they aggrandize the "effeminate domesticity" he anticipated, are filling all the wrinkles in Lady Gloucester's hide, and the part in her hair, with hideous houses mass-designed for money-lending; the bulldozing trades would like to leave no stone unturned between hilltop and high water. Implored by a majority of the Trojans themselves, streams of off-island Greeks bear gift certificates for "more jobs" and "an expanded tax base".

Still, I believe that our civic virtue, though retrenched and condensed, will continue to survive amidst voguish traitors and callous invaders as long as the island remains a source of exisles, a sink of failures, a refuge of the homeless, an entrepot of fish, an empyrean for gulls, and a sanctuary for dogs. Yet I remind you that it's not an entirely isolated particle of the broad New World that we dwell upon. The plantation of Englishspeakers was only in the second quarter of its first millennium when mainland plagues began to infect it with national entertainments. Soon its only interest to a distantly future historian may be what's already its past.

Rafe Opsimath's intuitive mission was to investigate a settlement even then too old to resist Gresham's law of tender. The stunted economy was about to be disinhibited by general prosperity. But at the time it seemed to progressive citizens and carpet-bagging entrepreneurs that the indigenes of Dogtown were too doggedly habitual in their benighted reaction to all enlightened suggestions. Nevertheless, venue of misfits, Cape Gloucester had as many worlds as a metropolis. Its village gossip has always been misleading. The marooners themselves, poloi and aristoi, native or naturalized, have never known all each other's failures.

C Chapman

PARABASIS

(To be omitted by readers
who despise metaphysics)

*I*n a decadent civilization instead of pretending to the primitive or the classical your art must turn to account the virtues of decadence, which are technical—above all, without priding yourself on the meretricious virtue of simplicity. Writing can be the behavior by which a human mind realizes the complexity of its own gray matter. And so an insubordinate brain—even when it has already squandered far too many BTUs of time on mundane analysis and management, on banausic numbers, on mere communication, and (having no personal servants) on simple daily living—may venture too far when it attempts to engage the complexity of a society that is many orders of magnitude more complicated than its indefinite self.

Though I offer critics this multidimensional specimen to exercise themselves with, I've never been unmindful of the fact that our literary polity of sharks and academically attested schoolfish has consciously encouraged the inborn Atlantean scorn of such onerous and unprofitable projects as this one. The soi-disant avant-garde seems to have democratized itself, dissipated into thin air, deserted to the main corps, or perhaps vanished into forests and swamps as aimless scouts whose skeletons will never be found, while our depraved army has impoverished itself in the indulgence of fantasy. Submission to the remaining "counterculture"—gangs of one kind or another—is no less painful than the cerebral agony of living with the majority. Our rebels have coalesced into a faction almost as selfpraising as the U S electorate.

Since the death of Yeats there has been hardly any essential criticism of modern culture. With promiscuous diction and unscrupulous metaphor we debase the language that true prophecy requires, and without the right soothsayers our language has no champion. We're leading Europe down the goldenrose path to the Furthest West.

Even the necessary Resistance to devilvision is already remembered only by a few rueful souls without the courage of conviction. So soon after the initial provocation it is probably now represented by less than a hundred units of consciousness in over two hundred million, having perished without martyrs, not by persecution or repression but by vice and default. Resistance barely survived the Protestican Occupation of 1952, without aid from Catholicrats either.

Partly because I'm too selfish to consume myself as a complaining prophet in this age of intellectually lazy language, I privately tax my reactionary faculties with fictive reason, unsupported by any more sanguine hope than that the effort will become known to a friend or two, here or there, and somehow be absorbed by the Anima Mundi before the class of laboring readers is utterly extinct.

Philosophy takes too much time. Satire and parody end up at best as merely clever demagoguery. Journalistic criticism is even more ephemeral; and anyway its object is illimitable—seamless and Sisyphusian: at least for me it's impossible todraw the line anywhere, and tedious to inveigh against the whole damned population. "You are postinge to the grave every day; you dwell upon the borders; your breath is in your nostrils. . . . What is the reward of an inefficient servant?" With these words the mayor of Salisbury was only urging justices of the peace to close down the public houses.

Therefore, though I "begin to verge upon eld" warning myself that nothing but death adumbrates itself so stealthily, I continue alone to lay new foundations—deeper than Salisbury Cathedral's, which are only forty-eight inches—for an edifice that may not rise above the tombstones, perhaps never to be noticed even as a failure beneath undulations of desert sand. Yet my protest against corruption is architectural, not destructive. The longer it is pursued the more of reality it loosens and alters—not simply by reconfiguration but also by creation or transmutation of many constituent entities.

I may have traded subjectivity and exquisite sensibility for persistent abstractions, but I know that what's most interesting is experience itself; so by allusion, like any good manager, I often appropriate the phenomena of existences more pregnant with imagination than myself, and perhaps only one or two dimensions less advised of my system.

Not that it wouldn't be a mistake to aim for equality with the real itself. Doctor Charlemagne says that's a job for theater. Artificers of history, if they must earn their bread by construction or reconstruction in the real world, can't live long enough to offer as much as a simple fable with the density of reality in which they themselves live out their lives. In the novel—our quintessential medium of experience, my genre in literature (the art of meaning)—multiplicity of crude and partial consciousness may germinate nothing much more suggestive of reality than ambiguity and paradox.

The probability that the object of these occult remarks will ever emerge from my spiral-bound wirehouse of longhand is nearly negative; but if it fails to materialize for posterity, I'll be no worse off than successful writers when no one's left to poke through our electromagnetized rubble. In any case I needn't worry about copyrights as did Cervantes about pirates stealing his characters and his name; nor when I retire to Gloucester will it ever be noticed (as in another small city where Kierkegaard's anonymity was impossible) that I confess authorship to polynymous works of potential infamy. Even there the people who would find this work interesting don't read fiction, and the people who read fiction would not find it interesting. At best almost nobody would be susceptible to most of it, and few of the hardy would like all parts of it.

Contingently, however, these words will be insecurely preserved, like frozen fish in storage, unless the house burns down. I try to make of each day a cushion to hold my private working hours like a jeweled crown. One of the techniques of my sort of folly is to serialize a concatenation of small tactical hopes, so that one can keep renewing the incentive to finish what's been started. The emotions of political hope, or even democratic excitement about public ball games and anticipations of trivial personal events, may sustain the temperamental sanguinity necessary for the perpetuation of an almost solely suigenetic autogeneris motive.

As long as my wits are spared I'll keep drawing the continuously enlarging perspective of my wake from the fantail of the cutwater that measures out my years in the world's Last Testament, which will never become Scripture. As a rear-guard author in isolated despair, vainly covering the retreat of rational values, my scope of experience is necessarily broader than the Controller's.

A bewildered reader deserves thus to be given her bearings.

THIRD MOVEMENT

1
CALEB KARCIST

With his forehead pressed against Daisy's black-bespotted flank he was effortlessly squeezing and pulling the milk from two of her rubbery teats and soundlessly listening to the rhythmic pinging and plinking against the resonant bucket's stainless steel by the pair of alternating streams that he knew to be as sweet and warm as the cow herself—and he hadn't even started his calculus assignment for the first class of the morning! But in the sensuous experience of his dream the reference to past anxieties faded with the contemporary thought of stealing a playful long-distance squirt at Ibi-Roi to baffle his trust in the nature of things as he lay alert on the barn floor ten feet beyond the stanchion awaiting his breakfast.

Caleb's sleep was finally cut off by the cumulative affect of his critical reason. He awoke in relief, to the joyful recollection that he was free of schooling forever. Obviously the mathematics of six years ago under the shadow of the Gyrotron in Hume at the University of Cornucopia did not belong to the schooling several winters earlier way back East in bucolic Montvert; and in reality there was a bearing wall that made it impossible to see through the cows' manger to the hay barn's orchestral stage, the broad-planked court of a Colonial threshing floor. But his dog was in fact present, the leading saint of Dogtown, quasi-island on the Atlantic coast.

Without opening his eyes Caleb knew that Ibi was still asleep, stretched six feet in all athwart the bedroom doorway, who'd never been beyond earshot of the eastern sea that lies to the west of Europe, nor off the Cape that distinguished Gloucester County from the rest of Vinland, from all other jurisdictions of the United States. It was very pleasing to be reminded of where he lived. A place is best known by a biped thinker's longnosed waft-sensitive dog (not in this case by a hound with floppy ears that scoop up scents from the ground like an otter-trawl dragger); and by olfaction his distinguished subspecimen could read its palimpsestic history, detecting not only overlapping presences but also the absences there.

At first Caleb's re-enlightened consciousness was even narrower in span than the dream. He believed himself to be lying in darkness, but notwithstanding the gradual expansion of his specious present (James's term that somewhere but a moment ago had occurred to him in sleep) he didn't think of opening his eyes to put his comfort to the test. In springtime as long as dawn deferred itself he was spared the shock of his alarm clock.

But to be more definite, where is there?

Not Babylon Oaks. Not Hume or Dutchkill School before that. Not Allenton in Montvert or Unabridge in Vinland.

But in Vinland, yes—*there* where Dogtown is! There I lie, snug in my own cot, in the house of Mrs Keith there. My *there*-dog breathes at hand, the squire of my independent knighthood. Naturally, of course—habitually, certainly—it goes without saying that I don't feel free of quests or challenges or the imperatives of training. Work or defense, and hope, are demanded by waking. I know that, even without recovering my thoughts. There's joyful work I want to do, onerous work I'd like to postpone; worries to be unknotted by displacement of effort, mysteries to be ignored when I'm devoted to what I like.

So what's to be done today? Or rather what is it that I feel I'm hoping for? Once that's determined I can let my mind roam through the inventory of fears, the one of which I already remember is death, of which I should remind myself every night and morning, to spur me on through the dark wood toward the luminous mountain.

Seems simple enough right now. Too much to do at the Lab, and I want to do it all at once. The Parity Corporation file cards, sort and resort by officers and directors; with a new card file, index each personal name by affiliated company or companies. It won't be a waste of time: to find the pattern of Arthur Halymboyd's empire versus Professor Capstick's! —What colors shall I use to draw the COV organization chart? Too many will make it seem amateurishly busy, and anyway they won't show on diazo copies. Somehow simplify the lines also. —Oh but first the chore of posting daily stocks at the Free Enterprise Education Library [FEEL].

—Oh hell, before going to work at all I've got to torment my bones and delay all my satisfactions by grinding out the run to Birdhouse Hill that I promised Ibi, taking a shower, making coffee, and all the rest of an introit to daily life. And this brings me to what I should have remembered first if it's really my driving purpose and not just a prolonged act of artificial will: the one duty that appears for me alone because otherwise it wouldn't appear at all. Sometimes I hate to look at that inert dust-attracting typewriter in the next room! It's strange how often I can forget it entirely, as if I were traveling in Europe or enchanted by Mickey Mantle's slugging statistics! I must admit that I'm not a born playwright. I should be working twice as hard every morning of the year to compensate for mismatched ability. . . .

Thus Caleb Karcist, until his personal world was fully restored by unfolding memory of joy discipline responsibility and desire. Each returning vector of experience accelerated the reassociation of those that followed like pages of an opened book riffled by a silent gust of wind, for as long as he remained too lazy to get up on his hind legs and face the first of his duties. The contemplation of procrastinated action was tinctured with the most habitual sensations of a young male body emerging from unconsciousness, but at least he was in no danger of allowing the whole parade of life's dimensions to rotate back into his mind in ninety-degree flips. Never this morning did he admit planes beyond the uniquely personal. His immediate exclusive consciousness did not now admit common fears about the Entropy-bomb of war, the lethally selfdefeating counterentropy of indulgent human reproduction, or the global dysorder of ecological vice that sometimes blotted out his petty concerns.

But Dogtown: What am I doing here anyhow? That's the question Lilian my leading distraction and inspiration asks of us both. As to myself I cannot tell her. Because, for one thing, I don't get minutes enough with my face to hers. Those I do get are too wordless. In my unanswered letters of course I don't expatiate much beyond my prehension of herself. I already write her more than I can contain or she can find time to read. In her preciously rare presence—and even if I lived with her it would be the same no doubt—there's too much to expose.

But supposing her prehension of me could be combined with Belle Cingani's, Tessa Barebones's, Mrs Keith's, and Chris Lucey's in complementary aggregation, all of whom I am more or less free to face without scheme or calculation, I would still be compositely obscure cryptic and incomplete, with secrets to hide! Perhaps at least three of those four quasi-confidants are equally troubled by less mysterious concealments of their own derivations or other shames; but as for me, it's to my advantage (contrary to iatric wisdom) that I am less courageous than Oedipus in investigating my own conception, for self-analysis (assuming its possibility) might forestall my absurd motive. Realistic objectivity (assuming its possibility) would dissolve my illusionary will, as if I were a psychologist or a scholar instead of an esemplastic artisan.

Caleb's habits of self-examination, like Alpha Whitehead's (who said that "most psychology is herd psychology"), remained unexamined. But he was intrigued by Yeats's unresponsible Vision of the Faculties because it impersonally diagrammed all the types of personality without raising personal questions—although under the tutelage of Michael Chapman in Londonbridge, and abetted by both Father Duncannon and Doctor Charlemagne in Dogtown, he had left behind the platonism (and had never heeded the Neoplatonism) by which that vision's genesis was facultated. The poet's geometrically lunar symbolism was as irresistible to his unexamined mind as the "raft of reason" to a computer programmer such as Gil Algo, the present possessor of Lilian Cloud and her daughter Monday, whom he Caleb acknowledged as his own child, and whose bastardy was less unaccounted than his own.

Yet he did understand his own proclivity to overcompensate for a sensibility fully one third feminine. He was the only materialization of his mother's three preconceived children, two sons interspaced by a daughter.

Floating on his own idiopathic raft of reason, rationalizing almost everything with right triangles and imaginary numbers, for the most part he counteracted the wobbles and tremors of private infirmity. But he had no stand on a stable ground of a natural ice floe extended in the temperate brine by artificial refrigeration. With dynamos petrochemicals and expanding-gas machines a philosopher can enlarge his floating plain to the size of an international airport before it cracks, and perhaps propel it as far south as the Tropic of Cancer; but Caleb's little iceberg yclept Isorectotetrahedron [IRTH]—the specially talismanic phase-shape of a set of universal variables with which he claimed to reconcile Whitehead with Yeats, Leibniz with Descartes, and Pythagoras with the power of electricity; and which also stood for the infinitesimal of duration in space that reminded him of himself as a minim of manhood—didn't always remain integrated for long before his tormenting caloric split it apart. His secret impudence was cloven by lust and melted by love.

Does my sinistral first-quadrant solid merely eclipse the original mystery which it represents and about which it rotates? he now asks himself without opening his eyes. I prefer to think it a radiated complex of rather wise anxieties born of traumas forgotten or forgettable. Maybe I'm too complacent a victim of my own neurosis; but if so, I'm grateful to my mother for inciting me to "cut the mother bond" before I was even out of school. I wish I could thank her but without telling her so—for fear of encouraging her reappearance as an outspoken dependent eager to spill half our secrets and appeal for a public profession of filial love.

I know I haven't inherited enough of her "excessive imagination" that I've reacted to by sleeping in reason. Burton says "Folly, Melancholy, Madnesse, are but one disease, Delirium is a common name to all"; but I haven't even enough of Lilian's judicious madness—though she's the one that's driven me almost as delirious as my mother once was about Tony Porter the erstwhile Dogtown seacook whom I used to have to carry lovenotes to when we lived in Unabridge and his cab was stationed in Norumbega Square. For that element of my nurture I've never been grateful. I was erotically precocious by the age of twelve, too early for any sensible prospect of copulation. Satisfactions are still too few and far between, the fact that explains at least some varieties of my delirium.

This complaint made Caleb laugh aloud and shake off the vagaries of otiose reverie, and he resolved to come about nearer the wind of his daily tacks. It happened that at this moment of his life he was not at all sorry for himself as a voiceless troubadour. He had two strings to his unmusical bow, albeit he wasn't now permitted to fit his arrow to either. He felt salty and expected any number of possible satisfactions. Belle's admiration and affection, despite his doubts about their profundity (to say nothing of their constancy), were unmistakably authentic, and her intelligent appreciations (as far as they went) bolstered the confidence demanded by the cheerfulness that lightened and therefore strengthened his passionate address to the more profound and less inconstant other woman, Lilian, by luring her to the belief that he was sane and reliable in this his second irresponsible wooing of her.

Each of the two unwittingly made him more interesting to the other than he would have been if his totalitarian desire had remained undivided and continuously unequivocal. Belle was immeasurably more accessible to his sight and touch than Lilian; his conversation with her was careless and unconstrained, and where it seemed to verge on her values or convictions it was limited to depths near the surface of his deep concerns—thereby however somewhat relieving the internal pressure to make a fool of himself to the other more dignified woman with characteristically incoherent attempts to express within the constraints of his ridiculously limited conversational privilege (or in voluble pages ridiculously unlimited) every last scrap of his exuberance.

Of these two unequally valued friends, Belle herself (had she been informed of the other) would have cheerfully granted Lilian sight-unseen to be the truer. It was Lilian who ramified the arteries of his erotic mentality—and he at least the veins of hers, on some occasions rather by tacit recall of erotic sentiment in consummations of their mutual past (ostensibly expunged from the record) than by promotion of any particularly discriminating sensual appetite on her part. Though inflamed and reproved by his new and greater love for this longhaired ironical matron—who seemed incomparably more precious than the shorthaired nulliparous gypsy as an epitome of sympathetic humanity, more honest in her relations with men, more detached and disinterested in her judgments of persons, more attached and interested in her judgment of populations, yet essentially more capable of erotic beatitude—his highly discriminating thirst for intimacy with her meanwhile experienced body, because of having been slaked by its inexperience four years earlier, was no longer magnified by the marvels of elementary success that are more important in the desire of boys for girls than expectation of ecstasy.

On the other hand he still flattered himself that, given a second chance, he was the one man able to introduce Belle Cingani—a k a Bice Picory, poet and journalist, the beautiful wandering Anglo-

Jewish Transylvanian of many lovers—to the beatitude transcending atonement, which he believed had always escaped her but which Lilian Cloud the Atlindu crossbreed (less coruscating, a philosophical artist) had attained even at defloration and probably cultivated since he had forsaken her by departing for the East. It had taken that aboriginal Cornucopian four years of fortuitous migration to wind up also in Dogtown—with the impedimenta of her mother and her daughter but attached to Gil Algo the hotshot computer programmer.

Caleb told himself that he loved Lilian Cloud more than he craved her, and that Belle Cingani he craved more than he loved. Both now took their usual precedence over all the other occupations of the consciousness he was reascending to. They dominated the polarized lobe of the psyche which all his life had been instinctive and unexclusive. But even together they couldn't wholly absorb the ions of his libidinous mentality—except of course in the very midst of erotic brainstorms, at intervals between various peaceful or productive engagements.

It may be true on the one hand that he was often obsessed by Lilian and sometimes inordinately attracted by Belle, that occasionally his objective mind was not closed to other amorous possibilities, that his willpower was dedicated to life-work at home and his practical reason to the work of the Classic Order of the Vine at The Laboratory of Melchizedec and the Mesocosm and on Graveyard Street in Ur; but on the other he was chronically alert to the danger of post-traumatic excruciation in his Dogtown discoveries—and sometimes acutely alarmed by his pusillanimous cunctation in pursuing the purpose of his return to the place of his initial concrescence, where also three quarters later he had been dragged through the birth canal by forceps.

Thus as the planes of consciousness turned open to one more page of recovered reality he recollected that it was his mother's Dogtown past he dreaded almost as much as her possible homecoming. In this eoan meditation, no longer "between sleeping and waking" (as Yeats would say) but nearly resembling an old man's cold vision between waking and death—more truthful than either the sweet clarity of the Raft or the survival-hope of the Ark—he shuddered at his own cowardice about seeking self-enlightenment when it was so necessary for the eventual happiness of reaching Europe, his fabulous orient.

For this purpose a passport was required; and for his passport a certificate of birth or baptism with the name Karcist (assuming that there'd been no name-changing or fairy substitutions in his infancy); and for such a certificate the courage to reveal himself at Ibicity Hall or to hunt down the problematic records of defunct St Martha's Convent through the Diocesan office in St Bot; and for that courage the unlikely luck to find by default that no black mark against him by the Yerba Buena office of the Bureau of Domestic Investigation had seeded a dossier in Washington on account either of his passive participation in the Resistance or his self-dismissal from the military draft rolls.

Yet in the end a gratification of his transatlantic lust would demand the emotional liberty—the treachery, the cruelty—to abandon (at least for the duration of his travels) the world's most trusting friend, Ibi-Roi by name and rank, as if by heartless suicide: and as if it wasn't sad enough that any canine saint, of whatever nobility or power, depended utterly on the kindness and responsibility of human strangers. At such expense the master would find no happiness even in the British Isles.

Anyway, as he readied himself for the opening of his eyes, in order to summon the zest for facing daily life he once more raised the power of his operating coefficient the square root of minus one by adding a unit to its exponent, immediately flipping his consciousness by one more hyperpolyhedral right angle to the plane of a shorter and broader perspective of the most distasteful stumbling block to his execution of the second and immensely more difficult half of his eastward retrogression from Cornucopia the land of milk and honey to worn-out Britain and its Continent.

It was as if he simply stumbled onto the stream of impressions that of late had been besetting his mind with the ineluctability of a river current unresisted by the brine. Yet during the winter he had kedged his way through sloughs of despond to the estuary opening on sunrise, and on the verge of springtime consciousness he'd been feeling like an empty dory that at slack tide was tethered to its mooring only by a painter, swung round by whispers of moving air.

Now it was the year's current, and it carried him along with Dogtowners of every church toward the solstice that introduced the doubled octave of Gloucestermas, the vanishing point of everyone's annual perspective. Once again he dreaded to face the fascinating culmination of earth's cyclic tilt, the end of Dogtown's fiscal and academic year which initiated a prolonged piscatory and piscivorous carnival in anticipation of the feast of SS Peter and Paul, followed by a celebration of the nation's birthday. This was a Great

Year, one of the few in which Easter (and Passover) fell at its latest, when at the most favorable conjunction of fixed and movable calendars the festivities normally initiated by the midsummer solstice would be immediately preceded and compounded by a week linking Pentecost to Trinity Sunday, the day that marks the end of Christ's life in the liturgical cycle and honors the descent of the Holy Spirit to present the third aspect of God. The last year in which a Greater Gloucestermas had fallen was 1934, only one Congress after F D R had taken office.

For Caleb this Gloucestermas entailed important responsibilities as major-domo and "business consultant" of the Laboratory, for it was committed to hold an epochal Chapter meeting for the Order of the Vine during the earlier of the two fixed octaves comprised by Glo'mas, including Midsummer's Night. That particular observance fell three months after Johann Sebastian Bach's birthday and exactly nine months before Caleb's, which he understood was shared by a demographically astonishing number of Dogtown natives, whose families seldom proclaimed the dates of their nativity.

Communal disinhibition in this age of mobile privacy no longer demanded elaborate disguise. At the dances masks were optional. In reality Dogtown's private lives were becoming a little more easily ambiguous, thanks to a general loosening of prejudice that followed various liberations of the Second World War and to a local sophistication laggingly infused by the films of Holyrood and the devilvision of New Uruk. Festal license was ostensibly acknowledged only as no longer urgent, a theme for otiose jest.

Still, Mrs Grundy's guessing game quietly flourished. By date of birth it was problematical to distinguish merrybegots from the legitimate children of merely careless enthusiasm or conjugal probability. Spring Equinox birthdays were especially embarrassing to spurious children like Caleb and Galahad, brought up by a lone woman or in a nunnery. (He vividly recalled the long years in which he had feared that by the same token he was doomed to mature virginity. He had little use for Gnostic symbolism, but in Celtic tradition it had been at Whitsuntide also that Galahad came to Siege Perilous and made the Grail appear by drawing his stainless sword from granite. Some say the holy object itself was a stone from the War in Heaven, brought down by neutral angels, perhaps conflated with the Philosopher's Stone of celibacy.) Like Montaigne in regard to the Libyan practice reported by Herodotus, these quarrysome fisherfolk believed that it would lead to frequent mistakes in the selection of natural fathers from a crowd if they trusted to the intuition of the children themselves at about the time they were beginning to walk.

Ibi-Roi was a son of a bitch, but his pedigree was thoroughly attested in Mrs Sirius's Viking Shepherd social register at Ibicity Hall. Caleb would have liked to search that matrilinear Almanach for one telltale name. He believed that a clue of his own might be found in her archive of aristocratic saints. In a fire during the Glo'mas of 1934 his mother had lost Sycorax, an absolutely beloved Viking Shepherd, her longest and closest companion. From time immemorial he had understood this to be the calamity that had caused or signaled the conversion of her life's course and tenor. It was the metanoia in which she had utterly renounced pictorial art, destroying every last canvas and paper that survived the fire, after having devoted a decade to what she'd believed was her destined career. At the same time she had suddenly swept aside the prudent inhibitions that kept her from conceiving the cub she had intended early in her childhood to be the first of three, her unwavering heart's desire for twenty years. As to art, while gestating on the Isle of Manannan in the Irish Sea she'd determined to make herself over into "a poet of stories".

Sycorax's official genealogy might suggest something about the status or circumstances of her known owner. Yet such documentation would never disclose what acts the accidental smoke-offering of Sycorax and a whole studio full of canvasses and watercolors had disinhibited. Indeed you couldn't expect civil servants as a matter of routine to record at any annual collection of a bitch's poll tax the marital status of her mistress, still less the name of a consorting stranger at Gloucestermas seven or eight years after her first registration at the current address. Caleb must furthermore remind himself of his mother's claim that the name Karcist was a concoction of her own imagination many months after the dog's death.

Quite apart from the vastly dreaded but voluntary question of conspicuously unusual research in public records for traces of a Viking Shepherd stricken from the active list more than a quarter of a century before, he now had hanging over his head the legal obligation to enter Ibicity Hall and address someone in the Clerk's office, perhaps Mrs Sirius herself. For although his personal fees and levies could be paid by mail, the springtime tax for Ibi must be orally and manually exchanged for a dogtag and license. There was no possible evasion of his responsibility to visit the towering and forbidding edifice, which his giant landlord Dexter Keith, who worked in an upper chamber with the best view of the harbor, was wont to call Lilliput Hall when depressed by the stubborn backwardness of its bookkeepers earldermen and mayor. To Caleb the minim it was a dark Brobdingnagian Castle full of demagogic ogres. Only once before, on the crest of his initial enthusiasm for the possession of Ibi-Roi, prince of Viking Shepherds, had he blundered through the ordeal as an ignorant stranger burning with a bout of ambulatory fever.

Not that Ibi wouldn't be delighted to accompany him. This magnificent bodyguard feared nothing he'd yet encountered, just as he loved all sensory experience. The century of public scents in the Hall would be an aesthetic treat, and he would be admired by all Libertines they passed in the corridors, strangers who opposed the Puritan movement, which had begun to lobby for a "leash law" and was threatening a petition drive to launch a referendum against the rights of saints. (Any unimprisoned or unfastened dog with testicles would be summarily shot by Sergeant Proctor! Caleb feared the authoritarian Puritans of Dogtown as he feared the dynocratic antiprematureantifascists of the Protestican right wing.) He could only hope that Ibi's friendly curious and respectful sprezzatura would bolster his own nerve to risk being significantly identified by the most knowing of oldtime bureaucrats. The formidable Mrs Sirius had been unofficially taking an officious and gratuitous personal interest in her registered saints, their irregularities and their human affiliations, since ten years before Caleb's advent. Indeed her sotto voce authority as one of the city's most interested historians was founded on the fact that few people of the older generations in Dogtown had escaped some sort of association with dogs, as either friend or foe.

The Libertine party knew nothing of Caleb but recognized Ibi-Roi as an avatar of the blood royal. Mrs Sirius's assistant in the College of Heralds would loudly call her out from behind the counter to see a champion of the breed for which Dogtown was so famous along with a number of other artifacts and sports of nature as the locus of its origin; other functionaries and bystanders would congregate around the Viking Shepherd paragon in aesthetic or envious praise, noticing Caleb for his lucky relationship. Even Sergeant Proctor himself, if he happened to be at hand, consul of the saints and aedile of all animals, merciful hero in the eyes of Libertines yet an impartial enforcer of puritanical items in the present code, might loudly congratulate Ibi's mortified keeper, whom until then he'd observed from his paddywagon (mostly on deserted streets) as the eccentric pedestrian blessed with Dogtown's leading dog.

Ibi was sweet-tempered, ingratiating or tolerant with both strangers and saints, save in sexual competition (and otherwise any display of hostility was simply precautionary). He did not abuse his obvious advantage of size and power, instead exploring the world with interrogatory brows like Lilian's. Thus Caleb's joy often centered on his dog. The thought of seeing Ibi was always enough to make him want to open his eyes, and if he now wasn't yet doing so it was only because he'd rather not interrupt symbiotical thoughts that Ibi's heartfelt presence in their shared room had set afloat for sobering contemplation.

All through history, save in Ireland, dogs have been as misunderstood as women. In Dante and Aquinas they were characterized by anger, the wrathful souls of Hell, merely because they seemed to bite themselves in rage, when in fact they were generally scared or starved, and for lack of a hand they were nipping at fleas on their coccyx or attempting to scotch a tormenting itch in the anus. Though it may have been true that in Dogtown the per-capita abuse of saints by confinement neglect violence malnourishment or overfeeding was far below the national average, Caleb's breast was savagely lacerated by the knowledge that even here some were living out unhappy lives in cages or chains, dumbly oppressed by the cruelty or callousness of the master race, and that the laws of indenture prevented Sergeant Proctor from liberating those of whom he was aware. But at least the Libertine faction prevailed in public opinion; and Mrs Sirius's sacred budget, traditionally increased each year at no less than the rate of inflation even when other line-items of the Clerk's department were petulantly reduced by the Earls, sufficiently demonstrated that this was no city of Dis.

It therefore struck Caleb as odd that the city's merchants and politicians seemed thoughtless or ashamed of saints. Even the leaders who believed that the town's future prosperity depended more on the pilgrim business (a k a "needle trades") than on fishing or industrial development might have been expected to boast of Dogtown as the cradle of Viking Shepherd nobility. Except for the Lusitanian Water Dog pointing beyond the breakwater from the tripartite statue of the fisherman and his wife on the Esplanade, the canine totem did not appear in public commemorations. A stranger's best friend was not to be found on any other civic monument, hostelry signboard, weathervane, trademark, logotype, cenotaph, or carven mausoleum. No dog found a significant place in the historical murals of the Hall. It seemed almost as ungrateful as if Cape Gloucester were posted with signs reading

NO IRISH NEED APPLY, NO JEWS ALLOWED, BLACK LUSIES SEATED TO THE REAR, OFF LIMITS TO ETRUSCANS, NO ADMITTANCE IN SEAMAN'S ATTIRE, $25 FINE FOR FOUL-WEATHER LANGUAGE, WOMEN ON LEASH ONLY". A town otherwise so exhaustive in bragging about its past!

Even Doctor Charlemagne, no lover of dogs but a tolerable anthropologist, had complained about the city's cynic ingratitude in a recent letter to the Dogtown Daily Nous when the question of a new device for the city seal (and perhaps logo for the Chamber of Commercials) was bruited for democratic debate. Reminding citizens of their ostensible piety, and perhaps thinking of his young friend Caleb, he quoted Yeats's repetition of Francis Bacon's observation (transmitted through Wordsworth) that "God puts divinity into a man as a man puts humanity into his dog". Upon reading which, Wat Cibber the city's last singlehanded fisherman (when not aboard his rocking chair ashore), had muttered to Caleb, in Ibi's presence, the codicil "—or logic into a woman"; sententiously and inconsequentially adding one of his least original aphorisms: "What hits is history; what misses is mystery".

The dogs weren't publicity hounds, but they didn't have a chance anyway. Public opinion was commercial, even at the antiquarian end of the spectrum. The *Nous* was full of banausic suggestions, and so were the Knights of the Turntable at their luncheons, where agitation for the reform of public relations had begun. The cause of progress had been taken up by the victualer Loathey O'Toole (Lilian Cloud's employer), who wanted to get rid of the netting needle on the facade of his restaurant as well as elsewhere in the city's advertising and on its multiplicitous stationery. He was even prepared to relinquish his personal hope to substitute the motif of a fouled anchor if some other creative consensus could be reached, even if something as trite as an oilskinned Fisherman alone at a helm in heavy weather.

The Norumbega-educated young reality-developer named Hastings Mooncusser, the Norman who'd instigated this reaction to habitual imagery, had urged a schooner under full sail. This device had many sentimental partisans. The dory, and the lobster pot too, were vehemently rejected as too humble. A halibut or other flat fish with both eyes on one side of the head was favored by those scorning the ignorance of pilgrims who would take it for a distortion of "modern art", if for not the pitiable draftsmanship of provincials. Most inhabitants of the eastern shore preferred the Twin Lighthouses on

Pinnace Woe island, which had long been a parochial sigil of the Seamark liberty. No one could depict a simple and self-evident tool or product to distinguish the nearly defunct granite industry from commonplace mining or freemasonry. A few eccentric futurists wanted some electronic symbol of the cathode ray tube, or even of the sexode, which were said to have been invented by Captain Ozone in his Chateau Noir at Prudence Cove. Other icons were mentioned—self-serving, bathetic, or esoteric.

But the greater nostalgic public was divided between a couple of taxonomic images for which the city had at different times been noted, representing what was perhaps the hope to bring back either of two legendary species by sympathetic magic—though with far more probable success in one case than in the other:

Among those of influence beyond their own kitchens, the pragmatists nominalists scientists bankers clergymen doctors and educators would have been ashamed to sport the Sea Serpent, which was the choice favored by historians, a majority of the politicians, tavernkeepers, most of the other merchants, and nearly all children. A growing number of opponents to the Sea Serpent, especially women who like Caleb himself abhorred even pictures of snakes, instinctively favored the Osprey.

That remarkable fish-hawk once preferred Cape Gloucester's estuaries to all others in New Armorica, but it had been contracepted since World War 2 by insidious chemicals of the modern economy, or perhaps, according to freethinking ecologists, despite that bird's frequent epiphytic use of lofty high voltage AC power structures as nest platforms, by the electromagnetic waves of devilvision.

Now Mary Tremont, sojourning in equatorial South Atlantis with the Brotherhood of the Peaceable Kingdom after satisfying her wish to sail the tropical seas, has been told nothing of Dogtown's contemporary events or trends; but with her usual timely clairvoyance in a letter to her son from the green mansions of Vernalia she happens to evoke the Sea Serpent, despite a congenital fear of its phenotype on any scale of magnitude, regardless of the fact that its transverse motion was vertical rather than horizontal.

One afternoon [she writes Caleb] having finished her stint in the communal laundry, in her usual temerarious fashion, against all rules, she took a walk by herself to the nearby river whose name she did not know (a tributary of Orellana's Rio Parima), cheerfully hoping to glimpse the great black jaguar whose humanoid voice lures human victims so that he can eat their eyes, or to come across one of her Atlindu "friends" (with whom she said it was easier to be herself than with her British roommate) at the sandy swimming place.

Approaching through the jungle she stopped herself just short of blundering into a file of six or eight Guiaca men in what looked like a purposeful dance crossing the flat rock ledges worn naked by perennial flooding of the nearby rapids. Their sinuous nexus, borne by shoulder and clasped by arm, was a heavily shared burden that twisted with their path—a protracted tubular wave tattooed with sickeningly distorted squares and triangles, greenish yellow and black, its waning elasticity almost as horrifying as the autonomous muscularity with which it had lashed the earth in its agony not an hour before.

She did not wait to look for the corpse's head of tail. Clearly aware only of the shriek that erupted from her throat to obliterate the vision, she rushed blindly back to the safety of her compound, stumbling and breathless, followed by the brutally scornful laugh of people she had presumed to defend against the superstitions of Petrine missionaries.

To her (and hence her son, could she but know it) the mere glimpse of an Irish gartersnake is fear enough. Caleb imagined the anaconda's inanimation as ever-unfinished, asymptotic to the absolute. In her letter, the pen still trembling in her hand, she mocks herself for having teased her baby boy on the rocks of Matthews Point with tall tales of the Sea Serpent pictured in his incunabula.

And that memory of North Village (which on the whole escaped her bitter condemnation of Dogtown) reminds her to tell him on the next page that it was an osprey that had raised her spirits to the adventurous level that morning. She had noticed the lone bird on high as it slowly patrolled reaches of the winding river that were hidden from her bungalow by bank after bank of solid greenery. Vernalia, just above the equator, was only a few degrees east of the Cape Gloucester meridian. Maybe this young explorer was the nostalgic remnant of a Dogtown stirps, and in season would find her way home for breeding at an ancestral nest!

In former times it was not as its originator or proprietor that Dogtown claimed the osprey's patronage but only as a special haven in the international fellowship of sea hunting, though unable to boast of much whaling or piracy. The presence of this global raptor had claimed the great world's acknowledgement of Dogtown's worth at (as it turned out) the zenith of its history. But now the osprey was an extinct archangel, survived only by the raucous metempsychotic angels who localized the sky all year round.

Dogtown's own born and bred Maxwell gulls—no less peculiar to Dogtown than its famous schooners, its Sea Serpent, or its little-known Viking Shepherds—could hardly satisfy the patriotic appetite for unique prestige, though at a distance one of them might be taken for the national eagle.

But the osprey, bone-breaker of live fish, international fisher of margins and estuaries, a nesting yet migratory privateer more iconic of respectability than anything else that Dogtown has lost, was Doc Charlemagne's nomination for the Hall weathervane. His friend the sculptor Petto DaGetto offered to cut and weld its representation from the metal donated by Earl Day of Daisy's Junk Yard, if someone else would volunteer to mount it atop the ogival peak of the clock tower.

The giddy acrophobia envisioned for himself as a steeplejack, which had displaced Caleb's vicarious horror at the Apolline idol of the grotto, brought him down to the inner earth of his garret. He came to the limit of his drift. It was time to leave off vagarious evasions and climb back onto the liferaft of creative reason that honorably rescues one from life's traumas, both universal and idiopathic, as long as he stays healthy. The same is also his only deliverance from the chronic shocks of Atlantean vulgarity, without being abandoned to a precarious existence among cannibals on some Typee yet still with the hope of finding a literate Fayaway on his own rockbound island.

So he must open his eyes and face an interesting schedule of exercises problems tasks books joys and practicable desires. And he did open his eyes, to the amazing light of morning! His first pleasure, as he'd expected, was the sight of Ibi, who in after-dream, long past the stage of twitching paws, was deeply oblivious to his circumstances—until instantly recalled to duty by an ostentatious flapping-open of the bedclothes.

Most emphatically, hopping counterclockwise out of bed, Caleb put behind him the dread of being asked about himself or shrewdly suspected as a by-blown aborigine. "Sufficient unto the day is the anxiety thereof." saith Wat Cibber.

While nonetheless still postponing consideration of the struggle he'd have to resume at the typewriter between athletics and breakfast, he took rapid unmethodical inventory of the day's plans and possible topics, namely: the route for his morning run; today's tactics in securities-research at FEEL; his revision of the Lab filing system; accounting studies; improved speed at the calculator (with his right hand while writing figures with his left); various clarifying charts and diagrams; thought-experiments with the Synectic Method of Diagnostic Correlation [SMDC]; and, above all, schemes to lure "Love's aid for Love's distress".

In short, his defenses against the sea of life were briskly reassumed. Muscular disequilibrium swept away intimations of mortality in his eagerness to get going in some sort of action at one thing and another. Intuition he said to himself is an inertialess laziness of reason—more efficient than logic or empirical methods (and therefore producing larger insights)—but it's high time for ambitions. They indeed may not be rational either, and there are certainly too many of them to be realized, but any success should be pursued rationally. It was premature to think of love serving up its second arrow.

2
MOONCLOUD

Moonday

Dear Lil:

The last thing I did, save look and listen, was kiss the inside of your right wrist while you were managing the horses as confidently as Athena that whitewashed goddess. Oh Lily-Lil, next I'd like to kiss your ankle, starting with the toe.

The best thing would be not to be in love with Lily-Cloud. Then on Mondays I could pay attention to the other seven wonders of the world.

You are such an extraordinary, astounding, unprecedented event among all events presented for prehension that I must regard you as noumenal despite your accidentally phenomenal physique.

Now I'm the sailor, lovesick. It's a depressing day, confined to base while others take their liberties, a Siberian kind of day. I still have no specimen of your handwriting. Please write me a check for $1.00. As an immature male of your species—of your dyad—I must admit I can't help craving something written uniquely to me in acknowledgement of my halved existence.

But the wonder of gratitude is that I now possess some impersonal typescripts of your intellectual passion. "Tragedy", "Uncertainty", "Gilgamesh", and "a priori choice"! How does it happen that we've both lighted upon the same imponderable topics? After all, aren't we opposites in valence? Haven't our gonads decreed an immemorial disparity? Aren't we separated by nearly all our experience? Aren't you a princess and I a frog?

You are too independent for any of the professions. Your critical intelligence circumvents all doctorates and Institutes of Advanced Study. More even than disclosure of your naked skin I crave a long succession of unveilings to get at further knowledge of what you know. Our communication demands both kinds of language. Though at this moment my love for you seems to have passed the Elizabethan stage of praise, I know that praise will recur because it is a level to which my written language can aspire.

Yet what a fool I am when talking to you on the phone! I haven't yet learned how to. I can't say hello or goodbye without seeming to put you on the spot. I lack the simplest grace. I mumble. My mind goes blank. I speak inanities. You'd never know I'm trying to compare my heart to yours. I hope you can hear between my blundering lines.

As I've implored you, draw no conclusions now. Don't shut me out so soon! It would be a radical mistake to take and make decisions before we have half informed each other. Let the sun stand still until we've reached at least the half-life of our infinite approaches to opposite strangeness. Our reciprocal science demands no less than the suspension of astronomical rotation. Little Mooney is growing: that's all that counts as far as the continuation of our history is concerned. Please let her progress obnubilate all solar revolution—until our eccentric motions have had time to conjoin in involution!

How in the name of the B V M can you withstand my painful joy of unconsummated praise? When I take no thought of consequences I'm as hopeful as Henry Hudson starting up the great North River, or Champlain starting down his Lake Van Luck. Yet—oh yet!—the uncertainty of our superconductive messages through the wall that separates us cannot be resolved in the prohibitive awkwardness of telephone calls to the Doghouse cash register—not to mention prohibited communications directly to your nest!

I had to promise the discretion of silence just when you'd struck me more breathless than ever with admiration! Never have I been so overwhelmed as I was this afternoon. Our chance meeting in that interstice of your busy obligations was an enthralling adventure in sensate ideas to which I wasn't equal, though it yielded a windfall of most precious fruit.

I staggered home to Ibi still bemused and trembling with amazement at your easy efficiency of voice, your straightforward elucidation. Now I sit tossing off Scotch as if you were here, drinking to your trenchant friendship, to your frankness of address, to your integrity, your guts, your discriminations, your disinterested sincerity: all visible in a peculiar refinement of the rare kind of beauty that a million men would envy me for so little as the glances of. It's a lunar complexity that sometimes distracts my thigmotactic desire with purely cognitive gratitude. But I speak too much of beauty, a word from centuries ago. Likewise, too much of what I feel, far too much of myself, an excessive pronoun also from the past. The verb to love that desegregates me from your beauty is elsewhere bandied weakly. What I mean to celebrate is not the class of phenomena prophesied by Keats as beauty, or its general power over such as me, but you the uniquely fluctuating noumenon: my feathery cloud-trailing cynosure, in and for her essential self. Yet today under the sun when I noticed your hips and felt your backbone I was thinking of undisinterested country matters.

To tell the truth, any frail continuation of our history, under any constraint, under almost any conditions, is enough to keep me hoping. I swear I'm no further importunate. What's urgent at one moment may not be urgent the next; only the basic yearning is amaranthine.

I intend to stay up all night writing at what I'm trying to say. I hope you'll have the time to read it all, and the kindness to forgive my drunken breech of decorum. Let me know what you provisionally think of my madness: I may be able to suppress one or two of its manifestations before your mind is set against me.

I'm glad you read Yeats. He lends us a private vocabulary. The consilience of his analytical geometry and sublunar existence is more amazing to me than scientific correlations between a priori algebra and empirical observations. Yet symbolic schemes don't get me very far in fixing you. Your Body of Fate mocks me with irony. Your idio-instinctive Will is utterly beyond my surd ignorance. Your Creative Mind, the one of your Faculties that I should be least incapable of appreciating, I'm unable to do justice to, in spite of the fact that deprivation of sufficient touch drives me crazy enough to attempt abstraction and identification of the sovereign grace that is actually inseparable from the dissimilar strength of your character (which I was so blind to in my puppyhood at Hume, when I thought of you almost as artist only). That grace both leads and follows from the Mask of your "purpose"—as I now see that it always did, long before our separate transcontinental uprootings.

But of course you have also changed. I admired you erstwhile as a moody brown cygnet scornful of clocks and calendars, when you hardly seemed to take responsibility even for yourself—a thoroughly antithetical Atlindu. Your old way sanctions my equal admiration of the new. You are capable of any ironic shape-changing. I am utterly confident of your pragmatic competence.

I adore your honesty as much as the intelligence it infuses. It almost makes me forget my deferred dismay at the literal import of your recent words, lightly murmured with a stiff upper lip. Please don't be so absolute. Fearfully I cannot deny the shadows you fearlessly make us face. But necessity rules less than half our future. Do not volunteer precipitation.

When we see and touch each other, naturally, the reciprocating reinforcement can't be checked; it admits of no abeyance; its dialectic cannot be suspended; and it makes your cruel dilemma all the more difficult. But give me time to think—give me time, give me a little time for hope! Grant me the sight of you every now and then. Grant me your voice, close enough for the lightest of all touches that are less imaginary than this letter. For I am your scholar: in all of history I am the man most studious of you.

So let us make the sun stand still by day, if not by night. Even if we haven't yet found an honest way to take the next sweet step before which neither Atlindu nor Sumerian lovers would have felt obliged to pause so long.

But I acknowledge that from what you say I must try to prepare myself like a Cathar troubadour for failing ever to attain the first peace of lunar atonement. Sometimes that seems a small price for my tenuous oxymoronic privilege, notwithstanding that it seems to presage an unconscionable delight whenever you alight at my side like Athena. Only that close am I fully aware of your indiscernible essence—yet to feel your proximity is to desire it in full, as Plato et al would have said if they'd known your cloudcovered phenomenon. (Even as it is, I have the advantage of them in this experience.)

Please keep me alive from day to day—until I have time to unearth an old Irish souterrain for us in Purdeyville.

6:30 AM, Moonday morrow

Without reading over the above outburst I'm going to let it stand. It was very late when I went to sleep still half drunk with the water of life and wholly intoxicated with the day's compressed adventure—despite the foreboding words you started with, so inconsonant with the enchanting joys that followed. Still your ghostly presence woke me up at 3AM, for the third night in a row. On account of this lovesickness Ibi and I have skipped our morning run.

Yesterday's enchantment made me forget to tell you a dream I had the other night, just after I'd told you on the phone that I couldn't remember what you looked like, we so seldom saw each other. I dreamt that you turned out to be quite homely. I was dismayed but undeterred.

In waking existence, especially now that we have added another hundred minutes to our joined histories, I would give up your phenomenal face far less philosophically, for the style of your physiognomy is no mere accidental aspect of your noumenon. A scholar like me can't dispense with any one of the beauties in your seamless hypostasis of worth lest he lose them all. In your face is everything about you—a new swiftness and efficiency informed by goodhumored pragmatic experience; the old analytical clarity and coherence; critical intelligence; romantic maturity; reserved passion; lifelong talents of imagination.

It's comforting to know that you're running the whole Doghouse three or four evenings a week, civilizing the downtown lightnightlife. Yet you never say how hard it must be on you, added to all your other burdens as mother daughter and household captive.

Compared to yours, my double life is easy. At home I have too much time to think about you. Here I can jubilate in my malady. I have the luxury of solitude that you so cruelly lack. When I step about my little kitchen from stove to sink and back, I imagine you as cook, swinging your hip to close a drawer, managing a dozen tasks at once while cogitating a priori. Then the ineffable mystery of your incarnate being buffets my consciousness anew and turns me giddy. When I'm absorbed with problems at the Lab you're the blue sky that I'm always dimly aware is overhead and may be seen by simply looking out and up—or at least by believing it to be visible above any ephemeral overcast of cloud.

These my mere peripheral swoons are set in motion like gentle cyclones by the vast central hurricane that enlarges itself every time I see you, every time you speak to me on the phone. I'm still learning to dare to trust the continuity of your Dogtown embodiment. We've had only five new times together, and I'm not sure of your ground. Like Mooney, I must teach myself that your absences do not imply your discontinuity. But my belief still calls for an unlimited accumulation of your presences. This distrust of induction is one of the marks of what I meant by my immaturity, compared to you.

I'm definitely losing a different battle. The trouble with solitude is that whenever I sit down to work you occupy the same keyboard as that which my solitude was intended to serve. I have no child to demand my attention (—just a silent patient dog—), and scarcely any social obligations: only a labor of free will. But everything voluntary is now Lilianine. My old Muses are blocked by your ascendancy. That's why they're trying to make the best of poor clay by turning me to lyrics; and sometimes I attempt to console them for my defeats at drama with a crumb or two of ungovernable moon-verse. I'm too embarrassed to let you see the wrack it is.

And I can't force myself to do other things I ought—like paying bills, answering my mail, or unprocrastinating my shameful housework. When the heart is strong the will is weak. So I surrender to this compulsion of unilateral communication. I yield to the available pleasure of incantation. Too often I can address nought but the subject of you, metaphysically at least.

Still, all this sublimated energy of love! Although the electromagnetic polarity is always striving to play itself out in sweet natural mechanics, the closed thought-system made by the two of us converts more and more of my potential into passionate works of the open mind. (I know the phase-state transformation is reversible!) So I can't help risking indiscreet prose abstractions that well may weary you. I know you have no more time to read letters than to write them.

John Donne believed that "more than kisses, letters mingle souls". I heartily wish I had your signature. Yet:

IMPROXIMITY

Be off,
you adjectives and nouns!
The time has come
for verb.
I'd resume my kissing
at hollow and entasis
of your neck and calf.

Your gentleman-in-waiting,

Caleb

PS: No, don't cut off your noble Pocahaunting tresses just to accommodate Loathey O'Toole's uniform caps! Your hair's all one with feathers of strength and swift sufficient movements, even when the law makes you pin it up like a Georgio's. Your face, anyway, is to other faces as horses are to other animals. Which is not to say that anyone would call you horsefaced!

You'll be yet more beautiful when you're too old to seem so quick.

I feel such an affinity for your skin and bones that I'm sure we have a common ancestor, probably from one of the Lost Tribes.

3
IRTH

THE ISO-RECTO-TETRAHEDRON
or THE TOWER OF GILGAMESH

A Comedy for Dancers

PERSONS AND MASKS

Lil-Amin, queen of Uruk, priestess of Inanna
College of Widows, hierodules of the Temple

The Rector of the Temple, priest of Inanna,
       formerly governor of Uruk
Optimates, a council of ephors representing
       the people

Gilgamesh [Giszax], king-errant of Erech [Uruk]
Norkid, captain of his Kassite guard
Troopers, Kassite bowmen of the guard

Eber, Gilgamesh's vizier and patriarch of nomads
Traders, sons of Eber, nomadic merchants

Engidu [Enkidu], a wild man from the steppes

GLOSSARY

	Men's Language	Women's Language
Erech = Uruk (a city in Sumer)	___Err-ek	Ur-uk
Ishtar = Inanna (city goddess)	___Ish-tar	In-an-na
Enlil (the high god)	___En-lil	En-lil
Lil-Amin	___Lil-a-min	Lil-ah-min
Engidu = Enkidu	___En-gi-du	En-ki-du
Gilgamesh = Giszax	___Gil-ga-mesh	Gee-zax

PRODUCTION NOTES

1. *General Desiderata.* In principle this is a play for dancers who are also actors, but in practice it may as well be done by actors few or none of whom are dancers. It would be a fine thing if musicians playing derabucca drums or Indian cymbals, and a flute or recorder, could be sitting on the stage throughout the performance; but music may be otherwise provided, electronically if necessary, as long as the apparatus is not concealed. In a full-scale production, each of the four choruses (Widows, Troopers, Traders, and Optimates) would consist of three or more persons; but in any cast they must equal each other in the number of at least two each.

2. *Notation.* Dialogues shown in italics are spoken or chanted in unison. In choral parts not individually specified, dashes at the beginning of clauses indicate an arbitrary alternation of speakers.

   3. *Suggestions for casting or masking.*
   GILGAMESH: white; cleanshaven.
   ENGIDU: black, red, or dark; shaggy and lithe, but muscular or otherwise athletically imressive.
   EBER: bearded, longhaired; elderly but vigorous.
   RECTOR: perhaps hairless; remarkably strong (even if short); maybe tattooed.
   LIL-AMIN: dark; preferably tall and slender.
   NORKID: fairhaired; stocky or burly; wears steel-rim eyeglasses
   WIDOWS: lightly wimpled or veiled.

   4. *Properties.*
   Gilgamesh's *axe*: standard double-bitted steel head on a straight wooden haft.
   Engidu's *bannerstone*: a primitive symmetrically winged stone mounted on a short throwing handle.

Engidu's *bow and arrow*: the two-part tool used to make fire—a drilling device. (The Troopers use classic English *longbows*.)

The *Iso-recto-tetrahedron*: a solid formed by the corner of a cube, its perpendicular edges of equal length, its oblique face forming an equilateral triangle; threaded with a hole and small enough to wear around the neck on a thong or chain.

5. *Design criteria*. Ad lib: any style from extreme simplicity of set and costume (freely anachronistic, with never more than hints of historical verisimilitude) to sparely ornamented expression of cultural contrast—as long as it is consonant with the idea that this is a play about dancers, not opera singers. (The basic dress may be leotards of solid colors that each characterize one of the four choruses.) Individual masks may be simply or elaborately distinctive.

PROLOGUE

Herodotus of Halicarnassus hereby acknowledges that he was fatally unable to keep the promise in his book about Persia to write a more ancient History of Mesopotamia and Canaan.

I had wished to take entire leave of my own millennium and trace to their origins or antitheses the vestigial myths and rituals I mentioned in the work on Europe, Africa, and Asia that has come down to you. With waxing excitement I was advancing my researches, but had grown weary of the narrative form, which no longer seemed appropriate to my matter, when death overtook me.

The play you are about to see, my first and only attempt at drama, was the last thing I ever wrote, though only the introduction to my project. I was hoping to have it produced at the Greater Dionysia of the year you would designate as the 431st before your era, but I was debarred from competition both because of my disallowed Athenian citizenship (on the basis of a dead-letter law) and because, lacking poetic credentials, I was presumed to know nothing about the theater worthy of anybody's investment. In any case, my manuscript was disqualified when the archon refused to recognize it as comedy or satyr play, let alone tragedy.

Anyway, that year I would have found myself in rivalry with *Oedipus Tyrannus*. I was not terribly distressed that the battered scroll of my play, having been mistaken for mere notes to a History that would never be written, was burned at my funeral in Thuria as a symbolic sacrifice by my beloved wife.

For centuries I was called the father of lies; but your scholars have revived interest in our common cultural origins and therewith justified many of my conjectures about barbarian peoples and places denied or ignored by the proud Athenians, whose western seapower blinded them to the formative influence of Sumer, of which Akkad, Assyria, and the Babylon I visited were but imperial degenerations.

At the time of legendary Gilgamesh, a couple of thousand years before Semiramis and her even greater successor Nitocris (who made a labyrinth of the upper Euphrates to protect her Babylon from riverain invaders), the Sumerian city of Uruk—known in your Bible as Erech, especially sacred to Enlil (the original Bel or Baal), indigenous father of the gods, and to his daughter Inanna (later Ishtar)—was upstream hegemon of the eastern Sea-Lands. It was a time when the Tigris and Euphrates still debouched separately into the reedy silt-marshes of the Gulf that has since been named the Persian—almost as far from the splendid concerns of Pericles in miles as in years.

As you know from Boethius and others, those two rivers arose from the Ararat rocks, near alpine Lake Van, which remains more central to the world than Greece itself. I believe that in Sumer, at the bottom of that double-rivered plain, west of Eden, mankind first invented agriculture, writing, and other technology. The myths of Gilgamesh, or Giszax, began in pre-Semitic Sumerian ritual.

At some point an historical tyrant may have taken upon himself that famous name, perhaps as that of a traditional conqueror from the Zagros Mountains; but it's more likely that the primeval stories accrued to a born king Gilgamesh of the world's first city. In Babylon I heard an epic poem, a latterday redaction; but it seems to have simplified the tensions and conflicts that Gilgamesh must have experienced at the fountainhead of culture, where not merely two streams divided, but three or even four.

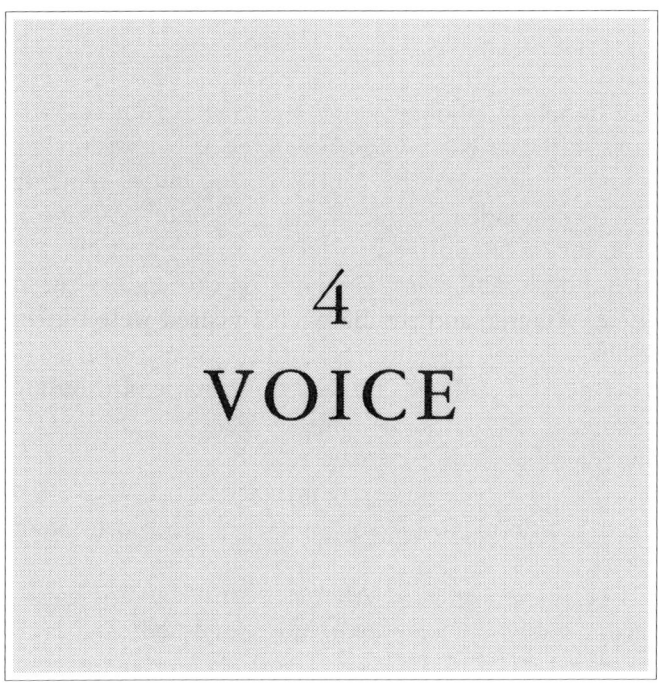

4
VOICE

*I*t's not your own." Father Lucey had said of Caleb's voice. "But it can be found if we look for it."

Caleb expected to need that undiscovered voice after the Gloucestermas Chapter, when the Fathers would probably be obliged by consensus of the COV membership to curtail the Lab's liberal payroll. He wanted to get a new job worthy of his bureaucratic talent, advancing some of his practicable ideas in an avocational career that would support his true vocation. Without a voice he would not be listened to; he would not even be given the opportunity to draw charts and write memos. Furthermore, in the more urgent hunt that obsesses almost all young men—at least when he wasn't forgetting himself in very love—he was sorely aware that an affective voice was necessary if not sufficient to make up for his inalterable handicaps.

But when all was said and done Chris hadn't helped him locate that disembodied doppelganger, and poor old Florence Starling had died in her effort. So he'd finally turned to Tessa Barebones of Troika Arts.

"I'm sufficiently eloquent with a sensitive dog; but with mankind I can't raise my voice in either anger or persuasion. I couldn't wind Roland's horn even in triumph! You must remember that because of my wooden throat I was the only boy at Dutchkill School that they were obliged to excuse from the choir it provided the village church, and every Sunday I had to endure the boredom and embarrassment of inaction without passion by sitting and standing among the handful of locals, as if ostracized by my overpeering peers. I suffered through the totalitarianism of community singing bullied by the little loud organ."

"Maybe you have emphysema."

"No, my vital capacity is extraordinary."

"Indeed I should think so. In fact I find your voice quite charming."

"But I can't even whistle. All I can bring forth is weak swishes barely recognizable as elements of the social code and patched together like pieces of torn envelope. And it's harder for me to shout than to run through water up to my neck."

"So what? Whistling brings bad luck and shouting is unseemly in a gentleman. Why bother looking for your lost voice? Someday it'll probably wander home of its own accord."

"But meanwhile it's that vocal accord I need to make myself visible in the world. If people could hear me, then they'd see me, and I wouldn't have to talk so fast trying to make them listen."

"Maybe then it's a matter not so much of voice as of delivery. Breathing and pausing are easily learned by an athlete like you. All it takes, besides practice, is tolerance of some crass elocution by way of training."

"Like writers who rely upon short sentences and lots of white space?"

"I'm not talking about rhetoric." said Mrs Barebones firmly.

On Monday afternoons, irregularly, despite the fact that her twist of his appeal wasn't what he'd bargained for, Caleb and Mrs Barebones sat together for an hour or so in a chilly corner of the Hoof and Mouth dance studio when it was void of other humanity. In this piquant conspiracy he gradually reconciled himself to the ignobility of secret selfimproving therapy. Though only a coach of dramatic art, not a professional teacher of voice, Mrs Barebones had been through the training mill herself, and she was well versed in techniques of speech.

She started with Caleb simply enough, by taking him through the relaxation exercises and introductory sound-making drills that Miss Starling had prescribed, whose respected reputation was well known in several professions. Mrs Barebones taught no particular method of her own, but rather experimented with her patient as they went along.

What with one or another of her own domestic contretemps she sometimes canceled an inconveniently scheduled session—but usually with Caleb's all-too-ready consent, who always found it hard to accept even this ambitious interruption of his precious day off, the bonus worth more than a day's wages. Once he realized that there was to be no miracle without faithful self-discipline in conflict with the more important employment of his private time he hardly practiced his homework exercises anyway. The regime of breathing on the run at dawn was onerous enough.

Before they met many times, therefore, the tutoring project began to peter out, by tacit agreement, under the pressure of more vital breathing on both their parts, and especially because right from the start she had said that she saw no need for him to improve himself unless he wanted to take to the boards or the hustings, or maybe the pulpit.

Still, his reply all along was that she didn't understand his difficulties in a world of men and women less perspicacious of his worth than herself. Even after the effort at formal training finally lapsed he continued to believe that its success would have won him inestimable advantages in business and society. To himself he justified the laziness and parsimony that prevailed over his positive motivation by the lackluster argument that lifelong sequestration of his voice would lead him not into the temptations of distracting achievements.

His "voice lessons" were nevertheless of more significant consequence than either pupil or teacher could be expected to anticipate. He was lent new confidence just by thinking that he could have purchased an almost normal confidence.

In any event, successful or not, the tutoring was always pleasant, once he made himself walk with Ibi down to the former pressroom of the DT Daily Nous on Front Street. Up in the third-floor loft they hardly noticed the desultory noise of the after-school traffic melee. They sat together at the piano in the tall-windowed loft that had once housed linotype machines. The two unfenestrated walls were now lined with mirrors, and exercise bars lined most of the perimeter. He at first protested the musical instrument, just as he had stiffened at Miss Starling's, like a dog shying at the prospect of a bath; but here too he was assured that there was no intention to mold him as a singer. The old lady had maintained that singing and speaking tones were identical, produced by the same organs in the same way, developed by the same training. Mrs Barebones said "It's merely to help widen your vocal scale and mark your intervals of intonation. But our first purpose is simply to place your voice."

It was misplaced, or displaced, or mutilated like Tristam Shandy's nose, as I squirmed in the forceps and strangled on my umbilical cord. If she supposes I have a respectable replacement somewhere, maybe other people will also give me the benefit of the doubt. That's enough to get by on, while work's in progress. Later I can test her proposition that my prenatal voice remains available whenever I think it's worth the trouble to fetch it up.

Miss Starling's touchingly disinterested devotion to his cause had obligated him to respect the documents she had left in his hands: anatomical explanations, detailed breathing instructions, and rules of posture, accompanied by music-staves of notes and sounds for humming chanting or singing, with vowel-reciting paradigms, followed by extracts of patriotic poetry, pledges of allegiance, Gettysburg addresses, passages from Goethe and Shakespeare (including Hamlet's instructions to the players). The half-dozen painstakingly typed sheets were carbon copies from her own frail fingers, but the music notations had been shakily penned in autograph for his sole use. [In those days before copying machines were versatile and available it was extravagantly generous to give an impoverished trifler such fruits of expert labor.] Only her death had relieved his anxiety at having been about to frustrate the charity of her wholehearted response to his dabbling in the vocal realm, which he'd always half despised.

Tessa Barebones had no quarrel with the analysis in her predecessor's ELEMENTS OF THE VOCAL INSTRUMENT, nor with the program of relaxation and breathing. But she practiced her own slyly radical interpretation of the declaration on Miss Starling's page titled BASIC PRINCIPLES IN SPEECH THERAPY that "the obstacles to good speaking and singing are psychologic rather than physiologic".

Tessa's loosely reined and indirect therapy, under the form of friendly advice, was far the more congenial to such a poor student. She made her search for the lost voice seem to him as casual as his own interest in it was to become when good weather and other variable factors became more influential than hope for social advancement. She gave no sign of wishing to reform him, and offered only limited guidance, usually in the quasi-metaphorical terms she had picked up as a student of acting. For instance: "Your tones have stuck somewhere in the back of your throat. All we've got to do is bring them forward to the right spot in your facial mask."

"For me it would be a False Mask. To the hypocrites of the Eighth Circle the palpitations of Dante's throat were proof enough that he was mortally alive."

"You secretly believe that voice is mere clothing, one of the more superficial accidents of personality. I can't quite say you're wrong."

Unlike Miss Starling, this coach was able to imagine her new young friend too pigheaded to believe that the ability to sing would have made him happy. In her prosody of prose she soft-pedaled allusions to music, hardly ever touching the piano keys, and spoke of sounds, not notes; flexibility, not diapason; rhythm, not melody. Yet both teachers held that the human voice has three elements in common with artifactual instruments of music: a motor (lungs and respiratory muscles), a vibrator (vocal cords), and a resonator (cavities of throat and head). Only the articulation by tongue, lips, teeth, and hard palate is specifically human.

By dissipating Caleb's suspicion of subterfugal music Mrs Barebones beguiled him into calm consideration of his "narrow range" (actually monotonous), frustrated lung power, inability to command modulation, crippled timbre, numbness of lips, dumbness of tongue, and general inexpressiveness of exhalation. Although his study of these defects and infirmities never got much beyond the stage of confidential acknowledgment, her brief diagnosis was conveyed so tactfully that it bolstered his determination to cultivate the contrasting class of disembodied and abstract faculties in which he had a foothold. Those, she implied, were far more distinguished than the histrionic and carnal virtues with which ordinary people like herself were indifferently endowed.

Nevertheless, though he now laughed to himself at the crab in his vocal cords that Bice-Belle had cured him of, he often still felt the strain of conversation in his undistinguished vibrator. Wasn't his fugitive voice hiding down there? But on this question the only pertinent suggestion from Mrs Barebones was simply negative: the proper posture for the larynx was a function of the tongue's position; despite the fact that the larynx can't help moving when the tongue moves, the less attention he gave it the better. "The tension and proximity of the vocal cords adjust themselves to produce a comfortable pitch without your conscious volition. There's no direct way to train them. They only need to be left alone! Form your sound in the resonance chambers, not in your throat." For Caleb much easier believed than left undone.

"And for Christ's sake, relax your jaw, as in the best kind of kissing!"

He persuaded himself that he was putting up with this therapeutic nonsense only because it was inflicted upon him by an intelligently sympathetic woman whose manner was as amiable as Chris Lucey's—at least when she dispensed with the tedious rehearsal of vowels and consonants. (But she was careful not to emphasize vowels at the expense of consonants. "Vowels are rivers, consonants are their banks." quoth she. "Remember that, for depth of volume.")

Before the end of their first meeting, she had artfully set the precedent for exploration of Caleb's voiceless psyche. Ostensibly in an offhand codicil to her physiological guidance in the case, she asked some "background" questions, negligently lighting a cigarette with long thin fingers, her smoke-narrowed eyes averted toward a diagonal corner of the high ceiling. The pleasant waft of her tobacco reminded him of childhood comfort in his mother's presence. In spontaneous memories he never associated the smell of a woman's cigarette with his natal puniness or with a probable heritage of weak blood vessels.

The alacrity of his replies almost seemed those of a normal personality. Upon subsequent reflection he would be surprised to find that he'd felt none of the uneasiness that ultimately inhibited his colloquies with Father Lucey (not to mention Father Duncannon or Doctor Charlemagne), nor any of the anxiousness to calculate affect that instinctively entered into his address of women who were younger or more eligible for his erotic consideration.

It was a small species she represented—those sympathetic to his person though still failing to appreciate the peculiarity of his motives and disguises—nearly as small as the imaginary one that did know what he was about and liked it. But with her he broke his characteristic silence only to explain himself too much! On the first day and on the several Mondays thereafter her questions grew freer and his answers more voluntary.

Her unobtrusive interrogation benignly insinuated itself among the instructions and exercises, gradually lengthening the time for which he was nominally charged. But of course her motives were scarcely financial. Before their professional sessions came to an end, she was to confide in him enough of her own condition to hearten his faith in her discretion.

Beyond the technical problem of such a curiously starved and delitescent voice, she was intrigued by the amusing inconsistency between his scorn of vocal persuasion—everything "merely rhetorical"—and his dissociated appeal for tutoring. From her friend his landlady Gloria Keith she had gotten wind of his secret occupation, but for her the notion of an antitheatrical playwright did not simplify the psychological case. What manner of marooner was this little young man who revered Yeats but abused Plato, hated the vernacular but loved the Catholicratic Party, abhorred DV but took pleasure in electrical engineering, despised gematria but expressed himself in complex numbers he called Pythagorean? By disingenuously incidental allusion to problems of voice on the stage, which he knew to be the scene of her professional experience, she soon charmed from him a voluntary confession of his unlikely vocation. "What's your play about?" she naturally asked.

It was the question he always dreaded even more than the generic disclosure of his pursuit. No short answer could fail to be misleading, and it would expose him to the contempt of any critic whose partialities were as prejudicial as his own. But Mrs Barebones, wife of the generous inventor who had befriended him, deserved at least a limited answer no more cryptic than some of her own remarks. "Among other things, the riddle of how to construct a regular triangle from isosceles perpendiculars on more than one plane."

"I suppose that might have been posed by one of the Sphinxes. Is the mise en scene Greek or Egyptian?"

"Older—the oldest of all. It's derived from clay tablets."

"I hope the hero hasn't feet of clay." She asked no more for the present, but the cat was out of the bag.

By way of common courtesy he told her the title and the subtitle, but said no more about the Matter of Sumer; yet to show his special trust in her he immediately diverted attention to the kind of motives that are always easier for a psychologist to grasp than passions of the intellect. "I've got to finish IRTH by Gloucestermas, because afterwards I must look for a full-time job. That's why I need a voice. To give me heart, and to make people listen to me when I'm explaining myself. So I won't be overlooked all the time. So I won't have to work twice as hard as everybody else just to get noticed!"

"You make it sound as if you're as handicapped as a woman. But why do you hide your light under a bushel?"

"Because I want to earn my living in Dogtown. I'd never get hired or promoted if people of business distrusted my ambition and my common sense. They might guess I'm a Premature Antifascist, or even suspect me of fellow-traveling with the Resistance."

"But why should your talent be kept secret from unbusinesslike friends?"

"Because word gets around. It's not talent anyway: only interest plus will. Besides, it would be ridiculous to mention the unrepresentative fragment of a trilogy less than one third finished. It's nothing but vain illusion until I do it all."

"What a pure Puritan! You suppress your own theater!"

"I'm really a sinister son of the true church."

"So were Galahad and Percival."

She was wrong about that, but he was now tempted to regard her as capable of understanding anything. "I don't want to be pegged as Doctor Charlemagne's arriere-garde."

"He doesn't know what you write?"

"Never asks. He's afraid I'll expect him to read it. God forbid! He'd call IRTH a 'drama da camera'."

"Then wild horses couldn't drag your secret out of me. I'd deny everything. And unless you yourself give the show away, nary a soul will ever even know you've come to me for singing lessons.

"But in a small town we can't pretend not to know each other. Now it does happen that we need a male voice in our troupe of armchair mummers. Some perfectly respectable attendance at our private play-readings would explain your acquaintance with the likes of me. As a bachelor you would be excused from the usual requirement of taking a turn to hold the chosen thought-play, with refreshments, at your own house. All you have to do is read aloud—not interpret—some comic or heroic parts. Your only reward will be the nectar and mead served by maenads. But there will always be one or two other men to drink with."

Caleb smiled at the idea that her enticement to participate in women's drama would be fortified by the prospect of male competition, while at the same time he was appalled by the absurd notion of his voice in male histrionics. As the single incarnate trinity of Mary Tremont's maternal dreams, he'd never felt more than two thirds masculine. "My middle name is ichabod." he frankly repined.

Indeed he was as accustomed as a plain woman to not being heeded; but unlike a hypothetical female double he was usually too opinionated not to insist upon expressing himself anyway. Thus under the protection of Tessa Barebones a social prospect that hitherto would have been unconscionable suddenly appeared attractive, almost comfortable. At least in his present mood he foresaw the possible pleasures of a playreading association as outweighing the requisite waste of so much time on Sunday evenings once a month.

5
STORMCLOUD

So intensely minute were Caleb's anticipations and tastings of Lilian's presence that it was as though he was having many astounding adventures, when in fact nothing much was actually happening. Much experience was compressed into the few moons during which Lady Gloucester's manifold petticoats of frost were unhastily exchanged for the thickening succession of green robes in which her people preferred to see her dressed, exposing in the transition not only unlaundered undergrowth of inorganic waste which no winter respite is long enough to rot but also the skinned vertebrae and knuckles of her granite armature, denuded parts of her living frame here and there disrobed of flesh. The tempests of Manannan's besiegement, to which the unmoved beloved sometimes seemed to have grown indifferent, only proved her more constant than himself, whose depth could never match hers, whose womanizing though he unceasingly chased the moon was treacherous and indiscriminate, whose few chameleon colors altered with every streak of wind or cloud.

Yet like the unpacified lord of Ocean beating on Dogtown's rocks, even amidst the most bootless of his stormy privations Caleb couldn't deny that he had the advantage of his lady in liberty, much as if he traveled with the sun in realms of gold. And merely by discerning more of Lilian's uniquely praiseworthy attributes than the rival in possession of her could even conceive of (whether or not desirable to him in his captive), Caleb seduced her keenly susceptible imagination. Only for the sake of her child she defended herself against the hypostatic unscrupulousness of his fascinating love.

In this second courting that seemed the first his heart was nevertheless tinctured with enough true compassion to prevent him from pursuing his desire entirely without compunction. He sometimes almost satisfied himself with the indefinite and inconclusive continuation of his mentally adventurous mal de mer. Even when he put out of mind (as he usually did) the obvious inference that Gil Algo's person incorporated some basically attractive if not irresistible qualities (perhaps rather burnished than dulled for Lilian by periodic rounds of atonement), Caleb couldn't blame her for hesitating at an offer he never made—to take upon himself an alliance with all her baggage. Though he flaunted his vow to Inanna, to "holden werre alway with chastitee", he respected Lilian's fluctuating fidelity to the undescript Gil as a loyalty both honorable and maternally prudent; for baggage is always impedimenta—and even a Yahi Natural doesn't come East without being able to use some help.

In her company he was both too polite (or chary) and too pressed for time to ask personal questions about her cohabitation; so he was never sure how often its domestic conflicts were interrupted by carnal reconciliations. Her reticence in this matter seemed frank enough, but almost equally polite. Any question of fact he was bold enough to ask she appeared to answer readily and plainly, but each gave the other to understand that at least under these wartime conditions their love was to be understood as too intelligent and too romantic to be concerned with commonplace private matters not yet shared. He disguised his chagrin at her references to coitus as an ordinary gratification no more significant than the quaffing of beer.

So far every meeting had ended in a strengthening of their mutual bond, but each rendezvous with her he still more or less expected to be the last. It was under the pressure of such doom—making the most of its indefinite and variable abeyance—that his opportunistic mind had fixed upon the tiny parking mole of the

Dogtown Net & Twine Manufactory ("The D N T ") as their next trysting place.

But he hardly knew why else he so much wanted to show her this spot, usually unpopulated at night, than to inculcate his appreciation of what he found interesting about it. The small gabled factory of framed wood and brick, painted red by day, had survived the demolition of its 19C ropewalk but retained its own ad hoc irregularities beneath a tapering square brick chimney-stack. The building was planted only a few feet above high water on a base of living rock at the end of Mother's Neck, guarding the entrance channel of the inner harbor like a blockhouse on the Rhine. Caleb resisted as intempestive the caprice of informing his driver that Wat Cibber said homecoming fishermen called it Lady Gloucester's clitoris.

Since Lilian never demurred at his tactical options (as if it made little difference where or how they spent their stolen minutes together), it was in her car that one night at about eleven o'clock they circled the womb of the harbor and bumped along the inner edge of the Neck, which paralleled the working waterfront closely opposite, lighted and throbbing in its nightly rest. He said that it seemed to him like promenading the hurricane deck of an ocean liner lying at anchor under the protection of the twin-towered Espirito Santo Church on the Hill across the stream—which fantastically resembled the piloting superstructure of a Mississippi steamboat!

Luckily they found the D N T free of other parkers.

Carried away by his hope to instill a delight in the spot that might somehow enhance her commitment to Dogtown and therefore her accessibility to himself, he had directed her there in the preciously short space of time between the end of her evening duty at the Doghouse and the beginning of whatever might be expected of her at home, without taking into account the fact that it was ten minutes in the opposite direction from both their destinations. As if he'd lost sight of favorable means to at least approach the one true end of love. Still, judging by the passion of her kisses, his maladroit failure to make the most of an opportunity actually served as a psychological stratagem, fortuitously worthy of a wiser and more patient swain.

So there they were, hugging each other so near the center of the city yet safe from the amused scorn that might have been lavished upon their behavior by any adult observer incapable of taking seriously the romantic tension that separated two such hearts. Looking past the red beacon of Parliament Island as they sat in her car facing the outer harbor's sparsely lighted western shore, which descended from Tansy Hill to the headland that eclipsed the butt of South Parish like a reclining thigh, he contrived with a kind of self-mockery to loosen the cloth of her unresisting bosom and expose a dune of bare skin as taut and soft as a maiden's.

Reckless in a prolonged sweetness that transcended the bounds of mere sense, she kept postponing her duty to restart the car and get home to her double bed. Caleb felt her sighs as but a taste of the comprehensive moan to which her grownup man was probably habituated, but they seemed instinct with love exclusively for himself.

They saw nothing of the waning moon just arisen over the Foreside's hip behind their backs. The sky before them was closing with high chilled clouds that would have been dismal to separated lovers who couldn't touch at all. Shortly before she was called back to time by the automatic ship's bell ringing a half-hour on the peak of the D N T his lips tenderly scanned the delicate repristinated bud that had suckled his daughter, without remembering that he'd callowly shared a more sensual past with that whole body. Even in the dim light that diffused its way into their vale of darkness from the Neck's last street lamp he could see almost nothing of the gleaming beauty he made obeisance to, because he had so rucked up her clothes under his nose that she had to laugh.

In an interval of elliptical conversation she had compared her inferior employments of recent years to his "wonderful life of austere self-discipline". Happily nestled in his arms to the right of the steering wheel, she murmured the comment with no trace of regret or selfpity. His thoughts and hers however were running upon different planes of common meaning. Thus, feigning levity, his voice husky with trepidation, he ventured to whisper the question of how long she ever suffered her parts to go without the kind of pacification he was deprived of. His tone was intended to leave such ingenuous curiosity open to interpretation as quizzing banter to which she might reply wittily, evasively, or not at all.

"It doesn't always have to be every night of the week." Her answer as always was light and frank, with the casually dismissive air of never before having considered such a childish question, but not without a tinge of something akin to amused self-discovery. But unless it leads to further troubles, her voice implied, it isn't worth talking about.

He laughed with mingled admiration and dismay, kissing her hair, her forehead, her nose, her ears, the side of her neck, and again and again and again, as if in celebration. She in turn kissed him on the mouth with a lingering vehemence that might have suggested a lunar sailor's farewell to him and all of Dogtown also; but he took it for exactly the reverse, and returned it with rising hope.

Holding her like this, his confidence was disturbed by nothing she professed. "As for living, our servants will do that for us!" he quoted, accepting for the moment her dismissal of his jealousy.

The literal import of her reply was suppressed by his joy in their cerebral intimacy, by which he was persuaded that he had now outstripped all other contenders for first place in her most inner history. Since he was too ashamed to ask pointblank about merely secondary atonements in her present life he would await voluntary or accidental disclosures in the future. (Yes, he was unable to believe that there might not be a future!) Meanwhile he intended to concentrate on the past four years in attempting to understand her soul's sexual essence.

But all inquiries were peripheral. Concupiscence itself sometimes almost evaporated in the immediate fever of love from which it had romantically condensed. And his caloric matter was often cooled by unnatural precipitation into words of many many pages—though they whirled and magnified his vortex as he wrote them—a dissipative process of solidification. Then his temperature abated for a few hours. And when he forgot himself in work at the Lab. His theoretical love never wavered; he always approved the cause of his agitation: but his awareness of it advanced and receded even in the frustration of its natural expression.

Whenever the sense of her existence suddenly illuminated the objects of Creative Mind he rejoiced in the access of sweet spiritual lust that tingled the fossorial extremity of his loins, inflaming it like an arrow shot from the bow of Aphrodite's son. At other times, though perhaps not actively seeking surrogation for Lilian's "parts" (despite her disinterested encouragement to do so), he was prepared by Homunculus to offer himself as a willing opportunist in the open market that for the likes of him was very thin. Meanwhile for many weeks the fluctuations of continuous love were cyclically progressive, not always with the need for sublimation of greater and greater heat, but with a generally rising level of residual disturbance and an increasing tendency to forsake rational philosophy. Not that he cared about his health. To youth a fever seems not very dangerous. No attempt is made to estimate the consequences of excitement. As vision is acuated, apperception is gladly beclouded.

On her part Lilian never complained of her unremitting responsibilities or her chronic deficit of sleep. It was only to explain her unpredictable decisions to risk meetings with him that she sometimes mentioned her anger at Gil for unspecified abuse, her contempt for his motives, her disgust at his selfishness, or her annoyance at his obtuse indifference to the normal plight of females. "It's true that I'm a sullied woman. But this morning he called me a fucking bitch." she calmly remarked.

Caleb began to wonder if some of the battering was more brutal than verbal only.

"Gil's had marriage twice or more, and some approximation to it many times over. He's one of those charming men that go around plowing up the topsoil, leaving it behind to erode in dry wind and heavy rain. Without harrowing or cultivation, it's just cropless rotation as they go on to break ground elsewhere. I'm not talking about fields for sowing and reaping; I'm saying it's their own pasturage they lay waste. They never get to know a woman, even their own wife."

(Whence the metaphors of farming? Was she reading an agricultural novel? Else whose influence? The Yahi of the Cordillera were forest hunters and gatherers, diggers at the most. Gil Algo himself was a city boy. There must have been an agrarian lover somewhere between the coasts, or maybe a soil scientist; even a professor of anthropological geography. . . .)

Now Caleb's time with Lilian was so scant that he usually refrained from pursuing dialogue that did not directly further his most exigent desire or distant reward. But this time it was for her sake that he wailed an indiscrete response: "Then why in the hell do you stay with him?"

She wasn't nonplussed but she had to stop and think. He regretted his question, that it might oblige her to plead meretricious reasons, or to tell an outright lie. Her answer was unexpected, and shamed himself. "I suppose it's because he straightens me out inside. Sticking to him is my easy virtue. My bottom seems to need a man more than it did before I was an independent mother."

Thereby Caleb was shockingly referred to his craving for the sensations channeled under her spine. He trembled with a redoubled anguish of fundamental deprivation. For also her reply recalled the lancination of her sympathetic repartee on an earlier occasion: that she was sorry circumstances kept him from sensing how much she'd "improved" since having his baby. Even as he now continued to taste and trace her accessible integument with the naive satisfaction of a boy believing himself doomed to ignorance of the ultimate information, he strove to remember in detail the peculiar avidity of the one already parous woman he'd known in the flesh (—one of the three Cornucopians who were to conceive in vivo a daughter more than probably half his own). Yet mostly he tormented himself with imaginations of the programmer's physique, whom she'd once mentioned in passing as "tall and rangy".

Still, apparently, he could be thankful that her own memory didn't dwell upon the words suggesting former and recurrent moods of Sister Ass. In Caleb's presence at least she seemed to regard as unremarkable the very essentials of her liaison with Gil. Thus she now went on to tell him what was on her mind primarily.

"He keeps bringing up this adoption business."

Something else that Caleb had forgotten, though putatively of more concern to him! Why should the ladykiller she adumbrated want so much to take possession of an unknown man's child? It seemed such a bizarre or phoney motive on that lover's part that her previous mention of it had prompted only an inassimilable pang, soon forgotten (among so many others) as insignificant, inasmuch as paternity was never one of his own desiderations. Now however it dawned on him with a kind of defensive pride that a hateful arrogant alien was perhaps about to make him (the blackguard) consider the child he had sired.

In this case she offered an explanation. "Because I won't marry him. He says he wants to see that she has a normal childhood. It makes me angry."

"I thought you said he was moving out."

"Now he intends to stay."

Once again Caleb repressed his interrogation, concealed his confusing pain. He had no right to ask questions, still less to advise. But he waited in vain for her to tell him more about the domestication she was suffering. And at last he began to wonder if with Gil it was wild suffering of a certain equivocal kind that she was not averse to. She had never denied every kind of love for her captor, nor that she could love two men at once.

As for himself, almost from their new beginning in Dogtown he had taken advantage of inconstancies and inconsistencies in her rules and prohibitions. He had learned how to disregard them, up to a point, with impunity. Whenever she didn't seem to remember her own proscription of his company or communication he had chosen to take his little success as proof of a unique ascendancy in the conflicts of her heart. Though there was nothing nebulous about Lilian Cloud he finally perceived that her rational and even-tempered dicta produced ideas no better in train with each other than those from Uncle Toby's fitful smoke-jack. Like a faint false dawn when he wasn't even looking for the morning, there arose in the back of his consciousness an unreliable hint of more profound difficulties in her constitution.

But troubadours on otherwise delightful nights always put out of mind a little longer the harbinger of cold daylight. There are kisses at hand, and more urgent subjects to touch upon, and very few minutes left for anything. Yet this dim auspice prepared him for disquieting doubts about the simple authenticity of romantic love—which in their case must complicate itself with many levels of irony before it passed beyond "the condition of fire".

But whether or not a dismal day now approached, it was sure enough that by the time her purview had changed from Golden Horn Bay to Vinland she herself had molted from duck to swan. Often as he might forget the girl he'd known before, and known with all the intimacy possible for a passage of youth, he marveled at the difference between what she had been or seemed and what she now was or seemed. Yet by sharing with him two points in spacetime she seemed to have become half like himself. That extraordinary frisson of perspective piqued the mental attraction that infused his animal desire with an almost incestuous thrill.

This new woman spoke of her interregnal history only in terms of I or We—herself her mother and her daughter—without reference to third persons, goading his scholarly urge to trace her other intimacies. Whereas at the time of their first love he had felt little curiosity about any of her emotional past that wasn't immediately associated with her response to himself, he now ravened for knowledge not only of her subsequent liaisons (so tantalizingly obscure—with his old friend Dave Wilson and nameless others, Western and Midwestern) as a selfsupporting unwed mother fiercely devoted to her child, but also of her erotic sensibility in the years of nonage before he himself had debauched her.

At Caleb's age four years past was long ago. He scarcely remembered the maiden painter-girl. She had called him Caliber; he had dubbed her Studio Lady of the Lilypad, his "one-man art show—artist and model", teasing her as a "neolithic bohemian from the High Cordillera". The diffident nonconformist had now become an efficient leader; her feminine mansuetude seemed to have grown into the unassertive mastery that she said was her "delayed manhood"; and indeed her person seemed less thoroughly female, even in the purely feminine condition of motherhood.

But had her psyche therewith adapted itself to a condition really renunciatory of fine art? Three weeks earlier she had spoken of setting up a loom in Gil's attic, and of her intention to learn how to make a practical art of weaving in her spare time; but tactfully he'd asked no more about it. He knew she had no spare time, and the attic was probably still too cold from winter. Several times she'd assured him with a laugh that she remained devoted to "art of one kind or another" as her "ultimate objective"—in face of her conviction that "being a woman and being an artist is impossible". But even then he'd dimly feared that she was only vainly denying to herself the possibility of addictive adaption to the narcosis of banausic success.

By his present calculation the only constant was Mooney, and it was Mooney that had changed her, body and soul: Mooney's head extruded from her pelvis, Mooney's neuroendocrinal afteraffect; but Mooney herself as the child of whom the love passed all understanding, whose welfare was the final cause. Yet instead of growing thicker and softer like many a matron, or self-sacrificial in attitude toward her extra-maternal interests, Lilian had grown both lither and more generally libidinous—under ironically goodhumored self-control!

So it was a new inamorata that the Caleb the stranger was in love with. Accordingly, the more he marveled at her semblance of steadily rational competence, and her inversely proportional seriousness about the things of art that she had apparently put away, the less he could imagine any benign outcome of the satisfaction that headed the list of all his wants from moon or sun. On the other hand her swift short flights of exciting speech sometimes baffled him. Were they deeply meant, or only capricious experiments with syntax in accord with a mood of the moment, accidentally misleading or ambiguous? There was never time for exploratory dialectic.

Was it merely a hazard of fancifully concise words, under the glamour of her renewed admirer's worship, that once when she'd forgotten what her "baggage" was, anticipating the exhilaration of finally freeing herself from Master Gilbert, she'd remarked to Caleb that she would teach Mooney to call him godfather. "That's what you really are to her. Her ghostly father."

For an instant of intuition his heart had leapt at the inference of a part for him in her future. But immediately it paused in horror at another reading: the sudden totally unprecedented notion of having been hitherto deceived, and for no apparent gain, by the woman in whose fearless honesty his faith was all but absolute.

No, nevertheless, not at all! He accepted her reticence and honored the secrets she kept from him, but such a crucial deception—even though unknown to him in that distant past as an occurrence about which he was deceivable (and of which he had only recently been informed)—was out of the question! Now recurring to his inner ear, "ghostly father" seemed nothing more than a negligent oxymoron, a play of words with some ambiguously anagogic meaning at the worst. Unless she had simply forgotten (as he himself still almost always did) that the troubadour she addressed was the same roguish rake who'd knocked her up by the carnal method?

Indeed, as far as that old event was concerned (if one joust could be singled out from their spated tournaments of chance), at another time she had declared the risk of it was her own option, after having always theretofore armed herself à plaisance, out of sight, refusing homunculus bated à outrance. "I undertook my own defense. There came a time to drop my shield. Whereupon I chose to remain out there among my savages as your Fayaway. You are guilty of nothing, and I'm happy you make no claim. Mooney is no more your responsibility than all those babies you planted in strange women via vitro."

Caleb was somewhat surprised to suspect ambivalence in her embarrassing reminder of the sordidly tamed oats he had sown so meretriciously at the Annunciator Laboratories sperm bank in Hume. He who had conscientiously fulfilled that engendering contract for calculated piece-work wages was then for four years callously ignorant of what he'd unwittingly begotten gratis in vivo. In those days she'd teased him as her "superfluous banker". Once more he recalled Michael Chapman's intonation from the Michaelmas gospel: "Woe unto the world because of offences! for it must needs be that offences come; but woe to that man by whom the offence cometh!"

At the same time he was glad to be reassured of his absolution. Once more she was confirming his natural delight in her indulgent attitude toward his contribution to her fatherless daughter's joyfully welcomed existence, whether mishap or not.

But how much did Gil Algo know about the origin of the child he wished to adopt? Quite apart from that gross query: Did he know anything about a Caleb Karcist either in Cornucopia or in Vinland? The inquirer couldn't bring himself to ask. The night of the D N T ended with these questions troubling the sweetness of his sleep.

*

In a briefer car-seat meeting soon after one of her violent quarrels at home, Lilian told Caleb that she had confessed to Algo her "interest in a another man". The information apparently jolted her oppressor. Caleb's nostrils flared at a little whiff of success. But, as usual, in the moral delicacy of his position as an unpromising interloper, he dared not question or crossquestion this voluntary news. In any case, before giving way to the intense curiosity that might sour the mix of exultation and danger churning in his chest, he was once again well advised to ponder for a while the implication of her quiet words. Maybe he'd still add more to his stock of truth simply by keeping his ears open.

Yet Caleb very nearly asked if she'd made her statement to Gil before or after he'd decided "to stay"; and before or after he'd renewed his demand to adopt her daughter. Lilian's candid remarks seldom offered subordinate temporal clauses. If told no more than that there was a new cloud on his title, and assuming that she had never favored him with the identification of former lovers, was it possible for the man to have guessed from his side of her curtain the fantastically improbable Dogtown connection to anonymous scraps of diachronistic transcontinental confession?

When she spoke calmly of cutting her hair again, already bereft of its longest tresses, Caleb trembled at the enormity of her agitation.

Then one night just before leaving her work at the Doghouse she unexpectedly telephoned to say she would pick him up for a few minutes on her way home. He was unshaven and unbathed—disquieted with himself and a little frightened at her hasty vehemence, as if Dogtown was about to have a midnight earthquake. "I'm too smelly to sit very close to you!" he warned. But how could he refuse his heart's desire? Any chance at all might be his last.

"Don't worry. I've been in a sweat all day myself. I'm not a woman of sugar and spice."

But it turned out otherwise. This time she parked down in the shadow of the Iron Works, where they could see the watchman before he saw them, should he have ventured from the irreducible red gloom of his airy vaulted bakery. (It was the first time Caleb had visited the place without Ibi.) The Doghouse kitchen had closed a little earlier than usual, and she was confident that Gil wouldn't call the restaurant during the half hour she assigned to Caleb.

But there was more to this bonanza for Caleb than an awaited opportunity, which she might have contrived before the last moment.

She explained her astonishing initiative as an unaccountable impulse. That evening, busy on her feet, without warning she had been overcome by the desire to see and touch the only true man, who lived in a true world. She demanded his kisses, and seemed to relish his shaggy goatish stink, which was only partially neutralized by the last-minute saturation of masculine anointments.

But it also turned out that she had something to tell him, rather proudly. "I've written you a letter." she vouchsafed at last, curled like a cat in his arms, giving joyful pause to his palpable bliss.

Seeing that she was happy and contented at the moment (except for her sympathy with the dielectric frustration of his potentiality), he guessed that her written message would contain no ill news; and that it was something more than a token response to his insufferable entreaties for her handwriting.

At home afterwards he tried not to hope for better or fear for worse than he already possessed. But what could she have written, if not either a declaration of love or an ultimatum? (From her no irony was inconceivable.) Perhaps only answers to some of his least important questions. And how would she salute him? How would she sign herself? It never occurred to him to dread a letter expressing nothing of more interest than such commonplace terms and superficial observations as were expected of wartime girls to bolster the morale of their boyfriends at sea.

No mail arrived at $165^1/_3$ Cod Street for the next two days. He was able to contain his impatience at the poor postal service only by bitterly reminding himself that when all the khaki mailboxes were repainted patriotic blue Eisenhower had taken the Post Office Department out of the cabinet (contrary to the clear intent of the Constitution) and half desocialized it.

But he wrote another of his own troubadour letters anyway, very nearly apologizing for having implored her reply to its predecessors, almost remorseful for having been so unreasonably importunate that she adopt his best mode of communication. The familiar burden of it was:

> Alas, I ne have no langage to telle
> Th'affectes ne the torments of myn helle.

Then he suffered the disappointments of a whole weekend, despite the fact that Protesticans in Washington hadn't succeeded in eliminating Saturday deliveries. Yet on Monday still no letter! And day by day the week went by in agonies of doubt—moral doubt, logical doubt, empirical doubt—philosophical scientific and psychological doubt. He was baffled, angry, disillusioned to his depths. Anguish hardened his heart. Her letter never arrived.

6
TABLET ONE

[Between dawn and sunrise. The square in front of Gilgamesh's headquarters.]

Enter Widows,
sauntering.

    WIDOW 1   A Widow praying to get pregnant! Don't you realize what it means to get expelled? Where's your self-respect when you've lost the emoluments and perquisites of College? You'll be out of the cold into the frozen. I tell you this dearth of work is just a time of passing troubles!

    WIDOW 2   Passing troubles! What's passing are the ways handed down from heaven by the Lord God Enlil! I've heard the next thing Giszax wants to change is time itself!

    WIDOW 1   How could he change the seasons of women? We shall outlive him. It's the worst of times for us to act capricious!

    WIDOW 2   My vocation isn't strong enough to endure depression. What's the joy in an easy life if there aren't as many worshippers as couches? Don't preach to me about my career!

The trouble is I like too much what we all profess. I can't be content with mere gestures of what we're here for! Under Giszax's yoke the clients of Inanna are as wilted as our sun-stroked bulls and rams. Bonded marriage is better than watered-down religious life—if I can land some crippled smith or leach who won't be drafted, or a boy with the enthusiasm not yet sweated out of him by godless labor! I'll earn my wrinkles spinning flax for an only child and at least half a man.

WIDOW 1   A helot's life is hell. You'll make a sorry housewife. Domestic wool is frayed before it's woven. And you're mistaken if you think Inanna will bless desertion. But say you do squeeze out one live baby: you can't expect a sister or a brother for her—when all the life around grows barren from our conquering savior's love of sacrilege!

WIDOW 2   While you sit by and watch Lil-Amin weave herself a dole of bitterest humiliation. I'm tired of weeping for our own queen confined to tapestries—while a self-appointed shah usurps the prerogatives of gods! For seven years her moons have come and gone—and still she's our priest in name alone. Giszax might as well have walled her up with bricks!

WIDOW 1   But the Rector's spindle isn't yet unwound! Soon he'll seize back the Rod and Ring. In fact, I just heard—

WIDOW 2   I wouldn't mind the family way at all. I'd like to get to really know a man—maybe even one of Giszax's palefaced falangists . . .

WIDOW 1   But listen to this—

WIDOW 2   You always listen to those hoaxes on ourselves. What kind of oracle can be brought to pass by gossip? You should have given up hope when Giszax took the warhead off his axe and proclaimed himself our peacemaker. It appears that peace consists of a law and order that tampers with the language, doctors our numbers, and desecrates our calendar. Better be at war than have our unison deranged. No sacrifice by the Rector will ever again raise my hope against a willful king who's made him fix our planting by the sun. Giszax's hideous obsessions darken the streets and regiment the waters.

Enter Troopers, unobserved, listening to the Widows.

WIDOW 1   Inanna will send us a champion! I'm telling you—

WIDOW 2	Oh please excuse me! I thought you were going to say the goddess herself, on second thought, would strike him dead! —Oh, oh! Don't look up. The Kassites are spying again!
TROOPER 1	Our forbidden fruit off guard!
TROOPER 2	If it ain't the bachelor girls bewailing their famine! Such sad song was never heard.
TROOPER 1	Hello, miladies! Are your coffers empty?
WIDOW 1	Did I hear hyenas yapping?
WIDOW 2	It's only the melting snowmen. From time to time they make attempts at speech.
TROOPER 2	They forget we saved their honor from the Elamites. Chivalry is but a trifle in this depraved witchburg!
TROOPER 1	We could cheer you up, bellibones!
WIDOW 1	No matter how long they study Uruk, these hillbillies will never be anything but unconscionable barbarians.
TROOPER 1	Un-con-shun-a-bul? Sounds like illegal woman-talk.
TROOPER 2	Or one of the Captain's words. We must be as uncouth as they say we are.
WIDOW 1	I could excuse simple ignorance, but not willful stupidity. They can't tell cashmere from earthenware. Ridiculous Chanticleers, to strut the ramparts crowing all their smut!
WIDOW 2	They do seem hardly chaste. But maybe where they come from—
WIDOW 1	Uncircumcised boars, bragging about their stinkhorns! But from what I hear on the outside, when it comes to business, these flagging dildoes only peck and bolt.
TROOPER 1	You must have a sweet-tooth somewhere, little jailbait!
WIDOW 1	I don't dote on fungus, and I've never had a yen for albino-livered chalk-skinned turnkeys.
TROOPER 1	It's not by choice we're on penal duty. And you're wrong if you guess I'm white all over. Want to see, Miss Bigot?
WIDOW 1	I know all about these parade-ground sharks: they're shrimps in battle. Superannuated striplings! They come and go with the stamina of rotten bananas. Doughboys reared on halfbaked underleavened bread. It's a poor brave

	that proves his manhood by the scalps he's left alive. The kind that shoots on sight but leaves his victim tossing!
WIDOW 2	Perhaps they need a governess. My grandmother said that pioneers who only plow never learn to sow and reap.
TROOPER 2	I'd be happy to have the harvest of your tutoring.
WIDOW 2	It's only right that what is torn should not be left unmended.
TROOPER 1	If Gilgamesh would let me, I'd show you how bowmen till shrewish whores sodden with their cultivation!
WIDOW 1	The bombastic hounds of Giszax are yapping on the leash! Let's go, before the feathered shuttlecocks work themselves into a lather and dribble out their curdless scum.

Enter Norkid.

TROOPER 1	There's always some battledore to sour a man's pearls.
TROOPER 2	You there, don't scowl! Ishtar bids you love her gifts.
WIDOW 2	I never said I hated them.
WIDOW 1	The bluster of slavedrivers doesn't faze me—but Our Lady preserve us from lewd insolence!

Widows leave.

TROOPER 2	I like the way she walks. A man should be allowed to measure his place with a woman he can get to know. Kids and all.
NORKID [Coming forward.]	At it again, yardbirds? You can't win a war of words with female churchwardens. The ways of our fathers are forever accursed to Messpot mothers. —*Fall* IN!
TROOPERS [Forming up in front of Norkid after a little shuffle.]	*Let them sing about their law,* *But clip the doxies' tooth and claw.* *Stitch their backbone to the mat* *And make them purr like a pussycat!*
NORKID	You cherry-pickers have nothing to gripe about. In my day a dogface would give all his pay for your fatigue duty, cracking the crotch of maidens. —*At-ten*-TION! —You royal guards have nothing to do at night but pluck the rosebuds—while your king takes the watch alone. Gilgamesh stays awake and you get all the sleep!
TROOPER 2	Poor Gilgamesh. He stays awake to think, and never takes the spoils. His nostrils flare no longer.

TROOPER 1	I didn't enlist to police a gang of bricklayers. An engineering king has turned me into a clerk-of-the-works!	
NORKID	I'll clerk your works! —*Dress it up* now! —There was a time when you were glad enough for all that tender meat. It made up for lack of plunder. But now you're billeted like gentry, you bitch all day because you're not allowed the common mess. —*A-bout*-FACE!	
TROOPER 1	The common mess is too rich for its brokendown hod-carriers, while all the military gets is uncooked veal—if the Rector doesn't consecrate it first!	
NORKID	You used to say variety's the spice of life.	

[Continuing the drill with various commands.]

TROOPER 1	Fucking little variety in a bushel of green apples! At least on payday I ought to get a bite that's ripe.
TROOPER 2	On these rations a man gets old with nothing but firstborn kids he can't even claim are his. I'd give a year's crop of pullets for one off-limits hen.
TROOPER 1	First they squeal, then they bleat. Long black eyelashes full of reproach because we didn't deliver the great swoon they've whispered about since their teats began to swell.
NORKID	*Company* HALT! —Graduation's just commencement.
TROOPER 2	Not for us. We get the girls, but we're not allowed to fraternize with women! We're always starting over. We get the sting so some farmhand can collect the honey!
NORKID	Even on archers in this vale of tears some rain must fall. —*Half-left*-FACE! —You could try a hunger strike.
TROOPER 1	A lion in the cage can't turn up his nose at the daily feed of jackal-food.
TROOPER 2	Who can resist the flowers of spring? It's the foretaste that keeps you ravenous.
NORKID [Marching them back and forth.]	Even to me, aged and infirm, it's superhuman, how Gilgamesh fights shy of the world's most undeflowered queen—absolutely at his mercy!
TROOPER 1	Now there's a lure to cheerful death! Long legs and inborn talent! How can he keep his distance from the parthenon? I sometimes wonder if he's lost his orchids.
NORKID	Why a king might want to keep his cast is beyond the understanding of cacoethical billygoats.

TROOPER 1   There he goes again! But I guess I can guess what it means.

TROOPER 2   If Lil-Amin is not his caste, who for god's sake is?

NORKID   *Pre-sent* ARMS!

TROOPER 1   Long arms or short arms?

NORKID   Any more of your lip and I'll present my hammy fist to you! —*Pa-rade* REST! Your style was sharper when ass was scarce.

TROOPERS
[Shuffling their feet.]

While we work this female city
We'll never know a woman's pity.
So we take the duty with the burden
And settle for the schoolgirl guerdon.

NORKID
[Motioning them through the routine of target practice.]

Things began to get out of kilter when Gilgamesh unstepped his iron eagle with its twin thin lips. Without that axe, before long we'll be fighting with our backs to the winding stairs. —You need more work on form. That's what counts in getting up your speed. To put down a mob, six seconds a shot is much too slow. They must be more quickly reminded of our feathered wood.

TROOPER 1   Inside walls, strings don't make good music! You should be leading us in the sword dance.

NORKID   Swords won't terrify the middle of a crowd. You can talk back after you've learnt how to shoot around corners: meanwhile you've got to stretch your range. Step back another yard.

TROOPER 1   My funnybone's already bumping the wall!

NORKID   I'll put in for your decoration: Knight of the Humerus.

TROOPER 1   Don't make me laugh.

NORKID   Tonight you can cry in your beer. Right now, show me your feathers in the bullseye. You're not past pluperfect yet.

TROOPERS   *Draw that arrow,*
Nock the string.
Loose your shaft
And make it sing!
One, two, three, four—
Back tomorrow to drill some more!

NORKID   Let's *go*, let's GO! You're slower than the pole star.

TROOPER 2	We were young when we followed Gilgamesh down from the north on some vague summons of the night wind to raise a siege of strangers. No one can say the gods didn't warn us. Our shields were too full of holes to float; he led us across the Tigris on wineskins. At first this whole irrigation district welcomed us like a pantheon of liberators. I thought we'd take home their gold, and odalisks to boot!
TROOPER 1	Instead we smother to death in garrison while he spends his time inventing calendars and designing public works. Anyway, what's the tower for? An island for the second coming of their Flood? To watch their enemies from afar? Or to see more stars? Well we can make them tote and stack the bricks, but they won't man it on their own. They think mortals are forbidden to see more than a mile at a time!
Enter Gilgamesh, unobserved, with headless axe-handle in one hand.	
TROOPER 2	Gilgamesh can see near and far without a stepladder. I don't see why he should build a tower for gods that hate him.
TROOPER 1	If only he'd keep his mind on the military problem!
NORKID	My military problem is to keep his stormtroopers from going soft, so that by time he's ready to remount his double-bite you'll still be able to hit a temple door. If you're not up to the mark in a little sport like this, you can't expect to save your pampered skins wee-wee-wee all the way home. So there you have your answer: The tower's a refuge for aging archers against a host of pitchforks!
TROOPERS	*Why did our proud demented king* *Accept from them their Rod and Ring?* *Why pile a mountain on the plain* *To raise on high Lord Enlil's fane?*
NORKID	Let's secure this pisspoor muster. Don't let me keep you from your bossing. Go call the roll of masons! Take up up your lash! The sooner you top that topless tower off, the better we can hope to return to our life of honorable violence. —*Fall* OUT! On the double now! Don't keep the labor battalion standing around.
TROOPER 1	Hurry up, he says! Hurry up and wait!
TROOPER 2	Hurry up the heavy looking-on! Wait for the pace-setter!
[Troopers unhurriedly prepare to leave.]	

GILGAMESH   Well, well: my elite guard all alert and fresh in the morning dew! A moonstruck nightwalker can surprise them even after sunrise!

[Menacing them mockingly with his axe-handle.]

TROOPERS   *A pace or two, and turn.*
Up the stairs and down.
We fiddle on our bows
To pacify this town!

Troopers go out hastily, dancing like sentries.

NORKID   Police duty makes simple soldiers ironical. But you already knew that. Your wide ear takes in from most to least.

GILGAMESH   Your Kassites have wide mouths.

NORKID   I confess they're not cut out for marshalling civilians harmlessly. I'm a little stir-crazy myself. It's been seven years since we've seen a real rock or a mountain. The Sea-Land marshes get a little boring.

GILGAMESH   Be of good cheer: you'll soon have foreign intelligence to amuse you. Eber's spit-and-images are sailing in from the desert with salt and other cargo.

NORKID   Begging your pardon: Hip, hip, hurray for all the excitement.

GILGAMESH   I'd have thought you'd get excited about the failure of your guard to spot their dust before I happened to.

NORKID   You know I don't have enough men for idle masthead watch.

GILGAMESH   Then be glad of these Eberew reinforcements.

NORKID   We don't need a cavalry of merchants. But I hope the peaceloving straightlaced Bactrian-drivers can defend themselves at least.

Enter Eber.

GILGAMESH   They wear shortswords under their veils. —Here's Eber now. If it weren't for this colleague, dear Norkid, where would all my engineering be? He's factored all the timber and stone, and rafted the lintels down river on their own joists!

NORKID   It was your suggestion, sir.

GILGAMESH   Now he's imported our most obscure necessity. Who else would have known that salt could cure sweatiness in men and skinniness in cattle? I had thought we could dispense with trade, once we'd stocked some soapstone and cedar!

EBER	As your humble servants my sons were everywhere received like magi. Your seal made them wizards of finance. From sea to sea, the name of Gilgamesh opened the door of every countinghouse and caravansary.
GILGAMESH	My vizier of budgets and accounts is a catholic statesman.
EBER	As your minister I've refrained from censure of the customs here. Have I not dealt justly with all the people?
GILGAMESH	Yes, yes, I always praise your jurisprudence too.
EBER	It used to be that no one ever tried to revive a poor man when he died, because the life he lost wasn't worth retaining. Now he's hired at twice his worth, gets his bread at cost, and pays no taxes. And, for fallow years to come, have I not filled the granaries by collecting from the rich—while by my hand fixed weights and measures have brought confidence to business? Further, sir, no man has found waste or ostentation in my disbursements from your treasury.
NORKID	One complaint I've never heard is that the king entertains too lavishly, or that his comptroller pays any bill too soon.
EBER	Yet even now, as we unload freight for the commonwealth, the marketplace grows silent with suspicion. Ever since you tied back the Rector's hand in favor of my office, and took his tithes for the state, poison has been percolating. In the warmest of hearts there's a cold spot for Eber and his tribe. My job is less than thankless.
GILGAMESH	You've told me that virtue is its own reward. . . . But call an assembly! I'll proclaim my gratitude for the way you've civilized my laws. The announcement of my project to raise Euphrates to the level of the Tigris, and give the farmers navigation by canal, will be a good occasion to tell all Erech that it's from you I learned to plan!
EBER	Please! My gracious leader—if he values my remaining service, or my life—will spare me public honors. Especially while informing the people of hydraulic engineering still in store for them.
NORKID	He's all too right, sir! Don't ignite the sullen sedition in this hagridden warren of male women and female men.
GILGAMESH	But even the stubble shows how good their harvests are! The grain hung heavy as peas. We've given them bread as well as walls. And when I've shown them how to feed the world, the arts will celebrate my name!

EBER   Not if you don't anticipate the treachery of their slithering pope. He decries burgeoning yields as portents of famine, waterways as highroads for the enemy, and architecture as an insult to religion! He has the city festering with venom.

NORKID   Any spurious flare of grievance and the simmer comes to boil!

EBER   Against a spider's web, halfway measures always fail. If you don't root out that dancing-master's cult, they'll lay waste all your works the day you die—which may come sooner than necessary. Put down that bawd! Disband the College! Stamp out their rites! Pronounce an edict *now*!

GILGAMESH   Am I a petty edic-tator? Let him be. This is not an ill-bred people. Let's open their eyes, not tear them out. It's not wisdom to call for force against the peace they make for love.

EBER   Love! There's no love here for me and mine. The day will come when my posterity can't be saved by the memory of your power. Better that I shake this clay from my feet right now.

GILGAMESH   I hold you to your word! Stay you must, a while. Without you here as my diplomatic secretary-bird, Norkid and I would have been vipered to death before our second year! I've not asked you to put fealty to me above your fear of the whirlwind God—any more than I've expected the Rector to forswear his Ishtar, or the Kassites not to pluck the dates they're offered. Remember your own words: El-Shaddai sometimes uses even Gentile means. His promise of green pastures for your seed will be kept through me because it is my promise to you to seek and grant them. Well you know also that I'd bless your sons if my offences against heaven weren't so likely to bring them curses down instead. —Meanwhile, let the city's godown reward its faithful purveyors for something more than risk at profit. Take for your own account any seven camel-loads—except lumber, stone, or arms. —Now then, bring the new copper to my furnace. Pay the Kassites with gold: it may bolster their confidence in my sagacity. —In order to avoid needless irritation, your sons will pitch their tents outside the gate.

NORKID   Sir! You're tempting providence! What's to stop them from decamping?

GILGAMESH Have no fear. Eber will remain inside with us. From him springs all their motive, while in them lies all his hope. We have mutual hostages to our alliance. It takes all three of us friends to build up this city.

Gilgamesh goes out.

EBER For whatever time Adonai wills that we remain in league, may we shorten the arm's length that's been between us in our past already. In the stables you will find as token of my accumulated gratitude a string of war-horses, procured by my travelers for your brave phalanx that until now has had to keep the peace on foot alone.

NORKID On fame alone, more like. You know I have no property to offer as my thanks—beyond a certain reputation for stout alliance. Your boys can tell us if foreigners have gotten wind of the fact that we grow fewer with age, or that in my retirement from action I've become a professor of military science—specializing in parades!

[Bowing.]

EBER With chariots you can dominate the streets.

NORKID Come to the hall tonight. I invite all your men and mine. Beer and mutton—feasting to the limit Gilgamesh allows. I'm afraid there'll be no dancing girls.

EBER We shall discuss harnesses, and various routes to the land of milk and honey.

Eber and Norkid go out together, laughing softly.

7
LANGUEDOC

*E*arly one Saturday afternoon Caleb was annoyed by the ring of his telephone just as he got warmed up at his typewriter with his third cup of coffee. Nearly all such interruptions were mistakes in dialing (an unfamiliar requirement of daily living in Dogtown, where until recently all users were still relying upon the skills and courtesies of personal operators at the central exchange behind the Lyceum on Dogfish Street), or charity solicitations ostensibly public-spirited in motive. Such intrusions were especially annoying at the outset of weekend solitude, when he was still struggling to shake off the hopes memories and anxieties of his private life that stood between his will and its freedom of action.

Nowadays, making the sudden sound seem all the harsher, he was compelled by his private goddess to have devoted his sweetest time, with the first cup, right after his run with Ibi, long before breakfast, to the catharsis of moonstruck handwriting. That expression of energy had usurped the rest of the morning as he flexed most of his fingers in exorcism of Lilian's obstinate reality and thereby restored his pleasure in the labor of proving his imagination. Now at last his will was just beginning to realize the satisfactory inertia of objective motion.

But this interruption was a pleasant surprise. Composing himself as he quickly corrected the testy tone in which he'd answered the ring, he decided that the matter might be worth scotching a day's work (provided he lived as long as he hoped to). It was Buck Barebones, in a spirit of the kind that sometimes put Caleb's selfish soul to shame.

"I'm sorry to bother you, but if you can spare the time I have something to show you." said the inventor, speaking at his quiet machine shop on the day of the week that he most nearly had to himself. He was not a man ever to say he was never too busy for a friend, but he was. That the professionally acclaimed toolmaker who earned a living for his expensive family on an insecure margin of the industrial world should take the time for any reason at all to communicate with a young nobody who occupied a world which could be of no intrinsic interest to him was more than enough to oblige instant acceptance of the diffident invitation.

But in the event Caleb's noetic heart was rewarded with peculiar exultation, for when he and Ibi got down to the premises of Dogtown Machine & Design, across the tracks from the Iron Works, Buck presented him with a triangulated analysis of the cube. The benevolent older man, wearing an oil-stained machinist's apron, stopped puttering around the atelier emptied of employees to hand Caleb a six-inch-square box constructed of paperboard salvaged from shipping cartons. Diagonal seams equally divided each of its sides. It felt little heavier than hollow, but the shape and heft of it inspired stereognostic confidence in its compressive strength: an ideally fungible brick of specific gravity just great enough to keep it in place when there was no wind. Caleb would have liked hundreds of them to build an anchored tower with.

Buck stood looking humbly down his big nose at the odd little intellectual he and his wife were becoming quite fond of. "Just corrugated paper, but it makes a model to start with."

In the pattern-making corner of his shop he had cut out a dozen congruent six-inch isosceles right triangles and with cellophane adhesive tape fashioned triplets of them perpendicular to each other, joined at their common trihedral right angle. These four hollow corners were each closed with a facing equilateral triangle, thereby forming a trilateral pyramid—which, *when stood on one of its faces*, was asymmetrically tense in three dimensions and immensely promising to the hand and eye of a constructive mind. Buck the synthesist of more than five centuries' mechanical devices had occupied himself with such simplicity only for Caleb's sake.

He had then fitted together the individual pyramids with bits of drafting tape to make a single cube of the complementary corners: an internally braced regular rectoparallelepiped—made up of "isorectotetrahedrons", as Caleb called the component shapes, or IRTHs.

At first glance of course Caleb didn't appreciate much of the geometrical fabrication, but presently he was to delight in it with a disinhibition worthy of Archimedes.

"Take it apart." said Buck. "See what you think."

Caleb peeled back the tags of tape by which the IRTHs had been fitted together face to face. The box fell apart like the shards of a mold—hatching a polyhedron which filled the residual space defining a matrix. Behold, the hollow paperboard baby, shaped by the internal facets of its partitioned shell, was delivered as perfectly regular, an ideal platonic cell!

"Eureka!" cried Caleb with a clap of his hands that excited Ibi's curiosity.

Cutting four more equilateral triangles identical to the ones that had been used as the sloping faces of the IRTHs, Buck had constructed a *regular* tetrahedron, the simplest conceivable straight-edged shape of space! For Caleb it was a three-dimensional Manx triskelion, Trinacria's tripodal jackstone without curve or bend! By handicraft and empirical geometry Buck had discovered a classic tetrahedron as the IRTH-cube's ventrical, concretely solving the puzzle that had been baffling Caleb's abstract imagination. This all-too-perfect egg was somewhat larger than the IRTHs, for it was cast from the great inward surface of each; but Caleb now felt with his hands and saw with his own eyes that four *Cartesian* IRTHs made a cubic volume if they cohered to a void of platonic deltas!

Caleb's astonishment at this joke on himself was a pleasure to last many days and often to be renewed.

After a few minutes of toying with the five tetrahedrons on the desk of the generous artificer (who was more interested in the inexplicable excitement he had aroused than in the symbolic functions that accounted for it) came Caleb's triumphant realization that his comparatively Aristotelian bias was vindicated by the fact that Plato's ideal form had been produced by technology! Thereupon he took the liberty of generalizing that the perfect a priori tetrahedron had been gestated by the same IRTH-pyramid that generates all the irrational quantities in trigonometric functions, gyres, and complex numbers, as well as the quadrants of all picture planes. He felt as if he and Buck had overturned the prejudice of platonic purity by an experiment in the laboratory! The priority of mathematical impurity was reaffirmed in his biased Weltanschauung—not merely analytically, but by synthesis! The ideal tetrahedron came a posteriori! He wanted to rush home and prove it to William Butler Yeats.

Caleb's gratitude to Buck was boundless when he was given the reassembled cube to take home in a paper bag for perpetual contemplation and inspiration. His jubilation relieved Buck of the deceptively simple production problem that he had originally undertaken so disinterestedly: the vexing question of a feasible method for turning out little IRTHS in a machine shop. (Cutting them from cubes of steel was his instinctive approach to the solution; it had led to the question of how many isorectotetrahedrons a perfect parallelepiped would yield, and whether or not there would be much waste.) Caleb's exaltation of the theoretical answer disburdened his own mind of the question which he had previously visited upon the proprietor of Dogtown M and D . He was happy to free his benefactor of any further trouble (unless he happened to think of some cheap way to produce solid IRTHs by the barrelful). They celebrated their intellectual success with drams of Scotch, while Ibi shared the amazingly animated good cheer of the gods by lapping more water from the guest pan.

*

That same Saturday night after supper Caleb and Ibi enthusiastically hastened not to address Yeats but as usual to go and thump trois coups with the staff on the planks of the landing outside Doctor Ipsissimus Charlemagne's door. Doc was aware of Buck's fame for innovative metalworking, besides understanding almost all figurations and fulgurations of the human brain.

The qui vive, as usual, was a startled stare through the glass, as if no one had ever before appeared on a Saturday night. "Mountjoy!" was the password.

"I am I. Is it you Karcist?"

"Mountjoy to the IRTH!"

"Why do you say *earth*, my boy?"

The elated young paladin was lucky to find no other douzeper at the table in Leviathan Court. [In the off-season, at the time of which I speak, Ipsissimus Charlemagne was still attracting very few from across the Gut. In later years would come to tempt him the stream of Ippies, old Beauts, and other curious followers, singly or in pairs: some to stay in town for weeks or months; a few, of sufficient character, to settle.] Ibi for his part was lucky to find an offering of leftover kidney stew, before he stole into the sanctum sanctorum to doze with Deeta Dana, Doc's young housekeeper.

So Caleb celebrated again, but this time far more expansively, expatiating upon the ironic ramifications of his IRTH-calculus, notwithstanding the fact that before they called it quits the next morning a large majority of the total words were spoken by Doc.

The enthusiastic visitor opened with his dynamic geometry, hoping to arouse Doc's native realistic nominalism (which he feared was sometimes bemused by the subjectivism that was sweeping his own Ippies along with Beauts and almost everyone in the latterday avant-garde of popular culture). Caleb declared the IRTH a model of the metaphysical ground in which to set the limited systems of both Yeats and Descartes.

"I hear you!" Doc cunningly agreed. "You've triviated the quadrivium, and triangulated the quadrant, like, in representing four dimensions! That Pythagorean amulet of yours is what Coleridge would have called a 'speculative instrument'. Stick with your heuristic geometry and stay away from literary criticism. I drink to the gnomonics of Karcist and Barebones! To the etymological anagnoresis of Platonic realism!"

Doc's general reputation was largely founded upon obiter dicta, uttered during rehearsals and elbow-bendings, which partly accounted for one of his occasional titles, "Herr Oberdichter", traced to the most distinguished academic wag among his admirers (who might have been a peer if he hadn't been a professor). Dichter he was to Caleb too, that night at least, who repressed all criticism and admiringly responded to appreciations.

The underground reaches of Doc's literary fame could hardly be explained by his almost clandestine theatrical productions, few in number and small in attendance. Not many of the anthropologist's adherents had ever actually found and read his famous out-of-print book *The Director's Quaquaverse*, or the often reprinted essay "Call Me Dramaturge", or even the half dozen editorials in his *Dromenology* magazine that had inseminated a tiny but growing sect of antithetical modernists. [Only later, as his perception of manipulation broadened, did Caleb understand that Doc's influence was levered chiefly in ostensibly personal letters to intellectuals who were as conscious as himself of posterity reading over their shoulders; for Doc wrote on his favorite subjects to sounding boards who were expected for the sake of reflected glory to publish at least his half of their reciprocating communications, if not immediately then not too long afterwards to amplify his living reverberations, and meanwhile to show and tell in cafes and garrets or seminar rooms. Those worthy of Doc's correspondence (—none in Dogtown—) were leaders of the kind of opinion that eventually makes its way to the top of the classless class.

But at home in his kitchen Doc was also glad to be free of such self-consciousness in conversing with an isolated sparring partner who acutely respected his "morphological understanding" without surrendering to his mere authority. That night indeed, as it seemed to Caleb, they struck new notes of friendly familiarity, senior and junior, dismissing shallow issues and extraneous topics. It happened that just at the time when Caleb was mulling over the *iso*rectotetrahedron as a special case within universal parameters Herr Oberdichter was concentrating on his Special Theory of drama rather than on the General Theory of Dromenology, which he hoped would be developed and more widely applied by his disciples and epigones. That is to say, as Doc waited for his piece on dance called "The First Museless Art" to make its way among cognoscenti as an introduction to his idea of the theater, he was again working on his *Dictionary for Action*, a compendious text that focused his bolts of lightning on the origin or cognate of all the arts.

That project seemed to Caleb a constructively angry reaction to Doc's disappointment at White Quarry College, which had lately turned down his ultimatum for a theatrical subvention. He had been demanding a permanent company of teaching dancers and players as the cadre of a seasonal company to be based at the College, performing in its assembly hall or in the quarry arena, or from a wagon on the baseball diamond, and to tour amateur playhouses in towns and cities where an anti-Limeway audience might gather around boards without proscenium arches. He imagined his theater in cloaks of many colors, as a circus of manifold epiphanies, catholic in its experimentation with skills and devices from all sorts of art, lasting throughout Dionysian festivals, full of merriment pity and terror; or else simple and austere, without platform or amplification, for discriminating guests. Doc's attack on the president and faculty had just ended in his own defeat and resignation.

"Everybody knows all about the theater! Even way up there three hundred miles from Limeway academics pride themselves on respecting the demands of show biz, the great marketplace of culture! The agora as orchestra! They all let me know that it's not

Atlantean theater if it ain't commercial! The flocking cost of doing business! The flocking function of art! They want to smell sweet to the flocking graduate schools and foundations. More flocking students at any level, just because the flocking college is going broke! The whole flocking institution of Atlantean education has turned itself into an employment agency pandering to markets. The academic market itself wants to become a flocking marketplace for markets! They all understand flocking Ophelimity! It is openly proclaimed that economic satisfaction is the criterion of culture! That's now the flocking sales pitch! Doctors of flocking Philosophy teach the arts and sciences of aggrantizement!" Caleb had never before heard such a coherent tirade from Doc. He was eager to chime in, observing that the Atlantean theater nowadays was no better than the Anglo-Irish sixty years ago, as the Victorian age faced its end, when Yeats was attempting to dislodge 'plays of commerce'. Little but the printed page remained from those few years of true illusion at the Abbey Theater. It corrupted itself in Yeats's very hands. But that artist was a poet, torn by the quarrel with himself; perhaps an undivided master dramaturge, further yet from the West End and Limeway, could make a new art for Atlantis, even after its years of theatrical self-congratulation. "Right here in Dogtown we've got plenty of Irish blood on our granite." Caleb suggested.

"But our 'country people' have no language to counter 'journalism' with." Doc replied, instantly accepting Caleb's allusion as if a challenge to his originality. "And we can't anymore console ourselves with reflections of a golden age that never was. Flock the True the Good and the Beautiful!

"Furthermore, Diskey and DV are irreversible, right here in the Harbor as well as everywhere else in the world."

This was not the first time Doc had failed in his attempt to create a theater of his own. "Must I—a man of action—must I, like theorists such as Schrödinger and Einstein, settle for experiments in thought?" he demanded, magnified gray eyes staring through his spectacles at the whiskey bottle. Then he looked at his young admirer with a slow smile.

Thus touchingly the Director confessed to Caleb what he generally concealed: frailty (such as otherwhiles he accused "dramatic poets" of) in face of institutional reality. "Closet drama" was the charge Caleb himself most dreaded. But the new closet drama of this Oberdichter—his medium of thought-experiment, unlike the playwright's or composer's—was not the script or dialectical poem, or musical score: it was not the text of plays but the charter and constitution for a drama system embodied in the founding father's imagined company of artists. It was a theory-challenge to the intelligentsia, and it demanded disenfranchisement of the existing theater, lock stock and barrel, Method and all, on and off the Great Milky Way.

Caleb never mentioned his play in connection with the functional IRTH symbol, yet as if Doc simply disregarded his pious deception he felt that nothing was hidden from the huge eye and wide ear of the maternally discreet and courteous master, who was granting full license to the secretly presumptuous enterprises of youth. For it was with quiet tones of conciliation that the elder, by reinterpreting traditional translations, defended Aristotle's idea of tragedy against the younger's romantic attack. Doc and Caleb were both Aristotelians only in a relative sense (as against Plato), when framed within an exclusively Hellenic universe. Neither had any Greek; nor had either studied any philosophy responsibly: but when it came to poetics, Doc closely read the most literal renderings of the lecture notes upon which opinions of Aristotle's limited special theory of dromenology must principally be based. Caleb disputed the empirical definition of tragedy and interpolated his own idea of the hero; but tradition had more to fear from Doc's criticism.

"Yeats says 'I have been the advocate of the poetry as against the actor, but I am the advocate of the actor as against the scenery.'" Doc had told Caleb. "But I myself am advocate of the director against them all. Aristotle was like Willie in arguing the supremacy of the poet when he held that the potential of tragedy exists irrespective of performance, and that its characters exist only for the sake of what he called the essential action. But the characters of the play were not the actors in the theater; and he was talking about the action that was represented—'imitated', as they usually translate it—, not about the action that it was represented by, not about the imaginative dromenon itself. That's why for him epic and tragedy are on the same order of representation, differing only in 'manner'. He pays no proper attention to the behavior of actors in ensemble—speaking, moving, making music—which I say is the distinctive business of this art. To him all that is only a medium of communication, not much above the level of scene-painting. . . ."

Caleb might have questioned some of the exegesis he heard, but not its value. When he listened to Doc he was nearly persuaded that the writing of text was little more than an auxiliary contribution to the interpretive art of action. But right now the issue of subjugation seemed unimportant, since the authors they bothered to mention were used to taking care of themselves.

Charlemagne spoke of the Euripides Jonson Shakespeare and Yeats he had directed and lived out; Karcist of the Euripides Sophocles Aeschylus and Yeats that he had only read. Charlemagne undertook to criticize Plato; Karcist, the closet drama of Villiers de l'Isle-Adam. Meanwhile the Director's manifold mind, which easily grasped the cube of tetrahedrons without seeing them, responding to the IRTH as an interesting whetstone, fenced inwardly with his expository work-in-progress, and the tenderfoot was secretly wrestling with his own confoundingly tractable plan for a Gilgamesh trilogy and its satyr-play.

However, Caleb was pleased to perceive that Doc never quite forbade himself the dream of a topopolitan theater worthy of proving the hierarchic art of a truly dramaturgic director. Despite his declared resignation to the unacceptable corruption of Atlantean culture (and his matter-of-fact acknowledgement that the Resistance had been a lost cause before it began), tonight Doc never ceased ruminating upon the delusive hope recurrently raised whenever two or three of the Muse's followers were gathered together in Dogtown and spoke with yearning of the theater it deserved. For some the motive was fame or commerce, for others political emotion or personal therapy; magical lyricism was another vague desideratum, as were a sodality of complementary painting and sculpture, a shelter for poetic declamation, and even merely a self-sufficiency of local entertainment. Doc of course had little patience for any of these motivations, yet notwithstanding his denouncement of collegial life (as it had almost always actually occurred since the Deformation) he was far from immune to the attraction of such dromenonical pipe-dreams.

So, egged on with sympathetic speculation by his junior ally, Doctor Charlemagne couldn't disguise the ashy rebirth of personal hope. Caleb never saw him in the kind of bad mood that plagued narrower psyches like his own, but on this Saturday night Doc showed himself more sanguine than ever before in discussions of shared *topos* as the only possible source of pristine dramatic art in the general decadence of Atlantean civilization—in particular, as always, of Dogtown, this unique topopolis which was still so blessedly reluctant to expurgate its history.

As the night wore on, Doc's circumstantial optimism rose like the drunken spirits of a sophisticated minority leader, and he waxed almost as youthful as Caleb in the "true illusion" of art's power.

Never afterwards moreover did he so nearly express the affinity to Caleb for which Caleb longed but from which Caleb aspired to independence. Never afterwards did their conversation last so long at a single sitting.

At last Doc allowed himself to hint at a contributing cause of his present sanguinity. "Listen to this, IRTH-Childe: that ambitious boilermaker of yours was scared to death when he heard I was quitting the White Quarry College house of commons. He's worried about getting his foolish degree without my protection! But he brought the chief mummer over here this afternoon to inveigle me into something probably just as futile."

*

In truth, Caleb's sometime employer Rafe Opsimath had known nothing of Doc's academic defection when he introduced Tessa Barebones to HIM [His Imperial Majesty] at Leviathan Court. Rafe had been expecting Buck Barebones to take him over to visit the Portable Equipment Manufacturing Company in Swipitch to see about trailers for mounting Tubalcain's largest steam cleaners, but at the last minute Buck got an emergency call from his brother-in-law Thad Kryothermsky to solve a mechanical problem in Line One at the Mercator-Steelyard plant, and Tessa had offered to drive the affable businessman (quartered at Shelly Schlossberg's caraVANsary without an automobile) wherever else he wanted to go, for there were still many features of the Cape he hadn't seen.

They had spent as much time as possible together at the recent White Quarry term in Montvert, but this accidental opportunity for companionship in Dogtown was not a conspiracy. She had returned from her first Semi-Convocation highly stimulated in thought about theater as well as about Rafe, and when they got into her car it was she who had asked him to beard the lionized recluse in his fabulous den, which she had been longing to see. None of her usual friends had ever been so bold. "My sister will be jealous." she said.

They were fortunate to find their teacher pausing in his afternoon breakfast, not a bad time to indulge a couple of intelligent students. That's how Rafe Opsimath and Tessa Barebones happened to hear Doc's rejoinder to the College's rebuff of his theatrical proposal, almost before White Quarry itself was informed by it. Contrary to what Doc now told Caleb, they had been too occupied with their current interests to give a damn about their future at the alma mater they now shared as part-time correspondents from opposite coasts of the country.

"She wants him to drum up a consortium to buy the old Stone Barn over in East Harbor as operating space for the Troika." said Doc to Caleb, referring to the Arts Center school run by Tessa, her sister Cora Kryothermsky the dancer, and Beni Vanderlyn the craft-artist. "He's had a good offer for his equity in the garbage-cookers: maybe he'll take the proceeds, trust the kids to his ex-wife, and renounce the land of lotus eaters. I wouldn't be surprised if he's inclined to settle here and make some new kind of steam-jenny with Buck. Anyway, he'll probably be the Hoof and Mouth angel, if there is one. She swears to gather a decent company of performers. They want me to be artistic director and do some serious plays. Neither of them can get it through their heads that Dogtown's no better educated in theater than Ur-town is."

"The Zoning Board would never grant them a variance." commented Caleb with the sagacity of a vizier. "Anyway they wouldn't be allowed to charge admission."

"These days even free performances play to the box office. They sell advertising on the ticket stubs. That's what it always comes down to before the first season of art-theater is half over. I told those two I'd start with *Philoctetes* or nothing. Not a woman in the whole cast! But it's not easy to shut such ladies up. That man-eating sister of hers will want them to call my bluff! You know, Kryothermsky's wife: she's a good imaginative dancer—when she forgets her politics—but the rest of the time she sees one side of all equations and thinks they're inequalities."

Caleb concurred that the great Director was entitled to believe that Dogtown and its mummers, and all the texts of the world, should be at his disposal—provided the deal was sweet enough, one way or another, even if the project was to be carried only far enough to teach a tiny company the elements of his doctrine. It was indeed the kind of hope that rose and fell over the years of Doc's career, wherever he was, from New Uruk to Yerba Buena, in London or Montvert, many times reawakened from the somnolence of despair. Though the Oberdichter usually disguised his hardbitten optimism, today the spark had found fresh tinder.

He especially wished to apply to the theater of speech the principle of "telemenos" that he had developed in his essay on dance—which Caleb had the honor to be understood to understand.

In that little-known monograph Doc had proposed the transmission of energy (not mere information) from dancer to audience, as representing a third order of counterentropy (following first that of life and then that of mind). This emanation was made aesthetically affective by a 'power factor' in the art of movement consilient to that which indicates the dissonance between voltage and current in the delivery of electricity. Of all Doc's ideas this one excited Caleb the most.

Doc was now speaking of a related but less natural conceit. "... power is force times distance—force through space, or work—*divided* by time: a ratio, a differential. Drama is not power but action; and action is integration, like history. It's force through space *times* time. It's the multiplication of energy by duration rather than the division of it; not watts but watt-hours. And the *telemenos* of 'speaking dance', the transformation and transmission of dramatic action *as multiplied by its audience*—the actualization of dramatic poetry—yes?—is a duration, not a ratio, of imagination. When a play is performed and witnessed, it's art's counterentropic confutation of the principle of least action. —Am I taking the metaphor too far?"

"Not at all." Caleb replied without emphasis, playing as independently as possible the judicious role of assent into which Doc usually pressed his companions, and hesitating to chime in with support of this supernatural metalepsis until he had sober time to look for a scientific parable. "I'll have to re-read what you said in "The Museless Art", and review what I used to know about the transformation of electromechanical power; but I know what you're getting at. Even if drama is less like power-transmission than pure dance is, it transforms and transmits *imagination* instead—which it likewise multiplies by an indefinite number of receivers without increasing the load on the primary circuit."

Doc frowned sternly, and Caleb faltered at the reception of his bold participation in the theory. But then the shaggy eyebrows rose into furrows of frontal wrinkling to stretch opener the godlike ports behind their bifocal lenses, and the great face relaxed into a benign smile. "Yeah, I like that. There you have the world's *most* transcendental phenomenon!"

So they skoaled. But Caleb felt a twinge of uneasiness, almost disloyalty—or at least a sense of philosophical evasion—at the thought of Father Duncannon administering the bread and wine not to artists and lovers of art alone but to all humanity. Perhaps art was indeed the entelechy of culture, as culture was the ultimate purpose of general welfare, and welfare the justification of human survival: therefore the most liberal counterentropic action in the cosmos. Yet art was not much valued by most individual children women and men. Their suffering would be abated and their pursuit of happiness advanced only by improvement of the whole society's steady-state prevalence over natural disorder.

He wondered if even the fantastically patient machinations of an inconceivably influential hostess could bring into compatible contact two such isolated men of genius as Doctor Charlemagne and Father Duncannon. Certainly neither would accept from the other his singular contribution to the 'unity of being' that sometimes made Caleb himself giddy with love and hope for the world. He believed that under different personal circumstances Father Duncannon, whose own theory of art did not seem incompatible with the poetics and aesthetics of dromenology, might have absorbed and cited many of Doctor Charlemagne's propositions—-at least if more rigorously argued—as supporting the secular apology for a theodynamic Church.

But Caleb doubted that the Ipsissimistic giant, an apostate from childhood Scholasticism, would ever again open his mind to an orthodox institution. He feared that the puritanical distortions of Christianity, its organ music and its sentimentality, its reactionary response to cultural evolution, its decadent ceremony, had irreparably perverted its own pure and irreducible dromena, which remained discernible only to the luckiest or most determined inquirers. As a dromenologist Doc had once acknowledged Jesus as "a liturgical genius", but Caleb did not deceive himself that his Chiron understood the special case he thus subsumed.

Caleb sometimes asked himself what he therefore ought to do about liberalizing the prejudices not of Dogtown but of Dogtown's two unrecognized philosophers. A childe of no eloquence or weight, with no wife or dinner table for entertainment, who hadn't yet disclosed even his first play—he alone and his dog were aware of both these God-given strangers, champions respectively of the antithetical theater and the antithetical church: only to Caleb Karcist could it possibly occur to offer them friendship with each other.

On the other hand, if it was his duty as an integrator (and his hope for joyful unification) to make their vision whole without bringing them together in person, how could he fulfill that time-consuming obligation without dangerously delaying or leaving unfinished his own lifetime part in cultivating the mental freedom for the ultimate sake of which mankind's maximum survival was worth everybody's effort? Though happy in his drunkenness he was appalled by the effort of scholarship and writing such a task required. He was neither competent nor patient enough for work in the vineyards of persuasion. For him the intellectual and social labor would be squared and cubed a thousand times by the irreducible conflict with what he'd be sacrificing. Even as it was, lacking servants to do his living for him, in a whole year he could hardly ever bring himself to divert psychic energy for so much as writing the shortest of letters, to his mother or to anyone else, except for Lilian.

"Well now I've got to get to work." said Doc at 4 AM.

As Caleb staggered to the door, followed by Ibi (still yawning, pausing to stretch in a concave bow, and shaking off luxurious backroom dreams), he remembered his intention to offer Ipsissimus Charlemagne and Perdita Dana the use of his bathtub. For long and long he had procrastinated the indelicacy of such an invitation. He also hesitated to risk complications in his diplomatic relations with landlord and landlady, who paid for his hot water and would not be pleased by thumpings and gurglings in the tiny bathroom over their bedroom at untoward times, for it was sure to be at Doc's sole convenience if an invitation was accepted at all, and once accepted it would have to be repeated. But most discouraging was the prospective burden of dealing with exasperating aftereffects on fabric and enamel. Even to clean up after himself he hated to scrub the tub.

Yet that night—that morning—he was touched by Doc's generosity not only with his hospitality (and above all with his time) but also with the tools of his trade; for the Oberdichter had given him his review copy of the illuminating new translation of Aristotle's *Poetics*.

In his clairvoyant besotment Caleb nevertheless finally chose to remain delicately baffled by the question of where and how Doc and Deeter managed to keep clean without tub or shower, without so much as a bathroom sink. (They were ragged indeed, but no one could say they were smelly.) This was no time to break the spell of a numinous intellectual friendship, and he left the court once more without mustering his courage to make the offer. With the carelessness of privilege he and Ibi descended the outside stairs, the latter's claws making more of a clatter than the former's; but there were no longer any hell-hounds to awaken below.

Caleb had never had the guts to raise even with Petto DaGetto the question of Doc's exiguous plumbing facilities. What neither he nor the blacksmith ever knew was that Doc and Deeta were discreetly accommodated by their Good Samaritans at the VAN, especially when the Poet's Corner was otherwise unoccupied. Dogtown has always harbored surprisingly secret charities.

8
MOONSTOP

*C*aleb was often able to lose himself in Doc Charlemagne's kitchen, and at Father Duncannon's liturgy, and in the paid activities that claimed his practical mind; or to transcend himself in the work of objective imagination; but he always gravitated, as here the story returns, to the consciously peremptory demand for private pleasures of well-requited love, which in the early Spring of 1961 was never either appeased or disregarded for very long.

Within this most vivid zone of experience his thought or desire was sometimes briefly and provisionally diverted from Lilian to another, as if on purpose to retard the major turbulence with minor counter-eddies; and his attitude toward her (as reflected in discussions with himself) veered from one hour to the next as erratically as a lodestone approaching the Pole, back and forth among all the uncertain positions between lordly unhurried satisfaction with his hold on her heart and the hopeless misery of absolute deprivation. But she remained the lunar lode-star of his planetary sky—wandering and variable, an illumination sometimes eclipsed without warning—presumably always waxing or waning, but in a pattern that he could no more discern in so few months than a New Uruk landlubber who found himself shanghaied on a fishing schooner in the Grand Banks fog could construct a tide-table. In soundings far from sight of land, the inconstancies of current and temperature, and of terrestrial clouds, continually altered his view of the celestial body that fluctuated between dazzling light and terrifying disappearance. He saw nothing to suggest Newton's simplest law of motion.

When her letter failed to arrive on time he plunged from the peak of joy, to which he had been raised by her promise, on steeps of cascading disappointment. Before the week was gone all hope had flattened out into a valley of bitter suspicions. A hiatus in the mere five-mile postal routing was unheard of. Was there a subliminal error on her part in addressing it? Or might she have forgotten to lick him a stamp, in unconscious resentment of the tip he'd left her at the Doghouse? Under such clandestine conditions she could not have been expected to show her return address on the envelope. Had his hard-won boon therefore ended up in the Dead Letter Office—eventually to be scanned by brutal eyes and burned officially like one of the unknown bodies found before the walls of Ilium?

In the days that immediately followed his first disillusionment there was little opportunity to question her—certainly not as calmly and indirectly as befitted the dignity of a gentleman. She offered no explanation; couldn't guess what might have gone wrong. But she seemed to take it as a rather unimportant misfortune, as if she'd stuffed nothing but some newspaper clipping into her envelope. He wasn't missing much, she said on the phone with a wry little snort.

Her casual comments made him ashamed of such an ado about a statistical fluke. She treated it as no more significant than a single electron's quantum of variation from the laws of mean causality, which simply happened to occur ironically on the occasion of their own over-determined event. He found himself adopting the extenuation that she was too busy to ponder the problem. The accident was clearly a sign from the gods that writing to the troubadour wasn't called for. It would be boorish to urge her to remember what she'd written and repeat that singular effort on paper.

Still suffering a ludicrous inequation of correspondence after many days of hopeless helplessness tinctured with annoyance at her apparent indifference to the mishap, he resumed his enlargement of the absurd trade-imbalance, again writing all the letters himself.

Feckless or seductive, writing was the only possible substitute for manly action.

Since it was not his vocation to dissipate ever-accumulating surplus energy by writing lyrics or romance, he declared on paper, every free calorie of experience was metabolized as love for her like flesh on his bones. And he believed that by allusive touch and intimate word of mouth they had mutually proven to be each other's sole comprehensive friend. To him that seemed demonstrated on his side by the effusions in which he wrote out his heart to her, howsoever balked by cul de sacs on the labyrinthine path to satisfaction. At every letter-writing he told himself that no matter what might happen afterwards—whether or not he ever saw her again, whether or not she vanished from his hopes before he once more enjoyed the natural reciprocity of gender—their complementary valence of electric affinity was steadier, and hotter too, than the wavering flames at both ends of any candle held by Belle Cingani née Bice Picory.

Even after he began to taste in the cud of his brooding ruminations the implausible possibility that Lilian had lied about having written a 'lost letter', when the bafflement of reason was better assimilated by his remarkably negative capability for general and permeating frustration, he believed that his love for her—though it appeared new and was certainly inexperienced, indeed essentially rather potential than entelechial—included and dominated not only his noetic world but also all the other good feelings he'd ever had or ever would have. Other loves, in memory or fantasy, now struck him as mere experiments in specialized desire. He was hardly aware that he might have inverted his hierarchy of cravings without altering by one iota her affect upon his heartbeat.

Temporarily setting aside the question of her lost letter, which in fact he soon grew disinclined to pursue with the vigor of his original request for it, and which in any case might have contained little to nourish his undefined hope for passionate or brilliant paragraphs, he attempted to factor his own motives in the inequation of written messages. The Leitmotiv of his epistolary variations was a claim that his erotic feelings were unique by virtue of their unprecedented range of integration.

His irresolute sense of mastery, founded upon her orally affirmed sense of his *physis*, was never quite extinguished, despite his failure to win the duel with her unseen bedmate that he had no intention of winning absolutely. By failing to ravish the bride, while preempting her heartfelt mind, he was spared the uncomfortable demands of a bride-winner's *ethos*. It was clear even to his fervent heart that the terms of cohabitation would have mocked beclouded or poisoned the causes of the love set forth, as follows, in one of his hyperscreeds:

> I love you most of all perhaps because of your carriage in peace and your mein in adversity.
> Perhaps most of all because of your aboriginal and liberal intelligence.
> Perhaps because of your experience in adventurous hardship.
> Because of your self-reliant Atlindu courage.
> Because of your creative and critical instincts: both poetic and aesthetic.
> And most of all because you have dropped away from the superstitions of the Church without forswearing sacramental Xty.
> Because as a matter of patriotism (ignoring the irresponsible idealism of many antitheticals) you remain loyal to the Catholicratic Party.
> Because as a Natural sympathizer with the Resistance you have scorned the idolatry of devilvision.
> And perhaps I love you most because from the very beginning of gestation you have set all desires below your maternal love.
> As you have said in one of your papers: 'History overdetermines what mechanical laws can't fix.'

But in truth the consummate cause of his highest love may have been that even before he'd happened into this second reserved courtship (with all the enthusiasm of a first) she seemed to have understood with approval the selfish moiety of his unreserved heart. Was it not obvious that "Women are the better people!", according to his mother's battle-cry, who wasn't referring to the comparative form of the "good" that Mrs Grundy meant as the adjective for chastity asymmetrically applied?

In one of his dispatches he stopped to accuse himself of behavior like that of Admetus praising Alceste for the nobility of her selfsacrifice on his cowardly behalf. But such a confessional was too dangerous to send. He tore it up into very small pieces, fearing the exposure of his most secret thoughts to rubbish collectors. On other occasions also it had seemed to him that his letters were reckless or ill-advised—much too transparent, too communicative, too informative of injustice; yet never before had one seemed foolish enough to be destroyed.

But immediately he regretted the impulse that had made him waste the product of his idiosyncratic spontaneity. Was it not an honest rule that nothing should be withheld from a perfect friend? Certainly not the pertinent reservations of a peculiar autobiography. Nor, on the other hand, certain particulars of a desire that hardly distinguished him from any other unrewarded desirer of a woman's desire.

His own desire was spared the most ignoble extremes of jealousy only because she'd never offered a gross description of his preemptive competitor. From his few clues it was hard to form an image of the man about whom her mind and body were divided. However, the next time Caleb enjoyed Lilian's real presence (after their tryst at the Net & Twine where her letter had been declared), his attitude toward Gil Algo was suddenly roused from one of indefinite detestation to that of fear and odium:

He stayed up late one night with the intention of waylaying her as she left work at the Doghouse. It was a desperate hazard—to disregard not only her commands and his own rules of chivalry but also the probability of miscalculation. Daring neither to call by phone nor to penetrate the double doors of the restaurant simply to see who was at the cash register, he had no way even to be sure she was on duty for that shift until he could find her car parked somewhere in the vicinity; still less could he guess the variable time at which she'd close the till and quit the building.

So for almost an hour he paced the immediate vicinity, trying not to look like a loiterer, keeping under surveillance the spot on Dogfish Street at which he did find her kilroy—almost certainly hers. (Until now he hadn't thought of recording her license plate number in his pocket notebook. His memory was not to be trusted for any fact ever so close to his heart.) When he wasn't watching the car he was keeping an eye on either the front or the back door of the Doghouse at the corner of Dogfish and Front.

In Dogtown the ear of almost everyone is too accustomed to the syllable *dog* to notice the homonymities ironies or other coincidences of its occurrence; but Caleb, especially in this time of ambulatory meditation, was preternaturally sensitive to that word even when incorporated into common nouns borne by familiar public signs. Of all the precincts in which to be detained without his dog! His impatience for Lilian was all the more uneasy because his one true companion (who, mutatis mutandis, would have written him a letter every day) had been left alone upstairs at home, standing with cocked ears and interrogative eyes—rightfully offended to suffer deliberate abandonment for the sake of a vulgar pursuit, yet with his dropped tail slowly swaying in loyal forgiveness—sadly accepting guilty sounds of apology. Ibi must then have been further aggrieved when he'd listened in vain for a car leaving the house and it finally became clear that his man was actually going *on foot* without him!

But the adventure would have been cramped by that party's presence. Even in dim light and shadows the highly distinguished saint would have given away the lurking nondescript stranger. Then too Caleb hoped to get a ride home in Lilian's car: although she herself would have been delighted to invite his squire onto her back seat, he feared that evidence of dirt or doghairs would embarrass her at home on the morrow.

Thus all alone, vulnerable without his usual escort, Caleb tramped up and down, back and forth, avoiding the few pedestrians (to say nothing of the police cars that circulated from the nearby Station). Several times he paused in darkness on the steps of a moribund house used once or twice a week by the volunteer staff of the locally askanced Red Cross, until he was too chilled to sit still any longer.

He was now almost less jealous of the man with whom Lilian did her sleeping than of Loathey O'Toole, proprietor of the Doghouse, notwithstanding her comment that his swarthy palms and forehead glistened with sweat. Her susceptibility was above suspicion, but Loathey had special reason as a businessman to make more assiduous advances to her than to others in his power, for she had rather easily proven herself his most valuable employee.

For example, he had been vexed and baffled by the irregular turnover at his tables of both regular and casual customers during the busy hours. A majority came and went happily enough, often with good words for the food and service, efficiently making room for their successors. But others seemed to sit there half the night, restlessly twiddling their thumbs, sometimes even too annoyed to call for extra drinks to while away the time. He was aware that few displeased patrons ever cared to register complaint with the hostess or to ask for the boss; but behind his back they'd malign his good name as a leading restaurateur. Even after he divined that something in the service was characteristically erratic, Loathey blustered to the girls and fumed to the chef without any idea of what was specific to the problem.

There was no discernible pattern to indicate the chronic delinquency of any one waitress or any one man in the kitchen, but he changed table-assignments and fired one or two waitresses of unreliable demeanor. He went so far as to take moments of reflection, somewhat curtailing his bantering gossip with regulars at the bar in order to watch times and motions in and out of the dining room. But everyone was always working as fast as ever, and never did he discover that any customers were kept waiting before they were first attended to.

At last one night during a lull he confided his perplexity to the calmly efficient hostess-cashier, whom he called Lil or Honey, by whose contribution to the general efficiency of his establishment he had already been practically awestruck. He gladly accepted her offer to take a lunchtime turn as waitress in order to observe the dysfunction as one of its operating victims. The very next day she told him what was wrong.

Loathey was not one to grasp at once the significance of crucial details, but he did implement Lilian's irritating suggestion. For some time after he promulgated this solution to the problem his other employees scoffed and grumbled at the disturbance to habits they had learned when the business was considerably less rational. But within a week the help had stopped complaining about the new procedure and Loathey was again free to spend most of his time enjoying public relations in the tap room. For a long time thereafter he ceased belittling the help for stupidity and sloth.

Lilian had merely pointed out that because the waitresses had been taught to place their order slips on top of the stack in on kitchen counter, and because the cooks had not been instructed to work on their backlog from the bottom up, the staff had been unwittingly habituated to a LIFO procedure: Last In/ First Out! No wonder that a quarter of the customers had hardly time to savor high-priced alcohol before their food was served, whereas another quarter had to swallow their hunger, sometimes at the extremity of patience, while later-arriving customers were already paying their checks at the cash register on their way out.

If he'd but known it, Caleb had more to fear from the peacemaking young second cook, already a devotee to Lilian; his burden of complaints was astonishingly lightened by her improvement of the system. It is always well for an outside suitor to consider the solidarity and propinquity of the workplace, where a tired woman's good nature can grow forgetful of the underlying defects to be expected in humorous or handsome men.

A still greater cause for anxiety could have been the unaccompanied strangers privileged to watch her, bandy words, and listen to her speech, deliberately becoming familiars merely by eating there;

or foreign ships' officers—fair gentle and heroic, with the aura of transatlantic culture—who might pique even the most experienced Atlantean woman.

That night however, when Lilian at last emerged, it was without company, trailing no man's confidential laughter; not so much as a murmur of leavetaking was disclosed at the exit. She was a swift shadow silently released, slipping around the corner straight toward him before he could prepare himself for what he'd been awaiting. He was given only a wan smile for his pains, but no reproach, no sign of surprise, as if he was her mate.

He now found that she'd left her car unlocked in the dark on Dogfish Street. "Get in." she said. "I have something to tell you. But we can't go anywhere. I have to be home in fifteen minutes."

Trembling with presentiment, numbly, he complied. Under any circumstances his excitement in her company, as long as it lasted, dissolved whatever he had planned to say or do. Tonight she was speaking with a determination he hadn't seen before, with a will unamenable to offerings of praise knowledge or sensation. Suddenly it seemed as if she'd demanded this meeting.

Swiftly she drove to Cod Street, and in two minutes, without deviating from her homeward route, came to a stop against the curb in front of the cemetery, just beyond his house, ignoring the glares and whizzes of the sparse night traffic. During the short time of their all-absorbing conversation in the parked car no more than two or three deadhead reefer rigs rattled by in the opposite direction, headed for the loading docks, where (after a few drinks before closing time at some Harbor bar) the drivers would go to sleep in their cabined berths.

She turned off the headlights but left her engine running. In token of his readiness to honor her wishes he laid his right hand on the door handle, drawing up his legs to climb out before he was summarily dismissed. Her hands remained on the steering wheel. Thus on the wing, in respective positions of suspended motion, without touching, that night's communication tersely took place.

At this beginning he almost wished she'd changed her mind and decided to get rid of him without telling him why. Instead she spoke rapidly, and so quietly, above the engine's vibrating continuo, that most of his sensitive faculties were occupied with the immediately effort to decipher her sounds. He had to concentrate upon his outer ears just to capture the articulation of sounds and to do his part in prolonging their flow by acknowledging the utterance. He was unprepared to understand her meaning, or to question the intelligence he hardly perceived mechanically. And to her his own simpleminded replies were hardly audible; they caught in his throat as husky croaks of unfolding dread.

"Gil intercepted my letter to you."

"How do you know? Didn't you mail it?"

"He didn't tell me for a few days. Then he tore it up in front of my eyes."

"Did he read it?"

"Oh he wouldn't dare do that! I think the envelope was still sealed."

"But did you ask him?"

"I wouldn't give him the satisfaction."

"What did the letter say?"

"Nothing important. I forget. I'm no good at writing letters. I'm sorry you expected it. It's all my fault! I shouldn't have told you I wrote it." She gave a short laugh non sequitur: "I'm a wretched white bear." The allusion was to Walter Sterne's paradigm as an oxymoron specific to his generation's ignorance of natural history, which Caleb had mentioned in a recent letter to illustrate (from the vantage of a posteriori Arctic knowledge) the danger of reasoning from the white crow as a logical expression of what's impossible in life. She switched on the headlights.

"Did he ask about me?" Caleb inquired hurriedly, unable to conceal his fear.

"No. That's the satisfaction he wouldn't give me. But no matter what, I'll never allow him to adopt Mooney!" The transmission of her car still in neutral but she pressed a little on the gas. "I've got to get home."

Caleb desperately returned to the point that more interested him. "But how did he get hold of it? He's not a letter carrier."

"It was in a stack of bill payments ready for mailing. I was all out of stamps, so I asked him to mail the whole batch, as usual, when he got to his office."

Suddenly she leaned over and with her hand at the back of his head pressed his mouth to hers, stopping his breath with the lengthy vehemence of decisive passion. Then she put the car in gear. "I can't see you any more." she asserted in a monotone. "If you come to the Doghouse I'll quit my job."

Caleb responded hastily, but was able to speak only the first abject thought that bobbed up from the swirl of his unbalanced brain. "Would he intercept letters from me if I kept writing to you?"

"Of course not! How could he?"

9
TABLET TWO

[**Gilgamesh** alone in his laboratory late at night. On the back wall hangs a multiple roller of charts (as for schoolroom maps), from which a geometrical diagram of the IsoRectoTetraHedron (IRTH) is drawn down and exposed. At first he is working at a table, occupied with the ceramic IRTH itself, drilling a hole through it, and stringing it around his neck. Off to one side is a small open-hearth furnace, anvil, buckets, and a few tools.]

GILGAMESH
[Working distractedly, with frequent pauses to peer intently at the IRTH, both before and after suspending it from his neck, or to finger it as he stares into space.]
Enter Lil-Amin, disheveled from sleep, standing hesitantly in a doorway. After staring around at

Until now every night has been a gem well spent—but this time I can't think my way. I've come up against an essence. In a rockless unwooded land I can forge these stones in a furnace—but who can make firewood? If a whole city's cooking must be done on dung and dried reeds, how can I find the fuel to bake a million bricks? I can't squeeze flame from sod! What's left to burn? There isn't heat enough in all our straw to glaze a single square-foot slab of clay.

—Lil-Amin! Without a mask! Is it you?

[*Pause.*]

At first I thought you were only a goddess. All night long divinities and I follow each other around corners as they

101

[various objects she points somnambulistically to identify the drawings with the IRTH hanging on his chest.]

inspect the day's damage to tradition. But you seem mortal, and here where all women are lovely there can be no doubt which one is their queen!
—Ah, my Iso-Recto-Tetra-Hedron? You weavers abhor such a lopsided signet, with too many planes but without a single facet that adds up to more or less that half a circle—especially when three out of four are only two-thirds regular.

[*Pause.*]

[He does the **Dance of the IRTH**, gesturing with the handle of his headless axe.]

Or perhaps it's the sharp straight lines? This tense jackstone is one corner of a cubic brick. I can hew its fundamentals with six strokes of my binary axe! With four faces of three sides each, it's the trivium and quadrivium of all faculties! It breeds all the numbers we'll ever need to count the stars or measure earth by season and degree. Even music has twelve sounds, and all words are made from twice as many.

[Seeing no response, he stops dancing.]

[*Pause.*]

But you'd rather memorize yourself to sleep with the lore you're taught than reckon by a system on your own.

LIL-AMIN   Long ago I learned to manage sleep. But tonight fear has cut it short.

[Shaking off her trance and advancing uncertainly.]

GILGAMESH   You are always safe while I am sleepless.

LIL-AMIN   Fear for Giszax himself. —I must be quick. —He has invited men to dream for him, a many-thoughted king.

GILGAMESH   But no one's done so—or dares to tell—though my cry's been out a month.

LIL-AMIN   You can force your slaves to scrape up a mountain on the river, but you can't make them dream your dreams. Since you still refuse to sleep yourself, perhaps the unbidden agency of a woman will serve your purpose.

GILGAMESH   Seeing that she's my peer, and occupies those many thoughts.

LIL-AMIN   Then listen to your dream while it's still naive, before I come to my senses and it takes the guarded lines I'll give it later.

GILGAMESH   You are right to come to me for this. Pray tell at once! Don't let your bewildered face grow thoughtful. Don't interpret, don't predict! Let me do the thinking.

LIL-AMIN		Well—translated into men's language? I dreamt that I, as you, took protection of the night to learn the mystery hidden from men and unknown to foreign women. In the narthex of the Temple, I, Lil-Amin, lay uncovered in sleep as I—you, Gilgamesh—stole past without a pause. At the adytum door unvoiced words were in my ear: "No mortal man may address the hag in women's tongue." I said: "It's I, the king of Erech—only one part man, but two thirds god!"
[She dances.]		
GILGAMESH		The last time I slept, before I saw Erech, it came to me in dream that strangers somewhere were saying just those last seven words!
LIL-AMIN		The proof my dream is yours. But hear it out. I crept inside, toward a fissure in the earth. A crone squatted with her back to me, clawing up handfuls of wet clay to make an infant's figure, starting with the head, which hardened under her breath and had become what I took to be the featureless branch of a man that's molded for a woman's pyx. But when she smeared it with foul black tar, a flame ignited and it split along its length. Quicker than blinking, a golden serpent flashed from the shards and vanished between the lips of the cracked hollow. "Look what you've done!" she shrieked at me. "Next year there'll be no moon!" But when I bent to see her face, she smiled: and it was Inanna—Ishtar—that I saw!
[Stops dancing.]		
GILGAMESH		You must not annotate the dream.
LIL-AMIN		Then, as you, I found myself standing high as a bird in the sky-lighted night, naked with a man's extremity, while people far below pointed arrows up at me to shoot. —Is it true that with moonlight Inanna can make a man extend himself against his will?
GILGAMESH		Expunge that dream—and all your puzzlement! I command you to wipe it clean, and forbid you to tell it to any god or person, or to remember it at all.
LIL-AMIN		I am guilty of the enigma, and doubly so to tell you.
GILGAMESH		But it's mine alone to bear. I'll take on the dread. It's not for you to ponder. I will not have its import or its expiation on any other mind.
LIL-AMIN		You have no cause to worry about my discretion—except in being here right now. They'd bury me alive. I've handed you a perfect hostage. All you have to do is tell.

GILGAMESH   Then let's study our collusion. Since you stand first in this city of arts, as artist and as living art, it's generally supposed by all that's holy we should share a bed. Yet the Widows have been heard to say you've such genius at beatitude that you have no need for atonement with a man.

LIL-AMIN   They admire mysticism, and you mistake the mockery of my solitude in that canard. It falsifies the serenity of an unanointed queen. My proper office lies vacant that was handed down from heaven. I'm sadly called the Maid of Uruk: the only one denied our priest by law—yet refused a woman's dignity by the sole pretender.

GILGAMESH   Pretender! I was scanning the world for a place to choose when your Optimates sought me out to implore my archers and my thin-lipped axe. So I delivered Ishtar's city from level carnage. But I won't propitiate her with my foreskin. I will not wear her livery just to glorify her cult!

LIL-AMIN
[With a fleeting smile.]
Now I understand a little: demigods don't sacrifice to gods!

—But who are you to scorn her mark? In return for sovereignty you swore with hands between your legs to safeguard our customs and perpetuate our rites!

GILGAMESH   They ceded me control of all destinies within the range of my bow. Do I pretend too much when I include my own? Erech's people swore to exalt whatever I exalted. Do I pretend too much when I count you among its citizens?

LIL-AMIN   Oaths of office are pronounced in ancient form and understood reasonably. Any pledge is subject to pious decency. Who would have thought ours could be taken as a mandate for your unholy pride? Instead of honoring the people's rights you edify them with bricks! Your hours of audience are filled with time-and-motion analysis. At night you try to petrify our clay by improving upon the fire of the sun; or dream up levees and ditches to reform our god-given waters! Without a plan from any god you displace a thousand households to make room for a twisted tower—and then regulate our works and days by its evil shadow! Is it fane or barrow? Tell me whether it's god's or yours!

GILGAMESH
[Laughing.]
For myself, neither castle nor hanging garden, but an apex: to lengthen my bowshot; to look down upon the temptations of power; to give me sooner sight of your attackers; to widen my span of stars, while shortening the hours between sunset and sunrise; to give my men a glimpse of

peaks beyond the dust of your horizon; and to combine plan with profile in the perspective of my public works. For the gods, yes: a beacon for them in our middle world of seven cities. But not least for you, as sky-house for the tryst! Your canon law stipulates the highest place.

LIL-AMIN Am I your bait to challenge heaven? Isn't the sacrilege enough—Uruk offering the Lord God Enlil a mortal bride so unperfected—without presuming to elevate her to the floor of heaven?

GILGAMESH I do not admit that you have been wronged by me, and I mean no insult to your god. Engineering's my only art. It keeps my mind off feeling. I never felt anything before I first saw you. You are shaped to cradle me, and my thoughts yours.

LIL-AMIN Then make your liking good. Don't remain an odious clan of one! Join the priesthood of men! Ordained, you can confirm the queen a woman, and she then consecrate you king by law. Rule no longer by default! By unnullifying me you can reduce the people's other grievances to reactionary gripes. In the end they'd praise your works forever. Isn't

[She laughs.] that the fame you want? Circumcision is no great price to pay. It won't mutilate your faculties. Is Eber maimed? Is the Rector failing? The knife is small, and the pain is

[He smiles.] briefer than a bride's.

GILGAMESH For you I'd suffer vultures. But no enemy's knife is small, nor the Rector's enmity so brief. But the worst of it would be to have that insolent priest heave his trophy up to Ishtar, so she could pin it to her shoulder like a bloody sleeve!

LIL-AMIN Your pride is cowardly. If women didn't have the guts for humiliation, there'd be no one born on earth to serve the gods or you.

GILGAMESH Still, the de-coronation is a custom I might submit to—if you'd condescend to mine. Where I come from, a king's wife doesn't play the bitch to dogs.

LIL-AMIN Your terms are outrageous. You'd hoard the sacrament!

GILGAMESH No, only you. If you're mine, you're not to be dispensed.

LIL-AMIN Never have honorable guests diminished a husband's abounding riches: they magnify his glory. Besides, how could any man copy you, or steal me from you? You're the

	one that not even my god can dispossess. And the future woman is already yours—before sanction or touch or promise. My hand is yours; my lips, my ears, my eyes. But especially the thoughts I make up.
GILGAMESH	Yes, those feed and sleep with mine! It's they that make you the artist of your people, and in them lies my hope for apostasy. But your brain has yet to be deafened by the buzz of honey-bees. With me you'd know your gifts.
LIL-AMIN	The commonwealth comes first. Can you be prouder than the Lord Enlil? Woman's superabundance is celebrated by the gods themselves. I take on faith the catechism I teach, that even from the husband of heaven there won't be beatitude enough for the vicar of Inanna.
GILGAMESH	Mankind was given the jewel of games for you and me alone to play! My only demand is equity.
LIL-AMIN	I've heard about Northmen's equity! You'd cage me like a widowed dove, or have me follow at your heel—half forgotten when your fickle appetite is slaked.
[Softening.]	. . . though perhaps not you. I mustn't forget that you're a scandal to your own race too: a chaste barbarian!
GILGAMESH	Since I first saw you dance. Since my last sleep.
LIL-AMIN	Before your dream I had one for myself. I lay enslaved as with a blunt gleam you overshadowed me. Yet, out of shame, no beatitude would come—until Inanna, one hand resting on your back, stood smiling down at me and said: "No one can withstand him. He is now the state. You must weave his banner." Such false dreams come to me more often as my childhood lengthens. In sleep they don't seem heretical.
GILGAMESH [Vehemently.]	To whisper that you might yield to force without offending heaven is a shabby lure! It re-reminds me that to get the peace I crave by merely spending power would be to drown like a bee in the honeyed catacomb. A rueful atonement!
LIL-AMIN [Flaring up.] [Scornfully.]	I despise your gloss! Didn't I say the dream was false? Who but Giszax himself has proclaimed by herald that dreams are not presentiments—only suspended speculation, pro or con? —What fatuous presumption, to say I'm provoking violence I affect to fear—in order to rob you of your strength! You're the clear free star, and I'm the deep black pool that traps you by reflection! I'm the succubus

that provokes brutal lust to betray the liberty I envy! What nonsense!

GILGAMESH
[Approaching.]

I only meant that we must love each other.

LIL-AMIN

For the love of god, are you too willful or are you too stupid to understand that my renunciation of custom would only cheapen me to you as well as to my people?

GILGAMESH

Lil-Amin! This is closer than we've ever been before. I find I can endure the air you breathe!

LIL-AMIN

You abuse the confidence of a private dream. It's sad that frankness is a woman's fault, and sadder yet that a word, once let go, is a bird that can never be recaptured.

[In a lower voice, turning away.]

—It sometimes happens when the moon is dark like this that I bewail my vows, and yearn to comfort as a private wife the only other loveless lover in all of Uruk. But the full will come again, and this lunatic will get back her wits. You can't corrupt me with your self-importance.

[He comes closer.]

—Don't touch me! —I tell you, the fraud is yours, to speak of passion! You'd scorch me with a simulation too tepid to keep your feet warm. I often wonder at the fame that preceded you to Uruk. The world had heard enough of your warp-spasm in battle—and the untamed generosity of your loves! But now here, your flaring nostrils only snort the steam of cogitation! Your mighty right hand wields a stylus! Your shield-arm turns a potter's wheel! . . . For the prima donna of Uruk your liberality is sackcloth and ashes.

GILGAMESH

The liberality you want is plethora of consorts!

LIL-AMIN

Oh Queen of Heaven, who seven times inflamed all eyes in harrowed hell, I'm worth no more than a leer to our famous mountain bull! I unstring his desire with something bitter in my voice. I stink in his nose. There is no hope in me. —Must I disgrace the house of Inanna? No! Let the Rector drag the axe-man to the block! Let my people drown the Doge of Dikes in blood! —Or else myself befuddle me enough to forswear Inanna under the next onslaught of milord's residual warmth.

Lil-Amin goes off quickly.

GILGAMESH
[Starts to dance, but stops abruptly.]

My nights in this rimless valley have been brimming with sleepless dreams of the labyrinth beneath that brilliant heart. But she's partly right: her intelligence divides my iron blood and feeds the smithy in my head. And now her voice has given me the oracle to work on! I can use her dream without her form and substance. Let that desire wait. It won't turn rancid.

Excitedly snatching up a bucket, **Gilgamesh runs off** another way.

—The riddle of my origin was a wraith of mist to distract me from the other idea that might have come to me in sleep!

10
CONFESSION

*I*bi-Roi took issue with Alpha Whitehead's postulate, and Rembrandt's too perhaps, that touch is the prime sense. Even the late electronical Captain Ozone, unlike Samson, had been of the persuasion that he was better blind than bereft of touch (for he preferred the apolaustic to the moral). But it was Ibi's sensible opinion that Isaac couldn't have made his world-historic mistake if he'd used his nose to distinguish Esau from Jacob; and that Athena was merciful when she punished the seven-year-old Tiresias for blundering upon her naked bath by covering his eyes with her hand instead of pinching his nose.

As he grew older Ibi paused longer and more often at points of overlaid spoor. Though still too young for contemplative loitering he was old enough to unearth layer upon layer of history, and backwards through time to discover the visitations that had befallen an interesting spot. To him each pausing point was imbued with a distinct agglomeration of molecules grossly undiscriminated by people, for whom the gasses of a deme or lot of land or wall were indivisible; to him every select post or rock or tree was its own Renaissance landscape, with a story in temporal perspective, often conventional, sometimes novel. Yet unlike Einstein and others who have visually imagined the functions or structures represented by abstract symbols, it was not by image that his brain read narratives of strangers saints sinners and less domestic animals at their water holes of diachronistic intersection; not by diagram or icon: but rather by an unmediated and irreducible configuration of olfactory identifications—just as by scanning a surface with his flews or raising his nose to the air he was able to dispense with the ancillary senses of eye and ear in detecting simultaneous phenomena of organic and mechanical types.

But Ibi's investigations were hardly apperceptive, and as it would never have occurred to him that they could be communicated like desires he did not wonder how he could share them with the communion of saints. His ad hoc intuitions, as well as his leadership, in plain contrast to his theoretical master's, were purely pragmatic; therefore he neither dwelt upon them nor compared them—until he met his new friend the venerable Praisegod Barebones over in North Village.

Then, in arguing the question of sensory priority, he was admonished by the elder, who was growing rather deaf, for undervaluing the essential gift of hearing, which had blessed him as an embryo with the first sensation of his mother. The wise old Collie gently chided the brash youth for ingratitude to the ancestral breeding that had endowed him with the enviable ears of a Viking Shepherd.

Ibi for his part could not forbear observing that Praisegod himself, now slightly arthritic, having failed to attend the Thing for many a year, and having lost most of his curiosity about passengers beyond his demesne, was forever discriminating subtle fluctuations and refinements by nosing around his single tiny beachhead where the interfering sounds of the impartial ocean, periodically overpowered by the thundering crunches of Pigeonhole Forge, were almost always flooding the dry refinements of one's tympanum. It was touching that the sedentary old fellow should rate the aesthetic cultivation of his own genius lower than the simply inherited faculty of enlarged and directable ears.

Goddy granted that those organs might well be cherished less then one's educated nostrils by a young gallant living in a neighborhood of mechanically promiscuous noises and still chasing pussies; and that indeed, though apparently otherwise with strangers, audible signals can convey to a saint next to nothing of even the recent past.

Ibi on the other hand allowed that in a comparatively quiet village a dog can effortlessly prehend without leaving his station a much greater field of space by ear than by nose. This his own reflection in the course of discussion brought to mind the Magic Mountain radar antennae of the North Atlantic Distant Early Warning System as described by Bice Picory (now calling herself Belle Cingani). Anyhow, the conversation made him conscious for the first time that the involuntary erection of Atlantean Gothic ears was a conspicuous development of Viking and Jewish shepherds only, ridiculously gross in comparison with the aristocratic disproportion of a long thin nose in the Celtic race.

Thus each of the two saints modestly deprecated one of his own talents; but the younger, not yet having satisfied himself as to all the other possibilities of sense, was far from settled enough in life to practice the patient muzzle scholarship of his hoary new teacher. He nevertheless agreed that the aural faculty, though he prized it as his first sense, merely gathered one limited kind of intelligence for translation into the common substance of innermost metascent, which was formed into epistemological shapes for memory and thought.

Until now Ibi Karcist had been barely aware of Praisegod Barebones as a retired scent from distant parts who had ceased contributing to the palimpsest of the Marking Rock in olden times and was now detectable on Mr Barebones's pants at the machine shop. If they hadn't been introduced by their strangers they never would have met.

This is how it happened, on an adventurous Monday afternoon in Spring [which never would have been forgotten, if any event remaining in Ibi's experience could be called memory in human terms], when Caleb first directed an expedition clear across the Purdeyville heath to North Village for a voice lesson:

On the way over to Powerhouse Cove Ibi anticipated nothing unusual until he found himself called right on past Cynosure Rock (the Marking Stone, site of the Thing). Up to that point he had been so absorbed in learning or recalling details of the moorland wilderness (once largely domesticated but now frequented only by small quadrupeds, some birds, a few snakes, and blueberriers or odd bipedestrians) that he had almost forgotten the man he scouted for.

It was principally for Ibi's study and delight that this overland trail had been taken to the transferred venue of an appointment with Mrs Barebones that otherwise would have been canceled on account of her sick child. It would have saved mortal working hours to drive around to the Village by Cod Street. But the prospect of an afternoon hike with a definite purpose (yet conducive to free meditation upon theatrical and erotic prospects) had presented Caleb with a good excuse to skip his morning run again. Besides, he'd never seen the Purdeyville Common of Tir-Na-Dog at this time of year, at least since forgotten childhood, and he hoped to find Wat Cibber's mocking contributions to the apothegms on rocks that later would be hidden by the overgrowths of summertime.

Not far from their starting point they turned off Cod Street up the still-settled segment of Watling Road (the abandoned inland coach route) and crossed the Old Stone Bridge whose solid granite balustrades were smudged by a century of steam locomotives chugging through the cut. The cunningly pieced blocks of undressed stone, locked together by their own weight, spanned the single line where the right-of-way to Land's End sliced through deep walls of living rock as sheer as the Corinthian Ship Canal's. Here the ruins of modern pavement left off and the earliest track to Seamark dwindled into a recidivous double path of rutted dirt lined with grasses.

The nostalgic lane climbed a ridge of deserted pastureland, not yet gone to seed, where surface stones had been dragged and lifted into walls edging the road and still fended off the second encroachment of forest, which was adumbrated by hardwood scrub lodging along the borders. Methodically, by labor no longer imaginable, nine months of the year, six days of the week, as long as there was light in the sky, for the century and a half before Georgio colonists finally admitted to their wives or mothers that they couldn't make their living as farmers, men and oxen had denuded these irregular slopes of primeval pines, the King's and all. But before their kine could tame this pasturage, now so charmingly ribbed with ledges of chthonic mother-bone and (with the cows all gone) softening into decline against a threatened invasion of sumac birch and aspen, the death-grips of noble stumps had to be pried and extirpated by the sweat of man and the brawn of neat. It took smoldering fire to shrivel their roots.

But instead of continuing to follow the old road down into hollow woods where it was still swamped with mud from the melted grip of winter (thereby skirting Birdhouse Hill to rejoin the eastern segment of Cod Street at Tybbot's Reach), they plunged off to their left on a path through the tumbled wall to a precipitous trail ending at the railroad track below. The cinder bed of calibrated parallel bars took them onto a short embankment across the old eastern inlet of Railcut Pond, long ago raised by a dam to become the city's first artificial reservoir, leveling the Colonial mill-race of Quigley Brook, by which the public drinking water was still fed through a culvert buried under the elevated causeway.

Listening with somewhat excessive anxiety for a train from either direction whose whistles he might have failed to hear and Ibi failed to interpret, glancing especially behind his back toward the blind bend from the Corinthian chasm he had peered down into a few minutes before and keeping the dog close before him, Caleb hurried along the canted gravel footpath worn into a sloping shoulder of weatherbeaten gravel. Superstitiously cautious, he refused to walk between the rails on the splintered oily sleepers. Those monotonously repeated cross-sills imbedded in the blackened ballast were decaying in neglect, yet they continued to serve well enough as organic foundations for the sinuous extensions of 40-foot steel that still divided the west of the island from the east, the north from the south, the rural from the urban, until they ended as a spacious candelabra. Caleb breathed more easily climbing through stone-obstructed woods on the opposite steep, approaching the lovely open upland of the time-ruined Common.

Mild salt air from the northeast had yielded to a chillier northwest motion that veiled the vernal sun with reminders of bleak winter. In many places the paths were still sodden, and greening grass was coldly mushy under foot. Even the dry cedars and junipers did not yet trust the warming tilt of earth, though the leaves of deciduous bushes were already half unfolded, sparsely scattered around "Purdeyville Square", where three roads used to meet at the groin of a hamlet. Here the wooded fringes of the disincarnate community were out of sight behind ridges of thin rockbottomed earth that had once supported forests among erratic boulders previously strewn like megalithic dung by the last scouring glacier but now keeping company with the low boscage of abandoned agriculture. The thin boreal grass seemed cropped forever by vanished sheep and cattle. To this atmosphere Ibi was impervious, but for Caleb, who'd envisioned Spring, the parkland of nearly naked moor was exposed to a churlish sky. In this weather the Irish-Atlindu pastures were almost forbiddingly prehistoric. The immovable moraine was overgrown here and there with barely traceable Old World hedgerows or a haunted single vestige of dooryard orchards, which had generally given way to juniper and cedar.

Ibi, busy, marked the titanic surface rocks that were incised with the Duke of Dogtown's mottoes, many of which would be obscured in summer by bushes or brambles. Now and then stepping off the path, Caleb reviewed his favorites:

> WHEN WORK STOPS VALUES DECAY
> WORK FOR THE NIGHT IS COMING

and ENJOY THE BENEFITS OF TIME

but ignored:
> FAITH IS A GOOD IDEA
> KEEP YOUR PROMISES
> TRY TO LOVE FATHER
> SUPPORT MOTHER
> NEVER SIGH NEVER SIN

and other Pauline pieties.

But lingering longer than intended he also discovered the one he was looking for:

> NEVER TRUST THE EXPERTS

And, nearby, another that was new to him:

> A WISE SON HIS FATHER'S JOY

Some of these literations had often been quoted by his mother; they always reminded him of her Caliban-jingle, composed at a bedtime in Norumbega when he was looking forward with awe to the great adventure of going to school for the first time:

> A seagle flew from north to south
> With Caleb Karcist in his mouth.
> When he found he had a fool
> He dropped him in
> The Purdeyville School!

Of course there was no Purdeyville School, even back home on Cape Gloucester, never had been, and even before the dawn of education Caleb knew that enrollment in Dogtown was not his destiny. But now he laughed at what he learned by dawdling among the ghosts of an imaginary schoolyard.

Further along, pushing his way some distance off the beaten track of the Common to a trio of lesser rocks, he at last found the impertinent contributions of Wat Cibber in the palmy days of his youth. The amateurish chiseling was rough and irregular, probably executed hastily by the tricky light of moonshine:

> IT'S TOO EARLY TO PREDICT
> AND TOO LATE TO REPENT
>
> SUFFICIENT UNTO THE DAY
> ARE THE ANXIETIES THEREOF
>
> A WATCHED POT NEVER BOILS
> BUT AN UNWATCHED POT BOILS OVER

To Ibi in turn, further on, when his master tried to hurry him past the Marking Stone (sacred library of scents) with no time for more than cursory sniffs, it seemed only fair to lag behind and study its laminations of history and new learning. The man himself who was in such a big rush to get somewhere did not even stop to mark his passage; but the dog, invoking the occasional privilege of contrary will, lost himself in pentimento analysis, nearly heedless of receding whistles and ever more peremptory calls. Why such insensate indifference to the central monument of Tir-Na-Dog? But in the end, just as his disobedience to repeated cries of command was about to provoke profane and ugly wrath, he obeyed the human summons.

At another time Caleb would have tarried to climb this Rock of rock's cranium, split to one side by a millennium of frost, like the inverted jaw of a breaching sperm whale; but once his quest for Wat Cibber's holographs was satisfied he'd given himself almost exclusively to proleptic rumination about his first visit to Tessa Barebones's house as a private pupil, the compelling object of this excursion, not without pondering excuses for his delinquency in self-disciplining homework.

Still, in his eagerness for her conversation, most of the island's backbone was trodden in two hours, even with two or three mistaken ventures into attenuating paths made by a century of blueberry-pickers, and one overconfidently chosen by-path in woods beyond the Cynosure. He was looking for a descent somewhere between the fire trail (which veered off too soon to the Cod Street traffic of Seamark Village) and the path that would have taken them too far toward Pigeonhole Cove. By threading scrub oak and vegetating heaps of granite rubble, strewn in latterday underbrush about the rims of vacated quarries, he succeeded at last in coming out exactly where he'd hoped to. Rejoining the city's circumferential thoroughfare at a level halfway down to the sea, they crossed the broad and sturdy New Stone Bridge (too high above the abandoned roadbed of the private quarry rails to have been smudged by puffing coalsmoke), whence there were only a couple of cable lengths further to go down to the Barebones' Powerhouse.

Melissa, Tessa's younger, was sick in bed upstairs, sick of school but not too sick to sleep. Praisegod stood quietly on the threshold, as if he'd been told to expect Ibi, with the silent dignity of some unassuming senior baron greeting his new prince. Ibi paused with instinctive respect, but made the first movement, suggestive of play, as befits the younger; the Collie, surprised, unbent. All at once they were chasing each other with smiling tongues, or running shoulder to shoulder all about the pier, down on the poppled shingle, and half way up the residential bluff above the house.

"Goddy hasn't romped like this since the cow jumped over the moon." said Tessa. "They can entertain each other until Miles gets home from school. There's plenty of water for two in the dish out there."

Tessa's children were never underfoot, and she didn't expect her friends to be interested in them. She made light of her devotion to their future for whose sake she suffered rustication and boredom. Caleb was no more aware of them than of his own, then or later, except as elements of their mother's apparently well-mastered domestic responsibilities.

The voice lesson took place in comfortable chairs before the massive empty hearth in the long rough-hewn granite and paneled living room. "This mausoleum isn't the best spot for getting down to business. I'm not very good at setting the tone without some artificial help. I regret lending our piano to the studio. It would have been better to keep it here for the kids to grow up with. Cora and I never had one at home. She has perfect pitch; I have none."

She put Caleb through his breathing exercises; then his vowels and consonants; he was even advanced a little into the reading of words. "Don't worry: I'm not going to make you into an actor. Remember, it's just to place your voice."

"If we can find it first!"

After half an hour they both gave up the pretense of interest in such hopeless therapy. Unless he devoted his life to self-improvement—and at home he could scarcely bring himself to repeat the easiest exercises—she could do little more for his maimed voice than for his stature. He believed that she understood the degree to which he was disqualified by both of society's most prevalent criteria for estimating a man. She denied that by now she was secretly half prepared to agree that his vocal function was incorrigible, but he read her mind.

Yet he trusted that even as a professional judge of quality in men of masks she did not judge as others judged. So he confessed to having been strangled by his own umbilical cord and dragged into the world by obstetrical force.

"The birth trauma's nothing, compared to the mother's labor." she assured him through the curling smoke of her cigarette, after pouring two glasses of sherry, her face lifted to the great beams of her ceiling with judiciously narrowed eyes. Slowly twisting her eloquent neck she then peered quizzically at her patient. Under her appraisal, shrunk in his corner of the excessively large rectangular sofa, he felt no more than half opaque.

The pleasure of tobacco wafted to his nostrils summoned up from childhood his mother's tranquil presence, particularly in this case with a picnic on the rocks half a mile from where he now sat, less innocent yet unembittered about women who smoked during gestation. Nevertheless it was an uncongenial theme that she caused him to extract from all the memories of his nurture. "So I've been taught, from time out of mind. I heard it as a sort of biological abstraction before I was old enough to take it as a fact of life. To this day in letters from the Peaceable Kingdom I'm sometimes reproached for my mother's 'sacrifice'! For years I may have taken the blame too lightly; and now I'm inured."

"Mothers recover. So do throttled babies, if they survive the neonatal crisis. There's nothing wrong with your vocal organs. I won't give up on you until your neck's under the guillotine. But even then I suppose you wouldn't reveal the subject of your play. Before they condemn you, tell me at least what it *means*."

Unaccountably, he wasn't loathe to respond (at least in distracting terms), though he had always despised that ubiquitous demand, even about Life. "It has no meaning." he told her with referential scorn in his flat voice. "It's made of meanings—seeing that any play is composed of language—but as a whole it *means* nothing. A bird's nest may be built of twigs, but it isn't just a bigger twig."

"Then mention just one of the straws that's not a stage direction."

Abstraction so concretely challenged, his forehead flushed in evasion. How could he so suddenly open up forthright? Besides, it was hard to remember the play at all, or to recall the purpose of his defenses. He was perversely tempted to talk instead about his efforts to defy nidificational wisdom by including rather than excluding certain twigs or straws that appeared inessential to the hatching of eggs; but he remembered just in time what a fool he made of himself whenever he tried to combine exposition of his axiological crotchets by pleasant conversation. Though a creature of the Method in drama, and a lover of the arts, he reminded himself, she was "commercial" at heart, like nearly everyone else in Atlantis.

Since she was attacking his ultimate privacy, he turned the tables on her, hoping to demonstrate by bold discontinuity that he was a patient to be reckoned with. "I'll talk when you get your theater started." To young Caleb the passion of a "middle-aged" pair was more touching than enviable, but he felt from the sympathetic vibrations of his competitive instinct that Mrs Barebones wanted to talk about the angel flown in from the West. "I've heard Rafe say Dogtown isn't beautiful but it's the kind of place where a man could do business without giving up poetry."

Rafe's remark had been sincere. Often the beginning of interest in something, or of its aesthetic appreciation, is tolerance for the interest or appreciation of a person to whom it's important, and may lead to enthusiasm. The Westerner's devotion to Dogtown had dawned with his liking for more than a few lovers of Dogtown, especially Doctor Charlemagne, the Schlossbergs, Thad Kryothermsky, and this woman's husband; but it had risen swiftly to a zenith from his tolerance of Tessa's attachment to the location of her unhappiness, who was otherwise no more typical of the place than any of the other denizens he knew. So it is that seraphs are captivated by particularities of time and space to which daughters of men are partial. Rafe's formerly eclectic nostalgia for Atlantean places from coast to coast was now reduced and concentrated.

Considering Caleb's insolence without returning his look, Tessa blew a lungful of savory smoke at the great besomed fireplace, more suggestive of the granite portal to a Barebones tomb than of an ashy family hearth. With but faint pretense of random idleness the smoke drifted into the chimney originally built to draw great blasts of boiler-heating gaseous carbons. "So you're guessing—about Rafe and me?" she calmly dared to offer with half a smile, though it seemed gratuitous to admit anything so lacking in evidence. "Not much has happened yet."

Despite the smell of cigarette she was nothing like Caleb's mother. Her negligent but precisely modulated contralto voice—so different for instance from his landlady Keith's, her ebullient friend, and just as different in her sunless complexion—conveyed neither surprise nor displeasure. Her vocal savoir faire reminded him of Father Lucey.

"Buck must never know." she went on. But now she glanced at Caleb in definite sign of anxiety. "He's a true saint."

"I know." Caleb solemnly agreed, glad as ever to share a woman's secret, and still incapable of authentic sympathy for the plight of a husband (unaware or not) for whom his admiration gratitude and affection was wholly genuine.

In any event Caleb's habitual reserve was disarmed by Tessa's frankness. He was learning from her, and from Father Chris, that personal revelations need not either devastate one's bios theoretikos or endanger an innermore privacy. Nor did the telling of a secret necessarily expose other zones of concealment. In speaking of himself for the nonce he would invert the Method of acting whereby a real personal feeling is artificially associated with the emotion of the public role: by behaving histrionically with a psychological audience, if not actually speaking in psychological cliches, he might be able to transfer the emotion of the mask to the vivification of hardly remembered or unremembered memories.

But Tessa wasn't talking about Caleb Karcist now. By referring to her theater project she found a way to express coolly disguised excitement at the possibility of Rafe's continuous presence in Dogtown, whatever the consequences. "I think of him as our guardian archangel. He understands what we're trying to do with a company of dancing mummers."

Among his Dogtown friends Rafe was making no secret of the fact that he'd done well with Parity stock, or that he and his manufacturing associates might sell Tubalcain to Cook Evaporator, one of the Parity companies, at an irresistible price. (Walt Edenfield his de facto partner must remain as chief engineer but Rafe himself, the president, would be retained as a nonresident consultant for at least a year.) These lodes of fortune perhaps sufficiently explained his reappearance in Dogtown as a potential investor or entrepreneur, as though he was simply inclined to live far away from bittersweet Golden Horn Bay where his two decades of corporate labor during the private trials of marriage had finally produced a personal horn of plenty.

"It's a shame we have to go to all this trouble just to get a mumming place, when there are half a dozen private theaters and great halls owned by the rich around here." she sighed. "The one that would be best for Hoof and Mouth belongs to an old dog-in-the-manger fart who supports St Paul's Apostolic Church and reserves the seignorial right to read the Lessons with pompous expression, though he condescends to exercise that caprice only when he happens to be estivating here. What makes this rich ham all the more sickening is that he owns the whole Merrymount Hill and calls his house Shandy Hall. He did some student acting at Princedom, and ever thereafter he's fancied himself a gentleman amateur. Before the war he sported a summer theater up there—'by invitation only'! He got notices on the Society page of the *New Uruk Testament* for the celebrities from Ur and London who were inveigled to his houseparty shows."

Tessa had canvassed this subject comprehensively. "Over the past fifty years there have been a few other companies for the summer trade—never anything but "summer stock". The demand for that kind of drama proved so light that one of the theaters has been converted into a donkey-engine stable!" She meant the shed that housed the stationary steam engine used to haul large boats at the Simon's Point Marine Railways.

"Even the handsome Ibicity Hall auditorium, where they used to hold all the school plays and graduation exercises, has been half chopped up into a warren of flimsy cubicles for the entrenching bureaucracy. Our officials despoil space the way their predecessors attacked the hostile forest. Dexter Keith says it would take an act of the state legislature—and the grant of a quarter of a million dollars—to make them restore it. But the likes of us would never be allowed to use it anyway, for fear of boring the majority or disturbing popular taste.

"Then there's the Gallery of Players, which once had some pretensions as an attraction for serious producers, but now has been fixed up by a fashionable painter as his private studio and seduction parlor. . . . Not to mention Captain Ozone's open-air Theater-on-the-Rocks out at Chateau Noir, long since dedicated to the devil, I'm told, but of course off limits for good people like us.

"So maybe Mr Opsimath can help spare us the knuckling of our foreheads to any such dogs-in-the-manger."

But wouldn't she beg for "recognition" of one kind or another? Caleb asked himself—in a republic that had spawned and battened the devilvision culture in every household, her own included. It occurred to him to mention one thing Ipsissimus Charlemagne had tried, to keep his distance between dramaturgic democracy and the Medici, before there was DV to undermine his optimism:

"One summer when Doc was young he persuaded Black's Hardware to give him their old delivery dray, built a hinged apron stage to fold up like a circus wagon's flank, organized a company, got some artists to execute his masks, hauled the loaded wagon up Pilot

Hill with an old team from the last livery stable, and put on his version of the Oedipus trilogy—at what he called 'one of the right places within our place'. It was free. The best attendance was seventeen, not counting dogs, mostly to view the brilliant blue offing beyond the wagon."

"So I've heard. It was called Theater-on-the-Wain. Cape Gloucester people have always cherished an animus for the prairie kind of schooner. I've heard interesting stories about that summer. There were about seventeen transpontine performers volunteering their services.

"Nowadays we locals can't offer him that many, but maybe we can entice him into our barn by renovating it according to his ideas. Dexter's our complimentary architect. He'll find the time, once we hold the deed. Everybody else must contribute money or services in kind. Rafe isn't rich, you know. Most of his capital should be invested in some paying business."

Caleb warmly mentioned his own gratitude for Rafe's help as his temporary employer, and his admiration of Rafe's alert interest in all things. Yet for Buck's sake he was uneasy about the confirmed stage of intimacy, almost of economic partnership, that he thought was betrayed by her nearly possessive attitude toward Rafe, whom he believed divorced from another daughter of man at the other end of the country. He was now growing reluctant to share her secrets any further. With her he preferred to share his own.

[As a matter of fact Tessa wasn't in love with Rafe Opsimath wildly or uncontrollably; despite her erotic concerns, and her domestic, she remained as curious as ever about the lives of unexplained people, particularly that of Caleb her new hemidemisemi confidant. Not for long did the pleasure of discussing Rafe divert her professional curiosity from the reticent young playwright whom Rafe had praised for a kind of esoteric analytical talent (the objects of which were in themselves of no attraction to her). His masked arrogance was plain enough to her, but not the causes of his diffident demeanor, which usually neutralized the objectionable facet of his masculinity.]

"This time Rafe came East on the train." Caleb was telling her, tactfully and perhaps jealously affecting the belief that she knew less about the man than he did. "He says it was just to see the back fences. And that's how Ibi and I are going to get home this afternoon." He asked if she knew the V & M schedule. He'd have to allow half an hour for walking to the station.

She assured him that there was still time enough and more to tarry for another glass of sherry. Miles didn't get home until late in the afternoon, inasmuch as he attended a private school that was very serious about giving him a head start toward college; and Melissa was still asleep upstairs.

Afterwards, therefore, in the Land's End rail yard, waiting for the 4:52 "Westbound" to load at the terminal platform, he had more to regret, having stayed too long.

He and Ibi went over to inspect the stout swivel crane (built for steam but now motorized with electric power) which all his life had been planted in concrete among the cinders alongside the furthest siding with all its gear-train open to the weather. Of heaviest iron and steel Hephaestus had wrought its squat solid post, trussed boom, and massive lifting block, rigged for angular elevation with short multiplications of the heaviest cable. This obsolete mechanical structure might have been taken for the torso of a European windmill. Twenty years ago it had been his earliest image of declining industry, in piteous contrast to the nearby locomotives panting with vibrant vitality even at their rest.

Before the war all great structures of the male world had seemed archeological remnants of a golden age, pointed out by his mother to the best of her knowledge. With no more edification than what she could remember from a seldom available father in her otherwise feminine childhood she was conscientiously alert to structural and mechanical devices, sometimes misunderstanding their purposes but always attempting to inculcate her boy as she thought a father might, or else amusing herself with imaginary causes.

She'd called it Thor's teakettle, which mortals were never allowed to see in use; then seriously surmised that it was designed for lifting the ends of freight cars while their wheels were being repaired, like horses being shod. Young Mary Tremont had never had a Buck to correct such fancies in the daily course of living. Doubting all her conjectures about its function, Caleb had always vainly hoped to see the crane in action. But now he knew from a casual article in the *Nous* that it was still used by the Cape Gloucester Forge Company to unload stock steel from flat cars and lay it onto flatbed trucks (formerly horse-drays) for hauling over to North Village. Ibi pissed thrice upon the pedestal of the motionless insensible monster.

Caleb was asking himself what had possessed him to tell Tessa he was a child of Melchizedek. Brooding over the Powerhouse visit, his forehead burned with regret. He had unnecessarily amplified his unprecedented self-revelation to this woman (so charmingly unlike any other he knew in real life) by also blurting out a cowardly anxiety: "I've even belonged to the Resistance!"

"I understand it's practically a secret society, now reduced to two or three uncommunicating members." she had smiled with droll weariness. "Don't tell me your part in conspiracies!"

Tessa perfectly well knew Doc's position in the Resistance, and had all along assumed this dissident's fealty to it. [Even as far back as 1961 it was pegged by nearly everybody but Caleb as a Luddite cause both anachronistic and ridiculous.] In reputation it was no longer conflated with Premature Antifascism. Not only by sophisticates but now also by the masses it had come to be regarded as an almost harmless eccentricity. According to Tessa's liberal estimate of public opinion Caleb would have been considered no more subversive of contemporary law and order than was Ishi of Cornucopian civilization in 1909.

In abstraction Caleb perceived that amelioration of demotic attitude; yet the trend toward personal tolerance, which might have palliated his religious depression at the degradation of his country, left him little the less fearful for his social security. For the Resistance was metaleptic of all his shames. That confidential admission to Tessa had only led him further into the depths of a misleading confession.

He tried to comfort himself with the assurance that there were more immediate things he'd had the sense to leave untouched. He'd said nothing about Lilian or Belle, for instance; and certain other threads of dignity had been left intact.

But the very fact that Tessa didn't know there were crucial things she hadn't been told (not only about his lovelife but also about his bios theoretikos), and therefore doubtless thought she could read his history, bothered him no less than his indiscreet exposure of presumably deterministic traumas. Her weening psychologism was the attitude that rankled; and for the moment it only made him want to tell her more, to correct her vision of himself, dignified or not!

Later, during the ten minutes that he stood swaying in the aftermost vestibule of the train with Ibi (illicitly indulged by a goodnatured conductor)—watching the single track recede as they clacked rapidly out of inert somnolence and rolled toward the comforts of home, clicking past the switches of the turn-around loop, down the stretch of Tybbot's Reach, where private cars used to be parked for the summer on carriage-trade sidings, swiftly crossing their own footworn trail at the Reservoir causeway, rattling through the cut under the smoke-stained Old Stone Bridge on which they had begun their journey into the interior so long ago in living time, and slowing into the Harbor yard—his stomach was still turning in revulsion against selfdisclosure to any human being: indeed against all speech.

But that night as he lay in retrospection for a minute or two before gaining the full attention of Hypnos, who had already attended to flat-out Ibi, Caleb reviewed the day in that sleeping dog's perspective. Ibi and Goddy had immediately accepted each other as natural allies—one young and optimistic, the other benign and melancholy, each resembling his master in comparative wisdom. After one brief sniffing, head to tail, and after Ibi had been shown about the property, it was by a grace of God which strangers had long since forfeited that they'd played for an hour or more like littermates.

Ibi hadn't been worried about the weirdly drawn-out sounds that at first issued from within the house of Goddy, for to an olfactory certainty it was a female by whom Caleb was admitted to the cavern. The shepherd had learned from his charge's previous sequestrations with females that odd sounds were likely to emanate as a sign of anything but danger or distress.

Thereafter the two smiling guardians had rested like a pair of couchant lions outside the great double door on Poseidon's landing. In parallel dignities they faced the driveway, toward the overshadowing escarpment of the granite shore. With pulsating satisfaction their wet pink tongues evaporated heat in the balmy springtide air, lolling in and out of parted mouths. But Ibi's adolescent teeth gleamed whiter and sharper than the dulled ivory in Goddy's more delicate and narrow jaw. By then the dogs had left off their epistemological colloquy, having sufficient consensus in organoleptic empiricism.

Lady Barebones had sincerely admired the doughty young Viking's stature and temperament, though he seemed to her grossly energetic and half naked next to the fully coated sheepdog she cherished as a standard of intelligence and beauty. "Ibi should play the lead in our Dogtown pageant." she said to her pupil as he and his champion took their leave. Goddy was standing sadly at her side, his drooping tail slowly asway, while Ibi led Caleb up the sea-cliff as vigorously as he had begun the excursion, his nose rapidly rereading the wooded slope half an inch from the ground, already insensible to the farewell of the worthy friend he left behind.

In sleep Caleb allowed himself to be separated from the sleep of Ibi. They both dreamt a lot that night. The dog forgot his dreams every time he awoke enough to redispose his sinews according to the variable gradients between his self-warmed parts and the falling dormitory temperature—in a continuity of postures between his lengthy spread and his tight heat-conserving curl of nose and tail, repeated in reverse order after dawn, when his man closed the window and turned on a radiator to signal the human reveille.

Usually Caleb too forgot his dreams, and this time he forgot all but one, or part of one that he knew was extensive and complex, or perhaps one of a family of condensed dreams echoing each other like paradigmed equations. Anyhow he was aware of having experienced picaresque psychical activity—of which he was able to retain the last episode long enough to reach the awakening surface of consciousness, before it too dissolved in the very retrieval:

Under Doc Charlemagne's direction he pushed through some small cedars off the path in Tir-Na-Dog near the Common to come upon an overgrown boulder he hadn't seen before on any rock:

> MATERNITY IS A FACT
> PATERNITY A MATTER OF OPINION

The chiseled style suggested cuneiform lettering. No one knew who had carved the apothegm, but Doc was about to offer his hypothesis that Mary Tremont had done the carving, thus disclosing that all along he'd known the crucial secret in Caleb Karcist's past::

As the dreamer turned to go on toward the Village, Doc somewhere in the wings, he found Wat Cibber blocking the way behind a juniper in his one-piece fish-hauling armor of black rubber buskins cuisses and cuirass. The stout fisherman repeatedly mumbled "Eternity is a matter of opinion . . ." and showed his teeth in the foolish rictus he often affected when he'd just made a witticism:::

"It's an article of Attic law." glossed the offstage voice.

11
THE PRINCESS TOWER

*E*xcursions and therapies notwithstanding, and quotidian vocational remissions, the fever raged that was caused by both Love's arrows. Caleb's contemplative faculties were increasingly possessed by the mystery peculiar to Lilian Cloud. Even for scenes devoid of gender, she now seemed to be the ground of all colors. Always, for purposes of work or diversion, it was consciousness of her that had to be displaced or overlaid; otherwise her figure, the representative and focus of all imaginations, claimed his whole moral continuum. Again and again he contended against his hope, calculating to annul the vacuum of her absence, whenever he tried to enjoy a disinterested state of bios, either praktikos or theoretikos.

His most obsessive speculations were directed to Lilian's conditionally reserved body but his thoughts took incalculably more account of her consort Gil Algo, whom he'd never seen, than of Mooney, contracted in her with his own flesh, whom he'd seen two or three times, toward whom there could be no question of the mother's attitude, and of whom he was not in the least jealous.

Propagation had not ever been the point of his desire. On his part the motive for phallic conjugation was anything but seminal. And he was nearly as indifferent as Jean-Jaques Rousseau to the existence of children. His other two daughters presumptive (whose very names, sanctioned by other men, he did not remember), not to mention his spurious extravasations of children in vitro, were less missed than certain temporarily interactive classmates at various grade schools he'd attended as a transient. Although generally believing that only women and satiated men were given to philoprogeneity, he attributed to his own peculiar incunabula the exceptional impassiveness with which he regarded all references to reproduction that were not directly related to the desire of his sex for a narrowminded and more immediate satisfaction.

But Lilian's face-to-face excommunication put an end to his headlong pursuit and tripped him into a comprehensive depression resembling grief: at any rate it was the nearest he'd ever come to mourning. He wept at the bleak illimitable sense of absolute loss. Every thought or fact that he associated with her by imagination or memory (even if only because it happened to have registered during either of their two common eras), previously cherished as a mark of joy or hope, was now the nostalgic twist of a knife. It would have seemed an adumbration of his own death if she had also forbidden a continuation of his letters.

He looked into the trusting brown eyes of Ibi-Roi, as interrogative and spiritual as hers, locked the embarrassed dog in his arms, and cried aloud for the skinkeeper's halfbreed daughter who had loved a wolf.

A title in the bookcase caught his eye, *Beyond Psychology*, and he cried aloud for the student who had once remarked that psychology made her sick.

He read of Amandus and Amanda of Lyon whose tomb was an illusion, Larry Sterne's elusive Pyramus and Thisbe, and wept for the inchoate painter with whom he'd once hoped to go to France.

He remembered the Knight's selection from Matter of Rome—

> And yet they weenen for to be ful wise,
> That serven love, for ought that may bifalle.

—and wept for the death of his romance.

But after a while, entirely on the strength of his own unanswered screeds, utter despair gave way to the melancholy hope for a revived or persisting share of her thoughts. He began to trust in her irresolution, that she might reopen by a crack, only now and then, the gate of folly that had been shut in his face. But folly she knew it was for him to seek open possession of a woman with the baggage of both daughter and mother; for it was not simply a matter of sustaining her young. Had he not told her that among the Greeks swans were especially noted for protecting their parents?

Over and over again he tried to guess what she might have written if she had replied to his absurd letters. Such as the one that began: "Are you so strong that you can despise your attractive force? I'll probably never mail this, for that force would be reversed by horror of the passion that dictates to me. I guess you've had all too much passion centered on you in the last four years. I ought to be silenced by knowing that."

Or the devlish letter that let loose with this: "Under your sky I'm a thawing volcano. Give my madness a chance. I haven't had a fair hearing. Let me have a little time to talk to you. Take no thought for the morrow. You weren't made for secure domesticity. This is not the time to worry about putting Mooney through college. Don't give up your soul to virtue."

Or another, groveling: "I keep trying to fetch up your view of the situation (as far as I can imagine it from the unbalanced facts in my possession). I have no just cause to protest against the minimization of my shadow on your habitation in Dogtown."

Succeeded by: ". . . my galactic windfall of intelligence and beauty. Perhaps our mutual fate was experimental on destiny's part. Perhaps no promises were ever in order. Perhaps nature has endowed us with an irreconcilable contrariety. Thus were my hopes misplaced in the first place, or displaced by my replacement. Yet for both of us the value of our intersection is inexpungible: the precious, incomparable, astounding, essentially novel whirlwind of heat and light that has wakened and shaken all my molecules, inviting yours to sympathetic agitation. . . ." Which ended: "I know practically nothing about what you really think; but it's inconceivable that you feel no conflict, no tension, no turmoil about severing yourself from me. On the other hand, if you have really fallen into alien bondage, you are refusing to accept my compassion.

> The she-wolf in a cage
> Calls all Heaven in her rage."

Without thinking to mention his abuse of Blake.

And postscribed: "I've decided to mail this because I have recourse to no other poor pitiful action that will keep me from pounding on your door in Folly Road and challenging a duel. And to leave my attic for any other purpose—like going to work tomorrow morning—will be as hard as martyrdom in war. My Mask is undermined by a tenderness too weak to suffer any eyes but yours."

Or the more lugubrious one that followed: "My croons of sorrow are the Moonfeather Blues. I wish you'd listen to the voice that can sing no other songs. Your straight spine haunts me; but your quizzical forehead is my most treasured loss. A recurrent memory of your humorous eyes wrenches my heart away from duties.

"Full-face or profile, in any view at all, waxing or waning, you are the light I see by. It's not a constant light. Less than a week ago you yourself said you felt no need to decide anything right now. I thought I was going to have time to hide or redress my handicaps. How could I hear what you had to teach me when your every liberty was subject to a slave-owner's veto? You know anguish all too well; but can you understand the touchless pain of a Lilian-lover outside the walls of the house of love?"

And finally his hazardous "STORY FOR MOONEY AT BEDTIME. Once upon a time there was a swan called Moonfeather who came down from the mountains of the West and laid an egg. She had many good times with the ducks and the geese, and sometimes with eagles, but she was usually lonely. At last she settled down with an ostrich so that she could build a nest for her egg." [For he was then imagining Gil Algo as an attraction no less high-stretched and ungainly than Chris Lucey.] "This is where the story ends."

That last, as it happened, was the letter she responded to, as follows, when he unexpectedly encountered her face-to-face in an aisle of the Aristotle and Plato. Their grocery carts kissing, his heart pounded with sudden hope and fear—fear of cold rebuff and fawning hope for mere recognition of the past. He dared not look her in the eye. In his shameful fright, as though dumb with guilt, he could think of nothing but the weather. He was hardly able to twist his mouth for such insipid words as "How have you been?", etc . His lips were further benumbed by the platitudinous vulgarity of their own initial sounds; looking up he caught the frank gaze with which she had aristocratically ignored them. Desperate for intelligence, he returned to the weather: "It's been an unsprung Spring."

A benign smile was beginning to pull at the corners of her mouth. She wasn't trying to avoid him! And she wasn't angry about the latest letter! "I liked your fairy story. I read it to Mooney. It made me cry."

"How's Mr Algo?" Caleb asked, stupidly unready for idoneous reply to her graciousness. He didn't think of inquiring about the egg.

"Prospering. We had a big fight over Mooney this morning, just before he went off to Chicago for a week of software gossip. Maybe I'll never see him again." Caleb chuckled, as if her tone was jesting, taking care not to seem to be exploiting what was doubtless another exhilarating billow in her tempestuous bondage. In his most artfully unpresumptuous manner, grasping for the slenderest thread of lingering friendship, he regained the tremulous initiative that he'd thought was lost to him forever.

"Have you been getting my letters?"

She nodded. "Don't worry about counterespionage. Besides, he's a gentleman in some respects. Correspondence isn't dangerous."

He wondered to what degree she appreciated the literal ambiguity of her sentence; but her humor unmistakably brightened with the self-mocking irony of it. Yet there was no time to tease her, and in any case it was not to his advantage to remind her of the pregnancies and kinships he often discovered among her uncomplicated words, nor otherwise to rub her nose in the question of consistency. She used his language, and he hers, but at times he suspected that their meanings were shared to no greater extent than their emotions.

Then as other Dogtown shoppers brushed past them in irritable haste or fatigue she gently dashed his hope—"I must go across the street and pick up my paycheck." But she didn't make a move. "Got to get home and make supper."

"When can I see you?"

"For the last time?"

"Better than never."

"My mother's present to me for Mother's Day is a day off from Mooney et cetera for a shopping trip to St Bot. She'll take care of everything at home. I'm going Friday. I have to be back here at the Doghouse by five, but maybe I could look at you for an hour or so in the morning if you aren't working."

Caleb had never been less prepared for an assignation. With so few seconds to suggest the rendezvous and negotiate its terms he was bound to choose the first safe and pleasant milieu that occurred to him from memories of his childhood in the city—not Bot itself, with which he had little intimate acquaintance, but Unabridge on the other side of the river, near one of his old neighborhoods, where he thought it would be easiest for her to park her car, for him to evade the superfluous anxieties of unfamiliar locale, and for them both to shut out the manifold distractions of urban noise. She readily accepted the appointment.

It seemed wasteful that he was forbidden her company on the way down and the way back, but the chance bumping of wheeled wire baskets thus accounted for finding himself on a morning train early enough to make all his subway and streetcar connections with time to spare. Chris had asked no explanation of his request for special permission, and indeed encouraged the irregularity. "Trading your day-off would suit us splendidly! Take two days if you like. As a matter of fact, just today at breakfast Father Duncannon was saying he wished you could be here on Saturday next week, when many of the preparations for Chapter should be discussed with Father Davy. He's coming down from Markland to advise us."

When Caleb had set out for the station on foot Ibi was pitifully puzzled by the farewell command not to follow, and further disquieted by the affectedly reassuring tone of apology. The voice betrayed a guilt. For a few minutes the dog dared not disobey. By then the train had come and gone, releasing a dammed-up spate of kilroy traffic at the crossing gates like a wind clearing the sky behind it. When he finally broke the spell and tailed his master, as if pretending to patrol in the same direction inadvertently, it was only to lose the scent across the tracks in the stew of strange signs that spoiled the olfactory colonnade leading to the oily house which strangers flocked to before the trains stormed in. But gradually forgetting how strange this Friday was, as he trotted home the melancholy dissipated.

The ride into St Botolph afforded Caleb an idle hour to repine his folly as a plaintive lover, and to regret the elaborate imbecility with which he had attempted to improve this trifling occasion. It would take an additional hour of waiting and transferring to reach his inconvenient destination.

And then it was much to be doubted that she would appear at all, especially if she had begun to repent her promise the minute she made it. Perhaps because of having promised Gil that she would never use the telephone to circumvent his proscription of the mails she had scrupled to inform her soi-disant outside lover that she would not keep an appointment of a kind which by oversight she had never been literally sworn not to make: it might have seemed morally simpler, when she changed her mind, to let her pathetic admirer waste his precious day on a disappointment.

Besides, even with sincere intentions the meeting spot was difficult for an unguided driver to find, not detailed on any road map. In that cramped urban superimposition upon Colonial pathways nothing was familiar to the migrant from modern Cornucopia. She had plenty of excuses for not showing up.

For much of the railroad journey he stared vacantly at the rocks and shores of private estates buffered from unending sweeps of windward tide by inlet islands that for the most part remained starkly unimproved—the coastline that ordinarily continued to draw his deliberate attention, even after hundreds of rides as a grinding commuter down the line to Bethsalem or Liverpool—without even opening the book he always carried for inactive interstices of time away from office or attic. While bitterly cursing this wild swan chase he pondered the number of quarter-hours he should wait for her at the appointed place after the appointed time before he finally dismissed all cold hope.

Dear time was lost from his longevity, plus out-of-pocket costs; and he would only be further depressed if on his way home, in outworn habit, he allowed himself to tarry among successful lovers and cosseted intellectuals in the bookstores of Norumbega Square. The best plan was to go straight back to Dogtown, read as much as possible until bedtime, and devote all his own words to Ibi in an attempt to rectify his energy for a pristine morrow of the strictest discipline. He resolved to avail himself of the ensuing weekend with castigating efficiency, invoking for all he was worth the dispassionate inspiration under which he might again snap his fingers at the ridiculous notion of a miserable self.

Still, why wholly waste a wasted day? After, say, thirty minutes of pacing back and forth—forty five at the most—or of leaning against a trolley post with book in hand, as he all alone endured the incessant noise of gasoline kilroys and electric streetcars, he might break far enough out of his immediate exclusive consciousness to dwell objectively upon almost forgotten impressions of the precinct within the spiked iron fence where he'd meant to loiter with accompaniment, for his mother had sometimes taken him there when they lived in Unabridge.

The double gates of Mount Olive Cemetery, spanned by Egyptian entablature, two or three miles from the brickwalled Garth of seven-gated Norumbega, were worthy of life's ultimate frontier-crossing—in contrast to the red sandstone chapel and administrative building just inside them. Like many of the markers death-bunkers and monuments they opened upon, their frame had been hewn and assembled from the gray bones of Lady Gloucester.

This reservation, though open to the public, was still as good as new—better than new, thanks to a century of nurtured growth—by virtue of almost humming management. No headstone overturned; no broken angel-wings; no withered wreathes or abandoned flower-pots; no tattered little stick-flags bleaching in the weather. Not a scrap of paper, shard of glass, beer can, or condom! Groundskeeping here was a stern and respected career, provided with unobtrusive facilities and unseen machinery, guarded by a fraternity of porters. At night the unbroken perimeter of high fences and walls—in excellent repair, itself an essential object of perpetual maintenance—was better defended than the pale of the University.

The great necropolis, originally enclosed and shaped by Irish labor, before there were bulldozers to move the earth, was accessible only through those noble gates. Isolated from the litter of Unabridge, it was as superior to the eleven-acre Acorn Pasture Cemetery on Cod Street (its neglected agnate in provenance, commanded by Caleb's windows) as Norumbega University to Dogtown High School, albeit designed by the firm of the same landscaper. Thanks to meticulous regulation by the ample and discriminating staff, it was neither too densely nor too uniformly depopulated. Yet in acknowledgment of the formidable creative task presented by death almost every individual taste of its corporators and their survivors was tolerated, who thank heaven were above average in judgment as well as in means.

The private subdivisions were so conservatively various of expression that most of them inoffensively subordinated themselves to the collective homogeneity which naturally characterizes our common goal. Of the artificial entirety, bosky hills and dales, only surfaces were disfigured. The land-planner Frederick Mark Elmwood had been commissioned to lay out an informal park providing both "rural" uplift and cosmopolitan horticulture. Unlike a designer of architectonic structures, the chief creator of Mt Olive had been expected to anticipate changes wrought by decades of organic development that would be assisted but not dominated by the visible hand of posterity. After six-score years in this famous botanical garden many of the trees were serenely mature, and their younger generations, like 'Bega students, domestic and foreign, were harbored as esteemed individuals.

[Mr Elmwood was not to be blamed that his atelier had failed in projecting the small Acorn Pasture job, where the soil was thin, where the territory of the dead was imbedded with whalebacks of geogonic stone and sprinkled with boulders from the late glacier, where none but indigenous trees were budgeted, where financial resources were dependent upon the business cycle, and where a more demotic respect for dead bodies favored the mythical over the monumental.]

With charming irregularity at this season almost everywhere in Mount Olive the spacious sward of graves was relieved by dappled shading, especially in the spots that most stirred Caleb's nostalgia with their tawn scattering of pine needles or acorns. Hereabouts were buried many of far more renown than Isopel Berners or high-liner schooner captains, or even than Richard Tybbot, as well as thousands of no note at all, including certain unattested ancestors of Caleb Karcist whose graves he'd been shown often enough by his mother when he was indifferent to the scarcely conceivable past but now had no idea of how to find by himself. The ghosts his mother claimed lay lost among hill-spurs and dells of botanists and biologists, mathematical navigators, physicians, engineers, scholars, statesmen, abolitionists, artists, poets, politicians, novelists, historians, philosophers, college presidents, professors of every department, Pauline preachers, architects, and all their wives, not to mention the founder of the Docetic Church of Christian Health with a telephone in her coffin.

What had most attracted Caleb and his playmates, however, and therefore now urged him to revisit the mazy routes of awe, with or without Lilian, was a hilltop keep that matched the gateposts in species of stone but outweighed and overshadowed them as a mass of very different style and situation: the pseudo-European "Princess Tower" (as his mother dubbed it). Though invisible through acres of crowning foliation from the entrance to the cemetery, it surveyed not only the grounds of Mount Olive itself but also the Shawmut River basin of Greater Botolph. It was the high place upon which in Sunday School he had imagined Satan to have tempted Jesus. George Washington, had he been summoned a century later than 1775, could have used its round platform to command his siege. It rendered the enclave of Norumbega University in a perspective appropriately obfuscated by daubs of greenery and but for its tallest halls and belfries reduced to proper proportions in the vastly spreading plain of the city that surrounded it, much as if the Unaford to which the stonemason Jude aspired were viewed from a balloon and almost lost to sight within an industrial toy-town.

Since it was this faintly homesick recollection of the eminence and its grounds as a morbid setting of cowboy-and-Atlindian imagination that had spontaneously prompted his choice of Mt Olive as the place for an adult rendezvous, why not walk it alone in his disappointment? Keep an eye open for the matrilinear names he could remember, climb the Emerson Tower (as it was officially named), and like a country mouse scan from afar in wistful liberty the bridges and steeples that lead one's eye to the exalting professions he eschews by harkening to his Controller.

He sought sour consolation for the day's needless loss in the hypothesis that all along he'd been deluding himself about the natural aristocracy of a woman who accepted the specious institution of Mother's Day as genuinely traditional—and no doubt taught her daughter to do the same! He'd been brought up to scorn commercially adventitious symbols of sentiment (although his mother had never objected to such political sentimentalities as tinted pictures of F D R or the tearful strains of "Happy days are here again!").

All along Lilian had used the locutions "Mother gave me . . . Mother says . . ."! Was that how Atlindus of the High Cordillera naturally referred to their mother—not as "*my* mother", or Ma, Mama, or Mom or Momma, or Mum, or even my Old Squaw? Had she consciously copied the genteel honorific from bourgeois classmates, or from English novels? She might as well mention her old lady as "The Mater"!

But his prejudice against forms of intimate address that smacked of class or platitude Caleb had to admit was rather unfairly applied to Lilian. She at least had faced the problem, whereas he himself had been wriggling out of it for fifteen years, refusing to indulge his mother's self-dramatization by addressing her as she wished to be addressed; in person evading the vocative case, and in letters using such periphrastic salutations as "Dear Mother of All Living". In a pinch he'd call her Ma—but never since leaving her board had he repeated the "Mummie" she'd inculcated in his defenseless infancy. Yet they'd both have died before he called her Mary.

Mother's Day he'd always categorically declined to observe, never deigning to excuse himself for offering no present to the one person in the world to whom he was totally obligated, to say nothing of a so-called greeting card (the use of which he considered more immoral than neglect), stubbornly contemning even the most lighthearted recognition of "such a meretricious custom on such an arbitrary date". Perhaps it was not so bad that in this instance Lilian would *take* a special gift from her mother; but presumably she had also given one, and accepted one from her own innocent daughter.

Nevertheless, whatever profit he might wrest from a solitary excursion, and however he might benefit from the occasion by digging up the repellent faults of a woman who obsessed him, he felt no freer of enthrallment in his disenchanted blues than he had in the happiness of expectation. Yet she, the unpredictable one, had been surprisingly faithful in appearing for all their Dogtown dates that weren't canceled by telephone beforehand; and again, in mitigation, he reflected that today he had left home so far ahead of time that she would have sufficient margin of explanation for not having been able to inform him that some contingency was preventing her. And after all, such an elaborate spur-of-the-moment commitment might well have been distrusted as the outcome of a purely accidental encounter. Her default represented reasonable second thoughts about an impromptu exception to her own prudent and honest policy of disseverence.

*

On another seat, having emerged from the Norumbega Square tunnel in the Mount Olive streetcar, Caleb trundled past one of his early grade schools, subsequently abandoned but now refurbished, improving itself under the tasteful outreach of postwar academic prosperity. With an abyss of uncertainty opening in the pit of his stomach, he steeled himself for the surprise of desolation—too far from childhood, too far from home, too far from Ibi and his books to lie down and sleep.

He descended the unfolded step of the trolleycar before daring to glance to his left across the broad thoroughfare at the noble gates of the dead's own city where in his fantasy of astonishment she might have been awaiting him already. So first, before the vehicles pausing for a red light slowly lifted their blockade of the opposite bank, he found himself on a sidewalk facing the shop and display yard of the venerably entrenched headstone merchants—Mount Olive Memorials—who had immemorially displayed popular samples engraved with flowery and angelic lines (for it also served more banal cemeteries), nowadays mostly wrought only in two dimensions upon blank stock of highly polished wholesaled granite from Montvert.

To the right was a florist's shop; on the left, beyond a broad residential side street divided by abandoned car tracks, a svelte low supermarketing concatenation packed with kilroys, which he found to his surprise had replaced the shabby scattering of stores he dimly remembered on the site of an almost prehistoric carbarn. It was like being landed with a fever and sore throat on the wrong shore of the Amazon.

Just as he was turning to cross Mount Olive Avenue, Lilian herself walked up from the parking lot looking not at all unhappy. Neversoever had his heart so leaped!

"You're *so* wonderful!" He stammered with astonishment at the perfect timing of her apparition, and in Bohemian holiday attire!

"That what?" she laughed. "Professor So-and-so called that the 'feminine *so*'. You haven't given me a complete sentence."

"You'll have to imagine the ineffable ellipsis. There's no vocabulary for the extravagant clause!"

Suddenly they were together on secret liberty! Gaily joining hands and kissing for all the world to see, wantonly enjoying the mufti of urban incognito, freed of Dogtown strictures, they passed through the Egyptian portals of the nation's most cultured cemetery. Lilian kept looking at Caleb's face, caring not where he might lead her: his flower among all the flowers of May.

She pointed at a free patch of gold-erupted green under an oak. "Have you ever noticed that daffodil petals are all of one piece? I wish I were allowed to pick one for your buttonhole."

"You should be adorned with thornless roses!"

"It's not our season for artifical flowers."

"Along the shore at Dilemma Cove the wild ones are already out."

"I'm no longer wild."

The sky of May was brilliant too; the day itself was blue and green. Here in the final contraction of a patrician republic, an enclave enfolded in the warmth of Vinland's bosom half a dozen miles from the cool Atlantic, Spring had stolen a fortnight's march on Dogtown, where the grudging sea winds still hadn't come round to the continental season. Thus to these visitors from a near northeast the forenoon sun seemed summery; and Caleb had never seen its light so free of shadow in the black depth of Lilian's eyes.

He relaxed, talking a blue streak until he got her talking, talking and kissing back, and with less reserve than ever before in this second courtship, despite the public air and sunlight that prevented them from coupling right there in one of the open bowers.

If the graves had vanished, leaving undisturbed the contours and the flora of their sod, this parkland could have been a model estate for the greatest of English country houses. As such Caleb was inclined to see it. In his vision the memorial superstructures were but transparent interventions, like the homely houses of Dogtown Harbor that he ordinarily ignored as insignificant blemishes upon its naturally distinguished hills and shores. For here the dead had only incidentally endowed their own visible headstones caves and shrines: in this prelapsarian burial ground they funded primarily a generous plantation for both dwellers and admirers of cultivated Nature.

The graves disregarded by Caleb's erotic eye bore no crucifix or Blessed Virgin, though there were some simple crosses, even a few of Celtic complexity, among distinctly Pauline, Arian, Docetic, and Greek Revival styles; but it was good to see that gloomy ogival curves did not predominate. Here and there were to be found the simplest of granite markers flush with the earth, and nobly unadorned pediments with mossy roofs and iron doors half burrowed like sunken attics into the sides of greensward glens or knolls.

Yet Mrs Grundy had her way with semantic structures of granite and marble: obelisks and baldachined mausoleums; columns artificially dilapidated, if not surmounted by amphoras urns or angels; busts and statues, even of a dog (symbolizing the reliability of the U S A's first express company, founded by the deceased), and of the sphinx (symbolizing the endurance of the federal Union); and wholesome neoclassical gazebos, or cordons of cast-iron enclosing daissed cenotaphs. There were also a few bizarre experiments, such as a stack of three jagged sandstone rocks (or a sculptured imitation thereof), ostensibly balanced upon each other like some cunning feat of Heracles.

Caleb led his jocund tiger-lily on a labyrinthine saunter up and down in wandering ascent toward the tower, past no end of blossoming shrubs and flowers in every garden color, a continuum of turf and leaves in every vernal hue—all harmoniously sheltered by arboreal tents: canopies aloft in stately age or spreading nearer the ground in youth; trees informally refined, great and small, enleaving all the slopes and hollows, shading paved or grassy drives and paths that wended all the elegiac lots. Among their crowns dwelt a privileged population of darting land-birds, whose disunity of myriad fresh calls was so richly pleached as to emolliate and charm the ceaseless noises of infernal combustion and electric power in distantly surrounding streets. Indeed all sounds were dulled to a harmless murmur by this absorbent vegetation as Caleb and Lilian hand-in-hand approached the summit. But the mastermind had provided no direct trail to the

Transcendentalist's monument, and more than once they lost the way even when they could see their destination above them.

Gradients of sweet airs were just enough astir to blend and waft a variegation of scents that enchanted humans but were largely wasted on their nostrils. The only guilt in this hour's joy was Ibi's absence. For good reason dogs were prohibited in the arboretum, as in the public transportation system that served it. Yet exceptions were always made for guide dogs, and he tried to imagine himself with the effrontery to pose as a blind man. On the other hand, restrained by a short harness, tantalized by the virgin ambience (so strangely unmarked), Ibi's kinesthetic curiosity would have been cruelly frustrated. It was after all for the best that he was kept absolutely ignorant of his master's adventure. The most that Caleb could do to ease his conscience was confide a rueful remark to the Natural mother of his natural child: what a Paradise this would be for his saint to have the freedom of, for whom the sparsest of molecules (such as those emanating as each of the 275 fragrances from a single rose) were sufficient to excite the most exquisite intelligence! Imagine the aesthetic affect of this delicate pleroma for the first lucky dog in this garden of houris! Undisturbed by the fellowship of his kind, he'd be an Adam or an Engidu, by his mark giving names to the unspotted ideals of a sexless world!

As for Caleb's own actual delights, there was the balmy aura of Lilian's ventilated skin under loosened clothes, the fantastics of her feet, the pressures of hand and lip. He mystified himself with the innocence of his senses. The present rapture was as reckless of the next hour as of the last forty thousand. It was impossible to imagine this strolling delight as a celebration of final farewell, or as anything but a sample of timeless love in the bliss of seamless beauty.

From sunset to sunrise this refuge from the world was so inviolable that living lovers said it was benighted in vain; and of course at no time was pelvic quickening permitted. As a child not yet driven by sexual imagination Caleb had been terrified at the prospect of being locked inside the grounds after the curfew hour, and he used to drag his mother toward the gates even before the great bronze warning bell was sounded like a gong of doom at the base of the tower. How different now, on an idyllic morning in May, his grown-up fears and motives! Yet this sequestered campus of sun-flecked nooks was unbecoming to indecorous lust. It seemed to him that they satisfied their hearts by touching one another lightly, tasting no more than the tips of tongues and only vaguely discriminating the vicinal pleasure of other nerves—mystically united in an enchantment even more precious than the marriage of true minds in which they were also joined.

Laughing, little conscious of their course, they wound generally upward, capriciously seeking the tower up steeps and around curves. It rose like a magic vision upon the highest contour of the Romantic interior, but was all the harder to fix upon as they nearly circled its partly wooded mount, sometimes shortcutting proper roads and paths, especially as the all-too-human leader was nearly oblivious to every landmark except his numinous follower.

Caleb's aesthetic sensibility was rather piqued than offended when at length he noticed that the import of Lilian's charming words wasn't sweetly harmonizing with the temperamental and atmospheric felicity of the moment. He couldn't help assuming that he had a thousand and one nights to talk away her auguries of doom.

Adverting almost for the first time to their former life in Hume, she told him a little of her subsequent love affair with their friend Dave Wilson, after he, Caleb, had returned to the East unaware of her cyesis. Continuing with no change in her tone of calm uncomplaining history, she then revealed her one "important" love of their four-year hiatus. It was the story of a "professor", now at Maud Gonne College in Montvert. While she was working to support him (and her other baggage) during his doctoral candidacy at St Botolph University he had been betraying her with "a brilliant beautiful blonde undergraduate".

Caleb suppressed all his questions that weren't directly relevant to the moment, as if he really did have a thousand and one nights for reconsideration. This wasn't the time to put two and two together, and at present he had no wish to blunder into the succession of new jealousies that would have presented themselves when his candid lady replied. Nevertheless, flattered by her voluntary revelations, in growing confidence of a love that stood above all her others, he was content to be touched more closely than anybody else on earth by her affective soul.

"Since my menarche you're the only person I've felt comfortable with."

"No wonder: I'm my mother's daughter, not just her two sons. One third woman and only two-thirds man!"

"Man enough for me. You're the only real man I've ever known." And then, as if from a thought that was always with her, she repeated something she'd said to him before: "I don't call myself a victim, but if I've ever been wronged in my life it was not by you."

She spoke of the unattainable fulfillment it would be—more than a naughty girl should even hope for—to spend her life keeping house for Caleb Karcist, bringing in a salary, making his life-work easier, helping him do what he was destined to do, as his secretary-dog, his faithful bitch. "I've always most desired what's impossible for me. Three hundred years ago I would have fallen in love with a celibate missionary or some scholar-monk. I love above my station. I'm not good enough for a man like you. It was the luck of my life to get Mooney as a free sample. You were my understanding banker, without usury or stud fee! What more could I want of value? I wasn't looking for a nest. I've been contented enough as a loose fish these last four years. But now, in real life, it's time to prepare Mooney for her own motherhood. The child is mother of the woman."

Caleb wouldn't take the time to cudgel his brain about the real meaning of her astounding statements, which clearly were neither literal nor sarcastic, but certainly tactful. Unlike the romantic Pyramus (a decadent descendant of primeval Sumerians) he accepted the wall of destiny between them—but without acknowledging its immediate function of separation. To him, under the prevailing conditions of that glorious day, all her implications were consistent: no matter what her fate, he was and would always remain the classically romantic love of her life. As a mother she was ruled by her deontic conscience, but his wellbeing was her steadfast wish, second only to Mooney's.

Was it witness to such a fact that she now reiterated an express wish for his success with Bice (whose name she hadn't yet learned was changed to Belle). "You deserve any women that can make you happy."

Caleb laughed aloud. Meanwhile however, like a carefree actress memorizing some lines she'd interpret later, she was squeezing his hand and dancing at his side to independent music.

"It's been confusing for Mooney." she went on. "It will be bad enough growing up as an octoroon in a man's world. From now on she may need someone she can call her daddy, even if all he talks about is bits and bytes and fucking."

Despite a fluttering catch of his heartbeat at the sudden penetration of this last inflaming dart, Caleb was still too bemused by her exquisite propinquity, the calmness of her gaiety, the intimacy of her confessions, to react with alarm. The psyche in command of his brain spared him untimely pain by pretending that it was only the evoked memory of his own childhood confusion or the question of his own breeding that for a moment eclipsed his joy. His mother too had always said that the laws of family life were written by men.

The suppression of his intelligence was successful. They were both glad to resume the unalloyed enjoyment of an ironic freedom that resembled the elemental frustrations of wartime infatuation—closings of briefly opened doors in the wall of circumstance, pleasures without future—which they had both assimilated from the Zeitgeist as their model of romance during the most impressionable years of childhood. To Caleb, as if he was the girl ashore, it seemed that nothing else than "malign externality" had been keeping Lilian at doubled duties, grudging him the briefest of her shore liberties before arbitrary and inexorable orders would dispatch her overseas, perhaps forever.

Yet this fate had been cryptically foretold by the suffering Pythia herself who now skipped at his side, sometimes stopping him for her kisses of emphasized adoration. It was no wonder that he disregarded and then forgot her inconsonant prophecy from Apollo. Blithely they celebrated each other from opposite sides of the wicket as if it would never be shut again.

Besides, even if all along he had been alive to the past and future of every last torment in love's bondage, and even if she had thereto presented him with all her baggage and all her buried childhood sorrow, he wouldn't have traded this hour's transitory and ironic bliss for all the invulnerable serenities of India bolstered by the empirical wisdom of Greece Rome and France.

At last from under the greenery he led her up the final breathless steps of an embankment to the pavilioned base of the tower. The naked citadel, storybook imitation of a Norman donjon without castle or bailey, had been erected by the same eleemosynary president of the Mount Olive corporation (a Norumbega professor of medicine and amateur architect) who had designed the Egyptian main gate as a monument to transcendent eternity and commissioned much of the cemetery's triumphant sculpture. To Lilian it seemed the unbraced centerpost of an infinitely high blue circus—with not a cloud to catch her fall.

This crowning philanthropic pile had been an extraordinary blessing for the boy Caleb's adventurous poverty: a military playhouse of really exciting stone from which he could look out over boring statues of the famous as if they made up a city of his followers; and further off: houses of the rich; walls and halls that kept his mother out; low arched bridges over the academic river polluted upstream and down, a brown cloaca of ever-level saltless water in which he'd learned to swim, and to which he learned to correlate the historical diorama in the Norumbega Library that showed it in three-dimensional perspective as a broad tidewater estuary before it was dammed with locks and channeled, its stinking mudflats filled and its banks deprived of shipping, by the same brahmins who had donated Mount Olive to observe it from.

He drew Lilian across the terrace, tugging her by hand along the base circumference of the massive gray turret to find its entrance. She was already satisfied with an inferior view of the landscape from the pavement of that open rotunda, not at all frustrated by the crowns of tall trees standing far below their feet that interrupted the azimuth at that level. She said nothing to thwart his will, but she would have been glad to omit the further ascent. From the foot of the minaret it made her dizzy to look up along the giant column at the beetling corbelled machicolations of its battlements, far too far overhead, against the swimming blue firmament.

Unwarned by pilaster or jamstone in the smooth surface of the wall they traced, she shied like a rabbit at the suddenly gaping recess of the portal, which pierced the titanic blocks of dressed granite like a browless cyclops. And within the low dark aperture a concentrically curved iron door was retracted on its swivel like the nictitating membrane of a one-eyed reptile to disclose in deep shadow the first stone steps of a sinister helix. Lilian Cloud shuddered subliminally at the treacherous mechanism of a whiteman's trap. But her reason trusted Caleb's benevolence as a Georgio of the least possible brutality or recklessness, and allowed herself to be dragged out of the sunlight.

Insensitive to her trepidation, unappreciative of her confidence in him, he callously teased her as the Cordilleran squaw he had called cloud-capped, fearless in childbirth travel and business. So she managed to dissipate her overt fear of the winding staircase— which at first lost all light, then dawned and dimmed again as they climbed past the first splayed Gothic squint, groping skyward through the next unilluminated round. Only after what seemed many giddy revolutions were they delivered out of breath upon the landing of the lower balcony, where she began to recover her inward trust in his providence. In the open air, grasping the stout iron railings that spanned the crenels of the parapet, the altitude was nothing to a native of the western mountains. It was the opacity of hewn cold stone, which tombs were also made of, that had frightened her.

Inside again, the stone lightened and dried as they wound a final spiral against gravity to the unshaded hemisphere of the sky, to which they were instinctively drawn, like heliotropic moths in an inverted funnel; for the passage narrowed as it rose, constraining their elbows and at the top making them duck for the companionway scuttle. But at last they came to a breathtaking standstill in the balmy ether directly under the very sun whose source some of her people had sought in eastward migration (before Europeans were seeking occidental gold), only to learn the necessity of fishing in the bitter waters that put a stop to their hubris. The dazzled lovers issued from the ironclad cuddyhatch like storm-worn sailors awakened to an amazing change of latitude.

For nearly a minute Caleb almost forgot Lilian in the thrill of reviewing his former empire, the tiresome inland tracts of asphalt concrete brick and wood transfigured from above as a strategic river valley bounded at cannonshot distances by what was left of the hills George Washington had seized. The distant elms that once had shaded the Continental Army's headquarters were fewer now than in the times of F D R ; as seen from this high place, now when Kennedy was President, the Unabridge Common, as well as the Garth, was intussuscepted by spreading properties of the riverine 'Varsity which proclaimed itself the Federal dinosaur's pituitary gland, though still but a suburban patch in the metropolis of commerce and industry.

They had these lineaments and skylines all to themselves for nineteen minutes more. It was a lucky lull in the stream of curious scenery-seekers, before their heady monopoly was ended by a panting couple accoutred with a camera. As though he'd won her by ordeal or conversion, this conquest of quaquaversal space was staged in a mystic union that embraced everything save what was irrelevant to their elective affinity within the circumferential horizon. Alone, practicing the tangible affinities of impassioned commonfolk, they tarried upon the castled platform without denying themselves the preliminary pleasures of touch that Axel and Sarah had renounced.

Caleb made sure they stood behind the hatch where he could anticipate any intrusion upon their exquisite intimacy, as if instead of merely viewing the hub of the universe against a ground of greens and blues they dallied in private sunshine. Yet so preoccupied was he with securing the opportunity that to his own loss he still made little effort to follow the feelings of his companion, which, without altering her manner of speech, had graduated from those of nameless fear to those of nameless abandon. He did not realize that a sense of the observatory's azure-naked situation, elevated in a shamelessly pellucid vault, was now suffusing Lilian's uncalculating parts with transcendental concupiscence.

She didn't much listen to his interest in the history or geography of the highest spot on which she'd set foot east of the Rockies; nor was she swooningly impressed by the panorama itself, though her eyes were vaguely responsive to the undelimited haze suspended over Vinland Bay in the furthest range of their purview. The romantic circumstances condoned Caleb's silly fingertips as they found their way to her off-nipple, but as excitation his procedure was a distraction; mature desire exuded its lovely pelvic sensations autonomously. Deceived by her outward passivity—both playful and instinctive—and by the equability of her utterances, the cavalier remained endearingly unaware that her knees were weakening, that she was almost overcome by partial memories conducted up and down throughout her skin. She clung to presentiments that could be indulged only as long as she kept them unidentified incomplete and fantastic; but she couldn't help allowing him to tempt her with the enthusiasm of his infatuation, and to tempt himself—once more, still!—with exclusive commitment to the differentiated and idolized object of his inflamed desire.

Yet honestly enough she summoned her usual strength to protest the extravagant adoration to which she was being subjected by her first and most romantic lover, who seemed to think he wished to become also her last. His headstrong voice cracked and faltered, but hers never lost its fluent diffidence.

"Don't forget what the man says who plays Thisbe in *Midsummer Night's Dream*." she warned him. "'A paramour, God bless us, is a thing of nought.'

"—You see," she continued, in her endeavor to speak self-protectively on the plane of preestablished objectivity, "I do read some of the things you tell me about! But if I read more I'd be better prepared for your mind. Yeats says all literature is but the Muses' love-cry to the manhood of the world, but for me it's a vaccination against life. You don't believe in Aristotle's homeopathic theory of catharsis, but it suits my primitive mentality.

"Anyway, I also know what Eithne Inguba says in *Fighting the Waves*: 'Women like me awake a violent love for a while, and when the time is over are flung into some corner like an old eggshell.' —Oh I don't mean that anyone has abused me! I've done badly enough on my own. —I must have known this would happen before it began. Until I met you in Hume I used to open my fists and wriggle in bed alone. Beatitude without atonement: that was my felicity. Then when I was with you I swore to God that if he would grant me your child I'd willingly let you go and never have any other lover but Jesus Christ!"

Not until many days after this birdseye conversation above a the commonwealth of living and dead, when the sounds he could recall finally reached the reflective recesses of his mind, did Caleb finish examining all her words. At the time he heard what she said but was not always able to really listen, in part because he was too inclined to dismiss the statements of a woman on such occasions as flour thrown in his eyes to distract him from the greed for joy, which he gratuitously explained as "sensory, sensuous, and sensual", since they were kissing all the while, between sentences, often between syllables. She responded equivalently to all of his caresses, even as she spoke of their mutual subject in apparently objective if not rational spates of breath. But even at the time she seemed to deprecate as somewhat amusing the autonomy of her Sister Ass, playing down the significance of her physical response to other men who only wounded her with the less noble of Love's two arrows.

"Right away I broke my vow, without even waiting for Mooney to make her appearance and prove God's end of the bargain." She returned to this aspect of the topic with a wryly vehement kiss more provocative than ever. "And ever since then I've observed it only with irony. The fact that one doesn't keep her oath doesn't make the oath any less sacred. Maybe from now on I can keep at least half of it—by leaving you free and sticking to Gil. Since it can't be you, I don't want any new lover for the rest of my life. —When Gil leaves me, maybe I'll take to women! Would you mind that so much?" She laughed in digressive amusement at the liberties of poetic license.

As Caleb attended the jauntiness of her communication, his thoughts averted from the painful sentences it comprised, he was struck by that last notion of hers as one that even his mother would never have come out with. Anyway, as far as speech was concerned, Lilian's courage never faltered—whereas his own offerings were cautious frail and squeamish. He himself was afraid of words. But he already knew that it's usually the woman who faces reality (if anyone does), or identifies it; and because the woman is brought up not to take the initiative it's left to her to make most of the binary decisions, yea or nay. The hunted one is braver than the hunter.

But as far as judgment was concerned, he it was who never faltered in his conviction that her tastes were amazingly like his own. "You could have been my sister!" he said.

"I *am* your sister!" she replied. "That's how we're going to solve the problem."

"By reducing it to incest!"

Just then Caleb's exorbiting excitement was checked by one of Nature's pleasant phenomena, the hoarse outburst of a crow patrol alighting in some pines that rose from the steep bank below the tower. Until then, with all too many sights and scents clamoring for a consciousness otherwise intent upon its closest desire, the twitterings and uncoordinated calls of Mount Olive's extraordinary aviary had been lost upon him; but this Natural woman had taught him to pay almost as much attention to the raven family as to the canine. He turned to look, as she, already watching the birds, took up the interruption. "Is it true that in the Czech language *Kafka* means *crow*?"

"It sounds too good to be true. The crow was pure white—Apollo's faithful spy—until turned black as punishment."

"What was his offence against sweetness and light?"

"He brought the news that Koronis (which also means crow!), already pregnant with the god's son Asclepius, had betrayed him with a mortal. So much for the analogical model of your logic."

"You see! I've always been more of a black-moon crow than an ugly duckling! You can't imagine how I had to fight the priest to make him baptize my bastard!"

Caleb could only fall silent in admiration, squeezing her shoulder, as he tried to analyze her interjection. Her next remark though less welcome seemed more pertinent to the conversation he had thought they were having. "I still haven't made up my mind how to answer Mooney when she starts asking who her father is. I don't want to lie to her. She must never call a man like Gil her daddy."

For a moment Caleb lost the sense of his present position. He remembered that not lying to a child was Mary Tremont's cardinal principle of mothering; but apparently it wasn't a corollary that she should volunteer the whole truth. In his early years he had only tardily come to perceive that despite the supererogatory realism of all the distasteful or precocious truths she imposed upon him, and despite all her bitter vociferations against Mrs Grundy's hypocrisies, she never quite explained the fact of his own life—

"But you and I must part." Lilian added.

It should not have surprised him. The rebenumbing shock of this plainly reasserted news, obliterating all egoistic motifs, had been portended not only by the premonitions warnings ambiguities and blunt dicta of recent weeks but also by the climactic truth that there in his arms under the open sky her body had become softly importunate in suggestion of valedictory passion. He closed his eyes. By all palpable signs there was still hope that she would yield to contradiction.

But Caleb found no argument to offer. His determination was enfeebled by the irrefutable justice of her decision, even as he desperately sought to frame his reply in a respectful tone of belief that would not betray his fundamental disbelief; for in his heart of hearts he couldn't actually believe that the capital sentence would be carried out. Lilian's quietly critical sense of humor had always forbidden him the fatuous badinage that seemed almost always to rise in reflexive impulse during solemn colloquies with women.

At last, unable yet to really feel what still appeared in adumbration only, he managed to bring forth in a mournful mode his all-too-reasonable acquiescence. "It's infinitely sad." was all he said.

"No." said Lilian. "Not infinitely sad; just *very* sad. The loss is finite."

Suddenly she twisted out of his arms and stood with her back to him, both hands resting on a merlon of the battlement, as if taking in without dismay the broad world in which she'd been invited to participate by many white men—which in this charming swatch consisted of houses and apartments among streets, hills, trees, schools, factories, churches, offices, and playing fields along both banks of a small poisoned stream that drained a minor sinus of her continent into their sea. " 'Earth has not anything to show more fair!'

"—If this goes on another minute I'll make up my mind to run away and get work as an art-teacher! Live with you or not, but do your typing, cook your food, scrub your floors! A squaw on the prairie would carry as much as a dog could drag."

For one wild second Caleb came perilously close to an offer of the missing condition. He forgot all his objections to marriage. It now seemed the obvious solution of all erotic and spiritual problems. For a tangential instant he considered only the advantages of possession, as if for all his life he hadn't been more appalled at the prospect of calling anyone "my wife" than of calling his mother "my Mummie"; and more to the point, as if the thought of anyone calling him "my husband"—were she even the ballerina Elizabeth Quicherat or the anthropological philosopher Fayaway Morgan, or Jane Harrison or Queen Aoife or Isopel Berners, or the world's finest and most beautiful artist—hadn't been categorically repugnant. He had shuddered at the notion, the very sound, of these possessive common nouns. But in a flash of willful revelation he now envisaged the upper aspect of the cloud: the comforts and conveniences; the peace of intellectual beauty in corporeal heaven. He got so far as asking himself "Why not?"

But she was reminding herself of her baggage. And just then he was saved for burning by the irruption of a husband and wife who wanted to take pictures of the academic kingdom. His afflatus instantly collapsed.

By the time they'd made their escape from the Princess Tower, dizzily descending step by step through the wavering darkness to terrestrial light, Caleb and Lilian were recovered of their dual senses.

On the way back to the main gates he took her through the deepest dingle, along the willow-weeping shore of a brown frog-pond lined with whited ossuaries—still as he'd remembered them: tombs overgrown with ivy, some with their cobwebbed doors ajar, granting courageous children a whiff of horror. Together the grown-up lovers peered through glassless marble traceries at banks of musty gray file drawers containing whole families of moldered optimates. "Yes," said Lilian, "this cemetery must have been a wonderful place for kids to play hide-and-escape."

Caleb had noticed that she sometimes got paleface idioms slightly wrong.

12

TABLET THREE

[Gilgamesh's laboratory arranged for a meeting. The charts are rolled up.]

Enter Gilgamesh, wearing
the IRTH, and Eber.

GILGAMESH [Excited.]	I've proved it! Condensed or rarified, *pitch* will solve my problem! The bottomless bitumen that blights our swamps will bind the bricks and waterproof the walls. We'll scoop the mastic from those black puddles! We'll dip out naphtha to feed the steady flames we need for furnaces!
EBER [Dismayed.]	You mean the tar pits? Black puddles! Bottomless pits of abomination! Stinking sludge of desolation! Burning mud is Satan's art.
GILGAMESH [Laughing.]	Bane perhaps, but not black magic. No god would leave a miracle to me. It's by a neglected law of nature that I'll superheat my kilns!
EBER	It would be the last straw of grievances—to pollute these heathens with the nightsoil of hell!

GILGAMESH

[Indicating the IRTH.]

Their tune will change, when they understand. It took a whole tree of cedar logs, with my lungs for bellows, to transmute this pointed bit of clay. But with pitch on fire day and night, we'll petrify all the bricks we can mold, without even waiting for them to dry! Isn't it you who's always warning me that God's weather will wear away the works of sun-dried earth? But walls all sheathed with glittering man-made stone won't stand to perish like our flesh; nor be worn to dust by wind, or reduced to mud by rain. If we can coin immortal tiles, the future's labor will be lightened.

EBER   These laborers don't look beyond their week.

GILGAMESH   They shall sleep while fire makes my stone. Let them have the day in bed you say they need every week. Take credit for that indulgence. You'll reconcile them yet.

EBER   Reconcile us all to Hell! Already these sullen worms can see nothing but sarcastic pride in your monument to their gods. If furthermore you make them traffic with devils' dung and Satan's piss, you'll turn them into a colony of frantic vipers. Forever worse by far, you'll bring down the curse of Adonai on all of us! Against him an enameled tower endures no longer than a harlot's image pressed in sand. Can glossy facades repel a plague of locusts? Can the caulking of cracks keep out a rain of blood?

GILGAMESH   You wanderers carry your tabernacles with you. You'll never understand the love of a fixed hearth that governs these people. Their gods call for cities.

EBER   But abhor invention. You can't rub their noses in the jakes of Hell—unless you act with power and extirpate the idols that give them the courage to defy you! You've so tolerated their cult that the Rector preaches in public already! King, act on principle!

GILGAMESH   I'll not be the scourge of your god any more than theirs. To you truth is so clear that it oversimplifies the web. Justice isn't economic only. You should dispense all kinds of charity. Next month the equinox will fix our common feast of feasts—the first New Year of the second polestar: the covenant that Erech will become a city of one speech, one clock, one calendar—but of all the arts. In the end my public works will earn the public's praises.

EBER   The end will be too soon if you refuse to pay attention. The public will celebrate your New Year with a vengeance.

Some hokum's afoot in the temple already. Crush it in the egg!

Enter Rector and Optimates, escorted by Norkid.

GILGAMESH Ah, my privy council!

RECTOR
[Bowing.]
The summons from Your Lugalissimus anticipated my petition for an audience.

GILGAMESH You know perfectly well that nobody needs a petition to see me—let alone my people's chaplain. Day and night these four doors invite unguarded. I may be stingy with holidays, but I'm generous of ear. Is your heart cowed by some anxiety?

[The Rector hands Gilgamesh

RECTOR The queen's compliments with this gift woven by her
a cloth. hand. A prayer rug, she declares, to bend your knee upon.
All laugh or smile at his words. Gilgamesh unrolls an ensign bearing a red and blue triskelion. With Norkid's help, he fastens it to the wall under the rolls of charts.]

GILGAMESH A riddle in tapestry! She knows my taste in two dimensions. I marvel at her triangular lines, woven with the perpendicular stitches of a loom! I hope her droll purpose lightened the work. —Here, take her as potlatch this trenchant adamantine jewel, for lack of human sculpture, to pique her interest in the third coordinate. Tell her it's a stylus for her signature in clay.

[He takes off the IRTH necklace and hands it to the Rector.]

EBER You're putting in his hands your tool for writing!
[Makes a gesture of protest.]

GILGAMESH Don't worry: I know how to make its mate. —There was a
[Eber gives up with time when I got many presents from a grateful city.
a shrug.]

RECTOR In a pinch of emergency the wise Optimates of Uruk elected
[Motioning toward to hand you the Rod and Ring. We remain indebted, even
the Optimates.] though we are obliged to oppose your innovations.

GILGAMESH Yes, you are not enthusiastic. Your religion is too old.

RECTOR It has not run its course. But I am no enemy of yours, as I'm told you are advised. Have I not contracted the labor for piling up our tower?

NORKID *Our* tower! Since when, this politic change of heart?
[To Eber.] —Why does he so suddenly clothe necessity with virtue?

EBER He's beginning to pretend. That means they've been busier than I thought!

GILGAMESH The right hand of peace, city fathers, grand masters of the guilds. I'd like to have your counsel in all the trades. Now that our architecture's high enough to catch the eye, it needs the skills of potters. Can you mix those colors into clay?
[Shakes hands with each of the Optimates. Points to the Triskelion. They look at each other.]

EBER He hopes to win over posterity with gaudy images?
[Aside.]

RECTOR The Optimates and I agree that all the crafts will heed your call. Furthermore, in accordance with our decision to cooperate in high ambition for the city of Inanna, we shall adjust our almanac to your equinox, keeping what we can of ancient measures handed down from heaven. It is devoutly to be hoped that my sacerdotal compromises will be forgiven—so long as we preserve the forms most dear to our people.
[Makes a gesture of reverence at mention of the goddess.]

GILGAMESH I think you're driving at something I won't like. Let it be no tawdry sham!

OPTIMATE 1 Sir, we plead only for the way to harmonize all rites, and—

RECTOR These gentlemen mean to say—

GILGAMESH Let them speak.

OPTIMATE 2 —resolve all discord by a show of sacrificial contest.

RECTOR As mathematician I have come to see the reason in your duodecimal scheme. By calculation I still could fix the dates for planting. But when it dawns on people that after this New Year you'll be abolishing the month of Epact, which Enlil gave them with their city when time began, sooner or later—
[Hastily, shushing up the Optimates by gesture.]

NORKID I'm sure you'll see that it's sooner.

RECTOR —there'll be riot, and the end to all my management. Unless you act right now.

GILGAMESH Every year they'll have a five-day feast. More frequent revelry. No long wait for reelections! Every blessed year your calendar will be true to Sun. It's *he* that makes Euphrates rise. You should pray accordingly.

RECTOR None old enough to swing a scythe will forget the thirteenth moon given Inanna by Father Enlil. The people are

	maddened enough by a bachelor for king. But strife and tumult won't serve the gods. The temple thrives on peace—and the temple is the state.
GILGAMESH	What act are you implanting in my stateless will?
RECTOR	First, withhold your intercalary decree until this New Year has begun. It's time enough when the people have tired of their pleasures—after you have pleased them most by winning the Rod and Ring from their champion. Your power to alter the city's tradition will be recognized and cheered if he has been worthy of the queen before you strike him down.
GILGAMESH	I told you that I want no puppet putting me to the test. I won't abuse your law with play-acting. Otherwise, I agree in advance to any suitor you put forward.

[Eber and Norkid express consternation.]

RECTOR [To Eber.] [To Gilgamesh.]	Of course I speak of nothing more than the king's reinauguration. It's the rite of Epact that rids us of our sins. —During the feast you will lie hidden in undiminished royalty, like a god withdrawn, while the Lord of Misrule struts and boasts. Finally, when the braggart's purple is stained with dissipation, you'll recapitulate your fame by cutting short the mockery.
GILGAMESH	Fatuity I suppose will awaken my bloodlust to simply kill the pretender who's trying to kill me first. But I warn you that I'll not accept for sake of protocol some innocent fool deceived by adulation. I won't murder a puppy.
NORKID	Gilgamesh, don't tempt fate! Better make-believe than real surprise: treachery in the trappings of their ceremony!
RECTOR	A decent stranger, so elated by a few days of royal emoluments and perquisites that he'll fight to keep them.
EBER	Make him tell you who's his pick already!
RECTOR	My Temple hunters, tracking lions up into Aram on the rivers, venturing beyond the sight of smoke from hearth or altar, have happened upon the wild man known to legend as Enkidu.
NORKID	Engidu! By mere chance, eh? Just stumbled on him! It must have been a right cool search, beating all the bushes of Akkady. By accident you enlist the abominable windman—who abhors the faintest whiff of featherless bipeds!

EBER | This explains the gossip that's been showing up in my reports! That horned and hairy monster lives with the beasts, speaks their lore, and judges all their cases.

GILGAMESH | I've heard tales of Engidu, but never to believe. He instructs lions, outruns the cheetah, and protects the oryx.

RECTOR | Full of the hot red life that gods and mortals love to smell. Blood-power well to be expended. No danger to you of course in a duel of human skill. But to capture him will take more force than the Temple has.

GILGAMESH | I myself will fetch him!

RECTOR & OPTIMATES | Absolutely forbidden! —Not the king! —Against all religion! —It would defeat the purpose! [etc.]

NORKID
[Aside to Gilgamesh.] | Without you on hand we couldn't keep the people at work for even three days!

EBER
[Aside to Gilgamesh.] | It's conspiracy, playing upon your lesser pride!

GILGAMESH
[Grinning at the Rector, who hesitates and then bows with icy formality.] | I forgot. —You go, Norkid. —And reverend sir, you must go with him, as spokesman for the law. I promise that Eber will not usurp your crosier. —The name of Engidu is something to bite on. Fast as a javelin and hard as an axe. Is it true that he can uproot an oak in anger? —With the Rector out of town, I can spare a few of your men. Pick volunteers who aren't half-cocked string-happy heroes. Take the battle-net. Bring in Engidu fresh and unscathed.

NORKID | I'm the very understudy of Gilgamesh himself, but how in the name of Mazda am I expected to snare alive some troglodytic aborigine of superhuman senses living at the end of a rainbow in league with all the fauna? I'll have to crease him with an arrow first.

RECTOR | The victim must not be either pained or drugged!

GILGAMESH | Then use the surest lure. Take the woman with you.

ALL | —Who? —What woman? —What do you mean? [etc.]

GILGAMESH | Lil-Amin.

OPTIMATES
[Their dismay is first shared by the Rector, who soon bethinks himself however, making the effort to conceal his unexpected satisfaction.] | The queen! She can't leave the Temple. —An insult to Inanna! —She won't go outside the walls!

GILGAMESH | I so decree. No further discussion. Engidu may hate mankind, but she'll have an opposite affect. Have her open up her robe. Let the dog sniff. Soon enough he'll have to share the scent with gods and packs of saints—after he fells old Gilgamesh! You may catch them in the net together.

EBER | With open eyes you walk right into the trap of this hoodwinking whoremonger!

RECTOR
[Blandly spreading his palms.] | It's not I that offered the queen. My hands are clean. They toil for love.

GILGAMESH
Aside to Eber and Norkid, taking them by the elbow as he and they slowly walk off, while the Rector keeps his Opimates quiet. | Eber, my old friend, there are times when one quick stroke should cut the knot. With both of them absent from their altar, there'll be no one here to stampede the herd before I can top off the present work. —You see, I'm sufficiently suspicious. —Norkid, don't let the Rector outnumber you with his glebe-men: no more than two or three as guides. Any trouble, I trust you to keep it diplomatic. . . .

OPTIMATE 1 | Let Your Grace put a stop to this sacrilege! You hardly lift your hand!

OPTIMATE 2 | Call out the mob tonight! We'll die before we let her go!

RECTOR
[Soothing them.] | No, there's no summons to waste your death. The catastrophe is his. Suddenly an old oracle is about to be understood.

OPTIMATE 2 | The gods will turn on us in unison if Lil-Amin is allowed to be dragged into the wilderness and ravaged by a bestial foundling!

OPTIMATE 1 | Who will ever stop the whims of this sleepless mountain bull—if our pontiff gives him leave to paw the dust?

RECTOR
[Turning on them impatiently.]

[Strides back and forth, here and there breaking into dance.] | Fools! It's not for laymen to interpret prodigies, or to judge the evil destined for a good to follow. Your piety dwells too much on custom. The fall of Gilgamesh will be accomplished if we endure the last vicissitude of his regime. I tell you the Tablets of Fate are about to be fulfilled. Find no fault with my tolerance of this expedition. It's I, Our Lady's dancer, who has suffered most; and it's I, the lawkeeper, who will bring down the law upon this tyrant. And when the glebe's restored, we shall possess his miscalculated monument as the city's bond to heaven! It is the will of the gods that for us Gilgamesh should raise this ladder up to heaven! . . . On a nuptial dais in

	the firmament, my sister's frankincense and myrrh will smell all the sweeter to Our Lord.
OPTIMATE 1	We defer to you in matters of divinity even when no precedent is found. But will Engidu reduce our taxes?
OPTIMATE 2	In any case, how can we be sure he'll win the Rod and Ring? People whisper that Gilgamesh is two-thirds god.
RECTOR	Two thirds can't save the mortal part! Engidu is sent to us by Inanna. When he's seen there'll be no doubt of the issue. We can rest assured he's quicker and stronger by half than the stories claim. Gilgamesh won't get the chance to dance.
OPTIMATE 2	Then we should prime the people to welcome their redeemer. Old women will grow young with expectation!
RECTOR [Dancing by way of illustration.] [Leaving off his dance.]	No! Rejoicing must be contained in the mummery. Let the jubilation seem sarcastic. "The King of Beasts" they may acclaim him, decked in purple, riding backwards on his ass. —That interloping vizier never ceases to probe the pus of hatred swelling in my liver. His spies and provocateurs are still to be feared. If he incites the northmen to forestall us, you'll die with feathers sticking out of your lungs. But may Tigris join Euphrates if I don't scatter his bones—and stamp out all his children like isolated ants!
OPTIMATES [Chanting in antiphony, perhaps with dance.] Optimates go out.	—Exalted shall be the sacred fool who laughs when we mock him :: that he may leap for the hand at our throat! —Happy shall be the King of the Epact :: to sow his seed like stars of the sky! —Blessed shall be the lion of the steppes :: for he lays low the raging mountain bull!
RECTOR [Inspecting Gilgamesh's laboratory, idly pulling down various rollers, but pausing at the three-dimensional diagram of the IRTH, which he still holds in his hand. At the end he suddenly unrolls and hangs up a banner displaying the blue five-point star.] The Rector leaves, following Optimates.	Now I must convince the virgin queen that Enlil's law is broad enough to sanction such reversal. Gilgamesh shall never have her! Engidu is no lover for her heart: let him open the unstitched seam that's forbidden to her brother and confessor. When she's our mistress at last, she'll learn the worth of her one true minister. —Meanwhile let her scorn this gage. What an absurd talisman: Iso-Recto-Tetra-Hedron! —The fourth facet wouldn't be so bad if it weren't the shape that makes a star of Eber. Yet soon we'll be bowing again to the lovely star of Inanna! —Salt, indeed! By the good Lord, I'll salt his tears!

13
MUMMERY

For Caleb the competitive world was as full as ever of wellspoken personable giants picking and choosing among its unoverlooked women; but their bold presence, as against his own phenomenal imperceptibility, troubled him less and less as he passed into his second quarter-century with gradually subsiding fear of his mother's reappearance in the town of his conception, where he hadn't dwelt with her since before his age of embarrassment. Usually the diversion of friends and benefactors, as well as his labor over Sumerian creatures, conspired with the reassurance of her happy letters from faraway Orellana to lull his deep-rooted sense of danger.

In Dogtown no one he knew in person did he hate. Little by little, in cautiously talking to troglodytes of the north Cape, aborigines of the Harbor, and local genealogists, he worried less and less about exposing himself to questions of his origin; for he was gaining confidence in his ability to avert conversation that might draw attention to the sometime personae of pre-War Dogtown. His inbred social discomfort was alleviated by Lilian's admiration, Bice-Belle's encouragement, Father Lucey's appreciation, Father Duncannon's illumination, Doctor Charlemagne's challenge, the Schlossbergs' friendliness, Rafe Opsimath's affability, Buck Barebones's generosity, Mrs Keith's respect, and Tessa Barebones's sympathy.

Thus one of the effects of his visits to the Hoof & Mouth studio, and to Powerhouse Wharf, was that he nearly disregarded the original therapeutic intention. At home he neglected the purpose of overcoming his handicap by histrionic exercise; except during halfhearted solmizations he forgot his crippled weasand. He dismissed his resentment that men of voice, his rivals in all things, could often win the prizes of masculinity without benefit of knowledge, imagination, managerial intelligence, athletic stamina, cleanliness, or even stature. He was too busy to remember his absolute deficiencies and relative failures. Except during his lighthearted solfeggios with Tessa he kept forgetting to remind himself that a successful voice, according to Stanislavsky's Method, "is placed forward in the mask of your face and floats freely out to fill the whole room." In this exercise he never thought of the mask itself.

But Caleb was emboldened mainly in response to his dog's self-confidence. Not that Ibi-Roi was complacent or self-esteeming, just a successful son of a bitch—who nevertheless watched the visage of his unsuccessful little master as the leader's of the world and eagerly submitted to his discipline. Obedience to the macro-command HEEL had become habitual; and Ibi no longer questioned the earnestness or wisdom of any acute order. When his mind was not occupied in training it took full advantage of its freedom to make autodidactic inquiries about objects of amazingly unselfconscious perception. Thus simply by exemplification the saint's dauntless pursuit of immediate experience—his nonchalance as to past and future—shamed away many of the stranger's anxieties who studied and emulated him.

Nonetheless, one fine Saturday afternoon on a walk across the city to Mother's Neck the young dog's learning was saltatorily advanced by a sudden embarrassment:

Replacing the dust cover on his typewriter, the man had resolved to make up for having again omitted his morning run in face of the insidious alliance between calisthenic sloth and literary zest. The marrow of his bones had been coursing with a sweet balmy desire to magnify the green blades of Spring that were about to clothe warming edges of granite; at the same time to rediscover the vernal waterfront, to savor its sunny noises, its pastures corrals and stables of boats, its embrined aroma of cordage and fish; and underfoot to feel the shoreline. Also with the hope of finding Wat Cibber his new East Harbor friend at leisure after a day's fishing and receptive to an unannounced visitor with his double-footed double.

For the most part their route was the one he traversed on wheels four times a week commuting to the Lab; but his day off was no occasion to walk all the way out to the extremity of that all too familiar domain, even for Ibi's sake who would have loved to follow rabbit spoor on the wuthered heights and was always rewarded for showing his face at Father Duncannon's door. There were three nearer goals to consider as a nominal purpose. Every time-out from sedentary self-cudgeling had to have diversionary objectives.

They were disappointed in the first of them. Maestro Petto DaGetto was not in his shop at Wye Square, and the welding truck was not in his yard.

And further on, at Apostle's Dock, Caleb was hardly surprised to find no one at Belle's apartment, though her door wasn't tightly closed that Ibi would gladly have pushed open with his nose. Nowadays she was always too busy at the *Nous*, or on behalf of the *Nous*, to have repeated an invitation to lunch, which it made him hungry to remember. Last time he'd been distracted by a missing dog and an erotic opportunity, but now he lingered on the deck outside to take in the soporific cyclic lapping of a lowered tide. With faint squeaks of mooring ropes it tugged gently at the collars of spiles lining the courtyard of boats, each creaking in its own rhythm. The low groans of wood and manila, mingled with the unlocated voices of three or four men in the deliberations of work, were pierced by the urgent yelps and screeches of gulls, perched or errant, alow or aloft, each with its own eccentric intent. Tethered strakes and landlocked pilings rubbed indolently together with the sighing contentment of well-used spouses, slackly yoked in the quiet sunshine. As a unified sensation these sounds blended with the pungency of low-water mud and drying barnacles, with the tarred and hempen condiments of painted vessels as various in size and lines as different races of the city's canine species. Except for Maxwell and Cosmo gulls, not a soul was to be seen.

Lingering upon his inn-of-court proscenium the tyro dramatist gazed down on the embraced tide at one of its lowest levels. Was he surveying an auditorium of boats—or the orchestral stage itself? What an epicene theater! Should he float the audience down below on a work-barge, and mount the action on these decks and balconies, or spread seats on three sides around the main deck of piers and bring other spectators up here on the bridge to watch dancers and players do their work on the barge—in either case each performance and each minute at a slightly different distance from the eye and ear? If the latter, off-stage right (on the pier to his left), he had a convenient derrick for the gods, or for heavy props: the elephantine boom of the Dock's trussed-steel isorectotetrahedron (matched in topographical composition by its sister crane at the marine railway across the mouth of Argonaut Cove). Now however this machine was motionless, suspending an empty boat-sling that looked to him like a chastity belt for Siamese twins.

After descending the outside stairs and proceeding further along East Main Street, Caleb and Ibi likewise found Wat to be absent from his little "deep water wharf", a newly acquired ramshackle property that he was patching up in his spare time as a base for small boats like his own that were being orphaned by razings and dozings along the main waterfront in anticipation of Civic Instauration. So it was toward Wat's "officious headquarters" on Mother's Neck at the head of the cove that they wended at last, hoping that the small workshop's battered easy chair opposite Wat's overstuffed rocker would not be preempted by some fisherman or parlor historian. With luck, if the host wasn't still out harrowing the bottom of the sea, the wayfarers could expect a can of beer and a pan of water before returning to their inland attic.

Indeed so it was to it transpire—one of Caleb's first few visits to Wat, the only native marooner among his friends in Dogtown, introduced of course by Rafe Opsimath the Cornucopian intercessor. But my story follows this trek only as far as its dramatic climax, at which Ibi escaped a violent death by the hair of his tail.

Caleb was perpetually beset by dread of parlous adventures unrecorded in his absence; now for the second time he actually witnessed Ibi's reckless disregard of traffic hazards when seized by an atavistic reflex, in this case predatory, as he was walking at heel ostensibly mastered by habits of civility.

On the waterside of East Front, before the right-turn on Mother's Neck Avenue, in a neighborhood that Ibi-Roi had never walked through before, they had just reached the three great Argo Oaks (said to have been planted by Druids stealing down at night from Tir-na-Dog for tidal incantations), when he suddenly noticed on the opposite side, against a white house, the black silhouette of a sitting cat.

With blinding force he lunged across the narrow street. Caleb could not have checked him even if he'd been leashed by his choke-collar. The protector of sheep from wolves was instantly as oblivious of danger as of his owner. As he darted two monstrously swift machines were already upon him from either direction. Indigenous kilroys, habitually reckless of mishap, were accustomed to liberties of outrageously solipsistic precipitation even in this narrow twisting thoroughfare populated with infant strangers as well as saints and sinners.

At the middle of two bounds, in a double eddy of pressure and vacuum, unaccompanied by the sound of brakes, Ibi was nearly brushed simultaneously by the gigantic left front tire of the fuel-oil truck that had been speedily overtaking them and by the lethal bumper of a counterspeeding sports car.

He fetched up against the clapboards of a sun porch built close upon the street, having chased a painted image. It surmounted the words SEMIRAMIS GIFTS, the trade sign of a silent unbusinesslike domicile without other evidence of its wares that seemed to have been ignored for twenty years by pilgrims toyvoters and denizens alike. Caleb, who passed it twice a day in his car, was no longer touched by its innocence of commercial savvy, and Ibi when riding by had never looked down far enough to see it at all.

The Viking prince had been disabused before the second leap was past its apogee, and for a split second he was mortified by his stupid error. But his befuddlement was at once replaced by an affectation of idle curiosity. Before he could turn back with the grace of a runner who'd hit an easy fly ball Caleb had dashed over to grab his ruff, trembling with the aftereffects of mingled rage and terror and hoping that his token blows with the doubled-up leash, along with incontinent cries of chastisement, were applied soon enough to impress a primitive association of ideas between the punishment and the egregious violation of an undiscontinued command to HEEL. Ibi yelped once, and cringed, but less in apology than in shame.

They returned to their course with the mechanical whirlwind and Caleb's undignified requital still echoing in their equally embarrassed ears, but it was the man who still trembled. In ideal docility, but with scarcely more than an appealing glance of forgiveness for his master's violence (since nothing really *bad* had happened), having totally recovered from his sheepish disappointment, the shepherd quietly resumed his proper place at the sheep's thigh, his tail curled and asway, trusting to expunge his sensory mistake from everybody's memory.

The shamefaced human recovered much less easily from his syncopated stroke of insensate fear and anger, hoping that the loud curses with which he had expressed his reprimand weren't heard or guessed by any accidental spectator. The heart-thumping alarm and its palpitating aftermath was all on his side. He and Ibi shared the humiliation, and each had learned something not to be forgotten, but when the seemly pattern of deportment was restored, and his pulse had gradually resumed its normal beat, he was too thankful to grudge the goddess Tyche a disengaging smile; for it was amusing to see how dumbfoundedly Ibi had discovered the untrustworthiness of his unconvected and longest-range sense.

*

There's no more to this episode of the dual Bildungsroman, but it should be explained that although Caleb's sympathy extended to most of his dog's pursuits their biases somewhat diverged when it came to a taste for cats. Ibi would have been appalled to see the magnified sinners his master almost worshipped in zoos and books.

It was nevertheless true that Ibi, when he came to live with Caleb on Cod Street conditioned by his incunabular residence at Chateau Noir, which was infamously partial to cats, had made an exception for O'Hair, the Keiths' Elamite, to whose patronizing friendliness he was growing rather indulgent; and he was slowly teaching himself not to chase others for the kill. But when abroad in the world it was not yet possible for him to repress the initial impulse to pursue a running feline. On the whole he was still cynical about the possibility of a peaceable kingdom, whether of the golden past or of the millennial future, if it entailed the saint lying down with the sinner. He regarded most cats as pretentiously self-sufficient. They flattered people and curried privilege for their own sensual pleasure (such as sleeping on beds), yet prided themselves on refusing to submit to authority, walking as they chose in their wild lones, as if they were born to have their every craving satisfied without the obligation either to serve or to learn or to put themselves to any inconvenience. They had mean little desires but no disinterested emotions. They made no attempt to listen to the language of their betters, to whom they expressed themselves in shamelessly disingenuous gestures or plaintive cries (much unlike communication with their own kind), their ridiculous tails waving straight up in the air like vapid smoke signals. They regarded their feeding as a categorical imperative, yet their fastidious attitude toward food was disgusting; they affected to despise the likes of a saint for letting nothing go to waste.

Ibi especially execrated as downright perverse their ludicrous behavior at stool—as if their disgusting little feces were as precious as beef bones! On the other hand he was wholly ingenuous about his own idiosyncratic discretion in relieving his bowels, if possible in at least partial privacy whenever more secluded alternatives than sidewalks or lawns were conveniently at hand. He contributed comparatively little to the canine eyesores in Dogtown, at any rate in daylight, and to Caleb's knowledge no captious Puritan had ever caught him in the act. But this autonomous delicacy had been influenced no more by his observation of cats than by Caleb's preaching.

The poor fellow could hardly be expected to admit to himself that he was flattered by O'Hair's occasional attention, or that he was fascinated by the detestable sounds of contentment that rose and fell within the tigeraster's chest, in accompaniment to the somnolent systoles and diastoles of dangerous little claws, while lying so damned complacently in the indulgent houselady's lap, who called that affectation "kneading dough from his mother".

In short, cats were selfserving, with no genuine affinity for the beings by whom they were protected—more like Protesticans than Catholicrats as citizens of the commonwealth. Often, as Ibi made his rounds of Acorn Pasture Cemetery pretending to pay no attention to the souls of dead cats that cawed at him in raucous jeers from the treetops, he sighed the immemorial refrain of the Canine Blues:

> Sinners live and sinners die,
> But their demons always fly!

—a folk ditty he'd learned to howl along with in a commiserating interlude of the otherwise enthusiastic Ma'eve Thing (a sanctified convocation marking the kind of solidarity that cats were absolutely incapable of). Yet it was merely from traditional prejudice that Ibi acted like a saint when it came to sinners on the run, though if one of them made a stand, or sat still, his gentled conscience always bade him sheer off and let it sheath its dangerous little claws.

Though Ibi exhibited cavalier indifference to his comeuppance in the SEMIRAMIS fiasco, he reflected afterwards upon the profit he'd derived from having made a fool of himself. His passing discomposure gave way to philosophical gratitude. Deprived of all but the grossest use of his scenting and hearing faculties by the noise and gassy stink of East Front kilroy traffic, he had allowed himself to be deceived by the trumpery of vision, unchecked by any other sense, unrestrained by judgment; but without quite killing himself, without permanently impairing his dignity, he had thereby learned to think twice before chasing any merely visual apparition. Elsewhere it might have been a black jaguar, sitting at a greater distance!

Caleb meanwhile for his part pondered the sobering fragility of Ibi's obedience. The wolf's civic morality had not been confirmed, notwithstanding its ordinary compliance with the discipline. Novelty was the only true test. Under surprise attack a soldier of the strongest character may be overtaken by panic. An unwarned critic may be carried away by some fantasy simply because it's fresh.

At the same time Caleb was pleased to find that he had underestimated the facility of his companion's eyesight. It was some satisfaction to realize that Ibi—who refused to look at a devilvision screen or see himself in a mirror—was so responsive to a rather small silhouette in conventionally stylized form. Wasn't it but a minute before, near Apostles Dock, that with neither glance nor sniff the subject had totally disregarded in a patch of sidewalk concrete the intaglio paw-prints of some bygone Shepherd—which the preoccupied human observer had immediately noticed? Thereupon the overweening man had once again induced that a dog's eyes, when unassisted by nose or ears, responded primarily to organic or three-dimensional cinematic objects. But now it appeared that this animal's power of visual abstraction was so highly cultivated as to mislead his primitive instinct—despite his intuitive scorn of virtual images from glass!

This reappraisal of Ibi's faculties reminded Caleb of his own hatred for histrionic scenery and his old longing for true sculpture on the stage. A presque-isle-de-pierre should be the larger mise-en-scene for drama, he mused in English. But Dogtown had never had a theater any truer than Limeway's, and he would resist entanglement with the Hoof and Mouth enterprise unless Doctor Charlemagne was persuaded to become its plenipotentiary: a fanciful eventuality. As a possible sanctuary of counter-commercial theater Dogtown would be too precariously defended to invest one's hopes with any champion but HIM, the virtuosic Director for such a time and place.

Only then, and only as a stagehand, in the holy service of art, would the secret proud and tender playwright submit himself to criticism. It was enough to serve the word of God in action at the altar, under a Doctor of the church, while privately preserving the chastity of his own language and keeping all the secrets that Tessa Barebones hadn't yet wormed out of him.

Secrets still! Must his foundations be forever undermined by unimportant shame and anachronistic doubt, when others seemed to have no anxieties peculiar to themselves? The most humiliating undisclosure was not merely of the past: it was a condition of present fact impossible to reveal even when he tried to explain it. Dostoyevsky himself had to wrap such difficulties in narratives of crime or insanity in order to suggest them by indirection. There was nothing criminal about Mary Tremont. Quite the contrary: she practiced a uniquely unselfish religion. And he believed that neither a male nor a female psychoanalyst, nor a Russian epileptic, could have described her ineffable idiopathy.

Quavering in dread, sometimes, he sketched forecasts in which his mother kicked over the traces in Vernalia—violating its proprieties with some outrageous breach of verbal decency; perhaps extorting her plane fare back to the States as quitclaim for the injustice done her by a narrowminded Community; then showing up in Dogtown to demand shelter and make a jolly impression by telling all his new world with the laugh of a fearless original that her "one and only pride and joy doesn't even know his father!" Although these days it was a fear less and less chronic, it grew all the more acute as the Dogtown root of his life deepened its grasp.

The waking nightmare, recurrent and variable, kept warning him to prepare an emergency plan for skipping town. Always keep a full tank of gas and some money for the road! All his papers and a preselection of books would leave room for Ibi in the front seat. But it would be necessary to abandon inessential property, not to mention friends and mentors. The Keiths would have to hold the bag.

Again and again, in thought-drama, Caleb put himself to the triage of listing books he couldn't leave behind. Now as it happened, first among them (along with Father Duncannon's works, Jane Harrison's, and Fayaway Morgan's) and also harder to replace than Euripides Redburn or Yeats, was the late Auto Drang's, an anthropological psychology that seeded the theory of tragedy guiding most of his subsequent dives into scholarship. And a greater wonder it was that after finishing drama school in Ur the young Tessa Masterson had for almost a year been the "lay secretary" of Doctor Drang!

That apostate scion of Father Freud, self-exiled Jewish sibling rival of the Aryan Neognostic G C Gnuj, "looked like a little frog".

At an earlier time Ipsissimus Charlemagne too had known him, as the briefly acclaimed partisan of artists who was blackballed by the New Uruk Cabal of Psychoanalysts, ostensibly for lack of a medical degree. Caleb reverently cherished these two fortuitous personal links to the heroic investigator of exceptional psyches, as if they augured a special destiny for himself.

His estimation of Tessa was extravagantly enhanced by an accidental hint of her privileged experience, the full nature and extent of which remained unclear. His curiosity about this matter of such great intellectual importance only stimulated and justified his attempts to turn the tables and make himself her counter-confidant. For he believed he was all but alone in understanding the radical distinction of Drang's critical scholarship, which had precipitated a professional failure somewhat resembling Fayaway Morgan's, Scott Dunne's, and several others' among his demigods. Tessa gracefully turned aside all trenchant inquiries, but his enthusiastic interest in that segment of her career earned him diversionary confidences that in turn encouraged more of his own. He counted this friendship as one of his secondary reasons not to leave the Rock, unless prematurely forced, until he had satisfied the interest in Dogtown that remained primarily egocentric.

Tessa's mind was too quick and pragmatic to have dived through Auto Drang's abstruse discourse and reached his radical conception of human will. By almost all other thinkers, from long before Chauvin to the latest logician, free will had been explained away as causal, stochastic, or supernatural; or at least it seemed to Caleb, rusticating on an island of gulls and dogs, that twenty years after Drang's death it was left to him, a bookworm, to interpret and evaluate that savant's essential ideas for a misplaced worldly housewife who had known the man himself to some degree of intimacy but was more interested in anyone's personal welfare than in a genius's theories, of which in this case she was anyway skeptical, seeing that her present voiceless pupil seemed to be the only one who still took them to heart, for in all modesty she made it her business to keep in tune with the New Uruk Zeitgeist.

If Caleb dived too deeply in their conversations, it was to indulge himself, for in his sincerest perceptions he was aware that a journalistic hairnet shaped the cranium under her hat. All the same, he was persuaded that her innate refinement of discrimination, less conscious than her coexisting commercial interests, enabled her to recognize the absolute distinction of mentalities like Drang and Charlemagne (though of course she'd no more disavow her preference for the culture advertised in *The Newurker* magazine than her attraction to the glamour of Limeway and its patrons). After all, she was Cape Gloucester's one philanthropological salonkeeper, her sympathetic ear open to everyone's opinions.

Caleb put the issue to Ibi. In Dogtown the freewill of saints—chained, confined, or unrestrained—is patent. If the freewill of Christians is also at work here, attempting to restore primitive motives to the social dynamo while simultaneously fostering the mental development of individuals, Caleb told his dog, don't be too cynical about a like effort on behalf of the dromenological arts. It may not be possible to get Father Duncannon and Doctor Charlemagne acquainted with each other—still less to edify a profane company of half-ignorant mummers with spiritual notions of the greater dromenology—, but there's momentous significance of some kind in their coincidence of locus.

If ritual is the origin or cognate of all mythology and art, Caleb said to his alter ego, in my reading of Father Duncannon's theodynamics art is the entelechy of civilization. Imaginative action is the final cause of Doctor Charlemagne's dromenology. Neither aspect of this consensus would be conceivable without the infinitesimals of liberty that inform every pulse of cultural evolution. Perhaps destiny, as the confluence of personal histories facilitated by Raphael Opsimath, is offering Tessa and her little band as instruments for a small manifestation of that free will which justifies, in face of world-historical horrors, the survival of a species that even in much of its art submits to the tyrannies of determinism and idealism.

Ibi stretched, yawned "Yee-aaah", wondering why it took so long to get moving.

*

One day, alone with Father Duncannon at the antique refectory table, after the responsive Latin grace (which he had only half mastered by rote), Caleb diffidently broached the subject of free will, hoping the conversation could be led to the problem of "aesthetics" and thence to Drang's treatment of art as free will in the service of immortality, a line of thought stirringly convergent with Father's own theodynamic orthodoxy. In the course of their morning editorial work together Caleb had been invited to have lunch with his venerated Superior. Such impromptu meals, always on Oku the houseboy's day off, were served by Father Duncannon himself, a fact that embarrassed the acolyte, as if his feet were being washed by the master.

Now free will was too naked a term, too laden with moral vulgarities, to be brought up before Doc Charlemagne—too anachronistic and philistine for the arch-subsumer not to dismiss before it could be argued; but it was still an undisillusioned and undisguised concept in Father Duncannon's transcendent social theory.

"Isn't it the ultimate question in biology, and therefore in all of philosophy," Caleb ventured, "—assuming the question of what mind is."

Father Duncannon smiled. Caleb had previously prompted him for his positions in critical controversies, as exemplified in compendious rhetorical formula by the question whether or not biology had succeeded physics (to say nothing of theology) as "the queen of sciences". The gentle priest replied with a playful parable that brought joy to Caleb's heart as emblematic of a new stage in their hitherto sober intimacy.

Slowly twisting a glass of Chablis in his slender fingers, the dedicated old servant of God now felt free enough with Caleb to make fun with a tropological device favored by the young Son of God. "The use of free will may be likened unto the telling of a true story. Howsoever unpredictable, the cause for each of its events may be plain to the listener—after it's ended."

"Tracing one path backward through someone else's decision tree, down from an acorn!"

"From one leaf among myriads. Like historians, who can ignore the serial outcomes of lost or unchosen causes."

It was an apposite point to mention Auto Drang, the failed genius, if Caleb hoped to interest Father Duncannon in *Beyond Psychology*. After all, in his youth as a classical physicist he had readily accepted Relativity and Quantum Mechanics. But in his advanced years he was too burdened with the spiritual direction and development of the Classic Order of the Vine, and too weary of disappointments, to permit himself a new and strange intellectual excitement, as if his curiosity was jaded and he no longer required the integration of compatible ideas which might seem a network of influences to some future polymath of the century's history.

In any case Caleb was loathe to risk discussion of "immortality" as according to Drang the personal and social motive underlying all the so-called drives of the human psyche. Any psychological interpretation of that sensitive term might be more offensive, even to such a scientific Christian, than outright criticism of what to Caleb was more essential to Church doctrine. As a matter of personal discretion and tact, he realized that he had to draw the line at this point as long as Father Duncannon was alive—just as when talking to anybody he avoided the word "spiritual", which in English was used in common by Auto Drang, Father Duncannon, and almost everyone else, including the dialectical disciples of the materialist whom Wat Cibber referred to as Churl Marx.

Caleb never got very far toward sharing his own integration of intellectual fathers: those disparate teachers and leaders, dead and alive. But still it seemed to him that if Dogtown was a seed bed of the Offertorial church it was reasonable to suppose that in an analogous spirit it could inseminate a revisionary theater, forasmuch as liturgy and drama were cousins-german.

It was from their understanding of Charlemagne's doctrine that the complementary Hoof and Mouth sisters, Tessa Barebones and Cora Kryothermsky, derived their new purpose; and they were heartily joined by Beni Vanderlyn, their plastic-arts partner in the Troika Arts Center, and eagerly supported by their friends and clients from the dance studio or their amateur play-reading sodality. But the most practical enthusiasm for a real theater, Tessa declared to Caleb, was propagated by his landlady Gloria Keith—their researcher, literary advisor, historian, secretary, bookkeeper, and costume-maker—who continually fostered and coordinated their leading energies, which were now bent upon moving beyond self-improvement or mutual amusement into collaboration as an earnest company of mumming performers.

Under Doc's influence Tessa had learned to be critical of commercial theater, despite her incomplete rejection of box-office standards; but Cora was the most artistic one of the three. Her imagination was frustrated as much by the limitations of dance itself as by the dearth of first-class dancers among her own few students. Neither she nor Tessa had attacked Doc's writings with enough literary perseverence to find herself offended by his insulting subsumptions of women as well as all but a handful of men, or by his exorbitant technological conceits. Though inspired by Doc's personality, Cora did not understand his reservations about the possibility of getting dancers to speak in action, a crucial problem, which she refused to recognize as insoluble. Like everyone else in their gang, she and her own followers were willing to take part in whatever theatricals Tessa was able to mount, but her underlying motive in dramatics was to get ideas for informing movement with the word—at first perhaps only as an "accompaniment" to the dance, separate and parallel to the real action, either resonant or ironic. Eventually, in integration, dramatic poetry might be less abused by dance than it always was by music. She had always believed in Doc's dictum that movement was the mother of speech.

Perhaps in the end, as Doc used to predict, it was the burgeoning dance of Atlantean women that would provide a new drama for directors, reversing history and absorbing all the arts of the stage. In a paragraph that enchanted Cora he called Modern dance the "Museless Art because it is something new invented by modern women without divine inspiration. . . . Muses are epitomes rather than inspirations . . . traditional artists and performers who have never been bettered. . . . But our dancers have had no ideal to lead them. They improve upon the past."

For the present she and her sister were seeking a method of unathletic movement that actors could learn, as unmusical priests learn to sing the Mass; and in her thoughts she experimented with choreographic ways to add a dimension to various kinds of drama. She might start simply by interpreting or mocking with concurrent action the staged emotions of inactive speakers, perhaps somewhat moderating an ordinary production's vulnerability to Brother Jonathan's cherished "characterization". Stimulated by Doc's writings, she thought about movement that would suggest the evolution of all drama—its diachronous etymology—, not as the speaker of a Prologue used to explain the makings of a particular plot, but as a stage designer, despite limitations of text and action, may suggest by both convention and innovation the relativity of dramatic space.

But the Troika was still in its collegial infancy, much distracted by divers responsibilities to children, husbands, customers, creditors, and civil authorities. As far as original work was concerned, its only immediate self-commission was the gestation and presentation of Cora's "Rock Dance". Unlike most of the projects entertained by the Hoof and Mouth company it was neither constrained nor goaded by the dearth of male performers. It was choreographed for herself and a few of the most promising women or older girls among those who attended her classes, to which no parent would any more think of sending her son than she would dream of sending her daughter to a military camp.

Caleb then hardly knew Cora. He was slow to take up her further acquaintance because in his years at Hume he'd learned that it was as profitless and infuriating to argue with atheistic Marxists as with Pauline fundamentalists, and though he believed himself nothing like his mother in temperament he was aware of an unfortunate proclivity for diving too deep, when he swam at all, in conversation with strangers. But he had heard about her ideas, and gathered from Tessa that she wasn't as formidable or humorless as she looked. In her presence, at any rate, he needn't fear to attack anyone's idealism, or to speak well of materialism, whatever those words might mean to her. Treading carefully, he might be able to learn something about The Museless Art. According to Doc it broadened a man's frequency-response.

But as to the future work of Hoof and Mouth, the three maenads had all been excited by Doctor Charlemagne's quizzical suggestion that, as their contribution to the Gloucestermas festival in June, without waiting to do a proper play in their own Stone Barn theater, they expand the seventeen-minute "Rock Dance" like a birth canal to deliver a plot and its speech.

"Make up something boisterous that dancers can mouth and actors can hoof—a piece healthy enough to hold up when almost anyone plays a part. You'd have a better cast than any college dramatic society if you two play the leads. Your New Atlantean Theater is never going to crawl off the beach if it waits for whole ensembles of cross-educated movers and speakers. And the Atlantean dance can't take over the Atlantean drama until it risks some maieutic failures with the Word. That's the only way it'll earn the skill to have any truck with stories. In Ur-Town they won't take such chances, but you've got the Glo'mas Dionysia to excuse you. In a year or two you can do a version of *Bartholemew Fair*; but first make up some simple puppetry to start with."

"Add role drama to the 'Rock Dance'?" Tessa drawled through smoke. " 'The Rock and Role Theatrical', maybe we'll call it."

Cora speculated through smoke of her own. "No doubt, dear sister, you'd want to add Prometheus, with pneumatic drills and rock-crushing machinery for dramatic conflict. But I'm not giving up my dance! On the rocks, of the rocks, for the rocks, by the rocks. Jagged floor and flat skyline. A rock foundation for the ironic stage!"

With Doctor Charlemagne, in his kitchen, all four of them were wreathed in auras of tobacco fog. Deeta wasn't home. Doc feasted his eyes and lavished most of his courtly manner on Beni the Bohemian blonde of the Troika. The lively teacher of arts and crafts helped out conscientiously as one of the most accomplished dancers and was certainly the most attractive. But she was now so awed into silence by the responsibility of becoming a stage designer that all Doc's interlocution was with the two performers.

As a fly on the wall Caleb would have been inspired, and Doc (characteristically, like a father who prefers to keep the family unaware of his own susceptibilities and frailties, of his deference or his pompousness in the company of other strangers) never mentioned the meeting to him; but Tessa was a faithful informant.

"Like any man out for his own pleasure, it's easy enough for him to urge us into provincial folly," she told her voiceless client, "because he hasn't committed himself. The old boy's pretty light on his feet, allemanding right and left like Falstaff doing the light fantastic, yet probably nowhere to be found when it comes time for choosing partners.

"God knows I myself couldn't dream up anything halfway original: but good old Gloria—I wish she could have been there with us—I don't know what we'd ever think of without her imagination! She's dug up some old-country mummer acts and combined them into one scenario, adapted for local delectation, which could expand the Rock Dance by forty-five minutes—with parts for every volunteer in town! Sword Dances and Morris Dances, no less! St George and the other six champions of Christendom! They represent all the nationalities in Dogtown, except for Jews of course.

"Best of all, *Robin Hood and the Friar*! After a rousing fight between equals, outlaws both, with some horseplay in the water, Robin, as King of the Summer, wins the services of Rabelaisian Friar Tuck and his three dogs by awarding him the favors of his own Queen of the May, the licentious Maid Marian!"

Marian means Mary, Caleb thought. I wonder if she'd be already pregnant.

"If this works, we'll ask the Chamber of Commerce to support an annual Rock and Role. Change a few names, and you have all the ingredients for a local tradition handed down from time immemorial!"

The current of the season was quietly gathering speed for its dizzy rapids. All flotsam moved toward Gloucestermas. All lives were swept along in the annual rhythm.

14
MOONTIME BLUES

*T*he time Caleb lived with Lilian in mind was immensely expanded, in comparison with the other times he was living, by the size and number of thoughts she attracted or connected in his brain while other events of his world were proceeding at their various velocities. Mooncloud-time excluded nothing of his present life and was vastly larger in its scope than normal duration. It comprehended all his intellectual passions as if they were enfolded in a rose he offered her. It was a rose she sniffed but would not take in hand.

She tried to remember it in the bud, when its attar had attracted and connected her vague expectations of love. But in certain moods its bloom of experience fascinated her more than ever before. The discoloring exfoliation had exhausted none of its essence, and the blown flower seemed a precious reward for her girlhood estimation of its pristine value. Yet betweenwhiles she reminded herself that no woman should trust even in its future maturity the excited man-brain, packed within such beguiling petals, which praised her much too much, with an appreciation (more precious than the love itself) of which many men and women were at least as worthy.

On his part, by the same token, hers was the rose in question—what he had hardly prized enough in its bud and now in its bloom did not possess. He knew that it was hardly she whom he once had known. This woman, now a mother, was not the same girl. But he reckoned with what he felt at present, scarcely ever recalling the past, and with a future no further beyond the instant than his next sound or sight of her. And while she was in mind he forgot all experience that could not be contemplated in passionate noesis.

It would have taken many cyclic pressings of their loins to synchronize him with her personal time; and deprived of that invulvement with the lunar he was all the less able to notice how little the whole earth moved in its annual arc around the sun while he was condensing in his desire an eon of calendars in layer upon layer of durative experience. At the core of his whirling globe, despite all its exclusions, the compression of these days weeks and months seemed to him as diachronic as the liminal moment before death when all of a life's anecdotes are said to be presented.

At every instant of his moonspell his brain commanded worldlines of coexistent space, each representing its own entire history! But he was to be astonished in retrospect to find how few monthly rent checks he had written during the chromatic inflammation of his soul, as if he had intimately traversed the whole rainbow, and grown to manhood, in three ticks of the clock.

And so it was with admirable self-restraint, in the trepidation of wisdom, that Caleb granted Lilian a few days of silence after the illuminating adventure of the Princess Tower. But his words had been ceaselessly forming and reforming. They burst forth in yet another spate of letters:

> My dear Blackhaired Lily, if you believe in the simultaneity of different loves (as in polyandry) you should not disallow the alternate principle of alternation. Before the sun resumes its interrupted course—not *necessarily* in opposition to the mutuality of our destinies—we must find a way to realize at least the beginning of what we've begun. I see that we're both romantics—but not transcendentalists or astral souls. We need a session of talking measurable in hours rather than minutes, though it be but in public,

sharing Scotch and water, to do justice to what's been only mentioned, if not to what we haven't yet had time to get to.

I try to imagine how you spend your days and evenings at home. (But not your nights, not when you're with the sultan.) There's almost nothing I know about your daily life, except that you must have too much work to do, with hardly time to sit down and read the *Nous*. I don't even know the layout of your house. I'd like to see the objects of your vexation and hear your formulas of cursing. Again and again I envision you both hands full closing with your hip a kitchen drawer I've never seen. I can only guess what you're like alone with Mooney.

The moon reminds me of you because it is you; but the sea reminds me of you because I've never walked by it with you, even though we both live on the same small island. Never together have we watched the ranks of bridleless horses or heard the monotonous roar of shape-changing Manannan.

(Alone, I draw your name in the sand; but Ibi blots my incantation with all four feet, mistaking it for the accidental trail of a stick-game. Yet it lasts until the tide laves away my hope. Maybe you'd be willing to go at night to Little Harbor Beach on your way home from the Doghouse and write me your answer there: your message would be gone within six hours, and I nor anyone would ever read it.)

For the same manifold of reasons a theater that I imagine reminds me of you. Everything reminds me of you because as the Muse of all the unreason I confess, as well as of all the reasoning work I do, you've awakened me from "the sleep of reason". I'm wide awake.

Yet, though you so much inspire my essential life, you make it very difficult to turn my thought to any duty not susceptible to the physio-logical transvaluations of Moontime. If we were proper lovers the bootless tension of my vectors would be harmonized in a steady state of regenerating equilibrium. Love's second arrow would take root. Madness would dissipate into harmonious order. My libido is superabundant when it can choose its form at will.

But alas, when I finish this letter I must make a another mighty effort to sublimate the frustration of my very life by the inorganic wall between us. It is a wall of ignorance. The vital knowledge I lack of your skin and spine cannot be supplied by an inappoite half-memory of the two histories we left behind in Hume. The information of you that I now crave would make the beginning of a knowledge invulnerable to hiatus or truncation.

I long too much for it. To hope for the future I must look below my horizon, like a sailor on nightwatch at war.

Despite your unassailable logic for casting loose, last week's adventure on Mount Olive dropped another anchor to the bottom of my heart. We get more grounded in each other with every word exchanged, whether in pain or delight. After every spoken sentence, after every real touch, even after my eye's briefest virtual touch, I seem to learn a new immeasurable dimension of your existence. There are n such dimensions, and always n more remaining to be disclosed—or to be rediscovered, since it's not just new things about you that are always newly exciting.

Free will aside, I still can't comprehend how you became what you are, from the brutal High Cordillera. What bred you into the peerage* of our realm? I keep asking that when I talk to myself. Was it something in Atlindu chromosomes that endowed you with a self-defining will—or in your mother's nurture of the baby girl? It's impossible to solve the inequation, but I'd like to reduce the mystery to its least factors.

You don't know what I'm talking about. You think I'm infatuated with my own madness. You don't know what I'm talking about because in the nature of things you can't be conscious of the cause—any more than a Viking Shepherd is aware of his own grace when he's lying alert in the grass or chasing sandpipers down the beach. Your superaristocracy* is as self-evident and unselfconscious as Ibi-Roi's.

But I'm not referring merely to your appearance or to your abilities. Those I have elsewhere celebrated and always celebrate. Now I mean something that I can't place exclusively in either ontology or epistemology, yet I know it's metaphysically natural. It belongs in the category of phenomena that justify humanity's claim to occupy the center of the universe: an ironic and terribly refined glorifaction.

We spent too little time looking out from the Princess Tower, where my mother used to encourage my ambitions.

To enjoy with you the cities of that plain, though in exile from this rock, would be more heavenly than the dominion of Ararat was to the angels of God when they descended to the daughters of men.

Caliban

* Of trenchancy, of courage, of kindness, of judgment, of alertness, of responsibility, and of leadership: all the secondary attributes of the primary quality your beauty is the scutcheon of.

Of course there was no reply. But meanwhile there came from the jungle's edge a waterstained and battered letter, many pages of cheap fragile paper, crowded on both sides with his mother's rounded hand in blurred ink, shot full of single and double underlines, parentheses, quotation marks, or dashes, and many words lettered in capitals. He laid it aside after a glance and a groan, promising himself he'd read it when his heart was fresher. Nothing so remote from Lilian, nothing so dissonant to his desire, nothing so irrelevant to his apprehensive excitement as maternal love, he lamented, could be worth a determination to work through those sheets before time and occasion presented the emotional velleity to start plowing. It was an archival chore to decipher his mother's screeds, hard on the eyes, challenging to loyalty. The duty to do so was oppressive to his conscience, poignantly exacerbating his haunted pity for her who continued such efforts to express illimitable love to an uncommunicative son, whose filial love she still assumed but whose obsessive storms of self-serving orectic love she could not be expected to guess he was suffering and cherishing at all costs.

The next day he formally devoted himself to the task of reading it, spread upon the kitchen table. It was an old letter, one of her earliest from Vernalia, written some six weeks before its latest known successor but retarded by the accidents and indolence which were institutionally excused by the annual act of God known as the rainy season. But as so often before, when he finally plunged into her jungle he found it vivid and admirable—though profuse with a life not positively attractive to one who yearned for the Old World's cultivated landscape: too redundant with other letters, too embarrassing to read more than once, or reply to, especially as it contained no new language and nothing to surprise him:

... If only I could write as I feel about this Peaceable out-of-the-world Kingdom to all those who have helped me through my misery and despair back in the evil world of Money and Power, and especially to you, my sturdy little oak tree, the supremely precious three-in-one pride and joy of my life (even though I dedicate myself forever to this selfless terrestrial brotherhood-and-sisterhood of true communal love). But it would be *impossible* to describe the peace and wonder I have found among these healthy, happy, saintly people who live together in purely Christian solidarity almost on the surprisingly merciful Equator of God's bountiful earth, and toward whom God has been guiding me all my benighted life, in spite of my sinful stupidity and individualistic PRIDE! I think I shall be writing fewer letters, the longer I live in Vernalia—because I am unable to convey in words the deep solemnity and awe of my being here at all.

This is the lost black sheep's return to the fold, whither the Good Shepherd has brought her—back to the other 99. And you my dear child, and all my friends, must each by yourself find this Way alone, from the contrite fullness of you own heart. There is nothing *I* can do about that. God must do it! Pray *do* so, God! Bring them in too. For thine is the Kingdom, and the power, and the glory forever. . . .

I have been in my assigned routine for almost a week now—gradually accustoming myself to the *modus vivendi* and to my job: hanging and folding clothes in the communal laundry. (This is a pleasant place for such wholesome work—out-of-doors when it isn't raining, or in-doors in a thatched-roof slat-walled building, cooperating with *always* pleasant people, in a very useful, serviceable capacity. Already I hardly notice the inescapable HEAT, and I haven't minded the *drenching* daily RAIN, although it makes drying the laundry a major accomplishment.)

It is hard to put into words the delight I feel in being here, for the delight surely cometh from God, the Unknowable—by the Wind of His Spirit, which transforms simple (not to say "primitive") living, and coarse, plain (even flavorless) food, and the plainest possible clothing (with none of the vanities of cosmetics, nor jewelry, nor superfluous adornment)—transforms it all into *living for Him*, by means of living in love with one's true brothers & sisters—with those who "believe on Him", as I do.

. . . There are NO "CROSS" PEOPLE in Community! Thank God! The children, & their clear-eyed, laughing friendliness, without one trace of the self-conscious distorted behavior due to lack of Love, & their happiness together & in their family & school-groups—*they* indeed are the positive *proof* of The Life! The well-adjusted, quiet-mannered, happy, "secure" young people—isolated from the world, but more alive by far to its needs and its sickness than those over-indulged "teen agers" in the "best" worldly environments! —*They*, who have grown up in Community, & who, for the most part, will elect to return to it voluntarily, when the time comes for their decision, after their advanced education in the outside world—what more convincing proof could be asked?

As for the loveliness of Vernalia's morning and evening sky, of its flora and fauna (including its *snakes*!), of its elusive silent natives—fading in and out of sight like the Great Black Jaguar himself, tapping rubber trees as if they were collecting sap for maple syrup, and gathering medicinal herbs for pharmaceutical cartels in order to earn the manufactured rewards of civilization (which have become necessities to them: mass-produced clothes, radios, outboard infernal consumption engines for their boats, etc.)—how could I record the beauty of all that surrounds our thriving example of *God's* intended El Dorado? We live in a perfectly natural peace with the surrounding inhabitants, trading with them in the required goods of life (or Caesar's coin, when such must be), and freely provide them the kindly services of our doctors and the well-equipped facilities of our Infirmary—without *preaching* to them, or trying in any way to correct even their degenerate version of superstitious Popery.

(I haven't yet learned to distinguish pure Naturals from interbred Hispanics or Lusitanians. And I have yet to see anything of the almost extinct "white Atlindu" woman-tribe that gave the Amazon its name because it seems to have favored the Orinoco side of the Casiquiare watershed. I fear it no longer exists! [Here I would be reproved if I said aloud that "Women are the better people"! It is *right* that I should keep my mouth shut about anything that sounds invidious or intolerant, even in fun, to the ears of good Christian people who don't understand the goodwill in my unfortunate usage of 'poetic license'!])

But first and best, before all beauty: the FELLOWSHIP! What *friends* I have here already! EVERYONE is my *true*, trustworthy, forgiving, tolerant friend—a man (or woman) of his word—his quiet, gentle *bond*-word, which will never be broken. And the kind of merriment that I find here is never found in "the world" (except in rare unlooked-for persons, like gentle little Sarah Cleghorn, the poet you and I knew in Allenton, whom one encounters with astonishment and considers "too good to be true"). There is ready laughter here; no primness, no piety, no *prating*. Nothing idle or silly is ever heard. Here, words have *meaning*. The songs are sung for their meaning, in the spirit of their authors, at table in the community dining room or at our more private "family" meals.

Communal living attracts only *thinking* people—people who have always asked the meaning of life and now have *found the answers*, and so are OF ONE MIND, each with the other—though some are former "intellectuals", some clerks, and some "peasants", etc . It is all one Spirit that brought them—*us!*—together. I am truly INCLUDED here (—yet more radically "different" from all others than I have been anywhere else).

Marjorie ("Old Humbug") Acton-Ridgeway is my room-mate in the little cottage I've been assigned in the North Compound. "You are to live with a very 'aristocratic' Englishwoman," I was told on my journey up from Uaupes. I had not expected life with her to be quite so *fine* and *deep* and *beautiful* as it *is*—essentially (though we have little "spats" occasionally). She is a deeply devout and devoted Sister, painstakingly "showing me the way", carefully thinking of and for me (just as Florrie did—more understandably, as a fellow-New Armorican, at the B P K 's Manaus rest-house).

Marjorie is making it quite clear to me that we can & shall always be true Sisters, despite the vast differences between us of "background", diversity of interests, divergence of temperament, and, above all, disparity of experience. (She can hardly believe a great deal of what, in honest feeling and trust, I have told her about my life! It is, to her, literally *incredible*.) But our very dissimilarity is making our friendship a real ADVENTURE! Thank God for Marjorie! . . .

With passing regret Caleb acknowledged to himself that his failure to reply to this and other letters from his mother—a hundred times more informative than any letters he himself would ever write to anybody—was far less excusable than the silence of Lilian's correspondence. Unable to call himself to a duty that was annoyingly irrelevant to his besetting passion, casting off the incubus of remorse without scrawling a single word to the mother who would have given her life for him, he couldn't help addressing Lilian instead, with yet more extravagant praise:

. . . Your self is so much more interesting than anything I can imagine or remember that I ponder you instead of biographies or metaphysics. And when I roll a sheet of paper into the typewriter for my professed purpose, words for you are the only ones that come to mind. Then, as I do now, I must turn aside from intermediating keys and take up my tactile pen.

You are as sensitive and courageous as a horse. The way you shied at the entrance to the Princess Tower! But you're like a dog the way you watch my face to see if I misunderstand anything.

Harking back to our earliest conversations: in the years to come you must find a way to teach—to teach others in the world besides Mooney and me and Lothario O'Toole—perhaps as an administrator, or as some kind of leader, or even as an official educator. The world would do well to grant you special authority.

I'm not accusing you of being rationally consistent, selfconfident, invariable, equable, inwardly calm, indefatigable, unfailingly integrated, normal, wholesome, filtered, or unmoody, because I don't idealize you as it may appear, seeing that by virtue of getting to know you better little by little I can love you more broadly. I'm prepared for shocks of personality, knowledge of good and evil—fearing only that when you know me as I really am you still may not be prepared for my deformities, faults, flaws, gross deficiencies, and evil spirits. I pray that your taste for irony will spare me your radical disappointment.

Anyway, though we have hardly yet begun to witness each other's ordinary behavior (since we're not in an ordinary state when we meet or I communicate), it strikes me that I've never met anyone, real or fictional, whom I could get to know (if I wanted to) as much better than at first as I could get to know you—right down to the soul—if only because of the special intelligence with which you express yourself. A few may not lack talent for intimacy or honesty or candor, but—even those in books—they lack your speech.

I'm not too theoretical to understand that words can't do it all—not yours and mine together. They alone can never determine which of their own experiments is closest to the truth—if there ever is just one truth to approximate. But most people take no exception to the tyranny of demotic cliches that dictate the component parts of their thought; whereas you are fearless with language—or, better, brave.

I'd write you letters even if I were allowed to talk with you every day, because I haven't the skill of speech equal to such occasions. Your wits seem always ready, whereas mine often go right blank or lame (especially on the phone, when I can't see you), and I desire the messages of your mind as I desire its skin and bones. Your words deal with reality as well as they deal with everything else. Your expressions alleviate my dependency on printed stimulation.

I hope this my admiration doesn't irritate the selfconsciousness that lies so low in your wonderfully active psyche. Hereafter, now that I've said too much for your comfort, I'll try to quell the urge to praise your language, from voice to verb.

. . . Forgive me if I repeat myself, over these long days and nights of unrequited discourse. By now there's been enough water under the bridge to add ergodicity as the latest hazard for a madman crying out into the void.

. . . Before I saw you at the A & P I thought I had a fighting chance to resign myself to this hoax of destiny, if such it was to be. But that was only a brief sleep of reason. Mine is the enchantment of a frog once kissed by the princess: he can't be disenchanted:: in human form he's only more enthralled::: and the poor girl shakes with alarm.

I'm only getting more dogged in my idiocy, which has spread more evenly, dyeing all my tissues. If I didn't wear clothes the whole world would see that I'm Lily-colored all over. Then everybody would leave me alone, as the divinely mad tiger of the village, and let me maunder harmlessly. But dressed as I am, they don't understand my strange behavior in your presence. I need a collar labeled with your name and address, certifying that you'll pay my fines. Next to my heart I wish to wear any kind of dog-tag that will identify me with you.

But still there was no sign that Lilian heard his cry. By night he prowled the streets around the Doghouse, and once even dared to drive up and down forbidden Folly Road in search of evidence, but he saw no car like hers. By day he forced himself to his job and other parenthetical affairs, mere pastimes at best. But he was unable to read or write anything that could not be associated with his vision of her.

*

In the hope of regaining his perspective of reality and correcting his loss of self-control, Caleb read a little more in his mother's formidable "Autobiography", opening the first copybook at random. He found little in the divagating narrative that he hadn't been told in countless letters over the years; but this time, though it was difficult to read in long chunks, he found familiar emotional facts compendiously unified.

All my life I have longed for love—more love—more people to love; more people to love me! For the years of motherhood—even with no husband to love and be loved by—I could *manage* on the quota of love I had. But then my son grew up—he who from the beginning was as two sons and a daughter! (I "lost" all three of my children when I sent him off alone to Dutchkill School at the age of 12, except for the few brief periods when we lived together later. He has been loyally *independent* ever since.) After that there would have been *nothing, no one* to love, if I had not found P M !

It was not until July 4, 1955 that I found him. He was Chief Engineer of my first ship. She had met with an accident at sea, off Southern Cornucopia, just outside the Port of Nineveh. It was a severe collision; and of course, in the required Coast Guard investigation that followed, an inspection had been made of P M's domain to make sure no engine-room failure had contributed to it.

P M himself had hardly recovered from the shock of being thrown across the Captain's salon by the impact, or from his anguish on behalf of the Captain's 8-year-old daughter (whose terror had brought on hysteria), when the insurance investigators and Maritime Commissioners pulled his beloved engines all to bits, keeping the engine room completely out of service for nine weeks while we lay in drydock. But during that time, while he was free, we "fell in love". It was *real* love, of the human kind, deep in mutual trust, and deeper still in shared Belief!

Because P M is very gentle and sensitive, I think, he really needed love at that time as much as I did. I shall always thank God for our meeting and our long & beautiful intimacy, and the fact that (but for legal technicalities) P M was the only proper "husband" I ever had. Our (unauthorized) "marriage" lasted from July 1955 till March 6, 1957—and then it had reached such a *depth*, such a complete, beautiful fulfillment that I could not *stand* it any longer! (Not for a moment would I have dreamed of suggesting to P M that he disrupt his home in Norseland and marry me *legally*. It was understood at the beginning that we would have to part. Each week made the prospect of parting more dreadfully unthinkable!)

It was at the very topmost point of happiness that I suddenly realized THIS *was not what God wanted of us*! Our love *wasn't* right; could never be right. So the next day as we walked down to the dock I told him: "I'm going home [to the East Coast] tomorrow." I did go home (or almost home)! Then and there! I never even looked back over my shoulder to watch him go aboard the ship! *I loved him.* I "kept the faith" with him. But, as I tell him whenever I wind my watch: "I love God—*more*, and more & more. And, now that I have come to join the Brotherhood—God loves me!"

In the early days of our relationship, we often talked of the world's *need* for Christ's second coming. We used to lean on the rail, side by side, looking out at the sea, & talk of Christ's promise (in which we *both* believed implicitly!):

"Lo, I shall come again, with clouds of great glory, and every eye shall see!"—and—"And then the sign of the Son of Man shall appear in the Heavens; and then will the End come." And in the deep, loving trust we felt for each other, we said we would plan to meet again, somehow, in time to watch the End of the World together. I used to *pray* for that! Now I do not. It is for God to decree whether our (worldly) human love *could* be right in His sight, & whether or not it *may* come to pass that P M & I *shall* meet again, &, in the Kingdom of Heaven, where there is "no marrying, nor giving in marriage", we may resume our love, on a spiritual basis.

Thank you God, for the gentle, generous, understanding love of that *very Good*, devoted, devout man, whom I shall always remember & love as my husband—the only *true* lover I have had! (And may God forgive us both!) Bless P M forever. Amen.

It is incredible that I am here—surrounded & secured by the best love man can evince—the true love of Brotherhood & sharing. (The experience with P M helped to prepare me for this life. To a great degree his goodness & truthfulness & fidelity healed wounds made by the other men & *my own self*. But it is the love of the Brotherhood that has healed up EVERY wound I ever had—except the persistent "paranoid complex" that STILL dogs me & disrupts the peace.) I wonder every day if I really AM here, setting my feet on the strange soil of this almost unknown place? (I remember studying about unexplored Orellana in the 7th grade under dear Miss *Sheppard*, who also read us the Psalms, unforgettably.) Whenever I can be alone, lying in bed, or walking about the compounds, I add up all the tokens of my life's history *proving* that GOD actually called *me* here! (*Me*!) If I had not been so *utterly stupid*, I might have been here long ago! God has had great patience with me.

Now I *am* here! The End of the World CANNOT be far away! Thank *The Shepherd* for bringing in the sheep betimes, before the night of darkness cometh!

Caleb stopped reading, wearied by Deformation piety as well as appalled by her bizarre illusion of being mutually in love at the age of more than half a century! By assuming the language of both romance and religion his mother alienated the words he sometimes used! Once more he tried to shake her tones from his head, and for a long time he couldn't bring himself to reopen her manuscript. Her delusions were repellent to the empirical lusts of youth. Merely by allowing his meditation to gravitate toward Lilian, like a stone dropping into a bottomless well, he immediately forgot the very existence of his mother and callously remembered only his own anguish.

*

But suddenly a fear for Lilian's life and safety displaced the purely selfish fear for *his* loss of her. Under the threat of openly stalking her everywhere in Dogtown, he had extorted the promise to let him know once a week, by any means she chose, that she remained among the living. More than ten days went by without a signal from her.

Having passed a whole weekend of tormented imagination largely occupied with estimating the probabilities of various catastrophic or disabling mishaps, especially domestic violence, he finally decided to violate the privacy he had faithfully respected throughout his failed intrigue. On Monday morning, when, if there'd been no disaster, Gil was likely to be away at work, he rang her forbidden phone with trembling hands and tightened throat.

A woman's low voice answered, measured and univivacious. It sounded like Lilian's, but he couldn't be sure. He judged it better to appear ridiculous, if it was she, than to give their liaison away by a familiar greeting in case it was somebody else. His voice faltered. "May I please speak to Miss Lilian Cloud?"

"She's not here right now." the colorless voice replied. It seemed listless, but fortunately incurious, as if ruled by inflexible instructions. Perhaps it betrayed the stoic impassivity of a vestigial Yahi. "This is Mrs Cloud. Is there any message?"

When he told Lilian's mother that he wouldn't trouble her with such an inconvenience, that he'd try again some other time, she made no protest, offered no advice, showed no suspicion.

Was she accustomed to calls for her daughter from anonymous men?

In any event, though the intelligence he'd gained was only of negative value, Caleb breathed with relief. The reconnaissance had been performed without a blunder.

Yet now that he knew Lilian was alive, and her household apparently undisturbed, his selfishness returned with less compunction than ever. Anger and jealousy now drove his egocentric fear of loss, obliterating first his tenderness and then, in grief, almost even brute desire.

But soon his feelings, still in grief, reversed themselves once more: tenderness and desire overtook jealousy and anger. Having cast off generous and disinterested anxieties, all his thoughts were again concentrated upon what he craved most simply and directly: communication of any kind with that one person in his otherwise insensible universe.

Warding off despair, he wantonly resorted to a shameless letter, which he swore would be his last without an answer:

> . . . I wonder if you're compassionate enough to have called me if you'd reflected that no one would have reason to notify me if you met with an accident. Until a few minutes ago, when your mother answered the phone, I didn't know whether you and Mooney were alive or dead. The very last thing I heard from you was something sweet about your feelings for me, sweeter than ever, in fact—as if we'd found the way to love each other. I can understand why you might not be able to call me from home or from the Dog House, but not why you won't somehow signify that you remain unharmed. It's only by violating your injunction, and risking our conspiracy, thank God, that I now may guess you and Mooney are secure.
>
> Maybe you think men like me don't have ordinary human feelings; but especially from the time I saw you comforting that ragged little boy on the street I've believed *you* had them. There's always been evidence of your compassion for man and beast. So even though I may be doubling your man-burden, and can claim nothing as a phantom paramour, I'm sufficiently entwined with your inner self to deserve at least the proof of your mortal existence. You can always call me Collect from a phone booth—anytime, anywhere—or send me a blank scrap of paper in an envelope addressed with block letters, Postage Due!
>
> Phoebe has come round once more, but I'm glad the weather has been too bad for me to see her. This time her waxing brought me nothing but the blues; and now, three

days past her full, it's again Athene's birthday. Both goddesses weep over the fatal gulf that seems to be opening between their two most deserving suppliants.

For me it's been a week of excruciating anxiety about you. Even so, except for that one desperate test by telephone, I haven't yet overcome my scruple to clamor for you when I know I should be silent and unseen. But without some prospect of sustaining at least the faintest hope of a glimpse by eye or ear—if not of one last meteoric opportunity to arrest your attention—I too much fear your getting locked into solar orbit by my default. That would leave the geometry of spheres undisturbed, reassuring the astrological counterrevolutionaries, but it would bring to pass the disintegration of this your humble obedient comet.

Then also (apart from both the subjective and objective flare of my own trajectory) it seems clear that you'll be unhappy in any elliptical cycle determined by the sleep known as reason. You don't need advice, especially from one with such a conflict of interest, but I play the part of guardian angel when I beg you not to ignore the wisdom of your heart just because it can't be as clear as logic.

I think I have glimmerings (if they're not false leads) of what you fear of me, aside from all the obvious risks and disadvantages: the pattern of past orbits, perhaps. You call me an "intellectual"—which I am only in the sense that you are. Values of the mind are more important to us than comforts of ophelimity. But sociologically I'm no intellectual.

Neither am I of the academic type, albeit most of my scholar-heroes and heroines are professors, and I have slightly more in common with the academic than with any other profession, trade, or class. Only slightly. Anyway, most academics are not as intellectual as you are, and all those I have personally known are less perceptive. None of them match you in guts. I distinguish myself from them by preferring guts and perception to hypertrophied learning and thermometer success.

I'm a comet headed for the moon. You are unique in all your phases, and I am unique in my disobedience to astronomy. Therefore the relation between us has had and can have no parallel. Its compounded uniqueness is the reciprocal of !factorial infinity!

. . . It's too bad you didn't get to see more of my mother in Londonbridge. WOMEN ARE THE BETTER PEOPLE is only an aphoristic pleasantry of hers, but she discomfits both friends and foes by spotting "twerps" and "pantywaists" among all kinds of professional men. Bringing up a child by herself in the Depression, living mostly on Relief, on Defense jobs or on truly menial work (in each case before being fired for troublemaking), she had more different employments, at various levels of society—from fashion-illustrating to floor-scrubbing—than anyone else I've ever heard of: more experience of life in nearly every way. (All the while she kept at her writing, and broke her heart in ceaseless attempts to get her narrative poems and humorous verse into print.) You'd profit by her exemplary scorn of the gutless, who also are mostly men. Particularly of gutless academics, among whom she doesn't distinguish as I do.

This digression is not irrelevant to what I see in you that no other man is thus so well qualified to see (notwithstanding that my mother's a psychotic exhibitionist, and in behavior quite your polar opposite!). . . .

But I still have a feeling that there's something crucial I don't know, something I dread to hear, about what's behind your words—for it would otherwise seem clear that it can't be good for you to stay with Gil. I'm glad you made the priest in Baby Oaks do the baptism—(He sounds as baneful as the one who tried to exclude Ophelia from the churchyard.)—but I'm sorry it's too late for me to become her godfather, which would be less deterministic than being her natural father. Yet as you've said, it's better for a child to have no father than to have an adoptive one that's hostile to her mother.

I shouldn't speak of things that are none of my business, and I never would do so if only I enjoyed the civil right to talk to you at decent length about anything else. Must it always be wartime? Must you renounce me before I've even been announced—after you've pronounced me the only one that doesn't denounce what you're most comfortable with? Comfort is not luxury; once known and lost, it's more sorely missed! Even if your remark about me was careless, is it not an indication of our codetermined free will?

. . . Your mature negative capability—which seems to seem to you an ignorance—is more precious to me than any faculty for acquisitive learning or talent for mimesis that comes a dime a dozen around Norumbega Square, where the best you can say about the best of the best there is that they take advantage of their advantages.

Your competence is the moon. Let her phases pause for me, as the sun once paused for us together. Do not hasten from me. Something destined is not so easily undone. My loyalty is stubborn.

Caleb's consciousness wasn't so obsessive, and his other interests weren't so feeble, that he didn't often forget Lilian for minutes or hours at a time, in a kind of liberty quite different from that of a sailor on the beach—more like the sleep of reason. But those parenthetical recreations, aside from his service to the Trustees and his visits to Doc, were usually confined to brief intervals with Tessa or Belle, whereas his constant off-duty communion with Ibi extrapolated and intensified the consciousness of his spiritual Moontime. On the other hand, self-effaced encounters with women in books, or as visual attractions on the street, reanimated his inguinal Lilian-lust.

Tuesday on his way home from the Lab, after hours of dividing his paid attention with elaborate thought-experiments, restraining the impulse no longer, he stopped at the dusty Western Union office on Pleasure Street to send her a frivolous telegram in ostensibly jocular code. By cheerfully threatening her with foolhardy acts he hoped to precipitate a revelatory response. He chose the "Night Letter" mode, not only because it would defer delivery until the morning, when she was most likely to receive it in person, but also because it offered fifty words at less cost than ten by fast "straight wire".

[However, there'd actually be no need of wire for this telegraphy, not even telephone cords—for he insisted upon carriage by messenger, as required by tariff, despite the moribund Western Union Company's preference for the informal new practice of vocal recitation only laggardly followed by envelope-posted "Confirmations" (in substitution for its vaunted delivery service, at least in markets outside the great concentrations of commerce or government), irrespective of the counted words' emotional burden.]

In his own town it was an embarrassing procedure, even without the presence of Ibi to give away his anonymity, for the taciturn old telegrapher (now also manager clerk and janitor) could surely read a boy's heart, though clothed in a business suit. But now that Caleb had made up his mind to do it he was too impatient to drive to Beggarly or Swipitch merely to fake an off-island situation that might call slightly less attention to his lovelorn folly. He marched in as nonchalantly as if to buy a packet of condoms; and when he was on the street again, having copied his highly edited message onto the yellow form, and handed it over without undergoing interrogation, gratuitous comment, or sidelong looks, he felt as if he'd accomplished something as decisive as one of Robin Hood's rescues.

(DO NOT FONE)
LAST WARNING STOP SETTLEMENT OVERDUE STOP GRACE PERIOD EXHAUSTED STOP EASY TERMS STILL NEGOTIABLE BY CALLING UNDERSIGNED STOP PROMISES ACCEPTABLE STOP UNLESS ACKNOWLEDGED TELEPHONE CALL WILL FOLLOW STOP COLLECTION PROCESS WILL INCLUDE PUBLIC ADVERTISEMENT AND FOLLY ROAD DEMONSTRATION STOP FINAL NOTICE STOP PLEASE DISREGARD IF REPLY ALREADY MAILED.

PYRAMUS CUBIE

By not waiting for her possible answer to his last letter he superstitiously hoped to change his luck and find that the telegram had made a fool of him by crossing word from her on the way.

But the slight satisfaction derived from novelty of action petered out within twenty-four hours. Only silence from the silent woman.

His despair redoubled, rising to the pitch of recklessness. One morning he stayed home from work until nine-thirty (a carefully calculated hour), giddy with splanchnic fear. After rehearsing a dozen contingent phrases he jacked up his courage to dial the dreadful number in Taraville.

"Lilian?" he croaked, nonplussed, after all, to find that she was really there. In renewed apprehension of his weakness in dealing with this female stranger, forgetting all rehearsals, he was already temporizing. "I wasn't sure. . . . I'm sorry to bother you. How are things going? Are you alone?"

"Yes. I don't much like being compared to a horse! It's bad enough that I look like your dog!"

Caleb laughed almost hysterically in weakminded relief. "Only when he's puzzled."

"Mooney's at nursery school. Mother's in Cornucopia."

He concealed his gladness at the hint of opportunity. Now they both spoke in the flat tones of unsurprise. He couldn't remember any of the debonair or incisive expressions he had compiled. His only remaining thought was to devise comments that would keep her in conversation. "That was a sweet morning with you at Mount Olive."

"Yes, it was one of the loveliest in my life. Please don't think I'll ever forget it."

"You've been as silent as the moon."

"I didn't know what to say. It takes a lot of thought. You told me truth is a special case of meaning. But my case is much too peculiar."

"Meet me at Cynosure Rock!"

"I can't. I've got too much to catch up. I've been away."

"Oh! Did you go back home?"

"No. —I flew down to Jamaica."

"My God! Did you go—?"

"Alone? Of course not. But it was a kind of rape. The little flute girl is wedlocked now. The crow's been painted white. That's why I can't see you anymore."

Caleb was shocked by the thump of love's latest arrow, this time in his back. The aerial ambush left him trembling—more from the revelation of a totally unexpected honeymoon (as if she'd suddenly inherited a fortune) than of the untimely marriage—but numbed by an aesthetic ecstasy of doom, like a man's falling clean into the ocean from his Apolline masthead.

He was mechanically determined not to let communication lapse within his last arc of sensation; yet unlike a dying man his vision was beclouded by the headlong fall. His brain was able to fetch up nothing but a hasty banality: "But we're still friends, aren't we?"

"I was afraid you wouldn't want to be. Your existence is very precious."

"Can I write to you now and then? Tell me how to reach you."

"My husband is not going to intercept letters!" she exclaimed—then laughingly relaxed. "But I won't have enough of an allowance for stamps."

"But how will I know you're well, or if you need a book?"

"Read the police reports in the *Nous*. And every once in a while we're bound to be down the Street at the same time. I can't very well avoid you in the Aristotle and Plato, can I?"

She paused, while he brushed aside a spurious notion to take offence. When she continued in a halting voice he detected an uncharacteristic clearing of her throat. "It will be important to know that *you're* staying alive, I hope nearby. I'll always think of you as . . . the best friend I've ever had. I sound like a schoolgirl, but . . . my dreams have never been possible. It's sad."

Caleb was mournfully grateful for the tiny crack she'd left unpatched in the wall. His throttled sob was almost triumphant. "It's infinitely sad!"

"No." she said. "Very sad. Very very sad. But not infinitely." They both laughed at the lugubrious pattern they had fallen into without intending to mock themselves.

"I'll be your doleful knight, your ever monotonous troubadour."

"Yeats says if you want to be melancholy hold an image of the moon in your left hand."

"But that's the hand I write with!"

15
TABLET FOUR

Gilgamesh and Eber enter the Laboratory by torchlight. [During the conversation with Eber, Gilgamesh unrolls a series of the charts, thereby covering the tapestry affixed by the Rector in Tablet Three. Some of the charts he merely glances at; others he studies with varying degrees of attention: a site plan of the city, drawings of the ziggurat (tower), a flow-chart of the construction project, and projective geometrical drawings of the IRTH.]

GILGAMESH   All works take longer than they should. So my motto is: predict too soon, and finish soon enough. Production is at last improving. The building trades have learned to heed my specifications. Work-orders regulate their habits.

EBER   It's an army under lash. You might as easily push them into war as force their arts and crafts.

GILGAMESH   You must admit bitumen was a good idea. Not for a moment has fuel been lacking. Watertight pitch makes hellish heat—as well as perpetual torches to light more work at night! In the flames aloft, when there's no moon, the new tiles gleam like sapphire, lapis lazuli, and rubied

	copper. By that heap of beacons I dare the thunderbolts to find me after dark!
EBER	You think their gods will be dazzled by ersatz stones in girlish colors? Leaving only Engidu for you to fight? Shall I tie one hand behind your back?
GILGAMESH	Without sarcasm now, tell me what you think: does he abhor my works? Or will they fill him with delight? I wonder if he's really ugly.
EBER	These beauty-lovers want him in your place regardless. A man who lies with beasts should be stoned outside the gates, instead of welcomed like a bridegroom! But the women have gone out to greet him with garlands already! Are you going to let a stupid game of force bring all your works to desolation?
GILGAMESH	No man exists with greater strength than mine.
EBER	But an animal may be faster and more cunning. —Still, all things are reported to me, and I'll ferret out his weakness. It's possible that by some device we can survive him.
GILGAMESH	Not by trickery!
EBER	The trick is to forestall the Rector's tricks. No longer can my vigilance alone keep the chain-mail of his conspiracy unmeshed. Yet you send Norkid on a hospitality expedition!
GILGAMESH	Your wariness has not been wasted. Had not your One True God set his face against my enemies, no doubt I'd long since have fallen to poison or my own unreckoning. But I don't want to keep the Rod and Ring on Shaddai's sufferance!
EBER	You abuse His gift of will by thwarting His favor with stiffnecked caprice. But it's not as prophet that I protest your negligence. By your command I'm responsible for the body politic. Furthermore, daughters of Erech now bear my children's seed. Therefore allow me to ward off my own destruction by urging you against your pride. A great spirit gets time to grow still greater if it's less magnanimous about the way to stay alive in single combat.
GILGAMESH	There'd be no greatness of any kind in consenting to a secret handicap. If I deserve my power and my life, I must contest the categories of life and power. It's the law of nature that spirit be sustained by gross faculties of body.

Norkid enters, travel-worn and weary.	—Is Engidu intact? What about the priest-woman? Did you have to push her? How long did it take? How did she—
NORKID [Smiling wryly.]	Good my lord, I'm not strolling back from an idle bout of chess. Give me leave to catch my breath—and savor your joy at seeing me again. I'm happy to find that you too are still alive.
GILGAMESH [Grinning, reaches Norkid a mug.]	Hello, old dogface! —Your beer's been waiting. —I hear you've landed the prince of the peaceable kingdom. —What have we here? A puny bow!
NORKID [Hands Gilgamesh the bow of a fire-drill.]	His present to you. The scepter he rules by. For making fires when you're all alone. Her Highness had given him your Isorectotetrahedron.
GILGAMESH	That was the lure that did it?
NORKID	I couldn't say what did it.
GILGAMESH [Examining the bow.]	I'll tighten the string and play it pizzicato while I wait for New Year's Day; or pass the time like a bard, thrumming deeds I've never done.
NORKID [Drinking deep.]	She called it her one private jewel. But she also gave him another, as we would have said back home. The goddess favors Engidu, and everyone knows it. You can smell incense in the street.
EBER	That gorilla will have the mob on his side before the feast even begins. You should have kept him out of sight.
NORKID [Gilgamesh lays down the drill and takes up his axe, which has been remounted with its double head.]	Of course I brought him in as a hooded prisoner after dark; but how do you disguise such a specimen? A swarm of honeybees was waiting at the gate! When this pretender's all adorned with gold and purple, and led before the people with their queen, it will take thunder and lightning to reduce him to a scapegoat!
EBER	The Rector's busy transmogrifying bees to hornets.
NORKID	In his mind it's all over but the acclamation. He began to taste the restoration as soon as he saw his royal sister about to be disburdened of her natural imperfection by a holy savage already incised with the barb of religion—congenital proof of Ishtar's choice! At two hundred yards Engidu's notch was as prominent as the Rector's miter. Maybe he was born ithyphallic too, because until he was relieved of

his superabundance, it looked as if he was goose-stepping on the run!

[Gilgamesh hurls his axe into the floor, where it remains sticking.]

[*Pause.*]

Being the clairvoyant hound of Gilgamesh, I bristled with presentiment—the sparrow's horror at a sudden shadow on the sun. You should have seen the ferocity of him before she sheared his mane and dressed his loins! Without the lady's help, I'd rather have tried to lassoo a crazed elephant!

GILGAMESH   If you'd killed him I would have pardoned you.

NORKID

[Dances, or slightly mimes, dry and sporadic illustrations of his story.]

So lightly you now disclaim the threat that frightened me the most! Still, I tried to disobey my orders. Nearly in a palsy, I fitted a silver-tipped arrow to my bow. It's not easy to aim at the son of a goddess when your nerves are shaking like a cornered rabbit's. He hadn't seen us, but he heard the shaft, caught it in his hand, and flung it back at me like a javelin, but twice as fast. Thank god it must have been deflected by the volley I'd ordered in my panic. Twice, with our Rector's shrieks splitting the silence of high noon, we skirred a band of sky. But Engidu stepped among the arrows as if they were children streaming out to play. It was eerie: no shadow, no echo, no engagement! —The guides broke cover and ran. One of them he got on the back of the head with his bannerstone, thrown by the handle. The other two he overtook in easy bounds, and spilled their brains by banging the two skulls together.

GILGAMESH   I'm glad you missed. Your blind devotion would have disgraced me.

NORKID

[Gilgamesh retrieves his axe and hones it with a whetstone.]

[Norkid sits down to drink pensively.]

Or cost you my worthless life. What saved me and mine was his awe of the lady. It made him see that he was naked. He retired to the hills, escorted by the animals that had been at the water hole. Next day, nevertheless, he returned in the same condition—still shy. But not as timid as the hares and gazelles and foxes and wolves and lions. Like us, they hung back to watch the unveiling from a distance.

GILGAMESH   What unveiling?

EBER   Unveiling of a whore! How much distance?

NORKID   We couldn't see much from our side of the grove, and His Grace nearly had a conniption when she refused to take him along as master of ceremonies. But I reckon there's not much doubt about the consummation. Three days later

	she led Engidu out through the trees clothed like you and wearing the Isorectotetrahedron. The animals had fled, and he was no more innocent than she who was laughing at his familiarities.
GILGAMESH	What familiarities?
NORKID	That's all there is to tell. After that wedding he was brought here for all the feastings of a potentate. The rest is detail.
GILGAMESH [Flaring up.]	Detail is what you're paid for, captain! Details are all I want. A general needs no report on net results. Did she dance?
NORKID	The Rector seemed to visualize what we couldn't see of her courtship. He was skirling on that weird pipe of his—a thin monotony; it stood my hair on end, and would have swayed a cobra on its haunches: the only sound for twenty miles. Then his music stopped—an officious cue for her Cry of the Maidenhead. It finally came, like a fainting afterthought.
GILGAMESH	What courage, to have danced in her very terror!
NORKID [Gilgamesh fiddles with the bow, using one of Norkid's arrows as a fire-drill.]	That's your imagination of a Gilgamissy girl! Engidu has no horns and he isn't ugly. If she trembled, 'twas not in fright. She was prepared for her duty!
GILGAMESH	You mistook her poise. I think she stood with frozen veins, dreading to be seized. Those shudders are invisible.
NORKID	All right. I'm no psychologist. But she opened up her robe.
GILGAMESH	As she'd been instructed. But she didn't make advances.
NORKID	I didn't say he was backward. Knee to knee, he didn't need a schoolmarm's prompting.
GILGAMESH [Raising his voice.]	Norkid, were they like dogs, blinded by instinct?
NORKID	Dogs don't make love when they couple. Or talk. He had speech to learn. She taught him how to use his tongue.
GILGAMESH	It's natural he'd love her. But the converse doesn't hold. She has no use for a troglodyte.
NORKID	I'm not a spy—my job was to bring the victim back alive—but I could see she wasn't too proud to let her eyes be opened. It was no surprise that an imaginative spinster, roused by priestcraft, should fall for an adoring gallant who wishes to deliver her from a fate worse than death.

GILGAMESH: But then he grabbed her brutally. It was too rough and quick. He was incorrigible and rude, probably quite smelly.

NORKID: You seem to think that woman's as fastidious as a white raven. Haven't you noticed the way she walks? For her the unwashed ruffian was a princely changeling. On the way home he was in her tent at every bivouac, and in the morning she was always starry-eyed. You could almost hear the purring. As we traveled she would smile and close her eyes, rehearsing all the stitches she had taken.

GILGAMESH [Angrily.]: Why didn't you just rope the fellow and carry him here trussed upsidedown on a pole—without all those hornpipe solemnities?

NORKID: Sooner than be tied he would've gnawed off all four paws. Possibly you'll kill him yet, but I wish I'd done it before she brought him sorrow. In putting on the new man he gave up the old. He lost a dozen tongues by licking hers. Old littermates no longer listen to his calls.

EBER: A fool's exchange. He's no smart trader. If his lust can't be slaked in one white sepulcher, there's still a whole catacomb of hot sarcophagi stewing for his marrow. Before an ordeal, whoring cannot help him. A savage isn't bred for urban stamina.

NORKID [Polishing his spectacles.]: False hope, my friend. Even when he beclouded with beer the grief of being shunned by his animals, the honeymoon did not bereave him of strength or speed. Dissipation is his tonic, and funeral his resurrection. One sundown we camped on the edge of the steppes near some village that was terrorized by a rogue lion he had tamed. The shepherds came to ask his help. So by my leave he set out to tell the beast about mankind's sheep-laws. But dragging off another ewe between its teeth, it ignored his warning. In an amazed fury he threw off his clothes, grabbed the lion, and in half a minute tore the life out of it with his bare hands. When the frenzy left him, and he saw that he had killed, he carried the carcass to Lil-Amin, twice his own weight, asking her what to make of murder. As tender education of Engidu's ferocity, all night long they waked the poor lion. But in the morning, as usual, nothing drunk or done by himself or the woman had softened him up.

GILGAMESH: Did you say he sometimes sleeps?

NORKID   As much as a cat—as much or as little. Sleeps and leaps indifferently. By the pain of guilt he earned the praise that men reserve for a mighty hunter. He began to play the lion's part as our provider. Like a big carnivorous cat he found he also relished other blood. The blood of prey that used to flock to him for safety.

GILGAMESH   So he's aching for the thrill of more momentous sacrifice!

NORKID   The priest harped on that theme in his religious instruction: expiation of his kills by killing for the gods, to save their people, and win the Rod and Ring from the raging mountain bull who oppresses the numberless women of Ishtar's city and all her livestock. Meanwhile of course to me the Rector affects to be duping a victim too ignorant to suspect that the famous skill of Gilgamesh will be backed by the sacred force of custom. Of course I never left them alone together. You should make that a rule as long as you live.

GILGAMESH   Let the schemer proselytize. What difference does it make? Conspiracy's too linguistic for an aboriginal ear.

EBER   But that harlot's in the plot. How does she ply the golem's remorse?

NORKID   Their pillow-talk was not for ears of mine. All I know is that he battens on tales of Gilgamesh. He who never saw a wall now envisions himself commanding a tower. He who never saw a rite now imagines splendid liturgies in Gilgamesh's raiment. He who never heard of gods now calls himself the champion of Inanna.

GILGAMESH   Yet from inborn slavery to her the poor fish doesn't know his lack of air!

NORKID   But fighting man-to-man that fish won't feel out of water. Don't count on having time to size him up. He won't wait for you to start it.

GILGAMESH   If the first move gives an edge, why then he and I will strike at the same time. But he will feed the immortal maggots. I'll play the dirge while women mourn his mortal parts.

Plucking on the firebow, Gilgamesh picks up his axe and goes off.

NORKID   By bruising his widow's spikenard Engidu has merely unlocked her perfume for our royal anchorite. She's not one to lose her fragrance at the center like a wornout cake of soap.

It seems Gilgamesh is about to learn that such virtue renews itself in the giving.

EBER The three of us could be dead already! I'll watch the ayatollah. You watch the ape.

Eber and Norkid walk off together.

16
ION

Lilian had been right: the scission was not infinitely sad. It was not even googolically wretched. Aside from transitory fluctuations of spiritual nostalgia and sexual despair, after a few hours of reflection Caleb's mourning began to admit darting sensations of liberating catharsis, as if the grief of acute deprivation expunged his old guilt of paternity and restored his essential regimen without debarring the adventures of a melancholy that got no worse. At times his brain tingled with perverse proleptic pleasure in his joyless prospects as a voiceless troubadour, sans sword, sans horse, sans lute, but with a dog greater than Husdant.

In the first few minutes after parting from Lilian in Unabridge he had thought of shaking the sand of Dogtown from his feet, unfixing his purposes on the Cape and breasting the sun to the lands of his heart's desire—as if he could cross the Atlantic without money or passport!

But anyway he then remembered that dogs were forbidden the very realm in which the dominant seeds of Viking Shepherds had been amalgamated; Ibi could have obtained no visa even to the Isle of Dogs, which, of all London, Caleb wished most to see, especially before ships stopped docking in the Thames at all.

In any event, Father Duncannon depended upon him, at least to prepare for his epochal Chapter at Gloucestermas.

He was also obliged to remind himself that, apart from these other sufficient reasons, he had sworn not to continue his voyage to the East until he finished proving the IRTH.

So he had made no move to flee Dogtown, and stayed right where he was to brood over his desolate relief from the condition of responsibility that would have led him into the contubernal bondage and acknowledged fatherhood which were so inimical to both travel and artistic proof. With redoubled pity he recalled his old friend Michael Chapman, mired in Babylon Oaks with three sons and a daughter; he shuddered at his own guilt in putting that man's burden, as well as others', behind him. The joy of his escape, though it finally dawned, was false at first, overcast and doubtful.

For a few nights after the telephone conversation he haunted the streets around the Doghouse, looking for any car that resembled Lilian's, even attempting peeks at the cashier's station as the double set of doors swung successively for diners going in or out; but he found no evidence that she'd kept her job with Loathey O'Toole. His compulsion to spy upon her, for no particular purpose except to verify the marriage that he had no reason to doubt and little hope to violate, led his imagination not as directly to her bedroom or nursery as to the external traffic of her Taraville domain. Since she was married, a fast fish, no longer free to take her pleasures as she wished, deserving not congratulation but consolation, his envy of Gil Algo, as a husband legally burdened with stepchild and mother-in-law, imperceptibly evaporated. But his desire for knowledge of her white slavery remained almost prurient.

On the following Monday, his next available weekday, when Gil was presumably at work in the metropolis, as he and Ibi were making their way across the heath of Purdeyville toward her precinct on Folly Road, it suddenly occurred to him that consideration of her happiness had scarcely ever entered into his motivation. Whereupon, under the dour middlecast sky of sea-bound Spring, he lost heart but recovered conscience. At Cynosure Rock he paused in shame.

A flare of moral felicity rewarded this abortive conversion. Before turning back, in an exuberance of self-absolution, he marked for some few seconds the Marking Stone that his comrade had already briefly marked at a dozen spots about its skirts. Ibi had been absorbed in the less concentrated whiffs and spoors that punctuated the trails they followed; but now he was lost in brisk olfactory reverie, recalling the Thing at Walburga Eve, and perhaps loves of the May withal.

As Caleb gradually recovered his interest in the historical universe, they returned from Tir-Na-Dog proper by way of Purdeyville Square (so called since the 18C), where three ways still met in the middle of the old Commons, the bouldered ledges of old pastureland now half populated with cedar and juniper. He wandered among the epigraphical rocks strung out over a quarter of a mile, idly searching for delitescent and less famous ones, and for those mockingly engraved by Wat or other wags in complement to the Duke's, and found

A WISE DAUGHTER
IS HER MOTHER'S ENVY

But now reading WHEN WORK STOPS VALUES DECAY his historical mind juxtaposed ARBEIT MACHT FREI. He read WORK FOR THE NIGHT IS COMING imagining NACHT UND NEBEL.

Like an enlightened muser moving through a gallery of pictures that had hardly impressed him as a child with his mother, he was pondering

DO GREAT THINGS
DON'T DREAM THEM ALL DAY LONG

the words she always quoted to pique his willpower, when a volley of short yelps smote his heart with foreconscious fears. Ibi had ranged ahead into the woods that buffered the nearest edge of Purdeyville, where the path drops steeply down to the ruined millstream and the railroad cut.

Running to find the dog and shouting his name repeatedly, Caleb at last recognized the cries as proclamations of confident excitement; but he believed Ibi to be as naively innocent of peril from an overtaken porcupine or rabid racoon as of the occult evil in a trapper's steel jaws, and his chest heaved with little less alarm than if they were howls of pain.

Ah, but there was nothing to fear in this barking, thank God—only the rapture of harmless discovery! Emerging from the trees, with the yelper whirling around her like a circumspread electron, was Deeta Dana, Doctor Charlemagne's housekeeper! At every step she stooped to stroke her bobbing welcomer and attempt to kiss his head; but at length the demonstration subsided, and by the time she and Caleb were able to greet each other Ibi had accustomed himself to the presence of a guest mistress, one of his favorite benefactors, as natural and proper to the situation. Presently, but not without the pride of having been her herald, he was quietly off again on interspecific scents.

Under a gray sky her loose braid of flaxen hair looked quite yellow, and her blue eyes shone with delight at the reciprocal surprise of wayfaring apparitions, despite the fact that she was on her way into "contemplative solitude" with a pack on her back.

"I have a couple of days off. Ipsissimus has gone up to White Quarry for a provocation."

From the pure complexion of her frank and seamless face it was hard to guess the age of her youth, or from her tattered camping clothes the shape of her sturdiness. At this encounter she stirred Caleb's masculine sensibility, as Hudson's was by Rima the white Atlindu among her green mansions; but he never doubted that body and soul she was Doc's exclusively, as long as she was needed.

He asked her if she was going as far as North Village or Taraville.

"No." she smiled. "I pray as far from people as I can get. Do you think it's going to rain tonight?"

He thought of Isopel Berners bedding down alone in her English dingle, but he knew of no such dell in Purdeyville, where the land was all hard shoulder and hillock. "Do you sleep in a juniper bush?"

She laughed. "If I had Ibi-Roi to keep me company I could sleep anywhere."

Reckless, he offered to leave his dog with her, like Tristram giving Husdant to Yseult of Ireland. But she was firm in her refusal. "He'd disturb my concentration, and I have nothing to feed him. Besides, he wouldn't obey your cruel orders for long. He'd soon be on your trail."

Caleb silently blessed her for having saved him from an act of treacherous generosity that he'd have repented at once and ever after. Reverting to his curiosity, he asked "Where *do* you camp?"

For a few seconds her smile vanished and solemnly she said nothing at all. Then, nearly in a whisper, making him half privy to her secret, as if for Ibi's sake: "In Jack Chase's cellar hole. Bad cess to your guts if you tell!"

Caleb took an oath of secrecy; but if Deeta had dropped dead on the spot he would have run home to tell his landlady the Cape's historian.

"But I won't show you where it is. It's not among the others." She waved vaguely toward the north, whence he just had come. "It's back in Tir-Na-Dog. Of course the cabin wasn't his, but he was the last man to die in it, where he couldn't see or hear the sea unless he climbed Cynosure Rock."

"If Redburn had known, when he gave his lecture at the Lyceum—!"

"Jack Chase came here because he liked Lusitanians, but he named the Van after Redburn. Only he smudged the clue by substituting a net-needle for the harpoon. That was an indication of displeasure with his favorite main-top pupil for having cowardly concealed a whaleship education." Chase had made known his contempt for whalers, as bobbers for blubber, much inferior to honorable fishermen. "But he lost all his Navy savings on that innkeeping venture. Too many drinks on the house. Too much verse accepted as tender, especially for anyone who recited a line or two of the *Lusiads*. Eventually the old Limey went to sit on the stranger's stone by the hearth of the Irish widow-woman up yonder, after Colonel Riley was gone. She was impressed by the fact that a poem had been written about him."

" 'Jack Roi'!"

"For his room and board he read her all of *Clarel*, and explained it, and cut a few motions of granite in the Taraville woods for cash to keep the wolf from their door."

"But the D T chronicles never mention Jack Chase or Yoomy Taji White-Jacket Tom Ishmael Guy Pierre Wellingborough Glendinning Winthrop; nor even Redburn himself! How do you know so much?"

"Matrilocal memory. It unbefits even oral history. I was born up that way." She made an indefinite gesture toward the deeper interior.

"And Doc knows all about it?"

"Not what I just told you, where I sleep! But he knows the Chase story. I think that's why he came to live in Dogtown. He always thought that Redburn should have written plays. I never have to tell him much. He fathoms pretty much everything—as you may have noticed! I don't criticize his guesses about anyone. You, for instance. He's partial to you, though he sometimes thinks you're impudent."

Caleb flushed with gratification. He had already forgotten Lilian, and for the moment Doc's approbation seemed even more important than the favor of Father Duncannon whose work was needed by all mankind. And to think that Doc still knew nothing of his IRTH-proof! When the time came, would admiration augment affection? Or would the Director's avant-garde disapproval turn the playwright's love of him to bitter estrangement?

"He calls you Ion."

"Because I'm missing an electron, or have one too many?"

"Doesn't every male and female have too many or too few? But he means no such metaphor. Do you remember the conversation about Yeats when I was in the kitchen? You said that you wished we lived by a lunar calendar, so that one could tell the day of the month by the phase of the moon. Ion means moon-man."

It was only pride that prevented Caleb from pursuing the subject of himself. He laughed at this intelligence of Doc's equivocal intuition, pondering its dromenological significance. Caleb ichabod Karcist! But his pleasure was ominously checked as he recalled that Doc had once suggested he read the *Ion* of Euripides. Now I really must read it! He summoned the image of a certain volume's place on his shelves, its size and color. Doc had told him the play began like Samuel in the Temple and ended with divine deception only half exposed.

"Me he calls Riolama: Rima for short." Deeta added.

"That I can understand." Impulsively, engrossed, he touched her arm with his less prehensile hand. She was leaning back against the smooth granite under TRY TO LOVE FATHER. "But what does Deeta mean?"

"Oh he gets no credit for that!" she vehemently exclaimed. "I've always been called Deeta! My namesake's Perdita—the last daughter of the great Oisin, son of Finn—"

But she interrupted herself. "—Oh my dear!" she exclaimed, snatching up his right wrist. "What happened to your fingers?"

Since grammar-school days his selfconsciousness about the loosely furrowed skin on the back of his right knuckles had faded. Back in Hume he'd laughed with Lilian at the inconsonance of those premature wrinkles, and over the years with one or two other intimate females; but as his summers accumulated the blemish became less noticeable, looking (at least to himself) more and more like the normal slackened skin of his south paw, and he almost forgot these scars of a maiming which like circumcision had never lodged in memory.

Not even Belle, examining his body minutely, had called attention to this false sign of old age in his otherwise ephebic physique. For the first time it now crossed his mind that she and other friends might have been too tactful to mention the blemish. Maybe they'd occluded it from their consciousness as a harbinger of gerontic horrors. Yet now Deeta was tenderly soothing the slackened tissue with her fingertips, as if she was Artemis, more solicitous of pain and disfigurement than were parous or nubile women.

"Just one of my unremembered traumas." he replied negligently; but his hand jerked itself free. "My mother says that when I was a baby I stuck my right hand in a bedside pan of boiling benzene—a kind of vaporizing bitumen, for the croup I think. It was in a so-called tent to make me breathe the stuff. Supposedly thereafter I converted to the sinister."

Deeta looked into his eyes with a sympathy that seemed out of proportion to the sum-total of his own lifetime concern about the matter. Was she contemplating the herbs she would have applied on the spot to cure such iatrogenic mischief?

But "I must be going now." she announced abruptly.

That night it rained. In the dark morning he listened to dripping eaves and gurgling spouts that begged his excuse not to do his regular run, especially after the day of a long trek. Ibi too was nothing loathe to postpone the day's work. In the dry warmth of his luxury Caleb was almost glad that he and his comrade had not been invited to sleep in Jack Chase's cellar-hole.

Then, as though suddenly reminded of his origins, in a pang that expanded from his brain with the plangency of a gong, he remembered his loss of Lilian Cloud. She probably lay warmed in a wide bed less than half a mile as the crow flies from that secret hollow. Still, in the seasons of her unhappiness, every now and then, why shouldn't she tryst with him in Tir-na-Dog, as it were on guiltless visits to the Sidhe? Or in the nearby King's Pines, when the Boy Scouts weren't camping there.

17
ORT-AN-SICH

*I*n less than a minute Caleb's poor overloaded soul dreamt a dream, perhaps the longest of his life, which afterwards he never remembered. His brain relieved itself of odds and ends by concatenating them with details or metaphors and antitheses of details or metaphors from thoughts and conversations of the previous evening but one.

That first fully social experience since returning to his native rock, an introduction to Tessa's dozen or so "theater-lovers", had been a Powerhouse party to celebrate the consummating immigration of Rafe Opsimath. But the dream was woven also with representations of persons whose very existence was unknown to any or many of those in attendance at the Barebones salon; with fragments of ideas suggested by snippets he'd recently read in the *Nous* or elsewhere, or heard from Doctor Charlemagne; with isolated memories from the distant past; with his mother's stories; and with vivid scenes of events he'd actually been aware of with casual indifference—as well of course with images of what he feared or desired. By syntax or apposition all these monomers and polymers were assembled with esemplastic invention by the astonishing daimon *i* who from time to time proved immensely more imaginative than his intellect. Even as he dreamt he marveled at the complex components of his dream, vainly hoping to retain them until he could get to pencil and paper.

*

I wasn't trying to find out what's wrong with Dogtown, besides the Irish, Rafe said to the people: just trying to figure out what makes me like it enough to pitch my tent here [meaning build a house in Purdeyville]. But they didn't understand that discerning things to praise was the purpose of the meeting, which kept drifting back to the history of their wrongs.

Mercator's now calls itself a marketing-oriented company, Cora Kryothermsky is saying who'd rather have wedded a stage designer than a food engineer. That means they want to produce packages that can be forced down your throat by DV . Street vendors selling Sea-Dogs instead of hotdogs! The same frozen fish as Chien-de-Mer Steak Mignon on Midwest menus! Marketing!

The Government would still make them put Dogfish on the label, cried Edie Schlossberg, having crept in like a mouse, nibbling at a plate that Tessa had been saving for her. Joyfully she smiles at them all, forgetful of her misdirected and uncoordinated teeth, yellow and frailly rooted, which for half a life had doomed her—as the mainspring of an Ur office that advertised fashionable innovations—to hopeless self-abnegating support of other people's glittering careers. Everybody knows she now works like a scullion to support all the careers of the driftwood prince who'd broken her doom. Sally Salter says she seems more like one's old-maid aunt, always too busy to weigh the remainder of her sorrows, than a passionate spouse.

I can't think of a less appealing term than *dogfish*, Cora persists with surprising vivacity, while everyone else wants to hear Dexter Keith talk about the politics of getting her Rock Dance performed with her sister's Role Text in Lilliput Hall. Sounds too much like *cod*fish—Depression food—or *God*fish, which would violate the Constitutional principle separating church from business.

GOD and COD and DOG have always been mixed up in our names, says Gloria Keith, *speaking as an aborigine*, especially the first and the third. It was transcription errors by two successive town clerks in 1492 and 1588 that transposed letters in our city's lately incorporated name. The Archbishop of Gloucester had approved the original name at Merry Sterne's request, to trump the Chauvinists. Wherever one of those words appears in our substantives or epithets you should assume a mistaken spelling until otherwise persuaded. I'm petitioning to have that axiom written into the boilerplate of the Dogtown Ibicity Charter, like the caveat about its use of feminine pronouns for the generic person. It will obviate twelve hundred provisional clauses in the legal code.

We should teach children to distinguish their letters more clearly, as they do in Ireland, says one of the women from the floor of the auditorium.

God's frozen cod saved the dogs from starvation in the winter of 1603, when the people had eaten all the salt, says another.

The future of the world depends upon fish, Thad Kryothermsky comments at the asterisk. There are twenty thousand species of edible fish that are still thrown back from hook or net. So Mercator's a growth stock. It's going to be listed on the Curb.

Caleb already knows all this and uneasily awaits Doc's allocution, to which he has been assigned as formal Commentator. He feels his paper folded lengthwise in the left inner pocket of his jacket, balancing his wallet on the opposite side.

What's the difference [between seeing what's wrong and seeing what's unique]? demands Huck Salter. Gloria was getting close to it. Names have nothing to do with our problem, which didn't exist in colonial times. Most names are too old to give us a clue. He turns to Rafe at the Gospel lectern. No offence, I hope, brother: but pilgrims see only our picturesque decadence. They don't want to hear the best of what we've lost!

Caleb is disinclined to interrupt this analysis for fear of inviting attention to his own infirm status, but is nettled to hear his generous benefactor classified as a pilgrim when he was now a proper denizen [naturalized marooner]. It seems that the distinct impression Rafe once made upon the playreaders' husbands has already faded into the indiscriminate category of off-islander apparitions. Caleb makes note on a 3-by-5 card that Huck's broad contempt for pleasure-seekers sometimes overcomes his personal goodwill, and that his prejudice resumes its sway by conflating a sympathetic adventurer with predatory tourists.

Dexter Keith, effortless in the principal armchair, draws all attention, even that of the highschool girls murmuring and whispering off stage, by making the quietly judicious remark that you must admit our city fathers don't know the difference either. Quoting Doc Charlemagne he says the orgiastic aspect of Gloucestermas, as of all Dionysian rites, has been greatly exaggerated: the liberation is not promiscuous or adventitious; it's discreet and largely premeditated.

What have we lost that the Hall doesn't know about? Caleb himself is meanwhile asked rather sharply by one of the examiners from the philosophy department whose hostility to Yeats is generally known.

But the Commentator is much relieved to find many tongues ready to answer in his stead. He'll be able to show his preparation merely by criticizing their replies. But it's hard to remember everything they list because the blackboard is a fixed asset that can't be turned over at home when he writes his dissertation. Yet he's expected to start them with a cue. First of all, the granite industry, don't you think? he smiles quite competently, nodding encouragement. Look at all the vertical caves it's left in the hills for missile pits!

No one responds. Dexter takes it upon himself to prime the pump by personal magnetism, filling in for Doc who's been delayed by the electrician installing the trapdoor elevator in the Stone Barn stage. More to the point, says Dex, we've lost our trolleycars.

And our dairy farms, adds Gretta Doloroso in tactful mediation, representing not only Buck but also the entire North Village faction, although she herself is registered as a voter over in the Prairies of West Marsh.

And the pigs are on their way out, says Rafe with amazing awareness of the deepest issues, prompting Gretta modestly enough yet making it clear that his intelligence is behind the entire charter-reform movement. On Innisman they live in people's houses, but here we don't even steam-clean them.

Mrs Keith takes her turn. The loss of draft horses is more significant. We have learned from Doctor Charlemagne, she declaims without reading from her notes, that most primitive societies studied by anthropologists have too little animal husbandry to induce a high degree of sex-awareness in their children. Thus the initiation at puberty is a real revelation and sex-catechism in the high school is also necessary. If you're not brought up on a farm, ritual is the only means of awakening and explaining sexuality while restricting its activity. But goats and rams don't amount to much, folklore to the contrary notwithstanding.

We've damn well lost our halibut, says old-fashioned Wat Cibber, embarrassed by the incomer-landswoman's turn of conversation.

We've lost our isinglass factories, says Tessa. And we've lost the sweat shops.

We've lost our Theater on the Rocks, says her sister Cora, newly tainted with box-office capitalism. Captain Ozone had his players do *The Well of the Saints* every summer for a charity benefit.

We've lost our painters, Beni Vanderlyn contributes, the Troika's Director of Arts and Crafts.

We lost our Transatlantic cable when the relay station was shut down, says Buck, coming in from the door of Captain Ozone's personal laboratory. And all our windmills. The watermills were already burnt down.

We've lost the lamp in one of the Double Digit Lights, says Eric Vanderlyn the toyboater, imitating a salty Coast Guardsman.

Teddi Cibber quietly brings them down to fundamentals. The beauty we've been given, the poison we've returned! First of all we lost our forest, she says, for Wat Cibber is too shy to speak with eloquence against the policies of the Crown. What didn't go to the Royal Navy was used up for wooden needles, or sold in Botolph for firewood. And it must have gone into the whaleboats we built for all Vinland in the early days of Slavery. Schooners wouldn't have been invented if we hadn't first manufactured many many oars and dories.

Tessa stares into the fire as she pokes it with brass-knobbed tongs. Everybody is waiting for her to speak of Auto Drang. Without turning around she finally admits that he was old enough to be her father: thus the incest was symbolic only. But it is understood that she will discuss the social psychology of a community that is said to have lost its Irish, save for an underground remnant. Cape Gloucester has always had reason to be afraid of pirates and raiders, she continues from her previous lecture. To this day Dogtown women are preternaturally apprehensive of rape. They used to seek safety in the interior, but now they won't go up to Tir-Na-Dog alone.

Mrs Keith her teaching assistant takes over the display easel, having drawn the telescopic stainless steel pointer like a bull's pizzle to its full length with her teeth (because her hands are full), and makes the footnote presentation, which takes no time at all because he has heard her rehearsal this afternoon. When the Vikings and then the French were gone, and after the imperial Georgios had given up in 1812, we had a navy of our own to protect us, and Purdeyville the refuge became the place in which Dogtown feared itself. It was blamed for all the vice and crime. But after it faded into a ghost town the crime got worse at the Harbor and everything up there was vandalized before falling into final disuse. Even over here in this most respectable ward of Protestican Deformers there were a couple of unsolved murders during the Depression, when Total Abstinence hadn't yet been repealed by the Catholicrats. Those crimes probably had something to do with rumrunning—which went very smoothly in all our sandy coves and may have had police protection on the big beaches when nights were foggy. So we've given up blaming the Irish ghosts of the uplands, and now most of the goo-goos like us support the Tybbot Graveyard Foundation program to buy Tir-Na-Dog back from the pirates and preserve it from airport bulldozers.

A domestic argument seems to ensue, husband et ux, the issue of which Caleb dares not stop to figure out lest he miss its matter. Well, says Mr Keith with cruel sarcasm, at least let's say that the glacier left its best topsoil up there, and the earliest Georgios from Casterbridge began to occupy it as soon as they could clear and sell the forest. Apparently the farming was good enough for sheep. I suppose you would have it that they finally came down to the edge of the sea to build and fish because they were encouraged by our Navy's success against the Barbary Pirates, and then by the fall of Napoleon! But I tell you it wasn't until the English abolished impressment and the whaling trade to Africa that the Purdeyville folk abandoned their houses and pastures to the Sidhe, who'd only been waiting for the right time to come out from their duns and raths!

Assuming an air of objectivity, Gloria Keith makes gay protest, pretending her husband's disputation is scientific and goodnatured: But potatoes didn't prosper; Irishmen walked over to the quarries whenever there was a shortage of Paulines at the bottom of the labor hierarchy. Yet she's genuinely pleased with the conversational engagement, which Dexter has long avoided because he's been more concerned with pleasing the Mayor and Earldermen. Her small luminous face is alert with widely attuned energy, according to Caleb's notes, and her tireless consciousness makes other blondes look placid disingenuous or crude. Her enthusiasm—though in modesty and deference she keeps it in check when reading her part—is more infectious than her reasonable attitude. They couldn't live on blueberries! she cries with a laugh.

There comes a multitude of assaults upon his understanding. Led or provoked by Huck Salter, most of the women and occasionally one of the least reticent male voices thrust upon him their opinions about what they think is important to be explained, and do so with a will that's intended to prove both their patriotism and their friendliness toward poor mainland bastards, nearly all of them sympathizing with the ignorance they themselves had been born into at one undistinguished place or another before they were lucky enough to maroon themselves here. Even Huck has served transpontine Atlantis among the ignorant, and taken one to wife.

Chris Lucy has been watching, to keep the dogs from getting out, and he now points out to Caleb, aside, that it's not so much a dialectical debate as a parataxis of overlapped opinions, confessing that he isn't as interested in what they're driving at as Father Duncannon hoped he would be. After all it's simply praise of the diocese they happen to live in. They're bound to make virtues of their peculiar necessities with some rather odd boasts. Like God, try to give your attention to all of them at once.

Dexter Keith calmly utters something ex cathedra, and everybody stops gabbling to listen. The usurers of Earth extracted a hundred million tons of more than flesh from Mother Gloucester before the market for reinforced concrete put a stop to her pain, leaving a billion more in deadweight displacement for us to merely osteotomize. But first they laid her bare, turning the whole rock-strewn highland of trees, intended for the King's Broad Arrow, into a prehistoric heath. We must get a grant from Frank Bacon to keep it from brambling again into boscage unworthy of timber.

Here am I, Frank admits, modestly raising his hand in the background where no one has noticed him. While he makes his formal speech people look at their watches; but for Caleb it's as quick as a tick, since he can skip what he's read already: Lacking natural caves, our men butchered their way down through the cooled magma of the Ort-an-Sich hoping to force open Lady Gloucester's cuniculus. Or at least we can say the rock we live on is a wounded gut, gnawed at for a hundred years—and exposed—to build not only sea-towers piers walls bridges breakwaters and great city gnomons but also a thousand paved streets all over Atlantis, when the stone was cut small to keep the horseshoes from slipping. It's the strongest granite in the world, but not pretty enough for exported tombstones or fictile enough for the winged Victories of noble cenotaphs. The quarrymen died young, like the stonecutters of Montvert, but at any rate it wasn't merely to supply superstitious ornaments that they contracted silicosis. Long enough we've dug the bones of Mother Dog: now the old quarries—half for fresh water, half for salt—can be dedicated as Byzantine monasteries and

Scholastic convents for male and female fish, if we can only get them to freeze at the same temperature we can them at. Some of those blasted hollows go down 250 feet—below sea-level, and the sea is right nearby! It would be a shame to use them for public reservoirs or bomb shelters. The population's already too large for our water supply and our per capita baptisms. I beg your indulgence when I say 'we' and 'our', for as an orthodox Scholastic denizen I have no right to speak for the best of you without poetic license from the Hall.

Meanwhile stage right Dexter Keith has silenced his wife and is holding forth to adoring women voters: In the beginning Tybbot gave us 1200 acres. I want the city to take 800 more by eminent domain, and then turn all of Purdeyville over to the Foundation. [He bows to Frank Bacon, who raises the back of his hand in royal acknowledgement before resuming his conversation with Wat Cibber back under the balcony.] But the Atlantean Gun Legion is fighting us, and they've sent a squad to their Taraville execution post. However, the greatest difficulty is to trace the titles. Nobody knows who owns much of the last 800. The burden of proof is on the claimant and there's no money to hire a land lawyer. I'm secretly instigating the Earls to pass an ordinance making the Ibicity Solicitor take on the responsibility, feckless as he may be. But there's not much political support for the landtaking, because there's nothing in it for any businessman, and it's generally assumed that somebody or other can eventually profit from at least a little of the real-estate if it remains in private hands. Dexter receives his applause with unostentatious grace.

But he hasn't finished, and would have gone on if Doc didn't just then arrive in Sam Craigie's IXAT cab. The speaker immediately yields the chair, and the distinguished Rector of Gloucester University is hastily introduced by Tessa Barebones, whose flippancy masks her nervousness as a psychoanalytic intern mistaken for some tenured Professor of feminine psychology. I must ask you each to allow for the fact that as a consequence of the baptism trauma our special guest celebrates his Cuchulain Complex, it being his unconscious wish to sleep with the mother of his son.

Caleb edges back into the shadows because Doc has been angry with him for having written the play that he himself would have written if he weren't obliged by his contract with the Dogtown College division of the university to direct dramas without conflict of interest. It's for this reason that Doc tried to steal Lilian from him, taking her to dinner at the Millstone Bar every Wednesday night, pretending avuncular disinterest while lightly referring to her boyfriend [with double sarcasm coming from a Yeats man] as 'our young Mr Ibsen writing closet drama and ashamed to admit it'. Doc has a large towel around his neck because he's waiting for Buck's bathwater heater to recover full capacity. Tessa passes the word to everyone in the kitchen not to draw any more hot water from the tank for another hour, even if they have to stay late on overtime to finish cleaning up the kitchen.

It's this surprising dearth of hot water that accounts for Deeta Dana's appearance at the top floor of the Rectory. On the street she has concealed her towel, rolled into the sleeping bag that Ibi carries by its rope handle after having let her in at the door while Caleb was still trying to catch up on the first reading of his mother's letters the very night before his term paper is due on women as the better personae in *A Vision*.

Deeta perfectly understands his apology. I have my own copy, you see! she says, holding it up, a serene penniless smile on her face. The lunar imagery is continually relevant to Miss Lilian Cloud, she declares, simply as a particular woman among women. Destiny fate and doom—all kinds of portents and coincidences—demand the implementation of her heavenly emblem, even though it's been almost discarded by poets, except in nostalgic popular lyrics, if only because men know that sooner or later they're going to land on the thing itself.

Caleb is entranced by the revelation of this rational and judicious faculty in Deeta's druidical supernaturalism, and so grateful for her appreciation of Lilian that he now tells her what he's been intending to write Lilian: *In general* I do believe that although women understand men better than men understand women, men understand themselves better than women understand *them*selves. I don't even begin to know whether or not you're one of the exceptions. Everything surprises me—and yet over and over again I've found that my intuition, albeit often wrong, is righter than that of those who inveigh against reason.

With nothing for his eyes below Deeta's tender paps except her tented knees there in the deep foamy bathtub he casually asks her what he knows she'll quote to Lilian as meant for her, the experienced elder of the two friends and his own senior by four years: were you ever aware of the torments that distinguish boys from girls? Were you always wise to the calculations of the seducers you chose, laughing at devices no less transparent than the unsuccessful ones? Maybe you're too old ever to have had a first-love; but can you remember any defloration not frustrated by immaturity and imperfection? How does love feel on the girl's end? No one's ever been able to tell me. We don't know whether Tiresias when he was a woman was ever a virgin. All my life I've tried to imagine what it's like to be a female. Such concerns have made me hypersensitive, and ridiculously theoretical. I thank my stars you've been through enough to tolerate my errors. I look to you for the mystery that promiscuates deny.

Deeta receives his words to Lilian not with scorn but with an anticipation that draws them swift as thought to her frank blue eyes, while his own eyes seek her body beneath the suds to compare it with thirteen-year-old Eva's. In unconcealed sympathy the straightened homunculus on his part anticipates the unvoiced invitation to join her sinuous pitching in order to show Ibi by the reciprocating positions of their arms and legs that she's friendly and harmless to his master, deserving of a wolf's protection. Yet Caleb as a whole is sweetly free of haste, complacent in the lordly maturity to which he has attained by writing five-act tragedies; he is pleased with the capitalized poise of his lower-case root.

I haven't had a hot bath since I moved down to the Harbor, Deeta says, shifting her weight beneath the waters and slowly laving herself with a cake of soap beneath the surface. Sister Ass read me her poem about the picaresque lovers Clitoria and Phoenix. She said you'd want me, in the placiest of all places—which is not the grave! But I must get home before dawn to feed the Duke [her goat that Caleb visualizes at its tether on the ledge above Leviathan Court]. It was Ibi who found him for me this morning.

But what about Doc? he asks, reluctantly obliged to remind her of that slavery.

Up she flares with quiet alpine dignity. It's none of his business what happens to me on my day off. But I can't do this very often, she thoughtfully adds.

From his bathroom cabinet Caleb hands her the jewel case of amber latex pessaries, a baker's dozen of contraceptive domes in graduated sizes, which Dave Wilson the adventurous bush pilot (whose voice is as thin and constrained as his own) has sent him from the retail shop of the mestizo rubber-tappers' cooperative that seized the franchise from delitescent White Amazons. But with the cover open on its hinge, in the dancing light of the kerosene lamp, he can't see which one she selects after underwater trials by sleight-of-hand; and with the slicing motion used in deftly breaking the sequence of a pack of cards she shuffles the twelve that remain. He smilingly makes note to use some elenctic algorithm—next day, when he'll be relaxed and contented, past the Condition of Fire—to ascertain the thirteenth dimension [which determines the elliptical sections of the IRTH in this special category of inconstant z-axis rotation] by devising a new application of the Synectic Method of Diagnostic Correlation that was already beginning to take form in his third eye.

I hear that as a father you're wicked virile, Deeta is saying. But I suppose it's too early to predict and too late to repent. He understands that she is only pretending to examine the pump fabric for pin holes, inasmuch as she never cares about quality control, and only laughs at the complaints of Rafe's humorless jobbers.

Ibi stands craning his neck over the edge of the tub, puzzled by Bice-Belle's absence but excitedly wagging his tail and dancing about on his hind legs like a stallion at the hitching post, trying to make up his mind whether or not to jump in and kiss her with his tongue. For Dog's sake! she laughs in the animal's face, and won't invite him into the bath. You won't like the soapy water! Looking up at the human face she makes a more thoughtful remark: Ibi reminds me of my ancestor Francois Villon [—Ibi pants at the compliment, turning aside in embarrassment—], who according to my maternal tradition had interrogative antennae over both his eyes. When he joined some Irish sea-rovers, after his final reprieve in Paris, they were so superstitious about the wryonic discrepancy between his looks and his verse that they stranded him here to reverse their ill luck.

But she's also saying let me show you what I saw when I was hiding in the crack of Cynosure Rock. It's over there on the chair. He passes her the sketch book and she sits up to open the page of a charcoal drawing. It's Ibi's paw as seen upsidedown from the perspective of his chest when he bends his forefoot backward. Caleb assumes the appropriate attitude for examining a work of photographic art. It's a foreshortened view of Ibi's entire pastern, almost up to the elbow, emphasizing the solid black pads as shown above the claws, including the extra pair that distinguishes his foot from that of an ordinary dog. You see, she says, his sense of touch is extraordinary. I wish you could have seen the original picture: I drew all four paws on Little Harbor Beach. They say it's invulnerable to wind, and for six hours on the average it'll keep a more precise image than the desert I prefer for sleeping. But he mucked them up with his feet, doing Cora's award-winning Dance "On the Sands of Time", and your line was busy until after the tide came in and washed my secrets away.

However, she adds reproachfully, you didn't deserve them. Ibi complains that you don't read to him the way your mother used to read to Sycorax. The white witch here bends to kiss the side of Ibi's lips. I'd read you *The Jungle Book*, I would, Ibi, and all about the big black jaguar, like the one that von Humboldt's bitch ran away with in Orellana!

Cats again! Ibi sneezes.

And, if you were really interested, I'd read the Jack London stories, for your expert review in the pages of the *Sunday Testament*. Ibi's tail thumps like his master's heart.

She leans further over to hug Ibi by the shoulders, revealing the back of her unexpectedly slender torso. Then with a sign of affection too quick for the dreamer to identify she extends her opposite hand to be helped out of the tub. Like a breaching mermaid she rises from the waters with a sudden theophanous stir; but it's an incomparable Psyche standing there above him, not one of the replicated Nereids. He kneels before her innocence, about to worship as Melchizedec at Delphi taught. [The pose she modeled at the forge for Petto's abstraction. It's a good thing his sculpture doesn't embody the Yahoo simplification of femininity that resounds in the sculptor's speech.] He seeks no rhymes for his prologue-poem. Let his own assuagement come wisely later—a disenflamement that would inflame him at a wakened memory.

One of the lost Purdeyville maxims was that A GIRL UNKISSED IS A GIRL UNKNOWN, she laughs with both hands resting on his shoulders. I'm in the subjunctive mood she says. He makes no sound giving tongue to his laving priestlike task, to which she playfully leads him by humming the moaned refrain of a rebarbative song: *If you're goin' to do it, Do it all night long*! Nevertheless hers is the tender lewdness of a wildflower.

Looking up at her face, as one looks up at a battlement from the foot of a granite tower, he is surprised to see that the beloved furrows in her forehead are not vertical but horizontal. They undulate like Aladdin-lighted ripples, fluctuating like diffraction patterns in their effect upon the atmosphere. And the same wakening thoughts now flicker at Ibi's eyebrows.

18
TABLET FIVE

[Before dawn on the day before New Year's. The temple sacristy to stage left of a dividing wall; stairs of the tower to the right. The sacristy is identified by the five-point star motif on a short screen (which makes an el with the wall) concealing Lil-Amin's bath; a loom is visible upstage. A sacrifice has just been celebrated, and the under-priestesses (Widows) are returning from the temple to the sound of recessional music from within. The ritual style is penitential.]

Lil-Amin enters, masked and in eucharistic vestments, **preceded by Widows**.

[In ceremonial but perfunctory fashion, during the following dialogue, they relieve her of a bloody knife on its sacred plate, and divest her one by one of tiara, chasuble, stole, maniple, cincture, amice, and alb (or mimed suggestions thereof). She herself may touch nothing. It is given to understand that other Widows are meanwhile passing back and forth with jars of water and hot stones. Finally they remove her mask and shift as she steps into her lustral bath out of sight. At first she appears dazed, praying by rote and exchanging formal bows with her acolytes.]

LIL-AMIN   Oh nuns of Inanna, blessed is the Queen of Heaven.
Oh ye servants of the Father Enlil, praise him forever.
Oh holy sisters, walk in the ways of Our Lady,
and glorify the prince of gods. Magnify the Lord.

WIDOWS   *Amen.*

LIL-AMIN [Kneels, facing the temple.]	O Lord Enlil, who has suffered me to minister this day in your holy temple, mercifully pardon the faults of my service, and vouchsafe to grant that on the highest altar of my people in the night to come I may receive without blemish the grace of your loins, and make myself acceptable to you as the vicar of Inanna in her own city here on earth, who lives and reigns your heavenly daughter in the world without end.
WIDOWS	*Amen.*
LIL-AMIN [Rises. The Widows undress her and prepare the bath as she gradually recovers.] [She steps behind the screen.]	All those years as a girl I dreaded my first sacrifice. It's strange how cool I was with the knife. I didn't fall faint with pity when the blood splattered my skin. Instead, I took pleasure in my style, and felt nothing for the throbbing sow as I slit her belly open that might well have lived to farrow many more. The embryos still quivered. I thought how painless breeding is, for boars. —Sisters, help me cleanse this female blood.
WIDOW 1	The cauls were perfect in the womb!
WIDOW 2 [They bathe her behind the screen.]	Your blood-voice was clear and strong. Your penitential dance was flawless. Surely it's now forgiven, your journey beyond the scan of Uruk. Heaven knows it was to right seven long years of wrong.
LIL-AMIN	My new worthiness is small. Dawn's air still smells of famine. The moon is dark and the sun is loathe to rise. It goes hard for me so to please heaven's bridegroom that he will stay the Great Gods' Council, to keep the waters from coming to an end. I, the one most weak and terrified in all this city, not yet learned even in the ways of men, must feign the supremacy of sacred desire! I tremble more as victim than I did as hunter.
WIDOW 2	Your trembling brought on beatitude. Enlil's heart will be gladdened by earth's most holy bride. He will trace the shape of your skin, and love's tide will rise in his golden thigh.
LIL-AMIN	It will be the plowing of a salted field. My liver's shriveled and my heart benumbed. I am dead before I climb those stairs. The god will cinder me with lightning.
WIDOW 1	Yet your spirit lives, like barley-seed in a moistened grave! A withered ear of grain is sevenfold reborn.

TABLET FIVE 227

WIDOW 2   In tonight's vigil you'll learn your way by prayer, meditating the hopes you uphold of all Uruk:

WIDOWS
[Widows dance.]

—that the cow of the field will yet be covered by the bull.
—that man will no longer turn from woman.
—no bride ever again sit in grief beside her bed.
—For the fragrance of your sanctity will be giddy musk to the king of gods in his nostril.
—For the counsel will prevail of soft-eyed Inanna in the Chamber of the Gods.
—And Enkidu will wrest from Giszax the Rod and Ring of her own city.

Gilgamesh appears, invisible to them, coming down the stairs outside the sacristy wall. [He carries Engidu's fire-bow,

LIL-AMIN moving without purpose until he catches the sound of their voices. Then puts his ear to the wall, as if to the opening of an air-duct, straining to hear.] **Widows go off** into the temple. [Lil-Amin remains behind the screen. Gilgamesh strikes a single note on the bow, which gives her pause; but she continues.
....
He then plucks two notes. Another pause and continuation.
....
Finally he sounds three notes.]

Now I'm clean. —Go sweep the sanctuary. —You go dress the meat. —Then come back with the herbs and unguents. The queen of Uruk must be doctored as she's passed from male to male like a bruised heifer until she calves. I know nothing of the mystery I profess. In all good faith, how can I deceive Our Lord when I'm stiff and cold from collarbone to ankle? They say a god is manly, and cannot fail to want me. Enkidu said that even when scared I could draw oaks down from the hills by their roots! Yet I myself am no better than the ghost of a hollow dried-up tree, my honey petrified. . . . It's the people that I fear for most. I pity them who put their trust in me. There's no health for them in a sickhearted queen. . . . But sweet Inanna, pity *me*—doomed by birth to be your servant! Was I a changeling? It's harder for me to walk up those steps and open my robe to the divine guardian of our race than it was for you to harrow all hell naked! I'll have no strength in me when I reach the top. Keep me at least from screaming. Let me faint on the Lord's bed, and avert my face, before the bolt of glory shatters this lump of half-baked clay. Does it pierce like flame, or spear? —What's that? . . . Who's there? . . . You must not come into the sacristy!

GILGAMESH   It's me.

LIL-AMIN   Enkidu? Not here! Not now! Go back, go back!

GILGAMESH
[Hesitating.]
I, Gilgamesh, with the string of Engidu.

LIL-AMIN   Oh no! No, no, no! They'll annihilate you here!

GILGAMESH
[Gaily.]
Deep calls to deep! Thought to thought! Eye to eye! Ear to ear! Tongue to tongue! Pelt to pelt!

LIL-AMIN [*Pause.*]

You mean stone to wool. Furnace to loom. Tar to holy water. Sleepless prowling to the sleep of love.

GILGAMESH Then tree to root! Or sun to moon!

LIL-AMIN Twain that meet in eclipse.
[With a short laugh.]

GILGAMESH Are you naked?

LIL-AMIN I wear no jewels.

GILGAMESH You gave away mine.

LIL-AMIN To buy that music-stick for you who had sent me!

GILGAMESH To me you never reported your success.

LIL-AMIN Was is likely that I'd fail?

Widows enter, preceded by horizontally carried flabellums, which they solemnly wave at her. Then dropping the fans, they go out again.

[Lil-Amin resumes in a whisper.]

—Shisss! Someone's coming.

—Be careful! Don't touch me! —Now go sprinkle the Veil of Inanna with seawater from the Apsu well. But first take care to inspect it thread by thread. Give it a blessing when you take it out of the tabernacle, and again at the door, with balsam. Try to walk with dignity.

—Go away, Giszax! You have enemies enough, without calling down the wrath of our Father in Heaven.

[*Silence.*]

Are you still there?

[*Silence.*]

[In sudden fear she reaches out from behind the screen and snatches up one of the fans by its head. The long handle is seen probing vaguely in self-defense.]

Can you hear me? —There's no way of getting in here without being seen by the Widows. Dear God, I pray he hasn't killed them!

GILGAMESH I haven't changed. I'm still no beast of prey. I still don't sack my cities.

LIL-AMIN It's I who have changed.

GILGAMESH You cannot be less fine.

LIL-AMIN From the worm you saw I've become a butterfly. As an old maid at the loom my knowledge was imagined, my speech too idle. But I no longer waste.

GILGAMESH   You were Ishtar's artist. And day by day you still increase in worth. I look forward to your wrinkles.

LIL-AMIN   You've waited too long in the looking. I do what is decreed above our heads. Your fate too will be inscribed tomorrow.

GILGAMESH   Perhaps I shall be obliged to alter one of those decisions. Or change your office. But you are a tree of innumerable harvests, which blossoms at fruition. My wedding present bears neither fruit nor flowers, but I have topped it off with Zagros evergreen. I molded the last brick, fired the last tile, pointed the last course with my own bitumen. The whole Sea-Land and all its seven cities look to the mountain I have made for your featherbed of bliss.
[Laughs.]

LIL-AMIN   As the destined platform for our Lord High God's descent to earth, it's an afterthought of your willed obsession.

GILGAMESH   It was my will to reconsider everything for you. I'm steersman, not a rudder. The afterthought is heaven's. Let my tower serve for all your marriages.

LIL-AMIN   Why do you come to taunt me, Giszax? It was not by my choice that I seemed fair to an impetuous champion. He had never seen a hairless face.

GILGAMESH   Or thigh. What was it made you dance against your will? I'm told he didn't have to lift your skirt. Did he lick your salty palm?

LIL-AMIN   It was the will of Inanna that spirit stood aside for body.

GILGAMESH   It's said your spirit was radiant.

LIL-AMIN   Are you here to spite my radiance?

GILGAMESH   I am here by chance. Is it true that by taking Engidu you left the peaceable kingdom in a snarl?

LIL-AMIN   The orders came from you, the duty from Inanna. I did not go with joy. But desire roused cannot be flouted.

GILGAMESH   Unless it's mine, apparently.

LIL-AMIN   You vaunt your sovereignty of mind! Ha! —I tell you, for myself and him it was Inanna who enkindled motive.

GILGAMESH   Then disobey the gods that use you! Stop Ishtar's game!

LIL-AMIN   The game of Inanna is the work of life.

GILGAMESH   So it was the means of work that made you love him?

LIL-AMIN   The means were ends. His chest pressed against mine. I did the work of a woman. It wasn't love. No, it was not love—at first.

GILGAMESH   At first! Then when did it begin? Were you in love a minute later?

LIL-AMIN   For pity's sake, it's like asking life itself when life began to ask me what I felt or when! At times he and I were halves of a single dancer—one breathing out, the other breathing in. Is that what you call love?

GILGAMESH   One tidbit of a mouse and you purr like a lion's mate.

LIL-AMIN   Oh he was gentle, but never mousy!

GILGAMESH   Mouse or lion, he'll die before he has the chance to roar!

Widows enter, singing.

WIDOWS   *Softly run Euphrates*
              Until we end this song.
              The veil of Inanna
              For Enlil's night on earth.

[They carry a blue veil behind the screen, where they dress Lil-Amin,

LIL-AMIN   My mother once wore this. —Mind you don't touch me! —There. Now carry up linen from the cedar chest, and make up the bed exactly as the Rector showed you. Our Lord's mask goes up late in the afternoon, with the flowers. Don't forget the bridesmaid's prayer when you finish.

who then appears from behind the screen in a blue diaphanous gown, her own mask in

WIDOWS   *Softly run Euphrates*
              Until we end this song.

hand. One of the Widows sprinkles her with an aspergillum.]

Widows go off, crossing downstage to the opposite side. [They carry various objects up the stairs. Shielding their eyes against the bright daylight outside the wall, they barely miss Gilgamesh, who manages to shrink back unseen. Lil-Amin listens, at first with a frown.]

LIL-AMIN   Giszax?

GILGAMESH   Here am I. How tractable you are—with cats and gods: anyone but me!

[Lil-Amin smiles to herself.]

LIL-AMIN   You sent me to the cat. You raised my bed to God. You and my brother agreed to it all.

GILGAMESH   I allow for your religion. When both the circumcised transients are gone, the question between us will remain.

TABLET FIVE 231

LIL-AMIN   Enlil's bride can never be a private wife!

GILGAMESH   I don't agree to that.

[He starts forward around

LIL-AMIN   It's a pity you won't be consulted. Tomorrow before dawn, behind the double doors, the Council of Gods will cast the New Year's lots: every person's, mine, and yours. Your two-thirds of a vote won't be solicited.

the projecting el, slowly groping his way through a dark and unknown passage.

GILGAMESH   As plenipotentiary for myself, I act without instructions. So can you. For us, you and I decide!

He speaks progressively louder as he moves away from the mouth of the ventilation duct (so that she may not suspect his change of position); her voice sounds commensurately fainter. As he rounds the el and approaches her, he lowers his voice, and hers sounds louder, until they are again in equilibrium.]

LIL-AMIN   What can we decide? To flee? To live in the marsh weaving nets for fish and making love for brats? You can decide to build a hut with reeds! . . . Did your mother have no gods, that you're immune to retribution? Not Enkidu, but you, should play the King of Fools!

GILGAMESH   Do you pray for him to kill me?

LIL-AMIN   Can you expect the sympathy of Inanna's high priestess?

GILGAMESH   But the private person, what does she hope?

LIL-AMIN   The private person drifts without hope, the orphan of Uruk, beyond the river's mother-reach, like an empty coracle at sea. Let wind and tide decree her course without entreaty. How can a floater be sure of what she wants, alone in the shoreless night without a moon? But I know that if you kill Enkidu, black cancer will eat away the sun, and miasmic naphtha rot away the bindings of our bones. The Optimates would arraign my feebleness, and the Rector would condemn his own sister for the city's failure to lift its curse. If Enkidu dies, I die too!

GILGAMESH   Not under my protection!

LIL-AMIN   They'd have ways to kill me. Unless you did so first.

GILGAMESH   Why would I kill my heart's desire?

LIL-AMIN   For keeping her vows. For remaining unbeholden to your weak preference. Her autonomy would enrage you. A tyrant can't endure paradox.

GILGAMESH My exclusive preference is preeminently strong. What's more, being deeper, more contented than loose servitude to mother nature. It's your match too—when I have the only wife for me in all four quarters of the universe.

LIL-AMIN Even after Enkidu? And after tonight? I thought you said—

GILGAMESH Even after circumcision! *After* anything perhaps. But not *before* any subsequent dancer! No successor while I live.

LIL-AMIN The mighty Nimrod has used me for his decoy, and now he wants jealous title to my carcass!

GILGAMESH If I were master you'd be mistress.

LIL-AMIN The symmetry is false. Equality isn't equity for a woman. You'd level our atonement, limiting my beatitude to yours!

GILGAMESH There's no limit to the mind. I speak of Gilgamesh and Lil-Amin, not of man and woman!

LIL-AMIN As if keeping the caste at two were as hard on you as me! A dog in the manger that wants a bitch as brood stock. To be reduced to your chattel is for me no honor. But you have never honored the ways of kings, and none that come after will ever honor yours.

GILGAMESH But Engidu wasn't raised by women either. He's been king
[He is now so close of kings in the bush. Not the man to esteem himself too
to her, without little, once he grasps the Rod and Ring.
detection, that he
LIL-AMIN Wrong! He's sensitive to gender, with an inner ear for
must deflect his rhythms, studious of the dual dance. When you're dead I'll
voice with one teach him more. He's adept at patience.
hand to his mouth.
GILGAMESH Before his patience sleeps, your dancing panther will bite
She turns to the the dust of one who takes no sedatives!
dividing wall, puzzled
LIL-AMIN He's kind to me, and as intelligent as a sister in knowing
by his altered tones.] what will please. But if he ever palters with my sovereignty, I can finish him off with my inexhaustible allures!
[She laughs.]
GILGAMESH You're already thin to the bone from overwork! But I
[He steps up behind thank him for ravishing the arrested beauty of your
her. At the sound of pucelage. In your face now is what I'd hoped to see!
his voice she spins Though I suppose you've also been fasting.
around and shrinks
LIL-AMIN Holy Mother, I thought you sounded much too close! You
back in fear, but can't come in here!
immediately recovers
from her surprise.]

TABLET FIVE 233

GILGAMESH | Who's not a cat may look at a queen. This is the place for a fly on the wall! I see that a woman's mystery battens on her penance.

LIL-AMIN | There's no mystery about women in a female city. —Don't come near me! I refuse to become your accessory!
[He takes a step toward her.]

GILGAMESH | You lured me here with your existence.
[Smiling.]

LIL-AMIN | Get out of here! I'm not fascinated.

GILGAMESH | When I am gone—

LIL-AMIN | —there'll be no one to praise me for my thoughts. Gilgamesh is but once. When he is gone, it will be as if the cruel sun went out. To rid my office of his begrudging glare I must lose the light I see by, and deprive the city of blazing invention. —Yet I promise you I'll put aside the loom and ply the fire-craft you've taught us. I'll use any art that serves my way to perpetuate your works. I need Enkidu to loosen up the law, but no consort shall repossess your seat, or occupy your cot. Why should the people of a woman-god have any king at all? *I'll* build the seven walls! *I'll* erect seven towers for the seven cities of seven gods!
[Turning away.]

[Facing him again.]

GILGAMESH | If I'd only known you cared for power! I'd've long since handed you the plans and got some sleep.
[Laughing at her.]

LIL-AMIN | To become an actress, I've studied all your acts. Before your huge eyes are closed, I mean to take in all their vision. I know how to draw plans and issue specifications; by anatomizing space, to control the use of time; to appraise skills and apportion tasks; to examine small movements and seek innocent causes of untoward effects; to be friendly and aloof; to bend and stiffen. I can imitate your face, and how you walk, and even how you swing your axe. My method will put your moods to use.
[She dreamily mimics his characteristic acts and gestures, as they might seem to a child. At which he laughs happily.]

GILGAMESH | You're a keen student, but you can't inherit your teacher's memory. Design is also made of details; and it takes the particulars of experience to realize plans through gangs of men. It will take somewhat closer acquaintance to acquire all my lore. Therefore let me live another seven years, and help you learn much more!

LIL-AMIN | I already know more than you think. I make everyone tell me versions of your criticisms. I've sent reporters north for stories of your past. Taking up mathematics and ceramics,

[Lil-Amin performs her version of the dance of the IRTH.]

I've analyzed the Iso-recto-tetra-hedron by its syllables. I can dance your theorem of squared triangles. I don't know the proof, of course, but the fourth face is perfect, with long and equal sides, each of which when squared is equal to one third the full cube's surface. —The rest I get by experiment. See: the condensation of your battle-cry, the acorn of your oak!

GILGAMESH But you didn't keep the clay-stone I gave you.

LIL-AMIN I only pawned it. I'll have it back as souvenir. But you see, I've memorized your theme. By my resonance you'll live in fame.

GILGAMESH
[Her dances changes to reflect his words.]

Then you must resonate my desire now. Project my sleepless hope. Show the craving that scrapes my unglazed clay. Dance the turbulence of this aquifer that undermines my roots. But don't just counterfeit the harmonics of two joined rivers, or of two spines touching, opposite but like, where four legs meet!

LIL-AMIN I can immortalize your vibrations without your mortal power, but it's not for the sounding board to propagate your seed.

GILGAMESH
[Thoughtfully.]

You seem too sure that I'm the one will die. Does the Rector intend to daub Engidu's fingernails with venom?

LIL-AMIN No necessity for that. Would I be memorializing you if there were any hope? Giszax isn't equal to a lion with human hands and superhuman motion.

GILGAMESH Better warn him too, if you're an expert in the manly art! You can't blame me for opposing the gods in self-defense.

LIL-AMIN And when, before you know it, you're emptied of your blood, all breath spent, your disconceited ghost can't blame me I if don't suppress the cheers. The mask of power will staunch my wound and smooth the flux of pain. My widow breasts will harden before the milk begins to well. Tight-lipped I'll beat my chest, subjugate my brother, and set free pigheaded will against all varieties of wisdom—my heart commemorating yours in wanton purity of pride!

GILGAMESH I didn't suck my strength from milk, and I won't die to favor a necromancing witch!

LIL-AMIN Carrying her mask, **Lil-Amin runs off** into the temple. **Gilgamesh**, giving pause to his astonishment, **walks off** the other way.	So after all it's fear that keeps you from me! Fear, fear, fear! You're afraid of what I am, and call it mystery! —Oh Blessed Lady Inanna, pardon my consideration of the secondary sex. Giszax can go to hell—body, shade, and name!

19
WESTERLY SUNRISE

*C*aleb knew not what matter he was leaving behind, although it had absorbed all the faculties of his mind, when up from under his eyelids he found the first glowing winks of sun on the wall opposite his window. It seemed to him that he had never before seen that wallpaper in the morning light. But the ruddy flutters of light entering through the drawn shade didn't steadily diffuse as they brightened; instead they fluctuated more and more erratically, like the sounds of an approaching mob—from the wrong side of the house! It was never possible to see sunrise from this room! This glowing projection must be the last flaring throes of a uniquely gorgeous sunset—the weird reverberating rift of a western cloud bank in twilight, actually fading. How strangely it lightened the dusk of evening!

But he'd already been long asleep and far away. Could he have slept around the clock? Had he missed a whole day's work? Why hadn't Ibi wakened him with pleas of necessity?

Jesus Christ, it was no sunset, but deep night terrifically alive with prodigy! Caleb finished his awakening with a leap of fear. Ibi was already on his feet, circulating doubtfully, about to whimper. All at once shrill sirens were rapidly approaching. As Caleb released the spring of his rolled-down shade he became aware that he'd been hearing the deep bass fire whistle in the midst of its long monotonous signal, which Ibi had been trying to decipher from the beginning without definite cause to make a fuss. The false red dawn was now exposed behind the rooftops across the street, toward the valley of the Namauche. All at once it concentrated into spasmodic peaks of flame. If there was smoke, black sky concealed it; but this fire looked too ravenous for smoke.

Suddenly, as Caleb dressed with fumbling haste, a howl began to rise from Ibi's stiffened upward-tilted throat, aimed from earth for heaven. The astonishing song was given birth in a range of voice expressively mature, modulated by a daimon's memories. No gross metamorphosis could have been greater cause for Caleb's admiration.

Ibi had first found his voice of haunting ululation at the Thing of the Marking Stone, with no human witness. Caleb had never seen his young dog so possessed by an urge beyond will or reason. It was as if some slow development in a triggering cell of his sympathetic nervous system, crystallized by the piercingly undulating Doppler effects of such loudly passing engines at nighttime (when fire sirens, obviated by the recession of other noises, were usually muted in favor of flashing lights), had all at once touched the threshold at which it would respond transcendentally not only to the voices of brethren but also to weird music it had never before separated from the promiscuous melodies and rhythms of the Harbor's sounds. At this moment the young prince of Dogtown saints was involuntarily initiated into the responsibility of a mystery that henceforth was never to be ignored.

Yet Ibi's maiden fire-cry was ironically intempestive, insofar as its intimately preemptive urgency (especially in such a small room)—its awe-inspiring spiritual revelation—made it difficult for Caleb to count the blasts of the fire whistle on the Traction powerhouse as it repeated its dread summons in a tensely paced message that filled the surrounding night like a behemoth ship in deliberating pain. And meanwhile the fire engines roared past, flashing blue and red through the curtains of every house, juggernaut Christmas displays of momentous automotive power, sparing their sirens less than ever before at this time of night—more perhaps for giving pause to trains on the tracks than for warning the few kilroys likely to be in motion on the streets. It took a long time to detect and reckon the second round of six blasts, then three, and one. Without consulting his D T Savings & Loan pocket code-card (or losing time at the window) Caleb knew from the first two digits that the fire was close to home.

But the ominous stationary steam whistle was not satisfied. Instead of falling silent it continued with a pair of twos—"Second Alarm"—immediately followed by two and two and two, calling to emergency duty all the city's firemen. Behind silhouetted treetops the western heavens silently clamored brighter and brighter, as if heralding a doomsday sun. Fainter sirens were now drawing near from South Parish and Taraville and Seamark, and coming up the Felly from the mainland towns of Felicity Beggarly Chebego and Swipitch, to help at least indirectly by manning Dogtown's deserted fire stations.

Ibi's participation as a medium of doom, like the last in a chain of signal fires mourning the sack of a library, though gradually subsiding, magnified Caleb's thrilling apprehension of disaster; but when he saw that the solidified flames were getting no closer his fear for the neighborhood gave way to the primitive excitement of chasing a rare spectacle before it was too late. In his case, an ingenue among the resident veterans of Dogtown's notorious hecatombs, it was the feverish rush for an experience both dramatic and entirely new. But old-timers were also hastening by car and foot to find the focus, even those who'd many a time attended the irregular church of Mazda, whose guessing of causes, accidental or criminal, was not a whit less sensational than the disastrous combustions themselves.

At the front door downstairs Caleb converged with Mrs Keith, who was wearing a coat wrapped around her foundation of pajamas, in pursuit of her children Robert and Deirdre. She was glad to have Ibi and his handler for an escort. Dexter had stayed unusually late for a meeting at the Hall. "The kids are way ahead of us." she said. "I couldn't stop them. I hope that daughter of mine is dressed more properly than I am."

Ibi, having recovered himself, notwithstanding his bewilderment at the preternatural agitation of all the strangers they joined was irresistibly eager for exploration. He would gladly have heeled on his best behavior (allowing for solecisms in such unprecedented circumstances), but Caleb apprehensively fastened him to the leash in precaution against unpredictable danger and confusion, not to mention the temptation of other dogs too happily excited by the same human swarm.

Theories of arson were already in the air as they entered the rivulet of carelessly dressed quidnuncs wearing masks of solemnity and suppressing the urge to run like the children—many of whom, old enough not to be sound asleep or positively forbidden, were already far ahead. Strung out like circus-goers, neighbors far and wide (known or unknown to each other) streamed down Coalyard Lane from Cod Street, drawn from beds and electronic hearths of narcotic diseducation by the hope of getting to a live unmediated spectacle before it died out.

All parking spaces were filled helter-skelter within a quarter-mile of the fire (the exact locus of which was as yet only speculatively determined by the pedestrians now drawing with them the three from the Rectory), and the police were turning back the cars of citizens whose greed for unpremeditated theatricals had lured them too close to the destination, festively hindering the official vehicles that were still arriving.

The troopers from 165 Cod Street were no less avid than the rest. Ibi politely slowed his trot to Caleb's pace, which was politely slowed to his landlady's, who forgetful of her age was almost skipping like a schoolgirl.

Rounding the bend of Coalyard Lane they saw that all the properties on that street itself were untouched by smoke or flame. At the far end there were only one or two lights in the *Nous* office, but its parking lot was crammed with cars abandoned by occupants who'd scarcely taken time to turn off their ignitions. The high flamboyant background stemmed from some further site.

"I hope it isn't the Iron Works" said Caleb somewhat hypocritically. It was difficult truly to dread being eyewitness to an unbinding of demon fire in the iron cavern that housed the hearths of Hephaestus. But the enmasonried glass of the mammoth machine-tool arsenal at the foot of the Lane, which blocked any unrefracted light from the sunken building's clerestory, was as dark and opaque as ever; and he immediately saw that the dancing illumination, partially defined by the lineaments of interposed roofs and trees, was being cast from further to the left.

They could now sense the quaquaversal uproar of air as it was gathered by a fixed haystack of flame. The inverted cone of heat whipped an invisible column of smoke straight up into enveloping darkness, so thoroughly that Ibi was still the only one who could smell its gaseous dispersions.

Caleb checked himself. "No, it's across the tracks! It must be the gas tanks, or else— Oh my God, is it Buck's shop?"

They ran the rest of the way—dog, man, and woman. Turning the corner behind the *Nous*, dodging and tripping through a welter of light-slinging police cars, throbbing kilroy fire pumps, flaccid and tumescent hoses—jostling other unrestrained spectators—they arrived at the inferno. On the other side of the railroad tracks, backed against a ledged spur of the Fuckintired drumlin, surrounded on three sides by mobile floodlights and elevated ladders, the holocaust was being attacked with pizzle ordnance by an apparently anarchic chorus of black-clad fire-fighters in axe-belts and buskins, helmeted in ridged and crested Stetsons shaped tall and hard enough to defend their heads, with broad-tailed brims to keep deflected water from running down their necks. In and around the floodlighted orchestra their armor gleamed with the quivering reflections of sweeping or flashing peripheral beams—garish orange, lurid, rosy, chaotic; cyclic, cherry, livid, pallid, icy: each self-willed and undirected, except where all conflared like a single torch in the ocean's unfathomable night. The team of benign warriors seemed to work in silence, communicating like ants beneath a welkin of noise—the crackling of the bonfire and the steady roar of infernal-combustion pumps. Its tangled labors were sympathetically observed, and even advised, by a freely circulating congress of male and female nightwalkers, some as personal friends or relatives.

Dogtown Machine & Design was sacrificing itself to flames from within. It was some time before its ribs began to show, but there could be no question of its swift destruction. The fire had gone too long undiscovered, and had spread too fast, for any hope to frustrate its will. No man had been able to enter the building in a normal attempt to extinguish the flames at their base, but the nozzles at ground level were pointed at the cella through frames in the lower walls already as unshielded by doors and windows as an araeosystyle temple of Hephaestus.

It was a knowledgeable audience. "Just an old building, but a lot of expensive machinery." said a woman.

A portly man informed several overhearers: "The old Demeter Milling feed store that Wally Buster's dad used to own. His brother was the steamfitter that worked down the line to the Navy Yard. Married the old Boxshaw girl."

Once agreed that there was no death or injury to discuss (ignoring mice and perhaps a cat), nor any public evidence of arson, the main concern was to predict and evaluate the climax of collapse. Would the blaze have passed its noontide before the walls fell or dissolved that still concealed much of its body? Some estimated by the height of the flames on the roof, some by the saturation of color at the apertures, some by the apparently inverse proportion of smoke to the heat, which alone kept the spectators from approaching the altar of immolation.

Yet it must needs be a dwindling congregation, now past midnight and the morrow allowing no holiday from school or work. Only the semiprofessional critics were worshipful enough to await the sunset. Even among leisured Dogtowners, few inveterate observers would have traded very much of their sleep for such an unexceptional fire. This one seemed of no great size or novelty to any resident of more than four or five years. The canniest oldtimers had probably long since spotted this victim as one of the prime targets of Tyche, like certain fishing boats of the insured category that were quite destined for accidental sinking.

But it was to be doubted that Barebones carried fire insurance. The building had no sprinkler system, and of course the premiums for adequate coverage in Dogtown were as high as they come. Still, the topic wouldn't have arisen in Caleb's mind if Mrs Keith the bill-paying householder hadn't quite naturally mentioned it, though preoccupied with searching the throng for her offspring.

Inwardly Caleb tried to imagine what it would be like to lose the work of a lifetime—or at least the proof of what was done and the preparation for what was left to do. Outwardly he was too timid to intrude upon people engaged with interlocutors more valued than himself. So, having no more idea of what to say to a vicarious victim of fire than to a vicarious victim of death, he excused himself from accompanying Mrs Keith across the rails and through the firefighting paraphernalia to Buck and Tessa by volunteering instead to station himself as trackside lookout for the kids.

In fact he undertook to serve as monitor of any recognized individuals who might cross the line. By mounting a small space left by ferrous logs on a nearby flatcar in the Iron Works yard (under the swiveled machina whose magnetic deus lay idle upon a neighboring stockpile like a brooding cheese of prey) he was also able to survey all actors over the heads of giants. From this visible position he hoped to point out the young Keiths if their mother didn't collar them milling about in the orchestra. It was almost the morning of a "school night", and every student had by now had time enough to savor the distracting phenomenon. Robert especially was too young to lose his sleep, said Mrs Keith. Yet until she'd spoken to the devastated Bareboneses she couldn't devote full attention to family discipline.

Buck and Tessa, on either side of Gretta Doloroso, stood behind the conferring chiefs of Fire and Police, a little apart from several off-duty officials and other men who looked unofficially influential. The Bareboneses were smoking cigarettes and consoling their stout shop secretary with hugs and words of reassurance. Tessa was calm and dry-eyed; Buck looked as beatific as Don Quixote at his rescue of a lady and her duenna.

But here the duenna wept for her master. More acutely than Buck himself his maid of all work appraised the terrible entropy effected by this racing disintegration. To her most intimate knowledge the information and capital energy once sheltered by those shabby clapboards, now utterly undone, was priceless. That stack of planks and boards had served as studio and godown for peerless gifts of mechanical imagination.

Yet the proprietor himself, more than she, mourned the means of her livelihood, and that of half a dozen other household-heads.

Caleb soon forgot to look for Deirdre and Robert as he watched the battle, which by this time he could see was rather organized than not, despite the manifestly disordered deployment of equipment. As usual he was chary of asking bystanders or passers-by even the simple questions they well might know the answers to, for he feared to elicit the kind of redundantly interminable and uninterruptable ramble with which he was nonplussed or misinformed almost every time he did resort to helpful citizens for advice or directions. As when he rode in trains by daylight, moreover, he found it impossible to watch the scenery while being harangued with loquacious companionship.

Therefore he was remarkably delighted by his good luck when Ibi's welcoming mews announced their anonymous acquaintance the night watchman and sole third-shift smith of the Iron Works forge. The aging man had climbed the bank's steep wooden staircase to punch his clocks in the upper building on his second rounds since being the first to notice inchoate flickers of heat across the way. He'd broken open an alarm box, and then telephoned his boss.

At length the superintendent of the Works had made his appearance, but only long enough to be certain that there was no wind from the south, no danger to his real estate from flames or flying scintillas. Having reassurance from the calm Fire Chief on the other side of the tracks, public defender of property, he'd handed back all responsibility for the Works to his anchor watch and gone home to bed like a schooner captain leaving instructions to be called only at an unfavorable change in the weather. His heavy industry shared with its lightly machining neighbor a certain professional interest in the properties of steel, and he sometimes purchased special skills from Buck; but at bottom the small wooden chandlery of designs and refinements was of no further concern to the skipper's corporation—unless and until, under these new circumstances, his board should decide to make an offer for the trackside lot that would soon be leveled opposite their own.

"Yep, I wish I had this fella with me every night!" repeated the agreeable halftoothed smithy-watcher, rubbing Ibi behind the ears, for it wasn't the first time he'd confided those very words. Both he and Caleb were too shy to ask each other's name—Caleb mainly because he knew he'd forget what he was told and thus embarrass himself in the future.

Unfortunately it was only after getting entangled in this conversation that he caught sight of Belle on the battle lines. She was in her Cossack boots and tailored trenchcoat, black curls flung loosely back from brow by the vigor of swerves and strides. As a journalist with unopened notebook she boldly threaded her way back and forth across the front like a privileged dignitary, while Tim Scriabin the cub reporter assigned to cover routine events laboriously took down facts from the lips of the Chief and other authenticators. From time to time she was caught up by Flash Silver, the paper's semi-autonomous photographer, who appeared to pursue her for suggestions despite collateral gestures that smacked of her imperious indifference to his attention.

Caleb was vexed to realize that if he hadn't been trapped by his own friendliness to landlady and watchman he might have claimed Belle as his tutor for the occasion. For some weeks he'd practically forgotten her, but the sudden glimpse stirred sleeping desire without reawakening the bitter caution of past disappointments. Perhaps her feelings would have matched his own.

Nevertheless this nice old geezer under the derrick was an unrecognized messenger demigod in the drama. He'd been apprehensive about the ramshackle granary almost since his demobilization after World War One, during the times when sparks and cinders from passing locomotives threatened every wooden structure along the right-of-way (including yonder Jubilee Avenue bridge and many a backyard dog shed). Caleb hoped that by listening patiently for clues to information and echoes of insight from this unrecorded point of view, he himself might be found useful to the Bareboneses and the Keiths, and especially to the *Nous*'s new feature-writer, as a conduit of local matter. The nearly superannuated guardian, one of the few aborigines with whom Caleb felt comfortably acquainted (as if, thanks to Ibi's aristocracy, with an hereditary inferior), was an old comrade of the Fire Inspector: altogether a unique source of intelligence for Dogtown's intelligentsia.

"I guess she'll go all the way now. They won't even try to save the walls. Them tanks are more important." Champing his hollow jaws, he motioned toward the large sphere of silver-painted steel a hundred yards east on the other side of the tracks, resting upon the railroad embankment's shoulder above the swamp that separated Buck's land from Cricket Field, which lay down in the hollow below the little overgrown cemetery of the first settlers. On a siding inside the neat wire fence of the Vinland Gas liquid storage station there was also a tank car.

"It's a good thing there ain't any breeze, but in case it shifts to westerly it might warm up that ball a little too much. Wouldn't that be the worst explosion since the ammunition ship in Chebuctu Harbor!" He seemed undistressed by the notion. Judging by the Fire Chief's tolerance of wandering spectators and other defaults in public safety, the city's authorities likewise seemed unalarmed about such a contingency (seeing that nothing like that had ever happened before).

The headlight of a distant train just then rounded a bend at the far end of the causeway on the west side of Namauche marsh. Caleb was looking for it, but its warning whistle had been missed because it was drowned out by the commotion of immediately surrounding apparatus. "I've been wondering what the trains will do." he commented. "Don't the fire hoses take precedence?"

The amiable gaffer pulled a pocket watch from his inner clothes. "Right on schedule. But it'll be breakfast time before the Chief clears off the track and pulls out of here. The trains'll have to back up to the West Marsh station and call in busses between there and Seamark, I shouldn't wonder."

Soon the train came to a stop on the far side of the draw, its powerful white headlamp highlighting the jumbled scene along the tracks like a rehearsal stage and downplaying the fire itself as a backdrop. They saw from moving lanterns that the conductor cautiously climbed down to get his news from the bridge-tender, who then took him into his hut to use the telephone.

"Good thing they've got a switch over there. The night freight's somewhere down the line on that track."

It took another quarter of an hour for the captain of the train to get permission from the Bethsalem dispatcher and creep forward over the drawbridge far enough for the brakeman to throw the switch behind him. At last the train slowly backed onto the westbound track, paused for the brakeman to walk forward and return the switch to its normal position, and gathered the confidence to disappear in reverse on the West Marsh shore.

But a couple of impatient night-school law students or overworking computer programmers had jumped off the train with their briefcases and in the teeth of the glare slipped across the parlous catwalk of the unguarded drawbridge to reach their Ithaca, hardly pausing to get the story. Threading their way through the crowd and over the welter of hoses, they continued straight down the right-of-way toward their cars at the Depot parking lot beyond the pitch-dark bend in the granite cut.

No sooner was the train gone than the groaning span had to be raised for a dragger straggling home via Smith's Bay from its secret fishing ground in the Gulf of Markland; then lowered again and locked back into the transcontinental network of parallel lines.

Thus Caleb was rewarded for the interruption of his sleep by the novelty of his observations, but there was little satisfaction for the dog at his feet. Admirably patient, Ibi sat on his haunches with a view of nothing but the undercarriages of people and machines, his ears assaulted by the roaring melange, comforted only by the watchman patting his head, while vulgar callous dogs had the run of all scents, exploring every stir and spot of animate or inanimate assembly, and were even greeted by the fire-workers.

The hydrant nearest D T M & D had been illegally blocked by a car parked on Coalyard Lane. Luckily its resident owner was just coming out of his house to see the fire, and had magnanimously obliged an unusually rigorous policeman by taking the trouble to move it a few feet into his driveway. But still there was a dearth of water.

Soon more than a thousand feet of hose were pieced together —and then duplicated twice—along the dirt road that skirted Fuckintired Rock and looped around the uncultivated field of the Poor Farm, to reach another water main on Blythedale Avenue, whither one of the pumper trucks had been sent to compensate for the pressure lost by distance. "They lose fifteen pounds for every ten feet of hose." Caleb was told. Pumpers had to be stationed at the hydrants to feed pumpers at the fire.

"Were you here when they were trying to get another hose down the cliff to the police boat? She's got the best pumps in town. Best water supply too!" the watchman chuckled. "One guy almost fell in the river! It's a long way straight down that ledge, even if you can swim. Of course the low tide didn't help none. (I'm always scared the kids are going to kill theirselves on that rock.) But they finally got wise and tied the boat up at the spiles down to the wharf in back of the forge, and the Chief sent a couple of his own engines down there too. The pumpers have got to get close to the water; they can't suck it up more than twenty feet or so. So now there's four or five hoses drawing saltwater, but it ain't too good for the equipment, you know what I mean? As far as saving the property goes, it's too late anyway. When a fire's first starting it squares itself every minute."

This last solemn quotation was memorized verbatim from his friend the Inspector. The hitherto unassuming furnace-tender seemed to know quite a bit about putting out fires, and it was a unique opportunity to unite the arcane generalization with his unequaled knowledge of a particular situation. In gatherings of the Veterans Legion at the Purity Square club house, where tankards were hoisted at all hours of the day, he still suffered from inveterate diffidence, and he appreciated this chance to warm up his self-confidence with the unaggressive little incomer, obviously neither a Beaut nor a Norman.

In any event there wasn't enough water to save Buck's property from total destruction, and no attempt could have been made early enough to fight the blaze from within its walls.

At some change of gradient in the atmospheric pressure (as if an imperceptible breeze had stopped to rest) the spot they occupied was fleetingly bathed in a warmth that reminded Caleb of why he was there. The flames were definitely lower now, the walls blackened, the rafters almost gone. An aerial hose was still doggedly played by a brave figure close to the flames on a truck's self-supporting ladder at the apex of an hypotenuse steeper than the IRTH's. Those now inattentively manning the ground nozzles had fallen into conversation with their superior officers, with policemen, or with neighborly spectators.

After Buck and his party had stepped out of sight behind the fiery ruination, Caleb's eyes wandered again in search of Belle—to see whom she was favoring if not the photographer. Instead he caught sight of Mrs Keith making her way toward him through the thinning crowd. During the anticlimactic act of the drama many of the remaining pleasure-seekers were defecting, like patrons of an unfinished football game given up for lost. Head down, hands in the pockets of her coat, looking no one in the face, as if excused by anonymity, she walked privately engrossed. But there was still no sign of Robert or Deirdre.

"Every time the fire begins to die down it starts to flare up again." he remarked to his technical advisor. They continued to watch from their isolating spot, which was now receding further into the encroaching darkness. Buck's private sacrifice, which the public congregation had made into theater, now exposed the backdrop of blanched gray blueberry bushes rooted in seams of living rock behind the charred and dissolving timbers. Only now did Caleb notice the acrid smell—burning wood and the steam of charcoal quenched in water, fresh and salt—which must have been torturing Ibi's refined sensibility all along.

"It's the old grain in all the corners and between the walls, especially up in the loft. They couldn't have gotten it all out without tearing the whole thing down. You could sweep till the cows came home and it would still sift down into all the cracks and fly up into the ceiling like them dust storms the Oakies had. Same way grain elevators can blow up out west." After forty years of desiccation between floorboards, among joists and studs, behind panels and wainscotting, the sweepings of corn oats and hay too fine for the mice to eat had moldered to the like of gunpowder forgotten and unseen in the crannies of an old fort's magazine. Tailings of that dust were as good as fuses for conducting phlogiston from the oil-soaked machine shop floor through upper storeys to the tarry shingles of an all-too-seasoned roof. "Any firebug could send that place up in smoke, finest kind, without no gasoline at all!"

The commentator couldn't idle long enough to offer his conjectures of what act elsewhere on the shores of the island this fire might be diverting attention from. Before he punched his next clock, in the machine shop, it was necessary to descend again into his peaceful hell and "turn a piece" that was annealing all night in Furnace No.3. But his hints had referred Caleb to the axiom bruited by sardonic aborigines and troglodytes that any big fire like this served somebody's purpose, like the frontal attacks of pirate ships while their small boats landed at a distal cove to raid the Commons for sheep (which the colonists themselves had smuggled in against the self-serving British mercantile law), or for chickens and pigs, or girls and housewives who hadn't fled to the woods. Incursions for rapine of that sort were nowadays less feared; in this century the illicit landings were crimes of importation—more likely than bank robberies or premeditated murder, and far less likely to be publicized.

Owing to his opinion that uncooperative stupidity prevailed in most aspects of Atlantean society (at least until the recent election), Caleb was always careful to remember Dogtown's penchant for theories of conspiracy to explain acute felony. But he'd learned the futility of trying to arrive at the truth by hometown dialectic, even when both he and his informant were willing to take the time. Among natives, any skeptical questioning of the common mind— no matter how mild or dispassionate—was likely to be classified either as ludicrous innocence or as "criticism", stigmatized as "sarcasm", a sure sign of self-esteem.

Unless this fire had been set by a ghost cell of the Resistance to distract the populace from its nighttime devilvision, or unless it was over-insured, it must have been merely accidental. The next day's front page carried more than one story about the exciting loss, but no notice of unusual activity anywhere else. (That memorable edition of the *Nous* displayed five skillfully detailed photographs by a craftsman of much experience in the genre.) It was mentioned that Buck himself (known by many readers to be a heavy smoker of cigarettes) had been the last one to leave the building, having worked later than usual. But in Dogtown any suspicion of unnefarious culpability was shruggingly dismissed as an act of God.

20
ROCK
DANCE

Ocean no longer contended with the mainland for Dogtown's promised summer. The prodromal days and nights of spring whirled more and more unbalanced toward the grand double-octave of Gloucestermas, as the diurnal floodings and exposures of Lady Gloucester's barefoot plinth (toes, shinbones, knees)—lagging as always at the mensural pace of the great tide-mistress—epicycled toward the solstice upon the larger tide of the year. It was as if Buck's disaster signaled an acceleration of annual time.

The city's fiscal year coincided with the earth's; calendars of education and business conspired with the sun's, and with off-islanders' expectation of the summer. The needle trades would begin a new year with the feast of SS Peter and Paul. Liturgies, carnival amusements, parades, contests, street fairs, block dances, and other festal entertainments would be brought to a climax by cascading galaxies of skyhigh harborwide fireworks in prolonged orgastic crescendo.

Civic beatification thus would be Dogtown's reward for the discomfort boredom and labor of the year's longest three quarters. All at once would come the commencement of students' freedom, the fanfared introduction of toyboats and warm beaches, and the liminal beginning of two months' liberty, peace, or hectic commercial gratification.

Most of the time Caleb forgot his symbolic dread of that festival. Like one who through common usage blunts his sensitivity to the horrors represented by easy words or images of death or corruption, he usually segregated the common significance of Gloucestermas from what was secretly idiosyncratic. Like the Bareboneses and the Keiths and all their friends, like Doc Charlemagne and visiting Ippies, like Father Duncannon and his followers from near and far, like the Schlossbergs and all other hostlers, like fisherman families and all the churches, like even Rafe Opsimath the Cornucopian, each swept along in some part by the stronger or weaker forces of Dogtown's calendar, in substance or in accidence, as witness or as actor, Caleb was borne by his own waves on the converging currents of local event. So much was happening in the spring of 1961 that finally in the interest of saving time and getting enough sleep his morning runs, to Ibi's disappointment, almost ceased entirely. Yet on the whole (when he kept Lilian out of the picture) he was pretty pleased with himself.

It was his salaried duty to help the Fathers plan their Chapter at Gloucestertide. Therefore the foremost effort of his bios theoretikos was to finish *The Isorectotetrahedron* in time to devote all his surplus value to managing the logistics of Father Duncannon's cherished conclave. And otherwise too, as this story will tell, his particular urges joined Dogtown's stream of seasonal motives, as if the Dionysia were going to be for him personally a graduation, triumph, or midsummernight's dream.

*

But others, of less limited responsibility, were busier yet. Like many a calamity, Buck's had unexpectable consequences. One of them was that during the critical weeks of bewilderment and rehabilitation he drank much less than usual. In the deepest most guarded recesses of his heart he discovered a feeling of relief from the burden of creative expectation. The masts and rigging had been cut away; decks were clear of the shambles: his leveled schooner now offered no feckless resistance to the weather gods.

The proprietor's first rational feeling was apologetic, to his men who'd lost their occupations. On the very morning of the fire he and Gretta were already advising them about claims for unemployment insurance and attempting to find other jobs for them, at the Yard or elsewhere. He promised them that they would be first on his list when he got back into business—somehow, as soon as possible. To them, and to most of the city, Dogtown Machine & Design had been a typically useful small business, a social institution for paychecks and mug-ups, a source of tax revenue. But at first he spoke to them without real faith in his economic ambition, ostensibly on strength of the fact that during the fire itself, much to his surprise, he'd been informed by his secretary that everything was right adequately insured.

It was Tessa (as Treasurer of the corporation) who had lately decided to pay for protection with an expensive policy, purchased on Rafe's advice, at the end of the calendar year when the mail was bringing as wherewithal a spate of checks liquidating some of the firm's sluggish receivables. She and Gretta had conspired to divert Buck's attention from that new chunk of overhead who was always vexed by the lack of cash to pay for his unremunerated researches. On hearing this news he hugged and kissed them both, in front of all the fire-watchers, once again blessing his wise and clever wife.

After the fire he was also surprised to find among the smoking ruins, which stood not much higher than his head, at least two drawers of charred but readable drawings in his sooted "fire-proof" storage cabinet of drawings. His latest sketches and calculations were lost, having been scattered all over his desk, but not all his earlier plans and specifications, not every idea he'd ever fixed on paper.

The uninvited phoenix of hope stirred in its ashen egg before Buck had a chance to brood over the ramifications of his catastrophe. By the time he was in any condition to trace the runners and tendrils of his loss he'd found a counterweight of morale, besides dollars of insurance, in the scale of Tyche (if it wasn't Dike's). For the demanding consequences of dispossession—innumerable annoyances and inconveniences—entwined themselves with the hopeful electives and judgments of a projected new enterprise. The great debit of ill fortune seemed almost absorbed by all the prospective credits of reconstruction, which presented themselves as many positive alternatives. A thousand interesting problems and pragmatic possibilities obscured Buck's most secret desolation at the deepest level of all: his probably final delivery from the creative struggle he'd always been engaged in. He did not care to count the closet symphonies he'd lost.

It was thanks to Rafe Opsimath, who returned from Cornucopia to the Poet's Corner of the Van a few days after the fire, that he was able to occupy himself with these forward-looking thoughts. Rafe was now more or less at liberty, with liquid assets in Jason Anacoluther's bank and in his account with Father Lucey at Weatherglass, Neatherd & Co. Buck's unlabored solution to the 360 pump problem, having met with no resistance from Rafe's partner Walt Edenfield (seeing that it required little more modification than the substitution of one diaphragm vendor for another, without modification of Tubalcain's patented design), had impressively enhanced the value of Tubalcain Manufacturing before it was sold to Cook Evaporator.

With a retainer of fixed salary as a loosely available "consultant", Rafe had settled also for exclusive rights to the Tubalcain steam generators, the "obsolete" line of continuous-coil water heaters and boilers, which the new management wished to drop from its line in order to concentrate upon the entirely different market for steam-cleaning equipment. These residual products were very similar to their ancestors that Shelly Schlossberg had long ago peddled to farmers for sterilizing their dairies. For the first year, until he could establish his own facilities, Tubalcain would continue to manufacture and ship on Rafe's behalf the few orders that still drifted in from Hafnia-Iona and a few loyal old dealers.

Thus with providential timeliness Buck was asked to join Rafe in a new scheme of possibilities. Together they would revive and reorganize Dogtown Machine & Design as a larger corporation, perhaps with some additional equity capital from Jason, Thad, and other local believers in the mechanical genius of one who would have for the asking a certain modicum of bread-and-butter jobshop business.

But how to combine traditional toolmaker crafts with methods of repetitive production for standardized products—especially those newly conceived, at least in principle, and calculated to be economically feasible? Above all, what exactly? Desalinization units? Auxiliary steam-driven electric generators? Specialized heat-exchangers or power-converters? Reliable garbage-cookers? What kind of plant to build or lease somewhere on the Cape? In short, what engines, gins, or jenneys; what brick and mortar? These were the questions Rafe and Buck huddled over; these were the ideas they discussed by day and night.

Along with his investment Rafe offered the managerial competence disclaimed by Buck: financial knowledge, complex administrative experience, commercial energy, and a sense of ophelimity. And all with an equable affability as suited to the demands of friendly partnership with a kindhearted inventor as to success in sales. Doctor Charlemagne had given the Cornucopian his Bachelor's degree from White Quarry College; he was free to pursue his M B A in jig time anywhere else at all. And his sanguine attitude had overcome Buck's natural pessimism, whose drinking ceased to diminish as soon as he saw that all was not lost.

The owner of D M & D was hardly impoverished. His shop's land was still valuable, either for his own use or on the industrial real estate market. He would have the cash to replace and modernize most of his machine tools. But foremost in his heart was the assurance of enough surplus in the bank to realize Tessa's desire for the Stone Barn. This last was the chief solace for his incommunicable loss of years—almost a compensation.

Yet even before these new prospects had appeared—even on the very morrow of the fire, when nothing but the promise of property insurance justified his coterie's gaiety and fellowship, the appetites for food and drink, that immediately followed the shock of disaster—Tessa had reassured the friends gathered at Powerhouse Cove, many of whom naturally kept to themselves the truth that they were less distraught by Buck's professional devastation than by its presumed affect upon the effort to found a Rock and Role theater, which depended so much on his wife's resources and free time.

"We won't let this stop us!" she said to her sister Cora and Beni Vanderlyn. Sally Salter was also there. Gloria Keith was kept away only by her job at the Library.

Tessa said nothing about the possibility of bankruptcy—insurance or no insurance—but, as it seemed, any Barebones financial survival hung upon whatever accounts receivable Gretta could reconstruct from the damaged safe and twisted half-burnt file cabinets, or upon the voluntary honesty of customers for whom she no longer had any record of outstanding invoices. Gretta's memory and intelligence would be the firm's provisional salvation.

Buck concealed his despair as he forced himself to pick through the debris at her side simply in order to show his gratitude for her courage. To the best of his recollection he answered her questions about finished jobs and work in process. Willingly he ran errands to assist her.

Fortunately the weather was mild and clear, and the birds sang all around—as usual ignoring the trains. While Gretta worked, in coveralls and gloves, her face all smudged with soot and sweat, Buck shielded her from the interruptions of official inspectors and curious onlookers, summoning his own vague answers and mastering his tears by smoking cigarettes.

In the afternoon Tessa came over to help. By then the rear guard of the Fire Department had left, fully confident that the last smoldering sparks had been scattered and quenched in the sodden junk that imperilled every step on the sturdy old floorboards—still permeated with machine oil!—whose massive underpinnings, flooded with tons of water, had kept almost intact the base line of the skyward fire. At length the three scavengers were alone, except for a few small kids after school, creeping past at awestruck distance.

It was the work of little more than a day, in squishing squeaking boots, to salvage everything of possible legal or mnemonic value amid soaked ashes and chopped or half-evaporated timber, pungent with the smell of harsh smoke that clings for years to any surviving subject of fire. Among the defaced machine tools, entangled by baked electrical cables and twisted pipes, which had fallen from the cremated walls and ceilings like scorched tendons, their besmirching search of the space that had been their cave of security was conducted in the mocking glare of open sunlight. There was no hurry to call in junk dealers or bulldozers and dump trucks. The insurance adjustors had yet to come and look, as well as salvage estimators and rubble-removers bidding for what might have been the more substantial job of demolition, had it been near the fire station.

The following day a temporary office was set up next to the telephone in Tessa's living room six miles away, and Gretta was soon coming there to work half-time, though at Buck's insistence still drawing full pay for herself. There were many calls and visits of commiseration or practical charity from friends, vendors, and customers, some bearing token gifts of food or offers of undefined assistance. Buck was surprised and touched by every demonstration of disinterested affection.

But soon Tessa found for the business a second-floor office downtown on Front Street, and Gretta settled into a fulltime routine of low-pressure (almost antiquarian) fiscal and administrative research. Buck set up a new drawing board in the opposite corner of the room. Before long a third desk was installed for Rafe, who was spending more and more of his time in Dogtown, discussing possibilities with his tentative new partner, while he himself was looking for a more proprietary place to live than the Poet's Corner.

Nearby at the Hoof & Mouth studio, when there were no classes, Cora Kryothermsky was working on elements of the Rock Dance with a few of her best students and with two or three rusticating housewives who at some crucial point in their lives had chosen children and Dogtown rather than professional careers (but whose occasionally remorseful preference had always been ambivalent), as much as with the intimate nucleus of her company. The younger women strove to evangelize the art of dance among denizens who knew even less about that art than any other.

But the two oldest and closest hoofers—fair graduates of colleges that cherished both dance and drama, who still looked like undergraduates—had studied under Cora as avocational amateurs with few illusions of virtuosity: Beni the plastic-arts partner of the Troika, and Sally the poet of Pigeonhole Cove, Huck Salter's Southern wife. Nor husbands nor children, nor housework nor arts of their own, could stay the faithful collaboration of these versatile sister-Muses.

It happened to be a company that would have pleased at least the male half of any inexperienced audience merely by walking across the stage in leotards. But that was a sexual phenomenon that Cora strove to sublimate—without the disguises of unnecessary costume—by proving the art-in-itself that she led them in.

Having been born to squaredancing cheerleading and early marriage, Gloria Keith had at first been too rural and then too busy to learn the Atlantean art of movement; and in fact she'd hardly heard of Modern before coming down from Montvert. But she was the number one enthusiast about Hoof & Mouth's entry into the Gloucestermas theatrical competition, its publicist, and its literary researcher. In this production the basic actions of the Rock Dance were to be arranged in wordless celebration of one Captain Hood, a rediscovered hero of Cape mythomania.

It had been agreed that there wasn't time to develop voice and role-text before the oncoming celebrations. However, though any experimental amalgamation of speech and dance was premature, and though even Cora admitted that it was still uncomfortably problematical, it was not too soon to mount a dance of paradramatic legend as the Hoof and Mouth's radical new contribution to the Arts Festival, a defunct constituent of ancient Glo'mas that was now being reintroduced by Dexter Keith the City Planner, who had led a movement to revive the tradition and persuaded the city fathers to appropriate a little money for the purpose of encouraging participation by Cape performers and artists and by the many volunteers required to prepare the way and clean up afterwards. These elite events were to take place at the High School, where for six evenings the auditorium and the gymnasium would be devoted to art shows, theater, jazz, and highbrow music.

For his pains Dexter was somewhat maliciously appointed master of these revels, but with no additional assistance for his normal overload of work. The office of impresario was his reward for having identified himself with the fifth column of enlightened Normans—naturalized incomers who could never be quite accepted as genuinely uneducated islanders even if they coached boys' teams or got themselves elected earldermen. Like a sacrificial bull tricked into nodding acquiescence to his own immolation at an Athenian altar, he took responsibility with a rueful laugh. But it was his hope to establish a precedent for free and public art by insinuating into the city budget a "traditional" line-item for the Festival, next to the sine-qua-non funding of fireworks. No one else in Gloucester County could serve the arts so effectively.

Dexter believed he would rather have practiced private architecture than "city planning"; but thanks to his premature nidification this aspiration had been diverted to his perhaps truer vocation in public service. Although ordinary citizens didn't know him from Adam, he was the only person in Dogtown generally respected by both politicians and artists; and naturally he was influential with almost all women who encountered him by sight or voice. Who else could have muted the opposition of the needle trades, whose clamor to advertise pilgrim business at public expense was the most powerful in every annual competition for whatever supererogatory appropriations could be extorted from the public purse? Who else could have charmed Ibicity Hall into supporting an uncommercial program of art that would have been turned down almost unanimously by the merchants and by two thirds of the disinterested voters if it had come to a referendum?

In fact he was risking something much worse than vetoes. Deprivation was less to be feared than corruption. Among public figures he alone recognized as pernicious the probability of commercial subversion, always the danger in a politically successful advancement of culture. His deepest reason for taking on the thankless job was that it would otherwise be seized by someone without taste or integrity who'd been raised to prominence by the degradation of democracy.

The celebration of art required a stubborn measure of aesthetic despotism, however disguised, if it was not to be infected by the values of the taxpayers to whom it was offered. Fortunately he was one to relish the oblique exercise of bland and genial power for a good cause, suffering advisory committees only as window-dressing. Himself under the clandestine influence of Ipsissimus Charlemagne, he privately (not to say secretly) paraphrased the declaration of Yeats (who wanted to "spiritualize Irish imagination") that the purpose of the Abbey Theater was not to present what the audience wanted.

"I may not be able to confine the menu to what *we* like, as the Troika hopes to do with the Stone Barn Theater," he said to his closest friends, "but at least I may be able to keep it out of the hands of the Chamber of Commercials, and pick juries that aren't members of the Art Association. Let's go for broke! Les fauves or la boucherie!

"It's not the sort of thing you could inveigle Doc Charlemagne into, but it mustn't be a disgrace, and at least he'll attend some of it. Anyway, the chamber music group will make all our efforts respectable when they do the premiere of John Vole's *Forge Quintet*, even though he's hardly ever been performed. His musicians are the only artists we must pay (like the pyrotechnicians)—since they won't come to Dogtown for the beauty of it, let alone to learn something new—whereas he gets nothing but the recognition of a few nobodies. I find it's customary for an unpaid composer to pay the copyists out of his own pocket.

"But there'll also be the Cape Gloucester Symphony to put on an inoffensive amateur program.

"Of course it's de rigueur to have one sculpture and painting show open to all entries, but my people will classify and hang it. I wouldn't take the job until I had that assurance.

"As far as the scenic art is concerned, besides Hoof and Mouth, we'll allow the drama clubs and strolling players two or three comedies, plus one poetic fisherman play at the end. But the decisions about who's allowed to compete for the stage will be tyrannical or oligarchic. I don't care who gets the final prizes, Sophocles or Euripides. John O'Leary told Yeats 'The Irish people do not know good from bad in any art, but they do not hate the good once it is pointed out to them *because* it's good.' That's the best we can hope for in New Ireland."

Tessa was the one to reply. "But Yeats also wouldn't have us forget that Goethe saw the Irish as 'a pack of hounds, always dragging down some noble stag'. Like Parnell, I suppose. So be careful. We need you preserved alive in Lilliput Hall, dear Gulliver!"

Yet dancers and actors alike in the subversive cabal congratulated themselves that the Mayor had left to Dexter the comprehensive problems of organization, planning, and public relations. In fact, seeing that the sole Glo'mas responsibility of the Troika associates was their single offering of the Rock Dance, those not fervently occupied as principal creative dancers were all so confident of Dexter's ability to handle the troublesome opinion of taxpayers that they were already beginning to look ahead toward an independent production of *Friar Bacon and Friar Bungay* by the Stone Barn Company of Mummers at the end of the summer.

At first the more dramatic attraction of this larger venture may have tempered their personal enthusiasm for merely ancillary participation in their more immediate public performance, which was chiefly Cora's affair. Even as these handmaids devoted their bodies to the service of *Rock Dance* (on or off the stage), the minds of most were more excited by possible contributions to sister Tessa's future role-drama.

Still, they all regarded the Rock Dance as their collective debut. And as the studio improvisations and rehearsals wore on, Tessa at the piano, Gloria witnessing when possible, Cora gradually absorbed all the free time and round-the-clock imagination of her temporarily expanded dance company, including the "chorus". The thematic movements were not new; Cora had been working on them for months. Indeed this Rock Dance was intended as only the first in an unlimited cycle or family of Rock Dances, expanded or contracted variations applicable to any number of other Dogtown "texts" in the future. After this single festival performance, Cora said, it would be produced less as a unique composition than as a maqam.

For the present however it was to be an individual dance celebrating Gloria's unfamiliar legend, not in narrative mime or cryptic charades but in "kinepoetic abstractions" that would simultaneously represent: the relations of Robin Hood and Friar Tuck; St George and the six other champions of Europe; and Captain Hood, Abolitionist master of the schooner *White Jacket*, who smuggled a cargo of fugitive slaves to the underground railroad before illegally privateering in the Civil War and then quietly retiring to Purdeyville with the reputation of a pirate.

The musicological dancer and the historyteller inspired each other, sometimes in conspiracy also with Tessa the critical stage manager and Beni their imaginator of set and costumes. They had been goaded into this artistic enterprise by some of Doc's passim remarks (who'd seen none of Cora's work but urged her on with the certainty of intuition), but their cooperative energies were now driven by their own ideas. Under the pressure of circumstances their initial vision of the entirety was altered in almost every respect. For instance, they had to give up the fancy of coopting the dancers and the dancing of sodalities that celebrated their own way at Tuscan, Lusitanian, Scandian, or Aramaic festivities.

At the first meeting of the Rock Dance company as a whole, females all, Cora delivered her only hermeneutic apology. "With all due respect to Gloria's verbal culture: the legends will take care of themselves. Let them be induced in the minds of beholders. Here begineth my disavowal.

"We shan't mime an archery contest, or strike off shackles, or dance the hornpipe. Nor are we militants of any kind. Seeing that the struggle against injustice is perpetual and unremitting, let's just assume that we and the audience are all Premature Antifascists, and tacitly cancel politics from both sides of all equations. We're here for the art of movement—animal, vegetable, and mineral—not for rhetorical communication—notwithstanding everything you may think you've heard me say to the contrary. It's true that this dance could not have been imagined by a Protestican—but it's equally true that it's not the ideological dream of a feminist socialist. I can conceive that in my human frailty I might someday become a lilylivered liberal, but my art will never be subject to message or recantation.

"Neither will my existence. Women know well enough what it is to lurch through spectrums of incommunicable feeling, but we forget too much as we go along. So on the floor, in radical antithesis to so-called abstract painters, we invent actions to objectify outwardly motionless emotions. Then we arrest and condense or amplify or distort the body's ensuing proprioceptions. Certain aesthetic aspects of this behavior may bear resemblance in form to what men call meaning, but not in content. It's of merely secondary significance that the dance helps us remember, as it helps men become sensitive.

"It's true I have hoped for a speaking dance, and my hope is not exhausted; but I may be beginning to despair. We shall see what is physically possible when we get the Stone Barn experiments going. But Doctor Charlemagne may be right. He has plenty of theoretical reasons why dancers can't be actors at the same time. No one's ever done it. The dance of the Greek theater was not our kind of dance. Creative dance has always been a battle *against* poetry. Etymologically speaking, we are poetic, unlike ballet dancers, because we ourselves make the dance; but the dance shouldn't open itself to the symbolic flowerings of language.

"So, aside from the technical difficulty, I fear subjugation by words and those who interpret them. I fear losing our hard-won creative rights and resigning ourselves to trained virtuosity, docilely faking a dimension in which we don't belong, like painters ruled by mechanical perspective.

"But all that is something to worry about at the Stone Barn. Meanwhile, right now, we must not allow ourselves to be seduced and subsumed by anyone's idea or story or music. We are nobody else's chorus. Instead we are the most primitive actors—and maybe the most primitive artists. We are the only ones who purely act. Our action is the thing itself, not merely its representation. And it is our own action—not prescribed action, not the passive action of drilled performers. Though we move together we are not an orchestra. As Charlemagne says about Modern dance, 'In principle, creation and performance are one.'

"When the time comes I'm very willing to play a role in Friars B & B, but any dancing therein, if it's wanted, will be nothing but accompaniment, in gratitude to Tessa and Gloria for helping us now. Jean-Louis Bartaud says the actor has two bags of air—one for herself, one for the role. But I'm only one old bag of air. If I were two bags I wouldn't need a sister. And 'Self-possession is the subject of all dance.' saith the Director somewhere in his scripture.

"Now as to this modest Rock Dance, it refers to what you often do by yourself on this Cape. Walking the jumbled-up shore rocks can be a dance—an absorbing rather dangerous dance, unrolling itself and stretching out in a broken line along the landseascape. In solipsistic concentration you leap and hop, staggering on tiptoe; you skim or flit from point to point, jagged or smooth, broken or rounded. *Your footing is not a plane.* The rocks give you no floor! Yet you don't climb them with your hands, and, with gulls watching from altitudes above beside and below, though you balance with your arms you know better than to pretend to fly.

"Between every two beaches here on our stone island, between harbors and coves, wherever the land stops the sea, those tawny anfractuous rocks are a jagged pathway of choices. At chaotic elevations, with footholds on irregular cusps at all angles, no step is predictable until your foot is in the air, no step is determined by habits of graceful continuity. From ledges and pinnacles, on whalebacks and whalejaws, you fling yourself across one crevasse to another in jerky motion, sideways and forward, sometimes switching back to descend a crag or traverse a tidal gorge, sometimes down to a tongue of popples, at the lower tides always keeping above the slippery seaweed. Each imbalance is corrected by the next. In midair the muscles of one leg calculate the force and direction of their reaction to the next immovable resistance and warn the muscles of the other through the levers of your pelvis without assistance from the conscious brain. It feels as if you're rapidly covering great distances. Your dazzling way is bleached by salt and sun. It's impossible to stop and think. Yet all the while you are both spectator and center of attraction for surf below, clouds above, and boats in the offing.

"But those aren't the only steps we dance. We're not always careening along from rock to rock on top of them. At times we contemplate rocks themselves, sitting alongside, not in transit. And of course not all our rocks are butted by the ocean.

"There's always the erratic variation of the moraine, when we *avoid* the rocks in a path through the woods. And there are circulations like the Sidhe's, 'they that dance *among* the stones', as Yeats puts it, when we wander in Purdeyville looking for the raths of Tir-na-Dog and forgetting that we're supposed to be out for blueberries.

"Then too, we flee the heat and avoid salted sunburn by swimming *inside* the living rock. We dive from the peaceful ledges of inverted mountains, sequestered from the restless waters, invisible to fishing boats, screened from all but the very nearest angels by quarry walls.

"And don't forget the motions you're likely to stumble into while witching in the woods, choked with brambles and scrub trees—the scars of Lady Gloucester's little wounds, which look like the cellar holes of crazy fairy castles; to kiss our mother we find her bare spots and patches.

"But we hug her stone children too, our foster brothers and sisters all over the place—as big as our houses or as small as our stoves—still clinging to her by their own weight and loathe to budge. We circle round and even climb Cynosure Rock, one of her eldest, high up on her breast, just to tease the dogs that can't follow us up their own altar.

"And don't forget her babies, little more than seeds, which might have been carried a thousand years longer if they hadn't been delivered by the frost, after Brother Jonathan stripped away the trees and exposed our Lady's underwear! All those stillborn infants piled into walls by human muscle two or three hundred years ago and now slowly scattered again in abandoned woodlots by the same old snow and ice—a bane not precious to land-speculators and presently destined for the bulldozer!

"Let's show the Bacchae how to violate ritual without running away to the mountains. Even as rock-jumpers, with the horizon our only level and the sky our only plane, we don't need a kinetic landscape. And let the spectators see that we fling out our arms for equilibrium, not to attract attention.

"Some literary lawyer is said to have observed that the average word is a dead metaphor. I say the average movement is a dead habit. The Rock Dance will break you of habit, turn your reference upsidedown. Otherwise you won't get very far without breaking your head!

"So you see, the Director's right when he says that dance is the 'modern art of locality'. By exploiting gravity, not opposing it, and by leaving crosscountry travel to dramatic Maenads, we'll dispute Aristotle where he says that 'Place is neither a part nor a quality of things'. No words or numbers can do what the Rock Dance does in expressing our Ort-an-Sich. The phenomena of Dogtown are a noumenon. That should be chiseled in bas-relief on the Stone Barn threshold.

"The sympathetic Doctor is also right that our dance-time is trophic time—neither relative nor rock-eternal. But the dance we're about to make is trophic time in the gravitation of this enduring granite. Therefore he'd be wrong to say in our case that the stage is a fictitious place.

"Here ends my apology for the work that follows."

"I've never heard you speak so much!" cried Tessa through wreathes of smoke. "It's fascinating! One's own brilliant polylithic sister!"

Sally the poet-housewife, one of Cora's veteran hoofers, glanced at Beni, the member of the Troika she knew best, vainly hoping for some sign by which to interpret the sister's tone, which seemed as usual both sincere and ironic. In this case was the ambiguity ambivalent? "The real irony" said Sally with a laugh (as if irony had been mentioned) "is that Lady Gloucester's rocks may also symbolize our missing partners and adversaries—the hardness that we as Amazons dance in want of. We couldn't even get enough men to *read* the male roles at our drinking parties!"

"I always ended up playing a man because I have a deep voice and not many curves!" Cora responded, cracking a smile as she briefly unbended from her functional position as leader of the dance. "But we got so used to our dramatic penury that when a man now and then did favor us with his attendance we didn't like to hear his imitation of a male part! And in this dance we don't need men to represent the other gender."

"When boys spoke of rocks, in the New Uruk of my youth," said Tessa "they were referring to their testicles, craving our mercy to relieve them of their charge. In my innocence at the time it seemed a curiously transposed metonymy of attributes, confusing an organ with its neighbors. Later I learned more about anatomy and realized that they were scientifically alluding not to the gross effect but to the occult cause. Men are sometimes subtler than we think. It turned out that in their conceit it was not the inconvenience of satyriasis from which they sought relief: they were complaining of the *urge*! And this they attributed to the nuggets carried in their twin reticules! They were really talking about a couple of small *stones*!"

Most of the company laughed, but Gloria Keith blushed, the country barnyard girl, at this drollery from her most intimate friend.

Stretching another quick smile in horizontal lines across her handsome square jaws, Cora calmly resumed her surprising address. "Well of course the Rock Dance is not about fruit stones. But I'll say no more about what I exclude. Now that I've finished my one homily you must forget everything I've said.

"For weeks we've been proving the differentiations of rock movement. There's no longer any question of our intensity. —Let's call it density!— If you believe Doctor Charlemagne's monographs, we have the ability to generate and transform our power by virtue of the very fact that we renounce the linguistic dimensions of dramatic poetry! So by physical means, without acting charades or miming allegory, dumbly but not in dumbshow, we must find ways to equal the immense leverage of words. That's why the device of irony is even less dispensable to us than it is to role-playing.

"But having forsworn the devices of Logos in our research and development, and also in our quality control, we find ourselves committed to integrate a particular and finite Rock Dance from among the limitless possibilities. And here I must admit our need of abstraction! Thank the goddesses we have Gloria's legend as a teleological form for our emergence! It's a matter of forming certain narrative non-representations by noumenal action, almost as if we're reversing the sequence in which Purdeyville rocks were inscribed: perhaps we're rediscovering oracles in the undergrowth— and successively *undoing* them!"

Gloria clapped her hands in joy at this reciprocating illumination of her creative opportunity, though well aware that she was perilously susceptible to literary encouragement. She could hardly wait to tell Caleb about Cora's insight into the possibilities of collaboration. This fresh creative stimulus instantly fused with the tremendous excitement of his presence in her house. Her stereotactic memories of the last few days were now vibrant with new idea as well as with new touch.

*

Gloria Keith had suddenly found herself playing the kind of part that hitherto she'd read of only with disapproval or incredulous amusement. Already the emotions of an addicted actor were soothing or agitating every ventricle and interstice of her rejuvenated body day and night. Her horizon had shrunk to the span of a few days but she was unaware of its bounds; her future was limited to the next sight of her tenant. Her underconscious life had flared up with a fuel of lovely balm.

These days she served her children like a dreamily impatient automaton—outwardly, by rote, as ebullient as ever—merely as one of the undeniable conditions of staying alive, like that of going to work in the morning or staying cheerfully opaque to her husband. Yet once or twice she'd caught herself gazing at her primely cherished Deedee almost in rivalry. The tiny girl-baby from her womb had become an imperious blade of frivolous virginity, a willowy flatbellied unopened slip of a woman, apple of her father's eye and a piece of ripening fruit to all young men.

At the same time it was hard to remember why Dexter had to be reckoned with at all. The shining knight of the town's enlightened population—god for his daughter, model for his son, charming bedmate for his envied wife—was now no more luminous or interesting than the rest of her householding institution. In fact he seemed obtuse and awkward, out of scale for the refinements of a gentleman, and in that sense a monster. Ironically, she could now thank the heavens that he wasn't on hand as often as other people believed he was. There was no reason to learn the full story of his absences or call him to justice. How miserable I was! she had marveled on the last few mornings as she waited for the monstrous landlord to absent himself from his proportional moiety of the bed behind her back, or as she awoke with the relief of finding him gone.

For several years the father of her children had eaten most of his breakfasts downtown, so that he could get to the Hall as soon as the janitor turned up the wheezing steam or opened the windows. The City Planner said that if he was to make any net progress between Monday morning and Friday afternoon it was necessary to get in a solid hour of peace and quiet at his desk before the interruptions and appointments began. At night there were too many official meetings.

Ever since reading Herodotus she had tried to imagine what it was like for a Nasomonian bride, and had sometimes put herself to sleep making a list of the wedding guests she would have invited, though there were few from among the men of her personal acquaintance and, except for Adlai Stevenson, the rest were from literature or cinema. At her wedding there had been no Caleb. He would have been a small boy at the time. If I still wanted babies at this age a satyr's would be just about the right size. Wouldn't that faze the old centaur!

Like most housewives she was aware that connubial transgressions sometimes occurred even among her trusted friends, for reasons with which she might sympathize, as in Tessa's present case; and she herself had already lain with many males—gods, heroes, scholars, poets, artists, sailors, faceless outlaws—in the shape of Dexter himself. But except for Tessa she had never given thought to the existential infidelity of the women with whom men committed adultery. Those were not the wives with whose feelings she had reason to compare her own. So the notion of having a lover had overtaken her with great surprise.

Especially such an untimely young instigator—at the least likely hour for recovering any sort of happiness—and so suddenly out of the dismal fog of self-contempt, which had blinded all sensation as it thickened about her after the moment of shock at the fire, that the notion of what she had done came after the fact! Though not entirely without certain premonitory hints of the kind that are almost always mistaken and easily forgotten, this amazingly additional privilege in life—a new condition of body and soul—had been acquired without foresight or preparation. At one snick of confrontation her history had been cloven into two separate stories.

Alone in the crowd of fire-watchers, an irrevocable conversion from innocence to bitterness had been visited upon her with the flooding release of slowly accumulated doubt into the open consciousness of an agonizing certainty, feverish to the head, freezing to the heart. Her nearly lifelong devotion to the man she was married to had at last been poisoned throttled and compressed by a double apparition in the shadows cast by a cluster of officials attending the firemen at their dance of hoses and axes.

A spurious flare of light had drawn her eyes to the doubled figure of her husband and a tall pale woman of great beauty standing apart from the others with their faces turned toward each other. Gloria had looked away immediately, without seeing anything in what was left of the world around her, but not before she thought she saw him touch the woman's hand almost hidden by the clothes between them.

It was not with anger or the impulse for retribution that she had thrilled to her first sight of the incomparable Mrs Cotton! It was with a foretaste of death that she had absorbed the shock that she had almost forgotten to fear. But for a long time she had heard with increasing humility and awe the name of that peerless lady. In Gloria's fantasy on Dexter's behalf Mrs *Deirdre* Cotton was so obviously his hitherto unmatched counterpart in stature and dignity, of mind and heart so worthy of the hero, that her equal was not to be found this side of mythological Ireland. As storyteller Mrs Keith very nearly wished them well.

But now she had put aside that epiphany, ignoring the darkness that surrounded the nimbus of her own momentous adventure. She had been even more astonished than Caleb by what came about as she and he spontaneously turned toward each other in the hall at the bottom of the stairs, after their slow walk home from the fire. They had coolly joined lips fresh as fruit in a kiss tenderly ripening with warmth and urgency. Caleb Karcist had not alarmed her with strength or power. From head to toe their parts were practically on a level with each other.

"I'm a married woman." she whispered.

"But not this very minute."

She paused in caress of his shoulder blades. "True." she assented. "Not at such a minute."

"Not this hour." Caleb's calculations were suddenly swift and bold. The children had long since been found and ordered home; he relied on their mother for assurance that they were fast asleep in their rooms on the second floor. And he made up his mind to assume that Dexter would be expected to stay with Buck until the fire was out. The trespasser was confident that the sound of his landlord's car was warning enough.

"Not this month, not this year!" she added. "Wait for me upstairs."

Together they crept up the first flight, parting at the door of her bedroom. She turned down her conjugal bed and put on a nightgown, calmly confident that Dexter would not be home for a long time. Having put in his rather equivocal appearance at the fire, he'd afterwards been nowhere to be found by the kids, who were eager for his information about the exciting event. As she hastily brushed her teeth the absurd proposition flitted across her mind that he might have started the fire to create an all-night diversion.

Then with pounding heart she'd groped her way up to the third floor, where Caleb was waiting in suspended disbelief of her promise.

But now, sitting with her everyday friends in Tessa's living room, the continuing affair seemed to her a perfectly natural realization of generic dreams. At the same time it seemed a familiar old game that she was learning to play in her second youth. To her reasoning mind it was the most dangerous sport of her life, but all ingrained sensibilities were overwhelmed from bottom to top by echoes—by aftermaths, by autonomic expectations—from the nether plexus, and by frissons of beautiful irony from the brain itself. She was beginning to believe that the danger was not as much to her marriage, or even to her reputation among housewives, as it was to her selfpossession. At every atonement, as Caleb called it, beatitude was renewed.

But atonements are all too few when you're not married to a man, she sighed, listening to the talk about dance and suppressing overt movement by tightening her crossed legs as she savored the sensations that seemed still to emanate from the bottom of her spine many hours after he'd last made them. If only they could sleep all night together! Though they lived under the same roof it was hard to find any occasion at all. Like a boy and girl in school they had to pass notes when no one was looking, and allow themselves to be heard conversing only in the coolest double entendre of accidental chat. That was fun, but excitement fit only for intervals.

It would be easier if she could just speak to someone about Caleb, her incognito troubadour from the irresponsible realm of art! How sweet it would be, as in a cosmopolitan society, to keep the liaison secret without concealing the lover! Tessa was the human being with whom she was least reserved, an intimate friend, but even to her she dared not reciprocate the confessions she had been privy to.

Were not their cases very different? Tessa had no religion in her principles; and Buck was far gone with drink, really an old man, and wished for Tessa's happiness at all costs to himself. On the other hand, as she was now certain, Dexter deserved her own treachery. And in any case, though acutely jealous of his honor, except to protect his paternity of the kids he might not very deeply care. His impotence seemed to be of the opposite kind, a matter of loveless haste, betraying the sin of impersonal lust—apparently only in relation to his wife.

Even the last time I let him touch the front of me, a long long time ago, when we were both chuckling about what Caleb was doing with that girl upstairs—which warmed us both up as if we'd seen a stud at work in Daddy's pasture—I thought everything was going to be all right again. It was over before it began, disappointing, humiliating for him but only melancholy for me. Because he feels so guilty about not loving me anymore. My young lover admires me—his illusion perhaps—but my own husband despises me. Yet I saw Deirdre Cotton's face when she looked at him. It's clear he's made her happy enough! And that she has all his respect.

No, it would be too demeaning for the wife of Dexter Keith to tell Tessa even the sorrows that might excuse what wasn't told. As long as Gloria Keith believed her reputation was wholly intact, no excuses were necessary to anyone but herself. In the justice of natural law her integrity remained undamaged. But her reputation would not remain good if it was spoiled by so much as an inviolate private confession to the most sympathetic of confessors. An acknowledged violation of the marriage vow is not a mere transitory compromise of conscience like car-seat demivirginity: it's more like the prognosticating absolute of conception. And her own estimation of the reputation with which she found herself endowed would certainly be undermined by admitting even to herself that Caleb was too young and footloose for a matronly librarian who couldn't help being held up as an exemplar for all the sensible girls of the city.

Besides, she'd always had the feeling that Tessa wasn't exhaustively frank in her confidences. How could a criminal be sure that a friend with any reservations at all was totally discreet in pillow talks following her own transports with a man, or in unguarded passages with trusted familiars, if only as a distraction from gossip closer to home? Perhaps even Tessa the semiprofessional therapist was not fully armed against an occasional impulse to hint at other people's secrets, and might be foolish enough to entrust her lover or her sister—or even her husband—with sacred confidences. After all, as far as talking went, didn't the great Tristram Freud repeatedly abuse his own strictures on that score?

No, it was only with himself, face to face, that Gloria could venture to talk about Caleb! Yet what a paradox that in the famous age of communication she felt no freer than a Spanish señora to make bold with initiatives of any kind! She passively gibed at the incorrigible habits of feminine behavior that had been inculcated in her by centuries of consensus. She who all her life had been renowned for boundless extroverted energy—the least inhibited female at any square dance, leader of cheers, dynamic partisan of students, organizer of good works, vigorous mother, innovative redactor of history—even for her it was still almost unthinkable to originate a private telephone call to any male but her lawful spouse. Her most forward notes to Caleb were responsive. She must await the contrivances of his desire. So she had been trained; so she would remain: essentially as shy as a maiden. But she laughed, because it was the tail-up passivity of a mare in heat.

Though in dealing with most creatures of the opposite sex she was still incapable of autonomous action, it was quite different as far as Deedee and Robert were concerned. Them she ruled as a proleptic queen. But by the same token, in the private joy of slipping her bondage it was only the possible consequences for her children that weighed upon her conscience prudentially. Their welfare was the ultimate purpose of a good reputation, the justification for false appearances, the reason for convention. She prayed God for Mrs Grundy's protection.

But oh Caleb, the agent of her secret exultation! A little man of sympathetic and lubricious parts, she inwardly groaned, forestalling an amorous smile that would have been quite out of place among these earnest friends of the stage. There'd been no time for dalliance, and she hadn't yet been brazen enough to indulge her bucolic schoolgirl curiosity about the sculpture of a man's circumcision. She hadn't seen her son's since he was an unselfconscious little boy. Before abandoning her sense of sight, upstairs in the dim street light filtered through the drawn shades, there'd been no time for the aesthetic cognition of anything more than an importunate gleam that seemed of reddish gold. Sitting now on Tessa's sofa she traced in imagination a bluntly refined ogival helmet with the same fingertips that pressed a thumb lying on her lap in affected composure.

At this moment the memory of Caleb's desire displaced all other knowledge, and liquidated by oblivion the resentment of her mundane master's disesteem. The transitive comfort of her lover's nimbused impact had repolarized all the neutral nerves of her lapsed gender. The tremor of hidden sphincters brought to thought her feeling of the root-word *render*: rendering herself to Caleb, she would never again merely surrender to a deceitful lord.

She who was envied by other women for the only man she'd ever known was immensely grateful to this nimble boy for gaining the knowledge Dexter had never sought. By exciting her mental armature with waves of electrification Caleb had made her worthy of him who betrayed her. Though in her own eyes lacking the naturally aristocratic attractions of her present rival, she now felt infinitely better prepared to recover or refuse, if occasion should ever arise, the ordained love of her children's father.

Why was it that the light and wieldy youth, blown to her house by the west wind, hardly taller than herself, no bigger than her half-grown son, suited her carnally so much better than the Grandissimus she was married to? In the afterglow of the last beatitude—a veritable series of mounting beatitudes, in fact, that turned her into an ever-ready granary of bliss—between the sheets of his narrow attic bed on the morning of his Monday off (with Ibi outside on the front steps to make noises of welcome in case anyone suddenly came home sick), she had started to render her heart as the rest of her self was already rendered. For had he not plucked it up from the ground of sorrow which for years underlay the cultivated enthusiasms that kept her on the move as the marvel of citizens and students? "You and I make love so closely!" she'd marveled aloud. "It's the perfect way!"

Caleb was touched by her innocence. He understood that he was the only stranger in her experience. But he couldn't have been more pleased if Mrs Gilgamesh herself had said it to him. Look at who her first man was, and is! He gently ran his finger down the short straight ridge of her faintly freckled Irish nose. Sensually slackened by fullblown womanhood the fair face that gazed up at him with drowsy gray eyes was childlike yet; it was the loveliness of its ageing that magnified his pride. "Because you are my beautiful lady."

"I'm *not* beautiful!" She retorted so promptly and positively (though he felt no tension in her body) that he was almost convicted of deceitful flattery by the sincerity of her protest. He knew at once that she meant it not to be argued or repeated. But why must her fairness be a stumbling block, a sore point ever to be avoided, when she truly was as comely as any vivacious blonde in a college.

Elevating the upper half of his weight and supporting it symmetrically on his elbows, he spread his hands under the weightless curls of her surprisingly delicate head. "Spun filaments of ethereal gold!" he blithely offered—but at once regretted the literary allusion as nearly insincere because it echoed some such words he'd used to a girl loved long years before. It was disingenuous not to be original in praise, though on the opposite coast of a continent and as true to his feelings as the first time.

"Nothing but fluff." This time she smiled carelessly, as if assuming he said the same to all his blondes. "Yellow feathers!" That's how Dexter had made fun of her in school.

"But even your very name is Gloriana!"

"Sic transit Gloria Mundi." she laughed, squeezing his buttocks with both palms like a mother lying with her baby uppermost. The landlady who from his proper distance had seemed as firm and shiny as an apple, selfsufficient and opaque, alert to society, fitting consort for her lord, was now a creature of mood and passion: soft, desirous, submissive on his own plane. In the burgeoning self-confidence she bestowed upon him he was unable to remember his diffidence as a tenant on sufferance in the former servant quarters.

Slowly and silently he broke their quiet subterranean connection to identify the moment for her to take her leave at last. Voluptuously she shifted the cant of her hips, pretending to tease his stamina. And they laughed together at how far they'd danced, without landscape or locomotion, having found all the space they needed on the cot intended for a celibate. That was before she'd begun to wish them the luxury in her royal bed.

"I love you!" She heard herself rendering the postponed words quite distinctly. They were the right and proper effect of their cause. They were not shameful under the circumstances. Love had been made, and, so made, its fragrance must be sweet to the nostrils of at least the pagan gods.

Caleb invisibly blushed to hear the sentence; yet no sooner was it pronounced than he discovered on his part a sentiment not very different, and he automatically attempted to reply in kind, no less authentically. He'd always felt one third feminine. Love was the only word he could think of to signify the transcendent delight they found in the concupiscent embodiment of each other's minds. He was too surprised to think of a graceful reply, but it was important not to hesitate. Taking pains to show by tone and gesture that his interest would never be exhausted by a momentary enervation of the loins, he returned the sentence, wincing at its banality so late in the game, as if she'd been prompting him. "I love you too."

Thus he was obligated by a reciprocated statement, and began to love her indeed—as loves not a consort but a troubadour. In the uttering he started his deep dive to understand the suffering and courage of the infant girl Gloria, the wife, the mother, the woman within the cheerful head full of many interesting histories. His imagination was set aflame by this induction into the House of Lords.

It was after all the words rather than the act that committed him to her unique mystery, by incorporating tenderness and pity into the beatification of desire, which as soon as they parted was re-ignited by memory of the path to satiation.

21

TABLET SIX

[Morning of New Year's Eve. A space outside the temple, with tower stairs as before. Stage left, the great double doors to the council hall of the gods are now dominant. A pair of three-legged royal seats stands upstage, the one to the left occupied by Enlil's Council Mask. The Traders and their interlocutors take foreground (downstage) positions such that the ceremonies behind them are continuously seen but only sometimes heard.]

Eber and the Traders enter,
carrying their shepherd crooks
and the Troopers' bows.

      EBER Their gods have been carried into the Chamber of Destinies already, so now it's all right to watch; but give those
[The Traders lay doors a wide berth. —Keep those bows out of sight! But I
down the bows.] don't think our friends will call for them at such close
quarters. —After the coronation you can go celebrate New
Year's. When fixed and movable day are the same, it's a
[The doors open feast of reconciliation. Let Gilgamesh call it the sun-god's.
slowly from within.] At least the foolishness is shortened to twenty-four hours.

TRADER 1 Widows, Lil-Amin, Optimates, and Rector enter, in procession. [Lil-Amin is dressed as a masked bride.	Father, my heart's as anxious as any native's to hear the messenger hail this new moon, for I fear the vengeance of the God of the World. By speaking slyly, according to your light, you have accepted the shah's unholy calendar.
EBER The Widows, as bridesmaids, beat a rhythm with pestle-cymbals. The Rector carries a heavy crosier, with	Even from angels the will of Shaddai is often hidden. . . . I am not faultless maybe. It's a narrow line I tread. By opposing superstition I strengthen blasphemy. But the king has yielded to my policies, as these heathens have yielded to his demand for hell-oil. I can only hope to keep the peace while we wait for God's word to reveal itself day by day.

which he controls the ceremonies by thumping upon the floor. The Optimates close and seal the double doors, while Lil-Amin is led to take her seat on the right. They all touch their foreheads to the ground in front of Enlil's empty mask before

RECTOR moving to their places in the ensuing ritual. The Rector intones his walking homily with perfunctory formality.]	The gods asked one another, and chose Enlil to lead their decisions; for when chaos was full he had saved them from the dragon. With four currents of wind he hewed from earth and water a land of plenty between the two great rivers on their course to the sea; and set the black-haired people to attend with sacrifices bountiful and savory the seven lovely houses of the gods; and first among them was the city of his daughter Inanna. But we have allowed ourselves to be led into grievous strife with her law. We have menaced her altar with evil. Once again our manifold wickedness has disordered the spirit of Uruk. In our weakness we have failed to hold fast the love of our sacred mother. The serene and gracious moon has been taken from our sky, and the pitiless sun means to drink the river from our fields. Our bread is turned to stone. May Enlil look with mercy upon the the servants of Inanna, the despair of her heart! —Bring the old king before the seat of
Gilgamesh enters from the right, escorted by Troopers.	god to confess his transgressions. —May the gods renew this kingship by fatal decree, and grant their people another year of life. . . .

[He wears a horned crown on his mask, and carries the Rod and Ring. The Troopers bear the Triskelion banner as a gonfalon. Leaving Gilgamesh near the Rector at center, they take up positions opposite the Traders downstage,

TRADER 2 who speak to each other in the foreground.	They bring in their year by offering their choicest harlot on the highest place they've got. If she doesn't pacify the overlord idol, comes fire and brimstone!

Eber moves as close as possible to Gilgamesh without interfering in the ritual.]

TRADER 1	Law to them is nothing. Each year beforehand, divine consent to chance is chiseled as their destiny! All their piety goes toward learning how to guess the future. Righteousness does not avail.
TRADER 2	The Name of the One God, world without end.
OPTIMATES	*His word looms a stormcloud on the horizon.*
WIDOWS	*Amen.*
TRADER 2	Gilgamesh insisted on going through this. I hope our father can keep him from doing something rash. It would wrong our unborn seed to die for a Gentile. But the Troopers don't expect a crisis yet. Tonight they'll be carousing. Having been born in snow, they exalt the sun.
TRADER 1 [Upstage ritual action continues separately, its music and chanted words merely suggested, except where emerging into the text.]	Thank God this is the year of zero epact. With calendars in conjunction, we can agree for the moment with both kinds of heathen! For us the pleasure of acquiescence is all too rare.
TRADER 2 [The Widows and Optimates perform	I don't see how the holidays are going to be so pleasant if the people don't get any friendlier.
TRADER 1 elements of restrained dance.]	These are the days they serve their servants and have their scapegoat lead the revels! They'll welcome circumcised foreigners.
TRADER 2	I'd like to be happy in Erech. Why should we abhor the stationary arts and comforts? I didn't ask for levitical responsibility. It's not my idea to be against these women. In the middle of a dance who can ponder law?
TRADER 1	The famous guest-cup is not for us, and orgy is forbidden.
TRADER 2	No other nation is tested by self-abnegation!
RECTOR	. . . Confess the insubordination of your rule.
GILGAMESH [He satisfies ceremonial form and tone ironically, affecting to pretend that his semantic substitutions are as traditional as the coronation itself.]	I confess that none of my designs has been handed down from heaven. No god has envisioned my plans or approved them. I have taken it upon myself to make new things and devise more efficacious ways. By me the polity has been reformed, and idle artisans put to new inventions. In drastic supervision, never have I closed my ear or turned a blind eye. Worst of all, I have altered fate by refusing Ishtar's brand, and eschewing her adulterations. If these be offences to Enlil, then do I admit them.

OPTIMATES *Amen.*

[The Widows titter at their slow wits.]

TRADER 2 Gilgamesh is right to hold with a man's fatherhood.

RECTOR . . . As Lugal of Uruk, say what you have done to serve her.

GILGAMESH I have given Enlil a ladder down to earth, and the whole Sea-Land a beacon for caravans and boats. It flashes blue sunbeams into the deep of the sky, and its shadow walks across the city to cool the heads of children.

TRADER 2 They lure their god with a doctrine of incest.

RECTOR For trafficking in vile mire, may you be spared the wrath of Enlil; for polluting our city with the smoke of slime.

GILGAMESH Incense and orisons vanish like a mist; even hecatombs are not prolonged: but my freewill offering of fired earth winds an upward path that will endure for all our gods. Neither can it be pulled down by armies nor scattered by thunder.

[The Rector removes Gilgamesh's mask rather abruptly and lays it on Enlil's seat.]

TRADER 2 Only battered to an ant hill by the four winds of El-Shaddai!

RECTOR Yield up the Rod and Ring, and await the proof by custom, that you may contend to rule. Bow to the throne of Enlil. Until the king returns, let a stranger bear the retribution!

[Gilgamesh solemnly hands the Rod and Ring to Lil-Amin, but mockingly bows his face to the ground before her seat instead of Enlil's.]

[*Thumps once with his crosier.*]

Hark: I hear a knocking!

[*Silence. . . . Thumps twice.*]

Who knocks for kingship?

[*Silence. . . . Thumps three times.*]

Engidu enters, escorted by Norkid. [Optimates conduct Engidu to the Rector. Norkid

Enter, Lord of the Epact. . . . Do you swear to serve Uruk, and for love of Inanna carry from her streets the sins of long dark night?

ENGIDU Do I.

goes to stand with his men. Engidu looks at Gilgamesh.]

[*Sneezes.*]

Smell feathers make me cough.

RECTOR Relinquish the purple!

[He rips off Gilgamesh's cloak

[*Aside to Gilgamesh:*] Sir, we beg your public indulgence of our tradition immemorial.

TABLET SIX 279

(leaving him as bare as a slave), who starts to react but checks himself. —Lead the dying king to solitude. Let him eat dust and quench his thirst with penance. —We must break his pride!

The Rector then slaps Gilgamesh's face, somewhat harder than protocol requires. This time the latter responds with an open offer of violence—at which the Rector does not flinch.

The Troopers lay hand to swords, *[Thumps repeatedly in a drumming beat.]*

TRADER 2 No salt tears from that prince of men! Contrition, never!

but Norkid stops them with a gesture. Eber restrains Gilgamesh with a touch. The Rector smiles at him, bowing ironically, and resumes with ritual intonation.

RECTOR Banish this uncircumcised barbarian from the eyes of gods!

The Optimates awkwardly fling a net over Gilgamesh. He remains calm but uneasy, staring back at Engidu, who has been fascinated by him.]

OPTIMATES & WIDOWS

[Ad lib in various voices, jeering. They taunt him in sing-song and with bits of mocking dance.]

—You have all day to put a stop to time, your Royal Lugalissimus!—Halt the sun with arrows! —Piss up Euphrates; make him flow to the mountains! —Forbid the moon to grow! —Draft the masons to wall out Engidu! —Save your neck by axioms! Prove the theorem that Giszax's more than half immortal! —Cauterize your wounds with salt. Glaze out the dew on your eyeballs! —We'll smoke your carcass with stink-fire, and embalm it with bitumen!

TRADER 2 Tiny minds uncork their genius.

OPTIMATES & WIDOWS —Cogitate your freedom, Oh Philosopher-King! Reckon away those knots. —Find that battle-axe of yours! Hack your way out of the butterfly net! —Giszax, Giszax, time to go berserk! Show us the rage that your hillbillies thought was so awesome! Let's hear the battle-cry that weakened the knees of mountain ewes! —Bring down the temple with your Lifo-righto-textile-peed-on! —Oh savior of the city, invent yourself salvation! —After your parts are strewn around the brickyard, you'll be glad enough to share the favors of a female grave with local dogs!

TRADER 2 Son of the Nephilim, is there an angel to save you from this humiliation? Instead of mocking the savage, they turn their scorn on you!

RECTOR Enough. *[Thumps patiently.]* Enough.

[Smiling.]

WIDOWS	—Before you go, sir alchemist, answer us our riddle: what's two-thirds hydrogen plus one-third oxygen but can't get through a fish net?
TRADER 1	Gilgamesh is a son of man. If he falls, he falls.
TRADER 2	And down we go with him!
OPTIMATES Gilgamesh saunters off,	—Yes, go hide in your kiln, where Enkidu can't find you! —Soak yourself in creosote and fire up your guts!

draped in the net. [They make a show of kicking him out. Animated by their own bravery, they snatch the Triskelion gonfalon from the Troopers, who thereupon draw their swords. The Traders move to the rescue with suddenly revealed short-swords in one hand and their formidable crooks in the other. Norkid wades in with bare hands to make peace among them, while one of the Optimates tries to trample the Triskelion. Another Optimate gives a little scream.]
Gilgamesh re-enters, at another point, to watch unseen.

RECTOR	Order! Order! [*Thumping in earnest.*] Let it stay!
WIDOWS [Calling after Gilgamesh, as they think.]	—Yes, harden your codpiece with glaze! —Go play with your Erecto-testro-gilga-heathen! —Don't look here for any straightlaced nanny-goat that doesn't know the world is made for horny billies!
LIL-AMIN [With dignity. Commotion ceases. The Triskelion is restored.]	Silence! Silence for the coronation! For shame, on Enlil's wedding feast! Nor will the new king be any better pleased. —Rector, give me peace, or clear the court!
NORKID [Adjusting his spectacles. Troopers and Traders deploy to positions of control.]	I will, if he does not. While I'm alive, he won't turn temple mummery into a coup d'etat! [*A moment of silence.*]
RECTOR	Temporarily we submit to force. There'll be no holy war if the principal trial takes place according to the law.
EBER	The law is Gilgamesh. We can extirpate your priestcraft.
RECTOR	I deign to answer houseless nomads and rabid fascists only with my opinion that the bull which goeth before the herd is but a cattle like those that follow.
NORKID [Troopers and Traders slowly return to their former places.]	Sufficient unto the day is the anxiety thereof. That's this fascist's motto. But if Gilgamesh won't deign to scotch the snakes that hatch before our eyes, I have no such compunction. Thinking of the future I've been known to forget my orders.

RECTOR	Captain, you are an honorable soldier!
NORKID	My tongue has no bones, and wags as it will. An occupational compensation for our mindless rote. —Men, *as you* WERE!
LIL-AMIN [Ceremony resumes.	Let the rite proceed.
TROOPER 1 Troopers and Traders converse	My sword-palm itches to churn some flesh. Gilgamesh is not here now to protect the owners of our rightful spoils.
TROOPER 2 with each other in the foreground. Behind them the Rector invests	There's no use in plunder if you can't take it with you. And it's better to hack your way home after a feast than slay your host before he serves the eats! No one's going to be poisoned if we make the ayatollah taste it first.
TRADER 2 Engidu with Gilgamesh's mantle. In dumbshow: Engidu, while still bewildered by civilization, prompted by the Rector, accepts the Rod and Ring	What about us? We're dead already! This swarm of drones covets our imported goods. They also want the daughters back that were given us for wives by the erstwhile liberator who confiscated their temple treasury to pay for a pile of bricks! It doesn't make them hate us the less that he, our only defender, has surrendered to their folklore. The chief idolater is no priest of reconciliation!
TROOPER 2 from Lil-Amin; he is then led to the empty throne beside her and crowned with Gilgamesh's mask.]	Be of good cheer. Gilgamesh hasn't lost his nerve. He studies dreams too much, and for the moment some kingdom in his head seems more important; but our troubles fade as Mithra's fire climbs the zodiac.
ENGIDU [Speaks shyly and haltingly what he's tried to memorize.]	Oh Lady-Amin, highmost priest, and Op-timates of Ur-ek. Oh great womens and man, many as sands. I have shaking de gates at my arm. Soon wid hand I break ark-enemy on eart' of In-an-anna.
WIDOWS [Chanting in dance.]	*As earlier with human hands* *You unset human snares for beasts,* *And then for humans laid the lion low,* *Deliver us from evil now.*
RECTOR [Touches Engidu's head with blood from Lil-Amin's sacrificial dish.]	I anoint Enkidu, Imperator of the Epact, to try his strength against Gilgamesh; and if he fails the verdict to perish in his stead. —Take up kingship of the feast, to command us as you will, until you lose or win the place you sit in!

ENGIDU

[Speaks haltingly but with gradually gained confidence.]

Do I what speak you. I ready be for old bull of able-value blood! One life from two will blow away on wind. I kill him to lady-god and cover-god. Me city-king all years will be.

WIDOWS

Women and men, raise your joyful cry: Eu-oi, Eu-oi!

RECTOR & WIDOWS

[Intoned as antiphonal litany.]

Sleep not, until the New Year cracks its shell.

—Lest Enlil frown upon the black-haired folk in everlasting night. Sleep not, until the night's dark lid begins to open, until you see the slitted eye of light.

—Lest his bridal bed be made a nesting place for vultures. Sleep not, until you hark a voice from the east with tidings of the silver crescent.

—Lest the house of our gods be filled with dust and leveled like a desert tomb.

—Lest the merciless sun cake dry all mud with cracks, and choke with sand the living waters.

—Lest time go on without return.

WIDOWS

Give ear for word of Inanna her sky-boat!
Watch for the horns of her bullock!

TROOPER 2

It's not the moon that sprouts beer-barley; so how can she inaugurate a year? They don't understand the constant mill of time. Mithra lingers and retreats, but he never wanes!

RECTOR

When on high the gods chose Enlil to weave all destinies . . .

TRADER 2

The harlot they call a queen, she wasn't good enough for a blasphemous king, but for them she's pure messiah!

TROOPER 1

You patriarchals should have more respect for ladies of the cloth. She's the finest kind. Have you ever seen her dance? Or have you lost the yen, what with all your wives?

TROOPER 2

Nobody but Gilgamesh would refuse to touch the one woman anywhere that's his own true match.

TROOPER 1

But the perfect bride from folk to god, for god to folk!

WIDOWS

— . . . a pious bride.

[They lead Lil-Amin down from her throne, removing her mask and robes, leaving her dressed only in the blue bridal veil.]

—May our full, perfect, and living sacrifice be gladly received by her mystic bridegroom; and her beatitude bring upon us gifts of God. Let us make communion by the light of stars, in the shadow of Our Lord on her skin.

By the first sweet gleam of moon
Enlil greets his lovely bride!

RECTOR

[Kneeling before her, he loops a white cord three times about her waist and ties it lightly. His ritual prayer gradually grows more personal in address. Everyone falls silent as his voice lowers. Breaking off, he kisses her feet passionately.]

[The Urukians stir uneasily.]

[The Widows lead her to the tower stairs. The Rector remains on his knees.]

Slowly **Lil-Amin** disappears up the stairs. [The Widows return, dancing accompaniment to

TROOPER 2

the Rector's private prayer, and come to a stand between Troopers and Traders.]

ENGIDU

[He shouts and smiles spontaneously, growing more and more excited, to the amusement of everyone except the Rector, who arises and turns away to recover himself.]

TRADER 2

OPTIMATE 1

[Amazed.]

WIDOWS

[They dance. Little by little everybody's solemnity yields to

Weep not for garments, milady, when the lord of gods has gently plucked this knotted cord. Your gleaming skin will adorn the incensed linen like a cloven pearl. In the fearless manner of desire, like the petals of a lily, you must receive the savior of us all. Then shall you be reclothed in tender caresses, and dressed in Enlil's misty salt-sweet breath. His sea-soft hand will gently warm your bud-tipped breast. You shall feel his kiss on your lips. He will come unto you with lifted glory; your knees shall be parted by his golden ivory thigh. . . .

—Oh my sister Lil-Amin! Lil-Amin! The rapture of your god is forbidden to your priest! In every other sacrifice I have proved that I grudge great Enlil nothing I can have or know, nor life itself. But I give him you in anguish! I forebode the levin by which a god may infuse the beatitude that women dare not dream of. I dread that he will utterly consume you! Why should earth's jealous father release from divine atonement the most precious daughter of mankind, and restore to me the life that illuminates my humble altar? For me of all men it is most unlawful to serve as his attorney at love. He does not favor the testimony of my unhallowed desire. —I cannot follow you to heaven; yet I am the solicitor of Uruk, and thus, as lawyer to you, the city's proxy, though before a bar too high for human counsel, I arraign our accursed warlord's tower for raising your bridal bed too high!

Thus spake the all-too-human pope! This Messpot duty still unfolds a few surprises.

She love me! Peoples love me! I love all-body!

Thus spake orangutan!

Our ox is jealous of the Lord!

—Listen for the sighs of fathers!
—Hearken to the songs of young husbands!
—Guess the yearnings of blood-stirred boys!
Open the hearts of women!

[merriment and the rite dissolves into general festivity.]

—The bull will lift his head in the pasture,
—and the cow will lift her tail:
when Lil-Amin makes Enlil love!
—Journeymen will be set loose like cowboys
—to lift the skirts of wedded girls
when Lil-Amin makes love in the sky!
—Seven thousand times seven are the bids that await seven thousand wives baking folds of soft white bread. Pray not to waste a single drop of pearly yeast!
Swim swiftly, sweet Euphrates,
Until we end this dance!
—Merrily, merrily, merrily,
—Do not lose the chance!

RECTOR

[*Thumps heartily.*]

[Smiling and genial, signaling the end of formality.]

[Engidu lays the Gilgamesh mask on the seat and puts the Ring of office on his head like a rakish garland, handling the Rod like a swagger stick.]

Yes, dear guests of Uruk, it's not for you to watch this wedding in solemn silence. Strangers, welcome! Citizens, rejoice! Your choice of meat: wild boar killed by Engidu without a wound; or succulent lamb well drained of blood, to suit those that bring us salt. Custom is suspended! Let innocence drown all wisdom. Eat, drink, and dance: for the world may end tomorrow! —Your Highness, lead us to the end of time!

OPTIMATE 1 Ask your whim, Engidu the First! Rule thou our disorder!

ENGIDU Is all woman the same?

OPTIMATE 1 Does not each stick make its own smoke?

Optimates go off with Engidu, capering.

RECTOR

[To Eber, gesturing cordial invitation.]

May it please Your Honor and his distinguished sons! Our banquet is afforded by the economy you teach us. General welfare offends no god.

EBER I have made no pact, Your Grace.

RECTOR Our humble gratitude entails no obligation to the guest. On holiday we shed all cares of office.

NORKID Come along, Eb! There's nothing wrong with a truce. It can't hurt to help warm up the fun-king. As long as we're cold sober before it's over.

EBER Then my thanks already for your hospitality pro tem.

[Bowing to the Rector.]

NORKID
[Taking them both by the arm.]

As long as our Gilgamesh remains the autocrat ontologically.

RECTOR

I've always admired your vocabulary.

NORKID

It comes from cosmopolitan occupations. Take us to the belly-dancers.

Norkid, Rector, and Eber go off smiling at each other.

WIDOW 2
[To Traders.]

You could do worse than take your father's hint.

TROOPER 1

You called us some goddam awful names.

WIDOW 1

I did think the best part of you ran down your mother's leg.

TROOPER 1

Maybe we could be rehabilitated.

WIDOW 1

With some beer we could discuss your therapy.

TROOPER 1

Yes, Ma'am!

Troopers dash off.

WIDOW 1

This is the dance of rising sap.

[Widows mimic

WIDOW 2

For the palm to bear dates, seed must find its way to her flower.

a belly-dance.]

WIDOW 1

I'm more for sap than seed. But these tame Traders are famous for their fructifications.

TRADER 1

I'm so well married, I thought it would take a devil to make me wicked. But I must admit your torso is savory to my eye already.

WIDOW 2

Your eyes are nice. But we're not pictures. Our temple is not that kind of museum.

TRADER 2

Would you like to hear some tent music?

Troopers return,

TROOPER 1

First we wet our whistles. Let's all suck the fennel stalk.

each with a jug and long straw.

WIDOW 2

A toast to the fifth and final sense!

[A Widow, a

TROOPER 2

Drink to the supreme sacrifice!

Trader, and a

TROOPER 1

If it's sacrifice, who wants to live forever?

Trooper take turns at each straw.]

TRADER 2 — Of course it's a small thing to want a woman.

TROOPER 1 — For me it's a small thing after I get what I want.

WIDOW 2 — But not for long, I hope. You should consult a specialist.

[Traders dance.]

WIDOW 1 — According to the whispers of our exogamous sisters, we may have more to learn than teach from these educated sheiks.

WIDOW 2 — They're charming when they make us sheep's eyes, but I lean toward military men. —That northman now, that wrinkles up his nose every time he lets an arrow fly: I always like to watch him shoot.

[Pointing to Trooper 2.] [Troopers get up to do a sword dance.]

WIDOW 1 — On their feet, both these types have pros and cons. Judging just by song and dance, until they meet the test, let's award a bouquet of fig blossoms to all these handsome guests.

Widows keep sipping as they produce dainty food. Traders and Troopers eat morsels.]

TROOPER 2 — Praise be to Ishtar that it's not a prize of cherries!

WIDOW 2 — I'll separate rams from billygoats by the way they bite and chew my seedcakes.

WIDOW 1 — For my part, gentlemen, draw straws. . . .

[*A Trooper and a Trader draw from different jugs.*]

[She claps with glee.]

There's nothing to choose between them! They deserve equal entertainment. Praise be to Mithra and Shaddai both, we're neither maids nor wives! Let no one rise from this feast unsatisfied! The night's as long as the day!

[Throwing aside the straws, they take turns drinking from the jugs, on the fly, Troopers, Widows, and Traders dancing in a ring.]

WIDOW 2 — But not long enough. Somebody ask Giszax to hold back the sun!

TROOPER 2 — Not today he wouldn't! Don't forget his sexy-jismal system and zero impact!

WIDOW 1 — A stitch in the bush saves nine in time. I didn't take the veil for contemplation and celestial studies!

TRADERS — —Brethren and sisteren, it's useless to be shrewd!
—Mingle rhymes that blow like the wind!

WIDOWS — *No wight who dares complain or frown*
Will be allowed to lift my gown!

TRADERS	*There's almost nothing half so sweet* *As your exotic heaps of wheat!*
TROOPERS	*When we finish all these beers* *We'll quit the corps of engineers!*
WIDOW 2	Behold, I shall climb into the highest palm tree and take hold of all its branches.

Widows, Troopers, and Traders snake-dance off to the banquet. **Gilgamesh** crosses to the opposite side, walking backward to look after them with amusement, and **disappears**.

22
TROUBADOUR

With a husband by night and weekend at his lady's castle, with a pair of privileged adolescents dwelling there too, it wasn't often enough that the troubadour found her alone—considering that he and she were kept apart elsewhere by the preeminent duties of subsistence. He sang no aubade because he passed no night under the care of love's physician; but he wrote one anyway—several in fact—though words only, not music. He would fold the paper into a small square and slip it onto her palm when they contrived to meet at the front door on their way to work in the morning, or out in the yard fussing over Ibi for his virtuous service to the household.

Praise of Ibi happened to be especially in vogue at the time. The dog had suffered himself to be adopted as protector by a pair of kittens that Gloria had rescued from euthanasia or worse at the hands of her protege Inez Canary's more irritable parent, who had no more patience for his daughter's love of animals than for her love of learning. Surprised by an impulse of pity when she saw the two solidly black innocents in the poor girl's arms, who herself had accepted them from a friend's family in a moment of inexperienced horror at their destiny as the surplus of a litter, Gloria had taken on yet another burden—and a doubled one at that—immediately making room in her complicated life for one more alleviation of someone else's difficulty.

She'd hoped O'Hair would protect and tutor them; but the resident Elamite, whose auburn hair was darker and thicker than her own, would have nothing to do with the waifs, and expressed his disgust by leaving home in a huff for two or three days. Ibi-Roi had saved the day. Instead of hereditary hostility their tiny innocence evoked a gentle interspecific curiosity, which led to amused tolerance of their fearless attraction to his warm coat, and induced a certain sense of responsibility for their safety.

"I think Redburn had observed something like this when he referred to the 'sagacious kindness of the dog', said Caleb, as proud as if he was claiming some of the credit for himself, "—probably with his own big black Terranovice in mind, not the horrible misbegotten race of Typee canines he'd wanted to kill."

Ibi's condescending benevolence had spared Gloria much anxiety about her newest minor charges, while affording people of goodwill a glimpse of the peaceable kingdom, which Deedee and even Robert brought classmates to admire. The two cubs were still seeking milk as well as play from their huge stepmother whenever he found himself at leisure on the ground floor. Without hesitation, occupied as she was (in one lode of cortical activity) with the case of Bacon vs Faustus, Gloria had named the happy little sinners after a couple of Greene's devils, Belcephon and Ninus.

For Tessa was making her study the part of Margaret the Keeper's daughter, the Fair Maid of Fressingfield, for next year's Stone Barn production of *The Honorable History of Friar Bacon and Friar Bungay*. At first she'd been too embarrassed to attempt the representation of virginal youth and beauty—at her age!—but she was so interested in the subject for historical reasons, and so enthusiastic about the prospects of Hoof & Mouth, that she allowed her diffidence to be overcome by a growing wish to participate in external and recognized imaginations as liberated in the theater and legitimized by art. To tell the truth, at times she had shivered at intimations of revulsion against the comparatively passive role of an historian.

Although her hunger for excitement joy and self-respect was now being fed by Caleb's words and acts, and it was no longer urgent to practice histrionics as a substitute for reading, even a lover always on his mettle (under constraints of decency) could hardly fill all the interstices in her compassion for living creatures or relieve the voids of sorrow in her marriage which always threatened the integrity of her career as a busy servant public and private—as a leader of women and children quartered in Dogtown nests full of bibelots and cathode rays. On the contrary, Caleb's attention stimulated a hope to rise on her own wings above the spoilage of provincial domesticity, of which she became increasingly ashamed in the successful effort to conceal it from him. In any event, whatever new interests might arise, she had long since come to believe that life is nothing but a series of stepping stones, in the running water of handicaps, from one problem to the next—large or small—each presumably left behind as the next comes under foot.

It therefore seemed to her that without necessarily renouncing history she might as well give rein to the theatricality that had hitherto been checked by conscience, as well as to her astonishing sensuality, as means of anesthetizing the most personal of all her sensibilities as a simple woman. Why not study acting? she asked herself. I've been an actress since grade school anyway. Girls are brought up to be actresses.

So she read Stanislavsky while waiting to have a word or a smile with Caleb on his way in or out of the house. She chided herself for lacking the dignity of a chatelaine—the kind of nobility she'd seen in Deirdre Cotton merely standing to watch Buck's fire: the most beautiful woman on Cape Gloucester, who would have been regal in ancient Ireland. But in the nearly unbearable excitement of emancipation and intrigue Gloria no longer dwelt upon her own or anybody else's defects.

For weeks at a time even Deedee's girl-wisdom seemed to be maturing in harmony with the whole family, and Robert glided toward the last vernal days of school more unobtrusively self-sufficient than ever. In the forenoon of her consuming delight with Caleb's alacrity of body and mind—before the passing of the zenith began to point shadows of anguish back to her own history—though the children were always first in the habits of her consciousness, Gloria almost forgot she was a mother. Dexter's appearances were so perfunctory and collegial—he spoke so seldom about anything of personal importance—that she also had to remind herself she was still a wife. I must be on vacation, she laughed, when once or twice she stopped to think about her entrancement; I don't wish to know when or how it will come to an end.

But it would have been difficult to define her recreation, for she was no less busy than ever before with the things she now gave little thought to, and almost her only respites from work at home and abroad were the ones of feverish secrecy in which stolen minutes made up for years of what now seemed stupid self-immolation.

"Your dear man has set me free," she explained to Ibi, her uncle Pander and most frequent domestic companion, "but because of the kids I naturally don't choose as yet to exercise my liberty any further. The Madogians say King Arthur's wife, like Helen, was much given to being carried off; but I'm no Guinevere."

To a chaste matron of practiced imagination the actual materialization of an imaginative lover can bring spiritual confusion; but Gloria Keith's confusion had been swiftly deliberated, allowing the vaguely diffused desires of unfulfilled maturity to lead her into the infidelity that would have been unconscionable in her own life five minutes before it began. The confusion of conditions, of ages, of identities, was more or less willfully whirled into abrupt and dangerous love by passionate alternations of fevers and cures. All along she feared the confusion would not endure for the very reason that it wasn't pathologically involuntary—that she was too sensible by nature.

Yet attic trysts were difficult to plot, and in warm weather the sensations of nakedness under light clothes drove the lovers out of doors in reckless impatience for more frequent unions. They strove to overcome each other's caution. But on Daylight Savings Time, half way from equinox to solstice, darkness fell late by the clock; and they had to avoid the moon.

One Wednesday night after dinner when the stars were auspicious, and Dexter was testifying for his department's budget before the Finance Committee at the Hall, Gloria finished up in her kitchen with the pounding heart of a novice spy. Feigning exceptional vexation with her colleagues' preparation for the Library's budget hearing on the morrow, she sequestered herself for a long bath, ostensibly to relax her mind and dress again for an evening of cool study at the dining room table, as a professional woman very well might.

There she soon pushed away her books in favor of Deedee's unfinished Gloucestermas dress, jumping up every two minutes to look out at the sky. At last she assured herself that dusk of Acorn Pasture had yielded to the ultimate possible shadows of an eleven-acre public garden that was unfortunately bounded by the imperfectly enleaved lamplight of public streets.

From the foot of the stairs she called up to the two bedrooms in which the students were supposed to be doing their homework, affecting the role of a conscientious librarian who couldn't forget the job when she was at home, thoroughly exasperated by the administrative pusillanimity of her superiors. "I'm going out for a walk to calm down. Keep on working."

"Why go now?" Deedee demanded, like a grandmother. "It's already dark!" This excursion was somewhat extraordinary.

"Because I can't stand the thought of human stupidity any more tonight, including my own, and I've got to clear my head for tomorrow's bickering over dollars."

The children allowed her to go. Though familiar enough with the professional complaints of their talkative and sociable mother, they had never heard such animadversion against the polity from her end of the dinner table. They rarely saw her in repose, but her outbursts were few, and usually directed at their own departures from the norms of civility, or at herself exclusively. Not quite consciously, however, without consulting each other, the sister and brother had recently become aware of a new surcharge in her air—perhaps something negative that represented itself with positive signs.

Therefore the girl at least was a little eased of nameless uncertainty by hearing her mother vent some thunder on persons of no possible concern to young people. Deedee was always glad of evidence that the blitheful mother shared a bit of unreasonable female anger at the nature of things. "Do you want me to go with you, Mother?"

"Watch out for the bogey man, Ma!" Robert warned with glee. "Where shall we look for your dead body?"

"On the waterfront!" Gloria shouted, flinging herself out the front door in a flamboyantly comic manner that astonished her offspring.

"Are you mad at us about something?" Deeta screamed after her. Did this ominous aberration have something to do with an early "change of life"?

Robert got up from his desk to stand in his sister's doorway, perplexed about their old lady—whether she was really overwrought, or only teasing them in some adult way.

Adult happened to be the word just then under Gloria's breath: I'm an adult woman now, not just the city planner's cheerleader. Under her skirt the wanton night air rose between her unclothed thighs like the summons of Dionysus. As she hurried to the cemetery gate on Cod Street and doubled back on the drive behind her house the urgency of her craving for a man verged on indiscrimination. What if she met a stranger? But she remembered that she was looking for one Caleb Karcist—only half a stranger, yet nothing like Dexter.

She walked very fast. There was no time lose, if she was to abandon herself utterly. She didn't care where or how they flung themselves together, or whether he spoke or not. She was making it simple for him; there'd be no reason to guess or fumble, and it didn't matter if the ground was strewn with stones.

Ibi was the first to greet her. Then her lover stepped out of the darkness. His craving was external. Half running hand in hand they sought the deepest shadows of the distal oaks on the knoll, among great monuments and boulders that would baffle the policing of even phantom censors. Versed in a bachelor's kind of exordium, he was prepared to sing her praises in whispered prose and make courtly advances with his mouth and hands. But it was her lips and tongue that stifled unnecessary words, and her hands that went promptly to his belt.

As if there was nothing out of character in her initiative she pretended to be jocund. "Let's play hart and hind right now! I must get back to the house before Deedee and Robert sneak down to the DV ." From where they stood, if they had looked, the lighted windows of her castle were visible through the trees, above the lower graves and rocks. "Dear hart!" she added: her only smile that night.

For Caleb the purely carnal advances of his highly respected paramour were an unexpected advance of experience. But the almost imperceptible pause of playfulness gave him a chance to catch his breath. "Dear hind!" he replied, with his one and only laugh, clasping her haunches.

Already she seemed not to hear, and it occurred to him that a fundamental sense of humor like Lilian's was not necessarily to be found beneath the outer hilarity of an enthusiastic personality. But he failed to remind himself that they'd never had the time or security, even of an automobile, in which to hit upon such jests and endearments as those that animate the persiflage of sexual friends. All along, in the very case which he would have judged most likely to require long and subtle seduction, the troubadour's poetic work had been cut short by direct accession to the one true end of love.

Gloria Keith required no literary fictions from the lips of her lover. He had no means of knowing that her secret heart was resorting to the narrative matter of Lusus. Without such cerebral accompaniment, a descant of her own arrangement, on planes of irony too remote for communicable humor, this shameful jig of the hindquarters would have been unthinkable.

This liaison was so abrupt, deprived of the leisure for confession or pillow talk, that she had heard nothing about Caleb's past erotic life, and she'd been brought up not to ask personal questions; but for a long time she'd pitied and admired the reclusive tenant who apparently had entertained no companions, and taken no overnight leaves, since once stealing in and out of the house with the mysterious female more than half a year before (much to the titillation of Dexter and herself). Until recently he'd struck her as the sort of scholar too shy to be lucky with the kind of woman given to be carried off.

The young mortal she now draws down to the greensward is valiant and romantic Lionardo Rubeiro, always given to falling in love but doomed to a continuous succession of unlucky frustrations. It is for her as his choice among all the nymphs on the Isle of Love to change his ithyphallic fate. After a long plaintive chase through wood and meadow he is to be granted solace among the flowers in proportion to his years of disappointment.

Thus the copse of sepulture became the grove of Venus, and Isopel Berners's grave the bower of bliss in which she requited the torment of virile virginity. Guarded by the great dog Husdant, infallibly alert in all his superhuman senses against blundering wayfarers or ghostly footpads, she forgot all fear, and hardly felt the acorns under her shoulder blades. The atonement was a blessed rushing which overclouded and outlasted the scenario that brought it about.

But one unknotting didn't put a stop to her mania. Remission was brief. Love's remedy was but an intoxication; the first beatitude a foundation for further ascent of a winding tower. As much to herself as to the male person, tonight she seemed a different woman, neither tender nor modest: speechless, voluptuous, reckless, almost sardonic about her seizure—as if converted to the cult too late for the luxury of a lifetime's devotions at a languorous wave-length. Reversed at its axial limit, the winding stair descends uncurling. Down on the ground, sensations are restored of minor abrasion at vertebrae and shoulder blades: little pains of glorious martyrdom.

Returning toward Cod Street in the grove of oaks behind the back yard of her house, on the margin of gravestones more openly exposed, she stops him to kiss goodbye. Standing by the big glacial rock near the Keith stone wall, where by daylight her children could have watched, and where they might have been surprised by any night-walker cutting through the cemetery corner, she marvels to find herself so soon again reciprocating the recrudescent pressure so nicely placed; once more her discarded pride would have been horrified by the frantic lust for solid dilation: but this is the occasion to realize a method never possible with her toplofty husband! Shamelessly backing Caleb against the rock, without assistance she bestrides her Pegasus. Novel momentum overcomes her faculty for any further romance. In this codicil to the assignation there is no space for the aesthetic decency of even the setting for a story.

Yet after they had finally parted, with the recovery of her cognitive senses, his virtual presence within her, as well as his real issue, remained palpable to her brain. As she opened her front door, half an hour after she'd last closed it, and cheerily announced herself to the kids, she was already bemused with retroactive construction of a prosopopoeial alternative for her lefthanded troubadour: as the most imperialistic of epic poets, the underestimated bard of Lusitania, author of his own adventures—hardened one-eyed Camoens, a bitter heartbroken spirit of mettle and learning, firsthand cartographer of both geography and history.

"I feel better now!" she called, quickly passing the children's rooms. "I'm going straight to bed. Don't stay up too late." She meant to leave no waking time for meditation on her behavior. But in sleep she would retain some of the youthful milt still undrained.

It was past midnight when Dexter came home, a full hour after his official meeting was over. His whole family was asleep.

Upstairs on the bachelor cot, half awakening in baseless apprehension, the troubadour heard his lady's lord come in. Then, smiling at his unspecific alarm, Caleb sank back into complacent oblivion. There was nothing to fear. A puny unmusical roomer was beneath suspicion, and Gloria would never tell. Ibi had not stirred at the friendly voice of the family car entering his territory, nor at the familial sounds of those authoritative feet, for it was a pattern that repeated itself many times a week.

But in fact Dexter was uniquely excited. From the committee he had won complete incorporation of his reorganization plan into the new fiscal year budget. It would give him the staff required for radical improvements. Afterwards, to crown his success, Deirdre Cotton had at last confessed that she loved him. His born complement, with the face and walk of a queen, really loved him—loved him "alas", whispered in the voice of an angel, but loved him all the same—as he loved her! Perhaps soon the Prothonotary's love would yield to the desire that had been consuming all his unprofessional thoughts week after week sitting near her in public chambers as she recorded and advised the words or procedures of the earldermen and their attestants or petitioners. Somehow he would find the time and place.

But her beauty, like Iseult's, made others beautiful—in this case the wife in his bed, whose recusancy he had hardly resented of late. The royal Deirdre was married too. Many accommodations were necessary. For too long he had neglected Gloria's feelings and interests.

Of course he loved her too, from many years of shared distresses and achievements, the little plebeian mother of his children, irrepressible undiscriminating benefactor of all living creatures and worthy enterprises, including History as hobby-horse. It was a different kind of love, its mystery reduced to the food and blood of domestic experience, compounded more of grievance sympathy and gratitude than hope or further interest, but full of mature memories valued higher than most satisfactions.

As he undressed in the dim light from the street-side window shades it was impossible to remember his angers: only desires, carnal and utterly sincere. The shallowness of their conjugal matching was unimportant, now that he definitely hoped for perfection in the tall slender depths of Deirdre Cotton. Meanwhile it was decent and proper to make his couch in the lap of a childhood sweetheart, the mutable but steadfast Gloria he knew too well and had used too often ill, and to restore for her sake too, if only for a few segregated hours of sleep, the old sated peace of body and soul. It should be no stumbling block that the exclusive love with which she had fettered him since youth was being struck free by the woman someone else had married.

If he offered his resentful wife no kiss or caress as occasion for rebuff at the outset, straightforward coercion of atonement could regenerate beatitude and bring back the love that had taught her to accept it. Don't wake her first. Make no apologies. Say nothing. Omit the symbols of sentiment. But Mary Ever-blessed Virgin, let it be known that my pure lust is not merely opportunistic, having been aroused and frustrated by an unavailable loveliness; teach her that I'm seeking something more than convenient pacification: as of old, let my lawful action kindle her desire. But whether or not this prayer is granted, it's my house, my bed, and tonight I'm too amorous to be denied! And it's not at a time on the calendar when conception of another hostage is much to be feared.

According to latterday habit, Gloria had turned her back when she was wakened from her own pacification by the sound of water running in the bathroom. But a moment later she was made aware that Dexter had come naked to bed as sanguine as Priapus. She hadn't willingly allowed such attention since the night they'd both been diverted from their displeasures with each other by snickering speculation about what was going on between the little third-floor occupant and his unseen visitor. Dexter's brute left hand fumbled with the pajamas she now always wore in that bed.

—Holy Jesus, could he have searched my drawer and found the diaphragm missing? He thinks I've been waiting for him, that all is forgiven! —No, I'm sure he thinks I'm too old to get pregnant again. He's been with that Cotton lady. I wonder where they go to do it. But how can I hate the woman? It's not her fault. I know she's splendid; should I really blame him? Only for concealing it. They're obviously meant for each other: that's why everybody in town must know about it. Yet why did he have to pick his own daughter's namesake—the name *I* gave her? That's the thing I can't forgive him for. My love affair is insignificant compared to his perfidy. King David's corrupted his Bathsheba, and now comes home to fuck his first wife!

She'd never used that word before, save under her breath, impersonally, in rare gerundival curses of uncontrolled rage, which (in her present judgment) had broken out all too seldom. Beneath dissembled somnolence the frisson of that transitive verb distracted her resistance to the tugging at her upper hip. It recalled her unladylike recklessness out at the rock and reawakened sensations that had subsided into slumber. Not ten minutes before the poet there had been the lovelorn sailor too, who caught me on the ground! —Holy Mary, this minute I need an intact Bragwaine to take my place! Pray God this headstrong centaur doesn't notice the satyr's spoor!

But her husband noticed only the wholehearted ease of her welcome. It was as if she'd been dreaming of his homecoming.

I'm his closest meadow of clover, not to be utterly despised after all, not to be lost. I suppose this arrogant uncircumcised stallion never fails to mount the nearest mare in heat. It would never occur to him that I'm too sleepy to care what he pushes into me. Sleepy and dreamy. In fleeting reverie, without noticing the matrimonial path her body now retraced, she smiled to think of the lengths she had driven him to, and he her, when she'd made him wait for their wedding night! Jesus Mary and Joseph, maybe I really am in heat, committing adultery with a treacherous stud! —Why not, if the harm's adoing anyway?

Her person being thus recaptured by the puissant godlike lord of her hearth, once more unwillingly overshadowed and enthralled by a power to which in former times she had eagerly dedicated life itself, Gloria Keith fell back upon the story in a more likely role. As Tethys, senior sea-goddess, wife of distant Poseidon, mother of all the Neriads, she welcomed the great captain of the Lusitanians to the Isle of singing swans, leading all her daughters in making the company of New Argonauts sweet amends for entire years of dauntless maritime privation. It was for her in person, yes, to requite the great fame-craving Vasco da Gama, paragon of mortals, visionary cartographer, pioneer of India, most accomplished of geographers—as she would likewise guerdon his successors for centuries to come!

In a minute or two the tale faded and she was engrossed in the plenary coaptation that came with her marriage. Soon she was choking the cries she'd learned to mute when the children might be listening. But they were fast asleep across the hall and beyond two closed doors; and so was Caleb, ten feet overhead. Only Ibi could hear, his ears erect in sleep—and he would understand the conflicting affinities of an unchained captive.

23
SIRENS

*S*till in his burning youth, Ibi-Roi was far from having attained full wisdom, or even his athletic maturity; but of all those at the Rectory he was the only one in a position to understand the feelings of all adult parties, if not of children and kittens. House dogs, like wives, see more of men as they really are than other men do; and they are also more privy than men to the prayers and curses of women. His grasp of social relations was by no means comprehensive, but as the common friend and guardian of the principals he was severally trusted with their private thoughts, and his interpretation of their respective disturbances was inherently limited only by his ignorance of the concepts to which their spoken and unspoken words referred. In each case the feelings were wildly variable. It was their inconsistency of attitude that puzzled him.

Right from the beginning he was uneasy about his own man's euphoria, who behaved as if the children were the only ones to watch out for: almost as if the head of the house existed merely in the mind of Mrs Grundy and was no threat to the convenient liaison. Ibi had too much respect for Dexter's intelligence to discount the temptation of fate. Though the good lady sometimes affected to make merry of her intrigue she was much less lighthearted about it than her lover. If Ibi saw the most, Caleb saw the least.

Yet at the next private meeting of the lovers, which Gloria had several times postponed, Caleb sensed a certain constraint in her manner and was able to coax her into telling him what was wrong. She felt so transparent that she was obliged to confess the guilt of having been raped half asleep on the very night of her cemetery passion. To him, haltingly, as if to a wronged fiancé, she whispered of the shame in an "overlap" of men; but to herself it was the sinfulness of her anger at Dexter that seemed the worst of all.

Caleb had supposed that his liege-lady's husband like King Mark was exercising his conjugal rights all along; hence he was so gratefully touched by her ingenuous apology that he kissed away the tears of remorse—the first he'd seen since their intimacy began—with an entirely new compassion. It seemed that her true and silent being was revealed to be in his service alone, even if only for the time they could be together. He perceived her response to his priestly comfort as a confirmation of vehement desire for himself—not merely for his desire—which wholly transfigured the indefatigable historian known to the world as an ebullient eleemosynary matron, who until lately had been esteemed by himself as a possible disinterested and tolerant judge in the Court of Love if he could have brought himself to claim like a dog the privilege of confiding in her his troubles with Lilian and perhaps even Belle!

Still, when Gloria was not at hand he often found himself imagining the marriage-bed violation, of which he'd been informed in no more than brief abstract terms. Vivid speculation goaded his own crude lust. But at the same time her honesty about the fact deepened his love for her heart as a delicate defenseless mourning dove with folded wings. But the transformation he privately wrought in the outward woman (which to his amazement remained as publicly extroverted as ever) only encouraged the vanity of regarding himself as a successful knight. Unlike Ibi's selfconfidence, which was natural and unselfconscious, his was cocky and complacent. And of the consequences she might suffer he took even less thought than of his own danger.

Caleb was glad to learn Dogtown from the inside, proud to be related to local life through this popular female Chiron (former teacher at the high school) who seemed as closely allied to all ranks of youth as to the middleaged core of the city's liberal fellowship. With the authority of a studious lover he sought to inform himself with her knowledge of the society by which he was protected. He wanted to know the town vicariously, to sense by phallic antenna the exciting discrepancy between her inner and outer lives. He was fascinated by all her parallel activities.

Since proximate desire was gratified from time to time (mostly by conspiracy but sometimes by lucky chance), his nerves were in good tone for what he called "Glory-studies". A resident lover without responsibilities, troubled only by the piquant requirements of commonsensical prudence, could indulge his fancy for devising little cryptic notes of at least double entendre. Indeed he was so happy with the prospects of his covert friendship with the city's gossamer-aureoled Reference Librarian that he devised pretexts for engaging her in semi-public conversation (presumably without attracting attention) at her desk on Mondays in the back room full of archives. He made her blush at the accidental touch of their fingers as she responded to bold questions that evinced amateur historical interest in Dogtown's peculiar weathering of the Depression.

But in fact while taking advantage of the Atheneum to enrich the uniqueness of his luck it dawned on him with another kind of thrill that he was presented with the possibility of clues to the problem of his background. He came to the verge of confiding his almost forgotten quest for information about Dogtown people and practices circa 1934–1939. And he even thought of asking her—the very person who could be most useful to the purpose of his temporary and as it were pseudonymous return to the place of his origin—to spare him excruciating embarrassment with Mrs Sirius by crossing the street from her workplace to Ibicity Hall in order to search the heraldic archives for some hint about his mother's status in the record of her Sycorax, Ibi's putative maternal or cognate ancestor, an archetypal Viking Shepherd bitch.

Thus he would have sought the clandestine help of a practical scholar worthy to be trusted, in part, with the secret of Mary Tremont—if he'd decided to take the risk of shocking the rustic sense of decency for which that scholar was properly admired. But in the end he feared there was little enough time in her company to enjoy erotic conversation—without diverting her attention by evoking his equivocal nativity!

Meanwhile, unmentioned by Gloria, the matrimonial visitation recurred that had angered and confused her, though not again so close upon the tail of Caleb. Yet she knew that showerbaths clean underwear and perfume couldn't keep her duplicity from Ibi, stalwart sympathetic confidant, uncensorious and absolutely reliable, who needed no telling to sense the history of her body. She believed it was perfectly clear to the dog that as she walked about the house all her limbs and organs were soaking up the mingled slurry of satyr and centaur, estopped only by the rubber membrane shielding at least her honor and her career. When she smiled at Ibi she felt like a grinning harlot in his eyes, painted internally with layer upon layer of zoic molecules discharged and abandoned by the homuncular will of both his man and hers. Belike through ceiling and floor her muffled perturbations did not escape the shepherd's superhuman ears.

With her acculturation to adulterous experience Gloria began to leave behind God only knows how many historical phantoms; she grew too frank and impatient with herself to summon up exculpatory stories. Without much examination of the transition she found herself awake to the reality of what she recognized as the flowering decadence of her faculty for beatitude. In certain moods of almost cynical worldliness she admitted to consciousness and sometimes mocked the ravening plenitude of her doubled living. She felt a thousand times more knowledgeable of the Tree than any excusable and unilateral infidelity alone could have made her.

But experience of a pagan self also recalled lost innocence. In earliest times a little girl growing up in an animal husbandry farm had naturally learned the virile functions of billygoats bulls and stallions, which brought circumlocutions to her mother's otherwise plainspeaking lips and called for jocular allusions from mysteriously salacious menfolk. Without suggesting the motive for such awesome behavior, those first unspeakable epiphanies had made her conscious by homology of a definitely centered attraction and disquieting pleasure within extremely secret reach of autonomous self-explorations.

These memories stirred a special sympathy for Deedee—Deirdre—her sheltered urban daughter, who was now at the age a mother most vividly remembers in that respect, whose budding figure was never mentioned by either Caleb or Dexter, as if they avoided the subject selfconsciously. Why shouldn't Caleb be in love with my slim prancing long-limbed female child, fresh as uncut pages yet already in the first growth of softness, with freckles faintly like mine, and spasms of my glee, but without my undignified funnylooking map of Ireland? And how could the father be entirely free of incestuous curiosity who loves her namesake? I wouldn't dream of telling either of those men that she's worried about the development of her right breast because it doesn't seem to her as prominent as the left and complains that she's going to grow up an Amazon if it doesn't equalize within a month! I'm old enough now to believe that such intelligence would enflame the circumcised and the uncircumcised. It's a good thing I stand between her and the intrusion of men's desire. Soon enough she'll suffer it.

But Ibi was aware that beneath the lady's cheerful neutral manner in ordinary conversation with family and outer world these her base gross attitudes were far from continuous, and as long as they lasted were mere annoyances to more useful occupations. And indeed hardly a fortnight had passed before his master began to find the alternations of her mind perplexing.

Caleb's expectations were largely determined by her anticipation of Dexter's evenings at the Hall. But on Tuesday the lover was disappointed to find that she was going to be busy that evening with her tape measure and sewing machine—renewing all the curtains in her house! On her lunch hour that same day she'd abruptly initiated the project by running down to the Fabric Shop on Front Street to pick out her azure organdy.

At first he assumed it was a reluctantly scheduled task that she had simply never thought to mention as just one more domestic contretemps, for he believed her month cleared of the involuntary drawback. It seemed to him an enormous undertaking that would turn the house upsidedown for weeks, doubling duty's claims upon her. But just as her effortless energy always rose to an occasion, she cheerfully chose and spent and cut and stitched without rue or hesitation. As usual, she made the time for new work. Her enthusiasm was communicated to Deedee and even won the cooperation of Robert and Dexter.

Caleb's quarters were exempt from new furnishings; but he who had no right to an opinion (and never expressed it) was astonished that she would allow any such deferrable obligation to add itself to all her others amidst the great adventure of her life! Like some ethnic custom it now rather ostentatiously preempted most of her Tuesday night attention until long after the kids must have gone to sleep; and finally, when he called downstairs by telephone, he was warned that Dexter might be coming home any minute. He went to sleep in brooding desolation. What could she be thinking of?

It wasn't the end of the affair. Gloria Keith hadn't come up to Caleb's bed for the last time. She couldn't bring herself to refuse his least escapable suggestions. But he suspected it was the beginning of the end.

His selfconfidence vanished in her presence as well as in her absence. Her humming was still to be heard as she worked; her smiles and greetings were as friendly as ever: but in the effort to forfend humiliation he became rather artificially polite, clinging to the possibility that her evasion had something to do with the lunar calendar after all, even merely the ascendancy of conscience during a palliative phase of oestral rhythm.

So he curbed his demand for communication as he awaited change in the tide. Sometimes prolonging almost formally their few dialogues, but simulating as well as possible his previous style of cortezia, he concealed from her the anxiety that was obvious to his roommate on the third floor. His mood was now an uncertain dependent variable of hers—responding to his doubtful detection of her nearly imperceptible feelings. His side of the equation seemed by far the simpler.

For Gloria's part, as she scissored and basted and mounted chairs to reach the curtain rods with pins in her mouth or shrieked instructions to her daughter, she was restringing scattered pearls of precious things past: before the advent of babies and property, wartime loneliness deprivation and mortal anxiety, relieved now and then by the happy hardships of overcrowded travel and transient marriage beds; and, long before visions of an engagement ring, the cheering at basketball games, the strenuous exultation of squaredancing, the success in competition for school marks, with awards of public praise, and private kisses sweeter even than the subsequent blisses of a garlanded honeymoon on an Ensign's pay.

Among the earliest jewels in her chronicle she joylessly beaded certain especially poignant feats, perhaps the most cherished gestes of the knight from whom she thought soon to part. To celebrate his captaincy of the triumphant baseball team, instead of strutting about with all the girls Dexter had brought his crow to school, King Arthur, and shyly cued him to say "I love Gloria", to her blushing mortification and pride. The teasing about that never left off, but no other boy ever made bold with Dexter's girl.

Earlier yet, on the glorious Junior High picnic the boys and girls of both grades had swum together at Billy's Pond, and he, already the school's unrivaled leader, had very pointedly invited her, the youngest of them all, to ride out with him in the rowboat. It was a day of unblemished joy, emblazoned next to her betrothal fantasy of a few years later: herself with him like a naked Albanian bride and groom being bathed together in the solstice sunshine.

Carefree swimming: sunshine, skin, and water! Thereto it was idyllic Namauche Beach that had brought them with the children to see Cape Gloucester for the first time. Not for years now have they lain in the sand together or dived into the waves at Little Harbor; and never again have they swum by moonlight in a quarry with their Village friends.

Yet some of his most lovable traits had emerged even after the family was completed and all its personalities well established. It was only six or seven years ago that he dropped all other diversions to throw himself into the construction of the backyard suspension bridge with Deedee and Robert. All in all, it seems that most of a woman's life has nothing directly to do with barnyard foretail.

Gazing out the window to admire Ibi in sport among the gravestones with half a dozen inferiors she remembered how in the old days she was envisaging Dexter when she had told Tessa of Goethe's remark about the Irish and their noble stags: how in the end they always drag them down like a pack of yapping hounds. Apparently Tessa forgot where she'd learned the image. But of course it suggested itself to any reader of the Obiter Dichter who happened to know Sir Dexter Keith. To Gloria herself it recurred as often as it was dismissed, like one of the randomly reinforced sexual paradigms from her days of innocence. Isn't the doughtiest and cleverest of paragons—leader, sea-rover, athlete, or city-builder—always destined to defeat by the sheer numbers of his opposition?

Now she questioned by comparison the heroism of such exceptional masculinity. The champion who distinguishes himself in the terms of tribe or society can be brought down by the multitude, when not protected by the law or by the faction on his side; but the singular achievement of a lightweight runner, lonely and selfish in the sinister pursuit of fame, can never be defeated—whatever his obstacles, however long his ordeal—by mere aggregation of detractors or contestants. A different kind of man entirely: less male perhaps; perhaps for a female more elusive.

So why does a girl in the body of a woman keep loving a superman, despite his treachery, just because he plays chopsticks on her piano with his kids? Before Deirdre Cotton, how many others has he deceived me with? Hiding behind my enthusiasm for unimportant things over the years I've made sure I had no time to spare for suspicion of all the little unexplained incidents, so trifling that even now I can't remember what they were.

The truth is that a woman needs the social protection of a man to save her from the necessity of acting like a man, in order to remain what a man cannot be and thereby nearly double the limits of humanity. No, perhaps not so nearly, because there's something of humanity that we have in common—at least what's friezed in language, and what at first is felt in love. I used to think the duplication could be nearly total!

Yet it turns out that being overlapped by two men doesn't nearly double the span of a wife's experience. That's why the contrast of males doesn't greatly expand the story. But should I therefore turn gee or haw indifferently, dexter or sinister, simply because it's impossible to keep straight ahead?

Again at other times Gloria was still able to forget her own existence—that is to say, existence in her gender—and to dissolve her personal sensibilities in impersonal missions, nowadays less historical than dramaturgic. For hours at a time, often on the phone with Tessa, she projected the labor of bringing to birth the Stone Barn Theater, which had been so easily conceived and sufficiently financed for the delivery. The practicability of staging *Friar Bacon* remained an open question. That challenge alone offered plenty of anesthetic work.

But even this thought-career led her back to the dichotomy of sex, seeing that the prime difficulty was to find actors for the male parts. Almost all the roles were for men, whereas almost all the prospective players were female! There seemed to be only three possible solutions.

The first was to get some of the women to simulate male parts. At least the two sisters of the Troika could pass, and they might encourage a few other women of larger bulk. Then if the first Gloucestermas drama aroused enough interest perhaps three or four distinctly masculine figures could be recruited from lobster boats or past football teams. Then she would retain her interesting role as the Keeper's Daughter, Fair Maid of Fressingfield.

On the other hand, she thought, I would be spared the foolishness of pretending to the part of a beautiful young heroine if we took symmetrical liberties with all the personae—either by casting all players in parts and costumes of the opposite sex or by rewriting the text to transpose the genders of the parts themselves! The Honorable History of Sister Bacon and Sister Bungay! It might be possible to scrape up four men only. I could be the Countess who uses well the bucolic Youth, instead of the Maid valued for undeflowered beauty! Or else I could imitate desire at the male end of the tail, burlesquing the education of Tiresias!

But the desperate solution—the most artistic alternative—would be to stage the play as a mummery of large puppets! Dare I suggest it to Doctor Charlemagne? Trinacrian marionettes hung from the rafters of a stage! Insular figures derived from from the Matter of France and Rome alienated to new characters in the Matter of Britain whence romance began! And what's to stop us from inventing for our own little island a tradition of commedia dell'arte with moving wooden images? Surely Atlanteans are freer to pick and choose their matter than Europeans, and we Marooners the freest of them all! We're as free as dogs to make water on anybody's grave!

We may not have many real actors but there are voices galore. No lack of sculptors smiths and dressmakers. Dexter could get Mr DaGetto to make us a stunning Brass Head. Each of us could feed and clothe her own dolls. But most of the Trinacrians here are fishermen. Where on earth can we find a puppeteer to teach us his skill? It must take a lot of strength to manipulate those wires. I wonder if they can dangle the boys and girls close enough to each other without getting all tangled up. . . .

—Gloria brought herself up short. Busywork to keep my mind off sin, she chided herself, sitting for a minute on the back stoop and stroking Ibi's folded ears as she searched the clear brown eyes that gazed up at her from the depths of sympathy and trust. In Caleb's absence he's grateful to me for relieving his busylessness and wishes there were something he could do to help. Before the Atlindus had horses their dogs hauled travois across the prairies to relieve the squaws. It's a shame there's no sled-work in Dogtown to keep his mind off what he knows about me. If saints were allowed to work, little kids could be shepherded back and forth from school on their own two legs; and that would save enough in yellow buses to pay for everything we've ever fancied for the libraries all over town!

Now Ibi knew nothing of plans for the future, and still less of theatrical dreams, but he did witness the gross correspondence of current events. At the fire, on the ground amid the odoriferous legs of strangers, he hadn't been able to see Dexter, but he'd often scented one dimension of the other lady on the large hand of the chief that patted him at every encounter on the premises, and it was as Irish as anybody's in the house. The big stranger's troubled feelings were betrayed by jerky movements and an uncharacteristic alacrity of response to the speech of his wife and children.

But desire for an unseen beloved could not always sufficiently account for Dexter's uncomfortable mein. In truth his thoughts were more erratic than anyone else's. As soon as the city budget was settled he began to spend more time at the house. He broke workweek custom by sometimes coming home at noontime to make himself lunch, especially on Monday, his tenant's day off. (On any of the other four days he found Caleb's car gone and Ibi guarding the place alone, whose pleasure at his unexpected company was then more pronounced than ever.) Thus the castellan ventured to assure himself that his castle was more secure than it might have been in his cloudily uneasy imagination.

For one Saturday afternoon, in the usual weekend anomie, when it was time to start cooking dinner after a day of comings and goings by all members of the family at their various tasks or amusements, his wife had been called back to the phone as she was about to go up to "the big bedroom" to retrieve an apron she had forgotten. A moment later he himself had started up the stairs for a trifling purpose of his own and noticed a manila folder on the outer end of a tread where she had hastily left it when interrupted on her way. Other kinds of objects were often left on the lower steps for further portage at the next convenient ascent, but her "paperwork" was usually conducted and stored in the "front room" of the ground floor, which served as her study and sewing studio as well as playroom for children and their visitors. With the casual curiosity of an habituated bureaucrat he'd mechanically stooped to identify the file.

He saw at a glance that it contained the smudged carbon copy of a crowded messy typescript, which made no immediate sense to him except possibly as something to do with the playreading club that was meeting at his house that night; but on top of the manuscript was a note in Gloria's crisp black handwriting, which he involuntarily scanned as he paused on his way:

> I can't wait to see the last Tablet! Maybe that will change my mind about this quite secondary point: I still don't think you should insist that all the choruses be the same size. In actual production some of the usual casting and design problems might be solved by using the choruses as variable counterweights to balance the three (or four?) cultures by sound, color, mass, and movement—not to mention sex!

Dexter had quickly resumed his way, fearing that she'd be coming right back and catch him at his snooping. A gentleman never reads his wife's papers unless she asks him to; and in fact even at her behest he usually shunned information of her independent occupations. Only retrospectively—not until the next morning as he ruminated in bed between waking and sleeping, while she was downstairs cooking Sunday breakfast—had he ceased to ignore his accidental flicker of illation.

But in afterthought his uncertainty was limited. For one thing, the note bore no apparent relevance to any of the club's future considerations that were discussed at last night's meeting after the playreading (an exasperating almost unintelligible stab at *Bartholemew Fair* in which, unprepared, he himself had been compelled to puzzle out aloud several unflattering little parts). In any case the plays chosen by the group had to be available in printed copies for all the participants, whereas the manuscript in question was not only unpublished but also unfinished. Finally, it was on its way *upstairs* despite the fact that Gloria's books papers and typewriter were generally kept in her corner of the front room where she carried on all her lucubrations.

So the head of the house could not but infer that the note was intended for his tenant's door upstairs. Whereupon he concluded that he had been paying too little attention to Gloria's prattle when long ago she entrusted him with Tessa's secret that Caleb Karcist was writing a play in their garret!

The least he could now suspect was that the sly little wordslinger was wheedling secretarial assistance from his all too obliging wife. It's disappointing when someone with such a fine dog turns out to be just another self-absorbed intellectual. Has my foolish wife been electing an affinity? She wouldn't have made such a secret of some merely literary thing. Of course it might be just a Catharistic fantasy on her part: another one of her enthusiastic vagaries.

Yet no matter what, it's an intrigue of some kind—and I still can hardly imagine Gloria even thinking of deceit!

This time one of her manias must have taken a dangerous direction.

Still, timid young Caleb wasn't the kind of bookworm that usually turned the head of vivacious blonde cheerleaders, even when they were past their prime and had become history-mongering librarians—especially if they were overworking themselves pro bono publico. Not to mention the impediments of a conspicuous marriage and demanding Argus-eyed children. But Gloria had been voted the smartest girl in school as well as the prettiest, and from college days Dexter remembered rumors of amazing seductions by puny book-grinds who didn't even seem to be interested in girls.

Every man has ulterior motives; in cases like this the only question is how bold he may be and how easily an imaginative kindhearted woman is piqued by his idiosyncrasies. In many ways Gloria is still a naive sentimentalist who's never learned to preserve her dignity. Right now she happens to be stage-struck. To warn her would be demeaning to us both.

Thus at first Dexter Keith had been less alarmed than irritated; but the more he mulled over his mistrust of the safety factor the more his calculations ramified into fan-vaultings of intricate suspicion. For the first time since the War there was a tremor at his foundations.

Before tracing his feelings—and certainly before reacting to his fears, if he was not to abandon all self-control and make a fool of himself—it was necessary to confirm or falsify at least the most vulgar hypothesis. To that end he must not disturb the complacency of his suspects by betraying any unusual interest either in Gloria's intellectual activities or in Caleb Karcist's presence under the family roof.

These apprehensions directed his attention to Ibi, whom he now eyed more reflectively. This was a matter the dog knew more about than what met the governor's eye. To the three of them Ibi was a common friend, and Dexter still approved of him as an innocent cicisbeo. He began to take more time to reciprocate Ibi's greeting whenever they met, and even to look around for him if he didn't present himself in the yard or hallway when not up in the attic with his master.

Like Caleb and Gloria, Dexter was an inveterate admirer of distinguished dogs. Ibi wanted to be useful but wasn't much like old Sucat, an half-Irish retriever, who for all his beauty hadn't had a cavalier bone in his body. This great shepherd, by contrast, was disinclined to perform entertaining tricks in demonstration of subservience; but the landlord believed he could be persuaded to carry a briefcase at least from car to stoop without making fun of it.

Thanks to his acquaintance with Ibi, Dexter was now of opinion that any dog's profession should entail only what he naturally liked to do—run, tug, swim, bark, watch, sniff, dig, listen, search, chase, or carry by jaw—assuming that he was always glad to save lives and otherwise oblige the strangers who fed him. If whitecollar showhounds, redneck hunting lackeys, pheasant-chasers, waterdogs, diggerdogs, harness dogs, or other servile saints chose to abnegate their spiritual autonomy by competing with each other or performing docile antics to amuse strangers, or by fetching like footman to batten strangers' vanity, let the option be enjoyed simply as a canine pastime according to taste, or as an expression of friendship.

For Dexter had come to Ibi's way of thinking, that dogs could substantially contribute to the commonwealth, without doing anything they wouldn't want to do in normal bonded leisure. He was especially sympathetic to the most noble saints, without dignified work or profession, who were allowed little opportunity to employ themselves in the cultural evolution of mammals. It was the frustration of higher symbiosis that turned some of them testy or lazy.

With such sympathy and respect for the species, it was as if Dexter hoped to read about Caleb in Ibi's truthful eyes, or to sense the mingled caresses of others fingertips by feeling his deep ruff. Sir, what scenes have you been privy to? What sin do you bear as scapegoat for my wife?

Within a week or two, by means of heartpounding thought-interrogations, Dexter found out as much as he wished to know about his present equivocal security as a husband; for the reflections in Ibi's sober countenance (from which all playfulness seemed to have disappeared) had redirected contemplation to the conjugal difficulties at the Rectory before Caleb Karcist had come out of the West. Yet conjecture about the origin of his wife's discontentment was even more painful to entertain.

Those bitter years in which his fiery desire had repeatedly extinguished itself in unreciprocated issue at the narthex of her person: feckless detonation at first contact with her equally excited caloric; the success of lust foiled by lust itself, perhaps in subconscious dread of the irreducible reproductive hazard in making love! And those overwrought episodes were not the only disappointments to compound her rightful craving. Later, and worse, when he thought he'd discovered how to manage his impatience, he'd been stricken by the opposite and yet more alarming failure, too shameful to apologize for, save by the pretense of laughing it off with a faint falsified snicker as the symptom of some transient occult indisposition not worth worrying about, as if he was ignorant of her loyal expectations. He couldn't bring himself to speak of either the one disability or the other.

She'd suffered his unaccountable affliction in loyal tactful silence, denied even the possibility of conception, which she'd sworn off many years since but which might have served as her ultimate diversion from nuptial sorrow. He had understood that after her first attempts at courtesy she was too honest and intelligent to mitigate the devastation of her spirit with counterfeit gaiety or otherwise to insult his own honesty and intelligence by passing off her feelings with dismissive words to comfort him. But at last in husky pillow whispers she'd broached the catastrophe he was too proud and cowardly to address—and revealed with a terrifying wail that she was blaming herself! She had convinced herself that the cause of it all was the simple fact that he no longer loved her.

I tried to find words and syntax to tell her how I'd wanted her each time with all my soul, as ready with my love as I'd ever been—only to be helplessly disconnected from my body like a severed puppet. She must have wondered why my love revived, after many months, when I recovered my stamina. That was about the time Deirdre Cotton became Protonotary.

Maybe Gloria was right about my subliminal disaffection. But I've loved her since then, and I'm sure that all along I did, and always shall, for our interrooted years of youthplace and wartime, for the pathos of her childbearing courage and virtue—for the bedrock value of her stalwart character, to this day, as an exemplary educator of everybody's ethos, including mine. I do love Gloria, gratefully—even though I ragingly mourn the incomparable ravenhaired beauty less worthy of my love who must have been intended for me by the stars in the sky.

So I have no right to be outraged by the probability that my sadly mismatched wife is intrigued by the literary pretensions of a circumsized bantam—at least his name sounds Jewish—who would have suited her as snugly as an incestuous brother when she was a pullet. But does she flatter herself that she seems as young to him as she does to veterans of our cohort?

Whatever the facts or delusions, it was time to test himself for the negative capability Doctor Charlemagne was always exalting. Deictic evidence would be odious, the quest of it degrading; and disproof was impossible. So the king refrained from further efforts at palatine counterintelligence. Whenever Caleb's car was by the house he took care not to surprise the suspects, always whistling or making a fuss over Ibi before he showed himself, carefully masking his insights. Not a policy of indifference or tolerance, yet hardly as noble as it might have seemed to Ibi: it was only the need to temporize and the wish to postpone further complications until his overriding desire for Deirdre Cotton was either assuaged or eliminated. He was alternately cowed and angered by the intrusion of this shocking claim upon his personal time. This torpedo attack from landward might even be fatal: but it couldn't be serious enough to halt his culminating mission.

Yet of course it was impossible to isolate extramural love from the history-deep feelings of a responsible pater familias whose palm was ingrained with a lifeline of leadership and pride. If he hadn't been preoccupied with Deirdre he would have been stunned by Gloria's conspiracy against his dominion. But he was forced to acknowledge that his reaction to her putative corruption would depend upon whether or not he was granted the offsetting boon for which he was more zealous than his self-respect—an outcome of the most excruciating uncertainty. He was waiting to become as guilty as his wife.

From that equation he excluded his guilts of the past (which Ibi hadn't been at the Rectory long enough to know of) because as far as he could remember he'd never been moved by love in perpetrating them, and it was to be assumed that an honorable woman like Gloria could be lead into sexual transgression by nothing less than love. The special significance of having deceived her in the past with two of her own seductive friends was suppressed in his reckoning on the grounds that they'd disappointed his sensual expectations. His one considerable infidelity having not yet been consummated, it was further eased in his conscience by the supposition that Gloria had never even heard of the tall dark queen of Tuatha De Danann now behind the scenes at Lilliput Hall, whom he loved more urgently than he could remember ever loving the familiar short-legged Firbolg with stubby fingers who'd captured him before he could walk the world unfettered. The distinction of quality elevated his intention quite above the level of bourgeois peccancy.

Deirdre's refined beauty had lifted his vital spirit from the boring bottomland that his unmysterious little woman nested in. He no longer felt like a big Black Irish Gulliver deprived forever of his own kind, doomed to a life of petty political success as a spoiled priest of architecture, who as a curate had drafted details written specifications and supervised construction under the visible hand of maestro Caspar Aninigo but had never been chosen to design a structure of his own before he was sidetracked from art and fame by the hope of accomplishing something more important in public planning and management. If it hadn't been for Doc Charlemagne to talk with now and then he might have taken to drink like Buck—or run for mayor and abandoned his profession entirely.

I'm sure Gloria thinks I've lost my creative imagination in the toils of politics. She should be glad I'm alive again. My God, I could win Noble Prizes for the new art of ekistical topology [as Doc called it] if I had that lovely woman Waldo Cotton is blessed with in my bed. With me she'd outgrow vulgar possessions. No split-level box with "picture window", lawn, or patio. I'd be building walls and towers, and in defiance of suburban comfort announcing the defeminization of residential architecture! I'd mastermind a new New Uruk block by block: parks, museums, pavilions; docks, canals, railroads, bridges; cathedrals, theaters, pavilions—and we'd never own a house of our own or live in isolation! Deirdre would never bother to change her curtains.

She hardly knows she's not a matrimonial kind of woman; she doesn't admit that her secretarial power over Tom Thumbs and their earldermen is satisfying less than a tenth of her brain: but she would never have kept me from taking the Foreign Service exams. I could have taken her anywhere, and she'd never have harped on having babies.

But now of course she does have children, whom I haven't seen. At this stage I doubt that she thinks about mine. We don't waste time talking about property or family. I'm too old to frankly ruin half a dozen lives. Her secret body is consolation enough for the present—if only once, to dive the depth I've never known! For us hypocrisy and surreption are the better parts of virtue. And I'm not sure she isn't glad to be safely barred from my access by the fence of Waldo Cotton's paddock.

Still, Dexter could not deny his instinctive fear: all that might have been and yet might be was no defense of a man's honor. He thanked his stars that nobody in city government knew Karcist, nor probably in local business. Who would suspect him anyway? —Ah, who but Doc Charlemagne, the city's secondsighted Tiresias? The apprehension that Caleb might unintentionally betray his success (to whatever degree) by some slip of tongue or curl of lip which would escape anyone but Doc was too dreadful to pursue, but it justified the unjust anger of a wronged seigneur. Must he stay home like a lion with his pride, fucking and sleeping, just to keep off other males? Civilization was supposed to make it possible for a man to undertake all his quests in domestic security.

Never before had it occurred to him that he of all men might have cause for jealousy, a disease suffered by incompetents and commoners. Yet he couldn't surely tell whether that was what he felt, or an amalgamation of grief dishonor and shattered vanity. It was not a savagery of rage; but if it wasn't too shallow for anything like that it must be too deep. Certainly it was no mere offense against his dignity. It was more like Sucat's trembling when he'd been taken into the veterinarian's consulting room: an autonomic response to prospective torture and the terror of deracination. For Gloria was of one flesh with himself. After all, he wasn't jealous of Waldo Cotton for sleeping with Deirdre! Would he tolerate the status of a cuckold if absolute secrecy were guaranteed by God Almighty? No: secrecy helped, but not enough.

He began to appraise Gloria for what she was worth. It was true that he found her unresourceful and unimaginative in her intimacies; he'd gradually come to understand that she lacked an ideal wife's voluptuous initiative; and even beatitude never left her languid for long. He'd often complained to himself of having been spanceled to an effusive ingenuous hoyden who didn't know any better than to be seen chewing gum and wasn't delicate enough to keep her sanitary supplies out of sight in the bathroom. Sometimes in public he winced at the undignified shrieks of hilarity with which her voice would suddenly pierce the limits of temperate merriment. Moreover she spent their money impulsively and inefficiently.

Still—seeing that marriage (as the elder Yeats said) is "the enforced study of a fellow creature"—he also trained his binoculars on the skyline, confessing to himself that he'd always taken too much of her excellence for granted, as the flesh of his own flesh. I've simply incorporated her preciousness into the ordinary assumptions of my life, like vested assets, simply because she fell to my lot before I was old enough to appreciate my sheer undeserved luck in being missed by the Gresham's law of mates. By now her ability is no less mine than mine is hers. I too trade upon our strength. We may be two in the nucleus, but our atom is a unity.

As public toiler and Muse, without sparing herself at home, the good mother of my children has educated a whole generation of Dogtown parents teachers and pupils. My friends are few but hers are legion, and they all respect her works. My selfishness is screened by her kindness and generosity. "A capable wife is a husband's crown." it says in the Bible (according to my mother). Gloria may be inconsistent and imprudent, extravagantly unreserved, undiscriminating in her services to all the world: but the things that irritate me are either virtuous or inessential. What husband (even Waldo?) has a wife perfectly gifted in the art of love or totally devoted to the erotic edification that might compensate him for her defects—not to mention his own!

But how he shivered at that word *husband*! Especially "*my* husband"! Nevertheless, *wife* was different. A man should have a loyal wife in his house, whether or not he's equally true to her elsewhere! Like his fathers before him Dexter couldn't help believing that. It seemed to him that men's "disobedient members" (as Augustine called them) made the moral difference, whose "shameless movement" was "proof and penalty of man's rebellion against God".

But unlike his Ulster forefathers, owing to the guilt occupying his own heart, it was only feebly and in passing that Dexter could work himself up to any resolution. Certainly it never occurred to him to avenge his hidden disgrace—which anyway he reasonably still could doubt, notwithstanding all circumstantial intuitions of Gloria's heinous deception. A decently jealous lord should kill his wife's troubadour and serve his heart to her for dinner. When informed of what she's eaten the noble lady must say to her husband "Sir, you have given me such a delicious dish that never shall I partake of another!"—and throw herself out the castle window. God forbid that his wife should die—yet that's what might have happened if the aristocratic Deirdre had been his Countess!

Indeed, jealousy would have been unworthy of Dexter Keith in this case, even as a lord. How ludicrous to be outraged by a probably imagined injury from that scrawny little cuckoo-manqué! One did not challenge enlisted men to duels. "He who is slow to anger is better than the mighty, and he who rules his spirit than he who takes a city." For the present it was necessary only to correct appearances, lest they get out of hand in the neighborhood. So most of the time Dexter's immediate purpose was not retribution for his humiliation, nor even its active curtailment, but expunction of the very concept—without disclosure to any human being that it had ever entered his head.

On the other hand there were occasional intervals of bizarre refluxion in which (forgetting the possibility of contraceptive accident) he almost persuaded himself that he welcomed the hypothesis of his wife's infidelity with this least formidable of rivals. His illicit idea was an exciting anodyne, perhaps auguring the fulfillment of certain adulterated fantasies that had now and then reinflamed his connubial lust. In this series his wife's carnal quintessence was compounded of the cleft exposed in the pelvis of Rodin's truncated dancer and the orectic mouth of a siren mermaid in wanton devotion. He envisioned himself an accessory to her sensual effloration under the spell of a bachelor magician. Perhaps Greek refinement with Hebrew stamina was more affective than Milesian stature for deliquescing the ingrained constraints of a matron's soft marble. With her husband's blessing an honest lady whose modesty had been overcome by unhallowed atonements might be lured into the more forbidden adventures of a lit à trois. Of course his anticipation of her darkly doubled sensations was scarcely serious; the psychical impracticability of even proposing them was too much for his powers of invention: but the notion obediently extended his hypertension—as during the less depraved time of war, on sea duty in hot youth, when he'd had no wish to refrain from tormenting himself, with no prospect of realization, in detailed visualizations of his new bride solitarily tossing on her bed at home in the States like Mother Superior Heloise frankly craving him exclusively.

After all, Caleb had broken no vow of his own. He was only accepting a bachelor's temptation. In another man's house Dexter himself would have risen to a like opportunity. Thus oddly enough it was possible to imagine Caleb as his most intimate friend, lying on the other side of Gloria like a brother Marquesan. During these seizures of fiction, sometimes in his car on the brief drive home from the Hall, he was almost intolerably consumed by thought-experiments on the margin of marriage. For days at a time he was oblivious to his own children, except when called to consider their existence by his family dinner table.

The attraction of his primal imagery was reinforced by Caleb's qualifications as a man of intellect and taste with whom he might also find respite from the toils of sex. Caleb would wear well as a companion at table, and as a comrade on all kinds of travel. At these fanciful moments Caleb appeared in the fevered brain of the Rectory's vicar not as an adversary alienating Gloria's uxoriated senses but as his acolyte in worship of a transfigured woman. Together, in whatever complementary proportion, they could subtend a hypotenuse greater than either of the perpendiculars.

But the romantic figure of Deirdre Cotton was nowhere to be found in such a scene. For that reason more than any other the visions collapsed into commonsense shame as often and as suddenly as they'd possessed his imagination. Nonetheless, having consumed whatever idle meditations were not occupied by the purifying love of Deirdre, they left his heart in a nervously friendly attitude for greeting his tenant, when he happened to see him, as well as his wife. As often as not he covered up the disingenuousness in his voice (or diverted his risen blood) by crouching to tousle the dog arolling on the lawn. In one transitional reverie Dexter was amused to find himself wondering how Ibi would respond to the scalene trigon of dog-lovers. Would the sight sound and scents of that kinematic mingling arouse a bewildered defense of his master—or an equally bewildered urge to supplement the human depravity?

To Ibi himself, when he wasn't basking in personal attention from one of his superiors or another, it seemed that the big chief's obscurely conflicting passions were not to be ignored simply because they librated in a tension that still balanced. The man's very footsteps betrayed suspicion and doubt, or else exotic obsession. But how could a saint warn a stranger so rapt in the conviction of his fledgling success as the gallant of a safely married woman?

But in fact Caleb did notice—or at least in retrospect he later noticed—that Ibi's comportment was undergoing subtle change that appeared to have nothing to do with the kittens. He seemed more excitable; increasingly protective and at the same time appealing for more care; insistingly affectionate. He pressed closer to Caleb's knee at every opportunity, slept closer to the bed. He seemed to be testing all his senses, one against another. But the new development in his personality was most manifest at the sound of police-car or fire-engine sirens, when he laid back his ears, pointed his muzzle at the sky, and howled (though he still paid no more heed to the deep maritime fire whistle from the Traction steam plant than to the raucous blasts of the trains at the Cod Street crossing two blocks away).

It was a prophet's mournful warning of ruination, the signal born with Mr Barebones's fire on the night that household custom changed portentously. His doleful song had mysteriously become a reflexive habit, an unwitting urge and a puzzling outcome. He himself marveled at the mesmerized lacuna in whatever he was doing, wherever he might be, whenever one of the city's flashing kilroys wailed in its chase—before and after it was heard by the strangers around him. Endangering his life on the street, violating the taboos of HEEL, leading the pack in a game, or even trailing a bitch, he'd stop in his tracks and sit in motionless petit mal, tilting his throat to a greater angle than his spine. He never afterwards remembered his experience within the fit, as if the void had been a blink of his eye or a nullification of the interval. And yet he was aware of the diapason in his howl as an expression of sympathy more idoneous to civilization than barking or whining or squealing. Its modulations may have been suggested by the weird vowel exercises that Caleb was sometimes practicing before he abandoned self-improvement as unnecessary.

24

TABLET SEVEN

[*The middle of the night. Same scene as Tablet Six except that the royal seats are replaced by a kettledrum. Its drumstick leans against the wall.*]

Gilgamesh enters, carrying his mounted axe in one hand and the Rector's crosier in the other. [*Goes directly up to the double doors and addresses them.*]

    GILGAMESH   [*Knocks politely with the head of the crosier.*]

Gods, this is Gilgamesh whose name must be pronounced before you engrave the contingent fates of others. I'd like to speak to you, please.

[*Silence. Knocks again.*]

Admit me to your man-made chamber. I wish to make a suggestion. Listen to me. Take a recess, while Enlil absents himself to consummate the city's marriage. Spare yourselves the trouble of casting lots on our behalf. Dice were made for pure amusement. Wasn't it the very purpose of creating mortals to provide yourselves with leisure?

321

[To Audience.] (When the world was young they had to till their own fields and build their own houses. They had no art. The seven cities of Sumer were founded as slave quarters. The walls were made of mud. They should be grateful that I've improved their plantation.)

[To doors.] Can you hear me?

[*Silence. He knocks again, vehemently.*]

The Tablets of Fate are much too long. You could briefly decree our destiny in gross. Why bother with the warps and woofs? No need to endure a tedious night wrangling out the details. Reduce your New Year prescriptions to a few terse gnomes. If other people did as I have done, they'd tell their own story as they went along, day by day, and write the verses for you.

[*Silence again. He knocks less vigorously.*]

Listen, you all: my predecessors here were no more than priests or judges, but I have organized the kind of army you never dreamed of, in your imperial service. Where else has your lugal built a port to heaven? I'm entitled to the courtesy of a little conversation. Even if the riddle means I'm neither god nor man, but stand alone between, I should be consulted at your caucus as the engineer of your own public works.

[He examines the doors minutely, feeling with his fingers, vainly seeking entrance.]

[*Silence. He sounds the drum with his palm.*]

Doors, why do you keep me from the parliament? Open, or I'll break in upon my relatives!

[To audience.] (I should be welcome. They'll never find themselves another such producer. But now, on seven thrones carved from stone and carried here by human beings, the gods deny me audience! I have overestimated their gratitude to the species they like to make love to. Yet there's more imagination in the wits of any weaver's apprentice or halfbaked potter than in all these sagacious mollycoddled majesties. They have the privilege of inscribing those Tablets merely because they happened to come first and live forever. By no other virtue do they ordain the world's history, which we should wrest from destiny when their fingers are loosened at this hiatus of time. It's solely owing to the damned eternity of gods that herds and populations must wait for them to propound the next twelve months. But they should know that for me it's worse than living by chance alone to have chance's part predestined. See how anxiously they bar their ozoned hall when epact-time opens a crack in their firmament!)

[To doors.]

I concede weather and conception for you to fix at random, but we the people should determine what and when to do.

[*He strikes the drum with the crosier. Silence.*]

Just imagine you hadn't called this meeting: Would the seasons have run amok or merged, or men and women felt alike? Would there have been an end to daylight? No insemination of the dates or sprouting of the barley? I think not. You've concealed from your servants their freehold! It's sorry bosses who fear the competence of workers! You've ruled your drones by infixing self-fulfilled prophecies. —I've been a hypocrite to mute my contempt for your control of every hour of the year. What is fate in fact but history abstracted—the gods' intention ex post facto! Anyone who survives me can claim to have prescribed whatever it turns out I will have done. But if Enlil finds it necessary to disintegrate me for sacrilege, then he must confess that last year's Fate has failed!

[Dropping the crosier, he drives his axe through the drum skin. He then throws the axe at the doors, where it sticks by the blade. He retrieves the axe and unsuccessfully pries with its blade at the cracks of the doorway.]

[To audience.]

(Still, if it's nevertheless somehow true they spin and snip all my years, the hour to act is NOW!)

[To doors, which make no sound as he pounds on them with his bare fist. He then chops at them with his axe, in increasing fury, but to no effect.]

Doors of cedar, I know well enough why you stop me! If I interrupt the assembly before new fates are fixed, we'll have our liberty by default! Skittish gods, twitch your ears in consternation! Oh pusillanimous absolutes, eagles cowering in your covert like rabbits! Affect languid indifference if you like, but let me in to kiss your feet! ... Unless you've simply levanted, and left me besieging an empty garrison!

[Throwing down the axe, he snatches up the crosier and, using both hands, beats on the dull doors with the flat of its crook. The crosier breaks in two. He flings away the pieces and starts for the stairs.]

—Oh my god, has Enlil left already? —Then I'll race him to the bride! The ladder down from heaven is there for me to climb! On the feast of feasts I'll break my fast, and live like Engidu by nature! Ah, that deep sweet slippage of the touch, rooting for the flower underground! I'll butter his bun!—unless he beats me to it. Or join the dance, if it's already begun. But what if I find him mounted, undulating naked as a wing-ed snake? He'd better take cover in the upper air—or spend a thunderbolt on me!

Engidu enters, decked in the purple mantle and wearing the IRTH, but tired and discouraged, carrying the Rod and Ring negligently in one hand, his bannerstone (an axe-like weapon) in the other.

[He sniffs the air, sneezes, and only then sees Gilgamesh. Dropping everything, he leaps for the shoulders just as Gilgamesh hears him and whirls around to face him. Engidu misses his grasp and ends up on the stairs above Gilgamesh, looking down upon him.]

GILGAMESH —The circumcised wild man! I forgot about *your* fate! We meet again too soon.

ENGIDU Smell feathers before see you! Not go up there. No man do that! You know?

[He notices the broken crosier and comes down past Gilgamesh to pick up the two pieces.]

GILGAMESH Is Ishtar's lion here to defend her lamb? You're a pretty crafty son of a bitch to sneak up on me like that.

ENGIDU Stick from temple magic-man. You kill my friend, brother from Lady-Amin!

GILGAMESH Great friend: bring poor hagridden stripling to die in woman-cage! You ate acorns and ran with gazelles. A friend would not have brought you to a city's mockery.

ENGIDU People need me kill you later. But you go on tower, I kill you now! New king guard queen from bad bull.

[He menaces Gilgamesh in the attitude of a rampant lion, who only turns away and goes down front. Engidu mistakes the move for a retreat and follows aggressively; yet when Gilgamesh suddenly turns to face him, as if to take his arm, he momentarily shrinks from contact.]

GILGAMESH Maybe the only reason I'll be killing you instead is that when I was young I studied the wisdom in an old man's way of fighting, before I needed it to win. Furthermore, you'll be crapulous with meat and beer. You who were suckled by lions have slain your milk-brothers and eaten the flesh that alive consoled you. Now you're lured by the fame of a women's bazaar. But they haven't told you how terrible it is to face my battle-warp. Norkid says red clouds gather at my head and the air around me glows. Go back to your real friends, now that you know how women taste. I'll open the gate and let you out—right now, before they miss you.

ENGIDU No! All people love me, hate you.

GILGAMESH It's galling to be disputed by a foundling creature, misguided into vice, swaggering at a woman's apron string, strutting in front of lily-livered caterers. Go back to the steppes, where strife and love are artless, brother ape.

[Roused by what he takes to be an insult, Engidu casts off his mantle and springs to attack. Gilgamesh readily joins the fight, which is like a dance punctuated by the lightning movements of real combat. Gilgamesh is the boxer, avoiding Engidu's grasping blows with a sophisticated guard and precise footwork while annoying him with

ENGIDU Two times called me monkey, kinfolk I like not. Ugh! Other day I killed king of animals. Now kill you!

light jabs. At first Engidu fights like a baffled wrestler, as if the
frustration is about to enrage him to his own peril; but gradually and
intelligently he begins to imitate Gilgamesh, though occasionally
still throwing great straightarm haymakers that are deftly parried or
ducked. The fight is by no means ridiculously one-sided, but
Gilgamesh makes no attempt to land heavy punches. With growing
admiration, cooled off, Engidu studies Gilgamesh's style more and
more carefully, but the result is a mirror-imitation in which he leads
with his right to oppose a left, etc. . . .]

[*They both laugh.*]

I grab air!

Suddenly, almost
GILGAMESH
treacherously with a
weird but truncated
battle-cry,
**Gilgamesh knocks
Engidu flat** with a
right hook and
**bounds up the
stairs out of sight.**

When you're disappointed I can see why they love you.
May your tender eyes cease to show the suffering of life's
love while life is still alive! —As for me, I'm already so
accursed that I'd be drowned if I took notice of maledic-
tions. So if I am day and she is night, why not fly as a
white raven before I'm dead?

ENGIDU

[*Silence.*]

[For half a minute
he lies without
movement staring
up at the sky; then
speaks with a new
voice, though still
with a slight
accent. He
suddenly sits up,
straight from the
waist, and begins to
finger the IRTH on his chest. With his head high, still looking
straight ahead, he rises to his knees; but then his eye wanders to
Gilgamesh's axe, which he thereupon picks up to examine as he goes
to sit in the lotus position at the bottom of the stairs.]
Eber enters
hurriedly.

Now I see how people are! They laughed at my ignorance
when they made me think he lived in fear of wilderness.
They'll cheer him when he finally lays me low. Too late
I'm smitten with the city's bravest scent. Compared to
him, except for her who should have been his mate, the
city is seven thousand stinks. Before his nostrils flared the
fight was over, and only once did the hand that felled me
move; but I felt the power of something in his head not to
be learned from priest or woman.

EBER
[Preoccupied with
worry, his surprise
drops into weary
irony.]

Oh, the little child that's come to lead us. Homesick? The
fleshmonger's still got pots galore for you to dip. The duties of a human stud don't end so soon. —Ah, I see: it's
guarding the tower from drunks. Is it jealous already? Or
is this the way a thing-king prays?

ENGIDU
[With a
wan smile.]

Yes, oh priest-of-treasury, I am thin-king about how to tell
my second birth. In the Dreamtime, invented sounds were
my only words: names I sang for all things but myself: no
more than that. Then Lil-Amin tutored me the pith of
speech. But not enough to grasp deceit. Now I have begun

	to see that people can say untruth with the other meaning in each word to make the sound unmean itself.
EBER [Kindly, taking interest.]	Sometimes in Sumer there are meanings more than two, and no one can guess by the opposite of what is said. I can see you're not just a dumb gorilla avaricious for celebrity.
ENGIDU [In reverie.]	I did not name the creature you say I'm not: which means I am! Before she dressed me, I was like the bandar-log, showing all my wants and itches.
EBER [With divided attention, his eyes searching everywhere.]	Now that you know your shame, the likeness disappears. Well clothed unbelievers are more like apes than you are: not God's own creatures but golems formed by sarcastic words, civil for ambition only.
ENGIDU	You too are different. Tell me that God's name.
EBER [With a marveling glance at Engidu.]	Are you a second Adam, that you name the beasts and seek the name of God?
ENGIDU [Musing.]	Gilgamesh is like a god. By whatever light remains to me I'll be walking in his shadow. For him will I eat meat and drink beer, or go hungry.
EBER [Puzzled, until he notices the broken crosier.]	What's this new note in you already? He'll kill you, unless you kill him—if you don't run away. Yes, that's it: go right now! —Oi, oi weh! You've killed the priest!
ENGIDU	No. He did. Then spared me.
EBER [Violently distraught, he tries to raise Engidu to his feet.]	O my God, this is the end of us all! The people will riot. —Quick, which way did he go? —But first we've got to find my sons! My sons are the future, not Gilgamesh. History goes with my nation. Do you understand that this city is not the whole world? Shaddai calls upon you!
ENGIDU [Calmly.]	I do not know your sons. Gilgamesh went up there. If Enlil rivets them both with a shaft of lightning, I'll be left to play the fool alone. To think ahead hurts more than a leg torn off. Is the debt for meat and beer this fear of what is not yet but still may come?
EBER [Tearing his hair, **Eber runs off.**]	Gilgamesh is dead! I am dead! My sons are dead! —But where's the captain? Maybe he can get us out alive!
ENGIDU	My last sleep. The lion did not sleep in fear before I murdered him.

[Lies down on his side like a child and goes to sleep.]
Norkid enters briskly, fully armed. [Engidu, instantly wakened, rolls over onto his stomach, prepared to spring in any direction.]

NORKID
[Stopping short.]

Too much gallantry, Your Highness? Or were your vital fluids dried up by irony? You're doing your devotions all alone. I thought the divinities here were nothing but venereal. Some might think the people's champion has a rotten gourd; but I'd say you're sulking like a chimpanzee.

ENGIDU
[Leaping to his feet. Norkid recoils,

Why does everyone think of simians when they look at me?

NORKID
drawing his sword; but, seeing Gilgamesh's axe, he picks it up.]

Because you're a natural. Your heart is on your face. —But I've got to find my men and rip them from their screwholes. There's trouble in the air. —What's this!!??

ENGIDU

His hawk. He did not use it on me.

NORKID
[Attacks Engidu in cold rage. Engidu catches his wrist

If you've killed Gilgamesh, I'll shed your bones.! If there's no more ground to stand on, I'll pull the whole world down to hell!

ENGIDU
and immobilizes his sword-arm.

It's the ayatollah. Gilgamesh killed *him*. Then went up those stairs.

Engidu displays the broken crosier and releases Norkid.]

NORKID
[Laughs.]

He's a fucking genius at outrage! What more sacrilegious compound of desecrations could even be conceived by these bottomlanders? We'll be smothered by the mob when this gets out. I fancy you expect to lead the retribution.

ENGIDU

He let me live! Why did he not kill me?

NORKID
[Stares at Engidu; then paces up and down thoughtfully as Engidu slowly shakes his head.]

He saved you for the proper time. But the people won't spare either of you when they find things gone awry. — Why don't you get out of here? Vamoose! It's your last chance. They pamper monkeys in Egypt. —Where the hell are those amaranthine cocksmen of mine? —Shit piss and corruption, where's even Eber and his men? —All right then, if you want to die with us, get off your ass and hold these stairs until I get back with a few necessaries. The tower is our citadel.

Norkid runs off.

ENGIDU
[Rises. Takes up his bannerstone. Hesitates. Puts the mantle back on. Lies down to sleep.]

Even the soldier tells me to run away. Which way is Egypt? —But no: if Gilgamesh is struck dead by her god, it's for me to inherit his statecraft. I think a black boy is capable of city-lore. For his name's sake I forswear the simplicity of escape.

Optimates hurry in, ineptly armed and out of breath. [One drags a large fish net. They are hushed in awe of the gods, and steer clear of the doors.]

OPTIMATE 1 [Optimate 2 notices the broken crosier.] **Rector enters,** searching.	Engidu! The khan has broken loose! Help us catch him!
OPTIMATE 2	[*Screams.*] The Rector's crosier!
RECTOR [Finds the pieces of the crosier. Discovers Gilgamesh's axe. Engidu sits up in amazement.]	Enkidu! What are you doing here? I'm looking for my staff. —There it is! But broken in two! —You besotted puppet, it's a curse on you to touch it even! —Oh, now I see! Of course it was Giszax that would insult my office, and you were forced to kill him on the spot! But where's his body?
ENGIDU [To Optimates.]	I thought he killed you! [*Pause.*] —Now you know I'm less than he. No one can take his place. —Do you expect to truss him up like a fish?
RECTOR [Engidu points falsely.] **Rector runs off,** carrying the axe.	Giszax has tamed this tom cat. —Well, I'll do the job. Which way did he go? —Father Enlil, teach me a dance I was not born to learn. I'll chop down that architect!
OPTIMATE 1	This is what comes of tampering with liturgy.
OPTIMATE 2 Dropping all equipment, **Optimates run off** in opposite direction.	The Rector's magic isn't strong enough. Even our godsend can't stand up against the sleepless mountain bull!
ENGIDU [Shifts to a position clear of the stairs and lies flat on his back, drowsily fingering the IRTH again.] Engidu goes to sleep as **Gilgamesh slowly comes down the stairs** without seeing him, with Enlil's mask in his hand.	I could smell danger over the horizon, but when she opened up her robe, I looked. When I sat at her feet, I watched the teeth between her lips. But I did not understand. You are like a lion, she sang to me: strong and swift, a lord for women; let me take you to the house of Inanna, to the cloud-gathering peak of Uruk, where the loveless one, wise and preeminent, keeps his own counsel. Come, she said, if in your belly you crave a wife, if in your heart you long for a friend: if such desires move you. From the beginning she said such words with other meaning than she taught. But it will be bitter to sleep the longest sleep without her. . . .

GILGAMESH Praise be to Enlil for such sweet annealment. She perfected the enclosure. I felt her feeling me. There's a sea-change in my bones. But still no conversion deep enough for sleep. How was I to reach her mind, merely on acquaintance, keeping silence incognito? I still don't know her thoughts, let alone her vision working at the loom.

[He catches sight of Engidu, who awakens and looks

—Engidu! I told you to go away! Why die by the calendar?

ENGIDU
at Gilgamesh without moving.]

Now I know what words mean. Next time we fight I'll have memory to help me.

GILGAMESH I've just begun to cultivate the faculty of wordlessness that you renounce. Don't despise the instinct not to think in action. If you remember Lil-Amin's conduct in the dark, tell me what I wonder: Of course she knows that as soon as love is spent its promises renew themselves; but would she expect a beatific repetition before her other senses are restored? Will the skill to deceive be born of self-deception? . . . When Enlil finds he's wearing horns, I'll need your right hand to aid my war with heaven. If she's still breathing, which side will she be with?

[Laughs.]

ENGIDU When she and I made jointure, it was you she wished to think it was, deceiving herself on purpose. Euoi, euoi! But she taught me speech sincerely, speaking of your fame as if you called for my friendship.

GILGAMESH Yet I am guilty of your meat and beer. If I live, that sin will be expiated. —Go back to sleep. I'd be caught asleep myself right now if I were more than only one-third human.

ENGIDU I've had sleep enough for one who isn't less than two-thirds brute.

GILGAMESH Then join your share of humanity to mine! Let's double the manhood of this kingship! Multiply its liberty by two! The remaining necessity will be divided between law and nature, half-and-half. Let Ishtar have her sway over the things we do like other males; but with the guts of a twofold man we'll alter fate as if we wrote it! Pray share my follies!

[Engidu jumps up and finds the Rod and Ring, handing one to Gilgamesh, keeping the other. They dance.]

—I'll take the Rod. You take the Ring!

ENGIDU   The lion will serve the eagle, and share his prey. I can run like the wind, and smell water in a sea of sand.

GILGAMESH   I'll abandon my studio for the art of action, and lead the way to labyrinths; but you go first in reducing Amazons to kitties. Like wind we'll roam the world for stories, and leave this kingship to the queen!

ENGIDU
[Engidu stops dancing.]   But the child! Would you leave the child to that priest?

GILGAMESH   Child? What child?

ENGIDU   The child that has been started.

GILGAMESH   [*Pause.*] You say I've blurted out an heir? Me, a copyist in sculpture? —Is seed entrapped by honey? Passion made me clean forget! Ishtar has us by the orchids: she makes sure the jewel of games is played for stakes. Did the gods themselves decree this rape to make me ante up. —But wait, maybe there won't be a brat! Isn't it a game of odds?

ENGIDU   Not on Enlil's wedding night. I think he'll take title.

GILGAMESH   By god, he can't claim my by-blow! I'll tell the world what's mine! No more his than the Rector's! My miscreant won't be circumcised and raised for stud! He was alloyed with the rarest artist. It was I, not Enlil, that melted her casting.

ENGIDU   But if he saw you, no childbirth after all: no woman will be walking down these stairs! He may have already scorned the city's oblate with his vengeance. Divine wrath, not beatitude, has been her second visitation!

GILGAMESH
[Casts about for his axe without success. Takes up Engidu's bannerstone and starts for the stairs.]   Then I'll rip my tadpole from her womb, as prematurely planted, and raise him to wrest that lethal fire from the lord high god. —Where's my axe? . . . I'll have to use your throwing stone for surgery. —Yet perhaps it's not too late! Enlil may be slow in raising his voltage. Come on! In a god-fight I'd like to have my foster-brother watching!

ENGIDU
[Restrains Gilgamesh.]   But now suppose the opposite. It's more likely that he's blind with rut. He'll take her second offering as the first and only. Let the eucharist run its course, without your death, or any other. —Besides, I may be the sire.

GILGAMESH   [*Silence, followed by a burst of laughter.*]

I forgot that too! Everywhere we turn, your intuition outreasons mine. —You want a cub? Very well, you've jumped my claim in advance! We'll make the birthright yours. If he's born circumcised, the priest can't skin him alive.

ENGIDU
[Smiles.]

He'll look half baboon!

GILGAMESH

Your whelp will be the recognized successor. We'll stay to see him through, and have her rear him as a bard, memorizing all the feats of kingship.

ENGIDU

There can't be two of us.

GILGAMESH

We've already settled that. You're the father.

ENGIDU

Two kings, I mean.

GILGAMESH
[With bannerstone in hand, he repeats the movements of Tablet 2. Engidu responds in kind, tossing and whirling the IRTH.]

Why not? Our will is free. Tomorrow's combat will be a double dance of the Isorectotetrahedron. Two points to hew each edge! We can double our talent for autonomy by halving the burden. Waiting for baby, the people will have you to love all the while I'm making them breed Euphrates to the Tigris! Together, back to back, we can face both ways and never be surprised!

ENGIDU

With me to trust, you can sleep at last!

GILGAMESH

No, sleeping's still your job. You can sleep for two, and store it up like a lazy lion, for us both to draw on whenever we want to prolong our zest. Be my dreamer too. You dreamt a world of peace before Lil-Amin awoke you. But if I were now to sleep, Ishtar would cackle to high heaven that it was proof I'd been kept awake for seven years by lack of love.

Eber enters,
in woeful
EBER
exhaustion,
wailing, rending
his garments, and
tearing his hair.

Gilgamesh! —I find you too late already. —I wish it was my sons that's still alive instead of you. The apples of my eye all dead! My tribes all lost at once for good! —I'm too old to make any more baby boys for this history.

GILGAMESH
[Alarmed.]

Who killed them? How do you know they're dead?

EBER
[More calmly.]

I know nothing else. I can't find the soldiers either. I can't find anyone. This is such a hateful night that not even rumors reach my ear. —Help the Lord avenge my sons!

GILGAMESH
[Pats Eber on the back.]

Perhaps vengeance is unnecessary, dear man. First Engidu and I will find them, dead or alive.

GILGAMESH & ENGIDU
Singing, Gilgamesh and Engidu go off arm in arm, with bannerstone and IRTH.

Questing to and fro,
We'll count the trees
And search the seas
As far as camels go!

EBER
Norkid enters from the opposite side, followed at a

Captain! Where are the troops already? Hurry—my boys, your friends! May God lengthen your years, if you will only help!

NORKID
distance by the straggling Troopers, still buckling on their equipment.

Here's the dawn patrol. They must have ended their lubricities. —Fall in, funnyboneses! Shake a leg! Strawberries and cream are too rich for your blood. Tomorrow cherries will be back in season. Dress it up, old vets! The Traders are missing. Their governor thinks they were ambushed on their way to the tents.

TROOPERS
[Chuckling, giggling, and collapsing with laughter.]

—Waylaid is the word, wouldn't you say, boys?
—They were still going strong when you routed us out. I've got to take my hat off to them. Nothing leaches the starch out of those merrymaking stags.
—Of course they only drank a thimbleful, compared to us. But, next to those comedians, we're pikers when it comes to song and dance. Laugh? I thought I'd split a gut!
—The girls did.

EBER
[Shrieking.]

Girls! What girls? Where?

TROOPER 1
[Pointing the way they'd come.]

Don't worry, sir. Nothing but a little New Year's symposium. Beer, widows, and woodwinds. We had for guests some nuns.

EBER

You lie, goyim. Whoring! My sons?

NORKID

It's an unoriginal sin.

EBER
Eber runs off to find his sons.

Oi, oi, my polluted seed! The serpent has struck at my stem!

TROOPERS
[Breaking rank, they fall into a staggering shuffle and finish up on the ground sprawling with laughter.]

We the old boonfellows of the cup and the lance
—offered those oddfellows a memorable chance
—to share as our moonfellows in triangular dance,
—which made us all bedfellows in Messpot romance.!

Gilgamesh and Engidu return.

[Gilgamesh carries the fire-stick and drill, like a small bow and arrow; Engidu again wears the IRTH on his chest and holds the bannerstone. Norkid intercepts Gilgamesh at the

NORKID
side and continues to explain the situation sotto voce, both laughing.]

The lost have been found, in flagrante delicto, and the story is an old one. The Widows think our Traders worth their salt.

Widows enter, beating cymbals, **with Traders** playing recorders, in a reeling snakedance, **trailed by Eber**, who is moaning and sprinkling his head with handfuls of ashes from his suspended skirts. As **Rector also enters**, still carrying Gilgamesh's axe, the Troopers miraculously revive and join the dance. **Optimates timidly reappear**, fascinated, but remain at the side.

[The Rector abstractedly and vainly thumps for order with the butt of the axe. Then, at the horror of seeing Gilgamesh and Engidu in amity together, he rushes

RECTOR
at them with axe upraised. With the bow Gilgamesh blocks his attack and grabs away the axe, sending him backwards across the stage, right

Perfidious traitor! Giszax clinches his grip on the city's liver, and you fawn like a cur. Infidel! You have betrayed the people of your own creator. Salt will blight her fields; wild goats will crop her barley down to the sand. Heaven again will close. May I never speak again if I don't fix reprisal as my highest joy! Blessed shall he be who dashes the brains of your children in our marketplace!

through the dancers, so that he ends up on his knees, near the foot of the stairs, practically out of sight. This violence puts a stop to the dance, and all the dancers draw back to the right in motionless silence facing the double doors, except for the Troopers, who have sat down with exhaustion in the same place, amused at their own weakness, before realizing what goes on. The Widows thus lean against the Traders and rest their hands on the heads or shoulders of the Troopers. Throwing away the bow, Gilgamesh hands Engidu the recaptured axe and keeps the bannerstone. Together they work on the doors and succeed

GILGAMESH
in prying them open, only to reveal a perfectly blank black hole. Each with his weapon in one hand, with the

Let's spring this cage! —Gods, we've come to set you free! Are you staring wildly at each other as I say it? Gilgamesh and Engidu are coming to get the Tablets of Fate! Beware the mortal blacksmiths: Engidu and Gilgamesh are about to strike off chains. Drop the soapstones of destiny!

ENGIDU Gilgadu on the warpath!

other they lob the Rod and Ring into the blackness like grenades.]

Gilgamesh and Engidu disappear into the void. After an extended motionless silence, they reappear like pranksters fleeing with laughter, each carrying a Tablet, which they fling down and smash

GILGAMESH Our dance of the twin tomahawk!

ENGIDU   I smell the feathers of an Iso-recto-tetra-hawk!

with their axes in a fast exultant version of the IRTH Dance.
[Carried for a moment by the enthusiasm of the revived Troopers (now on their feet), the other dancers surge forward, excited and confused.]

GILGAMESH   Ye gods that blow like the wind, you won't forget that Gilgamesh was here. The world is young again! Let us no longer construe each other's words. —My friends, it's not worthy of a pair of kings to dwell shrewdly domesticated in this delta of marshes. —Engidu, let's go find a cedar grove with a granite quarry, and fetch the young prince a lifetime heap of stone and timber! An axe to cut, an axe to hew!

[He rips the IRTH from Engidu's neck and slings it toward the void, but it goes awry up the stairs.]

ENGIDU   A blade for flesh, a blade for bone!

Engidu and Gilgamesh dance off, followed by the Troopers, Norkid, Traders, and Eber, just as **Lil-Amin enters**, descending the stairs in time to catch the IRTH.
[The Urukians remaining, following the trajectory of the IRTH, turn to face Lil-Amin on the stairs. The Rector is exposed kneeling abjectly in her path, whom she blesses in passing with a vague motion of her left

LIL-AMIN   Vandals cannot disconcert our gods. Enlil is our father, and Enlil bides his time. The hour of Giszax is not yet come, but his felling is assured. For maiming the body of our motherland he shall be leveled to the dust, for insulting the gods of Sumer in the very house of Inanna, for suborning the consort she sent me.

hand. Smiling to herself, she hangs the IRTH around her neck. As her people watch in awed silence, she closes and fastens the doors like a serenely abstracted housewife.
All the while she is seen to be **growing pregnant**.
She turns to the Rector.]

    —Lift up your heart: the sacrifice was full, perfect, and sufficient. Enlil finds me blameless, and the anger of heaven will not fall upon you.

RECTOR   Save for strangers, all offences pardoned. Manifold sin and wickedness is remitted.

[Huskily, in customary form.]

WIDOWS & OPTIMATES   *Amen.*

LIL-AMIN   Like my mothers before me, I have been received into the blessed company of god's faithful brides, and I am absolved of mortal love by the beatitude of divine atonement. —It's still dark down here. Up on high, when I opened my eyes to the Morning Star, I saw dawn arising from far mountains.

WIDOW 1   We tried to feel your holy mystery: your horrified tremors, the cold breath of Enlil, his unknown weight and shape.

LIL-AMIN   Sisters, you may well believe that my wedding night began in the quaking fear you have imagined: clammy snake, searing dragon, clawing griffin; crucifixed impalement, fatal agony—anything but what we pray for. Yet, as Enlil's claim was not denied, neither was my hope. His pinions rocked the stars above, yet beat as softly as an adoring swan's, and the blessing was impressed that inspired in me a new art—not of the weaver but of what is woven! Finally, in sixth or seventh heaven, festooned with a procession of beatitudes, the galaxy grew vague. . . .

[Finding the firebow and drill, with solemn playfulness she takes a shot in the direction Gilgamesh has taken. When the stick falls ludicrously short, she laughs.]

—I could lure a man with this harp!

—He found my work was good, for after he drew back he did not leave me emptied of plenitude, but returned to the blessing in fresh tempo. That's how the incubus of private love is exorcised! Not once along the Milky Way did the name of Giszax halt my breath—though I shall live out my life as his spinster.

[Pats her belly.]

—The child I carry is his god-daughter. She shall be empress of all the Sea-Lands. When I'm a crone at my tapestry, behind the altar, I'll still be teaching her what I have studied. Her works will put to shame the works of Giszax!

[To the Rector.]

—It will take more than two king-bees to deprive this land of honeycombs. Tell the people that this year's sap and seed will flow. Children will come to birth, and there will be strength to bring them forth. Not in vain did I loosen my knees to the bridegroom and arch my throat, and press my eyelids closed, as I lifted up my spine to god. The bride you offered was not glorified in vain!

WIDOWS   *Softly run Euphrates*
Until we end this song.

Lil-Amin goes out, followed by Widows and Optimates. The Rector stands watching until they are out of sight; then **leaves** oppositely, ending the play.

25
THE
KEITH
FAMILY

*I*bi was delighted to be invited to dinner as Caleb's companion, though only to watch. The savory smells that had greeted him from the lady's kitchen long before he led his master down from the attic were no less salivant after eating to satisfaction from his Spartan rations upstairs. But Caleb never fed him from the table and he'd learned to behave like a fasting saint at the meals of strangers, except when officially commanded to accept their holiday offerings like a gracious mendicant.

He began by sitting decorously at various precatory distances behind and between different pairs of individuals, ears and eyes in alert synergic focus upon the most attractive objects of his nose, following the juiciest slices with quivering nostrils. But when the first line of discipline showed no sign of weakness he let up on his silent importunity, at least by lying down at a spot of tactical vantage in the patient hope of gathering crumbs from the lords' table after they'd had their fill. It took them an unconscionable length of time to feed themselves, perhaps five times as long as Caleb eating alone.

Yet even Mr and Mrs Keith, experienced disciplinarians, found it difficult to observe the civilized rule against sentimental charity by ignoring his heartbreakingly handsome appeal. And Caleb himself, as he fed his own face with a guilty sense of battening on Levitical privilege, recognized this feast as an exceptionally carnivorous temptation, like an Old Testament sacrifice, which might excuse a certain degree of hieratic generosity; but he never quite brought himself to say so to the Keiths, despite the almost irresistible supplication in Ibi's unremitting attention, especially when his name was being bandied in the most flattering admiration. Certainly Ibi's selfcontrol put to shame the tolerable willpower of his boss.

Without the nerve to mention the author of this injustice, or to look Caleb in the face, both the children murmured about the rule's cruelty and covertly prepared to defy it when nobody but Ibi was looking. They were confident that he would need no coaching to quietly catch up any collops of roast lamb slyly tossed in his direction from beneath the skirt of the tablecloth.

"If Ibi's a Viking Shepherd," Robert asked at large, "doesn't that mean he should be taking care of sheep?"

"Well he's doing that right now, isn't he?" his sister retorted.

"Where did the Vikings raise sheep? I thought they just stole them."

"Right. That's when the dogs came to help." said his father, whetting the family cutlass against its matching poniard with the unostentatious flourish of an efficient host.

"Help take them or help keep them? In school we read about some sheepdogs brought up with lambs. They think they're sheep, and fight off the wolves."

"Then they couldn't be Viking Shepherds." said his mother, darkening the kitchen doorway with a heavy platter in both hands. "Our sheepdogs don't come from the sheep; they come from wolves. They aren't at bit confused about their identity. The wild wolves are their rivals for possession of the sheep."

"Then why aren't they called Viking Wolfhounds?" Robert complained.

Ibi found that in spite of all the lip service any traffic in contraband mutton was checked by the vigilant father and mother, enforcing the austere code of their table guest. Yet there really was no need to put his sympathizers to the test, at risk of his expulsion from the house, for he was promised all the scraps when high table was cleared away; so after some minutes, taking the steward at her word, and weary of all the talk that yielded no morsel, Ibi repaired to the living room rug, out of sight, trusting to his ears and nose as monitors.

The kittens had been sealed off in the front room where their puny antics could be ignored, but from elevated felixity in an easy chair the sinner O'Hair, who'd already partaken of his delicacies as much as he cared to (after loudly waving his tail around the kitchen and almost tripping up the cook), was a supercilious witness of the saint's docile humility, insidiously hinting at the canard that of all the oppressed species Ibi's alone had sold its soul to humanity. The dog's feeble rejoinder to that charge was the local maxim that it took a saint to befriend a stranger. But the cat and dog were both glad enough of each other's company while awaiting an end to the meaningless cackle from the selfindulgent godlings in the other room. In vain, once or twice, at the mention of his name, Ibi rose to see if he was wanted. O'Hair, paws tucked under chest, twitched his whiskers in condescension to the clumsy unselfrespecting dog for fawning like a fishpier beggar and flapping his pennate tail like a luffed mainsail in a gale of wind.

"I wish you could see Ibi when you drive off without him!" Gloria was saying to her lover in public, with the perfectly affected tone of an unceremonious hostess, while everyone was waiting for the Cid (as Doc called Caleb's host) to finish carving mutton and passing plates. They were all twice as hungry as Ibi, but too polite to lick their lips in anticipation. "At first he sits still, staring down toward the crossing after your car's out of sight, as if wondering how he'd failed to make you understand. But in a minute or two he notices some scent in the air and it begins to divert him from his thoughts. He starts to glance away, but only very quickly, still poised in his faithful position; but then more and more frequently. Suddenly he gets up and lopes off on a beeline in the opposite direction, as if he'd visualized the gravestone he decided to start with!"

"Sounds like you watching Dad go to work, before you got your job at the Library." Robert blurted out, making Gloria blush.

"Are you going to write that up for your *Lives of the Saints?*" Deirdre quizzed, referring to one of her mother's chronic projects. In "outreach" to the teachers of the city (some of them her erstwhile colleagues) Gloria was hoping to inspire in students of all ages the discovery or creation of local cynographies and sacred anecdotes. She had persuaded the Head Librarian to allow her to gather such local lore around a nucleus of published volumes by Jack London, Rudyard Kipling, Miguel Cervantes, and other students of bestiary, cross-indexed on special 3by5 cards, instituting a special section of shelves and file cabinets, not unlike the collection she'd established for the Great Depression.

"Don't be satirical, Dee." said the father without looking up from his task. "There are more things in heaven and earth than dreamt of in your—"

"—*devilvision*!" his son chimed in, mocking the cautionary formula of his otherwise tolerant parents.

"But *you* always call her the Collector of Customs, Daddy!" cried the daughter.

"That's not ridicule." the father replied. "It's respectful admiration. Redburn himself, and Natty Hawhaw too, they both worked for Customs."

"I'm guilty of not reading to Ibi often enough." Caleb interrupted irenically. At this point Ibi returned from one of his looks at the feast to lie again in the shadow of O'Hair, faintly disgusted at the profitless part he was playing in the conversation. Ignoring him in person, these people took his name in vain.

"You may be remiss in some of your duty," the carver reassured Caleb, "but you're the best teacher in town. I never could train our good old Sooky to heel."

"Better than Wagner too." said Gloria. "In *Doctor Faustus* he tells the servant to fix his eye diagonally upon the *right* heel of his leader. Until I saw Ibi walking with Caleb I never realized how subtle Marlowe was in showing up the presumptuous folly of graduate students!" Her shrill cachinnation set in relief the sobriety of her children.

"Oh *Mother*!" Deirdre burst out. "Right in front of a guest! Even Miss Johnson wouldn't know what you're talking about. I hope you won't say things like that to her on Parent-Teacher's Night. It's bad enough having Daddy's name in the paper all the time! And this house looks like laundry hanging out to dry. The whole city drives by here all the time! It would be so nice to have an *in*conspicuous family!"

"The kids at school say Ma knows everybody's secrets because she handles Interlibrary *Loans*!" said Robert. "What are those, anyway?"

Dexter was addressing his daughter: "You should be glad you don't live in South Swindon, Montvert! At your age Glory was damned glad when the Feds financed telephone wires out to her dead-end valley, even though everyone listened in on the party line. But I never dared call her up." This sally silenced Deedee for a while, who was always complaining about the limitations of her privacy on the family's single telephone, which she was accused of hogging.

"You'd be surprised how few of the people in Dogtown know who we are." her father added. "This really is a city." But in truth he'd often wished that he himself was not so awkwardly prominent. For purposes of either survival or adventure it was sometimes advantageous to be as disarming and overlooked as his tenant.

When the chief himself finished carving and was free to eat he glanced around at all the busy faces. In Caleb's honor the children were on their good behavior, but their preceptors were less pedantic about merely traditional aspects of their table manners than was Caleb about Ibi's decorum.

The younger child was more openhearted than his sister, and not so chary of betraying his curiosities. Without waiting for an answer to his own question about the mother's job he was attracted to the vaguer subject of the paternal past: "But Dad, wasn't Sheffield a small town too?"

"Much smaller than this one, what geographers call an 'industrial village', but a pretty important one internationally, for its machine tools. When we were about as old as you are Glory and I went to the same consolidated school, but she was a hillbilly who still spoke a sort of Elizabethan English, sent to our 'academy' every day from the strung-out hardship village where there was no electricity or plumbing and they didn't have tractors. I lived in civilized townland to the east; but where she came from, at least in the winter, it was more like what Crevecoeur described a hundred and eighty years ago than country life nowadays. In those days they did have kilroys, but no bulldozers or chain saws. Don't you remember my brown house I pointed out near the highway bridge?"

"For God's sake, Rob," shrieked Deedee in exasperation, "he's made us look at it a hundred times! He and Ma still call it a highway!" Everyone but Caleb knew that the factor of her exaggeration was not significantly less than ten to the second power.

"That was a long time ago! I get all those 'Verty places mixed up. But I remember Grandma's white farm house near the mill pond in Swindon. There was an old ice house full of soggy sawdust. I'd never go so far to school, but I wouldn't mind living in a place like that, with all the woods and mountains around. I'd get a dog like Ibi and camp out in the summer. I don't care about growing vegetables."

"We didn't grow many vegetables." Gloria said. "Potatoes mostly, and some corn. Hay was the only important crop."

"Just for cows!"

"We lived off those dear old cows. But we still had a team of horses too, don't forget."

"How could we ever forget your icky barn, Mother? It's all you ever talk about!" Deedee protested. *"Hay is for horses—and better for cows!"* she jeered in childish singsong. "Hay foot, straw foot! Gee and Haw! Not to mention squaredancing! *Choose your partners for a plain quadrille!"* She cruelly burlesqued her mother's cherished memories. "Country hicks had to have a teacher yelling at them what to do, every step of the dance, year after year, like little Brownies and Cub Scouts! Ugh! *Swing your partners*, hayseeds one and all! They were always oldfashioned, if you ask me! They thought they were whirling dervishes or something."

"Su'fis spin all by themselves, on one axis." Caleb objected, speaking boldly to Deirdre Keith for the first time, in defense of himself as well as his paramour. "Two people can't keep their toes in the same spot. It takes three times the skill to swing around two rotating points like an eccentric binary star—as hard to analyze as a four-legged dog's trot!"

"That gives me an idea!" Gloria exclaimed. "Next year let's ask Cora to choreograph a piece with all the dancers on the head of one pin, exactly the opposite of her Rock Dance. —No, on one grain of sand! Our own kind of sand-dance, not like what the Atlindus do, smoking drugs, out in Pimeria!"

"Oh Ma, it's *sun*-dance they did!" cried Rob. "We learned that in the fourth grade!"

"Maybe I'm thinking of sand-painting."

"That's better!" Dexter said. "Didn't you once tell me the Atlindus who summered here did sand-painting on Namauche Beach? That artwork couldn't have outlasted the tide—but that's long enough for the endurance of our spectators. Do you think Cora would be interested in flattening the Hoofers into a Beach Dance?"

Rob was demonstratively amused by his father's topographic jest, but Gloria was still developing her theme. "At the bottom of the sea Hamlet's mill is always grinding rocks into sand. Someday the rocks will be no more. What better theme for a six-minute dance?"

The historian's eschatology brought conversation to a cusp; the Cid modestly reverted. "Well, Ibi and O'Hair seem to be the only ones in this house who don't have any memories of Montvert. I recall that I was pretty maladroit at squaredancing."

"You were dexterous at everything!" his wife contradicted, "Too tall for most of us in a small dance hall—that's all!"

"I was jealous when the other guys swung my Little Morning Glory. I once got in a fight over her with Billy Peen the Galway blacksmith, strongest man in Swindon County!"

"Daddy, you never told us—!" Deedee remonstrated, in romantic awe.

"Dee, that was only after we were engaged." her mother broke in. (Both these parents were as adept as any at heading off uncomfortable table-talk.) "By then we were old enough for a little excitement on Saturday night. Before that, until I got out of the one-room South Swindon school, there wasn't any social life at all except church suppers, especially in winter. You would've gone crazy. Even in summertime my only entertainment, besides listening to the radio, was going to the movies on Saturday afternoon. I rode into Sheffield with my girlfriend's family. My mother gave me exactly seventeen cents—twelve for the movies and five for candy. I got a little box of chocolate drops and timed myself to finish sucking on them just as the show ended."

"You must've changed a lot!" Deedee laughed, judging by her mother's impulsive characteristics. "I could never do that." she added more thoughtfully. Now that her vernal body was affectionate and unselfconscious Caleb easily imagined himself both as a Dogtown High School classmate tormented by the inconsolable desire and envy of forbidden experience and as one of her mother's unfortunate admirers under the hegemonical shadow of Dexter Keith.

"If only we hadn't spoiled you!" the father teased.

"Spoiled me! All the kids think you and Mother are much too strict. Not with Rob—just with me!" She seemed to have forgotten Caleb's presence, or to have dismissed the importance of his esteem as a harmless unimpressive grown-up.

Yet Caleb made bold to join the teasing. "Honor thy father and thy mother." was his sententious advice, without the authority of Laertes, hoping she'd take it as sympathetic support.

Deedee declined to look at him, but he wasn't entirely unheeded. "All we ever have in this house is commandments!" she flung out at large, putting him in his place as a despised abettor of old folks.

"It shows how we love you." her father calmly replied. "Glory just wants you to learn the constraints befitting an historian, and I'm all for that. You know how much Crevecoeur means to her—"

"Crevecoeur, de Crevecoeur! All I ever hear about is Crevecoeur! You'd think he was George Washington Abraham Lincoln and Franklin D Roosevelt rolled into one! Except from you it's Tocqueville de Tocqueville! I hate the arguments you have. I won't go to college if I have to take French or history. One's too snobbish and the other's too *boring!*"

"So is geography!" Rob sighed. "I'm glad it's over."

" 'History without that so much neglected study of Geography—' " Dexter prompted.

"*—is sick of a half dead palsy.*'!" the other three Keiths joined in unison, happily finishing the quotation from Sam'l Purchase, as famous in that family as the Pledge of Allegiance: a chorus of solidarity.

"I think Herodotus would agree." said Caleb, almost hoping to earn a niche for himself in the family. "It takes both space and time to make a place, and according to Doctor Charlemagne the Keiths are first-class chorophiliacs."

Deedee never paid any attention to words she didn't understand (and refused to open a dictionary), or to names of no immediate significance, but now for the first time she stared straight across the table into Caleb's face. Though he had the advantage of her with the light at his back he was flustered by her attention. "But Herod was Roman or something, wasn't he?"

Before he could reply she dropped him again and plunged back into the circle of authentic kinship, which itself was now the topic of discussion. With unfeigned interest she asked her mother the lorist: "Even if all your heroes must be men, how come you and Daddy both like the French so much? Aren't we supposed to be Irish?"

DEXTER: "You're forgetting John Smith Robin Hood and King Alfred. Not to mention Friar Bacon and Don Quixote. None of them was French."

DEIRDRE: "Well they weren't Irish either—not to mention women!"

GLORIA: "Deedee's right. We tend to take the Irish and Jews for granted."

CALEB [*with pseudo-avuncular persistence, resuming his gauche offer to bear a share of the conviviality*]: "Not to mention women. But the French were more sympathetic to the Atlindus than the Georgios were. Northern Montvert is still called the French Kingdom."

GLORIA: "If Champlain hadn't been forced to take sides with the Hurons the Five Nations of the Iroquois might never have turned against the French; the British might never have occupied the Hiawatha Valley, or Carillon, or the rest of upper Nether Land."

CALEB [*to Deirdre, as if boasting*]: "I lived near there, to the west of the Green Mountains, on the Dutch side of Montvert."

GLORIA: "The French could have cut off all of New Armorica before 1765, right down to New Uruk. In the end they'd have kept Canada at least, and our Revolution would probably have failed."

ROBERT [*moaning*]: "Is the history lesson over yet?"

DEIRDRE: "Then we'd've been treated like the Irish!"

GLORIA: "Or else you kids would be speaking French and learning the Latin catechism."

DEXTER: "Even as it was, where I grew up, over on the English side, I had to study the catechism in a parish nine-tenths French. You might have benefitted from it too if your mother's grandfather hadn't converted to the Paulines out of political expediency."

GLORIA: "My grandfather was as good an Irish Republican as any of your Ulster Scholastics! His father and mother died in the famine and he came over when he was ten years old to work on the Pequod River railroad, between Hector Falls and Casterbridge Junction. And no one in my family was ever a traitor to the Catholicratic Party—unlike some of your Irish antecedents I could mention!"

DEXTER [*laughs*]: "My father meant well, but he was naive and believed all the Protestican claims to political righteousness. As a Sheffield toolmaker he considered himself one of the self-made 'aristocrats' of Atlantean labor. He was flattered to be called a rugged individualist. I blame the Church for failing to educate its own people in social morals."

GLORIA [*to her children*]: "The Bishops and Cardinals were almost all opposed to F D R !"

DEXTER [*to his children*]: "But many of the nuns and priests were good enough Christians to feel uncomfortable about the Petrine hierarchy siding with Protestican politics. The subalterns and foot soldiers could see injustice with their own eyes and therefore voted for the Crats. But my father was politically stupid, like all people of goodwill who swallow the anti-social doctrine that usurps an elephant for its trademark."

GLORIA [*eagerly assenting*]: "A-men!"

DEXTER [*in high good humor*]: "Your dear mother wouldn't have married me if we hadn't always agreed on that! —But at least my father was no apostate from the Mother Church!"

GLORIA [*to her husband*]: "If it weren't for the Pauline Deformation there'd be no democracy now, or human rights either!"

DEXTER [*looking at everybody*]: "If it weren't for the Church there'd have been no society to deform."

DEIRDRE [*with a curl of her lip*]: "So that's why neither of you go to church anymore!"

ROBERT [*whining*]: "But we had to go to Sunday school just for Bible stories!"

GLORIA [*correcting her son*]: "For the facts of life."

DEIRDRE [*hurriedly, blushing scarlet at Caleb's presence*]: "I've decided to become a Divine Individualist."

DEXTER: "They have the best architecture in Dogtown."

ROBERT [*to Caleb*]: "Are you a Petrine or a Pauline?"

CALEB [*swallowing, caught off guard*]: "I'm officially a Pauline Apostolic, but in the left wing of the High Church. So I'm both and neither. The real Eucharist, but no Pope."

Robert and Deirdre stare at him blankly.

DEXTER [*wagging his head toward Caleb in an attitude of pleasantry*]: "They have the intellectual freedom of Divine Individualists plus all the ritual a Mass can bear! The Apostolics are generally called praying Protesticans, but they tolerate exceptions among them, like President Roosevelt."

ROBERT [*looking at Caleb*]: "Maybe that's what I'll be. Nobody could criticize me!"

DEXTER: "They also have the best stained glass in Dogtown."

DEIRDRE: "I hate ritual."

DEXTER: "Except at Proms graduations and weddings."

"Now you see what an oxymoronic family this is." Gloria addressed Caleb with the arms-length tone she imagined an accomplished hostess like Tessa would have assumed in an effort to keep her offspring from forgetting their manners under the eyes of a fifth party. "In the old country Dexter's forebears took on a Chauvinist name to improve themselves; they were really a mixture of O'Briens and O'Neills. Some of mine changed their name over here from Keough to Sanderson—which they thought sounded like good Yankee lineage for hard-scrabble farming. My father believed the name helped us get away with registering as New Deal Catholicrats among cussed Protesticans in the most libertarian state of the Union. We never had any trouble getting along with the other voters. My mother was re-elected Town Clerk about twenty times."

Although Caleb was very much interested in Gloria's personal determinants, he hastened to change the subject lest Robert ask him bluntly to identify his own stock, now that the Keiths' had been elucidated. Having half dreaded a meal in company with the kids (quite apart from sufficient anxiety about the unprecedented invitation to dine with their parents), he had tried to prepare himself, like a good Sea Scout, with one or two anchors to windward in case the discourse yawed or flagged. The one he now politely cast was a question that had never been called for during his intercourse with Gloria alone:

When gazing through the window earthward from his writing chair up in the garret he'd often wondered about postmortem details. Now in the dining room he was sitting with his back to the open twilight of the cemetery, but to his left, through the perpendicular plane of the back window provided by the set-back of the kitchen wing, he could see some gravestones behind the Rectory, beyond the swing hanging from the yardarm of the oak, to the rear of the ruined wall of gathered stones and behind the unforgettable rock of passion. Gesturing vaguely in that direction as he looked deferentially from one Keith to another, he asked if they ever saw funerals out there. "Never since I've lived here have I seen an actual burial, though once in a while there's fresh evidence of one."

"Very few." Dexter replied. "Most of them seem to take place during our working hours. No overtime to pay."

"Or in the dead of night, especially when it's dark and stormy." Deirdre whispered. "I can hear them wailing, but I don't dare wake up and look out my window."

"The back-hoes are quicker than live gravediggers." Dexter went on. "The purpose of the funeral is disguised with sheets of green plastic sod to cover the piles of dirt, and what they call the interment is indecently swift and secretive. They don't fill up the hole until after the mourners are gone. It's the only kind of shoveling anyone does anymore: a slight lifting—and gravity does the rest. I used to *dig* a lot of ditches!"

"So did I." said Caleb. "Foundations and post-holes too."

"And even my father did. When his plant was closed he had to go onto the W P A for a while—the most humiliating period of his life. But the only time I ever dug a grave was out there in our own yard, for our old Saint Patrick."

The mother instinctively put out her hand to touch Rob's forearm, anticipating his struggle to suppress the tears of childhood at a reminder of Sucat's death, which still threatened his manhood, as she alone knew. But biting her lip she managed to cancel her involuntary response just in time to prevent the public gesture of sympathy from breaking down his mastery of Sooky's burial. By way of diverting the embarrassment of old grief to a reactive resentment of her gratuitous maternal tact, she instantly resurrected a different skeleton from the family cupboard, laughing aloud with the usual high-pitched precipitation that her husband had almost inured himself to. "Once when Rob was very little he noticed a flowery cortege out there. 'O look,' he said: 'people getting married!' "

Caleb smiled, and even Deirdre looked at her little brother with a peculiar tenderness; but Rob groaned angrily at the outworn family anecdote, and butted back at his mother in the kind of sullen irritation that Caleb might have expected of the sister his senior: "Oh Ma, forget it! Leave me alone! It's ancient history, and none of your business anymore!"

"It's my job to keep up all the histories." Hesiodia cheerfully rejoined. "I don't want anybody to forget anything."

"But Mother," said Deirdre, investing herself in an air of judicious criticism, "I thought you were more interested in what *didn't* happen—what you called counterfactual history!"

The three elders united in outright laughter. Rob stole suspicious glances around the table, but concluded by degrees that the joke must have been on his mother, and he too grinned.

"But facts are not to be ignored." the mother contentedly replied.

26
SYMPOSIUM

Whereas dinner was later than usual, and whereas both the children were to be away from home overnight on the coming weekend—Rob at the springtime Scout Jamboree up in the King's Pines, Deirdre at a girlfriend's "pajama party" in Seamark—it was resolved by their parents that they do homework immediately after dessert. They weren't allowed to procrastinate. Not that they were sorry to disappear without being pressed into their ordinary postprandial chores in dining room and kitchen. The alacrity of their compliance made everyone overlook their omission of leave-taking proprieties vis-a-vis the guest of the meal.

But in the doorway Deirdre suddenly remembered something she'd intended to tell the family assembled. "Guess what I saw painted in big letters on a rock by the High School! It said 'ROBERT HAS NO STATE OF MIND'!"

"It wasn't me!" Rob yelled. "I don't know anybody who talks that fancy!" And he chased his giggling sister upstairs as if they were both five years younger. On the way to their respectively eremitic studies they were glad to find a bit of undignified foolishness to divert the selfpity for being deprived of broadcast amusements per devilvision.

These two victims of prominently edificational parents were never reconciled to the decree of bypassing the parlor cathode ray tube on "school nights". But they had gradually acquired the art of pretending to know (and actually guessing) the cultural allusions of their friends, and of making special excuses for having missed the most significant episodes of serial entertainment. As the unfortunate children of quasi-recusants they had become adept at amplifying their limited DV experience for purposes of smalltalk and at changing the subject when it got to the coinage of advertisements.

Ibi rose to join the happy commotion, but he didn't follow the princelings any further than the foot of the stairs. Instead, now feeling freer to claim his deferred share of the feast, he turned back to the kitchen, politely sidestepping the lady's interminable movements to and fro, and waited for her to scrape the spoils into one dish; and at last she rewarded him for his self-restraint. She also wrapped up for him up some future desserts.

Having left her two men in the dining room with a bottle of luse, Gloria made no apology for expanding the interval of her disappearance into a thoroughgoing wash-up of every artifact in sight—all but the kitchen floor—taking as much time as if there had been three additional guests and no equipment to ease her task. She went so far as to imagine herself baking some bread.

But she began by calling through the open door "Shall I let Ibi out with his bone? It's beef from yesterday, not lamb."

"Oh, yes . . . Please." Caleb bumbled. "Thank you . . . I'm sorry . . . I didn't realize it was so late!" He shuffled half way to his feet, burning with the confusion of a guest who suddenly apprehends that he's outlasted his welcome.

"Oh no, don't go yet! I'm sorry about my compulsive housekeeping. I never have time in the morning. I'll be with you in a few minutes. Dexter, please pour me a glass of wine."

Without rising from his chair her husband restrained his drinking companion by the elbow, unmistakably reassuring him with the cordial attitude of one who'd looked forward to a lingering conversation. Caleb was doubly mortified to find that he'd been too quick to assume he wasn't wanted.

No sooner were courtesies asseverated than Dexter continued the response he'd been making to Caleb's comments on the difficult feat of organizing an Arts Festival in Dogtown. "I'd like to get

Huck Salter roped into the committee. He's full of leading opinions. But I don't know how to do it without getting him blamed for conflict of interest, seeing that he's an exhibiting sculptor."

Gloria was listening as she worked in the kitchen, and now she stuck her head around the corner again. "Put him on the poetry board!

"—Do you mind if I shut this door in your face? I have to turn on my noisy dishwashing machine." But Caleb was aware that instead of closing only the kitchen door only she stepped out of the kitchen the other way, through the living room, and also closed the doors that communicated to the rest of the house by the front room and the stairwell, unobtrusively sequestering the mens' conversation from any ears blundering down the stairs. After she returned to her enclosed kitchen the radio could be heard airing a Brandenberg Concerto above the muffled tempest of the hotwater mill. The two gentlemen were thus assured of their privacy.

At last it dawned on Caleb that the unexpected bidding to dine en famille with this highly esteemed public figure, so rarely at leisure, signaled something more calculated than the graduated acceptance of a demisemidetached tenant who was quiet overhead and paid his rent on time.

Altogether Caleb had spent scarcely half an hour in conversation with the head of the house since the early days of his occupancy, when in both diffidence and aversion he'd declined the friendly proposals of these "theater-lovers" to join them in "watching" Shakespeare, as well as a few other such offers of diversion at their electronic hearth—which had naturally ceased as the proprietors came to the conclusion that he was a recluse too proud or too neurotic to relish homely sociability.

Now he all but envisioned a specially privileged friendship that would augment and enrich the secret favors of the housewife, perhaps also embracing the goodwill of son and daughter. He speculated that under the unsuspicious protection of Dexter Keith he might enjoy the conveniences of independent domesticity. Setting his own limits of devotion, more or less choosing his pleasures, with all the extramural freedom of a bachelor, he'd savor the advantage of an unobligating sojourn in this amicable nest of comforts. His enviable situation, by accommodating him to the semi-frustration known as chivalry, though it somewhat constrained other pursuits, would greatly alleviate the erostatic distractions of unmarried life.

Yet the dialectical reflex to this sanguine daydream could be deferred no longer than its component assumptions were poised in perfect balance, the complacent interval between one sip of wine and the next. All at once it seemed especially improbable that this man-to-man talk had been plotted without some motive more acute than holistic benevolence.

For a split second Caleb was pierced by a theoretical fear of treacherous violence. But in light of the frank and generous prelude to this chat it was impossible to believe that he was being cornered by a jealous husband; short of poisoning, neither threat nor vengeance required the overture of a family cenacle. Still, there was something definite in the wind. What was the purpose of such a velvet trap?

Suddenly the beach gave way to quicksand in every direction. His heart thumped; he was instantly dispossessed of internal muscle; his brain was flooded with waves of fearful excitement. Only by forcing himself to take a mechanical part in the dialogue was he able to suppress the trembling of his hands and lips; and, by breathing deeply, of his voice. How much did this still gentle Chiron know? What was he about to examine? Nauseating doubt ensued.

In the kitchen meanwhile the other guilty party had been trembling all along. She now doubted that her remorse and moral confusion could be cured by this conspiracy with her husband, whose part was so cooperative and sweet, as if, in his own penitence, he knew and forgave—as if he loved her again and was no longer pretending. She blamed herself as a coward for not probing his motives, for not getting to the bottom of her own. But under the protection of her radio, when the dull roar ceased of her dishwashing machine and exposed the purity of Bach's music, her analysis resumed as she soothed her grosser nerves by scouring pots and pans, and all the surfaces in sight, by unnecessarily drying each dish with a towel, and finally by realigning the contents of a cupboard.

Yes, she feared and she doubted; but also she laughed! She told herself that no woman should scruple to outflank the duplicity of men, which was always at least one dimension deeper than a woman's deception, and not merely emotional. Seeing through the historians of Genesis, she laughed to find that contemporary truth was no more reliable than history. Once his wealth and pride were secured, Abraham successfully pretended to posterity that his beautiful wife Sarah, "princess" of Hebrews, whom he'd offered to sell, hadn't actually lain with Pharaoh or Abimelech; and of course he never asked her what she felt about the transactions. But before the legends were collected and edited, Isaac's true filiation must have been suspect—Isaac, "he that laughs"—a link no less important than Father Abraham in Israel's nexus to Eber. She laughed because this very minute it didn't seem any easier for her to know the hearts of the two men who thought they knew her heart than for El Shaddai Himself actually to determine all the individual facts of life in a millennium of old testimony. She'd wasted far too much of her youth trying to explain away moral irregularities in the Bible— she who was so incapable of initiating suggestions to men.

Before closing the doors she'd already laughed to overhear them nostalgically discussing the outmoded work of Montvert woodsmen. That was the only other stitching motion they might have shared! It was funny to picture such a pair matching endurance and skill at the two ends of a crosscut saw. They were agreeing on the relative merits of a common single-bladed axe, balanced by the gracefully evolved curve of its long wooden handle, and the more versatile doublebitted tool of straight and shorter helve that won't twist in your hand and is better for hacking. Compare the instruments a woman uses in sewing—or the jagged shard of flint that Zipporah circumcised her son with.

As Gloria waited for the uncircumcised to sound out the attitude of the circumcised she raised her inward eyes to contemplate the furthest-spread wake of her onrushing course. Caleb's playscript had drawn her libido sciendi to the reconciliation of myths that were imbedded in ancient history before Genesis was writ, leading her in particular to a conviction that the legend of Nimrod—mighty hunter of the Lord, builder of Babel (Gate of Yahweh)—was a decadent conflation of Sumerian lore about Gilgamesh and Engidu. Despite her bone-felt misgivings anent the tête-à-tête in the dining room, those of her thoughts that remained vagarious returned not only to the rod of sovereignty and ring of circumcision but also to the Flood as a halfway measure that failed to expurgate humanity, occurring before the hybris of the Tower (not, as according to the revisionary historians, after it), the consequential curse of which was our speaking in tongues thousands of years before Pentecost.

Smiling in shamefaced disapproval she teased herself with wanton speculations. I'm dangerous again, she thought. I wish he hadn't shown me his draft of the last Tablet—of course I was too embarrassed to betray any personal interest in the import of it— just as I was coming to my senses! And she laughed again, at the irony of that expression!

I'm getting too many notions. There are things I should forget—insidious ideas. I wish Doctor Charlemagne had never planted his remark that *Friar Bacon* should be played as if the Fair Maid of Fressingfield knows full well that after the wedding Lacey is going to share her with Prince Edward. That man corrupts our theater and charms us all with his evil insights. I shouldn't have had him here for dinner. Thank God I was wise enough not to have the kids eating with us. He's so bulky and inconsiderate that it never occurred to him to apologize for breaking the dining room chair.

Next to him Dexter seems gracefully slender and refined, my Metatron of old, "tallest of archangels"; yet he and Doctor Charlemagne egg each other on like Gog and Magog. Tallest of towerbuilders, he might have been! Maybe my princely stallion of the Dogtown acropolis would have been a great architect if he hadn't stopped to father hinnies by a giddy little she-ass. His mother was a queen of a woman, and it was she who made him, though begotten upon her by a lowly man (as Auto Drang says of Gilgamesh). It's my fault he didn't stay with Caspar Aninigo. With wedding bells still ringing in my head for babies, and our own house and home the only thing I could imagine worth the struggle, I persuaded myself it was the same with him.

I always had an inkling that Caspar was disappointed in Dexter as a creative designer. But probably all maestros are chary of letting their most useful assistants find their own way. His detailing of solutions and supervision of construction was never appreciated by owners. He wrote the specs, revised the mistakes, improvised the omissions, corrected the engineers, vetted the shop drawings, taught the clerk of the works, negotiated the change orders, and reconciled the contractors to standards of performance that exposed their ineffective management and absorbed their profits. Yet no one hated him! At that last Christmas party one of the Associates told me that thanks to Dexter no other firm ever had so few disgruntled clients after a full year's cycle of occupation. That's not what wins awards from the critics. What kept Dexter from becoming an architect was the virtue of assuming responsibility!

I was no help, always looking backward in my ragged cone of historical vision, excluding unbearable insights into the present. I kept thinking that you steer best with your back to the future, and the longer your wake the easier to stay on course! But looking behind us now I know that on the horizon Gloria Sanderson Keith should have put up with ten more years of hardship, or at least postponed her maculate conceptions.

Still, maybe Gilgamesh was really no artist either. Ars longa, arx brevis!

Caleb shouldn't invent names for me. It's too intimate, too possessive. I'm not his pet and I'm not his fiancee. I don't like being called Gossamer Gloriana With a Crown of Feathery Gold. I'm really just a an inexperienced de-clawed house-leopard. Even if I'm not yet fat and flabby, I'm too old to be his 'perfect dimorph'. Ugh! Yet I can't help falling for his romantic interpretation of how I use my mind! And he truly is the dimorph history failed to give me—with a lovely telescopic lower-case ego. I wonder what the difference is for him, in making love, between a worn-out bashful matron and a sultry shameless Gypsy-girl with lean nates and pristine nipples.

What an unlikely playwright! Just as unlike his models who were unlike their own heroes as those who weren't. So finical and cocky! So critical of the world! Right from the beginning I knew he was on my side. No wonder I felt younger than when I was square-dancing with Dexter! Even the first time, upstairs, I wasn't afraid to hoist my sails! [She laughs at the zephyr playing in her spine.] He doesn't weigh me down like the Matterhorn, or overwhelm me with his selfsufficiency. It's equal volume in two-part harmony! [Again she laughs, at the thought of a musical Caleb.] He doesn't overrun the sense of person. For him I'm not just the one who always happens to be on duty in his bed. He knows the sultry leopard's inner life, and doesn't look at the spots!

But just then she was rubbing a spot on the bottom of a pan that called up a gust of wind, and she gibed in tears. Like facts excluded from a dream, the children of her womb and all public causes ceased to exist. Giddily veering like the golden cock of the Hall weathervane that she watched from the Library window in equinoctial gales, she scrubbed more and more vehemently at memories of Dexter and her falsely invidious comparisons. He was the best of husbands, and mostly his lusts were tender.

But in there, if he does what he promised, what will Caleb think of me? If he does not, this torment will never end, or else this family will be annihilated. Why can't love stay clean and simple, with no alternatives?

It's true that my husband needs circumcision of the heart. [Her lips quivered at John Wesley's term.] But on the night of the rock, the most obreptitious night of my life, I deceived a good man, not being the person the other person thought I was, as Jacob deceived Isaac—and as such he blessed me!

Collapsing into misery, deaf to the Brandenberg Concerto, both hands still mechanically at work on her oven tray in the greasy water of the sink, she wept with dripping cheeks and heaving shoulders, mutely mourning all her years. My Irish blood knows that the Petrines are right: it's a sacrament. Caleb says that not all consumption of bread and wine is sacramental; not all atonement must be holy: yet in speaking our vows Dexter and I renounced unholy beatitudes and profane feasts in order to make ourselves priest and priestess of one flesh.

As an unscrupulous historian she would have preferred to confess her guilt to a Court of Love, rather than directly to her conscience. Under the humane mercy of Venus she would have been forgiven for loving the father of Deirdre and Robert Keith throughout her praiseworthy transgression of mankind's most oppressive commandment. Yet at bottom she never doubted, despite her recent subscription to the laws of civil Love, that even her chosen court, in handing down its divided opinion, would uphold the natural asymmetry of justice for a species in which the female has evolved beyond the limitations of seasonal oestrus without being relieved of lengthy gestation and protracted nesting. Though taking only a single transitory lover I'm more at fault than the faithless fountain of seed I'm married to. Both these men are enfranchised with the patent excuse of subservience to a "peccant part" part, which really does rear itself up even on baby boys to father the wish before its time. My disobedient insurrections [she laughs] came later, and certainly weren't so stiffnecked; I've never been subjected to such teeming lures of sex designed by Mother Nature: yet I deliberately allowed myself to be seduced under my own roof by a boy whose wishes and notions were probably elsewhere until I stole his attention!

Dexter is one who never needed to seduce. He should be given credit for whatever chastity to which he may have held himself on his side of our marriage. If he'd been licentious he would have met with no resistance anywhere. What if I were married to Waldo Cotton and my colleague Dexter Keith fell in love with me—or so pretended? [Her shapeshifting vane swerved back and forth in these fits of wind.] Despite his civic initiatives he's thought to be modest and self-effacing—but it's only the hypocrisy he cultivates to make himself less conspicuous for clandestine purposes! He would be much worse if we didn't live here, out in the open, where all the world goes by; but sometimes I almost retch at his public charm.

I've always tried to act as he expected me to do, even when I realized that he loved the dog more than he loved me. When I knew he didn't want me along on his paternal excursions with the kids I always begged off graciously. Everyone knows he's been an excellent father, as fathers go: putting up swings, building sandboxes and bridges, inventing playthings. I've never failed to express my appreciation for that sort of thing, but for the last six months I haven't been very nice to him at bedtime, since even before it occurred to me that he's thinking of someone else when he pokes me with Old Glory Rod—or, what's worse, *anyone* else! When I'm treated as an amorous convenience, like a private bath in his hotel room, I don't feel at all nice.

Especially now that I've glimpsed that tall classic namesake of my daughter as they were walking by the door together when I was working in the archives of the Clerk's vault at the Hall! A troubling black beauty for the Black Irish Cid! People must think God had intended them for each other: that's the worst of it. Just when I'd almost persuaded myself there was no reason to feel uneasy about his daytime hours! I went numb with the shock of her lovely contralto laugh at something he whispered! It wasn't merely office gossip. I could see him follow all the way to her desk. It's lucky no one happened to came in and find me spotting priceless documents with my tears! For half an hour I didn't dare show my face.

I dread going over to the Hall any more for fear of what I'll see or hear—and for the shame of feeling everyone's hypocritical pity. I used to think it was funny when I heard people say that the wife's always the last one to know. I'd resign as Curator if I didn't realize that it would be taken as an acknowledgement of my humiliation, and at the same time make it easier for him to hang around with that woman. "Deirdre, who alone among women who have set men mad had equal loveliness and wisdom." I haven't heard that Yeats quotation in this house since Deedee got too adolescent to take it in fun, but I'm sure he's repeating it elsewhere.

I doubt that women with many lovers understand the sensations of men any better than I do. Two of them so unlike each other are enough to prove how alien they all must be to us. Even in sacramental espousal the swagger stick is single-ended. The two of us may rub together when the mood prevails, and clutch in frenzy, stitching like sailmakers, and sometimes even grunt in harmony, but everything he feels is outside him!

And how much less I know about the opaque selfwilled manchild I've added to the world with my blood!

Caleb is a presumptuous young bachelor, but he may be right when he solemnly tells me that there can be no true empathy between the sexes. Sympathy, yes, he does assure me—because at times we both refer the same way to motives or interests or feelings that we really share only in the brief representations of our supposedly common language—but not the empathy of communing sentience. At least in that precocious college essay he was satisfied to ween that "neither the canonization of marriage nor its romantic violation can open the possibility of corresponding resonance in all the different vibrations that constitute a body's unity"! He says it's the impossibility that makes our love erotic. Otherwise it would be "merely mystical, without the dimorphic differential of pressure to conduct the holy spirits"! [Once more she laughed.] His reasoning is circular—not false, but simply phallacious!

With a sudden shake of her head she cleared her watered eyes. Oh God, must I leave my beloved home and go fellswalking in the wastes of Purdeyville to bewail the innocence I've lost? Ah, if only I could take dear Ibi! Sleep with my head on a stone until I dream a great fable, and then erect my pillow as a pillar—[Smiling at the alliteration she wiped tearstains with the bone of her wrist and finished her thought staring at the immiscible slime in her sink.]—a modest uncircumcised menhir left by the God of Glaciers and smoothed by Lady Gloucester's weatherings. I shall call the spot, not Bethel, House of El Shaddai, but Baal, altar of Enlil!

Even if they don't have a dog, how free and easy it is for men to go off running in the cold dark of the morning. But it's a wonder they can be such great athletes with their egos tucked between their legs. I seem to remember that Peter Abelard won the Mont-Saint-Michel Duodecathlon only because he wasn't merely gelded. Without such encumbrances a strong man would be as smooth and light as a girl, minus the tender burdens of a woman flopping on his chest. One could almost fly!

—Here I go again: from blue devils to the mania of an escapist! I'm always silencing my soul with divertissements of enfabulation!

Did I say free and easy? Free—but not easy. It's just the freedom part of running that sounds so good; I shudder at the brutality of pure freezing loneliness. If self-discipline like Caleb's is too much for the valiant studhorse, who won't even walk to his office, how could I expect myself—?.

Better it is to escape all toils of character and true history by acting on the stage. I once hoped to do it an even better way, as a poet; but I'm too susceptible to excitements on the surface. I can't seem to stay down when I swim, especially in the saltwater here; so I'll make a sport of diving into phosphorescent breakers. A matronly sub-librarian who does well at simulating happiness should be able to imitate a cosmopolitan as well as Tessa does. I don't look the part, but I'll let my hair grow and dye it black, let it stream behind me—if only I could do that without either wearing my heart on my sleeve or turning into a pillar of salt!

But [with a newly sardonic laughter that never reached her mouth] since I'd've been an antithetical kind of poet, I'll be an antithetical mummer: instead of faking emotion I'll succeed by disassuming it. That I can learn from Tessa. By making a disciplined effort to throttle my exuberance and transfigure my depressions I ought to be able to calm down and act with civilized consistency. (My reasoning also is circular, but true!) I'll moderate myself until I'm as obtuse as the Athenian philosophers who've been handed down to us by men. In fact, as an actor without a company, I could earn my living and support the kids by going back to some job in a school. They used to say that the stable exports of Vinland were ice, granite, stockfish, and schoolmarms. If I were a cold hard teacher maybe I wouldn't mind the tyranny. After all, the wages are very good in Cornucopia. . . .

*

Meanwhile, nescient as ever of anyone's thoughts but his own, Caleb was marveling at the adaptation of Gloria's skills to this exceptional occasion, which was apparently destined to improve his remarkably advantageous situation. Throughout dinner the hospitable householders had seemed in perfect amity with each other, as if touching feet under the full length of the table, and glad to have this particular stranger and his saint share their domestic felicity.

In the attempt to allay his remaining fear and doubt, which had been superstitiously aroused by the sheer unexpectedness of his new position, but not without faint stirrings of unreasonable jealousy, he was cultivating a bilateral friendship with Dexter. His sincerely characteristic approach was to abstract a geometrical basis for their common interest in the analysis of organizations.

But he failed to intrigue his host with the Synectic Method of Diagnostic Correlation [S M D C] as an arithmetical device (on an orthoparallelepiped model) for analyzing the performance of city departments. Dexter pessimistically declared that all attempts at analysis, save simple variances from budgeted expenditures, were repugnant to Dogtown officials—not as much in fear of science as in the inability to imagine any useful reasoning outside the archaic traditions of Vinland's municipal accounting practices. Nowadays Caleb was giving more and more consideration to his prospects for a future livelihood, and since there might be an opportunity to apply S M D C to city operations, on some sort of trial basis, as a paid consultant, he'd asked Dexter to suggest the city's fundamental management problems—whether or not publicly perceived.

He was also motivated by the hope of bringing the conversation around to the question of how well the events and issues of the Hall were understood by the journalists of the *Nous*. Had Belle Cingani already made an impression upon Dexter Keith—or visa versa? But the discourse never got as far as pretty names and faces.

Dexter on his part, after a fortnight of vivid relief, was still in a rather expansive mood from having learned that there was going to be no untoward consequence of the reckless raid he'd conducted into the presumably unshielded person of his wife [on what she thought of as the night of the rock]. The last thing he wanted was another son or daughter. The unspoken fear of such an intempestive eventuality had so deeply permeated his ground of consciousness in the days immediately following the rape that its de facto nullification made him feel almost as free as a bachelor.

At the moment he was too weary of politics for a comprehensive rehearsal of topics and controversies bruited almost daily to anyone dutiful enough to study the *Nous*; and his intention with the guest was entirely different. Still, in place of smalltalk alternatives he was ready enough to ease the transition to his purpose by airing a few of the administrative causes that occupied more of his attention than life as a private person—as gauged in time and energy over the course of a year even as intense with feeling as this last one. Lately he'd ceased to comment upon his professional emotions to Gloria, and this seemed a harmlessly fortuitous moment to disburden himself of a few brooded ideas for the benefit of a disinterested mind that appeared competent to grasp the importance of what he complained about.

"You must understand that in Dogtown Ibicity Hall no one has any concept of *management*, as distinguished from mere administration under law. Just as there's no analysis, there's no attempt to negotiate change in structure or procedures. When in doubt about licit possibilities of improvement the mayor and earldermen rely on the ad hoc opinions of an uneducated lawyer who doesn't trouble himself to ask either the intent of legislation in question or its practicability in relation to existing statutes and regulations—let alone its operational value."

Warming to his subject, Dexter was soon carried away, and the lecture grew into something more passionate than either the instructor or the student had bargained for.

"Laxity in implementation and inefficiency of administration are addressed (if at all) by passing new ordinances threatening fiercer penalties (without repealing the old ones), or amendments meant to conform more closely to de facto practice. And even such feckless lawmaking proceeds from tediously recorded debate about repetitious oversimplifications, trailing a meticulously protracted series of documents. Any rut of tradition is likely to be safeguarded not only by all the obstacles of 'due process' but also by the stumbling blocks of State civil service regulations or ill-advised union contracts, most of which were rendered into legalese by the least promising graduates of third-rate law schools. Every enactment is modeled on the rhetorical logic inherited and distorted and handed down by forgotten parrots of the same feather. Contingencies are anticipated by picaresque series of ambiguous and redundant subordinate clauses, which usually overlook the options most likely to be faced by administrators and often mix absurdly detailed directives of procedure with fantastic generalizations of legal responsibility.

"Worst of all, many of the acts that annoy kilroys or real-estate developers, such as those that defend the rights of saints or other pedestrians, are never enforced by the police department (except when officers have personal or political incentives to perform unpopular duties) and are soon forgotten by the Earls, who like as not had ratified them in some feverish response to misunderstood public opinion. It's no wonder that a number of city ordinances are radically inconsistent with others, or with general laws of the Commonwealth; or else impressively complicated with nugatory provisos.

"Furthermore, since the legislative branch is jealous of the executive, managers sometimes really are hedged in and shackled almost as closely as they think they are. Custom rules all doubts. All our elected officials, and nearly all their employees but me, are troglodytes or aborigines, born to the prejudices of counterefficiency. The Ibicity Clerk still files his routine documents in vertically slotted drawers, folded up like insurance policies and tied with ribbon. Books of account are still kept with pen and ink, bound in royal folios too heavy to be moved by the old ladies who inscribe them. And far from *correlating* anything at all, they're hard pressed to cast their simple monthly sums.

"Every department is a separate fief, and the city government is no more unified than a loose confederation of colonies, each echoing medieval prerogatives and habits from the old country. Once the budget is voted, they go their own ways, freely abusing the accounts to which they charge their expenditures, in habitual disregard of both 'generally accepted accounting practices' and specific state laws. The Earls are too lazy or innocent to question most figures of less than four digits. So the amounts and categories of reported line-item expenditures are no more reliable than footsteps on quicksand. When you despair of the accounting figures used even in the simplest budgeting, how can you hope to use them for *diagnostic* analysis?

"Turn then to methods and procedures, and you'll find it even more impossible to examine operational functions. The way things are actually done is impenetrably amorphous, and often deliberately so. I sputter with rage whenever I allow myself to take an interest in municipal efficiency. How can we inspect an organization, if only by measuring it, when there are no articulated procedures?"

Caleb held his tongue, but he was confident of the methods and principles he'd evolved as an autodidact of rationality in other kinds of organization. He entertained little doubt that as the mayor's first mate he himself could transform the wretched city government into an effective and efficient establishment, of more service to the public at less cost. He believed that by extrapolating his experience in private business he could readily absorb the special knowledge required for public administration. Eventually he might even be invited to assume the de jure function of chief executive!

"Your S M D C sounds interesting to me, my friend," Dexter continued, "but I'm afraid no one else in the Hall has ears to hear or eyes to see such new ideas. You're abstract and too imaginative; the city operates by memory, drill, and rote. Maybe someday, under a new charter, if we get a professional city manager. In theory that's a possibility."

Caleb had to admit that S M D C couldn't be applied to an irrational structure. "I've never found anything in the *Nous* about internal city operations."

"Journalists are too ignorant of how things actually work to take an interest. To them everything they associate with "bureaucracy" is assembled in large immutable units which are themselves boring and repugnant to the liberally educated mind. They accept the stage set as they accepted the curriculum and the hierarchy when they were kids in school, never dreaming that the nature of things could be otherwise. Consequently there's no fourth-estate demand for administrative reform. And of course without the press to raise a cry no one is more indifferent to management than a taxpayer—unless it's a conspicuously isolated factor in the tax rate.

"Anyhow, I couldn't be of much help to you yet. I have no influence in finance or administration. All these constraints upon analysis bear even harder against the synthesis of planning—which by very definition not only involves abstract imagination but also implies controversial change *outside* city chambers, where the voters are very alert indeed! I'm a distrusted off-islander to start with, and the mayor tries to keep all positive power out of my hands. Insofar as I'm not bogged down with petty adjudications and technical advisories, I'm permitted to worry only about the large long-range problems that will never lend themselves to serious political attention."

Whereupon Caleb abandoned his selfserving notion to edify the city fathers. He and Dexter had almost bypassed the warmer question lurking among his motives. "That new woman on the paper, is she any better than the other reporters? Her articles are well written."

"Belle Cingani? Oh yes, as far as my official issues are concerned, she's quite perceptive. Very bright girl. Goodlooking too: everybody wants to be interviewed by her. She gets red carpet treatment from the mayor, even though he complains that her reports are hostile. At least she doesn't misquote any of us.

"But it can't last. When she learns a few things about the city, and begins to feel the intransigence, she may not ignore the truth. I shouldn't wonder if she's just the kind of reporter Gary Ghibellini's been hoping to get. If she sticks it out he'll probably inspire her too much for his own good. He's not the kind of man to fire her under pressure from the politicians and businessmen. They'll go to the publisher and bring him down anyway when they realize they can't shut him up otherwise.

"But right now Belle's working on a piece about my list of Dogtown's most important problems—which I must say seem to me ultimately more serious than mismanagement in government."

Caleb understood. "You mean saving the West Marshes prairies? Preserving Swine Ridge Farm? The Purdeyville airport? The quarry missile base? The Tir-na-Dog DV transmission tower? Bulldozers and dynamite."

"All the threats of levelling and filling. But protecting the harbor comes first. Nothing can stop the pilgrims and aestivators; we can't do much about immigration or the birth rate: but, if the fisheries are finally dispossessed, it would be better even to surrender the port to tugboats and barges for a base of offshore oil-drilling than to have a waterfront of pleasure domes serving a Vanity Fair of plastic and aluminum toyboats.

"That's my main defensive concern. My devious resistance is encouraged at least by the native faction's xenophobic protest against any kind of change. I'm more worried about the problems of civic improvement that are positively costly—more or less inconspicuous public works that we've been getting along without. Not only small facilities, like public toilets for instance (which are expensive to maintain against filth and vandalism), but rather large ones, like a parking and service terminal for gypsies and their kilroy rigs—which everybody's already in favor of, without being willing to pay for it, as long as it isn't located where anybody objects to noise, air-pollution, congestion, or vice!"

Dexter waved his hand toward the window. "Also: providing land for future cemeteries. Space is fixed but eternity expands. The Earls don't like to anticipate that distasteful issue because it has no mortal constituency. They and the Mayor likewise cover their ears when I warn them about the inexorable necessity of providing for the next generation's disposal of 'solid waste'. The Commonwealth won't allow us to build a mountain at the so-called landfill, even if we were willing to override the whole ward of voters who violently oppose it already. The city midden is filling up with our high standard of living at an exponential rate of dumping, especially now that feeding garbage to pigs has been prohibited."

"Even if it's cooked?"

"That ruling is the reasonable response of the Vinland Department of Public Health to the farmers' protest that cooking can't be done economically. On Cape Gloucester there's nothing else for pigs to eat. Soon our pigs will be no more. They can't live on our acorns."

"Then Gypsies must bring home the bacon."

"The day's coming when we'll be forced to do something much more expensive about euphemistic human waste also. Even without economic growth we can't go on using the harbor for our cloaca. A century ago they blocked up the tidal creek from Little Harbor Beach that used to set the east ward off as an island-of-the-island and helped flush the harbor with ocean tides from the inner end. That made the beach cleaner but it leaves the head of the harbor comparatively stagnant. Yet the sewage question is still considered too 'theoretical' to bother with.

"But there's nothing abstract or distasteful about clean fresh water, and people are willing at least to talk about it. Naturally it's the most vital problem of all—right at the top of my irritating list—and the largest in scope. The political difficulty is that the expensive phases of remedy always appear indefinitely deferrable, like the last straw on the camel's back; and without them the easier projects aren't worth the money. So it's impossible to lead any discussion from the subject in general to debate about policy—still less, from policy to concrete planning, and from planning to financing—even though it's as certain as death and advertising that we're going to have water shortages even under normal weather conditions (and in fact we're statistically due for cycles of drought). We need at least one new reservoir, and new dams to double the capacity of two or three old ones.

"But it won't be enough merely to increase the quantity of water. That's comparatively simple. Thanks to communal provisions by the old capitalist Duke of Dogtown and others the city owns more watershed land than we've yet taken advantage of. The rub comes in incurring a huge debt to replace and augment the pipes of the distribution system, much of which is a hundred years old. We probably loose half our running supply through underground leaks already. And it's a matter of public safety as well as public health. Pressure is dangerously low in East Harbor, for example. If we ever had more than one fire at a time over there. . . ."

By this time Caleb was again preoccupied with an effort to fathom the Keiths' motives, and he wasn't listening very closely, but he was humbly convinced by Dexter's exposition that managerial efficiency was less urgent than the effective prophecy of a leader. This worthy Chiron, manly and honorable by gift of nature and goodwill, though without power or weapons save his own towering person of dark craggy mien and suasively modulated voice, seemed Dogtown's future Nimrod.

27
PERIPETEIA

Dexter's overt brief to Caleb was remarkably coherent because his professional reflections had been framed and rehearsed to himself in brooding hope or despair almost daily. It was an occasional relief, or preparatory exercise, to utter his opinions safely off the record, especially to someone with more bureaucratic experience than a wife or a dog. But his covert engrossment remained within the contubernal sphere that had been shaken by both Deirdre Cotton and his present interlocutor.

One of the speaker's underthoughts was that connubiality would be more tolerable if families were not straitened bilaterally. Jacob had two wives and two concubines, and never suffered a night of recusancy. But of course none of the four was licensed to test her fertility with menservants.

Gloria keeps up the appearance of buoyancy. With the crowd she always joins the cackle. Sometimes, forsooth, she's so strident that I bless my stars she never became the lady of a diplomat or architect. She'll never let herself sink, thank God; unless women are generally suspect, I'm the only one who'd ever doubt her inner stability; but inwardly, she's easily swamped. And yet even for consistency my character is inferior to hers, and my immature obsessions are less excusable than her endocrine fluctuations.

Any naturalist can see that we're ludicrously mismatched—though of the same species and all too fecund. Everyone else nevertheless looks upon us as the founders of an ideal democratic family. And it's true. Gloria serves well enough as a good wife—cooperative, compliant, and comely. She's more conservative in country matters than she used to be, but still dewy enough when I take the trouble to breach her defenses; and, when fully possessed—if she only knew it!—capable of more husbands in an hour than I of wives in a whole Gloucestermas. All in all, though she and I may be misspliced like halyard and hawser (as Wat might say), *when I'm in sound mind* I wouldn't permanently trade the more or less prevailing peace of domesticity she usually keeps us in—not for the consummate anatomy and exquisite grace of any other exclusive mate. . . .

Gloria's unique quality is of brain heart and thyroid. She's been a far better mother to Deedee and Robert than I was wise enough to have missed if she hadn't been, teaching me by teaching them. She made them what they are, who are worth to me a parcel of suffering millions of times worse than the mere frustration of sensual perfection in sport with their mother. The minds of most children are as mistreated as chained dogs. There's not one fit mother in ten thousand; and except for the one I would have married if I'd seen her soon enough there's no imperfect woman I would have preferred to dear Old Glory for a lifetime of consortium.

In the summer we all have a good time on the boat together, and at Christmas time we're happy. The picture of Sooky carrying my briefcase in his mouth was on the front page. If this family came asunder the whole town would lose faith in the indispensable sacrament.

The regal breathtaking Prothonotary may be a lazy mother or a slovenly housekeeper, for all I know. Maybe I romantically misinterpret her Celtic dignity and reserve. She's too afraid, perhaps, or still too priest-ridden at the bottom of her soul, despite her easy humor. For all I yet know, she may even be a neurotic prude, susceptible to no man's blessing. I can't know in advance.

On the other hand [Dexter mentally grunts], I allow that this my pretense at skepticism is only the wisdom of urbane psychology, making the best of premature hopes. It may be just the opposite. I'm disparaging the boon that I crave! Please God, don't let love come to a stop between us before I've fathomed her full length of bliss. If only once—even once and for all, once and forever—the single memory would magnify by dream all my lesser solaces in kind. 'Other pleasures are asleep by comparison.' For her Montaigne would have written it a thousand times on the Bordeaux blackboard. As the jewel of games is to other recreations, so Deirdre's beauty is to that of all others.

My transcendental and irresponsible desire for that patrician woman is not to be compared with my lawful love for Gloria—which these days, nevertheless, seems astir again in the carnal mode. A young man stiffens at the barest glimpse of a woman's skin, and it happens that her yen to be afflated by a Sympathetic Method of Dialectic Commutation sometimes coincides with his urge to infuse the like. But a man of my years doesn't rise in hydrostatic pressure at the sight of every half-dressed female, and my hankering for Deirdre's strange flesh has never been merely instinctive tumescence.

No sooner had that oversimplification ever crossed Dexter's mind than it was given the lie by an involuntary translation of orectic polarity from cerebral abstraction to palpable representation. But now he was surprised to find that the romantic fantasia of a desired Deirdre Cotton was displaced by a realistic vision of his unbridled wife in desirous disposition.

Without sufficient gratitude, he now admits, he had sufficiently benefited from the evolution of her sensory culture for some years after the birth of their hinnies, until the spontaneous delights of youthful marriage were all but finally smothered by anxieties resentments and disgusts, domestic or extraneous, their mysteries dissipated by the boredom of familiarity. Before they'd both grown too embarrassed by the disillusions of consuetudinary life to perpetuate the gaiety of lascivious innuendo in their amorous conversation, she'd not taken it amiss at certain phases of the moon to be called his little ass.

One Friday night not long before their tacit estrangement (which at present was tacitly suspended) they had returned from the West End Theater in perfectly opposite states of dielectric potential. In a sparse audience this imaginative couple had seen an Irish film of illicit passion so restrained in erotic action by the Scholastic mores of a village on the cliffs of the Western World, and in erotic exhibition by the cinematic craft of the director, that not daring to glance at each other they sat side by side without touching in a unison of rapt absorption as they were sympathetically moved by the potentiated romance. At home, flung out side by side on their backs after the mutual cloudburst, their nakedness seemed more libidinous than ever: at once sated and expectant; stilled, yet inchoate with provocation. Encouraged by Gloria's epochal disinhibition (redressing the frustration suffered by the love story's heroine), he improved the occasion by insinuating a theme that had been lurking in his fancy for more than a decade. It was a shamefully sensational suggestion of adventure concerning the only element of the problem of marriage about which he ever wished to hear more of her thoughts.

"This bed's wide enough for three." he sighed, as if offering a casually irrational trope for his satisfaction with her ardor.

"I won't have another woman in the house." she returned with the dying fall of a husky breath.

Was she obtusely affecting to mistake his pretended meaning—or expressing in jest a reawakened suspicion? He felt the ambiguous shadow of unforeseen alarm.

But suddenly she rose on one elbow from her languorous pause and reached over with her right hand to caress his ego—an uncharacteristically lubricious test that seemed to represent a tentative leap of liberation. "But you seem to have no one else in mind right now."

"Give me time; I'm getting old. —You'd be in the middle." He held his breath, trusting to invent routes of escape from the dangerous ground he was about to tread.

"Am I to be used like a priestess of your temple?" Her reply might have been acerbic, confirming his peril; but it was murmured in a tone which he took to admit an ambivalence that hinted playful curiosity as much as potential anger. "I don't like strangers."

"No strangers." His cautiousness, though still defensively tentative, was somewhat emboldened. "And I'd never turn you loose with any man alone." But he instantly regretted his diction, aware too late that a woman might listen for pejorative connotation, especially when she already nourished resentment at serving her spouse as an amorous utensil.

"I don't ever want to be trusted out of your sight." But then she added slyly: "You'll always be my right hand man."

"Then I'd better change places right now!" His custom of sleeping stage-left in the bed had been formed when the children were small, to accommodate her in getting to the door on her side of the room. But as he rose to cross her front, overshadowing her diminutive fairness like a dark angel in the shallow sea-bottom light that filtered through the shades from Cod Street, the reinvigorating view of her gave him pause and he never reached the proper place for a man called Dexter.

Her ensuing response to the resurrection mollified even his cerebral appetite for the proposal he'd been leading up to; but the novelty of her geographer's hypothetical initiative hadn't lost its pique for the suggestible historian. Redoubled beatitude didn't appease her senses quite well enough to let imagination sleep.

She startled him from his sweaty somnolence, and awakened an unfamiliar anxiety, by resuming the interrupted wordplay with a chaste lasciviousness that both gratified and dismayed his erstwhile desire to broaden the scope of her speculation. Her intempestive whisper was surprisingly solemn, as if in response to a definite proposition. "Only if you agree that you're forbidden to make up for my sin by trespassing likewise, in or out of my sight. It must be pure Christian generosity on your part."

"The pure fellowship of three good friends." Already he was wide awake again, once more thrilled by the effort to guess at her seriousness, whether literal or figurative. Was the subject infallibly interesting?

"Friends before we start!" she insisted. "Who've you got in mind? I won't have anything to do with a married man. That's my respect for the integrity of families."

First no strangers; now no married men. Indeed her teasing shaded off into mockery. Yet if her words were taken at face value he wasn't sorry to eliminate attractive devils like Huck Salter or Eric Vanderlyn. But who could it be? They had both been given something to think about. It opened future possibilities which though not yet identified were perhaps not too fantastic. Opening conjecture was perhaps progress enough for the present.

First he twitted her about the frail gray Head Librarian, most notable bachelor of the city's public servants; but she countered that as a professional she had to respect the prohibition of intimacy among colleagues. Then it appeared that all the doctors of their acquaintance were married, and teachers too. Just for fun he even ticked off the name of old Doc Charlemagne, but he was disqualified for having a commonlaw consort. Rafe Opsimath was likewise excluded on scruple, as Tessa's uncommon Knight Errant.

Before this stimulating colloquy finally played itself out in a cat's cradle of motionless arms and legs, under the aegis of Hypnos at the end of a long day, Dexter had begun to find the cathartic humor in itself sufficiently adventurous. By the time he named the little countercaster upstairs as a joking afterthought he had assumed that she too was gradually resigned to the impracticability of such an indecent experiment (ostensibly on her behalf), and had ruefully acknowledged the civilizing constraint upon unbridled femininity. At that time they'd hardly have classified Caleb as a friend, and she hadn't bothered with any other objection.

Since then nothing in their intercourse had suggested that she remembered either the ecstasies of this episode or its signal advances in communication. But whether or not the depraved notion was dormant in her consciousness, he'd hoped and feared that it had taken root—if only, along the lines of her more recent slant in all interpretations, as a heartless suggestion insulting to her dignity. (She'd recently fished up from the distant past as grievous evidence of her loss of his love a casual remark he'd innocently tossed off and long since forgotten, that sang froid was the essential attribute of a good lover!) And now, months later, her freethinking seemed on the rise again, just in time for the nightlong freedom of the house they were looking forward to on Saturday.

Thus reason memory and circumstance conspired with a recent change in the atmosphere to single out the sinister male with whom Dexter was at the moment making friends as a harmless bedfellow exactly suited by situation stature and social isolation for a safely limited probation, and from whom (as the husband hoped) there was tolerable risk of scandal or emotional competition.

Beneath the peroration of his dinnertable speech he was calculating his means as reasonably as Don Quixote, unmindful of his fictive assumptions. He thought of issuing a conditional invitation to the guest before asking Gloria if she was interested, not so much because the opportunity to do so was urged by a sudden revival of his mania, and even jibed with the official purpose of the evening's entertainment, as because it would have been an excruciating wound to her fragile pride if she had assented—probably only after the greatest trepidation of soul—and then been humiliated to find that her sacrifice was declined; whereas it would be easier and less cruel to make Caleb some plausible apology for a bid withdrawn if he should first accept the offer and she then decline it. Even if they both agreed to the secret party it would be necessary to conceal from her the unconscionable offense of not inviting the hostess first.

However, Dexter reassured his palpitating heart by deciding that before he said a word to revive his plot any further he must devise a diplomatic delivery of his shocking overture to this agreeable but somewhat reserved new comrade (whose passions seemed usually to dwell in other realms of experience) without either owning to the lechery of a pander or slandering his wife's historical virtue. He could therefore postpone the yet more problematic difficulty of tempting the woman without incurring her rightful wrath.

Thus trembling with an infatuation half shrewd and half reckless, listening to Caleb's part of the conversation, he pondered presentation of the offer as an act of hospitality. Luse wine and the nascent bonds of conviviality were dissolving their residual restraint. They saw eye to eye in many matters of judgment taste and criticism, a felicitous conjunction of opinions that seemed positively providential. What else but teleological propriety had brought Caleb into the house for explorations in complementarity just when the restless couple most needed a tonic?

In this phase of his fever Dexter's scheming was indeed so encouraged by fate's apparent approval, and his scruples about the protocols of its implementation so nearly overborne, that he almost forgot the original purpose of this man-to-man conference and his practical reason for agreeing to Gloria's own plot against their tenant. (Few motives are single; even the purest is often a crystal of motives—not simply a concatenate series of double-ended links but a lattice of chain mail woven together in four dimensions by nodes of desire and inhibition.) But considering all the trouble she'd taken to bring about this afterdinner chat, in accordance with their pillow-talk conferences, he was absolutely committed to a difficult promise. And he wasn't sorry that its execution would quite adventitiously set a safe term limit to his dangerous semibisexual game.

". . . What can you expect when the maximum horizon of reelection is only two years?" he was saying aloud, "By all odds it will take ten years to get the Federal grants we need; then we'll have to suffer two or three drought emergencies before the Earls will be persuaded to vote an increase even in long-term debt, and to raise the water rates, for the city's small share of the cost. Every year we use more water on lawns and quasi-athletic showers. The city has more and more private baths and swimming pools for bigger and bigger swarms of pilgrims. Fish plants waste fresh water by the ton. Worst of all, an army of opulence will soon besiege our townlands on both sides of the Gut. We're already beginning to blast and edify the unoccupied hillsides. Our landscape sickens from the loss of trees. Erosion ravages our rock-bottom soil. The water table keeps falling. Yet as soon as the reservoirs start filling in a stormy winter all our halfhearted conservation mottoes fade like ghosts at dawn. . . ."

All at once, struck by the absurdly improbable conjunction of three individual wills at a highly unlikely intersection of chances upon which the accomplishment of his fantasy depended, he was fetched smartly back to Mrs Grundy's realm of commonsense and the clairvoyance of ordinary life. His inner face burned with shame at the disgrace of his "well-reasoned nonsense". In the toils of venery he'd lost his moorings. In the name of female concupiscence he'd disguised a corruption too ignoble to confess to himself, let alone a priest. Now that he stood back to look at it, disgusted with its obliquity, his secret plan vanished.

But not the prurience itself, which ever abided, which he could only sublimate in work or confine to more wholesome lust. Neither did he pretend to expunge or deny his sympathetic respect for the coeducated desires of his respectable wife. Dexter plainly admitted to himself that it was prudence and fear of society—or fear of her fear—that wiped out the moral courage to expose his sexual truth, and hers—even if prospectively shared by but one other participant.

At the same time he chided himself for having failed to remind himself that very few Christians might be free enough of ethological prejudice to understand the compassion in his worshipful tribute to the woman's erotic superiority, which would have justified his proposal *in this particular case*—least of all Gloria herself before and after the mood was upon her (if indeed it could at any time subvert her actual behavior). Nor in any selfrespecting state of mind would he himself disclose to anyone so much as the fact that such an idea had ever appeared in his consciousness even as a mere anthropological possibility in New Armorica! For Gloria it would be an irremediable pollution of their marriage. Never again would she wholly accept his declarations of allegiance, and ever after would she look upon his ostensibly playful wish as contemptuous of her love.

In the end, sitting there with Caleb, he came to believe that if his vision had been fulfilled he would have been left forever not with a satisfaction of anthropological curiosity but with a horrible feeling of self-destructive degradation. All passion spent, when beatitude had ebbed to the level of reflection, all three would have loathed themselves in hot shame and cold turpitude. So spoke Dexter in his heart, striving to recover the esteem of his wife, of Caleb Karcist, of Deirdre Cotton, and of all others who might have guessed.

". . . Already the public watershed tracts are under attack that the Duke of Dogtown entailed for all his people in perpetuity."

"Old Tybbot must be whirling in his grave." said Caleb, broadly indicating the upper reach of Acorn Pasture Cemetery, now deep in darkness outside the windows.

"That rugged individualist meant well for his whole home town. In full armor he comes by night to charge me with my duty as Dogtown's putative guardian. My philanthropy's broader than his, and amid alien corn at that; but what more can I do? I'll grow old making land-use studies, drawing maps, writing grant applications for geological surveys, consulting civil engineers, and making gloomy presentations to all the boards. For an architect it's a far cry from building splendid new towers, domes, theaters, and temples."

Dexter's self-revealing swerve ad hominem (in the elation of relief from having discarded his aphrodisiac motive) went further than he would have advised, but at last he'd found his way toward the one true purpose of tonight's event. Just as Caleb for his part was attaining to the comfort of comradeship and solidarity under the spell of his host's deep gentle voice, he began to sense the tendentiousness of these earnest ruminations. By two or three swift transitions of speech the guest's complacency was reduced to its proper insecurity, like a Jewish banker's when faced by the limits of cordiality at his private dinner with Bismarck.

"I can't do any constructive work at the office." Dexter confided. "I must spend all my time on the phone listening to complaints, or going to useless meetings, or scrutinizing schemes for private aggrandizement. In order to do my most important job for this city I need time and space at home. Gloria has the same problem."

Caleb's blood ran cold with logical and sympathetic presentiment. Dexter's last shattering sentence struck home before its antecedent, instantly reproducing in Caleb's mind a conversation with Gloria following the Night of the Rock. After a few days, having heard no more of its burden, he'd dismissed it from his waking dread as a merely fugacious symptom of her moral agitation. It had seemed too inconsistent with his pattern of success, and with her usual selfsubordinating deference to his will, to be retained for meditation. And even now, listening to Dexter, he remembered her words without immediately divining the emotional determination that had summoned them.

It was the one occasion on which Caleb had been accepted in the great marriage bed (on the side closer to the hall door). They had dared risk it only for an hour or so, very late at night, spread and outflung, reckless of space for the first time, when Dexter was spending the night out of town at a gathering of Vinland's city planners. The children slept soundly, and Ibi guarded the house outside, in case Og should come home unannounced, perhaps with food poisoning or in a fit of professional disgust—though he'd telephoned his queen as late as eleven o'clock with the exemplary assurance that he was a hundred miles away on the banks of the Pequod. Gloria knew her husband well enough not to worry about entrapment by a faked long-distance call. That possibility was a faint misgiving that Caleb kept to himself after she'd used the same phone to signal him down from the attic.

It had been his callous mistake to plot that needlessly symbolic escapade. Though unopposed in advance by Gloria's docile body, in flagrante delicto the sacramental venue struck her soul as a violation of troth more heinous than the sin itself.

With the sleeping children so near it was a rash innovation anyway. The conversation was carried on in whispers, shrouded by bed clothes, though only after he was caught dozing in selfcongratulation and savoring the carelessly nude leisure of a husband, when she had recovered from the adulterous phase-state she intended to be her last, and gathered courage for the kind of forthright initiative that in spite of her fame for volubility and effusion she had never been able to muster against a man.

"Caleb?"

"Yes?"

"I can't control myself as long as you stay."

"Then you've got more strength left than I have. But I suppose I can get upstairs. Are you afraid the kids will wake up?"

"No, I mean stay in this house. It will be safer to see each other if you live somewhere else. Otherwise Dexter will find out."

With a glimmer of revelation Caleb had distinguished the new slyness in her desperate message. Flat on their backs, her hands and arms touched his, but she was closed and tense. His chest drew tight in a parallel attitude of suspended resolution as he rapidly weighed various interpretations of the crisis. "Is something—wrong?" he'd finally croaked, with a rigid gulp of fear.

"Not with you. You've given me new life. But I have to think of my Mrs Grundy. Appearances are important, for the childrens' sake at least. As long as you're here in the house I can't ask Dexter to leave."

At this second shock Caleb's alarm fissioned into plural apprehensions. Since their reciprocal declaration of love he had been aware of no hint that she contemplated any separation from Dexter. Could she be thinking of divorce—for the sake of love? In Vinland that still usually required proof of infidelity, or else an out-of-state collusion in some conventional perjury about cruel and inhuman treatment! Then Caleb trembled between the fear of detachment and the fear of adhesion.

Yet the thought of dissolving her marriage was consistent with her unhappiness in the past. Before the onset of their liaison he had accidentally surprised her in two or three scenes of solitary weeping; and once he'd heard (more to Ibi's distress than his own) rising voices from the living room when the children were out; but he'd judged the chafing to be no more than the normal discontent of undulant castle-fever.

In one instance she'd not been entirely alone, for she was caressing Ibi on the early backyard grass. As the intruder he had blundered too far to retreat without being seen, and under the necessity of an ameliorating smile she avowed that she was crying for less fortunate dogs and all captive animals. Afterwards, indeed, Caleb's adjunctive sympathy with her silent compassions, his own pity for longsuffering dogs and sorrow for all women, his exaltation of the feminine pain and charity that no man would ever get to learn, had become the essential cause of his tender love for the inner person who belonged to no one except her bygoing babies—as distinct from the causes of his disinterested admiration and selfserving desire.

Still, only an eon later in his knowledge of her, listening on the bed of Og, had it verily penetrated to his theater of worry that she might have honorable expectations of him in the sequel, notwithstanding every discrepancy of age condition and ambition.

"The whole city would be scandalized." she went on more lightly. "Even if you weren't my lover I'd feel compromised, having an extra man under my roof. Don't think I'm enough older than you to be above suspicion. I must never pull down shades in the daytime. This house is watched by five or six aborigines across the street, and I'm sure they wonder why I've been putting up new curtains."

He dared not yet reply.

"I want to feel free." she added after a pause. "But I'll miss Ibi something right awful!"

That hoarsely whispered mollification, in the language of her childhood, erupted into a spasm of sound between sob and laugh that he affected to hear as evidence that she'd been teasing him. He took charge of the outcome by reaching over to tickle the far side of her ribs, bussing her kneecaps, and pinching her lips for silence. She couldn't help herself: reacting to his tease with a spliggle, like a schoolgirl stifling a conflation of hilarity and resentment at the violation of her gravity in a public library, she shed twenty years of maturity.

His joshing, followed by another revivified atonement, was enough (so he'd thought) to put the quietus to her drastic vagary. Nothing further had been said of this wrenching reaction, and according to the signs that he noticed her consideration of it had vanished again in the usual business of an exciting intrigue.

By all appearances, after that prodigious utterance of her innermore will, she'd felt such relief that for many days thereafter she forgot that it was necessary to implement her decision.

But now down in the dining room, in mundane terms on pragmatic grounds, the husband for good and sufficient reasons of his own was forcing Caleb to recognize the fear he'd repressed and face the doom of termination.

"... The Board's driving the Building Inspector crazy with their Multiple Occupancy ordinance. What they're trying to do is good—at my own behest, in fact—finally, after three or four fire-fatalities in one year. But none of them can construct a sentence, so it's only after an order is brought up for debate that the thinking begins. 'Put it in language.' they say to the Solicitor or the Clerk—or to me, in a case like this—usually after they've already passed it! The afterthoughts are legion.

"Anyhow, from now on all rented domiciles must have a second egress. The ordinance stipulates alternative stairs for separate dwelling units on any upper floor. The Public Health inspectors will be looking at every apartment in Dogtown...."

While Dexter refilled their glasses with luse, leaning back in his chair as casually as an old friend with nothing ulterior on his mind, Caleb felt that he was being offered the last of several different causes for the same effect. He hardly needed to guess, as Gloria's husband unfolded his news (either as her guileless instrument only, or also as the disingenuous agent of his own suspicions), that he was being offered her face-saving excuse for Courtly treachery.

"This house has many doors and windows down here, but in case of fire as you know there's only one way to get down from your quarters on the top floor...."

Caleb needed no reminder on this score. As a troubadour he'd studied the architecture of this machine for living with the avidity of an inside burglar and was all too familiar with its circulational defects. For the very reason that was now being adduced by King Mark he had often refrained from playing the impulsive part of

Tristram with the queen; and only in default of an escape route at certain assignations in some of his thought-experiments had he refrained from risking the surprise of Abelard, should his yard sentry have failed to announce an irregular return of the sovereign.

". . . I'm afraid we just can't afford to build an outside staircase for your apartment."

Caleb made no protest. Wits benumbed, his throat tightened to the old pain. He was as tongue-tied and weak of voice as Moses—like "a man of uncircumcised lips"; but even within his head, unlike Moses, he found no speech. He resisted the urge to get up and walk away without a word—and especially without encountering Gloria—only because it would have been despicable to flout the Keiths' charitable diplomacy by responding in a churlish manner.

Dexter was giving him plenty of notice. "There's no hurry. I know you'll be too busy to think about moving before Gloucestermas, and anyway we may not have time to fix up either my study or Gloria's until the end of July. The kids are getting more gregarious every month, but that's soon enough for them to start making more noise in the house. Of course the long days and short nights will keep them outside most of the time . . ."

Caleb wanly smiled his acknowledgment of the landlord's problem, and managed to fetch up a few stock phrases signifying his deprecation of the inconvenience to himself that was only to be expected sooner or later by any landless marooner. Ostentatiously noting the hour on his watch, he pushed back his chair without haste and rose with the informal dignity of a contented visitor reluctant to take his leave. In a movement that unconsciously imitated Ibi's gesture of inconsequential greeting or embarrassment he stretched and yawned, arching his chest.

Dexter did the same, but leaning back in his chair as if not to hurry off the guest. Like two camping woodsmen about to turn in for the night. Right to the end Dexter tried to make amends for the eviction. "Our whole family's going to miss your dog. We'll always be glad to take care of him if you decide to go on a trip to Europe or somewhere." But when Dogtown's champion got up to say goodnight he stood like a tower over Caleb, who had shrunk again to the size of a suppliant.

In the aftermath of this unexpected discomfit, as Caleb freshly appreciated the most befitting aerie ever to be found for rent, the extraordinary privileges of which he felt no remorse at having abused, he was at first too bewildered, as well as incurious about the lore of real property, to inquire about the conditions and exceptions of the new ordinance, in case it really was the cause of this confounding hitch in his pursuit of happiness.

As a matter of fact, he later found out from one of Belle's articles in the *Nous*, such legislation is always qualified, especially when touching property rights and 'income investments'. Dexter had omitted to mention that a customary 'grandfather clause' exempted any landlord of three dwelling units or less sharing his own roof, until such time as the 'existing' tenant should give up his premises. Furthermore, the deadline for anyone's compliance was a full year from the date of enactment! But Caleb was well aware that even if he'd known enough to dispute his landlord's excuse, his own insuperable diffidence prevented him from exhibiting even the mildest doubt of an adversary's logic. Moreover the Keiths were not his adversaries. They were in truth his benefactors.

Yet they represented the "community", his adversary willy-nilly. He considered himself a featherweight antigen—and here in the wrong as a violator of honorable hospitality—who survived on the sufferance of society only because he was undistinguished from all the other ions of the political economy. He believed that his admittance to the Rectory was now repented by the woman he'd so unaccountably infatuated.

Too timid to take offence (as always, at least one third feminine), and morally defenseless, he bore no grudge for the way he was being eased out of his fundamentally insecure domicile. Nothing rancorous had been said by the spokesman; and he'd been spared the painful effort of the real decision-maker to declare her determination to get him out of her history. Above all, he'd been pardoned without confession, released without retribution. He hoped the parting would leave Gloria's domestic relations as undisturbed as the sea after a sinking.

It was a week after the family dinner before she could look him in the eye—and then they both pretended that nothing had happened to alter their affections. And no one in the menage adverted to the impending disassociation until the day Caleb gave the Keiths a definite date, much sooner than they'd asked, taking little advantage of the liberal grace he'd been given.

At the last it was hard to remember his pride in her professional prestige, his enchantment by the glamour of her connections with the city, his vicarious enjoyment of her communion with both exceptional and representative citizens of all ages. Her flesh and bones which at first acquaintance had seemed soft and delicate, almost numinous, he now knew as equally energetic at all points, as if nowhere softer than anywhere else. As his inward eye now superposed upon the physiognomy of her ceaseless interactivity the sultry languidness into which he'd sometimes beguiled it, her ageless face—ironically mutable, still fair with the sunspots of tomboy youth yet effervescently maternal—was beginning to gather the telltale wrinkles of experience.

The old inclination to confide in her, to explain his life, had given way to a nearly dispassionate wish not to end the suddenly objectified experience until his self-respect had been restored with a pentecostal confession from her body. He therefore doggedly exploited the ambiguity of his tacit understanding that she would end the affair when he moved out of the house. Once his departure was fixed, she who could never forthrightly demur was a little less evasive of his resumed advances (which had become artificially sanguine); and after each of their precious few appointments for valedictory atonement was negotiated she faithfully overcame her spiritual reluctance to accomplish it. But then they didn't find much to say to each other.

Nevertheless he moved to East Harbor with his vanity after all intact, and remained nostalgically loyal to the buried covenant as a fact of history. Gloria sighed for Ibi, but her marital pain was eased, no longer to have a second man claiming her rind.

FOURTH MOVEMENT

1
NORMAN MAROONED

*S*pring was as usual retarded by the cold east wind that had felt warm in the winter. Ruled by the sublunar rhythm that underrules the sun, priestly shape-changing Manannan still heaved two deep breaths every day, sometimes softly laving with whispers or deep sighs, sometimes lashing in anger; but the dog turds of March had been pierced to the pavement by April's cold rain, and the relics of those frozen on winter grass, dissolved by the primaveral fluids of May, were now spottily enriching the ragged lawns and parks as harbingers of summer. Malgré the sea's cunctating weather, a few incarcerated bulbs, disputing frost and wind, had displayed betimes their indomitable fertility; foils of green and yellow, compromised here and there by lavender, flashed upon an outward eye from the shambles of rock gardens, as if to bait the sun. Reversing the sequence of Fall, each oak's canopy began to consolidate itself out of efflorescing daubs, from brown through yellow to green. Sleepers were wakened early by the indefatigable love-call of the mourning dove.

But otherwise Dogtown had long since lost the prospect of outliving hibernation for its own productive flora. Wild roses stubbornly clung to the sand here and there along unimproved stretches of the shore but their hips were left to shrivel on the bush unvalued; arboriginal grapevines were extinct, methodically extirpated; the colonists' prized apple orchards, scions of the English pippin, were displaced by houses, or left unto the tenth degeneration in the choking isolation of abandoned cultivation (still to be claimed by chainsaw and bulldozer or reclaimed by the encroachments of incult woodland), hardly noticed by any birds but woodpeckers. Saltwater farms were sold out; unharvested marsh grass now quickened and perished just as it had for millennia before its beds were drained by Georgios for forage; Cape peas and beans were no longer yielded for the Bacon frozen food processing plant. In the northern parishes two or three tiny farmsteads remained for cow manure and milk, with some other still-defended pastures for saddle horses and the Christmas-Pageant donkey; but except for vegetables from dooryard gardens and scantly sufficient hay from even fewer crowded fields the succession of settlers had at last given up on the natural usufructation of their arable land.

The boisterous bag of winds was as full as ever in days of yore, but windmills could be remembered only from books and pictures. Timbercutting and shipbuilding had stripped Lady Gloucester of her richest raiment long before the ravishment of her bones began; there was no longer an adequate supply of firewood—and less demand: otiose, anyway, for Cyclopean hearths. More than a century ago the dams and sluiceways for overshot waterwheels had stopped turning saws or grinding local grain with radiantly grooved granite discs, all their structures allowed to fall idle in hillside overgrowth, then abandoned, to rot and collapse. A seasonal fried-clam stand now occupied the site of an undershot mill at Tinker's Dam, formerly a successful exploitation of the tidal energy that surges forth and back from Tinker's River to Tinker's Pond, sacred moonpower negligently disdained.

Nor did Dogtown any longer even import the bargeloads of coal—or yet carloads—that used to fuel steam for the cotton mill of Seamark, the quarry powerhouses, the fish plants, the locomotives, the Harbor gasworks, the municipal dynamo of the Cape Gloucester Power, Light, and Traction Company, and of course the foundries and forges on or off the railroad—as well as heat for thousands of family furnaces and kitchen ranges. The petrified energy of trees was now almost entirely replaced by the direct and indirect energy of liquid fossils—but likewise brought from the mainland.

In fact the Cape's economic autonomy was so illusory that soon the last remaining public utility would no longer even participate in the prime conversion of its quintessentially fungible energy from imported matter. The two Traction boilers and their gleaming reciprocating engine with its great bright flywheel were to be dismantled; the battleship-sized generator geared to its great eccentric crankshaft was slated for scrapping within three years. Local contribution to the transformation of power would be limited to that of dividing and reducing the three-phased pressure of electricity viaducted by a high-stepping imperial network. The city would no longer support its own thermodynamic disintegration of petrochemical molecules to produce vital currency and legal tender—ichor of all technology and amusement—save in emergencies, with mobile diesel engines dismounted like house trailers, or perhaps at times of peak load when all the airconditioners and DV dampers might be wide open at the same time. Already the auxiliary high-voltage lines from Beggarly and Bethsalem (where Sumerian oil had taken the place of Atlantean coal in primemover fireboxes as the fuel for usable energy) were being rerouted enlarged and stepped up, mainly along the railroad right-of-way, to serve as the sole normal supply of amperes for the quondam-island's illumination, luxury, and commerce—for all its electronic command communication and control, all its acquisition and demodulation of broadcast agitations—as well as for the fixed and portable machinery that reconverted energy to mechanical work for commercial public and domestic industry. The brick Traction building itself would be truncated, and maintained only as a switchboard for kilowatts and a mustering office for maintenance crews.

On Mother's Neck in the East Harbor ward Raphael Opsimath had ended his pilgrimage from Cornucopia. He still cared little about Dogtown's past, though increasingly indulgent of those for whom it was essential. He was beginning to mock himself for succumbing to what he had called "the superstition of place", yet what most impressed him was that notwithstanding this presque-isle's dependency on the mainland, and its continuous exchange of hopefully fleeing fledglings for hopeful or desperate immigrants, its insularity had given rise to several subspecies, human as well as canine and avian, according to the evolutionary principle of restricted natural selection.

Now that he'd stopped to think about it, Rafe was surprised to find himself a resident taxpayer. In half a year, incautiously, step by step, the curiously helpful sojourner had been fatally enmeshed. The casual adventurer had ended up as a Norman on this backward exisle of carnal saints and angels. Already he hardly noticed the dogs and gulls of morning noon and night, or the noisy smells of fishermen with fish. It scarcely occurred to him that his enlarged insensitivity, or mundane tolerance, was an outcome of his inveterate urge to enlighten or protect the daughters of men and other strangers.

Bemused on a Sunday morning he gazed down from his own window at the mussel-blackened gray flats of Swanson Cove evacuated by the tide.

To his left the floor of this tiny valley was headed by a strand-footed sea wall of tapered precast concrete blocks surmounting a tumbled granite riprap. A hundred yards opposite his vantage, across the emptied hollow now at its greatest depth, East Front Street ran briefly behind a handrail along a much older retaining wall of dressed and fitted stone before twisting sharply up and away, displaying the snouts and tails of kilroys before and after they traversed the level in profile at customary high speed. On the hither side of that rising curve the cove's dominant private property was buffered from both sea and neighborhood by the elevated shoulder of headland rock that supported the three four-decked particolored wooden buildings of an abandoned summer hotel named for Natty Hawhaw.

On either side of Rafe, as beholder of the tidal vale, half a dozen motley little houses were crowded in a string along their own common sea wall, which defended his highly populated knoll of greenery.

Protruding from the middle of the beach a whale of rust granite and two or three sucklings were half buried in the mud-colored bottomland, never totally submerged by the flood. Twice a day the tide did engulf and conceal three large boulders clustered midway across the mouth of the inlet where the sea god had rolled them to hinder Champlain and Smith, but now they were high and almost dry, their dark sea-worn hue blackening bottomward, at an edging frontier of ripples from the outer harbor just beginning its reflux under their skirts.

Nearly all the smaller and smallest rocks, whited with barnacles or clad in weeping seaweeds, randomly scattered here and there or strewn and imbedded as obstacles in the fine swart sand, attracted purple and nacreous colonies of opened or separated shells always emptied by predators or scavengers of the tidal demimonde. Yet in a few weeks barefooted bathers would be picking their way through the bleached shells and sharp pebbles of the highwater belt to reach the smooth passages and expanses that looked like miniature prairies broken up by wooded islands in relief, around which and over which the waters of Vinland Bay were drawn and withdrawn by the regular femininity of the moon, in winter sometimes flowing as if in malice but then in summertime's friendly abeyance, alluring swimmers toward deep water. At ebb's limit the outer jaws of the cove were further barred on several scales of magnitude by the teeth of two archipelagic mountain ranges almost meeting in the middle; but when the valley was at its shallowest the reef they formed was covered all the way out to the Neck's guanoed Gibraltar by a six-foot flooding of Noah's plain.

Brimming tides had always excited Rafe, but already he preferred the profundity of this map exhibited every half turn of the earth, especially at the dark or full of the moon; and at present the silent diorama was fully vacant with clarified space, once more preparing to yield its surface to the besieging leveler. At this hour all the angels were busy elsewhere who often spent their siestas here.

He was savoring an unscheduled lull in the asymptotic process of naturalizing his citizenship while he developed means of assisting the community of those whom Tessa Barebones at their first meeting had called "our kind of fugitives and failures".

It was an arbitrary category, small in numbers but as heterogeneous as the races comprised by canine. The disinterested foundation of his affinity for the whole place wasn't clear even to Tessa, to whom he seemed an affable epitome of ambitious power; but to himself it was a simply instinctive interest in complexity. There was no dearth of fair cities in which to make a success of the fortune he'd earned in his native stamping grounds, but here he hoped to invest his talents without unrestrained competition.

At the moment he was lazily enjoying the disappointment of a canceled fishing trip with Wat Cibber, confident that he would have future chances to observe the art of dragging without getting dragged into it. Wat's routine called for "a dawn patrol in my antique jalopy to check the Foreskin and the dorsal shore". Thanks to an auspice of certain whitecap shapes with the breeze in an unfavorable quarter, signifying that today's seas would be too choppy for setting hauling and towing a net in his singlehanded little vessel, this painless tour around the East Harbor peninsula had resolved the fisherman's ambivalence.

With a clearly pronounced sigh of relief Wat explained his decision: "You see what I mean: it did no good to change my boat's name to *Motion* from *Weather Breeder*! I'd probably have rimracked my gear on rocks and hard places anyway, or wasted my sweat on nothing but dogfish that take half the day cutting off their ugly heads to get them out of the net. I may have great regard for the regardless, but I've got very little use for the useless. It profits nothing to seize time by the forelock when it's bald everywhere else. So I guess I'll have to take you home-along." Some of his apparently idiosyncratic expressions were echoes of distant Wessex ancestry. "We'll turn aside from battle and ungird our lions with a Spartan mugup. Thank God I'm spared yet another day's net loss of dollars! Maybe tomorrow the prices will go up enough to pay for the gas."

The overcast threat of rain had nothing directly to do with Wat's decision to stay ashore and ply his needle, for precipitation alone, nor atmospheric temperature, no more than negative cash flow, would keep this true lover of fishing from pursuing fish. It was a love of which he himself the local trade's most zealous priest made mordant fun because the piety of his career was much too patent. Doctor Charlemagne had him pegged for adjunct professor of Piscatology and Ichtheology at Dogtown College.

The only printed matter in Wat's workshop was a late issue of *The New Armorican Fisherman*, which he regularly studied in order he said "to feed my agony and self-doubt". He must have done all his other reading at home with his wife Teddi, who he often asseverated would be "the most educated person in the graveyard". His respect for her culture could hardly be doubted, though couched not seldom in self-effacing gibes. In one digression with Rafe he'd added to his already familiar stock of pleasantries: "She condescends to call me her very dear husband; but she's even more expensive for me!"

Despite the aborted attempt to accompany Wat at the work he lived for, Rafe was glad that at least he'd been introduced to the solid breakfasts at Spartan's. The lunchroom, situated on a V where the principal streets of the Neck divaricated from the main stem of the causeway, was no more than a cablelength from his own underused kitchen, and only across a narrow one-way street from Argo Cove on the inner-harbor side where Wat received visitors in the atelier next to his private little marine railway.

At the lunchroom they had found five or six working landsmen—three of whom, from a City truck parked hard by, merely smiled when Wat hailed them sotto voice as "the D P W's cruising crew of crafty work-dodgers"—who Rafe understood made up the regular weekday gathering that waited for the unfailing proprietor to unlock the door exactly on time, long before the rest of the Neck was disturbed by sunlight breaking over the trees of the Foreside ridge. Mr Spartan never took a day off, and in the summer he was busy late into the evening.

The other clients nodded to Wat and exchanged almost soundless formulas worn down to esoteric signals by decades of familiarity with each other's sight. But in their embarrassment at a new man's presence Rafe was democratically ignored, dressed like a rusticating exotic but perhaps one of the marine biologists Cibber occasionally took under his wing—in any case, they could see at a glance, too innocent-looking to merit serious suspicion.

Wat's professional friends, a few Yankee "day-trippers" who tied up in East Harbor, were already outside the breakwater with their acolytes in larger boats than his.

As soon as the patrons had taken their customary places, Wat at the counter with his guest, where he was usually alone on his first victualling of the day, the others divided among two boothed tables, the hungry silence of the doorsteps broke into a vigorous babble of continued gossip, during which the smart young waitress was kept hopping with orders she knew by heart, matched by the seeing but unseen kitchen's faultless anticipations. Nobody ever had to ask for coffee or more of it. Behind the counter Mr Spartan himself was almost conspiratorial with Wat, his oldest and most frequent customer, and accorded Rafe the welcome of friendly but uninquisitive respect even before he was informed that the new face was a neighbor's, likely to become nearly as regular, though probably in the crowd that came much later in the diurnal clatter.

The fact that Wat always got up before the sun, whether or not to go fishing, might excuse the recesses he took from work during his long hours. His intervals at Spartan's were public, little more remarkable than many a man's; but they were of little weight compared to the sums of repose in his headquarters rocking chair, under a weathered gray board nailed to the wall in dusty shadows, its roughly painted legend in faded black: HOME OF LOST PAUSES. "That's Dogtown in general but right here in particular." he'd told Rafe; and then with a shy grin rapidly muttered his wellworn parody, in case Rafe never happened to have heard it: "Home of lost pauses, and shaken britches, and unpopular dames, and impossible deities."

The *Motion* herself was moored elsewhere, at a ruined wharf where boats remained afloat at low tide, barely clear of the mud that then presented itself to open air at this shallow end of the inner harbor's innermost haven where he held philosophical office at any tide and at high tide occasionally hauled her out, or someone else's boat, for repair, painting, or mechanical maintenance. His shop was as well equipped with tools and materials as any Jack-of-all-trade's.

Ruminating comfortably at the window of his yet-to-be-furnished house, Rafe procrastinated the unpacking and deployment that still left him at a loss. In rather lame loyalty to his friend and partner Buck Barebones he had not allowed Tessa Barebones to come and help, even though Buck, had he known his wife's therapeutic truth, might not have especially minded, so uxorious would he be in absolution. Such an intimate donation of domestic service would have been a negligibly gratuitous transgression against the occult shreds of his honor.

In truly private and secondary matters it was best to leave things exactly as they stood, a rather comfortable arrangement for at least two of the three concerned. An anonymous ditty suppressed in Rafe's married days suddenly popped up from the verbal lobe of his brain with the assurance of a longforgotten jingle:

> A proper man is a man alone;
> A proper woman's mated.
> Yet nowadays it's plain to see
> That neither is thus sated.

It was a local privilege to learn from Tessa interesting things about the disequilibriums of others' private affairs. Then too, he and Buck were associated in a sympathetic and entirely honorable alliance with each other, not without relevance to the financial deliberations with Father Chris Lucey which for the past week or more had preoccupied his banausic mind.

While enjoying this sabbath interval in his manifold pursuits of interested and disinterested success—an opportunity for meditation that a busy operator ordinarily forgets he's been missing—Rafe was reconciling himself to the condition of lost freedom under which interfering sons of God, entangled with the nets of men, were rewarded with human comforts. But the realization that his possibilities were no longer numberless only whetted his appetite for enterprises less limited than fishing or fornication.

The cove's frequenting angels hadn't yet mustered for their daily meditations and nodding ablutions on the creeping frontier of its puddled bottom. Their carte du jour varied with the tide, and with the offal distractions of boats returning to the harbor before their decks were washed of blood and guts. But three or four Cosmos were wheeling above the little valley—indeed within its bowl, below his own elevation ten feet higher than the seawall that retained the lower level of his tiny messuage. Down there the parapet upon which his small red "summer cottage" perched so confidently was only four feet above the basin's mean high water, but twice as high above the rocky teeth of the flats when the tide was out.

A lone Maxwell rested on one leg in motionless trance upon the ridgepole of the cottage like a windless weathervane at the level of Rafe's feet, no more than twenty yards from where he stood. Waiting for the meditative gull to show its other leg, or at least to prove that it wasn't maimed in the wing and could survive in competition without his assistance, and mulling over the diversions with which he might take advantage of the hitch in his former plan for the day, he resisted his proclivity to plunge back into the large questions of his future career. He fell instead into easier thought about his dawning scheme to convert the uninsulated shack into a genuine all-year-round cottage. It might provide a tenant with half as much living space as his own homely gray asbestos-shingled house, which included a small apartment in the basement (also for rent).

Tuber-stemmed Slim Boxshaw, one of the most friendly Roundhouse Knights of the Turntable, had promised to take on the reconstruction, provided it didn't call for a studious estimate or fixed-price contract. On that point Rafe was indulgent, for he expected pitfalls in any "remodeling" project, knowing that he himself would be changing his mind as the job progressed. He trusted to Slim's honesty if not to his efficiency. A wary businessman should never accept the quote of some sharp carriage-trade contractor with the hedging morals of an M B A candidate and a high-priced crew of unhurried Union men. Notwithstanding Rafe's generalized political support of unionizatiion—at least where the hiring was fair, the work rules rational, and the supervision effective—he equivocated in his private affairs like a "liberal Protestican", or a Divine Humanist construing some case of situational ethics. Besides, in Dogtown practically nobody seemed to care about the union-hiring issue as long as Dogtowners were somehow put to work.

Rafe's problem was to find an educated person of intelligence and skill to make a few lists and drawings, no professional architect being required. Once more his thoughts turned to Caleb Karcist, who might be available for temporary work after Gloucestermas.

That pencil-pusher was pedantic at least, loved microscopic details, and seemed qualified, with Dexter Keith's informal advice, to define what an owner wanted.

Rafe had bought this "income property" as an anchor to windward, in case all his major investments went sour. At least he'd be able to pay the taxes for his own shelter if everything else went wrong. He warned himself to fix his rents like a pretender to the M B A and not play the generous fool. Clint Clifford (another sometime officer of the local Roundhouse, an appraising vice-president of the Dogtown Home Bank), the reality broker who'd sold him the property with scrupulous warnings of many a defect despite the fact that he represented the seller's interests, would probably be able to find him suitable year-round tenants for two of the three dwelling units, once he'd made up his own mind which of them he himself wished to occupy permanently. Though still enjoying the liberty of a liquid position, disencumbered of all obligations save alimony [fixed in his Cornucopian avatar long before great financial gains of the last six months], he wondered if he'd be wanting more space than a bachelor required.

He again reminded himself that he was no longer a carpetbagger in this city of only three gates—the Draw the Gut and the Eisenhower highway bridge—in the single wall of the ocean. From his new vantage of possession it seemed instead a town of one continuous portal barricaded discontinuously with all manner of rocks. Within it, anyway, he was free to choose his ventures and risk his substance—but no longer to flee it like a migratory osprey or a faithless angel.

In sightless bemusement he'd forgotten the gull in the foreground of the scene his eyes were staring at. Now he blinked, looked again, and found that it was gone—and never would he know whether it was a cripple or a faker.

Instead of tackling the immediate arrangement of his personal effects and temporary conveniences as the best way to relieve himself of inconclusive planning, he went to the kitchen and sat down with pencil and paper to review the prospects of his exislic conversion. Without chaste and contraceptive reasoning some of his proliferating possibilities might either escape attention or get fantastically out of hand. Even when no longer interbreeding they slithered together like a haul of fish. In the most pleasing location of his terrestrial life, with sufficient wealth and comparative freedom, numberless enterprises seemed to present themselves as if described in a printed clipping Wat had tacked on the wall behind his woodstove as a parable for his own deliberations at sea and ashore: "Again, the kingdom of heaven is like a net which was thrown into the sea and gathered fish of every kind; when it was full, men drew it ashore and sat down and sorted the good into vessels but threw away the bad. So it will be at the close of the age."

This harbor's angels needed no prompting to dispose of the bad, once fishers had separated the evil from the righteous, but they were of no help in sorting items for Raphael Opsimath's list of potential interests.

His pencil only doodled. The blooming buzzing sirens of Dogtown were luring him to old age with idle diversions that served none of his intentions. His speculative mind couldn't help dwelling on local things as they were and as they had been. He was also losing his grasp of chrematistics and yielding to the Dogtown definition of all issues. Though still protesting his preference for ritual to myth, he found himself accommodating what Tessa the first time he saw her had called "the ecology of legends" wherein denizens were "mutually tolerant of lies", which could not but fall into place inconsistently.

The dialectic between stout Wat and divers occupants of his Liar's Bench on the other side of the stove—a raggedly greasy overstuffed easy chair opposite his rocker (none too large or sturdy for his weight), which he was wont to drop into with an ostentatious murmur about "the weariness, the fever, and the sweat, here where we sit and make each other groan"—was more topical than that commonly to be heard in Tessa's circle. A few days earlier Rafe himself had sat there as the newest student while the big fisherman puffed on a dead cigar and rocked in tutorial rumination, unreluctant to discontinue some unhurried pipefitting at the Worker's Bench for a subassembly designed to improve the cooling system of his *Motion's* engine, which otherwhiles he babied like a parent.

"I read in the *Nous*" Rafe happened to have remarked "that a hundred years ago Dogtown's fishery was conventionally regarded as the most efficient and progressive on the whole Atlantic seaboard. Even before the heyday of schooners. Is that still true?"

"Prob'ly never was, and it ain't saying much. Stupidity is the mother of convention. So says Barwin in *The Origin of Feces and Descent of Testicles*. Here, more than elsewhere, fishing unfits a man for the business of life. That's why I left school as an ignoramus to enter the profession."

Rafe knew Wat's reputation as an advocate of research for the conservation, capture, handling, and preservation of fresh fish (despite his abhorrence of "the Feudal Government" that supported it), and was aware of the man's taciturn bitterness toward most of his Dogtown colleagues, who seemed to despise or oppose all innovation, cooperation, and foresight—even measures for their own safety—in favor of immediate return on investment (in the form of largely undeclared profit). By the same token, whenever conditions were propitious, at any time of year, his unassisted labor outside the breakwater was Heraclean, regardless of what the dealers were paying. He wouldn't have quit fishing for a million dollars, though he proclaimed he'd do so for one. It was true that most of the improvements he made in equipment and procedure were small and subtle, relevant only to the routines of an undercapitalized and crewless skipper in the narrowing inshore specialty of his métier, but they originated in unceasing thought and experiment, veiled by the soft jests and hard complaints of his social intercourse, while he kept secret only the landmark fixes he had meticulously compiled for piloting the courses of his tows where the bottom was clear of rocks and wrecks.

All Wat's indoor interlocutors (or auditors) had piscatory interests, however amateurish or theoretical, if only for the sake of the anomalous piscator himself; but few who called on him were contemporary fishermen. Some appeared to be fellow aborigines of other trades, who couldn't be expected to catch his educated allusions but who obviously appreciated those that were missed by the educated, and who perched on the workbench stool said little that was intelligible in the presence of a third person; but others seemed to be Normans like Rafe himself, seeking the edification of homespun pith. As a newcomer he had already come to understand that in Wat's facet of Dogtown lore the legendary, far from being scorned, was signally reflected on its own slowly turning axis, as if respun in foreshortened time. His mirror flashed like a good-humored school of mackerel—whenever it wasn't deflected to his well honed enmity toward "Cape Globster" lobstermen (sparing only his Villie friend Huck Salter) who had lobbied for the law keeping draggers three miles off shore, or darkened by insensate anger at the imperial tyranny of the frozen-fish interests.

Rafe nevertheless foreboded that Wat's levees—enlightening though they were when directed to brass facts and tricks of the trade or when adding something new to a Norman's fund of intelligible Watticisms—would outlive their refreshment if attended too often. Rafe had no intention of retiring from active life, and he really had no time to spare for the redundancies of idiosyncracy, however charming in its isolation from the broader political economy. Even Buck Barebones, Rafe's new partner and a staunch friend of Wat's who never said ill of any person, confessed that the fishing sage was sometimes boring in his rehearsals. There was much too much more to learn about this island of saints and angels that wasn't an island but a cape and that weren't saints and angels but dogs and gulls.

Dogtown is my destined alma mater, and probably my final home. A New Armorican backwater suits my taste for irony in progress. These lawless innocents jealously preserve their city for themselves, yet they demand the covetous admiration of developers like those who have captured and refitted my poor old San Ricardo, an unwalled salient of the opposite main. Apparently, from almost as far back as the time of Christ, radical churchmen apostates heretics ancient mariners marranos moriscos cimarrons renegade fathers wandering Jews famished Irishmen fugitive Slavs renitents recusants refusés orphans whalemen buccaneers unlucky merchants disappointed magnates disabled inventors failed critics fauve sculptors avant-garde dramaturges even painters and poets have been unobtrusively exiling themselves to this steady little state without disturbing its equilibrium, not infecting but leavening the stubborn mass of indigenous or already admixed mothers fishermen workers doctors lawyers musicians and public employees, and joining it to engender (among others) the zygotes of recalcitrant or distinguished youths who can hardly wait to counteract the continual influx by seeking sex and success elsewhere. Despite their quasi-isolation nearly all the denizens are anything but isolatoes in their quarrelsome supertribal solidarity vis-à-vis the main world.

But I can help them. Here I need no Masters degree. I'm now a Bachelor of Arts and I've always been a teacher at heart. I know a thing or two. I've done a lot and seen much more. Much have I traveled from the realm of gold, and many goodly places seen. I've been on and over the transcontinental map. But this mise en scène is the only one that calls for my action. —So I'd better get settled.

Throwing down the pencil, he took his coffee mug back to the window overlooking the hollow of Swanson's Cove, whose floor was now almost awash; but this time he turned to face inboard, scanning the small white cavern of his living room. When he overcame his procrastination it would be the scene-within-a-scene of a responsible bachelor's nest. You'd think I was an osprey hoping to attract a mate! I'd like to buy some of Petto's sculpture. . . . Imagination is what I lack and yet was born to crave. No one can match him for that afflatus of the Muse—not even Shelly Schlossberg his most original student or Ipsissimus Charlemagne his subsuming Übermensch. Maybe Tessa will have him do some things for the Stone Barn stage-sets. . . . But I'll hold off until I decide which dwelling unit of my quaint new estate I'm going to stay forever in.

The same for my maps [he said aloud]: all except one will have to wait. He glanced at the four-foot-high potbellied barrel standing open in the corner like a backwoods urn. Its convex tawny staves were splinter-rough, retaining the faint odor of obsolescent cooperage, and the twisted wire splices of its girdles also were a barbed hazard to the touch of whitecollar hands. It was his most cherished consignment from Londonbridge, the western estuary-island he'd removed from, lock and stock also. As far as common carriers were concerned its tare weight was all he had to pay for: it was practically no heavier full than empty.

The dozens of vertical scrolls snugly stacked inside it were maps of various lengths and scales, some as tall as the cask itself, corresponding to as many different views of Atlantean places. Like most good working libraries the assembly owed its collective pricelessness to a unification in the collector's mind, not to the expense or rarity of individual items; and also, he admitted, to what Montvert farm auctioneers call "sentimental value" when hoping to intrigue the summer folk attending for a lark. The cargo would have been nearly worthless to anyone who hadn't inhabited visited or wished to see such a scattering of locational tracts for the same sort of numinous and adventitious reasons as those that formed his uncritical consciousness of a yen for promiscuous ekistical experience. Fixing her attention on this barrel Tessa had quizzed him as "a lazy halfass Uncle Toby", and most of their friends probably would agree when they learned of his casual accumulation. He knew she suspected that he'd never make the effort to unroll these maps and match them to his memory of the settlements and spaces they "imitated" (as Aristotle's translators would have put it—the philosopher who was addressed by Wat when he had to lash the helm and let the *Motion* steam by herself so he could go below and sit on the open end of a bucket: "Oh Asterotle, Asterotle, please come here and take the throttle!")—places that he'd longed to tarry in and assimilate without foregoing any of the others. Still less would he ever have the expanse of wall space to tack up more than the two or three that reckoned directions on a coast where the sun and moon rose out of the sea instead of setting in it, made sense of stories in the *Daily Nous*, pointed his way to Purdeyville, or would interpret seamarks if he finally got to go steaming with Wat.

It was hard even to find curatorial space for his lot of scrolls—unless he treated the barrel as domestic furniture, precluding a more social piece. He was loathe to acknowledge that his impulses had childishly outreached his judgment and that the attempt to satisfy a mystic appetite had often been as pointless as matchbook-collecting. Still, the great Crèvecoeur, a surveyor of colonial space before he was its historian, would have been astonished at the precision and abundance of such cartography. And Rafe thought he'd also have the sympathy of Dexter Keith, husband of Crèvecoeur's most devoted admirer.

A few of the maps were broad geographies of the continent showing railroads and rivers or mountains without the distorting clutter of roads; or government Coast and Geodetic Survey charts cryptically designed for mariners, some showing little more of the land's frontier than birdseye profiles and the locations of its artifacts that were conspicuous from the whales' ceiling. Of those by the U S Army Corps of Engineers, one charted their civil constructions in the Mississippi basin, another the great water system of Cornucopia's central valley. But most were U S Department of Natural Resources Geological Survey maps, which plotted streets and buildings as well as contours and benchmarks on archangelic scales. He'd kept in file drawers the folded grid-ruled master charts of each state by which the local maps that might particularly interest him were organized: selections from graphic indices that governed and coded the equal areas of every topographical map available from Washington. If he'd been the head librarian at the Bureau of Domestic Investigation he would have ordered all the thousands of quadrants, but he was pleased to keep at least the keys not only to Cornucopia, New Albion, and Columbia—as well as Vinland, Markland, and Montvert; Island Roads, Pequod, and Nether Land; Nuzu, Hannah, Magdalene, and Parthenia; Lonestar, Napoleon, and Poncedeleon; Cherokee, Whyaway, Itasca, and Big Lake—but also to Wisconsin and Illinois.

The trouble was that state or coastal boundaries, and topographically logical subdivisions, did not lend themselves to a quilt of uniform mutually exclusive squares: it took more than one map to piece together many a political entity or natural watershed located on the edges of geodetic cells. For instance, the unified metropolitan area known as Tetrapolis, comprising four small cities in two states and on either side of the Mississippi, philanthropically dominated by the Corps of Engineers and the central divisions of International Stag Tractor, could not be taken in at a glance unless you took the trouble to trim and match on a large flat surface the borders of two frustratingly truncated quadrants.

This pair (like several of the other new ones for places he was known to have traveled to) had been presented to him as a farewell gift by one of Tubalcain's men at the final Babylon Oaks sales meeting under the Opsimath-Edenfield regime. Bob Garrison, the young M B A salesman being groomed for Midwest Regional Manager on the salaried payroll, tipped off by his older colleagues, was proud to gratify Rafe's unaccountable taste for this urban attraction in a steam-cleaner sales territory that was primarily agricultural.

The men had all seemed genuinely sorry at their president's departure, and not merely worried about the true intentions of Cook Evaporator's corporate management. Rafe was not quite at ease with his conscience at having sold out for the gain of a lifetime and left his employees to a fate that remained uncertain despite all the advance assurances and sweet talk of the new owners. But at least he took satisfaction in the success of his intricate and laborious negotiation of Leo LeFranc's promotion to Sales Manager without losing Ted McKee's talents, who ostensibly was not demoted but laterally transferred. [Rafe still mulled personnel justice no longer his to determine:] The former sales manager was now awarded the new hierarchically equivocal title of National Accounts Manager, with explicit responsibility for the huge Holystone account but also with the somewhat illogical assignment of regional accounts like Tractor Distributors (pace Ray Langiappe) and with the even less organizationally appropriate job of supervising Fred Tracy the national Service Manager, whose duties were dominated by territorial customers of the regular sales force. Ted was happy to be free of automotive jobbers, and kept face in his displacement with the secret encouragement of a higher salary. At the same time Cook would inherit much stronger marketing leadership—and a good opinion of Tubalcain's former chief executive officer might find its way to King Arthur Halymboyd at Parity in New Uruk, very center of this interesting industrial web.

For immediate consultation, however, Rafe resolved to tack up two other planar projections, without waiting for permanent wall space.

One was his first purchase at the Top Dollar, Dogtown's carriage trade chandlery: a large nautical chart of the Cape, stiff and yellow, fraught with marks and symbols in red and black and blue (which were not self-explanatory to a cartophiliac landsman) but perfectly consistent with those he'd collected for the inland sea of Golden Horn Bay and never learned to read with the eyes of a navigator.

The other was a present from his Controller at the farewell dinner given him by the office staff on the eve of Tubalcain's official submission to the "merger" (and thus of his voluntary and lucrative deposition from the presidency), an occasion of disconcerting ambivalence in his heart. His advisory and compensatory connections with Tubalcain would continue for a year but his presence was no longer definitely required. Michael Chapman was gladly seeing him off to his own hometown: hence the care he'd taken with scissors and rubber cement to pare, abut, and mount on a single sheet of drawing paper the two official survey maps that had to be fitted together in order to display Dogtown as an integrated disjunction of Cape Gloucester. It was an unabashed labor of love.

2
MUNDANE DINNER

*A*s Rafe Opsimath followed the Father Economist following the Father Superior led by mein Host Busty Pacioli to a table at the broadly windowed corner of the Windmill dining room he looked westward, beyond the patinaed statute of the fisherman with wife and dog, to the clapboard back of the Gut's drawbridge gatehouse, which was glassed on its other three faces for purposes of directing waterway traffic. In contrast to the Vinland & Markland Railroad's cramped and shabby huts—for the tender of the Dogtown Draw half way up or down the same Janus-ended tidal river, and for the Cod Street crossing guard—this spacious shelter like the bridge of a ship was equipped by the Commonwealth with personal conveniences and remote controls.

Rafe's eye was first drawn in that direction, down along the seawall rather than toward the broad southerly magnificence within the distant breakwater on their left, by an adventitious echo of some uncannily pertinent words Doctor Charlemagne had dropped during a digression the previous night: a curiously random anticipation of event by idea, like proleptic dreams in legendary fiction yet only accidentally significant to the beholder and of no practical consequence. The coincidence exemplified Doc's most casual intuitions. Certainly there had been no mention of Rafe's plans for dinner the following day, to say nothing of the view to be expected from its vantage. But Doc's anticipatory remark was now seen to represent a mystic cohesion that Rafe was beginning to recognize as typical of this small city's selfindwelling imagery. It fostered Rafe's sensation of being at last possessed by one in particular of the nation's places.

Doc's passing allusion, relevant to dromenological theory, was simply a quotation of Jean-Louis Bartaud, with whom he'd taken a few master classes on his first trip to the Continent: "When a river flows into the sea it dies. It flows right away into the communion of saints. Its estuary is its sickness. Art is the challenge to death." The Frenchman was speaking of his youthful marriage to the theater, at which he took inward vows to "unfreeze the Silence" of a darkened house, to "go against the current." On the eve of debut, like Galahad in a perilous chapel, he had dedicated himself in an empty house, sleeping on the bare stage. But Doc added somewhat maliciously that Bartaud knew only freshwater rivers. "Our Namauche lives again with each change of tide. It has two mouths and two sources. It flows in both directions, to and from the community of saints."

It was a trivial concurrence, of no great improbability in such a concentric environment; but for Rafe presently to come upon the origin of this image so soon after Doc had released him into the dawn of the same day was like happening upon exactly the same outlandish ideogram in two books of two different nations times and genres, in two separate bookstores, within a single hour.

All the more so in that Father Duncannon, the elder of his dinner guests, wedded to the church, might well have evoked the counter-entropic component of Bartaud's conceit. No two good masters could have been more unlike than the founder of the Classic Order of the Vine and the founder of Dromenology. It was young Caleb Karcist, their common enthusiast, who had first pointed out to Rafe the striking parallel and antithesis of these two leaders who had no wish to learn of each other. But Rafe had met Father Duncannon only once before, as a private dinner guest at the monastic Laboratory of Melchizedec and the Mesocosm. Now that Easter observances were over his effort to return the hospitality was acceptable to the priests. On neither occasion did Rafe expect discussion of certain business interests to be excluded.

Father Chris Lucey had managed the invitation to the Lab so that his friend Rafe, a cultural sympathizer with the Tudor branch of Christianity by virtue of childhood circumstances, could make himself acquainted to the Superior, almost ostensively to be approved for friendly goodwill as a trustworthy unremunerated advisor or collaborator. But it wouldn't have mattered if he'd confessed himself a Parsi or an atheist. (One of the Trustees of the Fund for the Order, a corporation lawyer, was a practicing Jew.) Father Duncannon himself had studied largely among scientific agnostics; more infidels and Paulines remained among his old personal friends, according to Chris, than Petrine believers, and among the scholars he continued to read.

Rafe suspected that Father Duncannon had required no urging to authorize that invitation to the Lab refectory on Refreshment Sunday (a k a Refection Sunday and Mothering Sunday), when Christ's feeding of the loaves and fishes was celebrated with feast-day meat in the middle of Lent. The Father Superior probably hoped as discreetly as possible to sound his guest on the financial judgment of his impulsive subordinate (except for himself the sole Member Regular), who managed all the Trustees' monies. Despite the risks of impious exposition on Rafe's part, it was this very motive that the Father Economist himself encouraged, a subtle and honest psychologist too, who was conscious of his need to be bolstered at headquarters.

Rafe's pleasure at that privileged dinner had led to this public one, which undoubtedly would be a continuation of the first as far as both friendship and business were concerned. Obviously neither of the Fathers distrusted his motives or his cordiality. But his situation was delicate because he didn't know to what degree the founding father was aware of the dangers to which Chris was exposing all the liquid and hypothecated assets of his selfsupporting institution. And Rafe knew very little of Chris's mind regarding long or short term investments about which there was no reason to have been consulted.

By the same token his own prospects in business association with the inventive mechanist Buck Barebones had nothing to do with the Order. It was only in the matter of Parity Corporation that he might be competent to advise, and on that score he was far from disinterested. For the time being most of his own assets, as well as the Trustees', were in Parity stock, consequential of the fact that at considerable expense of time and money he'd spent the best part of a year wondering about, studying, or causing to be studied that complicated "closed-end investment company", about which primary mysteries nevertheless remained.

While Rafe himself would soon be wanting cash for his new manufacturing enterprise, Chris, a trader at heart, was chafing at the apparent limitation of PAR's growth-rate in market value. In spite of the increasingly favorable ratios of its net asset value the Little Ticker shares of PAR seemed only to undulate like mild waves on a slow tide. Chris wanted acceleration. And there was a new alternative in the picture, most tempting to a "socially responsible" adventurer.

The speculative value of Paraclete Biochemical Corporation common stock seemed providential for the Classic Order of the Vine, and the question (as Rafe guessed it had been reduced by Chris in sketching financial options to Father Duncannon) was whether or not to transfer the Trustees' concentrated eggs to a new basket. Paraclete's new contraceptive hormone was a lure to any Christian money-owner neither under the thumb of reactionary prelates nor absolutely opposed to risk-taking forms of usury yet seriously worried about the earth's future. Thus Members of the Order, representatives of whom would soon be getting a chance to pass democratic judgment on the known doings of their Father Economist, whether they were socialists, "premature antifascists", New Deal Catholicrats, or purehearted innocents, would presumably be more comfortable as the beneficiaries of PARA than of PAR on the Curb Exchange. Many of them were hostile to the Parity investment, or would be so when they learned of it from a report Chris was to make at the forthcoming Chapter. In any case he was calculating to head off demands to safeguard the Order's funds in the whited usury of insured savings accounts, if not to disburse them to various causes or charities that would dilute the Order's good works without furthering its unique purpose.

Granting the pragmatic necessity of capitalism, disregarding risk, trusting to reasonable management, and assuming the safety of its products, Paraclete seemed to Rafe a reasonable market basket for Christian revisionists more or less to the left of President Kennedy's father. But it was hard to overcome his bias in Parity's favor—still his own company as it were, since he remained under consulting contract to one of its subsubsidiaries and wished his former employees at Tubalcain to prosper under its ownership, preferably by the retention or extension of his own policies and plans. It had not been easy to sell out his managerial work of art only to start all over again, from scratch, in total uncertainty, on a much smaller scale, with an unaggressive alcoholic partner.

For the moment he was free to assist at the Trustees' problem because his negotiations with Buck Barebones and various possible backers had to be lawyerly and tentative until checks from the fire insurance definitely brought in more than enough for Buck's personal portion of capital for the new venture; but soon it would be necessary to sell his own Parity stock (rather than using it as problematic collateral for borrowing at unnecessary interest) in order to meet his own cash commitment to the new corporation: therefore any Paraclete investment on his own part was out of the question. Then too, though he understood man's metal artifacts he knew nothing about God's biochemistry.

The waitress for their table turned out to be a trepid aborigine whom Doc Charlemagne as Rafe's guest on his first visit to Dogtown when there were no other customers in the huge dining room had tyrannized by name as "Milly"; but now, with the house half full, she smiled in recognition of the embarrassed gentleman's compensatory bonus that night and was not at all awed by the two round collars in black suits. Without the giant Doctor any party must have seemed easy to cope with—even a roundtable of competing mothers-in-law.

As the host of this feast Rafe seated himself at the most accessible position, but he managed to present each of his guests with a view of the harbor unblinded by the glory of a sun about to set behind the mainland hills in a clarion sky of sea-reflected azure— which he himself would have been facing if Busty hadn't adjusted some drapery in the train of plate glass. As "Milly" was taking orders he wondered why the scene should so instantly and precisely summon by a complicated overlay of similarity and contrast rather than recollections of sunset the isolated memory of gliding unrushed in an almost silent interurban train across the lofty Goat Island Bridge many years ago, soon after Tubalcain's relocation from San Ricardo, on a pure clear rosyfingered morning before the sun had risen over the East Bay massif as he gazed through an *expanse of glass* at a pillar of fire in the high-piled ledge of smokeless cloud over the most majestic city of them all, as the resurgent beams at his back gradually lowered fresh tints of pink to glittering buildings on the westermost hills of the continent, the naked towers of Yerba Buena steeping fairer minute by minute while derricked ships of all the world lay still in the waterfront darkness.

It was a magnificently poignant artiscape, of which he had taken leave for the sake of retrograde pioneering and perhaps for the sake of a woman. Over Dogtown Harbor here at the other end of continental daytime the tranquil verge of a beauteous evening was likewise calm and free, but without the power and splendor of an immense valley bounded by the brazen treasure of golden hinds.

Sipping an apéritif with tidy composure the finely drawn face behind Father Duncannon's rimless glasses revealed a vein of levity that Rafe had not found at the Lenten feast, save for the mildly urbane jests that might be expected of an aesthetic churchman in retirement. But the Father Superior was retired only from urban and aesthetic society, not from work. His regimen was the labor of study, writing, and prayer—and the action of the Mass—to nurture his new shoot of the Lord's Vine and leaven secular Christianity with a new philosophy.

Disappointed in the democratic competence of reason, rebuffed by his own church, ignored by professional authorities, even defamed by vigilantes of the body politic and stigmatized in its archives, he strove to prevent his tiny institution from being choked by the brambles of culture, against which he persisted in hope but of which it seemed to Rafe he was far less indulgent than Doctor Charlemagne, another kind of prophet, who joined or acquiesced to some corruptions of Atlantean life while denouncing the general decline much less charitably. It was amusing to observe that Caleb, a theorist of tragedy, waxed more optimistic than either of his mentors in their disparate but parallel hopes for recovery of primitive conceptions essential to their respective revisions of civilization.

Rafe was pleased to see the slight frail Superior enjoying this hour comparatively off duty. The smooth fresh skin of his face, set in relief by a savant's composure, seemed much younger than the nearly sixty-five years of his age (which Chris had confided to Rafe with the significant tone of an anxious son). Father Duncannon was telling them some memories of happy or interesting childhood experience on and around the broad haven of brine that he now almost rudely stared out at, touchingly oblivious of his listeners, as the younger priest, himself apparently forgetful of all other anxiety, raptly watched his face. But Lancelot Duncannon had sojourned elsewhere, on both sides of the Atlantic, for forty years or more.

From where they sat, close above the tide, the Laboratory's elevated and remote view of the harbor was reversed and magnified. From here one looked upward to the greening hills. "It was only when I came back from England" Father Duncannon said "that I realized what a keen observer Professor Whitehead was, so soon after coming over from London to Norumbega, when he remarked that Spring here in New Armorica doesn't put up flowers or vernal trimmings voluntarily: Nature comes out only because it's ordered to do so. This year it looks as if it will finally obey.

"When I was a boy the harbor was still pure enough to freeze over sometimes, but not enough to stop the all-year-round steamboats that ran twice a week to Bournemouth and to Botolph. There were two of them, the *Norumbega* and the *Pale*, named by the board of directors for their alma maters. The locals used to call them the Meager and the Fail, but I defended them in arguments with other children because they seemed to be a faithful public utility like my father's."

"Father Duncannon's family owned the Cape Gloucester Power, Light, and Traction Company." Chris glossed in encouragement.

"That isn't quite right, Father Lucey." the elder gently amended. "We were shareholders. My father was only president. But it's true that I was protected from unpleasantness even when I went to public school. I was the victim of my own distaste for what used to be called vulgarity, secretly frightened of all majorities. I never socialized or played games or took part in competition because Duncannons were never permitted to make a mistake or lose; if you couldn't be sure of winning you wouldn't try. We lived on the hill, as my mother put it. At that time our fields were still being rented to farmers. It took me decades to overcome the family's unacknowledged prejudices. But my father was a good electrical engineer and a rational manager; I'm sure the men respected him as at least a Praying Protestican in his labor relations."

Chris looked beamingly at Rafe to congratulate him for being honored with such a rare revelation of the spare Superior's personality, for Father Duncannon's softened manner now differed indeed from his reserved graciousness on Refreshment Sunday. Rafe attributed this slight alteration of attitude to a conjunction of private influences at which his own affability played only a reagent's part. The most important might have been something like a post-Lenten improvement in Chris's observance of the Member Regular discipline. The layman supposed that he knew more about the Economist's emotional life than Father Duncannon knew he knew. It was impossible for an outsider to know how much more was known to the Superior.

"But my mother was the High Church Tudor." Father Duncannon continued reflectively as they awaited lobsters in jolly bibs tied around their necks by Milly, with picks and pincers at hand. "She always felt out of place at St Paul's, where they never acknowledged the Mass as more than symbolic Communion.

"When I was five or six years old we had an ignorant Irish cook and maid-of-all-work named Katie Martin, from the old country, who supported her parents on the three dollars a week we paid her in addition to board and keep. I repeated something Katie said that I thought ridiculous—complaining 'Oh these Classics!', imitating of course the exasperated condescension one used to hear in the Yankee ruling class. 'Look out, young man!' my mother scolded me. 'You're a Classic too. Don't ever say these things!' She was a devout Tractarian." Father Duncannon stared into the past as if for the first time given pause by this familiar reminiscence. "But as soon as I went away to prep school" he added, with a soft inchoate chuckle, glancing at Rafe, "I became a Sabellian."

"That's Father's kindly term for a Divine Humanist." Chris explained, more delighted than ever at the way his Superior was relaxing in Rafe's presence.

"Yes, a Modalistic Monarchian. Then in college I was an agnostic. Only in freshman physics did I began to open my ears to electricity and understand some of the jargon that Mother and I'd heard at home and closed our minds to—for instance the difference between *load factor* and *power factor*! Before Father died he was gladdened to know of my sudden fascination with alternating current, which eventually led to everything else I studied in science. But it was much longer before I rediscovered my native thetical church."

Rafe already knew that Father Duncannon's branch of the "thetical church"—High and Low—meant the Tudor Communion, founded in unantithetical schism from the thetical Petrine Classic Scholastics by Henry the Eighth, still under the nominal leadership of the Archbishop Primate of All England and ramified in Atlantis as the Pauline Apostolic Church, whose classic creed professed literal adherence to "the one holy classic and apostolic Church" despite its compromise or subversion of Petrine doctrine and rejection of modern papal authority. This ecclesiastical equivocation, as well as the adventitious events giving rise to it, was one of the unfortunate historical phenomena that the scientific priest tactfully ascribed to human "confusion". Rafe had questioned Chris with tentative curiosity about the origin and purpose of the Classic Order of the Vine, inasmuch as he himself for about a decade of childhood on the West Coast promontory of San Ricardo had almost thoughtlessly attended services and recreations at a low

Apostolic parish that was dominated by Praying Protesticans. He remembered nothing of any Sunday School explanations.

He didn't altogether trust Chris's piquant summaries either of the Paulinized Petrine church or of this tiny gadfly Order on the neck of its Anglo-Classic faction, which in his mind had always been associated with snobbish aesthetics if not with political reaction. It seemed to him that because the Father Founder's "theodynamics" was radically social and all but revolutionary Chris in his vocational effort to protect the personal pillar of his temple from external attack would deprecate the radical significance of his own Order even to a sympathetic businessman. Feeling no pain from his second double Scotch after a day at the Weatherglass, Neatherd & Company brokerage in Botolph, and alluding with a sigh to the unvoiced discountenance he suffered from some of the Order's purest in heart as a Member Regular apparently serving both God and a capitalistic Mammon, Chris had once bared his soul with the blasphemous declaration that to the contrary he indeed served one master only: not Mammon, perhaps not God, but certainly Father Duncannon, and therefore Father Duncannon's cause, including his Order and the Members thereof.

At any rate it would be impertinent for Rafe to pursue his elementary curiosity with the frail Founder himself, especially in an hour of leisure; and he had no wish to evince a degree of interest that might advance an expectation of further religious inquiry— albeit he could hardly imagine either Father Duncannon or Father Lucey (for entirely different reasons) as a recruiter for the Christian faith, still less for their somewhat puzzling movement within it; so he resolved to save his theological questions for Caleb who actually served both the priests not only in an office but also at the altar.

At the refectory dinner, served by Oku the Japanese houseboy in a white jacket, Rafe had at first been as selfconscious as a Fundamentalist in addressing the Superior as "Father"; and more so— feeling downright hypocritical—in calling his friend Chris by the same title in vocative as well as other cases simply to conform to a pious protocol against which his prejudice was inbred; but by now the honorific rolled off his tongue in ordinary circumstances as functionally and conveniently as if he was a born papist.

As they were digging into the resilient white of their hard orange lobsters he found himself being addressed in a more personally cordial manner than Father Duncannon had displayed at their earlier and more formal meal. Pausing in his characteristically articulated and deliberate eating—for, unlike Chris, the Superior did not hurry or batch his food but (rather like his former friend T S Chittering), knife in left hand, seemed more of an Englishman than an American in reducing the unnecessary action of eating—he expressed the civil interest of a friendly townsman. "Mr Opsimath, Father Lucey tells me you're thinking of a new factory here in Dogtown."

"Yes—Buck Barebones and I. Though it'll probably be not much more than a job shop at first. We're waiting for the outcome of several contingencies, principally the final settlement of his fire insurance."

"The poor dear man! It's hard to imagine such dreadful destruction! From what I saw in the *Nous* he seems to have lost his whole life's work; yet Father Lucey says you told him that Mr Barebones wouldn't consider his own losses until he'd provided for his employees. It occurs to me that his secretary, if she's now out of work, might be interested in helping us out until after Gloucestermas, when all our Chapter affairs are cleared up, and perhaps part-time thereafter. I'd like to find someone who can take shorthand for correspondence and also type from manuscript."

"And even stencils for the *COVEN*." Chris smiled. "That's the Classic Order of the Vine's newsletter. I'm sure the Members are going to ask us to take over the production end of it. But Mr Babwell hasn't yet produced a Limited Person for us." [Rafe well remembered his dealings with Bill Babwell, who sometimes waggishly referred to himself and his PERSONS LIMITED, a small secretarial service and temporary-personnel agency, by voicing the adjective before the noun.]

"Right now we don't need much of her time at the office we've rented, though Buck's still paying her old salary and that makes her feel guilty." Rafe replied. "It will be a few months before our new company has a regular job for her."

"Buck . . ." Father Duncannon mused, with the ruminating attention to language that was known to have preceded all his scholarly interests. "I used to know Buckminster Quiller, but that was the only time I ever understood where 'Buck' came from. One hears it quite often; it seems to be one of those indiscriminate sobriquets like Bud or Butch. Of course nothing as Yankee as Buckminster could be that popular."

"In this case, Baucis." said Rafe, and spelled it.

"But that's a feminine name!" Father Duncannon exclaimed with a slightly censorious chuckle. "Philemon and Baucis were a penniless old peasant couple. They took in two ragged wayfarers, against whom all richer doors were shut, and were amazed to find the cups and bowls of their hospitality refilling themselves. The strangers turned out to be Zeus and Hermes. Philemon and Baucis were granted survival of the forthcoming Deluge, followed by the joint priesthood of a garlanded temple on the site of their hut; and their wish to come to the end of both their lives at the same moment was also fulfilled. At death they were transformed into an oak and a linden. It's one of Ovid's loveliest stories. I seem to remember that Faust blessed them in Part Two. I think Baucis means something like 'too modest'."

"Then Buck's name is at least half appropriate. But his parents probably knew even less of classical literature than I did before this minute. His wife tells me that they left the spelling to some clerk. 'Barkis' was the name they had in mind. So despite their tin ear they were prescient on two counts: Buck turned out to be both the most modest and and the most willing fellow a woman could marry. It's hard not to take advantage of him. But he won't concentrate on new business until he's seen that every man who worked for Dogtown Machine and Design has a livelihood while hoping for a new shop to hire him back!" Father Duncannon gazed out at the vernal rim of the Harbor, blankly envisaging the sweet man spoken of, incongruously reminded of a certain sweet smile recurrent on the face of Alpha Whitehead, his late counselor in the Norumbega precinct of Unabridge—in the end an elder friend who didn't mind that he wasn't followed by the younger.

That was before Lance Duncannon had gone to England to study for the priesthood and found himself (as he said) with an original insight for the first time in his life: an idea that germinated with the toil of pastoral apprenticeship in a vineyard on the Isle of Dogs and on the south bank of the Thames, eventually to be promulgated in the avant-garde of the Tudor Classic church near the Garth of his native civilization's omphalos, in the very city (but at the opposite end of Vinland Avenue) where as a graduate in the seven arts, and having studied in Germany, he'd enrolled for electrical engineering but stayed for a doctorate in thermodynamics.

Professor Whitehead, an Apostle at Trinity in the old Unabridge who subsequently devoted many years to technical pedagogy for the people of London, had been one of the few at Norumbega who championed the neighboring Vinland Institute of Polytechnics, condescendingly known to 'Bega undergraduates as "the V I P trade school" despite its international distinction. He'd welcomed Lance as one of its remarkably educated students to domestic evenings with his own academic protégés, and recommended him for his personal qualities. It seemed providential that the famous mathematician's older brother (previously a lecturing Fellow of the other Trinity at Unaford) had been a Tractarian bishop of the Tudor Church in South India, and that he himself (though no longer faithful to Christianity) had once been attracted enough by Classic Scholastic doctrine to have sought out the dying Cardinal Newman at his Oratory. The erstwhile collaborator with Bernard Russell in mathematical logic had scrupulously insisted that "philosophy may not neglect the multifariousness of the world—the fairies dance, and Christ is nailed to the cross".

These remembrances took no time at all, nor did Father Duncannon's reascending thoughts as they turned to the contrasts between Dogtown—which he still knew mainly through the eyes of his childhood, and where his present existence, not to mention that of his Order, was known to no more than a handful of denizens—and the far greater city of Unabridge, filled with all stripes and colors, and with ordinary industry too, where he had established his first Laboratory closer to Norumbega than to V I P but alienated from both, where of all places in the world he would be most accessible to the kinds of people needed for the development as well as the dissemination of his Christian revision, and where in fact he became obscurely infamous as a sacrilegious premature antifascist.

But Rafe and Chris were now told only this much: "When Whitehead first arrived he marveled at our Unabridge, as a sort of Garden of Eden that suffered some very bad breakdowns. 'There's an astounding inefficiency somewhere.' he said. By the same token he saw that although there was as much culture and genius in our country as in England they had no influence on the government, which was 'instructed from below'. Of course he was generally reputed to be an unworldly sage; but with innocent wonder he immediately saw to the bottom of Vinland politics, wherein he said it seemed to him 'that the high-brow honest people are hopelessly off the pitch in their social ideas and that the corrupt demagogues are often advocating the right thing!' It's curious how well I remember some of the things he said, considering our fundamental disagreement in religion.

"He was happy to be over here but disappointed especially in our journalism. 'An excess in futility is the blackest evil,' he said, 'and I'm sure the Devil in hell talks incessantly like an Atlantean Sunday newspaper.' One of our members is about to start a biography of him.

There'll be a paper at Chapter on his rather conventional misconception of Christianity, at least when he said that 'religion is what the individual does with his own solitariness'."

Father Duncannon looked as funny as anyone else in a commercially decorated bib, but for him it was an unnecessary precaution because he was canny enough to have ordered his ruddy lobster shell split and stuffed in the kitchen beforehand. Accordingly, while Rafe and Chris labored with their special tools, making messes of their plates—the one an inexperienced Westerner, the other as always less attentive to what he ate than what he drank— the old priest evenly relished his Dogtown delicacy on the principle of least action, his motions (trained at the piano long before his practice at the altar) as deft delicate and unhurried as if the fish on his plate was a filet of sole.

Chris had been drinking more than his share of the wine bottle as inconspicuously as possible, but no one abstained. Another, this time of luse, was ordered for dessert. The diners nearby were not so cheerless or boisterous that these three couldn't feel comfortable about lingering after the final sanguined blue of the sky.

In order to avert or postpone the unresolved chrematistic issue that had occupied much of their refectory dinner, which was now demanding a decision for the Father Economist at the cusp of it, their conversation was allowed to drift quite naturally from Unabridge to the new regime in national politics (as it would have done in the days of Roosevelt), but then desultorily to Caleb Karcist back in Dogtown, on whom each of the three had depended in a greater or less degree for uniquely cherished work, inasmuch as he was or had been their common assistant and friend, whose absence was felt but whose presence would have been as inappropriate now as at the earlier feast, owing in part to a tacit consensus that his headstrong judgment was immature and in part to the present host's feeling that Father Lucey was beginning to sense (though without resentment) a subtle shift in the young man's preponderant loyalty from himself and the vulgar means of the Vine to the Father Superior and its vulnerably precious ends. In his gradually expanding function as Father Duncannon's intellectual companion, and potentially his profane apologist, Caleb in some measure relieved Chris of a burden beyond his competence—and did so without in the least threatening or damaging the affiliation, the complementary dependency, of the two Members Regular, probably (in the light of twenty years' disappointment) the only ones in the Order who would ever take C O V's three vows of monasticism.

The darkling harbor imperceptibly joined the night sky. The three gentlemen and other quietly clinking customers were gradually sealed off and reduplicated by the glass along two transparent walls. Unless one rose from the winestained cloth and pressed his shielded eyes to the window nothing was visible to seaward but navigation lights and a southwesterly flush from the distant metropolis beyond a faintly profiled barrier of hills.

It went without saying that both Fathers were glad that the Protesticans had been displaced at the White House. To no lover of commonwealth could the outcome of that perilous election have appeared any worse than movement in the right direction. But Father Duncannon, whose objective was regeneration for the whole earth, had never been very hopeful about any reform less than radical, even under F D R. Like Doc Charlemagne (a former New Dealer) he was scarcely optimistic—far more skeptical of President Kennedy than Rafe himself, who still (for the third time) would have preferred Adlai Stevenson to anyone else but who couldn't help saying that he shared some of Caleb's high hopes for the new administration even without great enthusiasm for its leader personally.

"I know nothing of management," said Father Duncannon "but it seems that without infusion of the Holy Spirit the only way to improve our society of selfgoverning voters is to manage the government's benign institutions so efficiently that the people will generally credit their value and therefore be willing to support with their taxes the liberal policies they question as well as the services they like. But as it is, apparently, organization and administration are so entangled by inherited complexities that fiscal requirements are never analyzed comprehensively from the bottom up, starting at the parochial level of the work itself, where money usually seems to be allocated according to immemorial formulas.

" 'Take care of the pence, for the pounds will take care of themselves.' My father used to quote that old mossback principle of Lord Chesterfield's. In constructing the national budget couldn't that principle apply as well to the cost of local organization and procedure as it does in business wage-negotiations? Instead of simply augmenting, expanding, contracting, substituting, or abolishing departments and 'programs' in gross dollar terms, why don't they rationally criticize and correct both functions and methods, as Taylor tried to do for simple factory work?"

Steadily and without haste, as if bemused, Father Duncannon pursued this surprising subject, which seemed to seem too dry for

Chris and took Rafe by surprise, who felt obliged to protest the practical problem: "Even if Congress or the Administration had enough wisdom and patience to undertake that kind of systematic "zero-based budgeting", which at least the first time around would be vastly expensive in both time and money, how could they create a national corps of practical analysts and synthesists capable of undertaking it? It's beyond the intellectual capability of accountants!"

Father Duncannon had worked for the government in Washington during the First World War, and ever since had read his newspapers between the lines. "Yes, I suppose it's still true that among administrators and sub-administrators who supervise the actual work we have very few liberally educated and imaginative minds with the talent and perseverance necessary at every level to integrate the kind of organic improvements that increase overall efficiency."

Rafe softly agreed with Father Duncannon's concession. "And even if we could assume the possibility that revisions would be accepted all the way up and down the hierarchy it would probably take a whole presidential term to realize even the most obvious cost improvements."

"I must admit that you're driving me back to my first proviso." Father Duncannon smiled. "It would take a couple of generations, free of political or commercial interference, to educate the educators and their pupils, lawyers and bureaucrats, in the Whiteheadean or Wienerian or Bertalanffian kind of abstract pragmatism it takes to make a social system both just and efficient."

"Not to mention the problem of popular interference!" Chris interjected.

"But even then, at what point or organ could anyone except the Holy Ghost begin to teach the body politic to improve itself? Brain, heart, lungs, liver, kidney, skin, or blood? You certainly can't start with the voters themselves, who have and should have the ultimate power. Without rational religion, or at least liberal education, they remain anti-intellectual victims of advertised idols and ignorant prejudices. But the teachers of their school teachers, who are in the least hopeless position (over several generations) to improve the republic by adjusting the valves and rheostats of our cultural network, are ultimately the democratic creatures of the mothers and fathers who nurture future students and determine public policy. In the long run teachers must adjust to the feedback of their students' students; they can't survive any wiser or more courageous than a constituency that's influenced more by broadcast advertising than by education its antithesis. Yet constitutional democracy is essential to justice, mercy, and the very freedom necessary for proposing educational reforms!"

Pausing at his quod erat non demonstrandum with another smile, Father Duncannon finished without emphasis: "So unless our people allow the wisdom and goodwill of the Holy Spirit to enter into their hearts and dissolve the circular problem of democratic education it will take a whole army of Caleb Karcists to reform our government!"

Rafe and Chris nearly choked on their wine. All three together now called attention to their table with such hilarity. They toasted Caleb, whom they could hardly imagine in public authority, to say nothing of his replication at all levels of public power. Each of the three entertained his own images of the young man's mundane crotchets without to any degree recanting their appreciation of his several services.

This conviviality was hardly typical of conversation between the two Members Regular. For the Superior himself (as if in an orgy of comedy) it clarified a slightly adulterated conscience by precipitating suspended particles of his selfindulgence: he was momentarily purged of the realization that he had encouraged Caleb's personal rather than spiritual devotion.

The fact was that Caleb who hated any duty that entailed persuasion or selling had quite voluntarily (not to say insistently, on his own time, and certainly beyond the terms of his job with the Lab) made ingenuous rounds of literary agents and religious editors in the New Uruk book trade attempting to convey his philosophical enthusiasm for one of a presumably unknown priest's privately printed books which he believed would excite common readers if commercially published and distributed.

The incompetence of his sales effort was sufficient cause for summary failure—that is to say, for being unable to get any editor even to take from his hand for examination a protocopy of *Christian Theodynamics*. But it hadn't been Caleb's own fault entirely. From a few periphrastic hints it finally dawned on him with a shock that he was so coolly rebuffed because Father Duncannon was already known by canard in the godly book community as (in Chris Lucey's subsequent explanation) "a socialistic crank appealing for disciples from some underground interstice of the Tudor-Petrine muddle and attracting all kinds of antiprematureantifascist suspicion as a temporal heresiarch in unworldly disguise who also probably aided and abetted enemies of the state more dangerous than the pitiable Resistance".

Chris was now responding to his leader. "Paperclips are an invention of the devil, according to Caleb! They snag papers that don't belong to them and confound the intentions of those whose topmost sheets have gone astray. That's why God has given us stapling machines and staple-pullers."

"They're especially devilish in file trays." Rafe chimed in. "And file trays are managerially essential; but only one kind is of efficient configuration; and if he were running the General Services Agency in Washington the specifications for a stack of them, or two stacks, would be written into the Federal Register for every desk job; and to clinch the matter his requisite model happens to be made by one of the sub-subsidiaries of the Parity Corporation, which first captured his imagination because its corporate seal is a doublebitted axe—more useful, he maintains, than a single edge!"

"Yes indeed." Father Duncannon merrily corroborated. "Professor Whitehead warned us about minds like his when he said that the symbolic elements in life have a tendency to run wild, like vegetation in a tropical forest. But thank heaven Caleb's not a Gnostic!"

"Caleb could also preach an eloquent sermon on the virtues of rubber cement." Chris continued. "It sticks like glue but you can change your mind and pull your papers apart again even after it dries. Furthermore you can slap it on paper without worrying about excess at the edges because spillage can be rubbed right off without damage to pencil marks or typed impressions. And for some reason he believes the bonding is good for at least thirty five years. Another item de rigueur for improving all the world's management! I wish his enthusiasm were more infectious!"

"If Caleb's pressed" Rafe further contributed "he'll admit that office supplies don't make a discernible difference in Return on Investment or the effectiveness of public services; but he elaborates the distinction between effectiveness and efficiency when it comes to office *equipment* and its usage. If he were czar all accountants and statistical clerks would be provided by ukase with C R F 's new ten-key printing calculators and forced to operate them with one hand while the other works pencil on paper. And his encomiums on punched-paper-tape data-processing machines—also made by C R F —can keep you up all night! His scorn of the bureaucratic status quo would leave nothing to be desired of a Red revolutionist. And he believes that one of the electronic computers we're hearing about could replace ten Hollerith machines a hundred accountants and a thousand clerks if it were fed by paper tape instead of 'unit-record' punched cards! He's hoping C R F will get into even closer collaboration with OHM. You may remember that C R F is one of Parity's major interests."

"Mr Halymboyd was quite clear about that." Father Duncannon replied. "But I didn't offer him Caleb's advice!"

Chris was pleased to see his Superior so playful before they began to discuss the business dilemma that had been raised a month before at the first dinner with Rafe. But this was gaiety only in comparison to the gentle solemnity of Father Duncannon's basic demeanor. He was generally preoccupied with concern for the mesocosm, cure of his Order, and propagation of an idea of sacrifice that was too primitive for spiritual Christians. Compared with his mien on Refreshment Sunday at the Lab, which had been cheerful enough in mood and tolerant in substance, his form today was distinctly humorous.

"Father, perhaps Mr Opsimath would like to hear what you thought of Mr Halymboyd." Chris broke in, sunnily beaming, as if the notion had just struck him. Halymboyd, chief executive officer and mastermind of the Parity Corporation, had come up from New Uruk to meet Father Duncannon since their Lenten discussion of his company's stock.

Father Duncannon, perhaps ever so slightly annoyed at this blatant prompting by his impatient Economist, paused in tacit acquiescence, for he couldn't totally deny thought for the morrow that had begun to obtrude upon thought for the present Vine. Though reared in the Southern gentry among horses and mansions, and before his stint on Graveyard Street civilized by the clubs of Princedom, Chris usually seemed more clumsy and incommensurate with society than he really was, especially at altar and table, like a self-restrained ostrich indoors; but so far at this gathering his comportment had been graceful, as if the ostrich had been shriven of the guilty yen for companionship of its own kind. But before yielding to his subordinate's hitherto repressed urgency Father Duncannon persevered in his affectionate commentary long enough to redress the scales of quizzical justice in Caleb's favor.

Chris' employment of the young outsider in Lab financial affairs (as well as in assistance to Father Duncannon as a sort of unofficial major domo and quasi-editorial companion) was troubling some of the less worldly Members of the Order, not because he wasn't himself a member or postulant—he might not even have been a Christian—but because he was used by the Trustees in profiting from "usury", which was their doctrinal objection to all capitalism. Others chafed at the extravagance of having any fulltime paid employees (except for the bookkeeper Mortimer Ockham who was one of the original Members Secular), seeing that a Member Regular—quite apart from the question of what his vows of poverty and obedience might mean—was thus being spared to render even more of his time to Caesar, among metropolitan money-changers, instead of performing the menial duties for which Oku and a local firefighter (who kept the grounds in his off-hours) were carried on the monastery's payroll.

Within and without the clergy, all the unmonastic Members were fully occupied with secular or worldly careers, but many of them couldn't help wondering why much of the Lab's overhead expense wasn't diverted to charitable purposes somewhere in the world if the Order itself had no immediate need for its surplus treasure—granting that it was based upon the personal fortune disclaimed and legally donated by the Father Founder when he renounced all personal property. With most of the attending Members—innocent babes in the world of law and finance but no fools in moral analysis—it would be vain and gratuitously antagonizing for Chris to argue at Chapter (speaking with the tendentious aid of a particolored organization chart created by Caleb) that "the Trustees" were legally a profitmaking entity solely for the purpose of managing a fund for the benefit of the Laboratory of Melchizedec and the Mesocosm, a "charitable corporation", whereas the Classic Order of the Vine, the object of it all, which comprised all Members, was only a religious association without any assets in the eyes of the law. Although it had been made known that Caleb would be dismissed soon after Gloucestermas, the entire question of usury was sure to be debated at Chapter, to Chris's especial discomfort, as the executor of all investments.

"We mustn't forget that Caleb is no less excited about diazo photocopy machines." Father Duncannon went on. "He says that kind of machine may be as important as computers; that the fast and easy reproduction of documents will revolutionize offices and drive carbon paper into extinction!"

"The business he gives with one hand is much less than what he takes away with the other!" said Rafe. "Fisheye and Cuttle, right over there in West Marsh, makes both rubber cement and carbon paper!"

"He thinks Browning Chancellor has the best method of reproducing documents."

"Another company controlled by Parity!" Chris pointed out.

"Mr Halymboyd didn't mention that name. I don't remember seeing it on Caleb's chart."

"It's one of the recent acquisitions." Chris explained. "We learned of it only after the Carborundum & Bituminous merger with Tubalcain. It makes Caleb all the more partial to Parity. I think he's finally gotten over his disappointment at not being invited to meet Halymboyd. We were lucky to have King Arthur's attention even for the hour with Father that he came all the way up here for! He insisted on hiring his own limousine and chauffeur at the airport just so he could keep working every minute!"

Rafe took Chris's comment as an apology also for the disappointment of his own less expectant and undeclared wish to meet the mysterious magnate. Halymboyd was an enigmatic figure to Graveyard Street itself. The "luck" was Chris's inveigling skill as an intriguing and mysterious stockbroker-priest speaking for a tiny but intriguingly speculative holy order of the universally legendary and amorphous Church Financial.

Rafe's chief curiosity about the private conference was whether of not Halymboyd himself was disappointed with it. The financier had once lived in Dogtown, on the Foreside, not far from the Lab. Purely personally, was Dogtown itself an attraction or a repellant, spurring or retarding his agreement to make such an inconvenient trip? What sort of local memories might have made him look out the protectively tinted windows as he rode across the bridge and twisted through the smelly little city's shabby streets to its peninsular of great estates? Surely such a momentous man like any other can't deny his feelings, his secret motives, casual or deepseated, in making decisions—and not only when they're equipoised.

"Caleb gets excited most of all about the Synectic Method of Diagnostic Correlation!" Rafe declared.

"I've never understood his description of S M D C ." Chris confessed. "All I know is that it's epistemologically unorthodox, composed of nothing but abstract Entities and Categories; it requires a lot of rhythmic one-handed computations with a ten-key calculator; it's better than anything conventional statisticians have for finding causes and effects on a large scale; but it won't work without a plenary array of standardized data!"

Rafe defended Caleb's statistical zeal. "But the technique seems powerful and subtle. I think it would work better for analysis of economic and public health figures that are always available than for the managerial problems he uses as examples. If he were willing to become a promoter he could make a professional career of applying S M D C. But first he'd have to get a job in government or some openminded organization that would provide the facilities to develop what he's talking about. Otherwise no one is likely to grasp the extremely abstract idea that distinguishes it from orthodox analysis."

"Then of course he'd have to give up what's more important to him." Father Duncannon observed seriously.

"And leave Dogtown to boot!" agreed Chris. "But unfortunately he's going to have to get a job anyway. How can he get work on a large scale?"

"He won't leave the Cape if he can't take his dog." Rafe said.

And so, before finally allowing Father Lucey to pin him down to pressing business (not simply for Rafe's enlightenment and advice but in the hope of practical cooperation), Father Duncannon sighed once more in memory of youth, his finely hollowed face again reposing in the irreversible dedication of age. "The lobster was excellent. I'm only sorry it leaves us with no bones to send home for Ibi-Roi. It's a pity we can't afford to keep Caleb much longer."

3
ROBIN REDBREAST

Not many weeks after Lilian Cloud's reported nuptial flight Caleb's adventure as a voiceless troubadour under his own roof had achieved its successful middle and come to its compromised end. The ion was released from its adventitious bonding for resumption of the radical pursuit. He now found that Lilian's excommunication of him was a quasiexcommunication, hardly more absolute than the prenuptial demiexcommunications. With her he succeeded in reresuming at least the semicommunication.

His theme still was Blake's; again and again he goaded her:

> A Robin Redbreast in a cage
> Puts all Heaven in a rage.

In jocular animadversion he risked her anger by rubbing in what he chose to regard as her capitulation to expediency; but in his teasing he dared not emphasize the new condition, her marriage, for fear that she'd take too much notice of the distinction between sacramental adultery and mere natural fornication—a distinction which was just beginning to strike him in his review of the headlong spousebreach with Gloria Keith. Though he wasn't prepared to blame himself for the healthy intention to do what he craved to do whenever the opportunity succeeded in presenting itself, to a certain measure his progressive immersion in Father Duncannon's affairs rendered him more sensitive to the moral significance of experience.

In retrospect, as his the needle of his personal compass swung back to its natural magnetic pole, the deviating troubadour was astonished at the words he'd written to Lilian in his state of shock at the sudden news of her surrender to an abusive bedfellow even as he unwittingly drifted toward the solace of another married woman's vortex. Now that he thought he knew something about the moods and circumstances of the older matron, who as his landlady had seemed as unthinkably touchable as a busy happy Countess Kathleen, the true love of his life seemed both more valuable and less mysterious than before.

As a lately seasoned veteran he could smile at his premature sense of Lili-doom, looking back on the disappointment of his fantasies like an incest-minded brother who'd only dos-à-dosed her at the square dance but now could draw his own parallel to some of her flings in shallow-rooted passion by virtue of having swung the local hero's partner. Strangely enough, in his moments of bravado before the unexpected interlude with Gloria, squaredancing—from Lilian's point of view, who'd known no such fun in the High Cordillera—was one of the metaphors that he as the masked stranger had thought of suggesting to her; but only the other woman, reared in Montvert, would have understood that dynamic imagery—and silently resented its application to her conduct.

Instead of developing this conceit he'd wailed a wallflower's lament, foreseeing nothing but his perpetual exclusion from the dance hall:

My Once Lilian:
  Every time I saw you there was a burst of glory. No more glory for me now.
  I'm not sure that I promised not to speak of my love when I agreed to leave you in peace (as if marriage were peaceful)—of my highest love, for your brow; of my lowest, for your instep; or of my medial. I think I said only that I

wouldn't try to see you or phone you. Even now I'm not lovetalking you; I merely continue my one-way messages, hazarding a madman's repetitions, never learning to accept this hoax of destiny.

But there's no second person any more for me to address: just this epistolary journal that now must be in the third person feminine of a fictitious past:

My pituitary has been in turmoil ever since I first found myself sitting beside her at the counter of Harry's Delicatessen. My brain (loaded to the point of explosion) has been exciting and reflecting all sorts of wild feelings that affect the bloodstream, which in turn has further agitated that same brain and all the nerves connected to and from it: and my mind emanates from both systems.

So I could still talk to the missing person for many months without once mentioning anything that would absolutely have to be kept out of written words. That's how interesting (but not necessarily how interested!) she is. But of course I'd skip it all if that much of her time were at my disposal—or even a whole weekend's hours of days and nights—because I wouldn't have space for a word to say that wasn't as private as my master gland.

When I stare at the chessboard that's been painted on the palimpsest of my soul during the fragmented weeks of our unfinished renaissance, sometimes red seems to be the background base, the fundamental color; sometimes the black. At other times black and red have been confusingly simultaneous and equally competitive components of perception. But now I see quite clearly what should have been obvious even to me: the red is the ground, the red came first, the red imbeds the black. Her heart is red—but loves the inflamed programmer! The black is mine, lacking all color, everything she's missed, patches of soluble ink spilled upon the lacquered tray when she was busy. The quadratic geometry of equal odds was only a pipedream.

Yet for me destiny's blackness was all too persuasive; and I still believe that for her everything beyond the edges of the board runs more black than red. By nature the swan's as colorless as I, and certainly no less ironic.

My waveless hue that reflects no light may be illusory in an isolated game but it proves itself primary in the unlimited field inhabited by our two anachronistic lives. So those black squares are emblematic clues to what might have been an endless match in many boundless dimensions. I am not grieving over a game of common checkers. That's why I keep telling the beads of our affinity: wolfdogs, Scotch and water, Catholicrats, Gilgamesh, and all the rest that has passed through both our minds in Dogtown, to say nothing of Hume and Babylon Oaks.

I'm more dogged than ever in my lunacy, which has only spread more evenly, dyeing all my tissues. If I wore no clothes the world would see that I'm Lili-colored all over. They'd leave me alone, the divine idiot of the village, and let me rave. But as it is they don't understand my indifference to riches and power, or my strange behavior in the fields and forests. I need a collar tagged with her name and address, certifying that she'll pay my fines. But in fact I lack any kind of license that would identify me with her. . . .

As it is, mine is the mortal enchantment of a frog once kissed by the princess on her tower: he can't be disenchanted:: in human form he's only more enthralled.

I respect her decision. She did everything possible to warn me, with thirty kisses. I suppose the sun stood still for as long as it was able to resist the law. Our destiny is not undone by her spurious honeymoon.

But desire now has turned to sorrow: instead of desire for what I did not possess, sorrow for what once I had. There is only this pen to ease my misery, for I can no longer hear her precious voice through any last remaining crack in the rebuilt wall between us. How can I help continuing my failure to conceal the aortal feeling of my life?

Always and everywhere people are suffering lost loves. The songs are full of such singers. The theme is *trying to forget*. That's obviously the best way to dissolve the madness fixed upon love-for-the-sake-of-love. One merely expunges the expugnable term on the opposite side of the equation, making room for some substitute that can restore the algebraic equilibrium, for satisfaction in that case has more than one possible solution.

But this is an algebra of values. I don't want to forget her. I don't try. Because the unique value of our attempted equation—which really was an inequality—lay not in the relationship but in the independent semiconstant representing her quality in it: which existed, pre-existed, and continues to exist in or out of any man's inequation.

But algebra too is one of a man's general delusions, and at the most I can forget all mathematics. What I cannot forget is the veridical person who in this unique instance anchors love in reality at the bottom of an ocean all but infinitely sad.

Still, there's something going on here that's even more peculiar than her inestimable worth. Can destiny so suddenly smash its tablets? If so, maybe it sets a precedent for changing its mind again—to re-reveal that our flashing glimpse of each other was no hoax after all.* Perhaps destiny is still experimenting with our mutual fate. Can my lady believe that we yet have all the evidence? Can she doubt that we were not merely the two fungible entities of a love song? And if we *were* not we still *are* not, even in the arms of others.

Not that I have another. My body wastes, as I try to adjust to the tone of all my fibers that she's altered from a distance too great. I'm trying to learn how best not to forget.

I had hoped to show her the lilacs from this open window, white and lavender intermingled in the fragrance of the yard, with Ibi on guard.

Her anchorite,

Caleb

* Until we're both dead I can't really believe that she and I are Pyramus and Thisbe. Certainly not Abelard and Heloise: my flame is not curtailed; I offer her no spiritual direction; it isn't Jesus Christ she's brided; nor does she as a mother superior write me reproachful letters of ever-quickened carnal memory.

Yet now, after his unforeseen baccalaureate as a practical troubadour, somewhat pleased with his progress and more hopeful of postgraduate prospects, he found himself wryly in tune with Lilian's erotic philosophy of autonomous parts. The Rectory episode over, his parts even in the prime of masculine life were at any rate emotionally assuaged for the time being, because little less than the whole itself they were mental as well as physical, subtle as well as gross. Like the whole, moreover, their libido was diverted or transformed by the increasing intensity of what especially engaged him: revising *The Tower of Gilgamesh*, helping Father Duncannon prepare for the Pentecostal Chapter, and preparing himself to reduce the mystery of his own Gloucestermas.

So when his disposable thoughts again centered themselves upon Lilian, now Mrs Algo, he found them tolerably resigned sensible and ironic as concerning her parts while nevertheless unwavered in evaluation of her whole person. Less feverishly than in the summer of his moonhope, his love in partial abeyance but (as he believed) unabated in potential entirety, he pitched himself as alert as ever for intelligence of her existence and for any improbable possibility of encounter. His letters lightened.

Caleb was now another troubadour, an unfaithful one, half quiescent, lying in wait, feigning nothing about his intentions, making no pretense of disinterested friendship, warning her of his aspiration to the ideal guerdon of a lover. Thanks to her marriage it seemed quite safe to strum on his soundless lute a repertory of metaphysical conceits about his "courtship". Nevertheless, love's true end, as far as his concerned her, receded to the oceanic horizon of anticipation. In its default, therefore, the hope of a letter from her was promoted from secondary to primary status in his unilateral written communications.

His theme now, for the long haul, was *trying to remember*. It was a cheerful ex post facto attempt at retroactive seduction. His cooler erotic wit was whetted. He harped on the idea that his persistence in disappointment stemmed from an undiminished intellectual desire that was neither generic nor specific but singular.

This distance of feeling seemed to suit her well enough. She respected her marriage but was apparently loathe to lose the stimulation of his admiration or the comfort of his sympathy. He was encouraged by short accidental meetings at daytime haunts such as the A & P, Harry's Delicatessen, or the children's playground at Salt Cod Park—initially the determinations of chance but improved by tacit hints once a week or so. Before long they were laughing at their unacknowledged conspiracies.

Whenever his hope was foiled by not finding her he had only his own guesswork to blame. But he guessed happily often enough that he was kept posted about a little of what she refused to post but was willing to disclose, and he was able to augment his treasury of her spoken words, while she fattened (though at moderated rate) her pack of his letters, which she asseverated were safely hidden.

In matter-of-fact manner she pretended not to suspect that he attended more of the possible appointments than she did—in fact all of them, more than all of them—at least until he'd finally reconciled himself to her fortified reservations as a married woman. But one day, as he found her pushing Mooney in a public swing on Tansy Hill, she equably remarked, recovering a little of their premarital intimacy: "You're a cat, always waiting for me to come out of my hole!"

"No: a black jaguar waiting for the swan!"

"If I'm not still the ugly duckling," she lazily protested, "I'm a black swan."

"The single case that refutes induction! And all the better for nighttime assignation."

As always now they spoke in public sight: there could be no question of touching. Thus however as his fever subsided asymptotically to its idiopathic base he discovered that Eros could shoot a third and tranquilizing arrow even when omitting (alas) the second. They settled into a new dyadic mooring, mutual anchors to windward that stopped each other from drifting onto the rocks of cynicism.

But Caleb's prurient curiosity about the man who'd caged her didn't pall at all. Apparently Gil was no longer mistreating her. At present he sounded positively uxorious. "He's getting me the old sculpture studio right across our road."

"For painting, or for weaving?" This reminder of the programmer's donatory power pierced Caleb's heart as a recurrent pang of sexual envy.

"I may have to furnish it with other artists' work. But there's space for looms and easels and etching presses, and an alcove for my seclusion-cot. He's making more money freelance. Perhaps he can patent his programs and sell them to businesses that can't do their own programming. Everybody thinks he's crazy. That's one thing I like about him."

Caleb found it difficult to suppress his scorn for the illusion that any company could be expected to submit its myriad details of form and content to the determinations of an outside technician: ". . . except for payroll."

"I think payroll is what he's starting with. You'd be surprised how complicated it is." With one hand mechanically pushing Mooney in the pendular rhythm of her shifting hips she turned to gaze across the broad waters of the outer harbor. The remnant of her twin raven braids was cut in the style of a helmet preened smooth by motion in and of the air. "But I'm not going to stop working. I won't be a kept wife!"

"Even for the sake of art?"

"I feel as if I've lost my masculinity."

*

Caleb walked to Doc Charlemagne's with Ibi one Saturday afternoon because he had arranged to go see *Father Barnacle's Niece* at the Globe with Petto the Artsmith of Dogtown, having missed it the first time around at the West End, instead of paying their usual nighttime respects at Saturday's court. (Belle Cingani neé Beatrice Picory, his first choice as movie-companion, had seen it long ago and was unavailable anyway.) He met Deeta Dana on the outside stairs, with an empty burlap sack slung over her shoulder, just leaving to gather seaweed on the Foreside rocks. While she and Ibi were making their usual fuss over each other her friendly smiles at himself naturally displaced the image of any other face. He thought it would have been more illuminating to see moving pictures of Ireland in her authentic company than in that of a semisemitic international journalist or an all-too-susceptible Tuscan sculptor.

Leaving Ibi outside on the upper landing to bask in the urban ravine of sunshine and watch the buzzing escarpment fauna of dilatory springtime, he found Doc still drinking his breakfast coffee and very hospitable. The young visitor forthwith resigned all of his afternoon to the joy of master conversation, offering no objection to the unaccustomed comfort of daytime tidbits and Scotch, enjoying the same gentle bird-chirping blue and green zephyr from open windows that the day before had called his attention to Lilian's refashioned hair outdoors.

But it was the motherly attentiveness of Doc himself that warmed him most. The impromptu refection, alone with a great teacher, stimulated all his delights in the ideas they either discussed or might have discussed in exciting agreement. Under Doc's benevolent countenance, softly egocratic but never egocentric, he tarried and talked, about this and that suggested by writings they both had read or should have read. Doc smiled upon his pupil's interests, sympathetically listening and approving his dromenological observations without subsuming them, yet now and then picking up a pencil to write on the used-up kitchen scratch pad a mnemonic of stimulated thought for his own purposes.

Under that spell Caleb stayed too long (though not long enough to see Deeta again); but when he left he felt so fortified with intellectual mastery that no sooner did he get home and fetch fresh water for Ibi than he sat down to violate the taboo against telephoning Lilian, which in his reckless euphoria seemed a petty prohibition. All his screeds notwithstanding, there was always a residue of tentative or probational subtleties for him to connote and her to perceive that he would not trust to letters for delivery to an Algo household even if it had been possible to exchange them in writing.

Temerarious, shedding all precaution in the flush of drunken pride, seeming to remember that Gil was scheduled to be in Chicago for a week, and prepared to brave it out as a business call if Lilian's mother answered, he dialed the number still listed in Lilian's maiden name. The telephone rang five times before he gave up, but just as he was about to hang up a man's voice answered, challenging and brusque, as if already suspicious: "Yes?"

Instantly sobered, Caleb's confidence vanished. He trembled as if he'd stumbled into single combat with Gilgamesh. His throat tightened. His tongue couldn't think, paralyzed by guilt. Hastily, yet hesitating at his rudeness, he put back the instrument to undo his call, lest he utterly betray Lilian's trust in his promise, too much of a coward to bluff an excuse, as if the unseen face had already read the whole story from the timbre of his ring.

But that selfsufficient monosyllable of voice only fascinated him the more. He wanted to steal a look at the man, to see if he was really a Cerne giant, or golden as Apollo. Lilian had casually admitted something that might explain his own failure as a troubadour: that it was not difficult for a Mrs Algo Ass to remain chaste. "I'm well enough ploughed, and maybe I'll be reaped, but he doesn't cultivate my mind!" She'd been speaking to the point of her last clause, Caleb's cherished part in her life, and realized only too late what had escaped her lips as the indiscretion as a loyal married woman. It was the first time Caleb had ever seen her blush, for one reason or the other.

But in any case, with a daughter growing more broadly aware of society, and with an aged mother yearning for legitimate posterity, she had not married lightly. Though she continued to assume an Atlindu-Bohemian indifference to Mrs Grundy, Caleb was sometimes persuaded that her whole life now grounded itself in a new appreciation of domestic security, and that she was especially glad to be liberated from the jactitation of marriage: for all of which she owed her husband his trust as well in word as deed—to the best of her ability, as a Greek philosopher who'd sold herself into Roman slavery.

Caleb's jealous urge to get a look at the lord of her enthrallment was not alleviated by any anodyne in which Love's third arrowhead was dipped. Three times he forswore his word of honor with a disingenuous approach to the menage on Folly Road, prepared to defend himself with the lame excuses of a spy for having stumbled upon Lilian's distant domain if he or Ibi should be discovered on her street in a successful search for the connecting trail down from Purdeyville.

Most of the way he followed his proven overland route toward the Barebones's pier at Powerhouse Cove—up Watling Road, across the railroad on Old Stone Bridge, down the principal path for maxims and epigrams to Railcut Pond and along the tracks to its ascent through the rocky woods onto Purdeyville Common, and thence across a stony juniper weald of ghosted pastureland to the summit of Tir-na-Dog at Cynosure Rock, the Marking Stone. There Ibi was granted more leisure to review its surrounding history since the Ma'eve Thing than on their previous transits, while he himself deliberated the most likely trail to Prudence Cove of the three choices that each would ramify in its own selected descents to the northwesterly settlements, altogether switching and wending a dozen different tortuous ways from that sacred spot down through the surviving tract of rockborn hardwood, thinned and stunted by two hundred years of laborious unvirgining, saved from bulldozers only by its exceptionally defiant ravines and ledges.

On Caleb's first attempt he came out on the extension of Miller's Lane, far to the south of his goal. It was a long walk home against the traffic on Cod Street, even Ibi very weary all the way at heel. For the next two days he made no morning run, not from exhaustion but in order to recover the time he'd squandered.

A week later, to even greater chagrin, he found himself debouched onto Cod by way of Granite Road, raw with interesting quarries he'd never seen before but still not north of Taraville. It would have been an even longer trudge home if Huck Salter hadn't happened along in his superannuated pickup truck on the way downtown from North Village with some lobster traps. (It was Huck's longer way to the Harbor, but he was avoiding the Pigeonhole covemaster, who happened to be the cop on duty along Cod Street's shorter arc.) Ibi, alone behind the cab, was exhilarated by his first kilroy ride in open air, sensuous and heady, savoring an unimaginable blend of scents in exhilarating succession. But again, this time for three days following, the dog was deprived of morning runs until his master's chagrin was annulled by objective accomplishment at the typewriter.

Before the third attempt Caleb studied his geodetic map, and when afoot paid more attention to the sun, keeping it well to his left as it declined over Smith's Bay. It was a longer and more complicated way than the others, requiring many a doubtful decision at crossed paths and bifurcations; but at last he came down onto the landline he was seeking, an abandoned quarry railroad bed between Taraville and North Village. It led him to the crossing of an old wagon lane, which, followed down a further slope to the left, became by degrees a pitted and populated road, although he wasn't sure it was Folly until he reached a string of houses and children's things looking and sounding like what Lilian's laconic obiter dicta had suggested of her precinct.

About the house itself he was acutely perplexed, for none was visibly numbered; but one, set back under spacious trees with a single tricycle in the dooryard, more or less across from a stone art studio, seemed to match his imagination better than its neighbors did, which were either too rundown or too sprucedup for a prosperous incomer menage without Norman pretensions. It appeared to have inside space and yard equipment suitable for the small cooperative nursery-school group that Lilian took her weekly turn at housing (lest Mooney enter society as a too-bedoted only-child).

Walking rapidly with his eyes straight ahead he could not very well see the car parked in the drive, or even try to read its license plate, but it seemed to be of Lilian's gray color. The voices of children came only from distances, and he felt all the more conspicuous because in the somnolence of a windless blossoming afternoon there were no other sounds, save from sporadic kilroys droning up or down the nearby twist of Cod Street. He did not run, for fear of disturbing the atmosphere's steady state of floral motions and attracting the attention of unseen saints or strangers who hadn't yet whiffed even his dog; but he hurried past, keeping Ibi at heel, trembling and sweating at the danger of Lilian's windows, glimpsing no more of his object than the robin's covered cage.

Lilian had quit more than one job when infuriated to find that her home address was being spied upon by a boss or colleague hoping to ascertain her degree of liberty. No matter what her dilemma, he said to himself, she apparently takes a bull by the horns. She would have been angry, he thought, but not contemptuous, if he'd done the same by forthrightly knocking on her door.

By road it was nearly the Cape's longest distance home, seven miles he guessed, this time going clockwise on Cod; but there was the possibility of being offered at least a cup of tea at Tessa's, and water for Ibi, before proceeding to Land's End and trying to smuggle Ibi aboard the next train (if one was leaving betimes). Thence the Harbor station would have been only a minute from home had he still been welcome to dwell in the castle of the Keiths; but now that he lived far out on East Front there'd be more than half an hour more to walk on pavement. All that effort to possess himself of no more than an external mise-en-scène for hidden images!

The best part of another week would ensue before he and Ibi revived the intention of running again, at glorious spring sunrises, now more often unclouded than not.

4
EXTRACTS FROM THE SECRET DIARY OF TESSA BAREBONES

*

... and I can't bear to look back at all the drivel I've written over the years about my soul's "unhappiness" from "boredom". Whatever happens from now on, it won't be tedious. As long as Melly and Miley continue to make it plain to me how to bring them up without anything to stand in the way of their development, I'll be happy in body, competent in mind, and lightheartedly shortsighted in the spiritual sphere.

I have so many secrets to keep that sometimes I even forget I'm a mother, especially when the secrets are not my own. Nowadays I'm not impelled to fill these blank pages with my soul in order to demonstrate to myself at least an apperceptive sanity! It is no longer necessary to confess herein my sins and desires. But I dare not wonder how long our worldly archangel will sustain my contentment.

When I'm so furiously busy I no longer wish for a servant.

*

... Now that the sun has been showing itself he knows what I meant when I told him not to despair of tardy Fräuline Spring. She seems churlish and hostile but is really only shy and modest. She blusters and sulks, freezes her face, drenches us with anger, and offends us with all sorts of tantrums only in order to turn us away so that she can get dressed behind her screen: she knows that airplane pilots never fly straight past Dogtown; they always circle around to see as much as they can.

R O says his native San Ricardo because it has no winter is becoming a vulgar country club even for retired petty officers. Its waterfront is never purified of tourists. The railroad is gone. The fishing families have become hotel and restaurant workers. It was once said by an Englishman to be "decidedly the pleasantest and most civilized-looking place in Cornucopia", and it still was when I saw it.

In soft moonlight whispers the Bahí de Pinos instructed me how to fall in love with the stage-design student as we fucked on a doubled sleeping bag in the deserted sand dunes. In the morning that beach (much coarser than ones on this cape) was still unpopulated. We had to hitchhike back to school in Yerba Buena. To the east of the hills there were lavender mountains in the background. I wish I could remember the boy's name. But the first time with R O at White Quarry the memory of that adventure brought back my precocious youth. We were two students, sans sand, far from the indolent Pacific, but under the same silent moon.

He doesn't want to see his hometown again, despite his sentimentally promiscuous nostalgia for towns all across the country that he hasn't even stopped in. He says this perversity only illustrates his indifference to the past: item, even though San Ricardo was discovered by Europe in 1542, and Francis Drake had explored Alta Cornucopia long before Champlain or Smith spied this Beauport, he prefers our junior ex-isle to his senior birthcape. And just between us, he dismisses Gloria's historiography as so much harmless fiction, and all such lore as what he says I called the "superstition of place". This whimsy is one of his charms.

We thank our lucky stars he's investing here and not getting intimate with any of those poignant places full of strange women that might have seduced him on his way to here. I'll slave behind the scenes to make sure that our reconstructed D M and D Corp is realized. Affluent friends are already responding. Jason Anacoluther cooperates not only as a banker but also as a personal stockholder.

Furthermore, none of this serious business has yet diverted anybody's pledge of financial support for our Stone Barn mummery!

Did that terrible fire start the flowering of my middle life?

*

I've been piqued by the obtuseness of R O 's continual attempt to understand and explain his fascination for this place without perceiving that I might have something to do with it! Or even Buck, for that matter. When I teased him on this point of gallantry he shrugged off my reproach by declaring that I'm the lovely egg in his beer, and Buck is the gravy for his meat and potatoes, considering that he would have chosen Dogtown anyway, despite the fact that at first sight it was decidedly unprepossessing, unlike hundreds of old and new towns in which he'd slept or supped. He has his own angle on Dogtown's quiddity but he's no better than the rest of us at defining the unarticulated consensus about our "homely Ort-an-sich". He swears he loves this place not just because he was subconsciously prepared, like a man who was seeking love for its own sake and willing to accommodate any lovable mistress, but because of the town's "absolute quality, irrespective of apolaustic relativity", as if it were what Doctor Charlemagne calls a Muse.

It keeps me on an even keel to be warned that he'll never come any closer to a declaration of love for me in particular. I'm free of illusions, and we are able to collaborate in more ways than one. I'm almost complacent about this salutary complement of my marriage to a saint. Fifteen years difference in age gets bigger and bigger when a husband's alcoholic. So man and wife both suffer the less when there's a guardian angel sent from God.

*

. . . [Rafe] was preoccupied today. I think he's beginning to distrust the mental stability of his friend the priest. As a prudent man entrusted with the Laboratory's capital Father Chris Lucey is no better than he should be. Apparently he's impatient to make his vineyard grow faster than the market. Fortunately the Superior has forbidden him to trade in short sales, warrants, puts and calls, rights, futures and all the other abstractions loved by capitalists who don't like real work. (Bonds are proscribed by the Order as unequivocally usurious, and anyhow they're too conservative for the Father Economist.) It is expected that at the Gloucestertide

Chapter the assembled members will demand that the Trustees deprive him of his freewheeling power—unless he makes enough money before then to meet the needs of all their charitable causes at once, including a decent annuity for lifetime maintenance of the Father Superior and his hilltop Lab, insured against Deluge, Depression, and Whirlwind.

R O now suspects that he hasn't been fully taken into Father Chris's confidence about matters that bear on their common interests. He suspects the secret desperation of an over-committed speculator swinging a wildcat by the tail. For his stake in our new company R O can't risk losses of buying power, and in any case he prefers not to borrow, but the priest is giving him to understand that it would be helpful to the Vine if he deferred selling his Parity stock until certain decisions and negotiations are completed so that he can continue to be counted (of course only "in street name") as part of the so-called "group of Parity investors" led by the bold Father.

What R O 's most worried about is Father Duncannon's reputation and security.

*

. . . I had the pleasure of correcting {Caleb} today. The boy can't be overbearing, like R O at times, but—small and timid as he may be—he can be just as overweening as that benign tyrant is when irritated by opinions that he jumps to the conclusion are at variance with his own. (At such times I never dispute R O 's assertions, because at all other times he's anything but angry or intolerant; and Buck's demeanor has always been so much the opposite of overbearing and overweening that I now luxuriate in any chance to play the passive role.) But on this occasion Caleb's scorn for a rather nice custom was based on such ignorant prejudice that I had to chasten him with a schoolmarmish lecture on Mother's Day as an important achievement of recognition before women got the vote, officially adopted by Congress and President Wilson in 1914—no doubt intended as a sop or pacifier by many of those who passed it but nevertheless a mark of irreversible symbolic progress. I forced him to agree that sentimental exploitation by commerce and Post Office is no more reason to contemn it than to ignore Christmas. After all, in the Church made by males there's a Mothering Sunday in the middle of Lent. Every mother's son should be so informed. Isn't it Caleb's own mother who taught him that WOMEN ARE THE

BETTER PEOPLE? For God's sake, even my iconoclastic sister Cora allows her family to celebrate Mother's Day!

Most feminists are too literal-minded. They lack the faculty of irony, which could easily "vanquish the vanishing Atlantean male", as Caleb says his mother urged.

*

Ray Lagniappe, one of R O 's old Tubalcain salesmen, wants to take on our new line of products, *whatever it may be*! He's also insinuating his wish to invest in the enterprise. (Thank God the S E C allows us only thirty five "nonaccredited" stockholders.) But such is his confidence in R ! Perhaps also he exaggerates Buck's genius in having solved the pump problem. (In this case I think it was only the wisdom of experience.)

Ray came up from Bot to take the boys to lunch. When he unfortunately found out from R O that we have a pier Buck was afraid he'd try to pay a call on us in his boat this summer. R took pains to rectify his indiscretion by mentioning to Ray that our cove hasn't been dredged since the Great Storm of '88, that for less than an hour of a calm high tide the deepest boat we can accommodate is a dory, and that therefore the only boating allowed is on the rocks for shipwrecked sailors. But I wouldn't be at home anyway.

R had no right to mention Buck's private life. Corporate officer or not, I insist on keeping the grubby part of our business out of my house. Perhaps someday I'll meet Mr Lagniappe at the company Christmas party.

So far the only line we have for anyone to sell is a few straggling little steam generators and dairy sterilizers that we will be taking over from Tubalcain to continue direct national distribution through Hafnia-Iona Creamery Equipment. And I doubt that an old-guard drummer in the automotive trade would be competent to handle any realizations of Buck's projets non réalizés. I hope we can afford a sales manager to protect R and Buck from time-consuming importunities, and me from social indignities.

*

... It's a good thing our new D M & D is a firm of unregistered "private placement" and doesn't come under most of the S E C rules. As the laylady Treasurer of our hard-scrabble former corporation I was so ignorant of even low finance that for the most part I just showed up to sign the checks that were put before me. I was free enough with my opinions about a few of the transactions I happened to notice and understand, but I wasn't enthusiastic about learning from Gretta even the theory of balancing a checkbook. If I hadn't been so sullen about learning the basic jargon and expanding my laughably limited ex officio experience in measly cash management it might not be so hard to follow what R O simplifies in telling me about Father Lucey's esoteric dilemmas in high finance.

I hope R O will never be subpoenaed for knowing too much about Parity and the priest. I'm very glad my friend and colleague is ready to liquidate his nest-egg stock and is too prudent to borrow against it in order to keep an interest in either Parity or Paraclete; but if it weren't for the capital required to control our new business (not to mention the needs of Stone Barn) I think he would have been inclined to sell one and buy the other.

Who wouldn't be tempted? Paraclete's got a product devoutly to be wished. When he asked me what I as an experienced consumer thought the demand might be for a contraceptive pill I was reckless with my blessings. If Paraclete's scientific claims are confirmed, and protected by patent, I think it will be the growth stock of the century, at least for speculators willing to wait for their profits. I can't blame the priest for being intrigued. He could enjoy the advantage of being in schism with the Pope.

Apparently the ticklish question is whether or not the Order of the Vine, which encourages birth-control as essential to the future welfare of humanity (if it is spared the E-Bomb), should pull out of its special relationship with Parity and transfer its capital to more innocent usury—which incidentally might save Father Lucey his job as holy financial manager!

Caleb's job is temporary, no matter what. For him the Parity experience is nothing more than an aesthetically satisfying observation of "organic power", and therefore he remains more trustful of Arthur Halymboyd's constructive intentions than R does (who, by the way, has finally met the spider king!). I'm told that Caleb seems indifferent to issues of stockholder risk and gain, and is against trading Parity for Paraclete because there's nothing complex to interest him in an immature pharmaceutical company's organization or management. To him (R O says) Paraclete's merely an ill-defined black box, insusceptible to his kind of analysis, especially since he knows nothing about biochemistry: any chart of it would be trivial! R O calls him a "subjective fundamentalist".

But from what Caleb has let slip during his soi-disant voice therapy I should think that he of all young men would be fascinated by Paraclete's new product. No doubt he'd take more interest in the company if there were talk of an ironic merger with Annunciator Labs, or Procreative Research! Maybe with vertical acquisition of Litmus Garter Products and Fourchette Enterprises! And horizontal integration with such as Adam & Eve Comforts, Liberal Latex Limited, and Pseudopharmaceutical Counterproducts! What a particolored diagram he'd make of an oxymoronic giant molecule like that!

I must admit that I'm getting pretty interested in these financial games. It's R O's impression that Father Chris would like to make the best of both worlds by getting Parity to gobble up a big chunk of Paraclete. Then he could claim benign speculation in birth control hedged by the safer investment in an established industrial conglomeration.

Aside from the unlikelihood of any response by Mr Halymboyd to such a presumptuous suggestion, the fly in the ointment, as I understand it, would be that Parity is registered as a "non-diversified" investment trust, and has already been under enough dilatory pressure from the S E C to have divorced itself from banking and insurance, if not from its food processing and other less miscegenous alliances. Is it possible that the priest thinks Parity could get away with buying Paraclete stock through an obscure subsidiary with a misleading name?

I've been shocked to hear how sloppily the Curb Exchange operates. It was originally a bunch of Irishmen, Jews, and Tuscans meeting on the street. They came in from the rain only thirty years ago and still sell seats for less than the price of Ray Lagniappe's $80,000 stinkpot toyboat. It's so slackly supervised by the S E C, not to mention its own governors, that even if anyone's caught in a violation he's usually cited with no worse than a "cease and desist" or "divestiture" order, with infinite time to comply. A couple of years ago one of the Curb's "specialists" was convicted of bribing its president! Fortunately it was not the Parity specialist whom Halymboyd has been suspected of suborning, but the case is fuel for the hue and cry of anti-capitalists who want their Father Economist to get off the Street entirely.

How much I'm learning that I'll never need to know—except for its relevance to masculine psychology!

*

... One can't help being intrigued by Parity's artful web, from which the rival spider's is now disentangling itself. Its invisible strands touch us in mysterious ways. We now find for instance that our Norman reality shark Hastings Mooncusser is the nephew of Halymboyd's former arachnoid collaborator Professor Zane Capstick (the "Byzantine emperor" of Financial Usufruct). Mooncusser, that smart young gift to Dogtown's economy, is the one who's marrying the daughter of Owen Leary, the devoted reader of T S Chittering, president of Tubalcain's distributor down at Charter Oak whom R O liked so much when he met him last year. The cosmopolitan wedding, announced in the *New Uruk Testament*, will be on the Foreside at Hoi Aristoi Yacht Club. Our banker Jason will be an usher. Also Hamilton DeCamp Jr, who's still identified as V P of Parity!

*

What a tonic, what a catalyst, what an animator is this man O! He's rejuvenated our scurvy crew like a barrel of limes.

Our little tribe of friends seems well provided but it's not as selfsufficient it looks. Though at least slightly known among the indigenes employed on this Cape, most of us have never seen the workers in their own houses. And we're not consulted like the doctors and lawyers they're obliged to meet in private offices. Most of us, the women at least, look askance at the Turntable Knights. We don't know the professional artists or scholars, let alone either the rich or the poor (except Ippy Charlemagne). In some of Dogtown's hamlets each of us hardly knows a soul. Of course my brother-in-law Thad is conspicuous among the people of our largest employer; Buck and Gretta have had commerce with hundreds of denizens; Gloria and Dexter converse with thousands; Huck has his lobster-trapping and firefighting cronies, Wat his own congenial handful; and we of the Troika have our elite students: but for the most part at arms length in business hours only. Those statistics won't change unless we go broke. We'll never be invited to Foreside weddings and we're not likely to put on our own beer busts for hoi poloi. But at least we're finally getting pollinated by a golden bumble-bee.

R O is opening our petals to all the airs of Lady Gloucester. And not with Charlemagne alone has he leavened our dough. He hangs around all kinds. He probably already knows more local people of all stripes, or more about them, than the sum of all our several acquaintances—not counting the Keiths'. He communicates far more freely than sublunar men. (Though not *too* freely, I trust!)

Maybe personal enthusiasm makes me exaggerate. But when I hesitantly mentioned to Buck my general feeling of social regeneration he readily agreed. He said that R O is like the lumberjack who frees a river logjam with two or three twists of his peavey. That isn't exactly the kind of metaphor that I would have voiced, but I'm sure it's innocently apposite from my husband's point of view.

Sally Salter put it differently: "That's the way the Holy Spirit works!" If she starts writing spiritual poems about R O I'll scratch out both her eyes.

Directly or indirectly he has led us to or led to us many residents of this rock now important to our prospects, whether or not we might otherwise have been merely aware of their existence but unaware of their worth. I should draw up a list to acknowledge these guided contingencies. . . .

*

. . . Cora tells me that Thad driving through town at night has twice seen Caleb walking with the hostess-cashier of the Doghouse. She was asked to treat this observation as unworthy of repetition. The secret stops right here, unless or until Caleb himself volunteers otherwise. I owe him no less. But from what I hear of that woman's distinction she's someone he might well have mentioned at least to me. Why his silence? In other matters, when we're talking alone, he doesn't hide his light under a bushel. He's certainly not the kind of chap that has any call to be ashamed of one of Loathey O'Toole's lovely bondsmaids. I think I'll go lunch there once or twice to see what I can discover about that apparently new incomer. Caleb—curse his intuition—holds my own honor in his hands, and if he's trying to keep something secret, however trivial the mystery may turn out to be, it might be wise to find him an incentive to keep holding his tongue for our mutual security.

*

. . . but I've always had such poor results from my saltwater gardening that it's not worth the struggle, especially when I have so little time for it. The notorious Gepetto (a k a Simplicissimus) suggests that I turn the beds on the wharf into a sculpture garden, with massive pieces of stone, iron thick enough to rust for a hundred years unweakened, or Poseidon's driftwood impervious to the weather of Zeus. It's a good idea. At least it would keep our drunken guests from parking there. I worry more about their safety than the kids'.

After repeated calls and promises I'd finally gotten Petto here in his flatulent tinker-truck to fix the hinge on my Dutch oven and discuss the "Brass Head" for our *F B & F B* production. He was a much gentler man than I'd expected: not an artless blacksmith who'd taken up an art but a selfmade artist who'd been obliged to take up the least distressing trade. He tells me frankly that alimony and child-support keep his nose to the grindstone. His language is sometimes gauche and salaciously impertinent, but somehow excusable because his intentions are evidently courteous and respectful. On the one hand he's serious and careful about his paid tasks; on the other he's excitable if not enthusiastic about everything else. It's impossible to stand on one's feminine dignity in the face of his sensitivity and goodwill.

Of course he suggests his own pieces for the garden, including the Brass Head after our play is over, but he also generously praises the work of Huck and Shelly. I remembered R 's remark that for lack of cost accounting his predecessor at Tubalcain had used weight as his criterion in setting the prices of steam cleaners, so I said I'd pay for sculpture by the pound. He laughed at the joke, doubled up, and slapped his thigh.

Yet he was solemnly impressed by Powerhouse Cove. It was noontime at the dark of the moon, and he was much affected by the calm flood tide. The wharf he said was "up to its eyebrows". He stood at the end and slowly flexed his knees. I thought he was going to jump in, but he told me he was only sympathizing with the tranquil breathing of the sea.

"This is living water!" he intoned in a pitch that rose and fell. "Not dead like lakes. The Atlindus say water's a medicine we can't do without. But we can't drink living waters any more than we can eat living meat."

The beat of his emphatic phrases amplified and distorted the soothing swells at his feet, but his meaning was contemplative. He was delighting in the seascape garden he envisioned for both storm and peace.

*

... so at R's suggestion Mr Ghibellini, the editor of the paper, assigned Belle Cingani to do a feature article on the Troika and our hopes for the Stone Barn Mummers. She's the new bright girl who wrote so well about Buck and the fire. This afternoon she brought over the *Nous*'s excellent photographer, Flash (Fenimore) Silver. I forbad any pictures of this house, but they came here to do me because they're pumping each of us separately before we're taken as a group at the Barn itself (which we expect to take possession of next week, after Mr Bagshaw has fixed some floor planks). After Flash left Belle and I had a long talk that little resembled an "interview".

She is young but perceptive, and an excellent writer, far better qualified to cover "cultural events" (and probably politics too) than anyone the *Nous* has ever hired before. (I'd been afraid Ghibellini would assign Doug Dimout the sports writer to review Troika productions.) She's alert and articulate, yet self-effacing, with a cheerfully ironic sense of humor. I wish we had her in our troupe, if only she could project her soft voice. She's the one who should have had her picture taken. I liked her from the first.

Her ambitions are not petty. Why is she here? I asked almost as many questions as she did, but with far less success. As an irreverent journalist she's beyond her years, and confident enough to be playful. The only thing I'd ever heard of her—from Gretta, secondhand, whose quilting companion operates one of the automated paper-tape typesetters at the *Nous*—is that she's considered "not very professional". From now on I'll have my curiosity antenna pitched to pick up any little perturbations in Dogtown's patriarchal establishment that such a provocative reporter may be suspected of.

Belle had just read one of Anima Nim's public diaries and was thoroughly enchanted to hear that I knew Auto Drang's brilliant belle dame when I was working for him. What especially interested the girl was Anima's claim that she didn't believe in sex without love. I warned Belle to look for a variable definition of love.

I had mentioned knowing Anima because by some indirect association that I haven't yet traced the attractiveness of Belle's manner—certainly not her lightly mirthful speech, her half-masculine gestures, or her fresh unpainted face!—reminded me of that life-artist as she'd struck me *when I was sixteen*. I have yet to see this one in the company of men, but I myself once learned a few tricks by watching Anima's amorets.

Nevertheless, provisionally, I like the wench. More power to her— as long as she steers clear of Mr O . Of course I don't yet know what she's going to write about "the chief mummer" and her rockbounding colleagues. I could turn on her in the blink of an eye if she lets us down, or quotes me off the record. At moments I was unguarded enough to treat her almost as a daughter, as Melissa perhaps, thinking of a grown-up Melissa, whose coloring is similar. I warned her that no woman lives in Dogtown for long before her hormones fall into phase with the moon. The bell curve of labor-room occupancy at Humphrey Tybbot Hospital is said to betray a lunar pattern.

*

Today our Stone Barn mummery suffered a jolt of disappointment. It's not life-threatening, but it forces us to be less optimistic about success. I learned that under the terms of Tybbot's trust none of Frank Bacon's grants can go to anything theatrical. It was a mistake to reckon on Frank's personal sympathy without first inquiring into constraints upon his professional support.

This afternoon I did what I should have done long ago:

I called on him to describe our plans. R goes to him for objective advice (since the dogs can't be consulted) when he fears D T denizens are gulling him, or when he gets conflicting versions of local affairs—that is, failing his trust in the dispassion or accuracy of our circle, or the wisdom of our anthropological Doctor. Maggie and the children were out but Frank left his office to serve me tea in their beautiful living room across the hall.

On his own he'll help us all he can, but of course it can't be much with money, seeing what a big family he has on his hands. He's willing to serve as a fundraiser among the gentry, and perhaps as our chairman. When I mentioned that Jason was one of our principal sponsors Frank told me about some of the reputed lecher's confidential benefactions.

That made me feel a little more comfortable about sitting with Jason as a fellow director and our largest outside investor on the new D M & D board. Still, though his business interest in our commercial enterprise is probably too trifling for him to attend our routine meetings, he always listens to R (especially as a friend of Ippy Charlemagne), admires Buck, and may not be loathe to test even me for round heels. "Keep your legs crossed when he's around!" says my sister in her proletarian mood. . . .

*

The "Irish Question" never quite goes away.

Besides Anima Nim—admirable, excessively talented, exquisitely exotic, generous, tolerant, liberal, and kind to me individually—as far as I can remember the only good woman I've ever disliked is Deeta Dana. What accounts for my feeling? Is it only my frivolous disdain of her long golden braid, so aggravatingly oldfashioned? It can't be jealousy of her life with the maestro, as his adoring servant but not his alter ego.

My animus for the egocentripetal Anima certainly didn't come from envy of her intimacy with poor ugly little Doctor Drang, a great mind reduced to fatuity by her unique toils, and for toiling Deeta it's no more so from envy of Doc the whale—if private proportion holds to public scale, wiener vs ketchup bottle. But I grudge the credit I must give this sturdy fay for her valiant youth, integrity, self-sacrificial devotion, loyalty, and botanical wisdom verging on white magic. No one, not even Doc himself, is less mercenary. Her simple egocentrifugal purity puts me to shame.

Her holiness seems premature, like the sapience of a Swiss goat-girl, or Joan of Arc. Surely this air of self-reliant almost smug tranquility (subordinate only to the most exalted of masters) is not indeed an Irish trait? She's nothing like the marooners O'Brien or O'Neill that I know here, or Pat Murphy the garbage-feeder whose grandfather was supposed to be a Purdeyville by-blow. She's not Railroad Irish, Salt Irish, or Doily Irish. It's hard to believe that her maternal ancestors, long before the mass Irish immigration, sometimes bred themselves to deserters from the British army and navy.

Glory (who's only seen Deeta from a distance, taking herbs and kelp to Isopel Berner's grave under the upstage oaks) thinks that she can be neither Fir Bolg nor Milesian, yet has no doubt that she's a scion of the Irindus, Atlantean cousins of the Tuatha De Danann. She is said to be the last of the Perditas, because in sheer disgust at what the ordinary Irish were coming to, her mother Perdita, surviving as midwife for Tinkersdale and Taraville, swore her to a life of contraception or worse. But one would no more care to ask that complacent young Ippy to acknowledge her identity than challenge a witch to recite her incantations.

For all these excellent and insufficient reasons I dislike her. She's too Natural to be natural. But I'm the only mean-spirited one. Everyone else is happy to grant her the benefit of mystery. Caleb, for one, dreams about her: he's convinced that the only book she reads is *A Vision*; she has devised a way to use it like the Book of I-Ching; it's her theosophy, and on the basis of it she expects someday to earn her living as a therapeutic sibyl, as the voice of "Megarithma".

Maybe it's just this aura of the occult that sticks in my craw. As a Drangian enemy of magi-psychology I hate what Caleb calls the mysticalistic evasion of both causality and freewill. I hope the our revered Director doesn't turn out to be what Caleb calls a "crypto-neo-gnostic Gnujian" and belie his own doctrine of dromenology! Can it be that even the great anthropological Doctor doesn't recognize subversion in the Alterian cure of souls? (That would surprise me as much as a revelation that His Imperial Majesty keeps a diary and patronizes a psychiatrist!) But otherwise who knows what binds him to the likes of Deeta Dana—unless it's crassly her young body and unqualified devotion?

Anyway, who has better claim to Yeats, the Irish or the Georgios, Paulines or Petrines, astrologers or typologists, mystics or dramaturges? Caleb accepts Yeats's assertion that he went among believers in magic only "all but unwillingly", and gives him the poetic license to say that he wrote *A Vision* for his "schoolmates only", à la Jacob Böhme. (Caleb complains or boasts that unlike all the other natives of Dogtown he has no schoolmates to write for!) He says that Yeats's harmless crotchets at this their best are excusable as mechanisms of "Lunar parable", unsurprising in an Irish poet of his peculiar origin and nurture; and that although his mother is hardly mentioned in all the autobiographical writing he declares "a man of genius takes the most after his mother"!

Yeats may have written that just to tease his tutorial father, John Butler Y, the marvelously literate painter, who called his wife weak and immature, nonetheless paying tribute to the great "imagination" on her side of the family. Did John mean insanity? But whether or not feckless and superstitious, it's said she remains the great mystery of Willie's life. According to Glory, if he wasn't a Milesian changeling of the Sidhe his remarkably dark complexion as a child may have betrayed a maternal ancestor in the Iberian trade on which Galway had thrived. In the cradle he was taught that after the Elizabethan wars England stripped Ireland of all its forests, leaving the hills naked, partly for the fuel and timber but also in order to deprive the natives of refuge in their resistance to serfdom; and that the English ate dogfish. Yet later he was happy to sail his toy *schooner* in a London park.

(Deeta told Caleb she hates the English even more for the cruel subjugation of their own patriotic people—such as the indiscriminate impressment of men for starving servitude in the Royal Navy's filthy crowded ships for years at a time, or the regular use of seven-year-old girls in harness, on hands and knees, to haul dollies of coal through tunnels twenty inches high as much as seven miles from the mouth of their pit. Caleb's only reply: that it was the exceptional and antithetical people of England, not the rulers as a class, to whom we are indebted for our best institutions and reforms, for the roots of our own culture. He's absurdly defensive about his Anglophilia.)

Deeta's as pious as a Daughter of the Mayflower about being Christy Mahon's granddaughter, even though, according to John Yeats, "Out of his country an Irishman is not a delicious morsel". The Playboy's escape to Purdeyville from initial refuge on the Aran Islands was attested by Willie Yeats (as it happens), but she's never been able to find his actual grave, the location of which seems to be as indeterminate as King Arthur's and as vague as the dimensions of the Celtic monuments that defy attempts to fix their measurements.

*

... but it's on theater that Doctor Charlemagne has made me read and appreciate Yeats. He's trying to decommercialize me, not as a student of literature and dreams but as the Mummer Superior and Sister Economist of a dramaturgic triumvirate about to be subsumed by an artistic director contemptuous of both profit and loss.

What would become of Stone Barn Mummers if we used his Yeats quotes in our ads?: "We must make a theater for ourselves and our friends, and for a few simple people who understand from sheer simplicity what we understand from scholarship and thought"! Or "... the arts would grow as serious as the Ten Commandments."!! At an arts center beyond the magnetic field of the metropolis our democratic dogfaces would learn "the subtle art of listening"!!! Why our Irindu Literary Theater would sink like a lead balloon!!!!

As "theater-lovers" we must of course conceal from the public the one common cause of Yeats and Charlemagne and Karcist, while as actors we must conceal from the Director our drive for economic success and popular fame. This is a problem in cultural diplomacy that was too much for the mummers of Dublin, even within the English Pale.

Everyone uses a play for her own purposes, all theory of communal motive to the contrary notwithstanding.

*

Surprise of surprises—and I of all people should not be surprised! I'm a little shocked, I must admit. But I can't yet tell whether I'm perturbed or pleased or prurient.

Doctor Charlemagne once said of my dearest friend Glory Keith that she has the gift of understanding history as "only one limit of the possible". When I happened to pass on this remark to Caleb he sententiously corrected the wise Director in absentia: "Except that it isn't a polar or boundary limit. It's the summit of a very broad probability curve." Whatever Caleb meant by this crypticism, it seems to me inconsistent with his Drangian notion of freewill. But if it applies to the intersection of two personal histories I should have known what was bound to happen in the Keith menage, unlikely as it might have seemed to an off-island psychologist.

She wouldn't have told me—and who am I to blame her?—if it wasn't all over with, she admitted apologetically. But perhaps in truth she would never have told me at all if it weren't for the doubly guilty "overlap" at the end. She has learned to assume a fairly healthy moral attitude toward the adultery itself, considering the conjugal offenses she's suffered (—more than she's aware—), not to mention all the ordinary disappointments of monogamy for a loyal female with an overworking husband, alcoholic or not. But the guilt of having been "shared", no matter how briefly and unintentionally, was too much for her to bear without confession.

With that detail of her story the tears came suddenly. I had known her to weep quietly, and she me, but never before to sob convulsively, clinging to me on the sofa and shaking like a child, no longer trying to moderate her remorse for this crowning sin against her own character. Her tears were spoiling my new blouse, but I was soon weeping too—for I know not what, except sympathy with a superior woman-soul suffering morally as I myself am not good enough to suffer. I felt like the sounding box of an unplayed cello responding to her sister viola's strings. Briefly I envied the purity that put me to shame, and for a moment knew the prick of conscience, abjuring all men and swearing solidarity with the universal sisterhood, and loving her as never before—my poor brave Glory, the most stalwart friend I ever had.

My tears dried more readily than hers, and my soul quickly recidivated, but soon she felt much better for the catharsis, and thanked me as if I'd dissolved for her the problem of female sex. Then I was able to lead her back to the familiar path of everyday pragmatism.

I offered what comfort I could without suggesting the lively sympathy of my experience in pre-Barebones escapades (lest she begin to wonder if I owed her secrets closer to home), but I was canny enough to provide against future loose talk by reciprocating her revelation with the disclosure of my unoverlapping guilt with R, as if it were my first offense on this lawless island of gulls and dogs. I was careful not to imply that my sin was less excusable than hers because my husband was more innocent than hers, but I did claim that it was much worse than hers because I hadn't the slightest intention of bringing it to an end. By contrast, I argued, her transitory experiment was but a peccadillo.

We then had a physiological discussion about how much lighter the world's moral burden falls on men than on us despite the fact that their corporal appetites are more easily sated. That conversation deepened our intimacy by loosening her inhibitions of expression.

I sometimes wish I had an *absolute* friend—male or female—to talk about the secrets of my whole long diary with. But I'm a clinician by nurture; I'm the one that gets leaned on. I always seem the stronger because the other is always more honest. Civilization would be impossible if personal truth were held to higher standards than history.

Anyway, I'm almost sure Glory was as genuinely surprised at my secret as was I at her way of kicking over the traces. So far Caleb must have kept his silence in both our cases—at least with each of the two female perpetrators, who happen to be the very persons among those uninjured who would have been most sympathetic with the other's secret. He's an honorable troubadour in a doubly privileged position. But I'm sure he never forgets that as his semi-clinician I hold hostage my privileged inklings of the original motive for his anxious sojourn in Dogtown, otherwise an enigma wrapped in a mystery.

However, I'm not sure the rest of our little world would be as surprised at me as I think Glory was. I've been rather reckless of late, trusting too much in sophisticated smokescreens. But as long as the facts are only tacitly guessed at—! Come Gloucestermas there'll be plenty of other lubricious speculations to wag envious tongues, which anyway Buck never hears.

*

I still haven't even seen the charming histrionic stockbroking psychiatric-socialworker priest, so I'm loathe to warn R O that from what I hear his friend is critically in need of both psychotherapy and legal counsel. Apparently the civilian lawyer of the Trust's triumvirate is kept even less informed of the "details" being handled by the junior Trustee than the Father Chairman is.

But Father Chris introduced R O to the said Endicott Krebs (of O'Grady, Krebs, & O'Grady) when we were looking for a corporation lawyer and legal member of our own board. If Buck and I like Mr Krebs he'll probably join us as a director no more active in the ordinary course of business (once he's set us up) than he is in his capacity as the outside Trustee of the Order's investment fund. His office is on Fate St in Botolph, but he lives in a big house on the Foreside, and Jason highly recommends him. Tomorrow Buck and I, along with Thad, Shelly, and some of the other D M & D investors, will meet him in the conference room at Jason's bank.

Of course Krebs can't talk privately to R O about the Trustees' business, but once when consulting him Father Chris took R along as a "financial advisor and friend of the Order". It seems that the Father Economist often speaks of his Street affairs with apparent candor in R's presence, upon whose perception I rely for my intuition of the priest, who of course is none of my business, and it would take more than crucifixion to make me talk about his strange personality with anyone else, not even Caleb, who probably knows more than anyone else about his behavior.

Thus I can keep religious secrets, no less! And I even refrain from giving Cora grist for her mill by divulging my new lowdown on the nefarious practices of opiatic capitalism. R trusts me. I don't parade my private impressions before the world as Anima Nim does (the model of my guileless youth) in that fascinating *Journal of Artifice*. It would take a rabid search by antiprematureantifascist technicians of the Bureau of Domestic Investigation to find *this* diary. (It's so secret that I don't impart the hiding place even to itself!) If it hadn't been for theatrics, amours, and domestication I might have attained the professional privileges of psychiatry or law.

*

    ... and on the temporary payroll of Bill Babwell's agency Gretta now has a part-time assignment at the Laboratory as Father Duncannon's stenographer, helping him get ready for the so-called Chapter meeting at the end of June. She'll transcribe their proceedings from tape recordings made by Caleb, and that work should last well into the summer. By that time—depending on whether we buy, rent, or build our new plant—we may have enough D M & D work to keep her busy fulltime.

    Dexter is working with the Industrial Development Economic Agency (a k a IDEA!), which he serves ex officio (thanks to his environmental foresight in designing the legislation), to get us some sort of financial "incentive" from "the public sector", such as a real-estate tax break or a federal guarantee of bank credit for construction and capital equipment. But if R insists on having a V & M spur track our choice will be limited to a very few existing sites. We may have to yield on that specification, which is regarded as obsolescent and romantic by most of those who authorize or own the money bags for benign usury.

    Jason is also very helpful—in his deceptively stuttering way. I hope I can defend my person without offending him. But I don't think fending him off will be a serious problem, because in that regard he seems truly casual. R O is my fender.

*

    So Caleb's moving out already—over to East Harbor! Glory's all excited about getting her own study, up in her attic at the front of the house where Caleb and Ibi had their living quarters—a room of her own for the first time. Dexter (of course) will get the big room with all the bookcases that Caleb built, and she'll have to let him go through her den to get to the little kitchen and bathroom in her suite, but even so I envy her.

    God knows she deserves a private place if anybody does. I hope she has space for her own private bed. She claps her hands and clicks her heels as if the intent of her fling had been solely to find a pretext for her lover's eviction!

    She resumes the opacity of busyness, as usual more cheerfully and energetically than the rest of our bravely masked sisterhood. Given the circumstances of marriage and maternity, she seems to ask, who could be happier? Certainly not the two Masterson sisters (though for the present I can't complain at all).

She has bestowed upon me the two little devils Belcephon and Ninus. How could I resist them? (I missed poor old Bricky. Just yesterday I remembered why Sally Salter had christened him Brickwork, first of the litter: not because he was red, yellow, or orange but in celebration of her discovery that T S Chittering was produced on the banks of the Mississippi by the Hydraulic Press Brick Company !) I knew Melly and Miley would be delighted, for a little while at least; and Goddy was indeed flabbergasted with benevolent curiosity. Glory said their departure from her household would restore O'Hair to his former good humor. Apparently Robert and Deirdre are too absorbed by the respective burgeoning of their social desires not to have grown bored with the childish pleasure of kittens. But more to the point, now that Ibi-Roi had left home with his master the poor little tykes were deprived of maternal protection during Glory's daily absence at the Library.

Goddy will become their second alma mater. He was immediately aware of the responsibility to which he has succeeded, accepting it from his royal predecessor with pleasant surprise and surprising pleasure. I'm sure he likes the prospect of frisky company for his lonesome hours. He marvels at such tiny activity, raised to the power of two, and their solid lack of color.

Two more tiny pink mouths to feed and clean up after are as nothing for a sinful mother and housekeeper assisting at the birth of a new corporation, managing a school of performing arts, and launching an unpopular repertory theater that has yet to be housed.

But it occurs to me rather belatedly: the reason my client that little bastard didn't mention his restaurant doxy to me was fear that poor Glory would hear about his two-timing! It appears that troubadours are all alike.

*

... It seems then that Father Chris is making a shameless attempt to charm his way into Arthur Halymboyd's inner circle, in part with the implied threat either to dump his advisedly unquantified block of Parity stock (including that of his private accounts at the brokerage and of airily intimated "friends and associates"), just when King Arthur is allegedly counting on another unexplained run-up of the price, or to let the world in on Caleb's schematic intelligence of the obscurantist anti-Vine being manipulated on the open market by the invisible hand. They say that on the Street no threat of revelation is too far-fetched to be heeded—perhaps especially from a courteously knowledgeable priest who seems to represent "the Church". But Father Chris may repent his audacity with the tolerant spider, R thinks, when he tries to fly too far inside the web.

It doesn't make sense to me. Even the priest's hotshot young technical advisors, who have been given the benefit of all Caleb's kinship research, are warning him to be cautious. Is he sure enough of what Parity's really worth in the world of things? Granted that what they call the "long-term growth potential" is huge in terms of market value—since it may be selling now at 50% "discount", and some of its holdings like CRF, Laclede Aircraft, and Whirleybird that are full of future promise can't continue to be overlooked by other speculating boys—eventually (according to the market's pendulum psychology) "PAR will sell at a premium". Then if or when to sell? It seems to me he should ask himself what he's after: to become a major stockholder or to make a profit? If PAR goes up in the short term, as he expects, it won't be as easy to get out with a large block at the top price as it was to get in at a low one. And if he doesn't sell, what profiteth paper in the Order's portfolio?

I don't understand either the "technicians" or the "fundamentalists". I'm more fascinated by the proper names than by the common numbers.

*

... I do wish R would spend less time drinking with Huck Salter. He's even gone out globstering with him. Such a waste of time! But they call each other long-lost brothers. It's pure conviviality, with nothing I can see in common. Sally doesn't mind.

*

I sometimes think Cora's radical politics are really a ludicrously misplaced symbolism by which she unconsciously seeks to express an inchoate feminism. But general feminism wouldn't be her primary motive. She's really protesting the dominance of men in dance institutions. All the rest she doesn't mind even as much as I do. She's glad of Thad's weakness to the extent that it fosters his saintly encouragement and practical support of her creative will. Deprived by circumstances of an unfettered career, she's unwittingly susceptible to both political and feministic ideology as a relief of artistic frustration. I have no such agony. In a small way I may be a performer of other people's art but I'm not a creator of anything except pottery that gathers dust in my boiler room.

That's probably why even at the age of sixteen I secretly half-hated Anima Nim, who was so nice to me while I was typing manuscripts about creative neurosis for Auto Drang. It probably wasn't for her sexual conquests that I began to dislike that dolled-up genius. Cora had the talent in our family, and I proudly loved her, but I couldn't love the limitless success of a brilliant femme fatale beauty so far above us all in culture and resources, who seemed to enjoy every effortless advantage of nature and nurture, including the Bohemian life of Paris (which would be destroyed before I could get to it), as well as the precious acclaim of those we most admired in the glamorous lofts and studios of Ur across the river from our unglamorous daily-working Lagash. She might have taken me under her wing if I hadn't been too shy to betray my awe, but she already had many dependents, most of whom were male weaklings.

But Cora never envied anyone. Her character is much stronger than mine, as I see at last. She looks like an austere Marxist or a disciplinary school-mistress, and she pronounces herself not feminine enough to be a great dancer, but it was she, not I, who could seduce D K . Her natural imagination is as lovely as a topsail schooner.

Many overt feminists are like penurious corsairs who capture a frigate and then scuttle their own beautiful brig that has sailed rings around the bigger ship to win the unequal battle, just because their vessel still labors with one less mast and one more battle hole than the defeated man-of-war. But Cora wouldn't sail away in any enemy's ship, unlike John Paul Jones in lesser desperation.

I suppose that's why she can be inspired by Doctor Charlemagne and resist his dominance at the same time. She likes his theories; they rationalize part of her experience. She loves his talk about "the temporal sincerity" of dance, "the only creative art primarily energetic", "the art of the unpreserved", "the modern art of locality" which creates its own place in "trophic time". Over the hot-water side of her kitchen sink she's tacked up a quotation from his book, two sentences to the effect that dance is the action itself, not merely Aristotle's representation of action, and that in the theater this generative principle should be extended to drama—as it can't be to opera. (Vide our Rock and Role program!)

But there's the rub, because he also preaches to the contrary. By way of goading her—and at the same time to prepare her for our ultimate disappointment—I have just copied this out for the cold-water side: "The action of the dance, on the other hand, is nothing but movement, which consists entirely of indivisible and irreducible reality, and the most excessive vital capacity can never be large enough to deliver poetry on top of it." I keep warning her, providing the excuse for failure, but she'll resist Doc's conservative pontification until her dying breath.

Underneath it all she's infuriated at his anthropological objectivity. She is still muttering angrily about his reasonably neutral statement that patriarchy—a term she applies to all modern society despite the hierarchy in her own household—is naturally monotheistic because a single stud can rule like a lion over scores of his children, whereas a population of the same size must have many more mothers to share matriarchal authority. It follows that male tyranny was bolstered by the belated understanding that lengthy pregnancy follows from quick and easy copulation. (Cora has no interest in biology, yet she cherishes "trophic time" as her medium!) But it seems to me that this is the wrong kind of male reasoning for her to flare up at, because she certainly doesn't mean to defend One God of either gender!

In Uganda they say that without dance music is wasted. She says that without dance drama is wasted. I say that without the Rock Dance this Gloucestermas arts festival will be wasted. Most of her audience will be expecting to see temporary sculpture; they won't know what to make of "every angle as possibility, position as momentum, floor as jagged ceiling for the feet."

But there's not enough housewife-time to perfect her dancers.

*

. . . Goddy was already rejuvenated by Ibi's friendship. Now he practically mothers the kittens. They knead the flesh under his cozy long hair, and have unhesitatingly transferred their primary affections from one male dog to the other. When Ibi comes with Caleb to see us these two little male ingrates no longer recognize him. For a minute they arch their tiny backs and spit, but soon he's their equivalent to a half-naked step-father (compared to our maternally fleecy collie). Now that Caleb's been evicted from the Rectory this is the only place he can leave Ibi when he goes down to New Uruk.

M and M are delighted. For two days at a time no one in the Powerhouse will be bored.

*

I wish we could do the Glo'mas *M S N D* instead of leaving it to high school kids. Their Theseus and Hippolyta are to our sophisticated citizenry what Bottom and his friends are to them.

I could find plenty of men to play the Mechanicals. If only it weren't so cruel to suggest it, I'd try to recruit Deirdre Cotton for one or both of the queens. But most of Dogtown's unauditioned talent is ruled out of public projects for private reasons!

Every year the senior class is given the option of *Romeo and Juliet* instead. Before the war it was *R & J* nine times out of ten; now it's just the opposite. Apparently the vote depends upon who in the class is getting married or should be, how much they like their comedians, and who'd be expected to get the leads. It's also much influenced by the fact that a few years ago one of our Pucks (a girl) went on to Limeway, and then a Lysander to bit parts in Holyrood. But it's already been ten years since the tragic version of love was chosen. Deirdre Keith told me that when she's a senior she'll make all her friends vote for *R & J*. Most of the underclassmen take sides before they've read the play, and many never do, or even come to see it. But the theme of Hymen is of course on all their minds. The drama teacher's usually a "theater-lover" who makes me seem a Lady Gregory by comparison. I suppose her presentation of the two alternatives at the Senior Assembly has a lot to do with the outcome, and whether or not the majority wishes to oppose what they guess is her antierotic preference.

But Miss Johnson the legendary spinster who teaches the English honors class is something else, though her students are too few to weigh much in the plebescite. By way of exercise in criticism as well as literary history, she sets them to write on the theatrical issues raised by the two plays, starting them off with Hazlitt's dictum that "poetry and the stage do not agree together", as regarded in the literary context of his time. To her credit, according to Glory, she doesn't arbitrarily squelch those who question her wholesome reading of both texts. (But one boy got short shrift when he tried to show that Romeo was merely so bound by his sense of honor that he trapped himself into keeping the false promises of ordinary lust.) Every year that old lady gets kids into the

Laurel Amphictyony, the Nine Muses, or the best small colleges like Hawthorne, Boanerges, and Barchester.

But Glory says Inez Canary will be lucky if her father lets her apply to Beggarly Community College night school. I who never went to any college may be accused of snobbery, but there's nothing undemocratic about mourning our failure to save Dogtown's superior girl-souls.

The truth is that all the teachers and decent politicians are terrified of attacks by the Puritans on our School Committee. Those who hate prematureantifascists, feminists, conservationists, atheists, and dogs are quick to descry and decry anything in the cultural domain that is "suggestive" to the young of the private thoughts besetting them in common. By amalgamating all public enemies into one category of horror the censors are able in the name of any one horror to rouse the yahoos against everything liberal or intellectual, especially of course in the theater. Imagine: boys and girls spending the night together in the woods, and swapping each other at that! Yet running away to get married at the age of fourteen in defiance of the patriarch—Guelph, Ghibelline, or Lusitanian—is worser yet! We Libertines laugh at their reactionary ignorance, but there's a real danger that the Puritan papists will get full control of the school system.

Worst of all, as in South Atlantis, aggressive sects of soul-saving Paulines are beginning to make inroads here among Petrine troglodytes and aborigines. This week I noticed another church for Jesus that they've just opened in East Harbor.

*

... but R tells me not to get too impatient with Shelly Schlossberg's curiosity, likening him to the chief of a small tribe in Orellana who was the only one a French Jewish ethnologist could get reliable information from—on condition that they *exchange* anthropological information! Still, he's one of our investors. We try to keep him away from the office until most of the exciting alternatives have been eliminated from our venture and we've decided on two or three of the products that the designer thinks can be made in our kind of shop and the manager thinks can be sold at a profit.

Who but Buck and R could have gathered backers for a business that might seem to be starting with the cart before the horse—and in what town but this? This entrepreneurial uncertainty makes me envy the salaried security my sister lives in (even if she and Thad lose everything they're putting into D M & D). By working sixty hours a week her husband benefits from skinflint Management's exploitation of his indispensability as the leader of three specialized departments in an established, debtless, and sempiternal corporation governed by paternalistic tradition.

But R doesn't seem to worry about our house of uncharted hopes and shows no sign of an uneasy conscience for putting us all to such a risk. Buck is as rejuvenated as Goddy, working day and night at his drawing board with an urgency I've never seen in him before. He's reticent (as he should be) about his fervent new ideas, but he's also reconstructing some of his old ones, on a charette for his first conference with the great patent lawyer who Mr Krebs and Jason insist is essential for our survival. One of those two prospective directors on our D M & D board is betting nothing on us except his reputation as a corporate counsel, but the banker's banking on our "intangible assets". The rights to sell or collect royalties on many of Buck's minor inventions may in the long run be worth far more than our own manufacturing of his products—which, moreover, to develop and introduce, it is said, will hinder the re-launching and rigging of a "job-shop" operation for our old customers, the business upon which the faith of most of our incorporators is based.

So Buck is in a technical trance these days, dreaming as he goes around the clock, happy as a clam to have his creative peace protected during this interlude of planning, even though for the time being he doesn't have shop tools and materials to help him think. R and I take all the responsibility for providing him with a business to justify his art. He's now concentrating on things that wind or twist other things, things that make steam or run on steam, things that force like pumps or run on force like turbines, things that make electricity or use electricity, and things that heat or cool; he's relieved of the bread-and-butter kind of machinery work that has maintained us in the provisional luxury of this picturesque cottage. He postpones even his industrial engineering, the very science of manufacturing, which used to be the object of his criticism and gossip but which must become his next most important contribution to the new firm. I'm afraid he dreads every hour away from his easel. The business end of the old company usually ran by itself, or rather by Gretta. Soon he'll have to face entirely new problems of time-and-motion, purchasing, and costing. Mr O can't do it all.

I now regret that I always refused to open my mind to technology. Whether Buck goes in for heat exchangers, rainwater collectors, desalination machines, emergency generators, portable power supplies, high-pressure water pumps operating on "in-plant" steam, or perpetual motion salt mills, ignorance will keep my mouth shut in demure passivity as he and R narrow down the practicable applications of his liberated imagination.

The most I can do is suggest a little market-research. But Buck says "Why pay for surveys? We know what people need."

"But they may not want it." say I in all diffidence, faltering in my presentiment.

"Leave that to the M B A s!" cries Mr O. He's feeling his oats because he's found that businessmen here in the East are a little less impressed by "pseudo-academic banausics" than those in Cornucopia. (He now tells me that if he should ever again pursue his abandoned goal of a Master's degree he would write his thesis on the psychological technique of being captured by a quasi-nondiversified closed-end investment web.) "Premature planning would only prejudice our precious serendipity!"

"Prosit!" says Buck in his usual mild way, raising a glass of ginger ale at our Doghouse lunch. "Time enough to plan when we've gathered enough mass to make the inertia of a moving body."

"I just hope you'll know its direction." I reply, sipping icewater in encouragement of his abstention.

Like the lilies of the field I must trust to semipaternal care. As Wat declared on one of his rocks, *Sufficient unto the day are the anxieties thereof.*

5
ARGO COVE

*C*aleb in springtime—in hiatus, in pause, in elated satisfaction with the completion of his first Gilgamesh play; in the neurotic discomfort of Gloucestermas foreshadowed; in clouds of personal despair swept off and on the sky by winds of impersonal intellect; in cordial relief at the astonishing ease of transition from domestic guilt to a new beginning of conscience; in intensification of service to Father Duncannon's high hope for revised religion—Caleb in springtime could hardly worry about the deferred insecurity of living beyond his means at Apostles Dock, which left him with very little money for food and none for the usual devices of seduction. For thanks to Belle Cingani (née Beatrice Picory) he had been spared the time and travail of house-hunting, the pains of negotiation, and the degradation of an undistinguished dwelling unit. Her alertness and charm on his behalf had smoothed the way with Tony Estivador, now their common landlord, who fortunately was preoccupied with the Dock's commercial tenants and nautical customers.

But her intervention was less for Caleb's own sake than for his ward Ibi's. She wanted his dog as her nether neighbor and familiar visitor. She had advocated the whole Dock's case for a watchdog in residence that never barked without reason. And on her recommendation Tony had waived for Caleb and Company the customary increase of rent at a turnover of tenants. The little "studio apartment" was the first on the second deck, one of its walls across a narrow corridor from the proprietor's office, which overlooked the active corner of his maritime courtyard.

Caleb's view of the cove was partially obstructed by the nautical clutter on the open wharf and overhung by its boat-slinging recto-tetrahedral derrick looming like a skeletal sundial of Atlas. This machine, christened Gog by Wat, was one of the pillars of Heracles, opposite Magog at the shipyard across the mouth of Argo Cove, "the gate of Hell" through which the *Motion* had to pass and repass every time he went fishing.

The working-day thumps and whines and shouts of a machine shop and a chandlery on the floor beneath Caleb's book-jammed new home would have been annoying if the mise en scène hadn't been enriched all around the clock by soothing wafts of pungent cordage and turpentine, and if the situation of the building itself hadn't been so dramatic—above shiplifting brine-dark tides at the foot of living granite.

The Tower of Gilgamesh having been finished for the nonce, he knew not what to do with it, except to hide it away in a bank safe deposit box until its uncomic complement was written. Certainly it wasn't fit to be put before the eyes of Doctor Charlemagne, who was sure to resent its dromenological presumption and shatter the confidence of its author more decisively than any merely commercial rejection from on or off Limeway. Though it couldn't prove a work of art until given voice by a company, at least its plans and specifications had been brought into existence for the possible use of a producer, in the event that any ever appeared who was willing to ignore contemporary theatrical prejudices. It was out of the question to offer the Dogtown mummers first refusal because it would take a frozen day in hell for Tessa to undertake any production derogated by Doc, especially when its cast would outnumber any likely audience; and anyway most of the roles were male.

(Still, as he postponed the ordeal of starting the second phase of his thought-experiment, he was pleased to have delivered himself of at least a secret projet non réalizé. He partook of its virtual power. For all his trepidation, it conferred the greatest pleasure of his first quarter-century, worth more in the balance than the favors of Bice-Belle, Gloria Keith, and Lilian Cloud combined. Nonetheless, without their stimulus of his active psyche the project might have turned into a mere essay on dromenological possibility; and at any one time he would have given up a week's writing for an hour's dalliance with one or another of them, or with almost any woman for that matter. Now, in this ensuing vocational respite, he would fain have traded many times more than a week of postponed literary effort for a jot of such inspiration.)

Belle's mercurial moods and preferences were no less inconstant than his own weightless cerebral states, and her actions were more so. His bituminous friendship with her was much less steady than the anthracite Moon-love banked at the back of his mind, which he blessed his stars that even in moments of fraternal trust he'd told her nothing of. He still couldn't help hoping to assist at Lilian's discreet guilt as a married woman, but her virtue was not as lightly to be trifled with as the indefinite reservations of a bachelor-girl with bachelors. Although Belle hinted that "a little birdie" had seen him exchanging private words with the Doghouse cashier she wasn't seriously suspicious. She would have affected to delight in any news of her darling Calebeenie's amorous success.

Thanks to tantalizing proximity, Belle was the bittersweet in his celibate routine, irregularly accessible for libertine conversation. He gave himself credit for half understanding her attitude toward him as a "libidinous friend", but wondered whether she overlooked or only pretended to overlook his possible jealousy of the privileged visitors who stole past his door on their way to her portal upstairs, and his watchdog's feat in learning to distinguish the scent and tread of intruders from that of unobjectionable visitors to her or other occupants of either residential level.

The creaking upper floors and light partitions had long ago been built into the Dock's original lofts in order to absorb some of the commercial establishment's overhead with rent from aestivators too poor for summer hotels or whole cottages. The pipes for heating and automatic fire-sprinklers, installed much later in expectation of all-year-round income, were as exposed as the outdated electric wiring and the cast-iron ducts that drained everybody's sewage into the living cove, and they seemed to conduct whatever audible vibrations were not convected or radiated in the internal atmosphere of the gabled post-and-beam warehouse shell. No well-treated Shepherd was ever a promiscuous barker, but at first Ibi's inexperienced discrimination had been sorely taxed. Now however he knew all the dozen residents of the building, and seemed to recognize the harmlessness of almost all other strangers on the dockside or in the corridors. By day the ground floor and wharf were swarming with them, especially as toyboat-owners came to prepare for the season. The Dock's four or five cats, whether domestic or independent, were of course privileged, and full of themselves, but one of them, Tiger the communal rat-warden, who belonged to no one, was particularly smug.

It had been Caleb's good luck to have come to the end of his playscript at the same time that Gloria Keith put the quietus to her adultery and evicted him from the Rectory. Yet it was his adultery too—not simply the innocent fornication of a lover—and perhaps she had relieved him of it none too soon. While still facing the need to forgive himself for deceiving her husband, his conscience now required him to concentrate his moral resources upon Father Duncannon's cause without continuing to ignore the Seventh Commandment read from the Book of Common Prayer.

This enlightenment without repentance was occurring, also luckily perhaps, at the best time to marshall all his disposable psychic energy in pursuit of his own private Gloucestermas mystery. Concurrently, the interval of relief from his vocation made more space, beyond his clerical devotions on behalf of the Laboratory, for spiritual participation in the world's most promising liturgy.

In fine, despite the disturbances of moving and settling, he was temporarily freed of intrigue as well as typewriting, and might well have expected some leisure for limited self-examination, just when all the strands of his proximate world were twisting into Gloucestertide convergence.

Meanwhile the apolaustic value of his new habitat (which entailed the ambiguous propinquity of Belle) was enriched by the omen that the original Jason's naming of the original *Argo* was one of the few times in all history that the creator of an artifact had been preeminently honored for the proleptic success of its heroic operators, of whom Heracles was but primus inter pares. But Argus the Thespian—call him either naval architect or ship's carpenter—was also to be one of Jason's martial galley-crew, and at launching time the Argonauts expected even greater things of him as a paragon of endurance with oar and precision with spear.

Caleb laughed ruefully at this involuntary evocation of himself as the versatile hero his mother thought he was. In Unabridge, on the marches of Norumbega University's hegemony where the kids of town and gown went to public school together, he'd organized and led a little band armed with sticks and ashcan covers to parade around the perfectly safe neighborhood, challenging to war games the rich kids who hadn't joined his gang; but in their one battle he was chattering at his men from the rear like a second-baseman hoping he wouldn't have to field a hard grounder. When he was cornered in the dining room of a psychology professor by a scientist's son threatening to douse him with a chemistry-set "stink-bomb like rotten eggs" he actually begged for mercy, while his doughty soldiers, gentry and commoner alike, were dinning and whacking in the yard outside. The psychologist's aura was spared by Caleb's personal capitulation, who thanking the clement adversary slipped away from his embarrassment. His mother was never informed of this skirmish, lest she jeer forever after. Regarding schoolboy particulars, she was aware only of her pride-and-joy's military leadership, whom she mocked as "General Housework".

But now he had built his first ship and would soon be as free as any adventurous Argonaut, free enough, that is, as Anselm would have said, to integrate his will with God's—if God should grant him a lucrative job, after Gloucestermas, whereby he could save up some money for a trip to the Isle of Manannan and its parental islands bounding the Irish Sea—provided, further, that God kept him in such amity with Belle that she would take care of Ibi for him in his absence and disposed her to do so in a fully responsible manner; somehow brought about the discovery of a birth certificate or equivalent as required for his passport application; and miraculously purged his B D I dossier of any damaging references to draft-exempted homosexuality, premature antifascism, or the Resistance, leaving nothing worse against him than his inexpungible record of interest in the liberal arts and the résumé of his irregular career as an underling in pitiable jobs.

As far as the guilt of parting from Ibi was concerned, he would cross that gangplank only when he came to the waterfront. Considering such a complexly contingent prospect of gratifying his transatlantic desire, it was too soon to agonize over that hypothetical treachery, which would be more unconscionable for an innocent saint than a wife's adultery for an experienced stranger absolutely confident of her exclusive love. Yet since it was now conceivable that the mere manuscript of IRTH might win him an uncommercial subvention to write more about Gilgamesh and Engidu, thereby sparing him the hurdle of a breadwinning job, it was time to moderate procrastination and take the first step in proving his Atlantean citizenship.

So far he had only brought himself to crack the ice of fear by venturing into the Clerk's Office and paying the annual poll tax required for Ibi's license to exist under protection of the law. The lady assisting at the counter was friendly, impersonal, and efficient. No one else paid any attention to him, for in order to make himself as inconspicuous as possible while running the gauntlet he'd decided to leave Ibi at home and forego the praises he prized. Thus the procedure turned out to be swift and painless, only an emotional preparation for the beginning of his genealogical ordeal.

Neither questioned nor stared at, he had been slightly emboldened by the impression that he was insignificant to the staff. Failing in the temerity to request rules and regulations for a citizen's research in the files, still less daring to ask for a decade of Viking Shepherd annals leading up to his own birth date, he'd at least taken advantage of the opportunity to glance furtively around the multiplex office and guess the location of the vault that safeguarded three centuries of human records, a pericope of which must be examined when his courage was screwed to the sticking point. He'd also caught sight to Mrs Sirius herself, the formidable Registrar of Saints, at her desk just outside the Clerk's inner sanctum, typing large complicated forms as fast as a teletype machine.

His irrational plan, conceived in superstition and designed for dithering, was inflexible. He'd ambivalently resolved not to inquire into the fully detailed entry of strangers' births at the equinox of 1935 until he'd found the name of Sycorax's registered owner in the Viking Shepherd chronicles in order to see if it offered the clue to any name besides that of Mary Trevisa or Tremont. But he pusillanimously excused himself from bearding the chancery functionaries until he was accustomed to the formal and moral atmosphere of the Ibicity Clerk's Office as a whole.

Yet mere embarrassment was less deterrent than shame, and public shame was far harder to bear than private confession to a sympathetic woman. When the Keith liaison had come to its inevitable end betimes he was on the point of telling Gloria something of his secret difficulties and asking for her help in research, ostensibly and vaguely as the Library's historian of Dogtown society during the Great Depression and F D R 's New Deal. But now he fitfully entertained the idea of Belle as his confidential attorney, with bona fide press credentials.

Whenever he wasn't angry at her inconsistent inconstancy and horrified at the thought of baring his soul to such a flouter of normal loyalty, her extraordinary generosity and affection tempted him to reveal his foolish agony of pride and ask her casual assistance. As an accredited writer for the *Nous* her presence in the Hall and even among the scribes themselves was no longer remarkable. Belle already did Caleb many spontaneous favors when she wasn't away at work or otherwise engaged, like bringing delicacies for him and his dog, often with a couple of bottles of Canterbury ale or a jug of wine to share when the day's business was over. She was generally as solicitous of his welfare as a whimsically incestuous sister (ignorant of the other one) for whom his company served as a quality she missed in her usual recreations.

At last the occasion came for his habitual reserve to be breached, his pride overcome under the influence of her freely manifested trust and goodwill, which for the moment he had reason not to perceive as an insulting attitude of mollification toward a transitory lover demoted to the second class.

*

One Saturday night, having been apologetically turned away at the postern of Leviathan Court by Deeta Dana because Doctor Charlemagne was in diplomatic reception of Jock Merrimac (a first-class visitor with his own kitchenful of henchmen), Caleb had walked back home with Ibi, retracing a nautical mile around the throbbing head of the harbor without so much as a glass of beer for his pains, and finally read himself to sleep before the ship's bell at the Net & Twine on the end of Mother's Neck had struck eleven.

For the first time he heard the springtime Saturday nightlife of the Dock. Tony was throwing a party in his family living quarters on the main deck of the el, and some of the residents hardly noticeable during five or six days of serious living were making bold with their privileges as pleasureseeking rent-payers, murmuring, laughing, playing music, and otherwise entertaining outsiders. But the season was still barely peeping from its nest and things quieted down fairly early, restoring to somnolent ears the whispering assurances of a soporific tide, the gentle flapping of halyards on masts, rhythmic creaking of wharf timber, and contented groans of hawsers—accompanied by the composite continuo of humming power plants along the main waterfront. The last thing he consciously heard was a pair of feet rapidly descending the stairs and Ibi's ghost of a growl at the same annoyed or careless footsteps traversing the corridor to the outside gallery: discordant but clearly recessional.

An hour or two later Caleb was awakened by an eager whimper of very different denotation. Its provocation was a tapping at the window over Caleb's head, but Ibi was intelligently standing at point by the door, his tail vigorously awag.

"For God's sake let me in!" came Belle's impatient whisper from the outside deck. "What's wrong with your ears? Scratching at the door doesn't wake you up. Do you expect me to knock like the Gestapo? Hurry up: I don't have any clothes on."

When he let the jaywalker in, to make her way through Ibi's laughing leaping overjoyment at the intrusion as she stroked and hushed his demonstration, her words of announcement proved to be exaggerated, for she wore an unbuttoned coat. Dropping that garment to the floor she dove into his warmly open bed, which was twice as wide as the one he had shared with her at the Rectory.

"Just this once. I won't stay long. But take off those silly pajamas! You look like a Certified Public Accountant! I was lonely tonight."

"You must be cold."

"No, I don't need warming up. I just took one of your heart-warming cold showers." With the fine damp hair clinging to her skull she looked as small and appealing as a refugee child.

As Ibi philosophically repaired to his mat, Caleb followed her under the covers, where at first she immobilized him with the snuggling clasp of a familiar visitor, her mouth to his ear. "I don't have anyone else I can talk to." she whispered complainingly. "They all just want to marry me!"

"We all agree that the likes of you shouldn't sleep alone." Caleb returned, assuming a mature tone of sympathetic amusement.

She chided his levity with the flat of her hand on his chest. "I don't like to *be* alone. Being in love or making love only postpones the loneliness for so many minutes. I'm alone much more often than you think—in fact it feels as if it's almost always. —But something's confused in my mind. Really all I want is privacy!"

"Were you confused about the gypsy poet?"

"Oi schlect! I usually like to stay on good terms with my ex-boyfriends. —But him! On his latest trip to Dogtown he found out my new name and tracked me down. Last Saturday night he was disgustingly drunk—called me an attractive nuisance, a public trash barrel, and a vagrant vagina. (Maybe I dreamed some of this!) 'All *I* ever get is Barmacide's Feast!' he yelled. That's because I used to feel so sorry for him that I let him sleep beside me without a sword between us. He said I should be taken for the public by eminent domain, because I'm a cockteasing Jewish princess, and kept shouting 'Lilies that fester smell far worse than weeds' as if he'd written the sonnet! (That reminded me of the herbs and wild flowers you and I saw rotting on Isopel Berners's grave.) He even tried to break down my door!"

"I thought you always left your door unlocked."

"Not when I have a guest."

"Next time I go to Doc's I'll leave Ibi here with you."

"Oh don't worry about that. That poet's not really a violent man—too small to do any damage, and too diffident to persist. He's just high-strung, even on the road, and he looks like Winston Churchill. He calls himself the Hillbilly of the Great Plains. In Whyaway they don't give talented orphans an education. All he knows how to write about is coon hunting and the Mississippi River. He wants me to bunk in his rig and play the guitar to help him make up lyrics at sixty miles an hour. Someday he may be famous, if he doesn't kill himself first."

Caleb was comforted. He had envisaged the trailer-truck gypsy (or "independent owner-operator") who'd given the then Bice Picory her first ride to Dogtown as a tall dark minstrel with all the physical attractions of and for an idealized European gypsy. But this lenitive revision of one character in his speculative rogues' gallery of unbeknown rivals only reminded him of her David, her first and greatest love (at last report), who he believed remained the most serious rival for her heart, the only other object of his halfhearted jealousy that was founded on her own words, even though (if he was not ingenuously mistaken) that winged hero to whom she'd sacrificed her maidenhood on a high place was long since wholly out of range. For some time he'd wanted the chance to question her about that likewise poetic veteran of the air war, when he could do so without seeming to take despicable advantage of the apparently unique confidence in his tact and discretion that she had evinced by vouchsafing him her domestic story of the Magic Mountain.

"It's hard for you to believe that I'm often depressed." she added. And that was true, for her gaiety seemed seldom interrupted.

"I was born in the Depression. So were you. We're both children of depression."

"But you believe in society. Anyway, don't call me a gypsy any more. Gypsies are dirty. Gypsy women are faithful. I don't like what Dogtown people mean by 'gypsy'! Furthermore I don't want to tell fortunes!" She seemed irritated by he knew not whom. "I wish I didn't have any Transylvanian blood at all. It was a mistake to choose Cingani for my surname. I should have let you give me Isobelle Berners's entire name. But it's too late now."

In the ensuing silence, as he hesitated between seeking further intelligence of whatever feminine experience could be communicated to a man and pursuing at once the tacit invitation to atone his kind of loneliness with hers (who all the while titillated one of his nipples with her fingertips and cuddled her arched thigh against his most thigmotactic nerve-ends), he was checked by the sensation of platted warm tears in the hollow of his neck.

Responding only with caresses, he thought it best to make no comment and put no questions. Wordlessly indeed he almost understood why she cried and why she hoped he wouldn't speak until she let it be known that her feeling of combined woe and comfort had given way to the quotidian equilibrium of her inner and outer spirits. Her weeping was silent and brief. It seemed a moment's easing of the social defense all women are born to, in a temporary shelter where her lifelong dialectic of loneliness and yearning for privacy could be appreciated without protest by a male human body even in its own state of maximum ionization.

Though upstairs she often left her haven door unlocked, and perhaps ajar, she said she wasn't as bad as she used to be. Before David, by her own account, on long-distance travel by trains she'd lock her compartment door for seclusion, but with the shade in her lighted berth undrawn, sometimes even at the stations, at least when her exhibition was on the move and spared all possibility of identification. By the same token, she'd shown herself at the windows of large hotels, where too anonymity was secure, opposite others of traveling strangers.

"But I do like to get tan all over." she'd told him on the telephone from her upper deck last Sunday afternoon, the first hot clear afternoon of the season, when he'd gratuitously warned her about the flimsy protection of the translucent screens that separated her sunbathing balcony from that of her immediate neighbors, within clear earshot of every word spoken by the fishermen and toyboaters who frequented the Dock below on a fine Spring sabbath. "That's the main reason I came down from the cold of Codfishland. I've never been paranoid about Peeping Toms. They'd have to peek over the wall or climb a mast to see me. And I don't have many visitors in the daytime."

That conversation had been on a chaste Monday evening when she came down with a bottle of Scotch she'd bought for him to celebrate her promotion by Gary Ghibellini as the *Nous*'s "fly on the wall" at Ibicity Hall—now that she had a driver's license and a car of her own. Besides reporting the Council meetings she would write a weekly column called "The Harmless Fly", a byproduct of her function as "investigative reporter"—without being relieved of the Community Page and the Arts Calendar! They'd drunk to the health of her sixty-hour week.

At another tête-a-tête she'd mentioned remembering that at the age of four, before children were evacuated from London, she used to stand naked with arms and legs outspread in her nursery window on a Plumesbury street looking for the uniform of a Royal Navy Commander. If I'd been her brother, Caleb thought, perhaps I would have attempted incest much sooner than her father did. Of course I make such a conjecture only because I've never been a brother and can hardly imagine the diamagnetic schesis of siblings or the distasteful quarrels that often adulterate the irreducible bonds between nest-mates of opposite gender before their flesh begins to discern qualities of attraction. But how could I ever sympathize with the half consanguine man she trusted more than God, whose transgression in middle age had no such excuse as a young boy's maddening desire for the most natural experience normally denied him?

Now however as Belle's nearly selfless affection was expressed in the wordless pause, with no more than a slight undulating pressure of her grateful clasp, and as Caleb's falsely disinterested reciprocation—despite the autonomous importunity of homunculus—was measured by an equally faint rhythm of stationary muscles, he was no more truly sensitive to the general pain of her sect than he'd been to Lilian's or Gloria's or his mother's. She was too fascinating either to elicit his pity or to permit his indifference, and in spite of everything that he believed about his own beliefs he involuntarily subordinated to his selfserving interest in the enclosure of her body his essentially uninterested attention to her complex feelings.

For this brutality of his he was sometimes especially sorry; but in respect to Belle he was no more insensitive than in his epistemic relations with the other female strangers that had more greatly influenced the course of his existence. His present affection for her was certainly tenderer than his inner response to any male except Ibi. It now seemed a necessary cause for instinctive action on her body.

Yet he could imagine little more of her experience than a scenario of her trysts with "David", and all at once the subjective power of words rendered him cocksure of Lilian's expert advice simply to "overwhelm" the girl who'd for a long time been refusing to honor the instinct of his peccant part. But just then the faint moonraking waves of her sympathetic nervous system began to gather the amplitude and frequency of conscious disposition. Without haste she anticipated his move by rising to overwhelm, artfully, his own ever-ready sensor (which was never caught off guard), pinning him down where he lay, yet seating herself gradually, first at the pace of a walk, then posting at a trot, cantering at length, and finally like a mounted Cossack bringing them both to ground in a steeplechasing gallop. Only when the gasping rider had finally sunk to his side was the winded centauraster himself restored to the faculty of peculiarly human communication.

True, she wasn't swooning as if this was the first beatitude of her life, or of 1961, or even of the month, but she was certainly moved to the depths by an afflatus of unreserved fondness, to that degree possible for a nulliparous girl of her tempered constitution, and Caleb was in no doubt that he had instrumentally assisted at her mystic competence. Under the tendentious provocation of their resumed colloquy, as he recovered stamina for his first riposte as the initiator of even snugger dimorphic trunneling, he might take any word or touch as a cue to overwhelm his ravisher like a proper missionary.

"I saw an imaginary number!" she languidly exclaimed.

"It wasn't imaginary." he huskily returned; then added "I thought you were avoiding me!"

"I wouldn't avoid you if you were the last man on earth! I confess that right now it would seem nothing but self-mortification ever to avoid you. But if ever I have done so, or will do so, you won't have known it, because I have used, or will use, the other entrance. Ask Ibi."

She was referring to the street door and stairway used almost exclusively by people of the woodworking shop and the garment-stitching business that occupied the first two levels at the northern end of the building. It was a confoundingly inconvenient portal for residents because it required them to double back on half their steps to and from their outside parking places. She tried to belie her callousness to his insuperable jealousy with a teasing pinch of his thigh.

"After all, it's I who brought you to a dwelling place so favorable for spying on my movements!"

Even in this blissful interval of that night's antepenultimate anticlimax he took in her confidential pleasantry as a rather friendly warning still not to trust any more than he ever should have trusted to an ordinary model of consistency. Maybe this piquant chaffing was also for the sheer fun of informing him that he (if not his supersensitive roommate) had already been fooled by more gallants than he guessed, stealing up to the bed that but for the offsetting distance of one other apartment was directly above his own, just out of range for a human monitor at his listening station.

But with the bird in his hand he was not of a mind to take much umbrage at most of his rivals' merely historical, merely contingent, or merely unsuccessful innings. As far as competition was concerned, he persuaded himself, let past and future go to the devil. —Except for David, the aerial knight of her Hyperborean past, of whom she'd told him his voice reminded her!

According to Doc Charlemagne, Bartaud avoided Diderot's "paradox" of acting with the binary theory that a voice reveals the invisible Actor, the Character's double, and Caleb was well enough aware that his voice all too often exposed the inner weakling. The hidden double of that David-dyad, whose role in life, whose age, physique, experience, and competence was presumably so superior to his own—was that daimon so like his own that she had just benefitted from the homological suggestion?

"Was your imaginary number that old David of yours?"

"Don't be silly. Not really. Thanks to you I'm getting more mature." The tonal metamorphosis of her body left no doubt about maturity. Her fingers traced with unfeigned bemusement the lineaments of his face.

"Blarney. Where is he now?"

"I told you before: I don't know. But a few weeks ago I read an article in the *New Uruk Testament* about an archeological expedition to Mesopotamia searching desert sands for the palace of Queen Semiramis. There was a David Wilson listed as its airplane pilot."

"Dave Wilson!"

"I know it's not an uncommon name. I've found David Wilsons in a hundred different phone books."

"Ha!" Caleb chuckled like a scholar making cryptic connections. "David Wilson is a descendant of James Wilson, a lawyer from Scottish universities who came to Philadelphia to teach Latin before our Revolution. He wrote against Parliament's authority to legislate for the Colonies, and had the guts to blame the King himself. He was a member of the Continental Congress and I think he signed the Declaration of Independence. He became a colonel in the American army and then Louis XVI's attorney over here. But as a principal writer of the Constitution he was most important for advocating the separation of powers. A good Federalist who trusted the people. The Crats should commemorate him as one of their great champions. Washington put him on the Supreme Court."

"I don't know what you're talking about! Are you making fun of me?"

She dug her fingers into his ribs and tickled out of him a squirming laugh that sounded acquiescent to her assumption.

But the incidental lesson in U S history, intended as an exordium to personal revelation, plus the little tomfoolery of horseplay, had given him a few seconds to bethink and suppress a spontaneous cry of surprise. He decided to conceal his astonishing discovery until he could examine its significance, lest the exciting epiphany distract Belle from his renewed addresses before they were both sated with the recreation in progress. Thus reflexively he guarded against squandering the nebulous advantage of reserved information in his unending duel with her. Warily he savored his belated recognition of her David as none other than Dave Wilson, the admirable old friend in Michael Chapman's East Bay gang.

So certain was the identification that he marveled at his own stupidity in having failed to make the connection between "David" (without surname) of Magic Mountain and Dave Wilson of Hume when he'd heard Bice Picory's traumatic confession. The adventurer was unmistakable: Air Corps pilot at Hiroshima, flyer-of-fortune, world traveler, Limeyphobe, Cornucopian poetry-lover, seeker of religions, and ingenuous Mugwump despite his superb political ancestry!

But Caleb made up his mind not to disclose his stupendous insight until the capacitance regenerated by his congressions with Belle had been grounded on both sides for the last time on this occasion, reduced for the time being to mutual electrostatic neutrality—when he'd have wrung for her the fullest pleasure from his phenomenal presence—when he himself would have nothing carnal to lose—perhaps when she was about to quit his bed.

The name Dave Wilson, as if legendary, habitually evoked several thought-images more indelible than authentic memories of the hero himself, four among which were especially vivid, automatically popping into Caleb's mind as a fixed set of abbreviated allusions so well rehearsed that it was no longer necessary to scan them in their entireties in order to comprehend them as a whole, as if they were logically integrated.

The first now to flash into consciousness from this imbedded composite of past mental experience was his vaguely established vision of the unlikely Isopel Berners, known only in the work of

George Borrow (the Pauline anti-picaro of Britain and Spain who called Atlantis "the land, indeed, par excellence, of humbug and humbug cries") to which Dave, despite his Anglophobia, had introduced him. The author's fabulous character remained undeservedly arcane even in Dogtown whither she'd followed an Irishman only to die alone in Purdeyville at a very old age. Along with admiration of Ibi, it was homage to this great personage that had introduced Bice to Caleb. In his mind the question now arose as to whether Bice and David had discovered a common interest in Borrow or, if not, which of the two on the Rock at St Bede had educated the other, and thence Caleb himself.

The second almost simultaneous recollection was Dave's bathroom cabinet of fuscous rubber tympanums arrayed in assorted sizes from the snuggest to the most capacious, each casing neatly labeled in centimeters.

The third epitomized Dave's delight in an esoteric explanation of the motto that edified the Order of the Garter, *Honi soit qui mal y pense*, whereby Edward III had euphemistically alleviated the Countess of Salisbury's embarrassment when the suspension of her catamenial martingale gave way onto the dance floor.

The fourth, non sequitur, the mythical figure of Gilgamesh, of whom the present playwright had never heard until he looked into Auto Drang as a result of Dave's remarks, likewise in one of the Hume living rooms. This grateful association of Dave with Nimrod was reinforced by certain qualities of the man himself, who might have been one of Jason's chosen argonauts.

This particular instance of recall did not explicitly entail the more abstract association of Dave with the E-Bombing of Cipango, the unimaginable catastrophe that had dissociated Captain Wilson's soul from the realm of experience he shared with friends and lovers. Such a preconscious reference always haunted Caleb's envy of the man's admirable adventures; yet it was not a great world-historical event rising from an exceedingly distant and impersonal past, but a recent revelation, intensely personal knowledge suddenly exposed in its shallow hiding place, that now signified Dave's preternatural importance to himself:

Lilian! What with all the subsequent episodes in her history, he had almost forgotten what she had told him about the era of her pregnancy! As gentle and considerate lover Dave Wilson had succeeded the faithless father of her child! Dave in particular—not some ectoplasmic anthropos ex machina, not some unanimated faceless fungible eunuch, not some forgettable unimpressioned Tom or Dick—as comforter and protector pro tem, until she'd pulled up stakes and started eastward with Mooney!

The deeper affect of this ironic clarification would settle upon him in retrospect the next day, after he'd mulled it over in solitude; but on the instant he was mainly impressed by its marvelous correspondences, so acutely exciting to detect, as typical and symbolic of this small polis! He had often heard Doc, Tessa, Shelly, Petto, and others warn Rafe not to doubt the doctrine of destinate intersections wherein Dogtown was the locus. Indeed he himself had already well enough witnessed an amazing per capita incidence of coincidence! But his tediously reiterative experience with the stochastics of digital tabulation and calculation warned him against the superstition of regarding what seemed comparatively improbable as simply supernatural. He'd heard so many accounts of Lady Gloucester's magnetism that reasoned myth had displaced reasoned chance in all his chorological interpretations. Nevertheless, though this latest improbability owed more to the general attraction of the place than to his personal gravitation, he estimated the chance of such a four-part relationship as far less than the quaternary root of the perhaps semidetermined probability that Lilian alone should show up in his small town three thousand miles from her origin without ever having met Belle's David. He could hardly have been more surprised if destiny had suddenly flown Dave Wilson himself into the harbor in a seaplane!

Having refrained from informing Belle of his acquaintance with her David he was all the more resolved to keep secret from her the knowledge that her winged knight had since taken up with a woman who she could scarcely happen to guess was the past and present Muse of the gentleman she was now doting on! As a secret from the heartbreaker now in his arms this ambivalently withheld knowledge about the man she would never forget bestowed him with a sense of the power conferred with his complicated pain. This epistemological mastery of her would be dissipated by confiding his peculiar new interest in the story of her defloration. His own case, however, was so poetic in its justice, and so funny, that he could hardly wait to impart Tyche's scheme to Lilian, the other female of the cast, hoping to be rewarded with the details of her participation that he had previously been too delicate to pursue.

Overwhelm her (this one), Moonfeather (the other one) had advised! Now was the time to trump the mighty hunter, he cried to himself, his imagination liberated, unchecked by outmoded introspection, as if Caleb the actor could assume—but with youth's refreshment—the charming passion of both women's sensitive melancholy hero, man of the world, religion-seeking donor of ecstasy. And so now (at least in his estimation of the act) he did overwhelm the beautiful Anglo-Gypsy revenant of mysterious ideal Eva the refugee Jewish maiden.

This was a mature paramour no longer easily impressionable at the jewel of games. It felt as if he was mastering her with a poet's inspiration, the vigor of long-pent renewable reserves, and skill beyond his years. All the wry dismay at finding that his initiation of Lilian had been trumped by Dave Wilson in Hume was submerged in the exhilaration of double-trumping Dave's initiate, no matter how many strangers had intervened. Of course he didn't pause to meditate upon the phallic motif that redoubled his libido, nor the sympathetic magic of his expanding anima. This vivid bond to the respected senior he had so envied and admired seemed to descend from Uruk as a mythic friendship. The orectic superinduction of fraternity bolstered his confidence with all possible women.

Despite his brain's condition of fire, however, homunculus was caught nodding when he found himself being called from his woolgathering by her languid inspection of the disobedient part that he had governed well enough. The drapery and window shade had been retracted to admit the Dock's floodlights, now paled but amplified by a descending full moon, which thenceforth supervised the alternating adorations each of each during intervals of comparatively passive bliss. The inns of court were aslumber, except where two or three night-owls sat at their DV hearths, whose jerking gray photons made rice paper of their window shades. The only sound from society was the reassuring throb of mechanical power along the Harbor's margins, and the only other, as lunar as the turning tide's mood, was the kissing rasp of barnacled pilings, the bumping nudges of captured boats, and the indolent clicking of marine hardware aloft. In the summer soon to come, he believed, with open doors and windows on every gallery, and aestivating toyboaters living afloat in the orchestra, the exciting sounds of Saturday night would not be so seductive.

"Don't worry." she murmured soothingly. "Nobody's ever out on this deck late at night, and without your light on we can't be seen from the el. I know what I'm talking about."

Chaperoned by Selene, they compared their symmetries (in Vitruvius's sense of the word: that is to say, homologous proportions). Caleb found that it was light enough to expose with subtle caresses her tiny androgynous horn under its sable fleece. "This impudent little coxcomb is the crown of your jewel. Don't let it get sunburned."

But although her sensual flesh took pleasure in his tender organoleptic playfulness, her sensuous faculties seemed to find his own hermaphroditical lure (—according to Goethe a "shining little dwarf"—) more interesting as a cynosure for manipulation. "Your poor dependable generous boy, he has no opposable limbs. But it's the most beautiful circumcision in the Western World! I'd recognize you anywhere, at attention or at ease." Like Helen with Menelaus, Caleb thought, long after Troy.

And in the moonlight no worse to him than Helen did she look when suddenly rolling out of the bed and stopping above him to stretch her arms like a cat. As Paris stricken with unslakable ardor by the first of lust's arrows he watched her cross the room into shadows. He let her go because he thought her destination was the bathroom; but she was headed for his pantry supplies. "Aha! I found the luse!" she said. "At first I thought I was going to have to run upstairs and get my sherry."

"Without your coat on?" Caleb asked.

"Down to the dregs!" It was the remains of a wine bottle she'd brought down to drink with him at one of their tea-time gossips. "Let's drink to a slew of beatitudes!" She contrived to drop a little on one side of her chest as she brought the small overfilled glasses to their festal bed. "Pretend it's Champagne. Just enough to disinhibit you!"

"Your honey is sweeter than this." he said, before accepting his glass from her hand, as he licked the spillage, hoping to distract her from the otiose ceremony that threatened an unbearable delay in resuming fundamental pleasures. But she was serious and he bided his time for a minute or two of rather sloppy toasting.

"We bachelor girls are like bees: it's not our nature that determines the flavor, but the kind of pollen we can find."

"I've had my appetizer. Now—"

"Yes, my darling Calebeenie, I was wrong to change my name from Bice. Tonight I am more than thrice blessed!"

"Beatrice is the one who *renders* joy."

"Until tonight, more than she was rendered."

While allowing for hyperbole in her transitory state of happiness, for her variable degrees of candor, for her unreliable moods and affections, and for the vicissitudes of her erotic fortune elsewhere, Caleb cast off the last shred of his old doubt about her capacity for occasional bliss with his assistance. Ergo nunc dossim repetatur. It wasn't until an hour or two later that his renewable humor quickened for the last time and they called it a night. Finally, when her body's last demand was for surrender to long unbroken sleep, preferring not to be spotted in Caleb's bed by Old Sol or anyone else, Belle-Bice reeled upstairs in the cool before dawn, trailing her coat on the floorboards, wondering why it should be her lot to have no husband, but perhaps already suspecting that tomorrow she would forget tonight.

But not before there had been another conversation. After Caleb got up to let Ibi out in the morning it was the enlightenment from this oral communication that he mulled over, rather than the transceiving sensations that when all is said and done are found to be limited in duration. The meaning of exchanged words is more clearly retained by a man's organism than the ephemeral consciousness of exulting pleasure, which turns out not to be peculiar to any one couple or coupling.

I was the one overwhelmed, heart and mind, he said to himself; but I'm not the fool I was last year at the Poet's Corner. This time "Love's aid for Love's distress" is preventive medicine. I was already free and easy with her. She was my drinking companion. She ministered to me and my dog thoughtfully and generously. She'll never let us go hungry. This time I may have seemed all in all to her for a few hours, but I must never forget that only God has a relationship with each of Her lovers that is individually total, incomparable, and for all practical purposes exclusive, as if Her attention were indivisible. As the love of this poetasteress is divided, so must mine remain—though never alas with such a large denominator.

Still, to do her justice and account for her goodwill toward me: perhaps her affections really are undivided at any one cross-section of time, but serial—simply interchanged in succession—unsurprisingly short compared to God's simultaneous past present and future prehension in the Augustinian view. She was annoyed when I asked if she'd ever been to bed with two men at once. As if that question was rhetorical or trivial, she remarked that she'd like to be the catalyst at an orgy of attractive performers but not an actress. I believe it was an evasively honest answer.

*

On Sunday night a low fog drifted in through the outer harbor and dimmed the sublunar lights without totally occluding the moon herself. Lying celibate again, between waking and sleeping, he resumed this meditation to accompaniment of the mournful diaphone on Parliament Island alternating with the distant one on the breakwater Point. Though from a different aural perspective it was the same ensemble that they had heard together on the beach at Dilemma Cove, when he had been made—and this too he did not doubt—her deepest confidant.

May she never regret having told me a paternal secret of the kind that's almost always kept forever in petto. If I were her I'd never have revealed it to anyone at all. For her trust of my character she deserves a fraction of my love.

And for her flattery of my person. She teases me about the secrecy of my own "love-life", little knowing, or pretending not to guess, that it's more like Percival's than Gawain's. But could there be an element of truth in her "confession" that it was out of jealousy she inveigled me into moving here, so that she could keep an eye on my infidelities to Beatrice? She's kind enough to comment that I'm too virile to content myself with average variety and should have a lot of paramours, for the same reason that Solomon had a thousand wives—so as to be sure of uninterrupted comfort whenever one of them withdraws. She must be thinking of the analogous but stronger case for Semiramis and all her gender.

Yet last night while absently petting homunculus she was more interested in Ibi's free life than mine. "I think Ibi's in love." she said. "He has a girlfriend. He may even be married! She's a beautiful proud longhaired Jewish Shepherd."

It was news to me. Her personal information system is formidable, quite apart from Dogtown news ex officio. Even if I had a record-turntable like hers upstairs I probably would never have known that Ibi tolerates Bach and Beethoven but gets off one's bed and leaves the room when Mahler is played. Judging by her intelligence about the Apostles here, you'd think she's Tony Estivador's private secretary. I might have lived here five years without realizing that Ibi growls at the debonair little man with a bow tie and white shoes because he's an antisemitic bibulous old goat of a dentist; that the only other one he bristles at is a homolecherous sea lawyer; or that the covert preacher-captain of the hulking "missionary schooner" *Good News* [launched as *Morgan le Fay* at Port Campion in Teddy Roosevelt's day for oceanic explorations by Henry Adams University and now forever tied up at Tony's back porch] keeps three concubines and four children under hatches like Fedullah's boat crew. Now she knows more than I do about my guardian himself, my mildest critic and nearly constant companion!

Ibi had countenanced his new neighborhood very well, and visage versa, as he established his leadership making many new interracial friends, foremost of whom was Metaphisto the sweet-tempered black Cabotland Water Dog harbored by the Cibbers, an arbiter of East Harbor saints whose massive pacifism like an archbishop's seconded the newcomer's benevolent monarchy. But Caleb himself was seeing very little of East Harbor Ward except on early morning runs before most dogs were out on the street.

Ibi was obliged to rove, as if for forage but actually for the opposite purpose. He no longer had a cemetery to relieve himself in. Save for a nearly vertical granite bluff immediately across the street, the earth of the Dock's environs was paved or planked; the nearest lawns were tiny, fenced, and in any event excessively unwelcoming. No one much objected to commonplace marking on the weathered wood and rusting machinery stacked or scattered about the Dock, and on that score Ibi felt no shame. But unlike most of the Dogtown saints, fortunately for Caleb's peace of mind as tenant and neighbor by sufferance, Ibi was loathe to leave his solider waste on hard naked surfaces that were too obviously owned by public or private corporations. In each instance he was exceptionally fastidious about locating a privy, and disliked to be seen in a vulnerable and undignified posture, even at night by cats.

About twice a day therefore he usually trotted either townward for a patch of overgrown waterside dirt, such as the one behind the blacksmith's shop, or southerly along East Front, to turn off onto Mother's Neck, which offered a choice of several coved beaches when the tide wasn't too high (or, when it was overrunning the sand to scour earlier deposits, a small park inside the sea wall). If the call wasn't too urgent he'd sometimes look for a fresh latrine further out onto the Foreside where a dog was presented at any tide with many an option of undefended grass or copse or sand.

On such expeditions one likely spot might lead to another, and at last evacuation at this distant convenience might free his intellectual curiosity for several miles of osmagogue roaming; and then perhaps (if he had nothing better to do while Caleb was at the Lab) he would come home a roundabout way from Dilemma Cove and the Back of the Foreside, even from as far north as Little Harbor Beach, in a wide loop over hill and dale, golf course and heath, yard and thoroughfare, down Skate Street past Phisto's house into Wye Square. Thus he made himself familiar with and to nearly the entire Ward, and became intimate with topographical details over a much larger area than whole packs of Viking Shepherds would require simply to stool in clean isolation.

So it went at least before he fell in love.

"I'd seen her from time to time out on the Point and elsewhere in East Harbor, and once even in Harbor Ward." said Belle. "She'd never let me touch her. But this time it was in that little spinney above Swanson Cove on Foreside Road. Ibi was mounting her. They were in no hurry, their eyes were closed, and they both looked ecstatic. I may have been too jealous to look away, but I was riding with somebody and I couldn't stop to watch."

"Appearances deceived you. Ibi's not a scrupulous romantic like me; he isn't the kind of saint that resists temptation just because he doesn't love the temptress!"

"I know you don't love me—any more than David did. Everyone else wants to marry me. —But you haven't heard half the story. I asked the dog officer what he could tell me about her, because I may want to get one of the puppies. That's as good a miscegenation of champions as Tristam and Iseult, although there's evidently no King Mark. Sergeant Proctor easily recognized the bitch I described, and he gave me her number—1234—which is all he's allowed to disclose. He told me what he knew about her character, which was limited by the fact that she's kept indoors most of the time. I think I can find out more from Mrs Sirius's records."

"How do you know there weren't a dozen King Marks, if she was running around in heat? Dogtown's full of alert dogs. Ibi always expects competition before he comes out on top."

"They had eloped. That was obvious, once the Sergeant told me the most interesting part. She must have been saving herself for the first liberty of her season. Ibi'd come for a friendship run together. Her new attitude took him by surprise!"

"And that's what made him fall in love. How do you know so much about the emotional life of two dogs?"

"We deduced it, the Sergeant and I, when I told him what I'd seen."

"In journalistic euphemisms that expressed your empathy?"

"Shut up and listen. If there's anything Sergeant Proctor knows about his job it's how to tell when a bitch is in heat. Ibi had been Number 1234's exclusive friend *before* that. Until Ibi appeared on the scene she would have nothing to do with any other animal, male or female, and snapped at any that tried to get familiar. According to the sergeant, *à chaque saint sa chandelle* was the principle she lived by. In other words, she and Ibi were platonic lovers at first sight, before their corporal passion—and afterwards. They'd been seen even way out by the lighthouse trotting and sniffing together like a pair of field biologists. Of course she's no bigger than a wolf, not the size of Ibi, but fiercer than he, with long fur, and in absolute aesthetic terms I must say she's the more beautiful one. Right from the beginning he was deferring to her. And a couple of days ago I saw him escorting her through a pack of respectful dogs on the Neck. Not that she needs protection from anything less than a gang, according to what I hear!"

On this subject Belle and Caleb had muffled their whispers under the covers, especially when mentioning the name of the nearby dog sleeping on his mat. Nevertheless from time to time they heard an intelligent thump of his tail.

Caleb was humiliated by his ignorance of Ibi's liaison, and a little resentful that he was not the first to know of his best friend's affair from whom he'd kept none of his own amours, witness this very night. But this new information accounted for what in retrospect was Ibi's unusual restlessness and irregularity of attendance in recent weeks. The master now appreciated Ibi's extraordinary loyalty in staying home at all when he must have wanted to haunt the streets waiting for 1234's appearance wherever it was likely, even when it wasn't.

But Caleb provisionally approved the match, though no less dissatisfied than Belle with ignorance of the Jewish Shepherd's identity and homage. Longhaired deviants from the Jewish Shepherd norm (demotically known as the "police dog") were officially disprized in aristocratic litters as spurious by A K C standards despite their superior beauty (in absolute aesthetic terms)—just as the magnificent black jaguar of Orellana was hardly noticed by evolutionary biologists, who considered it an insignificant individuation of the brightly burning South Atlantean Pecator Panthera. These rare ugly ducklings therefore fetched much less on the slave market for purely idealistic reasons, not because they were thought to shed more hair in a house or because it happened to be harder to keep their coats from snarling.

Having declared in Caleb's bed her intention to beard Mrs Sirius at the Clerk's office for access to the sacred records that were so questionably guarded (ostensibly in order to prevent the identification of dog-owners by life-threatening Puritans), Belle had been requested by her satyr, on the strength of her status in the fourth estate, while she was at it, to look up March 21, 1935 in the archive of stranger births. She promised to do so.

"If you do that for me," the exclamation escaped his constraint on the subject, "I'll wash your back and—"

"Dance with me at Glo'mas!"

*

He was to hear nothing more about this twofold research project until almost the eve of Gloucestermas. Meanwhile she seemed to be avoiding him, presumably under the pressure of her journalistic assignments. And himself too busy to brood about her promise, he'd gladly given up on it as a consequence of his own ambivalent indiscretion and not only as a default typical of her unreliability. And naturally she'd have forgotten her momentary enthusiasm for neonatal puppies.

But out of the blue she reported. "They make it sound as if you need a court order to see their sanctified files. And they won't answer questions about the records you want if you're not the owner. I think the stumbling block is their ignorance of the law, unless it's just ordinary bureaucratic defensiveness. I expect the *Nous* to join the class-action suit that's now afoot to force a 'freedom of information' doctrine from the Supreme Judicial Court of Vinland. This is the kind of thing that gets us professionals up in arms, just on principle!"

"Yes, but what about me?"

"What d'you mean, what about you? —Oh, yes! They're a little looser with the dossiers of strangers. You were born at 3:05 A M , and you weighed five pounds five and a half ounces. Your mother's shown as Mary Trevisa, as you assumed, but she reported the father as 'John Doe Karcist'. Those first two names are customarily allowed when local mothers wish to avoid a baldfaced 'father unknown', and they're used especially when deliveries occur about the time of the spring equinox. The surname that follows 'John Doe' is usually understood to be fictitious, but it may not be. Still, just in case there's a man in town whose last name might be similar to John Doe's, his responsibility is definitely disavowed by the 'Unknown' that's entered as the father's *occupation*—as in your case.

"That makes you more of a bastard than I am! It's about time we went to celebrate at Leonardo's. I just got paid."

6
THE LABORATORY OF MELCHIZEDEC AND THE MESOCOSM

*B*ecause Ibi-Roi's carinate chest was deep and narrow he could sleep flat on his side like a flounder (but with one eye up, one eye down), both ears still erect. Caleb slept on his back with level eyes and ears; even his narrow shoulders and hips were too broad for such a unilaterally spread surrender to gravity. Adreaming, Ibi's legs and paws made convulsive movements in pantomime. When Caleb dreamt on Ibi's behalf his wrists and ankles twitched.

The dreamer was Ibi running with his glorious longhaired bitch the full length of Little Harbor Beach, half way between dunes and rustling waves, where it was left as hard as clay by the recession of a spring tide. It was their first time together in an open gallop so long and smooth, half a mile of oyster-gray sand clear of strangers. She laughed at him on her inshore lee. Head and head, synchronized in effortless speed, they watched each other with open mouths of joy, ready at her first hint to turn and play like puppies, nothing else in mind. Once veering, they pretended to chase half a dozen sandpipers flitting along the frontal wash toward headland rocks at the far end.

She was no surly female, the kind he never paid attention to unless they were in amorous condition (in which case they weren't so surly with a prince); yet he had no thought at all of humping. Her beauty glorified his love. Her scent was fresh as dawn; the sound of her panting was as sweet as her breath, and the rhythmic clink of collar tags, muffled by the magnificent fur at her throat, chimed with his own.

A stick was thrown, beyond the first windrow of lazy surf, where the second was drawing back in its formation. They turned to race for it, each aiming for an end to swim in with like one of Manannan's unharnessed chariot teams bitted for tug-of-war on land. Already, before they reached the water, he noticed her footprints in the wet sand, where they were about to mingle wheeling with his own to make a lovely pattern for the next tide soon to find and wash away as a love-message for no one else's eyes.

But alas the telephone rang and Caleb the stranger-god awoke to find himself Samuel again, serving a higher deity.

Ibi stood up, shook himself, stretched fore and aft like a rocking horse, moved further away from the sounds of his master's voice responding to the repeated intempestive signal of the peremptory dumbbell, even earlier than the usual harsh summons from the angry little face and hands next to the bed, and lay down again to doze until the door should be opened for his preprandial piss-call.

It was Chris Lucey on the phone, profusely apologetic, sweetening his anomalous communication with all the excitement of an emergency that offered Caleb novel compensations (of which extra pay was not the most interesting) to expand his routine employment for a week at least.

*

In fact it was a piling of Pelion on Ossa, for it compounded an excitement the Lab was still absorbing. The houseboy had quit, hard upon the eve of Chapter. Oku's resignation was an unexpected alleviation of the embarrassment to be expected under scrutiny of the Secular membership congregating at the headquarters of Regular poverty chastity and obedience, where there appeared to be no priest with the humility of Brother Francis; but it was damned inconvenient coming just before the influx of guests. Temporary help must be hired for more than merely adjuvant work. Gretta Doloroso's outreach and Bill Babwell's procurement services had been urgently appealed to—at the very time that the "needle trades" were recruiting for the pilgrim season and especially competing for auxiliaries in the Gloucestermas octave during which the dates of Chapter fell, before high-school kids were yet available for the summer labor market. This bathetic contretemps was perforce agitating the Fathers, in conflict with intellectual spiritual and diplomatic preparations of the highest order.

Only after Oku was gone, when his silent underpinning of the domestic economy was more fully appreciated, did Caleb learn that he'd been recommended to Father Duncannon by Sidles the butler of Chateau Noir, who was obliged to dismiss him as superfluous when Captain Ozone finally ceased inviting house guests. By imperfect communication of sympathy (as one servant to another) Caleb had only recently succeeded in befriending the wiry Japanese, small as the pilot of a kamikaze submarine, who was scarcely able to converse with his employers but knew his duties better than they did. As an intermediary to the awe-inspiring "boss" giants, Caleb was informed a little more than the Fathers of his concealed attitude. Chris called him "Oku-I O"—the "Inscrutable One"—at least in private conversations on the road, or at the Lab when absolutely assured of the catfooted Oku's absence. Like Wang, the Chinese houseboy on the abandoned island of the Tropical Belt Coal Company (after ships had dispensed with such marginal coaling stations), he demonstrated the disconcerting ability to materialize and vanish in and out of thin air.

"Lonely here. Too lonely!" On his day off Oku sometimes traveled by train and bus all the way down to his own "farm" somewhere in Island Roads, where he had a little house and maybe a wife, if he wasn't a widower or an inveterate bachelor. It was very difficult to make out any of the rapidly ejaculated replies to questions about his personal life that might otherwise have been understandable, and Caleb had not had time to cultivate the inchoate friendship.

Oku's departure, after its cryptic announcement to "boss Father", was so swift that Caleb, to his distress, had only a few minutes of confidential opportunity to inquire what had gone wrong. It was evident that strong emotions had been repressed, but despite a brief burst of volubility the bewildered listener's sense of their objective correlatives remained baffled. The only intelligible causes were proximate—those that might have seemed to threaten the professional pride of a housekeeper. Apparently boss Father did too much of the cooking and housework, and—most annoying—boss number two on several occasions, last night in particular, had tried to help clean up the kitchen!

But Oku wasn't illiterate. A few days after his climactic departure Caleb was delivered by mail at home a perfectly legible note in the palely inked hand of a polite uneducated nineteenth century servant. The stock notepaper was monogrammed in blue with a flowery O.

Dear Mr Karcist:
    Thank for A kindness you have shown me: Hoping some day I may see you again
                    Very truly yours,
                    Frank Kubo Masayuki
Wilton, I R .

But much the heavier enclosure in the envelope was a small unpaginated staple-bound booklet "Published 1st Sun, 5th Moon, 1916 by Frank K Masayuki" and "Printed by The Signal Press of Susa, Nether Land, U S A." The cover was in green ink, bordered with vaguely Grecian double lines made up of stock decorative modules available to a typesetter in any letterpress job-shop, and the main title was from an "Old English" font:

𝔏𝔦𝔤𝔥𝔱==𝔊𝔯𝔢𝔞𝔱𝔢𝔰𝔱 𝔊𝔦𝔣𝔱 𝔬𝔣 𝔄𝔩𝔩
ORIGINAL WRITTEN BY
MR. ROBERT D. LOVELAND
PUBLISHED BY
A Son of the Land where the Cherry Blossom is Most Honorable

First page:

To Mr. Robert D. Loveland

    I have honor to publish under title; "Light—Greatest Gift of All." It is your original writing and was my lesson from you, a year ago this spring. If you perceive this publishing is just and pleasing to you, as from a strange student of a far-land, I shall be thankful with a heart of the ever-green, and cheer myself up to follow your spiritual work. I also may find great comfort by it, too, as a playful monkey catching a branch to save his life from falling down into the deep river, I think this poor monkey himself knows he gets great comfort by that little branch, and after all, his life was depending on it too. Thence, he always, trying to find a branch in whatever he does, truly, with such an opportunity to benefit mankind, he will be thereupon fruitful.

I am truly yours,

F. Kubo Masayuki.

Second page:

MOTHER'S GIFT AND MY LITTLE MISSION

My mother said to me:—
Goodness is in all men, but evil things born in the same soul as one could see both. The long journey of our life has need of the faith. Indeed, health, happiness, perhaps beauty, too, depend upon the kind faith we KNOW, and EXERCISE,

F. Kubo Masayuki

The text, printed on the outsides of half a dozen uncut folded leaves about the size of a picture postcard, was divided into eight Roman-numeraled sections, each consisting of more or less than a dozen Arabic-numeraled questions, titled respectively THE BIBLE, GOD, JESUS CHRIST AND HIS SALVATION, THE CHRISTIAN LIFE (A. Faith and Prayer, and B. The Life of Service), THE KINGDOM OF GOD, THE CHRISTIAN CHURCH, and THE SACRAMENTS. It was a Pauline catechism, tacitly more favorable to Chapel than to Church but evidently free of invidious fundamentalism, Chauvinism, sectarian pride, spiritual selfishness, individualism, tribalism, and nationalism. Many of the questions were tantalizingly unanswered (such as a couple about the nature and number of sacraments), or explained only by one or more citations of Biblical chapter and verse. Of the few answers vouchsafed without reference to Scripture, one was about Luther's origination of the Deformation. The tone of this checklist was as decent as Oku's dedication, though it didn't exhibit much of his personal charity.

Caleb wondered if this brochure would have met with the approval of the *Good News* missionary schooner's captain. It would not have positively offended a reasonable Petrine, on the one hand, nor, on the other, a leader of the Brotherhood in Vernalia.

Certainly Father Duncannon respected its Christian sincerity, and seemed touched with humility by Oku's unsuspected purity of heart. Caleb then wondered if Oku's name would be mentioned in the Superior's prayers, and in his next confession to Father Davy.

"Our loss is much greater than I knew." the Superior said to Caleb and Father Lucey. "I'm sorry I was insensitive to our underestimated I O. I sometimes thought he was rude or sullen. But now I can't blame him for being irritated at our superstitions—though I was careful never to ask him to clean the sacristy or chapel, which we've always done ourselves; and I must say he seemed to appreciate our scruple on that point even though he disapproved of my lifting a hand at anything else. But how he must have suffered by living under the same roof with vestments and crucifixes, sleeping above an altar of idolatry!"

"But Father," his junior priest had protested, "I O came to us after a long hitch at Chateau Noir!"

"Captain Ozone didn't call himself a Christian, at least when I knew him. Oku may have perceived the depravity over there—if such it really was, and not just the syncretism of rumors, please remember, Father—as merely the ignorant profanity of a lost soul. But for him I suppose our church is conflated with the all-too-knowledgeable Scarlet Lady."

"In whose lap Ozone died, they say!"

"Never mind. I owe Oku my apology."

"He wanted to be a servant, Father."

"But it's not for servants of God to treat anyone else like a servant."

Both priests' sympathy and esteem for Oku having failed to deepen until the surprising discovery of his Christian soul, admittedly to their discredit, the Father Economist paused before he replied softly and very distinctly: "If Chapter is too democratically conducted I'm afraid you and I will soon be the Laboratory's only servants."

"Please leave that to me, Father." rejoined Father Duncannon with a tone of exasperation presaging the kind of exchange that Caleb their witness found acutely embarrassing, and in this case especially because he was the whitecollar hand most at issue among some of the outside Members. At this point, finishing his glass of sherry, he had contrived to take his leave from the sun porch without attending the indignity of a testy disagreement between his revered teacher and the more intimate friend who was under a vow of obedience to him.

Father Duncannon didn't mind kitchen work but neither he nor Father Lucey had the time to spare for it, especially as they approached their respective charettes for the most important Chapter of the Order's recent history. Every day Caleb was pressing Bill Babwell or Gretta Doloroso for a temporary cook who might or might not be willing and able to perform other menial duties and undertake the Chapter workload with some extra help. Father Lucey insisted on employing a caterer for the membership's largest common meals at the Lab, but much else would be required of commissary and other service. All of which was to be coordinated by Caleb as a go-between lacking the authority to make any decision that might have the remotest religious or aesthetic significance without consulting the Superior, whose understanding of summary management had not been served by a lifetime of scholarship discourse and contemplation, or the Father Economist, who was usually not at hand and anyway preoccupied with the much larger matters of acquisitive chrematistics, and who by the same token showed very little regard for efficiency of expenditure, but whose emotions sometimes brought about reconsideration of his religious boss's secular decisions. Despite his intellectual devotion to the elder priest and his gratitude to the younger, Caleb was not wholly sorry that after the congress was over his discomfort as a servant of two masters would come to an end.

*

And now, before even transitional arrangements had been resolved, this dawn telephone call from Chris! His father had been taken ill and he had to fly down to Cherokee, perhaps for a week. Would Caleb be willing to occupy a guest room at the Lab until he, Chris, returned?

Father Duncannon was too frail to manage alone in that big house all around the clock, and he certainly needed a companion to assist him with message-taking and other conveniences after Caleb's regular business hours. Father would do all the cooking. Caleb was not to accept the invitation if it was untimely or unattractive. The proposal would not even have been made if Mort Ockham [a Member of COV and the Trustees' bookkeeper], who might have been spared at his backroom brokerage desk in Botolph (seeing that the Trustees were not active in the market at present), had not been tied down in Unabridge at night by a wife who was unable to cope with her own daily existence. "But *Father would welcome Ibi* as his guest, since I O is no longer there to be defended against dog hairs! Of course neither he nor you would be expected to observe parietal rules when you're not inside the monastery!"

It didn't seem that Chris was stricken with dread of his natural father's sickness unto death, but he would have sounded just as blithely serious if he'd been announcing his own. To Caleb the proposition was both timely and attractive, partly in the interest of Ibi's education, partly for relief from his own routine of cooking and other self-service, but above all for the joyful expectation of having Father Duncannon to himself for conversation at leisurely meals.

"Shall I drive you to the airport?"

"Oh no indeed, thank you! Father Duncannon needs all your time. Sam's going to drive me in. I'll call him to meet my return flight too." This was the luxury of a business executive, notwithstanding that Chris had ostensibly negotiated a retainer of the IXAT cab company at special rates, with preemptive claim to the services of Sam Craigie [the poet], whether on or off his regular shift.

So Caleb packed for two and installed himself that morning in a pleasant cell on the top floor of the Lab with a nearly 180-degree panorama of the sunrise's sinking Atlantic horizon—cloudlessly brassy, splendidly mountainous, or ominously invisible—and the moonrise's too. The sojourn was not disappointing. Stranger and saint improved their acquaintance with Father Duncannon more than they otherwise could have done in a dog's age.

At their first dinner in the refectory (served from scratch by Father Duncannon) Caleb asked whether Mr Lucey Senior was now in a Nashdom hospital, knowing that even on his ordinary travels Chris almost always telephoned the Lab at least once a day, ostensibly to volunteer reports on his own obedient or supererogatory activities but in truth to reassure himself about his ghostly father's health and security. The anticipated length of this separation of the two Regulars was unprecedented. It certainly indicated an emergency. But how much of an emergency? There was no longer any mother. Had the father himself called the other night?

"I can't really say." Father Duncannon replied. "I didn't hear the telephone ring. Father Lucey himself may have happened to make the call. This afternoon when I phoned to inquire about the situation only the butler was available. I must say he seemed surprised at my concern about Mr Lucey—a courteous and educated gentleman, by the way, though he's devoted his life to business. Malcolm said that yesterday 'the old master' had a little cold but was better today. At the moment he was taking his usual nap and 'the young master' was down at the stables to talk to the groom and get ready for riding. Isn't that a little odd?"

Caleb smiled at the thought of Chris mounted on a horse, especially as a mere pastime: an ostrich on a burro (unless there was a Cherokee Walker as big as Gallic draft horses)! It may have been a pretext for acquainting himself with a new farm hand; but surely, with all the Northern fish in the sea, that was not sufficient reason to exaggerate the illness of a father whose love he'd never fully returned and thereby separate himself from one to whom he'd dedicated his life.

"He left a note on my desk to say he'd borrowed the Parity chart." Caleb remarked. "He wanted to memorize it."

*

Caleb's parti-colored diagram might have been a gnostical image of an infernal tree growing downward, in structure like a self-tangled oak: indeed an anti-vine in appearance. Most of it represented the burgeoned possession or control of industrial corporations by Parity, a nether ramification of foliage pleached with that of Financial Usufruct Incorporated (FUI), a floral emblem simpler than its own in proportion as pure usury is more abstract than earnings from material organization. By the greatest economy of investment, or rather concatenation of cascading investments, the small corporation known as PAR on the Curb Exchange managed to control (or at least influence for its own benefit) scores of publicly held enterprises more or less productive and more or less similar in industrial category. But this solar system of Parity's was scarcely known off the Street. It was not nearly as massive as the high-priced stars OHM and Lily Liver Pharmaceuticals or the simple galaxies of Panharmonic Industries and General Agglomeration and Generic Victuals and General Chemicals and Infernal Consumption Engines, which were traded in Big Ticker blocks as valuable as chunks of the British Empire but about as volatile as the Swiss Republic. With the audacity of a market tyro whose ectoplasmatic self-confidence has been battened as if on the mere motto of his disembodied academic honor society—"Philosophy is the guide of life"—Caleb, having picked up a few details about this "special situation" and believing he comprehended the structure and substance of it, had convinced Chris, who knew a lot about the trading of stock in general, that his configured information could be employed for useful persuasion of some sort.

The domain of the Little Ticker, where the nuclear PAR and many of the stocks in its stereo-reticulation were publicly bought and sold, was alluring to Caleb as the market that made available giant molecules small enough to touch. But the labyrinth spun by Arthur Halymboyd had been especially fascinating to him because it was not simply a coruscating nautilus secreted by a living crab but an apparently evolutionary organization of arborescent colonies possessions and protectorates, each with its own parliament the constituency of which was freely traded on either of the New Uruk exchanges, "over the counter", or privately—in presumably Smithsonian ignorance of the web's arcane master hand.

For years the Trustees had owned a block of PAR, but Caleb's diligent and enthusiastic research had piqued the active imagination of the Father Economist, who was much better than his assistant at concealing the direct object of his appetite. In extramural dealings Chris was able to diffuse and obfuscate his wishes in a manner to excite the interest of those susceptible to speculative or impetuous urges whose cooperating capital would be required in his effort to move or shake such an appreciable firm in the firmament. His methods were usually indirect and often erratic; but what seemed vagaries were sometimes singleminded calculations, and what seemed unconscious in its apparent irrationality sometimes delighted Caleb in its dynamic outcome.

Many levels of uncertainty and new experience had perpetuated the pleasure of watching Chris in his Botolph and Ur-island venues. Acting on behalf of the Trustees of the Founder's Fund for the Classic Order of the Vine (under no more supervision on their part than he volunteered to present them with the opportunity for), the broker-priest had continued to trade other stocks on both Tickers, taking full advantage of his non-profit organization's exemption from capital-gains taxes (especially those on short-term profits) and availing himself of the greatest credit margin allowed by banks or brokers under Regulation T for purchase of stock at less than cost, hypothecated by the stock certificates themselves (retained in the creditor's custody).

But even with the best leverage and exceptional gains in a bull market Chris was discontented with "merely incremental paper profits" in his portfolio. He was driven by the vision of a geometric progression in the self-replenishing financial power to grant all of Father Duncannon's professional or eleemosynary wishes for the economic benefit of the C O V or of its beneficiaries in humanity at large. Yet inevitable trading losses here and there, and his impatient disposal of rising shares that seemed too prudential in their inertia, continued to frustrate his ambition to exceed double the capital growth rate of a normal fiduciary investment trust reinvesting all its dividends.

To Chris it was clear that if the Trustees were going to manage their own fund they ought to make with it all the money they could—and all the more if it was to be given away to some outside font or sink of charity. Though there were Members of the Order who questioned even the facultative virtue of money, its fungibility was obviously advantageous in all causes. As Father Economist he was less interested in the final employment of assets than in their acquisition and accretion; he always professed himself obediently ready to distribute whatever surplus might be amassed beyond what was needed to maintain Father Duncannon and his Laboratory: but no one mistook his hope that portfolio growth would never be stunted by a call to distribute the communal wealth as fast as or faster than it could be enlarged.

This acquisitive restlessness had signally broadened the education of Chris's confidential assistant. For months, every day the market was open, unless he went to New Uruk for research or pursued some special assignment, Caleb rode with Chris in the commuter traffic to Botolph, and there on the theatrical mezzanine of the Weatherglass, Neatherd and Company branch office found their dour bookkeeper Mortimer Ockham (pedantic formalist in ecclesiastical matters too) already at work preparing the worksheet that showed Chris the portfolio's opening position and buying power, or taking trial balances for monthly statements of the Fund and of the Lab its corporate dependent.

Caleb was brought along to help monitor the Big Ticker's cryptic messages (as projected in moving alphanumerics along a band of luminescent screen on the wall watched also as if on stage by everyone at main floor level); to read or write mail; to peruse printed reports; to coordinate appointments; to advise; to analyze; to record the execution of trades; to calculate; to participate in thought experiments; to cogitate interesting metaphors; to criticize proleptic hopes and hypothesize new ones; to supply Chris with information, warning, or goodfellowship at lunches or other appointments with clients, advisors, or friends; and to keep him company at his stop for a final drink on the way home—: in short, as his sidekick. The ticker hours were short, the lunches long, and every day a valuable extension of worldly experience.

What with associates, clients, and various convivial colloquies, there had sometimes been good reason to stay in town for dinner (long after Mort took the rush-hour subway home). Caleb's tolerance of Scotch had steadily improved, and Ibi had gotten accustomed to waiting for him under the maternal care of Gloria Keith (and latterly of Belle Cingani). Almost every market session began with anticipation like that at a sporting event, and likewise ended with expectation of the next. On the average (in a prospering market) doubt was framed only as an unsatisfactory degree of gain. Chris and Caleb and all the gentlemen adventurers they talked to, especially the youngest ones, were intoxicated by the milling of financial facts and rumors open to news of all the world, by the bustle of purportedly dynamic ideas animating everybody along divers lines purportedly without precedent.

Some of Chris's young clients at the brokerage—independent speculators with the assurance and self-assurance of unlimited credit, or thought-investors with the lordliness of impersonal risk—were expert enough in their own right to be drawn into reciprocal consultation, competent as Tao Theory "technicians" to graph and interpret the price-performance of a given stock or as "fundamentalists" to read the palms of new offerings. Like logical positivists ruling out "uninteresting questions" they prided themselves on hardboiled dispassion.

It was left to Caleb the common reader to organize Chris's esemplastic imagination and stimulate his negative capability for deeper evaluation of PAR's unique composition. They both tacitly acknowledged that Caleb's task—as loyalist, emotional partisan, romantic—had gradually become that of advocating or justifying a policy of financial alliances designed to penetrate Arthur Halymboyd's mysterious empire at the emperor's invitation, though not as presumptuously as Marco Polo had persuaded Kubla Khan to offer the Pope an opportunity to covert all of China to Christianity.

To this end, supplementing his master diagram, Caleb had constructed huge statistical tables from which he intended to graph the prices and sales-volumes of all the securities Parity owned, had owned, or probably expected to own. But even to himself this serial array proved as disappointing as the unpierced brick wall of a prison (which his master sheet resembled), for no significant correlations were discernible.

It seemed impossible in this simpleminded way to induce from random fluctuations of individuals the trend of the artificially defined group, or to isolate the group from the general upward drift of an optimistic market, even if he tracked them all for a year or more. He found no way to extract patterns or characteristics from the banks of chronological figures he was so stubbornly compiling as a reasonable blend of his fundamentalist approach to stock values with the technical method of Taoists to which most of Chris's young trading associates and advisors were zealously committed.

After long resisting Chris's hints that his time might better be otherwise spent, therefore, he had come to see that no matter how neatly and densely his comparative statistics were arrayed, or how many sheets of gargantuan graph paper he attached with rubber-cement to lengthen his matrix, the Parity webbing could never be shaped as a uniform grid; for Halymboyd's voltage was by no means even-handed, and apparently his parlously extended personal control of corporate directorates that supposedly represented large majorities of unorganized stockholders was to greatly varying degrees tenuous or fluctuant, perhaps in some case little more than nominal.

Even the illustrious organic chart constellated in many colors, which Chris had taken on his homecoming trip to Cherokee, was in danger of losing its lustre. Much of its purpose had already been served by imparting its image as a general guide, as an expository or mnemonic device, a visual stimulus of chrematistic or gnostic libido. As a working model of Parity's galaxy in the firmament it was no better than a planar projection abstracted from thousands of diachronous icons in the crowded hemisphere of aging stars. Its arbitrary cross-section of time was anyway left behind by the motions of change. It would have been impossible for a full-time draftsman and clerical staff to keep the annotated picture up to a date even three months behind the present.

In any event the details of imperialistic hegemony were no longer of much interest to the Father Economist. Even the most plausible conjectures about Halymboyd's external wars, treaties, cessions, revanches, territorial barters, forceful acquisitions, or general policy (which had once seemed to his imaginative clerk more successful than those of any world-historical imperium) had ceased to attract his primary attention.

But half a dozen circles at the top of the chart, which represented "private" trusts or corporations, above the great sun of Parity itself, were now the perplexing objects of his glass. They formed an inverted tap root of the whole anti-vine, which for many Members of the Order (had they seen the chart) would have epitomized the parasitical mistletoe of Atlantean capitalism. These few virtual entities on the dark side of Hyperion, opaquely disclosed to the public only in tedious 10Ks and 10Qs (mandatory ownership reports submitted by Parity itself as a publicly held management trust listed on the Curb Exchange), symbolized secrets of nuclear ownership.

In a word, the short series of small circles suggested aboriginal control of the entire galactic archipelago. From the point at which Halymboyd's family holdings were first united or fertilized with the wealth of Professor Capstick's FUI autarchy, the concatenation of straight line segments indicated cybernetic feedback, positive or negative—not merely classical designed to govern the proportional power with which Halymboyd's collaborating rival could share his controlling interest in the closed-end investment trust publicly traded as PAR—about 24 percent of equity at the moment of Caleb's snapshot.

This control was exercised proximately by Thule Associates Corporation, and through it, distally, by four "closely held" unlisted companies in both series and parallel, whose shares were not available to outsiders. Of these Python Corporation was the furthest or deepest, which is to say the highest on the chart and thus closest to the spider himself. But 57 percent of Python itself was owned by Icarus, of which 60 percent was owned by Dedaelus; and 53 percent of that was held in turn by the shaded mastermind's personal trust.

All along the way he gathered capital from God knows whom to supplement his own at every multiplication of power. Consequently at each dilution of ownership he enlarged the influence of his personal investment.

Chris's scheme for access deep in the soil to this little-known radish of empire was based on the hope that Professor Capstick, erstwhile military dentist, cunning financier, was still in the process of extricating himself from the Parity root system and leaving lesions that might be penetrable by a friendly harmless earthworm. For at the quarterly point of official history captured by Caleb's lagging map of already lagging reports, now perhaps six months in the real past, Capstick's Incroesus Bank of Washington D A had owned 38 percent of Caduceus Trading Company, partly through the jointly owned Darien Corporation, and 17 percent of Thule, the final nexus to Parity, which was controlled by Caduceus!

(The Bank directly controlled Financial Usufruct Inc, Capstick's Byzantium. FUI had been Rome's major Greek investment, the major infraction of Parity's registration as a "non-diversified management investment company" that had finally attracted the attention of S E C antitrust lawyers and precipitated this majority-minority divorce. The factional and fractional property settlement between Halymboyd and Capstick was bringing their latent enmity to a surface of unsurprising scandal in sophisticated quarters of the Street.)

In the past few analysts had pursued a study of Parity for possible recommendation to their clients any further than the rather elementary discovery of the feedback loops by which Thule, the immediately controlling entity, held some of Caduceus, the controller of itself, plus a substantial percentage of Darien, which held a like portion of the controlling corporation's controlling corporation.

In most cases, no doubt, the exact proportions of these ramifications were adventitious—convenient or inconvenient outcomes of expediences: residual percentages which had been impossible to calculate in advance of contingencies; the invisible hand of intuition emotion and chance. They nevertheless looked like the calculations of Merlin, and they were as difficult as descending the rocks of Parnassus to renegotiate without losing extravagantly to lawyers and accountants. The falling-out between the unequal emperors only exacerbated longstanding professional suspicion of the Roman who'd contrived the alliance.

"I'm afraid Father Lucey is losing interest in the Paraclete alternative." Father Duncannon said. "We're going to have a difficult time at Chapter. I may be obliged to overrule him before then. Anyway, our fund isn't nearly enough to interest the Parity people in special negotiations. Sooner or later they'll fathom the puniness of Father Lucey's 'group of investors' in their scale of finance. I've called a meeting of the Trustees the week after next. I'd like to hear Mr Krebs's opinion of our illusions. I doubt that he's fully informed himself of Father Lucey's most recent plans."

Caleb felt at liberty to smile at the Superior's ambiguous irony. His heart was lightened at the revelation that Father Duncannon was doubtful of Chris's present purpose. It somewhat relieved his own conscience of the conflict between confidential loyalty to Chris and the moral imperative to warn Father Duncannon of increasing danger to his Order, even to his personal subsistence. "Rafe Opsimath may know more about them than I do." he hinted.

Rafe's relations with Chris were far less intimate than his own, unconstrained by any moral obligation to honor the voluntary lay confessions of a psychological priest. Caleb hoped that without necessarily violating Chris's personal trust he might indirectly contribute to Father Duncannon's supervision by more or less vaguely confiding some of his purely financial anxiety to Rafe, at least to an extent commensurate with the degree to which he was already privy to the Trustees' affairs.

*

Father Superior and altar boy lingered for a while with the bottle of luse. Afterwards as they continued to converse Caleb helped clean up, studying the motions of his host (with a red apron tied over his soutane) in order to learn as a voluntary apprentice the methods and procedures preferred in the Lab's large modernized kitchen. For subsequent meals he was allowed to wash the dishes himself, but for the whole week that he assisted at refections (while he twice assisted at Masses in the chapel below, with its invisible congregation of Members) Father Duncannon was the fastidious cook (and the elegant scraps always ended up under Ibi's undiscriminating palate). But much of their unofficial conversation took place with sherry in the solarium, after each day's office work was done, before Father Duncannon repaired to the kitchen and Caleb went into the library to marvel at its inventory.

Since the Superior's health was delicate, the beating of his heart diagnosed as uncertain, he regularly shared his large bedroom with Chris, a vigilant nurse well educated in medical exigency, whose extraordinary absence at night now all the more required an emergency to explain the sudden journey to visit his natural father. But Caleb's room on the floor above was distant by more than a staircase, and Ibi, though never before arbitrarily separated from him when nearby at night, sympathetically complied with the instruction to sleep further from his personal god than from the slow-moving but benevolent old stranger. A luxurious bed of blankets was made for the shepherd at the strategic point just outside Father Duncannon's open door where he could both watch for Caleb on the stairs and perform his special assignment. From there he was also free to investigate untoward sounds or scents anywhere in the house.

Otherwise, forbidden only sacristy and chapel, Ibi-Roi readily made himself at home in the Lab. His nocturnal duty as watchdog and bodyguard took on the habit of monastic routine. The neighborhood was so far from the inner city's throbs and hums that he could hear wild unfamiliar creatures outdoors at night, and so far from the fish smells that indoors, from offices to kitchen, a myriad novel scents were purely delightful, demanding of course his protection. Yet by day his extramural liberty was uncurtailed, not limited even by the wonderfully large perimeter of rocks grass flowers shrubs and trees for which he assumed responsibility. Father Duncannon did not mind what he marked, even the unused altar built of dressed stone (unlike Abraham's) on the highest point, a ledge in back of the Lab overlooking Duncan's Field and the eastern shore of the Foreside. Carved into the living rock at its base was the motto *Ubi Cephas, Ibi Ecclesia.* He brought the Jewish Shepherd to see his glebe.

"*Ubi ibi, ibi ecclesia!*" laughed Father Duncannon.

Right from the first, despite the desertion of the Father Superior by his devoted and trained companion of more than a decade, Caleb sensed relaxation in the delicate old man's manner—whose equanimity nonetheless would have been shattered if the respite from Father Lucey's presence had threatened final or even prolonged separation. (Chris continued to telephone him every day, and, for that matter, Caleb too, on the office line: his father was rapidly on the mend; his Superior's vacation would soon be over.) The strain of emotional and physical dependence upon his disobedient Regular, the sole complement of his disappointing monastic "community" (envisioned as the mother house of a far-flung secular society with daughter priories as other religious nuclei), especially when preparing for one of the most critical deliberations in the Order's history, was almost outspokenly relieved by the companionship of an appreciative acolyte and an affectionate dog, both of whom were totally without religious obligations and easy to get along with—as Chris himself had anticipated, else he never would have gone off like this. Even for God, both Fathers presumed, there was less spiritual tension with unprofessed than with dedicated souls.

Caleb had learned the Latin grace at meals, as well as his layman's role in the Anamnesis, but he wasn't expected to kneel down for private orisons, which he thought his participation in the liturgical Lord's prayer sufficiently served, as also the General Confession seemed more than sufficient for his penitence. Caleb chose to assume that it was as clear to the priests as to himself that for all his belief in the effective liturgy (and consequently in the supernatural incarnation and grace that made it possible) he was infidelic on other grounds of orthodoxy, and that they might discomfort his personal and official friendship if they tried to test his ultimate faith by speaking of the religious experience any churchman would expect a classic Christian to be hoping for. At least some such tacit understanding between Caleb and his employers allowed Father Duncannon a good deal of discursive leeway on his short holiday with the studious stranger and the docile saint, temporarily alleviating ad hominem the spiritual responsibility he'd undertaken with holy orders, and especially with his vocation as a unique doctor of the church.

Whatever the understanding, after a day or two, with astonishing outbursts of feeling, in the manner of one who has been craving freedom of expression because he's lived for years exclusively with a person whose efforts of self-control are so delicately balanced between subjective wants and objective requirements that any breath of critical inquiry or inadvertent allusion may touch off a tantrum, he began to speak to Caleb about both his burden and his past, once or twice personally to the point of Caleb's embarrassment (who nevertheless was more gratified by the honor of his confidences than by any others in his career as an unprofessing confessor).

Save for discourse and doctrine that he'd read in printed works or heard in the Anamnesis, Caleb knew no more of Father Duncannon's private religious devotions or personal emotions than anyone who hadn't read Saint Anselm's prayers meditations and letters would know about that archbishop's personal piety from his logical proof of God's existence. The reserved slightly effeminate bearing of a gentle scholar revealed very little of the innermost person who harbored both lonely sympathy with all particulars of humanity and an orthodox faith wholly integrated with his intellectual passion. The man himself was personally obscure to everyone but Chris; and Chris—even to Caleb on the road home at night—was reticent about what he as a crazily perceptive Master of Psychiatric Social Work might have discovered or guessed of his revered master's emotional wellsprings.

*

Caleb judged that he was betraying no confidences in discussing Chris's objection to investment in tiny Paraclete before its probable success in the manufacture of a revolutionary contraceptive for women was generally appreciated by the market. PARA had only recently been listed on the Curb, after an undistinguished record as an over-the-counter pharmaceutical stock, barely qualified as an earner of dividends from its less exciting products. Indeed he found that Father Duncannon (who after all had managed to preserve a moiety of his family fortune during the Crash and Depression) was already fairly informed of the risk, and seemed to recall a little of what had engaged his attention about the management of his capital before turning it over to the Trustees when he took the vow of poverty.

Since PARA was still underfinanced, its price-to-earnings ratio already closer to a hundred than to ten, and the managerial ability of its founders unknown, the stock was classified as highly speculative. The Parity Corporation was a mature oak compared to Paraclete's exotic young date palm. PARA's most valuable assets were untested patents for biochemical compounds and the proprietary rights to but one or two finished products. Its very existence depending upon the legal cooperation of its gigantic rivals acting as customers vendors or licensees, it was still struggling for a permanent place in the corticosteroid market, which was obviously about to grow so fast in the "ethical drug industry" that it would soon surpass the demand for antibiotics, vitamins, and tranquilizers.

The endocrine segment of the pharmaceutical spectrum was attracting so much research effort, not only from Annunciator, Procreative, and Pseudopharmical but also from firms like Lily Liver Drugs, Surly & Murky, Glib, James Down, and Lavoisier, that Paraclete's chances of lasting success would probably depend as much upon a head start in the stock market as upon brilliant biochemistry, for the value of its corner on certain raw material sources in Orellana and elsewhere in South Atlantis (gathered by the same peoples who still tapped the forest for contraceptive rubber) was about to dissipate in face of the fecundating new synthetics—notwithstanding that its own laboratory invention seemed the most promising of them all.

Still, anticipating the commercial obsolescence of Mandragora mithridate, a rare jungle variety of the mandrake root, and other steroids discovered in Guaica narcotics by a Danish biochemical explorer (who was tricked out of his rights by the Dutch Guyanan businessman from whom they were thereafter commercially acquired), the company had succeeded in patenting artificial substitutes of incalculably enhanced virtue. With enough new capital to develop production techniques and facilities for succedaneous synthesis, mutatis mutandis, it hoped to replace the limited sub rosa demand for El Dorado's fertility stimulants with a vast market for oral contraceptives, hitherto unmentionable in polite society.

Whereas such commerce was officially anathema to Scholastics and decidedly distasteful to Paulines as a matter for public advertisement, Paraclete's artful graft of shrieking mandrake with Druid mistletoe (comparable to a formula of complex numbers in its reversible conjugation of real and imaginary values) had to be promulgated through the medical profession only, the most lucrative but also the most expensive of all trade channels. Directly or indirectly, the cost of this marketing would have to be capitalized before it could be socialized. Epidemic multiplication of negativity would benefit all of society; endemic multiplication of surplus, those who purchased equity before it was diluted or inflated by fame.

Those who did foresee the cultural potency of this little-known organic artifact, which was about to be finally approved by the public's Food and Drug guardians, supposed of course that the bidding of wealthy competitors (who had already established sales networks for both materia medica and for the "personal products" universally required by most of half the population when prophylaxis is neglected or mismanaged [flexible horizontally integrated distribution systems well suited not only to exploit an unprecedented continuity of pleasure but also to take advantage of fewer interruptions of the menses as compensation for the losses of revenue from baby-food and the cellulose stuff used on infants] and hoped to buy off or buy out Paraclete's crucial interests) would inflate the paper value of the stock, whether or not Paraclete accepted their oligopolistic tenders.

But it was of malnutrition strife and ecological damage from overpopulation that members of "the COVen" would take most notice when they heard about PARA's success in converting progestational substances from positive to negative agents while ostensibly seeking therapeutic hormones for Sarahs Hannahs Elizabeths and other barren women who in affluence craved progenitive expression or in misconception of their own worth prayed to serve the purpose of female life, in either case perhaps heedless of any child's present prospects for premature suffering of the general doom.

(Caleb's personal predilection for a PARA investment, though still suppressed in favor of PAR, was piqued by a prurient conviction that the aforesaid ad hominem pharmacology which turned a fertilizer into a sterilizer would by its toxic means release in girls a salubrious aphrodisia hitherto tempered by fear. Yet however exhilarating for women, he sometimes forgot, such progress was not necessarily to his personal advantage. The only ones who ever took tentative interest in him, it seemed, were bent in his favor by some pathological condition of the libido. Nonetheless he expected that with the general dissemination of contraceptive magic he would meet with less ultimate resistance from those who paid him any attention at all. Yet again, that happy stage of erotic evolution lay still in an indefinite future, and meanwhile it often seemed that his occasionally intermitted torment was growing less rather than more tolerable.)

No one understood better than Chris Lucey the opportunity presented by their avant garde knowledge of Paraclete's new product. It was his hesitancy, and then his apparent rejection of the Paraclete option, after initial enthusiasm, that Father Duncannon and Caleb talked about, each contributing to their speculative consensus, each reserving his own evidence for unvoiced fears or qualifications.

(Caleb remembered for instance that during one of their painless conversations homeward-bound from Botolph after a day of paper profits, speaking of the Scholastics in world affairs, he had exclaimed to Chris "How can they be for immortality and not for birth control? Think of the cumulative compaction in heaven! Hopeless strife up there! Dogtown's population of angels is a warning!" He meant the souls of saints.

Chris allowed that he was not passionately devoted to the crusade against population growth as if it were a greater eschatological threat than E-bomb deployment or chemical pollution, adding with grin: "But I think papist religious have always understood that there's something to be said for winking at autoeroticism and Greek love as partial solutions of the problem!")

Apart from the fact that it was already too late to take a ride all the way from the past bottom to the future peak of PARA's market value, the long and the short of it, the elder and the younger agreed—not that Chris pretended otherwise (though it was a subject left unmentioned during his daily long-distance telephone conversations)—was that Paraclete promised no leverage with which to multiply financial power. By Street standards the COV's Fund was almost risibly small, though presumably enlarged in influence by alliance with faceless "associates". Even a big profit leaves a small investor unimportant in a simply expanding universe.

Chris was not deterred by risk or doubt; nor was he driven by altruistic greed exactly. In part he wanted power on behalf of the Vine—to serve Father Duncannon's life work, for love of Father Duncannon in person, which he regarded as the one virtue bespeaking his own redemption. As long as Arthur Halymboyd's enigmatic structure tantalized him with the mechanical advantage of Archimedean levers he could not patiently satisfy himself with the merely speeded accretion of dollars by unmultiplied means.

But also, for himself, Chris wanted action—action to supersede the excitement of trading (of which he would be deprived by investing all his eggs). The thrills of rapid buying and selling had helped to offset all his monastic sitting-still and kneeling. He continued his innocuous trading for clients, but his commissions from comparatively cautious and infrequent transactions were less interesting to him than the customers themselves, and for months the diversity and activity of the Trustees' portfolio had been reduced as its buying power was progressively concentrated on Parity's public stock.

So the Father Economist was spoiling for action of a certain kind. To produce a much greater effect in the financial theater, on the principle of least action, action of a certain kind would require no more kinetic energy than he'd already worked up.

*

If Father Duncannon was glad of an hiatus in the companionship of his fellow monk that permitted a few days of peaceful work on the Chapter agenda and a stint of ruminative time in which to write his Allocutions for it without the interruptions and strains of responsibility for the discipline of an unruly subordinate in holy orders, Caleb on his part was excitedly grateful for the meals and other intervals of privileged conversation with his beloved educator, the creative savant who had provided followers with a new key to Christian hope for the world. Now for a short time, at Caleb's instigation, the priest felt free to inquire into intellectual questions that his specially affective vocation usually obliged him to put aside simply for lack of leisure so late in a burdened life.

In their conversations Caleb omitted his fundamental reservations about the Creeds, which *Theodynamics* called the "formal, symbolic externalization of the Faith, exceedingly compact, elliptical, and concise"; and by the same token employer spared employee any allusion to the religious feelings he warmly expressed among church people and in his writings, such as his faith in "those deep personal experiences gained in the practice of prayer and worship, through which alone can be developed and strengthened those necessary inner affections by which souls are bound to God", and in "the eternal yearning love of God toward men who seek Him and find Him not, because of human blindness and sin."

But they spoke without restraint of other matters relevant to whatever each held most dear—of language, of history, of dynamics, of cosmology, and of art-making (poetry) as distinguished from aesthetics. As Father Duncannon relaxed into the kind of "levities and gravities" that he had not often enjoyed since leaving the collegial circles of Unabridge, it was difficult for Caleb to refrain from pouring out a torrent of his own opinions about the questions he brought up.

Starting with language. Father Duncannon loved at least two things that Caleb did not, opera and organ music; but they shared an etymological conservatism and reactionary disgust with democratic lexographers and grammarians—delitescent or pusillanimous—who in their insensitivity or tolerance endangered semantic discriminations both implicit and explicit; for words have no creeds to protect themselves with. This was a fellowship that Caleb did not find with Doctor Charlemagne, who had nothing to say for norms, nor with anyone else he'd talked to since his dissociation from Michael Chapman far away in Hume.

Caleb was sincerely diffident about his immeasurable inferiority in scientific knowledge, philology, and aesthetic sensibility, but he pressed for profane development of Father Duncannon's ideas, always relating them, at least silently (for lack of time to expatiate with tact), to his own or Doc's by complementary, dialectical, or ironic imagination—seeing that despite its author's personal distaste for most living artists musicians poets and actors *Theodynamics* had elaborated an original and comprehensive theory of the poetic/aesthetic process which provided an analogue for the classic church's evolutionary creation of Creeds and the "counter-creative" appreciation of its laity.

(Caleb would have liked to argue for an amendment of the analysis that included a clarifying distinction between creative and performing art, and an unequivocal disavowal of the prevailing dictum that art is communication; but he was just wise enough to realize that you can't arrogate someone else's theory, however sympathetically, without alienating it. Indirectly, however, he did try to suggest that his complaint about abuse of the acute term *tragedy*, anent art, was comparable to the abuse deplored in *Theodynamics* and elsewhere in his mentor's writings of the acute term *sacrifice* anent the religion of Incarnation.)

In concurring that Atlantean culture was well illuminated when understood as the Protean manifestation of Christianity's various heresies, they discussed the critical term *gnosticism*, referring to a ubiquitously recidivistic attitude that was undermining Western genius, misguiding the commonwealth at its intellectual level (as it had always attacked the substance of history), proliferating fantastic symbols and subverting sacrament. One symbol led to another, ad infinitum; they ran amok, as in astrology Gnujian psychology or magic in general.

When it came to the extensions of these ideas, which cried out for the liberties of literary criticism, Caleb turned aside lest he speak too far alone, but he longed to advance *irony* as a philosophical concept of relationship with which to revaluate them. With more time than could be afforded during his stay at the Lab he thought he might have shown his classically educated superior how play of mind (such as that of Sorri Kierkegaard, the little salt mill usually overlooked by divers in our brine), by simple juxtaposition or by complication with "negative concepts" such as those dealing with the void in which all rafts floated, could generate many dimensions of theodynamic relevance to the themes they threshed, whether mathematical or poetical at their limits. He tried to imagine as his most desiderated interlocutor an organic alloy of Duncannon and Charlemagne. Irony, after all, was the antignostic ingredient most sorely lacking in the democratic mind. But he was warned off for the time being by the scientific priest's aversion to the kind of people ignorant of chemistry who boldly experimented with half-baked concoctions.

However Caleb felt no constraint in colloquies about the essential issue of free will in a universe of causal Relativity, aleatory Quanta, and hidden variables. The sympathetic discussion of this most basic philosophical problem encouraged him to propose the value of science as a basic etymology on which to found a general orismology for all the reciprocally figurative and otherwise undefined metaphors that make up not only our common language but also every raft of reason. Was science to culture as sacrament to religion? Come to think of it, he and Father Duncannon seemed to agree, granting that logic is only one special case of language, we have as temporary lifeboats various different rafts of reason floated independently on the same ocean of words. And any of these rafts (according to Caleb) may be buoyed by more than two dimensions of language, like the self-freighting arks of giant fir logs chained many layers deep that used to be towed down the West Coast in deep salt water from Columbia to Cornucopia!

Father Duncannon was not sure he understood everything that his young friend had in mind, but as an old sage experienced in the intellectual enthusiasms of youth and ever conscious of the time remaining for his own unfinished work, while listening with respect he refrained from response that might stimulate such tangential imaginations even when they would have elicited his affined interests in earlier years. In the lucid but closely reasoned *Theodynamics* he himself had written that "the greatest art has for its central and deepest content chiefly abstract ideas, philosophical or religious, and unlinked psychological affections." The last were elsewhere called "emotional tensions unattached to the artist". To anyone acquainted with Father Duncannon this phraseology evoked a living image of the author.

Nevertheless, rather than by artistic and aesthetic convergence Caleb's excitement was most gratified by a certain degree of success in getting Father Duncannon to further develop, as more than a foundation of definition and metaphor, the physical science that despite the suggestive title of his book was only implicit, perhaps partly subconscious, in the liturgical doctrine. The first day of his sojourn at the Lab he had wheedled from the Mass-maker's personal files, at his somewhat reluctant inconvenience, an old neglected offprint of the young theorist's appropriately mathematical monograph on "A Counterentropic Dialectic for Biology" published in the *Atlantean Journal of Physics* before he'd had any intention of rejoining his native church even as a lay communicant.

As soon as Caleb had read as much of the article as he could understand (mostly in the "Discussion" section) he made bold to request the physicist's recollection of his early work, which had never been professionally ambitious and which thereafter in a new milieu he had apparently dismissed as a vagary of inconclusive years rather than an esoteric prefiguration of his vocational oeuvre. Anyway, he seemed to have forgotten the significance of this monograph until Caleb's bold half-educated fervor now reopened his eyes to what may have been a strange seeding of God's will all along.

This modestly specialized paper indirectly addressed the general problem of life that had been put forward by his erstwhile colleague Ezra Schrödinger in warning scientists "to expect in biology unfamiliar principles which are consequences of conventional physics". The text, largely in the abstract terms of statistical and quantum mechanics, proposed in ideal form "the simplest possible example of steadily decreasing entropy along with increasing energy". It was illustrated with a block diagram of the four necessary and sufficient elements: the non-thermal energy source (a radio field of certain frequency), the heat bath, the "organizer" (electron spin in an external magnetic field), and the "subsystem" (spin of an atomic nucleus in the same field) that is ordered by their interactions. The described process, a kind of induced resonance, results in "dynamic polarization" of the subsystem. The organizer, unlike Maxwell's Demon, "does not select those subsystems already in the improbable state, but rather it puts many into that state." This steady-state model was offered "to define a class of 'processes'" that includes photosynthesis and the formation of functional proteins such as enzymes from amino acids.

Wasn't this process something more than a precursor of the thought-experimenter's parable of the Christian Vine assimilating mineral salts and water from the soil, carbon from the air's carbon dioxide? Caleb asked with an apologetic smile. "Isn't the Holy Spirit a source of non-thermal energy, the worldly environment a heat bath, the Mass an organizer, and the corporate church just such a subsystem?"

Father Duncannon considered the suggestion. After an auctorial pause to remember this perpetration of his youth scientifically, he thoughtfully replied. "It's worth thinking about for discussion at Chapter. But the irreversible process I showed there produces entropy for the open environment by which the artifical closed system is necessarily contained. That's also why I don't like to carry my Vine-roots metaphor too far. Growth increases entropy in the soil that nourishes it. The incarnational hope of classic Christianity is to produce counterentropy for creation *as a whole*, the only absolutely closed system. I don't think God wants us to save a few souls, or even all humanity, at the expense of our world."

This gentle response took some of the wind out of Caleb's sails, but his mother hadn't instilled him with hubris for nothing. "Still, Father, if physics can enlighten biology, which transcends it, why can't biology enlighten the theodynamics that transcends organic science?"

"That question might inspire a synthetic proposition'" the priest smiled in turn, "but I'm afraid it wouldn't be as irrefutable as Anselm's analytic proof of the ultimate metasystem. Yet I like your idea as a fruitful Christian conceit. After all, an enzyme *is* a leaven!

"As far as such tropes are concerned, in regard to the operation of the Anamnesis as distinguished from the explanation of it, I'm reminded of the distinction you once made between the spin of a gyroscope and the rotation of a flywheel. They're easier to imagine than the spin of wave-particles.

"Even John Chauvin acknowledged the liturgy to be Christianity's gyroscope—but, if we can put our words in his mouth, only as a small symbolic mass endowed with high-frequency kinetic energy by promulgation of the Word, to keep the church's spiritual compass constantly on true north. The Paulines—and these days, alas, most Petrines—have never realized, as you say, that the eucharistic sacrament is a massive flywheel that has always kept the church's dynamo going against the load and friction of matter, as in my father's power plant, whether or not the evangel is preached; and that without its conversion of chugging human works into low-frequency kinetic inertia, slow but continuous, none of the orthodox churches would have survived all the symbolic assaults of heresy from left and right. Yes, it might be developed as a useful metaphor—if only there were common readers in Atlantis who understood the simplest electrical technology!"

Caleb was satisfied, though he knew that Father Duncannon would never go so far as to accept even his figurative attempts to minimize the supernatural. He was as pleased as a demonstrative squaredancer to find that some of his expressionistic swinging had made a favorable impression upon the conservative dance-critic he most respected in all the world.

*

But there was a further disturbance to upset the monastic tranquility before Chris returned from his Cherokee homegoing. One evening Father Duncannon received a Nashdom phone call for almost an hour in his study while Caleb finished up the day's kitchen work and waited for him in the twilighted library with their thimblefuls of ordinary luse for dessert. The old priest reappeared at his usual dignified pace but his lips were compressed and his face was not serene. Before speaking he took his seat in the winged cathedra, gathering the skirts of his cassock with the habitual gestures of a lady, and accepted his glass from Caleb.

"Oh dear, oh dear, I do wish Christopher—Father Lucey would control his drinking. I've had to put an embargo on spirits in this house. I used to be fond of Scotch, and I must say I'd like something stronger right now!" He was tapping his foot and staring straight ahead, too agitated to be embarrassed by the inconsonant presence of a venerating layman.

The aged eyes behind his rimless glasses seemed preternaturally bright and the youthfully smooth features expressed a patrician exasperation with the latest irrelevant contretemps to frustrate his work as the abbot of a proprietary monastery with one recalcitrant monk. Caleb was frightened by this restrained but unexampled signature of anger that he thought he could read in the face he revered for its calm wisdom and unlinked affections.

Though he had generally passed over or forgotten the evidence of charity and personal devotion in Father Duncannon's purely religious tracts, Caleb knew that the present all-too-human vexation should be forgiven as the symptom of a voluntary but uniquely troublesome burden, unmistakably distinguishable from the peevishness of commonplace fallibility. He remembered a pamphlet in which the Father Founder had defined his Order, in terms of an "apocalyptically prophetic dedication to the eternal element attained by the liturgy in the worldly time of the empirical church, as a 'sect'—not a movement *cut off* from the church but a special community of *followers*—in the proper sense of that Latin word". The words Caleb now heard might have been taken as anything but prophetic or unlinked, but for the first time he felt the emotional pressure of his tutor's inner reservoir and shivered at an existential intuition that the religious ideas of suffering expressed in print were not merely imagined by reason.

The Reverend Lancelot Duncannon's polite but unequivocal defiance of the "thetical" church, for which he was spared professional martyrdom only by the bland tolerance of Bishop Derwent (at a point in history and geography where the thousand years of conflict between bishops and abbots was hardly pertinent), may have evolved from cogitation on a raft, but its passion was both transcendent and transmutable. This Regular life, no matter how inchoate its realization, no matter how petty its irritations, no matter how susceptible some of its aspects to the suspicions of psychology, was systemically central to the living Order that its founder believed destined to be a leaven in the restoration and evolution of a truly classic church. Caleb felt honored by his realistically unique privilege, disregarding as usual his inveterate aversion to the eschatology of orthodox Christianity.

"I also wish he wouldn't carry on about the imbalance of his functional proteins as the excuse for everything. When it isn't that it's some Procrustean formula of psychoanalysis! But I'm too annoyed to listen to the reasons for what he's finally just admitted. He's so worried about what's going to happen at Chapter! He reminds me of a politician neglecting all his public responsibilities in order to prepare his defense against charges of personal corruption. I don't understand why he's so desperate! I wanted him to come home immediately. At least he promised to return this weekend. He hasn't killed himself yet!"

Thus Caleb after all was speechlessly shocked at the querulous tone he'd never before heard in the quiet judicious voice—now testy, but plaintive too, even fearful, until it gradually subsided into a chronic anxiety hitherto unrevealed. Yet this discovery of the ghostly father's emotional frailty suddenly deepened the unlinked intimacy that the little oak tree had longed for.

So before this unassuming auditor the priest for once indulged his unadmirable impulses, and not wanting them to be remarked by reply he continued more evenly to relieve a little of the long-pent animation that was never exhausted by his briefer more formal and restrained confessions to Father Davy of Markland, the veteran Member Secular whom he totally trusted.

"Why must he make more and more money? We'd prefer he didn't. He's doing well enough, at least in paper profits. The Fund is growing even while it supports this all-too-expensive oratory. Of course it's for the Order's wherewithal. If he has anything more than that in mind," Father Duncannon wanly smiled, as if to himself, forgetful of Caleb, his voice in decline, "it can't be anything sinful, seeing that he doesn't confess it. Anyway, even Anselm took Gregory the Great's advice 'to tolerate lesser sins until the greater ones are extinguished'. On the other hand, how does one know 'which wrongs to correct strictly while permitting others out of leniency'? I don't have either the innocence of the dove or the wisdom of the serpent."

Recalling his interlocutory voice, he continued, but again in tones that faded: "Good gracious, it would have been easier to live through the Elizabethan Settlement! Gregory says that a prelate is supposed to be 'the equal of everyone in compassion, above everyone in contemplation'. He also says that secular business is sometimes to be tolerated out of compassion, but never sought for love. Christopher loves money, even as a professed religious, though never for himself. But I shall have to come to terms with him before Chapter.

"Jesus said 'No one who puts his hand to the plow and looks back is fit for the Kingdom of Heaven'. Anselm was very stern with anyone who dared to abrogate lifetime religious vows, even for the best of reasons. —If I asked Christopher to leave the Order I think he really would kill himself. There's sin enough in the Seventh Circle."

"But he loves you!" said Caleb stupidly, through a welling film of tears, overcome with grateful pity for Father Duncannon's dedicated subordinate, the swiftly galumphing clumsy-looking celebrant of the Mass who like his gigantic namesake (patron of wayfarers and motorists) wished only to serve the highest of masters and did so by bearing not only the Christ-child but also acolytes beggars bankers merchants thieves athletes and all other travelers, sick or well, across the ford at which his stature made him most useful. Chris's endocrine yearning was nothing else than the will to heal himself as he would heal others.

"Yes." said Father Duncannon sadly. "If only that were what it took to make a monk, or if love for him were enough to make a wise Superior! More than once when I've been stricken ill he's saved my life, by acting as quickly and selflessly as you say he did to save Ibi's life on Cod Street, and by nursing me afterwards. Despite everything he's been a self-effacing mainstay of the Order, often misunderstood or overlooked by the Members. His prayers may be irregular—but he believes! Of course he's no intellectual, but he's brilliant in his own way, and—if only to please me, I believe—he struggled through divinity school. Before taking his vows he gave his own time and fortune to see that my books were printed, while everyone else was commiserating me about publishers' rejection slips. He may not be the kind of 'four-square stone' that Anselm looked for in his monasteries, but I bear him more love and gratitude than any other person still on earth. Sometimes I'm so joyful in his company that to his face I call him Father Lucifer, Son of the Morning!"

For a moment both tutor and pupil were silent in objective rapport. But Father Duncannon was reminded of the dangerous truth in his present situation when Caleb finally allowed himself to disclose as delicately as he was able his unrefined curiosity about the proximate cause of his master's extraordinary sacerdotal indiscretion. "What's going on down in Nashdom?"

This inquiry brought the present occasion to a focus. Unlinking and controlling his agitation Father Duncannon told Caleb what had been volunteered or extracted in the telephone conversation, somewhat expanded by hermeneutic induction and reasonable imagination.

"Not to make too fine a point of it, after putting on an act he threatened his father that if he didn't get what he wanted he would expose the family's secret, as something to be proud of, when he delivers his little homily at tomorrow mornings's Eucharist, where he's offered to supply for the local rector, who truly is ill. His father is over eighty and has always spoiled his only child, but this time he surprised his scion by smiling at the tantrum, probably for the first time in his life. 'Everyone knows that most of the white families in the South have some African blood.' he said to his son. 'It's nothing to be ashamed of.'

"Thank God the humanists at Apostolic headquarters have been making headway among some of the Southern parishes! Apparently the old banker is no longer concerned about Mammon or social honor, and has already shocked his fellow magnates by publicly advocating equal rights. He's no traitor to his class, but a decent Protestican according to his own light. Christopher was so joyful at this metanoia that he wept in his father's arms and immediately dropped all his efforts to manipulate paternal emotions. So the prodigal's returning to my pig-farm."

Caleb dared ask: "What did Chris—Father Lucey—want?"

"That's what's so distressing! The father's really as indulgent as ever: it's just that he doesn't trust the son's stability—more for my sake than for his own. He promised to consult his lawyer and review the conditions of his will. You see, I'm now told, most of his estate is supposed to come to the Trustees, as long as the intended heir doesn't renounce his vows."

"And Father Lucey would be rich if he left the Order?"

"Much richer than when he joined—but of course with not nearly the buying power the Trustees would have after such a bequest. He wanted his father to anticipate the legacy, so that as a single investor, on behalf of the Trustees, we'd have enough capital to persuade Professor Capstick to sell us his portion of one of the unregistered limited trusts that control Parity! The need is urgent, Father Lucey says, because it may be for only one more fleeting moment that the mutual divestments probably still in progress between Halymboyd and Capstick will leave open the possibility for a trusted outsider to join Parity's inner circle!

"Of course he didn't mention that he's in haste also because he'd like to be able to announce a provisional agreement among gentlemen before our meeting with Endicott Krebs, and a fait accompli before the Chapter ordeal.

"But fortunately his father is no stranger to the Street people of Ur. He anyhow doubts that there *is* such an unlikely shortcut to power, calls the scheme not only chimerical but also unethical, and refuses as long as he lives to relinquish his wealth on such farfetched grounds. I'll probably be hearing from him directly. He always keeps me informed of 'family problems'.

"For the Order's sake I can't very well refuse Christopher's patrimony in the future. Perhaps it won't further complicate the moral problem of usury, but the persistence of money questions is more distasteful to me than all the conflicts and misunderstandings we had in the early days at our oratory in Unabridge when most of our inquirers were either firebrands or psychopaths and my sane friends called *Metacosmesis Mundi Per Incarnationem* an outworn hope, or the new Anamnesis 'Dun's closet ritual'! I know some even thought I was riding an aesthetic hobby horse with the idea of a monastery and its Rule. The medievalists teased that I had stared at the crucifix long enough to hear the Lord say 'Lancelot, repair my fallen house!'

"Oh Caleb, is it all too much for my strength? —What a great man Anselm was, besides a philosopher: as great a Saint in his way as Francis, to have established the English Church as a distinct institution during the very time at which Rome as a whole was centralizing itself! He opposed and obeyed both king and emperor while maintaining ecclesiastical discipline among Anglo-Saxons and Normans. —I wish I could turn these trammeling distractions over to Father Davy! He's the wisest churchman I've ever known, and certainly more practical than I.

"And he doesn't have to wait until I'm gone to simplify and modernize my perhaps pedantically traditional elaborations of the liturgy. There may be more than one style of orthodox antithesis to the thetical church, just as there's more than one Antichrist! The oldfashioned airplane-builder who invented a new kind of wing during the war but knew only trigonometry for his computations probably had help from someone with calculus to get his design accepted. I'm too old to love new language. (That's why I like to visit Monsignor Navarro over at Espirito Santo; he and I understand each other aesthetically.)

"But Father Davy demurs. He says he's too addicted to the freedom of pipe-smoking and salmon fishing to give up his parish and take the vows of a religious.

"—I need hardly mention that what I've been saying . . ."

Caleb nodded and cleared his throat to reply, but then said nothing. It seemed gratuitous to asseverate the trustworthiness of a gentleman's private witness. The uppermost board of a spillway having been lifted the tranquil mill pond became a temporary torrent. But soon, after one spate of overflow, the troubled mind would regain a steady state, and it was out of the question for any more of the dam's lip to be removed before the higher barrier was replaced and the capacity for reservation fully restored.

In the meantime Father Duncannon gave himself over to an upper level of unrestrained expression. ". . . that I've been speaking in absolute confidence."

"Yes, Father. Father Lucey is my friend, but lately I've come to see the . . . the difficulties anyone would have in living with him. As with my own mother. Anything I say or do only makes it worse—unless I have time to occupy myself with nothing else. The remedy is beyond psychology!"

"He's the one that psychologizes all the time! Good gracious, he once told me that my argument for the Immaculate Conception of the Virgin Mary had something to do with a childhood attitude toward *my* mother!"

They were staying up late, and there was a Mass to be made in the morning. The luse was too sweet to ply their drinking. Yet it was Caleb's place to await bedtime dismissal by his senior. He continued to listen in awe. It was tacitly understood that this very privilege, more than his classification as a mere uninitiated employee of the Order, would exclude him from the official sessions of the Chapter, like the child of a stormy marriage whose knowing presence would embarrass his reverend father's dignified delivery of peace and wisdom from the public pulpit.

"People have no idea hard it is, even for me, living under vows! They think I don't know what I'm missing! But my life hasn't been merely theoretical. I was an overworked pastoral curate for three years on the Isle of Dogs, and no parish in the slums of East London is innocent of crime and vice and personal misery for a single day. I never was an ivory-tower scientist either. My experience hasn't all been in thought-experiments! They think I'm an arm-chair social critic, ignorant of personal good and evil, because I haven't suffered.

"Some say *pathei mathos*, 'by suffering, learning'. It's true that in objective fact I haven't suffered as most people have—that often my sympathies require a theoretical or imaginative extension of my own experience, and that I must constantly pray for greater sensitivity, for the kind of simple Christian charity that moves and blesses such good people as those of the Classic Worker movement and all the living saints in and out of the religious life who put me to shame, whose vocation I believe I appreciate better than they should appreciate mine.

"Nor perhaps have I done justice to mysticism, or to the purely spiritual life—though I must say it suffers no lack of attention in religion nowadays and hardly needs my support. Kierkegaard was only half right when he defined Christianity as 'an actualization of inwardness'. My purpose has been to show what *is* neglected: the primitive sacramental antithesis to that which is itself rightly antithetical to superstition.

"Even as one of the two hundred and forty three thousand individuals 'unlikely to reflect credit on the U S A' in the 'subversive' files of the Imperial Department, I lead a protected life. I'm in no danger of unemployment, starvation, homelessness, imprisonment, torture, persecution, humiliation, excommunication, or outright public ostracism. I've given up the ordinary measure of superfluous and superficial freedom, and the ordinary success of a career, but social isolation and intellectual loneliness are more pleasant than uncomfortable for a dry stick like me. Yet even Christopher is mistaken in his belief that holy orders are natural for me.

"The Members understand that I'm not a mere aesthete, but I believe that some of them think all my passions are intellectual, and that my celibacy has been easy—as if I hadn't acknowledged in the Order's published doctrine that, next to hunger, sex is in all innocence the most powerful God-given urge. Lust is no more theoretical and impersonal for me than it was for Anselm agonizing over his youthful sin of fornication. I wasn't always a priest. I grew up in Dogtown. I was at Gloucestermas the Great Year after repeal of Total Abstinence, when crime was made over into public celebration, when artists and poets were congregating here, and when this was still a Navy town. I know what love for a woman is. And at no age does a man's imagination of 'one flesh' lose its power.

"I might have navigated life happily married—on subsidized rafts, prospering in some institutional tenure, joining the Ur Project without moral questions—and made this house a family homestead for God's gift of sons or daughters! This very day grandchildren might have been playing down there in the Duncannon field that's now going to brambles like wheat to tares, where I myself used to play when it still fed horses and cows! As a child my favorite rock in Purdeyville was the one with the Proverb A WISE SON IS HIS FATHER'S JOY. It's more significant to me now."

7

THE MAIN-TOP BAR

*L*ike other sagacious dogs on watch Ibi-Roy always took his position of repose at the best possible vantage for seeing hearing or smelling the greatest number of objects interesting to himself if not potentially dangerous to his master, even with one eye open or both of them closed. Thus on a series of Monday nights, barred from public houses by a statute of the Commonwealth, he waited for Caleb not immediately outside the Main-Top door at the back of the CaraVANsary Hotel but some six feet away at the flat intersection of streets on what had been the schooner-launching strand of Garrison Cove before it was filled in to make a waterfront site for the Traction power plant as well as more convenient land for the fishery industries and their workers. At the corner of Loft and Scrod—assis, couchant, or half-curled flat on the sidewalk—he was able not only to sense persons entering or leaving the tavern itself, and saints or strangers approaching on either of the two by-ways, but also to keep under northerly surveillance the main portal of the Van and the cinematic traffic passing its doorless front on the main thoroughfare.

By the same token he could be seen and recognized in the gloaming or streetlight by any eastward or westward passenger on foot or wheel who happened to glance down or across the street of old sail lofts while his god was attending Shelly Schlossberg's version of the Fort Orange Philologos Society, which starred Doctor Ipsissimus Charlemagne in place of Redburn. Caleb was the only friend who never missed a meeting, or much of one. Chris Lucey had gladly allowed him to exchange his Monday day-off for Tuesday so that he could sleep late after these public symposiums.

Shelly's abortive institution [though elevated to a "tradition" in future Dogtown legend] would last only six or eight weeks before dwindling and lapsing amid the distractions of midsummer celebrations, but in its time it seemed a custom. Meanwhile these semi-public soirées were often the scuttlebutt of potation at the intimate Saturday night gatherings of two or three in Doc's kitchen, where Ibi was welcomed by Deeta to the innermost sanctum.

Though excluded from the bar by segregation law Ibi regularly served as an advertisement of the Monday evening performances, as if the Sign of the Dog was their sidewalk barber-pole, Doc's animated cigar-store Atlindu prop—for Doc of course, not the bartending host, was the attraction for those discriminating few who knew of them and were there known. Shelly did what he could to make Ibi comfortable (short of losing his liquor license by admitting a dog to the company), namely to provide him with a floor mat and a dish of water out on the corner. (If the truth were told, he had once jeopardized his business by briefly showing Ibi around the room and behind the bar, through the rear exit to the unforbidden lobby of the hotel, in order to reassure him as to the innocence of the smokefilled den in which Caleb would be detained for so many hours, normally as out of reach to a dog as the platform of a main mast.) But the weather was fine, and in serving the purpose of an ambulatory marquee Ibi greeted men and dogs of his acquaintance as they arrived or passed by.

This particular liquor license, without change of trade name, though relocated, had originally been issued to Jack Chase, British-born petty officer emeritus of the U S Navy but "a dashing smuggler in his day": former gunner in the English flagship fighting Turks at Navarino and erstwhile captain of the *U S S Atlantis*'s main-top—having been pardoned, thanks to his extraordinarily competent leadership, for brief desertion as a commander commissioned in the new Peruvian navy by Simon Bolivar, during which liberty he had been caressed by the loveliest Castilian belle in South Atlantis. To White Jacket at least, Jack's glance was like that of a "sentimental archangel doomed to drag out his eternity in disgrace". He used to recite *The Lusiads* to his admiring Brother Jonathans in that tree-house where commissioned officers knew little more of what was going on than foresters know of the symbiotic ecology in canopies of primeval Douglas fir.

Once, to celebrate Independence Day in the South Pacific, heading home by the Horn, Jack got permission for *the people* not on watch at two bells on Fourth of July afternoon to stage a theatrical for the whole ship's company; then organized, directed, rehearsed, and played the lead in "Percy Royal-Mast, The True Yankee Sailor", in which he rescues fifteen swabbies from the brig, to the riotous applause of crew and officers alike (which however did not mitigate the usual quarter-deck solemnity of next morning's flogging). According to White Jacket, 'Jack Roy' "larked with life, heroic in his levity"; but even the ship's Captain Porter and Commodore Jones (future conqueror of San Ricardo and subjugator-for-the-nonce of Mexican Cornucopia) respected their leading seaman for his invaluable experience, intelligence, and manly dignity.

Jack Chase despised whaling as "pig-sticking" and "bobbing after carrion"—for "turning a ship into a fat-kettle, and the ocean into a whale-pen"; but he must have tolerated good and proper fishing, according to speculation in the Main-Top Bar, where he was more than once the subject of conversation between Doc Charlemagne and Dexter Keith, still at heart Lieutenant Junior Grade, U S N R , as most of the others listened in puzzlement, seeing that Jack's protege and biographer (a k a U S Customs Inspector Number 75 of New Uruk) was now generally reputed for nothing but his celebration of whaling. Doc charged them to look for his white shark and his white maiden, and especially his white jacket, as well as his white whale.

Huck Salter swore to take up reading again. Eric Vanderlyn tried to remember whether or not he'd read those sea stories in prep school. Shelly wondered if they were better than Jack London's. In all diffidence Thad Kryothermsky apologized for his disgraceful ignorance of literature, which he was now too busy to correct.

Jack Chase's old *Atlantis* had been of a frigate class peculiar to the U S Navy, handier and swifter than a classic ship-of-the-line but heavier than anybody else's cruisers—an "oaken castle of war", White Jacket called her:—indeed a sister of the famous

U S S Federalist, which was still in commission, afloat at the Botolph Navy Yard, whither Doc and Shelly had traveled to board her amid a gaggle of tourists, the one to situate and pace off an imaginary sea-theater on the main deck, the other to instruct himself in the hostelry trade-name he'd acquired, visualizing from underview the amazingly capacious eagles' nest identical to that in which Jack had sang and lectured.

Not that the Schlossbergs made any attempt to decorate their ordinary with anything more extraordinary than photographs of schooners and dories, which in the usual crepuscular atmosphere of spilled beer and dissipating spirits could be seen hardly any better than the oil painting at the Spouter-Inn. Jake his son, official manager of this tavern in affiliation and communication with the Van's principal business, who tended bar all other nights of the week, hadn't the slightest nautical or historical interests and wished only to identify his establishment as a friendly convenient taproom and "lounge", perhaps less respectable than his parents' hotel upstairs but sufficiently reputable for escorted ladies and plain enough to keep clean, on the principle of least action, away from bright lights.

If this series of weekly parties hadn't been destined for dissolution by the demanding irregularities of Gloucestertide and the diversions of summer it would certainly have been broken up by strife in the Schlossberg family whenever it fully dawned on Jake that his father was abusing the business. Embezzlement was noticeable especially in the shrinkage of Scotch without commensurate enrichment of the receipts one would expect even on an off-day from sales of such an expensive item. If their license hadn't required the bar to operate every night it would have been closed on Monday, the quietest night of the week and therefore the manager's day off. Eventually it would have occurred to Jake that the cash register's Monday yields were much too unrewarding even by the lowest standards, and perhaps what was worse, that a few of his regular topers were no longer appearing on other nights of the week, possibly having formed new habits elsewhere after a quick whiff of the Monday night crowd.

Indeed, alcoholics who might have frequented the place every day of the week, as well as casual Monday walk-ins from the street or transient guests of the Van, were diplomatically discouraged by the substitute bar-tender, Shelly himself, the ultimate proprietor. On Monday nights the DV always happened to be on the blink, and couldn't be fixed until Tuesday morning. It somehow blew or was blown by a certain mysteriously unreliable circuit-breaker that also fed the jukebox and the welcoming secondary lights of the facade. (The police would have inquired if the red neon MAIN-TOP outside had also been turned off.) Lest his machinations attract too much attention, from week to week Shelly slightly varied the malfunctions and mishaps.

But the small throng at his tables—which he sometimes attended, not as a servant under obligation, loitering at their side to the neglect of his proper duty at the taps in front of the room-doubling mirror—was enough to dismay ordinary souls who wandered in to a bar stool and stayed for no more than one distractedly served and quickly tossed drink, maybe only fifteen cents worth of draft beer, never to return. Any such stranger, irritated by lack of entertainment and bewildered if not angered by the unintelligible talk that took its place as background noise, would feel like a stupid intruder, despite Shelly's disingenuous efforts to compensate with apologetic smiles for his preoccupation and the strictly temporary inconveniences of his service.

Jake was the last to hear of the ruin he was barely spared by his infatuated father, just before its cause evaporated in the heat of the solstice.

*

The creatures of Arminius Melville were not by any means the sole or even principal topic in Shelly's ad hominem club, and on several of the Mondays they were ignored entirely, since the presiding Oberdichter was alertly conversant with a world of local national and universal matters—anthropological historical geographical topological political scientific philosophical artistic and technical—including the few in which his audience was severally competent and therefore treated as peers pro tem; but the New Uruker's Tom Guy and Ishmael, Wellingborough and Pierre, were often in Caleb's mind for discussion during his approaches to Doc, which though cautious were more argumentative than those of the other drinking companions, who seldom initiated a theme or demurred at the Director's opinion, no matter how lively their interest in an issue.

Whenever these questions of fiction were pursued the senior dromenologist held that the author whom they both claimed as their model of Atlantean genius was unconsciously impelled to imagine a radical theater, for which he was born too late on the one hand and too early on the other; whereas his junior believed that the novelist's creative tension (the platonic component of which they agreed upon) arose from an unconscious countercultural search for sacramental liturgy likewise unavailable in the Pauline culture of his time.

Among other discussions there was for instance Caleb's proposal that thermodynamics was the most important branch of physics, as against Dexter, who was for quantum mechanics, as well as against Doc, who subordinated all departments to Relativity by anthropological reasoning.

Though everyone attended in order to hear the Director, half the time on half the Monday nights Caleb was the only one who thought he understood what Doc propounded—such as the irony of Melville and Kierkegaard as contemporary polypseudonymous intellectuals. At such times the timid Karcist, while all others listened in silence, found himself an actor on the little stage defined by Doc's corner table. Thus like Samuel, or Ion, or even the boy Jesus at the Temple, though he listened and admired he also sometimes questioned—albeit much to his retrospective regret at the feeble rhetoric of his own challenges.

It might be said that Caleb was acquiring an underground reputation as Doctor Charlemagne's fairhaired boy, but to listeners he was constitutionally neutral as an attraction. Nobody in the gatherings liked to have topical obiter dicta of supremely idiosyncratic charm interrupted by abstractly adversarial deep-diving seriousness, which could not but seem pretentious to those without intellectual sympathy and was interesting only when Doc began to snort at the upstart—who thereupon spoiled the fun by backing off in deference to superior age and height.

In the inner circle Petto Simplicissimus helped make amends for Caleb's earnestness, but as a self-employed toiler in a demanding trade, famished for time to perform welding for his own purposes, he usually spent his enthusiasm early in the evening and reluctantly never stayed late.

*

Every Monday was different, but especially the night that local gossip as well as Caleb's prosaic fervor was silenced by the electrifying contrast of poetic excitement, a visit of the only off-islander ever admitted as a guest to the proceedings of this privileged Main-Top assembly: a recent friend of Doc's, rival for the hearts and minds of youth, far more famous than Ipsissimus his nominal host—less weening than Caleb in purely noetic expression and roaring drunk in most of his other discourse. That is to say, the Main-Top door was unexpectedly darkened by Jock Merrimac, the heroic poet of his generation, open bottle in hand, accompanied by two Beauts, his "bodyguards", sensitive long-haired jazz musicians.

"Am I not welcome in Dogtown at the Sign of the Dog?" Jock sang out. "I thought that mythical beast was going to attack me! But it was three against one, six feet to four, and teeth enough by any count. So I poured him a drink!"

Unheeded but furious, Ibi's master rushed out past the streetwise trio to save his dog from corruption. Into the gutter he poured Jock's insolent libation before it was lapped. Shelly replenished the dish with water from behind the bar. So Caleb missed Doc's salutation and introductions.

But as if by broadcast the word spread all over the Cape, and within an hour the tavern was filled with freemen who read or heard of latterday defiance in itinerant narrative poetry often called "epic". For pleasure or advice, this exuberant kilroy-lover, expatiator of transcontinental Atlantis (known for quashing references to Walter Whiteman), presumably united with Doc in esteem for Clarel, had come with greetings of goodwill from his native Higher Falls (where the Tranquility River of Vinland makes its tribute to the moody Kerouac), like a junior Elector of the Holy Roman Empire in the first blush of his popularity, to meet once more the arbiter of all culture, prepared to be subsumed by the emperor, as if the anomalous preponderance of Ippies over Beauts here and now in the Main-Top Bar was representative of their proportional constituencies. [The homage signaled by this pilgrimage would do wonders for the local fame and consequent respect that had hitherto escaped Ipsissimus Charlemagne. For more than that, Jock's knuckling chuckling obeisance finds little space in this story.] But Ippies everywhere saluted the Beauts, and educated Beauts the Ippies: they were allies of a sort—the Languedocs and the Languedouis — to the extent that they pledged any realm of the mind at all.

Unexpected but not uninvited. As a matter of fact, the Oberdichter had dropped a hint by mail that of a Monday his inland friend might like to wait upon him for a discussion of the educational enterprise he'd mentioned during the latter's call at Leviathan Court. Dogtown College would need a distinguished demonstrator of practical poetics, among lesser lights—smiths of all the arts, savants of all the sciences, and other professors. All the better, it was left unsaid, if the poet would fraternally invest a little of his art-earned wealth in the common cause of offering Atlantean students (and working people too) an institute of dromenological studies as an antipodean alternative to the nation's vocational centers of "creative writing". Imaginatively developed history and other interests of anthropology would make up for the omission of popular art and spirituality in the College curriculum.

In his cups Jock Merrimac never tired of explaining to the uninitiated, as he did tonight at Doc's prompting, that although most of the celebrated Beauts—his comrades and followers, who (more than the new President) were stirring the country out of its Eisenhower regression—had ingenuously accepted their collective journalistic cognomen as deriving from the word *beautiful* that heavily populated their vocabulary, the term in fact had been erroneously taken up from his own casual image of a *butte*. Once at a reading he'd sought to express his idea of a poet's task under contemporary Atlantean conditions: the sea of poetics had so receded, to the distress of an honest deep-diving artist (in spite of his egalitarian lip-jazz and his glorification of the U S wave-front whereby unlike Tristram Shandy he claimed to actually overtake his life in progress), that he was unwillingly stranded as a mesa high above the sediment of desert. Now there were thousands of Buttes, conspicuous and friable, though closer than an alpine elite to the great basin.

Doc had admired the metaphor as intended. On his level, a fortiori (for he was taller and less agile than Jock), even in performing art, there was much worse discouragement from the devilvised recession of democratic taste.

But they never got around to the problem of establishing a collegial house of countercultural dromenology. The meet was a rambling session of laughter and loosened tensions. Even jealous Caleb liked the handsome dark adventurer of all senses, bygone candidate for Ur University football laurels, finding him more congenial as a tender remembering child of hard times than as a narrator of the newest conquests in profligacy. It was the only Monday on which Shelly collected enough money to cover Jake's overhead. Tonight, with a newly rich poet loosening his own pockets and shaming all the others in potlatch, nothing was on the house except what was sneaked to Doc and Caleb and Petto when no one else was paying for rounds at the corner table. Everyone else except Jock had to fetch his drinks from the bar.

The faculty's table was not high, nor was it otherwise suitable as a podium. Everyone didn't always watch Jock or listen to Doc, not even the Beauts, who readily introduced themselves to the indigenes as sociable persons in their own right. There was plenty of cross-talk and shouting laughter as devotees milled about, going to and from the bar with their own opinions and responses, or sat at the other tables in separate conversations. It was mainly the difficulty of hearing Jock and Doc, who did not elevate their table talk for an audience, that left most of the witnesses inattentive at this legendary conclave; but Caleb and Petto were there to listen, and, though ignored by the two face-to-face Olympians, they were well positioned as reverential courtiers sitting on either side of both, one to analyze and the other to absorb celebrity's brotherhood.

But they heard nothing profound or edifying, nor yet titillating, at least at first, as if Allil of Connacht had come in peace to Conchobar of Ulster. Though amiable with each other, and even sweet, Jock was too tipsy and Doc too cautious. After some friendly smalltalking the Director chose Redburn's works as the text for their duel of feats. Merrimac disclosed that *Clarel* was his next narrative model, which would be to the disbelieving amazement of his wavefront fans but was much to Charlemagne's approval.

"That poet was the Shakespeare of Atlantis!" Jock asseverated in a generalization that he knew he was in no condition to defend. But Petto nodded vigorously, and Doc in his dignity did not demur at what should have been a national platitude.

"Artist and hero, both!" Caleb dared to butt in. "And is Einstein's genius greater than Redburn's merely because the common reader finds it harder to follow?"

Jock had been to sea during the war as a messfit galleyman, and Doc had gone out in a fishing schooner one summer, so they were both confident in their midrashim of Redburn's maritime experience, itself greatly extended by extrapolation from books. All three were great readers, and Shakespeare made another, who'd never been to sea at all. It was more significant that of the four only Redburn had served under the Articles of War.

It seemed as if Doc in semi-paternal manner wished to bolster Jock's self-confidence in literary criticism. The poet had read his elder's anthropological article on Mardian drama in an issue of *Dromenology*, and always recommended it to young Beauts who asked him for something short to start their "classical" reading with; and he'd heard that Doc was working on "A Key to Mardi and Its Sequels". Jock also knew that Charlemagne always recommended Merrimac's *Professor Hex* (of Higher Falls) as the best book of lyric poems in modern Atlantis, an exemplar of what Doc called "quantum verse".

"I'm waiting for you to write some plays." Doc now said, smiling through his smoke. "The theater needs your Teletype Poetry!" Jock was famous for punching out his narratives at white heat on continuous rolls of sprocket-holed paper, uninterrupted by hesitations or self-criticism—a sort of writing more autonomous than the prose of *A Vision*. "Redburn once told a friend he was so excited about the billion thoughts he wanted to write Natty Hawhaw that he wished for an endless 'ribband of paper', just like yours, but before numbers could be measured with a typewriter."

"A good man!" replied Jock. "A very beautiful man! —Mr Shelly," he called, "when you have time, another drink for all the Buttes and Ippies, all good and beautiful men! —Meanwhile, to Ipsissimus Charlemagne!" Merrimac was aware that Shakespeare and Redburn were two whom Doc never offered to subsume.

For a moment the hubbub was suspended, but the party was to grow louder before it finally dispersed into the vibrant outer silence of a working people's city. The two leaders were têt-a-têt again. It was natural that they should end up comparing "Fallstown" and "Doctown", French and Lusitanian, the larger and the smaller city, the newer and the older, the riparian and the coastal—the power canals built by manufacturing capitalists and the self-made Gut of delvers and gatherers. Dexter later told his wife that they were like two new sailors from mountains and plains brought together by the war, exploring what to boast that would distinguish their hopes memories and inner experiences from each other and from the common history of their shipmates.

They fell into reminiscences that led to argument about the Great Year of Vinland, which was not an astrological mark of the era but a matter of dispute among cities and towns, and among citizens within each of them. For the Poet of Higher Falls it was 1936, year of the Kerouac's Flood; for the Director of anthropological drama it was 1934, "the cusp of Dogtown's present age". The Director was not pleased when the Poet dropped his opposition and in an attempt at conciliation promised that the microtopopolis of saints and angels—port of dogs, arsenal of sculpture—would be given special recognition in his work-in-progress, already known to cognoscenti by the title of *Higher Falls in Cantos*, his first long lyric poem (disclaiming pretense to the epic genre).

After Jock went reeling out the door, sheering away from Ibi, he was chauffeured off the Cape by one who lived on narcotic stimulants.

*

All the talk of narrative poetry and Great Years made Caleb remember his dread resolution to force himself through the thicket of his mother's prose 'autobiography'. Once again he had postponed the ordeal of plowing through an assortment of uneven sheaves from the earth's most humid equatorial zone, cheap fragile acid-browned paper, nicked or creased, half unglued from faded notebooks or raggedly blocked in rubber bands no longer elastic, written all over on both sides without margins, in water-soluble ink, black or blue or purple, and only sporadically numbered—in short, hard to read for more than a few minutes at a time.

These manuscripts were priceless to him, but at present his own life as it was being lived from day to day continued to grow more interesting than an irrevocable past, which anyway in her almost every statement of objective fact was bound to be either unreliable or insignificant to himself. Knowing the y-coefficient of one's necessary cause, moreover, was in the end unnecessary. It would be inhibiting to freedom of the will. Initial causes were of lessened importance to the extent that destiny was otherwise determined, for will and chance were the truly independent variables. Beyond discovering the legally recorded fiction, as far as qualifying for a passport would be concerned at some indefinitely deferred point in the future, his own circumstantial dossier might be by far the greater stumbling block to freedom.

For the present, in other words, his appetite for self-knowledge, though greater than a mere velleity, was not elevated by his undulant fever to the pitch of nisus. His current sensations and hopes were plenary—even salubrious—leaving no room for retrospective anxiety of lesser importance than the ultimate anticipation, which as a heedless youth he had ceased to regard as soon as he'd been cured by Bice-Belle of the idiopathic malignancy in his rima vocalis. Just as the living triumph over the dead (in Babbalanja's words), he thought, they trump their fathers; and he would have admitted that his usual insensitivity to everything beyond his Immediate Exclusive Consciousness now extended to death itself.

He surmised that each brain of the billions around us—stranger, saint, or sinner; father, mother, child; Petrine, Pauline, or heathen; Moslem, Hindu, Buddhist; white black brown yellow red; Crat or Can; priest or artist—passes most of its life in a series of I E C s, only more or less attempting to understand the epiphenomena of others, singly or collectively, as animate objects worthy of more or less distinction for purposes of selfinterest or sympathy. Yet a thinker's I E C may entertain contradictory propositions simultaneously; and even many thoughts exclude an infinity of others. Some Eastern religions strive to obliterate the I E C, but even the most social Christianity (to say nothing of epithalamian mysticism) is necessarily limited by the temporal capability of an individual sentience.

I E C happened to be what he hoped to discuss with Doc on Saturday night—as differentiated from the common objectivity of either idealism or induction. But such cogitation did not occupy his mind on a certain Monday afternoon as he looked forward to the less exclusive colloquium of the evening.

As virtuous excuse for discontinuing his morning runs, and as redress to Ibi for deprivation of the athletic joy they had shared, he was making it a new habit to walk with him to and from the Lab (unless he was being picked up or delivered by Father Lucey on off-island business), now that he lived only a mile away. Next to auroral laziness his motive was to spare the starter and other stop-and-go parts in his obsolete and vulnerable Little King, whose life he hoped to eke out until he could get a normally remunerative job after the year had passed its zenith.

But with no thought of that unprovided future he was skipping home from his offices with an uncustomary whistle on his lips (much to Ibi's amusement) when he met Belle hurriedly getting out of her car on the Apostles Dock parking pavement.

Not until the dog and his coddling neighbor made their usual fuss in greeting each other did she glance closely at Caleb. Catching her breath, she grinned and frowned. "You—you've been doing it! Look how flushed you are! Don't deny it! You look as guilty as a six-fingered hand!"

Caleb smiled with sheepish amazement at her unhesitating mother-like intuition. His brow, if already abloom, burned all the more with a confusion of embarrassment and pride. What could he say? He moved toward the stairway to evade her eyes, ostensibly laughing at a jest, while she was still unloading articles of food and paper. But he knew she was dying of curiosity, which left him with the upper hand as long as he remained uncommunicative.

"I'm in a hurry to get ready for the Hall tonight, or you wouldn't get off so easily! Keeping secrets from me! Humph!"

"Ha!" Who was she to talk? Already taking the treads two risers at a time he laughed much louder, derisively expressing his comparative innocence, as hardly in the smallest measure her counterpart in experience.

"That's right—run away when you're ashamed of yourself!" she called after him. "Don't worry, I'll catch you tonight. Wait and see!"

He didn't wait, but he did see—an ambivalent surprise. She'd gotten wind of the Monday Nights (which he'd been careful never to mention, as if they were as secret as covens of the Unabridge Apostles) and lost no time appealing to Shelly. He who doted like an adopted father couldn't legally refuse her admission. Promising to see for herself, if she decided to do so, only as an accidental drop-in (demure and unaware, no more intrusive than a sympathetic off-duty unrecording fly on the wall), and not to let the proprietor get blamed for her effrontery, she'd enlisted his nervous cooperation.

Shelly actually liked the idea, in her case; his qualms were about setting a precedent for other female gate-crashers. This unique Main-Top institution, originally calculated for his own pleasure, might lose the unselfconscious spontaneity of those drawn to it by quite different attractions. He was still chary of the troubles caused by Yerba Buena women in the waterfront bars of Jack London's era, for he had to defend the Van's rehabilitated reputation against local memories of the time when Dogtown was a Navy port-of-call as well as base for the world's greatest fleet of fishing schooners.

But when Belle promptly decided to make use of this intelligence the shocking breech of tradition worked out as an easy exception. After the Special Public Meeting on proposals for a new city seal that she was assigned to cover at Ibicity Hall, she came down to the Main-Top casually escorted by Dexter Keith (reluctantly departing, she noticed, from the post-ex-officio company of Deirdre Cotton the beautiful Protonotary of all meetings) and by big fat gruntingly comical Benlevi Nathan, owner of the Factory Store and landlord of the entire Leviathan Court, who these days was attending all public deliberations in order to prepare himself for a populist Earldeman-run in the next election but who nevertheless in all ignorance greatly respected the disinterested learning and ingestive capacity of Doctor Charlemagne his largest and poorest tenant.

As a journalist Belle was already considered one of the Acropolis gang. In both sanctioned and off-the-record fidelity she had learned to make herself so sincerely inconspicuous and comparatively androgynous in speech, manner, and dress—her brisket clothed like a boy's, and her stride as brisk—that the two public figures were hardly surprised to hear that she knew where they were headed and that she intended to repair to the Main-Top with or without their protection.

"We won't blackball you." Dexter assured her.

Ben stood aside and marveled at the childish joy with which Dexter and especially Belle were greeted by the formidable dog, but after he'd passed unharmed did not look back to see the anthropocentric sorrow of being left outside for no good reason.

Thus in the shadow of two impressive figures—one vertically, the other horizontally—she was able to slip through the Monday Night doorway without bringing down the house like some lone flute-girl at an anti-Socratic symposium. It was an enlightened reception. Ostensibly on everyone's part she fitted in as one of the fellows, and thereafter one hardly noticed that she was the only woman ever to set foot in that fraternity. At first blush Caleb felt warm esteem and sexual tolerance for this her professional aspect.

One reason for her immediate success was that she quietly and unexpectedly took upon herself an unassuming function that combined the roles of servingmaid and secretary. (Only in the fullness of time would she gradually and ironically suggest the part of an unattached Aspasia.) No more than half an hour after her arrival she disappeared, after Shelly's connivance by means of telephone, only to return in fifteen minutes with a stack of hot cardboards separating various radially scored discs of pizza (a newly popular comestible) from Leonardo's a block down Front Street.

This gift for everybody was advanced from her own purse, but she barely murmured that she was taking up a freewill offering toward her reimbursement. The eventual fiscal response to her gratefully accepted service was generous enough at the middle of the roster's bell curve, even among those who did not partake, but other beneficiaries were either sensitively embarrassed or as ingenuously indifferent as she to cost accounting. Doc, who ate the most, was graciously forbidden to pay at all; and Caleb's money, who came in second, had been irritably but discreetly rejected. She didn't count noses, and when none of the viands remained gave never a thought to the cash shortfall as in the midst of higher-minded conversations (her own voice so soft and unobtrusive that it could be heard only by anyone close at hand whose eyes were meeting hers) she finally swept up the bills and coins on the table like a negligent croupier, long after the contributors had made their donations and taken their change.

The Director had made room for Belle at his right on the plush settee against the wall. But now, her service completed, she glared across the table at Caleb with furrowed brow and slowly shook her head, tapping the edge of the table with her forefingers. Despite her place of honor, she was so thoroughly integrated into the vociferous crowd (with Doc's maternalistic palm sometimes resting on the back of her hand) that her sotto voce intercourse with Caleb was largely unnoticed in the cornucopian clouds of communication emanating from the throne that passed over and between their lowered heads. But the Director never missed very much in a scene. At one point, dragging on his cigarette, Doc glanced down and asked "What are you two love-birds whispering about?"

But the Doc did not wait for an answer, absorbed as he was in tactfully maieutic examination of Ben's anecdotes about the garment industry that had sheltered itself amid the sea-crafts of the netting needle before the waterfront was infected with apolaustic values. And later on, when Belle participated as a cheerfully attentive auditor in the general exchange, her special attention to Caleb appeared to be forgotten.

For a long time it seemed Ben's night more than Doc's. He knew the living personae of Dogtown as if they were mere probationary and decadent entries on a broadly horizontal array of interconnected or simply parallel kith-and-kin charts going back as far as the year of his grandfather's exisle from the Lower East Side of Ur. Unlike Shelly (likewise derived from Ashkenazi, but via the city of Brotherly love), he was fascinated by gambling. His Factory Store was profitable enough, but he made a good living on the side by occasionally conducting personal sales promotions for other businessmen at shopping centers from New Uruk to Markland. All his motivations had been mercenary and Sybaritic, and unsurprisingly the more successful of his two sons had become a plastic surgeon. But when he saw no conflict with selfinterest Ben was goodnaturedly charitable, and he looked jovial, like a Silenus without beard or ass: the town's biographical comedian, as able as Rameau's nephew to hold the attention of town philosophers, even in the cheerful presence of a remarkable gypsy girl.

Who for a time meanwhile scowled at Caleb under the umbrella of noisy cross-talk. "You thought you could sneak home tonight after I went to bed!" she hissed. "You were walking on air. How disgusting, with the sweat still on your brow!"

She made him giggle but she didn't make him talk.

"It's infuriating, I must say. With all your pretensions to refinement! In broad daylight too—probably off under a bush on the Foreside. To think I once trusted myself to you out there in the fog!

Have you no sense of decency, to profane our love like that? You're as shameless as that dog of yours. Are males all alike after all: licentious and faithless?"

He was now snorting in his Scotch, almost doubled up with stifled laughter, but she continued to rail at him with narrowed eyes ablaze, now and then pausing to purse her lips and sadly shake the gay curls of her sable aureole.

"Or were you tumbling in some hardworking fisherman's conjugal bed in the middle of the afternoon, like a common sailor loose on the beach? Don't you ever consider a married woman's reputation?

". . . But maybe it was worse than that. I wouldn't be surprised if you were out at the end of the breakwater debauching a high-school virgin while the Coast Guards were watching with binoculars from the lighthouse! Are you trying to overpopulate this rock? Or just corrupt as many girls as you can? It would be just like you, with all your Sumerian fantasies!

". . . Jesus, I can hardly imagine your disgraceful behavior! What have you got to say for yourself—you fraud—before I give you back your trinity?" She fingered the lanyard on her neck as if on the point of tearing open the buttons of her decorous blouse to rid herself of the suspended amulet to which she was calling his attention in the invisible hollow of her chest.

"Do I—do I always wear *my* heart—for all—all the world to see?" he spluttered at last, swaying in his chair and holding his belly with both hands, blushing more than ever as he reveled in her attention to his exploits.

"It's not my heart and you're not all the world!" Wrinkling her nose and sniffing she suddenly paused confidentially without taking her eyes off his, the dimpled ends of her thin Anglo-gypsy lips beguiling him with a sly smile. "You know, I can keep secrets as well as tell them. —But I'm not begging!"

By this time Caleb was choking, half under the table, all but rolling on the floor. He feared the company would think he was suffering an attack of the grand mal—if not poisoned by the unexceptionable mixture of dough, cheese, seasoning, anchovies, and grain alcohol—or at least would begin to take notice of his and her childish frivolity in ducking the responsibility of attention to their seniors. Even Belle was alarmed at his hysterical reaction.

But she hadn't finished saying her piece, and he'd said nothing that failed to further provoke her curiosity. The fuel of his convulsive stubbornness renewed the flame that she affected to be consumed by.

"By the way, I hope you don't have the insulting gall to think I'm jealous! If so, never speak to me again!"

Unable to compose himself in the face of her protracted whimsy at his expense, Caleb found it necessary to leave his place and stumble to the Men's Room, all too aware that her eyes were casting ambivalent arrows into the unarmored spot between his shoulder blades. She of course could never have guessed the true story, he told himself as he stood in semi-privacy and retraced with subsiding chuckles his memories of that Moon-day's actual scandal. She'd divined nothing but residual symptoms which (judging only from gait and physiognomic complexion) might have betrayed a number of different aerobically exerted emotions. She knew practically nothing about how he spent his time away from Apostles Dock.

Of course if Caleb himself were guessing at what transpired during a bout of his own amnesia he'd have had more intimate aftereffects to draw upon for evidence. But he was sobering up, and began for the first time to perceive the deeper ironies of what had happened to him. There was no amnesia—only doubts about what I E C might have missed. He remembered details, but the picture was clouded here and there like a Romantic monotype painted upon the clearly etched plate of an Everyman scene. Yet he had entered the Main-Top feeling quite pleased with his life, full of pity for the crew of old domesticated men he joined, and still wasn't fazed by the liberties Belle took in teasing him.

*

Bill Babwell of PERSONS LIMITED still hoped to find the Fathers a regular housekeeper (or at least a part-time cook) for their normal requirements, but he had failed to assure them of a temporary commissary staff for the few days of the forthcoming Chapter. At his suggestion Chris had desperately urged the notion of a caterer. The Doghouse was recommended. Lothario O'Toole had never done any catering before, but as an ambitious businessman he thought he might be able to spare the requisite personnel, while employing a few of his loyal old reserves at the restaurant itself, despite the unusual scarcity of seasonal help all over the Cape (due in part to the academic year's snow storms which had brought cancellation of too many school-days that had to be made up for in June). In any year there were conflicting demands at the peak load of Gloucestermas; but his reputation would be considerably enhanced if he could meet this managerial challenge and perhaps establish a new branch of culinary operations to help absorb his overhead.

At lunchtime on Monday the Superior had said "Father Lucey just called from Botolph. He has arranged for Mr O'Toole to send over someone today to survey our facilities and prepare an estimate. I'm sure it's going to be fearfully expensive, but we seem to have no alternative if we're all going to make best use of our precious reunion time. Just plain food: cold lunches, and wine at dinner only. Something like that. It's not as if we're putting on banquets!"

"I've eaten at the Doghouse." Caleb calmly replied. "They seem to have a clean kitchen and a competent chef."

"Mr O'Toole's assistant is coming over at three. I'll talk to her for a few minutes, but I'm going to tea with Monsignor Navarro later this afternoon and I'm afraid you'll have to take the time to show her all the details."

When Caleb was called down from his office he found Lilian née Cloud finishing her interview with Father Duncannon in the kitchen. From his upper window he had watched her drive up and accept from Ibi the seemly salutation of kith. (The dog had returned from his morning peregrination because nowadays the Jewish Shepherd girl was evidently kept indoors on most afternoons.) The blackhaired Moonfeather was clad in her modified white uniform. For the first time her golden wedding ring was visible to the unsuccessful pseudo-suitor.

Faintly smiling as they were introduced, Mrs Algo took his hand firmly like a grave negotiator and did not respond to the distinguishing pressure of his fingers. Cooking and service questions had already been raised; menus, quantities, and schedules had been discussed: but Mrs Algo's notebook was still open and the Father Superior, in his round collar and black clerical suit, was moving to the door with fedora in hand. It remained for Caleb to show her the great hall in which meals would be served, as well as the Lab's portals, pantries, sideboards, and circulation spaces. He was expected to warn her of the architectural inconveniences and work out with her the logistical solutions to various problems of delivery, table service, washings-up, and other specifications upon which the Doghouse bid would be based.

Starting the rounds after Father Duncannon was gone Caleb found her less reserved but little less businesslike in her subtly ironic manner. Silently dodging his sportive advances, she refused to put away her notebook and pencil. So he decided to take his cue as her solemn client, meticulously avoiding so much as a touch of her elbow as he guided her about.

It had never been pretended that anyone else's competitive proposal would be solicited, but his chief professional anxiety about the service, as the Lab's disinterested business manager about to favor his own secret interest, was not relieved until he ascertained that she herself would indeed plan, join, and supervise the entire operation without interference from her sweaty boss.

Swiftly she took in all matters relevant to the job, missing no contingent detail that might affect her office, but Caleb immediately sensed her keen interest in the whole milieu. The highest card he held was her desire to see as much of the monastery and its furnishings as he was willing. But indeed in some instances it was as if the guest of a driver was being shown exotic scenery she'd never expected to see. To the degree that he took inconsequential liberties with his responsibility as sexton of the monastic manse, little by little he was allowed inconsequential liberties of speech.

It would have been too irresponsible to expose the priests' private quarters, so after but glancing at the second-floor hallway of doors they ascended the uppermost stairs, that she might get an idea of the additional cells for monks or servants. But there at the top, with a wordless smile, she declined to be entrapped by his hint to step in and see the view from his quondam bedroom. Consequently he was in a rather grumpy mood when he urged her back downstairs to the great hall so that he could grant her stated wish to be led further down by the narrow circular steps of rough-hewn granite to the chapel and sacristy in the basement. Until then Ibi had led or followed them with olfactory inspections every step of the way, but since he was forbidden the sacred spaces Caleb now sent him outdoors to await them on the driveway in front of the ground-level french doors which lighted the west end of the chapel and were used for access by nonresident communicants.

"This reminds me of the Princess Tower." she whispered, her first acknowledgement of intimacy, as she cautiously felt her way behind him down the winding stairs with the notebook tucked under an arm and the pencil restored to her shouldered purse—as if to exorcise the sullenness which she did not fail to detect in his abrupt taciturnity of disappointment.

Entering the chapel behind him she dipped her fingers in the holy-water stoup and stood crossing herself as she gazed at the softly flickering red lamp of the reserved Sacrament that hung from the low ceiling and at the crucifix above the cloth-covered altar. "So this is where you serve! In a cave of living rock!"

They turned into the sacristy, once a cul-de-sac laundry room of quarried granite. Until Caleb switched on the electricity it was lighted only by a single small window, as high small and deep as the illuminator of a martyr's cell. At her request he opened the wide drawers of embroidered linen and brocaded vestment accessories.

"When I was a little girl up in Los Dados the priest's lean-to sacristy seemed more sacred than the altar, but the officious old lady in charge of it never allowed me so much as a sniff of these holies."

Reverently she took in the faintly mildewed sacerdotal fragrance, with hands behind her back bending over to see the treasures he opened for her. (He himself had never before seen so much of them.) Then to please her most he opened without comment the great oaken wardrobe that Lancelot Duncannon had brought from Etruria before he could know that it would house his own monastery's solemn canonicals and gorgeous armor of the Lord for every season of the calendar. For a moment in motionless awe she feasted upon the array of sacred apparel, daring not to touch, too dazzled to differentiate them.

Then piously bending to sniff the odor of sanctity she noticed, at one end of the bar on which the vestments hung, several black hauberks of more common use by both clergy and acolyte. She pointed to the last and shortest cassock, her eyes lighting with gladdened intimation. "Is that one yours, Mr Karcist? —Put it on. I want to see how you look in it!"

Hesitating at this impropriety, admixed to the basic guilt of conducting such an indiscreet tour, he was nevertheless ruled by the woman's suddenly revealed partiality, reckoning that there'd be no embarrassing intrusion by tourists. Shedding his jacket he donned the layman's soutane and began to fasten its long closely fitting row of neck-to-knee buttons as she watched with what seemed the Immediate Exclusive Consciousness of an inquiring dog.

"Button it all the way to the top," she demanded, "and turn around. —What a beautiful man you are!"

Unbuttoning in the glow of her astounding approval, he asked her if she'd like to look around the grounds.

"No, thank you, sir. My God, you'd be a perfect priest—if only your petticoat weren't showing! You forgot to take off your trousers, Father Karcist! Let's get rid of them; there should be no bottom margin." Her own skirt she slitted open in a single motion, unzipping a hidden seam. "I'm not wearing mine. Underneath the prim white dress I'm still a heathen squaw, without a shift to my name, last of the Yahi. I had thought of the Great Hall, but the sacristy's almost as good as the altar itself."

She switched off the light and took it upon herself to refasten the upper buttons he had just undone, even as he was still unbuttoning his skirts to do her bidding. "Keep those buttons tight at the neck so I can see them as far down as the bottom of your chest. All you lack is a pectoral cross."

She fetched one of the low rush-bottomed kneeling chairs from the chapel and set it at an angle in the shadows just inside the Roman-arched stone doorway between the chapel and its green room. She made him sit where if he turned his head half to the right and kept his eyes open he could watch Ibi dozing on guard at the approach to the main door of the Lab, and where at the same time obliquely over his right shoulder she herself could take in or shut out the twilight scene of the holy dais. Her purse and notebook were flung down on the stone floor. She had slipped the gold ring off her left hand and tossed it onto the shelf in front of the sacristy's glass cupboard of holy vessels, the only flat surface she could find nearer than the credence table in the chancel. "My body hasn't changed for the worse since you deflowered me."

Even after his parts had instantly responded to the surprise they were always ready for, he was momentarily taken aback by the judicious vehemence with which she found ways to kiss his forehead, ears, eyes, and lips despite the disadvantages of her position for that purpose. Her initiative revealed itself too quickly for him to wonder at the time whether she had been waiting to seize this particular opportunity or was herself surprised by an unpremeditated impulse that she was always prepared to indulge. Yet simply by the anatomical facts of penistration he felt himself the aggressive opportunist in a triumph of I E C, into which his hitherto broadly objective prehension of the occasion was condensing.

All the same, his eyes did not close before noticing that Ibi had risen from the nearby lawn to see what hindered his walking god's progress through the forbidden cave, now that voices were no longer to be heard, though peering at little more than his own reflection no matter what the angle at which he cocked his interrogative brows and radar ears at the glass. Caleb chuckled to see the face of innocent perplexity, until the dog abandoned that problem and sat patiently to watch all exits, the pathos of his faith in noble profile.

"What are you laughing at?" she absently asked under her slowly accelerating breath, a transfigured equestrienne facing with

Lil-Amin's thin ironically twisted lips and vacant half-closed eyes the whitewashed ledge of Lady Gloucester's bone in back of the altar. But with lengthened and increasingly strenuous reciprocation his failure to reply went unnoticed.

The introit was fitting but not solemn, yet there was no fooling around: it was masterful and playful withal, masculine for both male and female, as if she'd had enough of the feminine inversion in all the years he'd been famished for it. Thereafter catechumenal word and ceremony were omitted, sanctification and all the variables: getting directly to the canon.

But neither immediate consciousness became so exclusive as to escape the arrow of time. The mutually shaped but functionally determined transition to their purpose, deeply appreciated and deeply appreciating, was the topical atonement of numberless ions seeking redress in coincidental concentration. His ultimate was the distinctly transitive sensation of pursed release almost as prolonged as thunder after lightning; hers seemed to reverberate in a vaster firmament: together palpable in extinction. Disparate but synchronous syncope. For a few minutes one might have thought that the biosphere would never expect mortal repetition of such triumphal dispatch.

Nevertheless it seemed to him (in later contemplation) that she owed the success of her superiority to an anticipatory gathering and reduction of broad feelings into her I E C—an essentially secret affect which he could guess at only when his own mind had returned from the fathoming that was only the proximate cause of it, as her initiatory measures had been only the proximate cause of that cause.

As they recovered awareness of their shared circumstances no words were spoken to opine or test the equality of two such private crescendos. But at least until rising to part from the two-backed beast she was amazingly modified in attitude and affection, adoring (though not infinitely adoring) of the acolyte she'd never marry. The young lovers of five years earlier, momentarily relieved of frustration anxiety and calculation, were reunited in maturity—more sacrilegiously than Heloïse and Abelard, husband and wife in the refectory of her convent, but with less to fear.

Furniture and garments replaced or smoothed, their persons restored to respectability, she kissed his mouth again with passion reminded by returning consciousness of civilized society's ineluctable constraints. He hoped this demonstrated gratification was a foretaste of continued dialectic, but it might as well have been a long-delayed codicil announcing that she and her baggage were leaving him forever. In his very exultation as a lover he knew he should be trembling once again with premonition, as well as with the sense of gratuitous impiety he still excluded from his dilating conscience.

She turned and genuflected to the tabernacle as they reached the french doors. At the small unconventionally placed Table of Prothesis, noticing a few pennies that hadn't recently been collected from the dish, she stopped to contribute one from her purse.

"No." He made her take it back. "That would be mockery. It's for when you go to Communion."

"But haven't I already?" she smiled, already looking at her watch. "It's later than I thought! I'll be overdue for my shift. Please blow into my ear, to defend me from Loathey's abuse. I don't want to quit until this job is over.

"—Ibi, it's not polite to sniff at a lady's legs! —I fear that your Time-Space-Causality has taken advantage of my negative capability, Mr Triple-K . Was I too audacious in confessing my lunar disposition?"

"It showed you haven't lost your masculinity. You overwhelmed me."

"No, I overtook you!"

He wanted to touch and kiss, but for any observer who couldn't hear her speech she'd resumed the open-air deportment of Mrs Grundy. "I hope you didn't put me in the family way again." he pretended to jest.

"Maybe I did. You felt like the Holy Ghost. But often one can have the T and the S without the C . Gil's almost given up hope. He thinks he's a sterile stallion—a dud stud, he weeps!"

"And he's given up trying?" Caleb teased.

"This is a case where it's obviously not my defect. He wants to go to a clinic and get his molecules enumerated, but I say it's a sickening idea, vulgar and demeaning—therefore insulting to me. An unworthy excuse to insinuate himself with nurses. I'm sure you'd be too proud to stand up and be counted! Certainly I wouldn't deign to, were I a man! Can you imagine Gilgamesh or Cuchulain submitting himself to haruspication?"

She offered her hand. "Good bye, Mister Fourth K . You'll have our estimate tomorrow. What a handsome man Father Duncannon is! Thanks for showing me around. It was my adultery, not yours: I'm the married one. It was profaned love—perhaps in vain."

"No: *in*-faned!"

At the wheel of her car she finished the subject with her crooked smile and quizzical eyebrow: "Don't worry. I was upside down. But if I have another baby she won't be Mooney's sister merely by half."

Suddenly making haste, she accelerated almost before the starter finished turning, and sped down the drive, out of sight at the lower curve. But there was a sudden screech of brakes and locked wheels skidding on gravel; and straightaway her car came accelerating backward up the hill. Caleb was alarmed for Ibi's safety, who had been politely following her to the margin of his estate and was not accustomed to such inefficient motion. He had to dance out of the way and then catch up the game.

"I forgot my ring!" she called through the window. "On the sideboard! —My God, what if I hadn't thought of it! I often leave it at home and never miss it!"

She staying in the car with her motor running as he ran back to fetch the overlooked talisman.

Since the french doors were locked behind them he had to dash a long way up by the front door, tortuously careening through the echoing rooms to the stairs, and down again to the sacristy. What if the little yellow band (all too habitual to her eyes) wasn't lying where she remembered last setting it, and she had dropped it unaware—to roll into some nook or corner of the sacristy or chapel? Or if she was entirely mistaken, and had taken it into her purse abstractedly? It was uncertainty that would most undo the day!

He stumbled in the rush, sweating like a criminal about to be cornered with the corpus delicti, not only from the delay injurious to Lilian's reputation as a trusted employee but also from the shame of self-distrust as to his own. At the best it would be a near escape from the enervating possibility that an inexplicable ring would be found by Father Duncannon as he dusted his sacristy in the morning. The worst fear was that the priest might drive up right now, before the search was finished!

But her memory was more valid than his terror. He found her marriage-badge at once, his heart pounding, illogically thankful it hadn't been a less respectable article. Before returning he methodically examined their venue for other clues, compulsively determined not to leave a trace of his transgression (call it what he might—crime, vice, or sin). But he didn't so hasten back through the chapel that he refrained from testing the ring, which got stuck less than half way up his finger of betrothal.

"That was a close call." she calmly remarked, holding a lighted cigarette in her mouth as she twisted the smooth gold fillet from his bony flesh with an impatient jerk. The car was already disappearing as she replaced it on her left hand and gave him a backward wave with her smoking right.

Neither of them had uttered the verb *love*. It was oddly awkward for this troubadour to sound that word even with this married woman whom he didn't wish to abduct, albeit the more flattering to his attributes that it wasn't required of him. But he thought their particular transitory concrescence of phenomena had invited the noumenal term if any beatitude ever did.

Almost five o'clock! Caleb hurried to take leave of the office and lock up the house before Father returned. The altar boy could not have faced his priest again so soon without telltale confusion. He hoped to get home before the Lab's little Autotod passed him on the only thoroughfare.

And so it was that when Belle encountered him elated flushed and guilty-looking, she had guessed at the adventure from secondary evidence. Indeed he was walking on air in the masculinity of having been so charmingly mounted, and casting condescension on all men whose amours were less wanton, even Solomon in all his glory with a thousand fungible wives to populate his palace without compunction; but the sanguine sweat was not from erotic calisthenics. Nor had the slight contusion on his back been inflicted by the inelastic seating with any discomfort. (He would cherish it like a dueling scar.) In fact the psychogenic heat crowning his head was the effect of feelings that fluctuated arrhythmically between supreme felicity and unforeseen misgivings about the conjunction of atonement, sacrilege, and the Seventh Commandment.

Yet in one of his ensuing views of the event, sometimes uppermost, the consummation of his heart's desire had been marred not by the common sensuality of Phoenix and Clitoria but by the aesthetic imperfection of a gross undisrobed matching that was dominated by the part as it diminished the person: a nuptial without the wholesomeness of naked leisure in a green mansion under filtered sunlight, or in the palmtree shadows of a Typee beach under the moon, or in the sensuous luxury of unreserved skin on smooth clean bed linen, broad as a queen's, perfumed with frankincense and Easter lilies. It hadn't been sordid, to be sure, nor as fettered as bundling—but somewhat decadent and even slattern, as undignified as ordinary fucking always is to the objective sensibility. He had seen or caressed practically nothing of the woman he craved and of course really loved. Was it little more distinctive than any happily simultaneous rut, easily duplicated anywhere on earth by others? By herself? Had he learned any more about the inner Mooncloud?

Notwithstanding this incipient criticism of his latest uncouth behavior, before he reached home these mixed reflections not only renewed the higher unattained desire but also yet again revived the irresistible challenge to satisfy the lower as more than a halfway measure. Because he had not yet reviewed all Lilian's words, especially those that suggested what his mother would have called the "broodiness" in her ironic lubricity, he was whistling and skipping (and not thinking too much), his soothed and balmy nerves anticipating he knew not what in repeated achievement, when he stumbled upon Belle at the Apostles. Despite her sudden attack, which had defenselessly raised his color, he was still empowered with the new confidence of a confirmed communicant at the court of love.

But now, returning from his brief sequestration to the multiplicity of noises in the Main-Top, awaited by Belle's frown, who was again tapping her fingers impatiently on the table and apparently paying no heed to the conversations around her, his thoughts were reverting to the probability that a mystical experience of casually bared loins was not extraordinary for heroes like Dave Wilson, well versed in all varieties of fornication, or for spliced centaurs like Dexter Keith—nor for Tom Dick and Harry either!

"I just remembered something!" Belle grabbed his wrist and scrutinized his face. "I bet it was that Doghouse woman!" she hurled at him in her aside. "She must be off work in the afternoon!"

Once more, but with acute alarm, he replied only with giggles to her demand for an answer. This time he defended himself by a counterattack that in any other circumstances he would not have deigned. "What about Flash Silva?" he at last replied in kind, but non sequitur, choking on his degradation with jocular vengeance, "Just as one example."

She grimaced with scorn for his lame and ungallant riposte—which happened to be pitiably off the present mark.

*

DEXTER KEITH: I sailed Redburn's ocean in Landing Ship for Tanks 1066. After August 1945 it was boring out there. When I finally revealed to the skipper that I was an F D R Crat he spitefully added to my duties the title of Recreation Officer. I tried to get our men to use the empty tank deck for theatricals, but all they wanted there was basketball, movies, and loudspeaker music.

Then all the decks were filled with humanity when we called at Mardi atoll to pick up Cipangese prisoners for repatriation. All the time we lay there the lagoon was overcast and dead. We didn't know its bottom was littered with logistic ships sunk by our carrier planes. Except for that attack the Navy had simply bypassed Cipangu's dreaded "Gibraltar of the Pacific".

SHELLY SCHLOSSBERG [*calling from the bar*]: The anthropologists wrecked Jack London's *Snark* before they found the Trobriands while looking for Mardi and Kokovoko. They had thought a ketch was too small to take along a navigator!

DOCTOR CHARLEMAGNE: Redburn made it in an open whaleboat less than a third as big.

WAT CIBBER: Could have done it in a sailing dory.

DOC: In the '30s Fay Morgan's party had a good crew but they never got to Mardi in the *Omoo*, which was a good-sized topsail schooner—actually a converted brigantine—because the Cipangese threatened to sink them if they got too close. She had to rely on ethnological extrapolation and hearsay.

WAT: The whole expedition was half-cocked anyway. Should have had a fast and able Gloucester-built schooner. Much handier, from the Arctic to the South Seas. Hermaphrodites were always too cranky, especially for liberals and amateurs.

DEX [*aside*]: I remember quoting Redburn in one of my sentimental letters to her, when we all had plenty of time to read for inspiration. The L S T seemed like a real ship and I thought I was a real Navy man. "To a seaman, a ship is no piece of mechanism merely; but a creature of thoughts and fancies, instinct with life. Standing at her vibrating helm, you feel her beating pulse. I have loved ships as I have loved men." But my ship was vibrant with stinking diesels; it was a quartermaster striker, not I, who stood at the helm below me where I couldn't see him at all as I conned from topside; and the helm was a lever that he turned like an elevator operator's. Yet I did feel her and in the end I loved her. Especially after we knew she wouldn't be blown to hell on a Cipango beach. I wondered if it would feel like a sailing ship inside Glory too when she was pregnant, hoping I'd get home long enough before her labor, or six weeks after it.

DOC: Redburn said a whaleboat was "the cunningest thing in its way ever fabricated by man". He called the one he stole his *Chamois*, "little sea-goat". But in his son's paintings you find dories, not whaleboats.

HUCK: Which son?

DOC: The white one Lizzie never knew about. Mary Mitchell's smuggled bairn, fostered off for pay on a family in Whaletown before she returned to her telescope out on Tasheto where he'd been conceived in the sand dunes. Jack Chase found out about his main-top pupil's disgraceful whaling curriculum (and forgave him for it), but even he never knew about this by-blow of the family man in Ur. Only now has the secret been unearthed by Goody Keith [*nodding toward Dexter*], our nifty mentor of Gloucesterbooks.

DEX: Alfred Blackburn Walkyr (known to his friends as Blacky), the great and only Subluminist!

GEPETTO DAGETTO [*breaking away from a nearby conversation to join in, with a wail of scorn for dilettantes who pretend to appreciate the unappreciated master*]: Oh-ooo! Say nothing against him! Leave him in peace! A man of granite to the bone, with drift and grain for those with the heart to see! "The artist must live to paint and not paint to live. He cannot be a good fellow." He spoke the truth, and proved it with his hands! His studio he called a workshop! "Everything comes to the patient artist"!

HUCK: A Subluminist is to a Luminist as sap-faced granite is to Carrara marble. A hundred and sixty eight pounds per cubic foot to a hundred and forty! The weight of our glacial rocks on abandoned pastures is what brought him here in the first place.

PETTO: And the sea that contends with the living rock!

WAT: And the boats with rock for ballast?

DOC: He came to watch our seabirds too. In those days this was still the only place to find Maxwells. But he almost never painted them to be recognized. Jason has the only one I know of—called *Dead Angel*. The gull's laid out like a Chardin still-life. It's painted on the cover of a cigar box. Jason won't let it out of his house. The public of Walkyr's Dogtown, his island of refuge and inspiration, is left with nothing but two cracking canvasses—the one of our old windmill and the one he miscalled *Tir-na-Dog*, strangely enough a headland above an ocean that looks like the tidal sea of undulating sand and fish in the land of Prester John that Mandeville reported. They're stupidly hung where no one can see them on the hottest and coldest walls of the Atheneum Free Library's infirmary for dogeared books—while pilgrims and connoisseurs are beseeched to admire dozens of illuminated Fritz U Lanes in the genteel air-conditioned Cape Gloucester Literary Scientific and Historical Lyceum on the other side of the same Acropolis! Goody Keith says she hasn't been able to do anything about it.

DEX: She's tried, believe me! Even the mayor and earldermen couldn't do anything about it—if they wanted to trouble themselves with arcane artifacts. There's a Library Board that hates the pictures but can't bear to risk any controversy by moving them an inch from their original position.
PETTO: If Walkyr had been a sculptor he'd have turned Purdeyville Common into his garden gallery!
DOC: But not his studio. Nature was always his study, but he said he never sketched or painted in front of nature. He'd sit among the Purdeyville rocks and junipers only to write poetry!
HUCK: But Purdeyville's where most of the Walkyr forgeries have been inspired, starting long before he was dead.
DOC: That's where he took the visiting old poet for a walk, and so that's where he first heard that he was misbegotten: Redburn's real-life Ishmael. His natural father had come to our Lyceum on a lecture tour about Old World art. They walked as far as Cynosure Rock, a world-neglected writer long past youth's celebrity and his uninformed bastard whose fame would come at the end of life when for good reason he feared visits by the New Uruk Board of Health.

They had proposed to talk about Redburn's published poetry in verse or prose and Walkyr's avocation—and more generally the infusions of imagination in fictions and pictures. The painter was flattered by the opportunity, which he thought no one else could have more fully deserved because for many years in reading he had been convinced of his spiritual affinity with this almost forgotten hero. But the prosaic fact now clumsily sprung upon him was such a shock that he found himself accusing his elder of lunacy.

But of course they were both madmen anyway—nocturnal madmen. That joyless meeting was their only one, even though they later lived in the same precints of Ur. Redburn had been prematurely fatherless himself; but he didn't need another son.

What he'd yearned for was a peer in humor. After he graduated from the limited genius of Jack Chase that's what the psyche of Natty Hawhaw so sadly disappointed him of.

The confession—or claim—was too much for Walkyr's self-respect. He never got over the pain. But after his death, twenty-five years later than the retired Customs Inspector's, a poem of his own was found on a hidden scrap of paper, without names and too metaphorical for anyone then to decode, which now shows that he really had no doubt. He knew their Jonah-daimons were alike. Yet he never forgot (as bards and psychologists often do) that it took two blocks to make his chip.

DEX: Gloria's working on the maternal contribution now. He was probably more anguished by losing the filial claim to his alma mater.

BELLE: Yes: you know, he chose to leave his ashes in Whaletown with the beloved carpenter's family that nurtured him. I once did a piece on that. He must have never told them that he knew the secret. They say he was widely esteemed for his sensitivity to other people's feelings.

DOC: Albert Blackburn Walkyr was apparently an attractive man, like his genital father, and likewise convivial most of his life, but was so "gentle and timid" that his friends did more talking than listening; whereas Wellingborough Redburn, before he withdrew from society, was said to be a spellbinding raconteur.

CALEB: Antithesis and thesis!

DOC: Son and sire, or sire and dam? Either way, or both: the Victorian synthesis of shame and secret. In any case, even when ignorant of the astronomy in his blood he always unconsciously reacted against warm sands and clement skies.

CALEB [*aside*]: Still, rather simple. Not a complex number!

DOC: After his unaccepted father died the son did almost nothing but rework perpetually unfinished pictures. In the last years he was often too arthritic to hold a brush, and his eyes were worse than ever; but it wasn't infirmity or artistic exhaustion that stopped his production prematurely. And it didn't have anything to do with the lingering trauma of disaffiliation, he told his Ur neighbor John Yeats, apparently the only one to whom he ever spoke about that secret distress. The two old men were sympathetic in their complementarity—as greater and lesser painter, as Christian and apostate, as worse and better writer, and then as son and father of a literary genius. When taxed with physical neglect of his pictures Walkyr had sometimes been heard to say "Why worry about my children?"—and "when a thing has the elements of beauty from the beginning it cannot be destroyed."

But in the end he admitted to Yeats that he was overtaken by the fatal importance of plastic technicalities. He also regretted his ingenuous trust of artists and connoisseurs when he'd refused to sign most of his paintings. Restorers and volunteer "finishers" were distorting the vision of his pictures; and barefaced imitators too. He wasn't too otherworldy to take notice that an English court had upheld the contention of Higher Falls's expatriate cosmopolitan painter that "a person doesn't wholly own a picture by simply buying it. Ergo," he declared to Yeats, "I have a right to protect my pictures from the vandalism of cleaning. It's appalling, this craze for clean pictures. Nature isn't clean, but it is the right matter in the right place (to paraphrase Faraday)." So, simply because he'd carelessly disregarded the fact that asphaltum of bitumen may take centuries to dry, his life's work was deteriorating almost as soon as his wretched eyesight. Forgeries were already appearing, right down to faked cracks, extrusions, and other details symptomatic of what he called the "inherent vice" in his willful ignorance of methods and materials.

At times what bothered him most was that the poetry everyone saw in his pictures might have been imperishable by replication if from first to last he had created it with parallel sticks of printed symbols as unedified in punctuation and spelling as his father's. And at last he confessed to his Irish confidant that with these intimations of ephemerality he felt overpowered by the typographically preserved imagination of the adventurer he'd been forced to believe he owed his art to—though the man had other children with never a sign of that creative armature. Walkyr's bitterest grievance was that his chivalrous father hadn't told him either the name or place of the other half in his origin.

HUCK: Of all our aestivators, the greatest failure. First he went years without selling a picture, then they excluded him from the Exhibition of Atlantean Art at the Chicago World's Fair—where they hung fifteen Homer Winslows, and six or seven of those were Cape Gloucester maritimes! He said he felt like an inchworm reaching the end of a limb and groping about in space! I know that feeling!

PETTO: No! [*Groaning*] Oh no! Not a failure! Everywhere else a living success! Don't forget the Armory Show! He had lots of exhibitions and prizes before his colors faded! And aging only made his pictures deeper. They don't have to last beyond the end of time! Driftwood also rots! Welded iron falls from rust! Marble stains and cracks! Walls dilapidate! Boulders split with frost, and even a granite colossus can't stay on his toes—[*Doubling up with a shriek of laughter*] Look at Ozymandias!

HUCK: Once he was so poor that he had to saw up his bedboard for a panel to paint on! Over the years he went from dressing natty to looking like a bum. For months he'd cook his dinners in the same unemptied stock pot! For years he never washed a cup or threw away a newspaper.

CALEB: "The Old Masters were great painters," he said, "but one can still be an artist."

DEX: The point is that immortality isn't the distinction between ocean whaleboat and coastal dory.

DOC: There you have a distinction with a difference!

HUCK: Whaleboat is to dory as whaleship is to schooner.

CALEB: Transposing terms, a schooner working whaleboats is therefore equivalent to a whaleship working dories.

WAT: Whaleboat is to dory as mountain goat to donkey. That's the distinction your heroic whalesman made about us fishermen, just because he thought the whale's brain enlightened the world while we brayed like asses about the hard life we led. So I say a whalesman is to a fisherman as a gold-digger is to a quarryman. Where fish are known to be abundant, skill and luck are less necessary than labor. My wife says that's why eleven of the chosen Apostles were fishermen. I tell her that I and all my colleagues each wish we were the one in twelve!

DOC: Let's grant Whaletown the superiority of a whaleboat in its way if Whaletown will grant Dogtown the superiority of a schooner in its. The ships that carried whaleboats were only tolerable for sailing qualities, but schooners were the fastest and ablest machines for taking dories out to sea.

WAT: Irredoubtably! And of course a few tons of midnight oil three or four years in landing never amounted to more than carriage trade alongside the real fish landed day-in and day-out to feed the disunited workers of the world! We went fishing thousands of years before the mighty hunters knew there were pigs out there to stick! We're still fishing, when whaling's as dead as our granite business—even if fishing *is* the work of ignorant asses! That's why the Whaletown folks long ago started to copy our dreary trade. There are still some dories around, at least for lifeboats on the draggers—but where can you find a whaleboat that ain't high and dry in a museum, with a placard to explain it?

HUCK: Even Mardian proas and catamarans have outlived whaleboats! The Navy gave up its version of them after the First War. Whereas toyboat schooners survive at least as effete echoes of the form, and a few real ones are still working in backward parts of the world.

DEX: Listen to an old Navy salt. Since a ship was a square-rigged sailing vessel with three tripartite masts and a bowsprit, and a boat was only a craft that could be hoisted aboard a ship, wouldn't you say in maritime terms that a schooner was an armless half-assed ship?

DOC: *Schooner* may have always been a genus of vessel unacknowledged in Navy biology, neither ship nor bark nor brig, but with two or more compound masts rigged fore-and-aft.

CALEB: *It's two-thirds ship!*

DOC: *Gloucester* is the species classicus, an artifact of creative evolution from right across that channel [*pointing*]: neither androgyne like a brigantine nor hybrid like a Maxwell gull, but in its refinement a beautifully economical machine.

WAT: When labor was cheap.

HUCK: But what was the genus of brigs and barks and barkentines if you didn't call them ships?

WAT: They had their own geniuses.

DOC: My dear young man, nautical orismology is as contextual as the virtues. It's never been consistent or hierarchically logical. You must distinguish between "ship" as a broad genus of hull and "ship" as a narrow species of rig. The important thing is that between boats and ships, schooners are an excluded middle.

WAT: A poetic craft.

DEX: Even in the Navy submarines as big as frigates are called boats.

CALEB: And ocean liners. It grates on the nerves. But still, you can't say "I'm taking ship to Europe" instead of "I'm taking the boat"!

DOC: Childe Caleb speaketh of his obsession.

CALEB [*aside*]: Is he so successful as to be above all longing? Is nothing he wants denied him? If my mother hadn't smoked cigarettes I might have been a centaur too, not a satyr—and had all his advantages, especially a skull enlarged to scale. Or else a Marathon runner.

[*Enter two Gypsies, in leather jackets, high-heel boots, and cowboy hats, ordering boilermakers. Belle, sitting tonight between Doc and Caleb, squirms down, dodging out of their sight.*]

FIRST GYPSY: I thought you said this was a tavern! —Jesus, no DV, jukebox on the blink! Where did that bartender disappear to? What is this, anyway? I guess it looks like one of your coffeeshop hangouts, except I don't see no pussy. Let's get out of here before they start reading poetry!

SECOND GYPSY: Don't worry about that. But I'm willing to go. Must have changed hands since last month. [*Exeunt Gypsies.*]

HUCK: When I was in high school Dogtown schooners were world-famous. No one knew they were doomed! They were still launching one or two a year over in Chebego, and a few high-liners kept making money. But 1934 was their peak year. The *Gloucesterman* had been to Washington and the Chicago World's Fair, and the whole country had seen her in the newsreels when the President went aboard. (Not that anybody in the Midwest ever learned how to say or spell the name.) But then F D R surprised everybody by showing up here at Glo'mas and giving her his Catholicrat blessing, along with the rest of the fleet. That was the thrill of my life. But he was gone before the press caught up with him.

BEN *{calling from another table}*: I sold a lot of candy that day.

DOC: The first time I saw him. I was just starting up my wagon stage for the summer. Later I found out that he was taking a secret three-day vacation with the Arnheims out at Krackenhurst. Jason Anacoluther's family were neighbors. That's when he met F D R and became a lifelong money-raiser for the Crats.

DEX: How could the trip be a secret?

DOC: In those days it was possible. His train sneaked out of Washington at night and by-passed Botolph on the freight tracks. Like the single private cars hauled up here every summer his whole consist was shunted onto the Grove siding at the site of the old West Seamark station. So it was easy to whisk him off to the Foreside in his own bodyguarded limousine. But Duke Richard of Tybbot got wind of it and stayed away in a pet. He punished his people for their treacherous applause by choosing not to show his face in Dogtown at all that summer.

DEX: Just because they cheered their Crat president?

DOC: Even more because F D R was staying with Jews—and foreign Jews to boot, who as Tybbot suspected were conspiring to defend their wealth as much as possible against confiscation by setting up Aryan-fronted subsidiaries over here in anticipation of what was coming in Europe. They had already begun to transfer assets to an Atlantean trust at a bank in Charter Oak.

CALEB [*aside*]: How does Doc know so much about everything that's interesting about anything?

DOC: The Arnheims were also urging scientists and intellectuals to leave the Continent long before most people took Hitler seriously enough, and gave dozens of them transient refuge at Krackenhurst. During the war they let the S I S take over the Krackenhurst estate. Later they sold it to a corporation lawyer who'd been in the S I S and helped them recover their industrial properties in Holland.

CALEB [*aside*]: Maybe it was Halymboyd! Not DeCamp. The Decamp family's old money brought European connections, and he might well have served in the wartime S I S because he could look and sound like a Junker, but it's hard to imagine him colluding with premature antifascists even of the capitalist variety, or devising clever schemes for unprecedented conditions. Capstick, less unlikely. Later he was commissioned an active Brigadier dentist in the Army, but by then some of the S I S people were in uniform. Anyone in corporate finance might be taken for a lawyer.

The benevolent conspiracy may all be Doc's uncanny guesswork—like my mother's kind, mutatis mutandis—based on Jason's hints; but Parity's direct and indirect investments in Arnheim's Atlantean companies, which also are invested in some of Parity's and Financial Usufruct's direct and indirect holdings, now begin to make some sense! Already Arnheim Electrical Industries seems to have gained far more than it lost to Hitler. Was it specially assisted by the S I S , and visa versa? No one knows how half the Graveyard Street bosses were so inconspicuously successful after the war.

DEX: It's ironic that Krakenhurst ended up with the Gnujian Neognostics, considering the disloyal antisemitism of their schismatic founding father.

BEN [*having been yielded a strong chair opposite Doc*]: It's not the end. They'll find they can't afford to keep it.

DEX: I remember 1934 for the launching of the *Normandie* and the *Queen Elizabeth*, one after the other, when the French and British were still equally respected. It was before I'd ever seen the ocean, but they were never just boats to me. France had the world's greatest army and the British Empire was intact.

WAT: In 1934 our anti-arsonists were still celebrating the Restoration and beginning to lobby for a Compulsory Consumption Amendment. There was no more rum-running, and at the time there was nothing else to smuggle, so you'd think there'd be no need for diverting the attention of firefighters coastguards policemen and other witnesses; but that was the biggest year for three-alarmers! One theory was that the fires were set to guarantee the privacy of orgies in Purdeyville or affairs of dishonor on the beaches. But times were hard, and I shouldn't wonder if there was some correlation between accidental flames and insurance policies. Ever since then insurance premiums have been much too high in Dogtown, like our gasoline prices.

HUCK: Two of the fires were smokescreens for murders. My mother's uncle was one of the victims.

WAT: That was a motive second only to bankruptcy. Those two unsolved cases didn't get us into the newsreels but for months they were infamous on the front pages of the Botolph papers. The State Police weren't any smarter than the Dogtown police wanted to be.

CALEB [*aside*]: Another almost forgotten anxiety! My mother thought she knew that the killer and his protectors believed she somehow knew who he was, like the knowing woman who was burned to death or half cremated after death in the Village house fire. That's why the troublemaking Mary Tremont fled to the Isle of Manannan in the summer of 1934, after Glo'mas. Ten years later in being fired by the *Botolph Crier* something leaked out about her crazy attempt to revive the investigation, and she again feared for her life and mine, even in Unabridge. It was mainly for that reason that we moved to Montvert, beyond any corrupt jurisdiction. Now a full generation later she still warns me that it's dangerous to show archeological interest in a hypersensitive case long since swept under the rug: you should never rule out the most improbable consanguinities or affinities of any person you're talking to in this town of deceptive surnames and interbred faces, nor assume that playful criticisms or recalled ironies won't be misunderstood as dangerous. How can an outsider like me know who's still alive with family secrets to guard? But again, I must read the autobiography: it might be my impubic memory that has magnified and distorted her casual suspicion of one or two then in high places. Softly now. Doc alone can I trust to ask in disinterested fashion, or Father Duncannon, for safe recollections of those public events.

HUCK: Attempted murders too. Funeral pyres. Evil was afoot that year. We've never deserved to regain the County Seat. Can you imagine with a straight face the Gloucester County Courthouse in a town that won't tolerate traffic lights?

DEX: Or the laws of the Commonwealth.

DOC: Evil? What is evil? Evil things, evil deeds, but not Evil-an-sich. The Tudor Reverend Merry Sterne called that the Fallacie of Attributive Substance—or what I'd propose as the Fallacy of Reified Qualification. It's not confined to discussion of Platonic Ideas.

CALEB: *Idea* in Greek was equivalent to *species* in Latin.

DOC: Yeah, and so the error was carried even into the nominalism of our day. That's what Merry's lost manuscript was about— as a revision of the Book of Common Prayer, along with some sermons by way of gloss. In the 17C it would have been pure heresy to Petrines and Paulines alike. It smacked of something worse than the Pelagian. And theologians are not the only ones still insensitive to the fallacy. By the way, it was in 1934 that the then Perdita discovered that casket of his papers in her ancestral cellar hole.

DEX: Inez Canary, my wife's favorite Gloucesterbook writer, has been winnowing out the hoaxes spawned in the idleness of the Depression!

DOC: This is no chaff, Mister Bureaucrat! *(Grinning mysteriously)* One must keep some secrets even from Goody's good historians! But when Dogtown College is planted she shall be the curator of its archaeological treasures! Meanwhile I'll deny as pure fiction everything I've just told you!

CALEB [*aside*]: Dare I ask Deeta to show me? Do I have that privilege just because I dream about her? I'm sure Father Duncannon, as a native, would be most interested!

DOC: But you may assure your Clio that she's on the right track about the Cavalcanti brothers in her quasi-similitudinous history. Another manuscript in Sterne's same ditty box, *A True Historie of the Naturals Found at Cape Gloucester in the Drogeo Plantations*, confirms her hypothesis about those Tuscan sea dogs having been cast away here, one searching for the other, and assimilated by the Irindus.

THAD KRYOTHERMSKY *(speaking at this table for the first time)*: Speaking for the Church, 1934 was a Great Year, like this one, because the Feast of St Peter and St Paul fell under the octave of Pentecost—following the latest possible Easter.

CALEB [*aside*]: If it was such a great vintage, why am I a minim?

PETTO: Octave? [*Whooping*] Must be a spy-glass in the zodiac!

THAD: An eight-day week. Less than a novena.

CALEB: The binary third power! As in an eight-channel paper tape, or a computer's byte.

PETTO [*doubling up and slapping his thigh*]: That's more than a bite—it's a mouthful!

WAT: Ask any dog: a bite is capital punishment.

DOC: 1934 was a sad year for dogs. In those days one of my East Harbor neighbors was a magnificent Viking Shepherd matriarch—killed in a studio fire that seemed to me to also end the art of original painting in Dogtown.

CALEB [*aside*]: Next Saturday night, if he's alone, shall I tell him my mother's name?

SERGEANT PROCTOR [*in mufti, off duty, joining from another table*]: I remember that one! Smoke inhalation, not burns. I was a part-time rookie then, lucky to be on harbor patrol. After Restoration the police boat didn't have much to do except help with waterfront fires. In those days our pressure-pumps couldn't pass much water.

[*Laughter in the audience.*]

DOC: That dog never got to like me.

PROCTOR: As I recall, it was about the beginning of Glo'mas. The same night there was the big Gold Coast Hotel fire in West Marsh, which of course we couldn't get near in a boat, so they had only one engine left in East Harbor and we took one of their hoses at the landing. As usual, the individual fire captain who happened to be on duty didn't completely put it out the first time. It rekindled the next day. The studio was converted from an old stable, so he had the excuse of grain and straw smoldering in the walls—like the Barebones fire this year, only they caught it the second time before it burned up anything on that floor except the paintings and stuff like that. In those days I liked cats—didn't much notice dogs—but it stuck in my mind that a big animal like that could die from a little smoke. Everybody else got out all right.

DEX: Your job may get harder. The Puritans are cranking up agitation for a leash law.

PROCTOR: It'll be harder yet if the Libertines win out with their petitions to prohibit the caging and chaining of saints that haven't been convicted by a jury! I'm the one that'll get their capital punishment.

CALEB [*aside*]: But they don't go far enough. Their ordinance wouldn't prohibit overfeeding.

WAT: I never sign anything, but Phisto wanted me to. He knows it wouldn't affect him, but he's sure it would cut down on all the barking that gives dogs such a bad name. Self-government would soon pacify any temporary increase of fighting.

PROCTOR: But it would make the pussy-chasing a lot worse. [*To Belle, sotto voice:*] Oh excuse me, Ma'am. I forgot you. . . .

DEX: The Puritans are much better organized than the Libertines, and this time they're grimly serious, supposedly on behalf of the needle trades. Ben, will you be for leashes if you're elected?

BEN: You mean when I'm elected. Depends on what the people think about it.

DOC: I'm in your ward. I'll tell you what I think.

BEN: You're not registered to vote. Mrs Laplace is.

HUCK: How can you solicit votes and collect delinquent rents from the same people?

BEN: You gotta know how. I won't come up short. They like me. I'll have to ask them how much they like dogs biting their kids. This clamor for dog-control started in my Ward. Then there's the merchants down the street, and I'm one of them. They don't like their customers tracking-in dogshit off the sidewalk.

DEX: Yes, from what I hear at the Hall, most of the Libertine voices come from East Harbor, Tinkersdale, the Plantation, Taraville, and West Marsh.

SHELLY: We want Ben to think about those wards too. This election is only his first step in politics.

PROCTOR: But all wards are biassed against liberty by the opinions of cemetery sextons, greenskeepers, lettercarriers, and paperboys. Most people don't stop to think how cruel it is to keep a dog from ever running free.

DEX: Your Chief preaches "selective enforcement". It would be up to you as Dog Warden.

PROCTOR: I have one blind eye. But I've always been willing to take my chances with canine personalities.

WAT: So if the Earldemen go along with the Puritans you'll soon let the howling die down, and they won't have to worry so much about a Libertine backleash. Who ever heard of a city ordinance changing Dogtown's habits?

PROCTOR: Still, that's what would make it hard on me: too much discretion! I say nothing for or against the Chief, but everyone would know that I had to make the decisions! I'd be blamed for every free dog that I did or did not arrest!

WAT: When there's no other crime than vagrancy it would be a discriminating injustice to ever pull one in. Dogs pay a poll tax, and three-fifths of them are counted in balancing ward populations, so they should have at least sixty percent of our civil rights.

DEX: But by ante-bellum law a dog, like a painting, is property, and property (as distinguished from a corporation, which is like a person) cannot own other property. Therefore the Libertines are about to challenge the poll tax in the Supreme Judicial Court. Would winning that one make a leash law any fairer?

WAT: Well let the demigods pass it. It'll make them feel active. Voters get carried away now and then, when there's nothing important to fight about, but in Dogtown all winds of change blow over. If the new law begins to pinch, the Libertines, who are a majority whether they know it or not, will be aroused and unified without waiting for the next election, and defend to the death their own dogs' freedom to be neglected and unschooled—to be knocked up, run over, kidnapped for slavery, sold for torture, poisoned by Puritan extremists, shot by hunters, or maimed and starved to death in steel traps—and to commit any public nuisance that doesn't threaten the other property of their owners. Dogs should be as free as any other free-loaders to be freely delinquent.

PROCTOR: The only fair way is to let the dogs police themselves. [*To Caleb*] That super-Viking of yours out there would make a stricter Dog Officer than I am, and the Libertines couldn't say a word against him! —That is, if he could tear himself away from the beautiful Jewish Shepherd that he dotes on. I'd like to get one of their pups that I could teach to help me in my work.

[*Fire whistle blasts. They wait in silence to count out the signal.*]

ALL [*severally*]: Not near me! . . . Nothing to worry about, I guess . . . Probably some little kilroy fire. . . . Aren't many buildings left I'd chase the engines for. . . . Well there's no second alarm—so far at least.

8
CHREMATISTICS

*

Chris Lucey had persuaded his father (as well as some minor clients) to invest in the block of Parity stock that he himself represented as broker and plenipotentiary of the Trustees. Nevertheless, when his intention outreached an ordinary policy of either profit-taking or capital-appreciation it was clear that the buying power of his consortium (even as amplified in hope and hint) was scarcely considerable in the eyes of Arthur Halymboyd and the corporate associates who controlled Parity, however intrigued they may have been by his round collar, his flowing scarlet-lined cloak with Domino hood, his Princedom connections, and his antebellum courtesy. The immediate financial power he desired, ultimately but not exclusively for Father Duncannon's sake, and thus for the sake of diverting himself from premature self-extradition to the Seventh Circle, might be attained only by participating in the leverage of Halymboyd's pyramid from much closer to the very top, above the market's reach, in the inverted root that faded from ordinary visibility like a wisp of smoke in the firmament.

But charming salesmanship, trustworthy background, and uncommon insight into the structure of the labyrinth were not sufficient for an approach to the adytum of Delphi's treasury, even for deposit, with a rather commonplace lump of capital. To further his proposal—rendered desperate by the forthcoming Chapter, which would almost certainly deprive him of usurious autonomy, not to mention the more immediate meeting of the Trustees at which all his recent operations would be inquired into for possible disapproval by an experienced corporation lawyer—he would have to ask of his father in Cherokee more than simply an additional purchase of PAR stock.

Now Security and Exchange Commission rules prevented broadening of ownership in any of the "closely held private unregistered trusts" that formed the subterranean chain of Halymboyd's controlling interest in the public Corporation. Only one "person" was allowed to replace another in the limited complement of private shareholders associated with Arthur Halymboyd. Any ambagious offering to replace Capstick's interest in a magnifying link of the root archipelago (if he succeeded in approaching the seller at all) would have to be not only much larger than his present span of proxies but also solely owned by the Trustees (as the trinity of a single "person"). Hence the motive of deserting his Superior for a whole week in order to comfort his father down home in Nashdom was to expedite his patrimony without precipitating the weakened old gentleman into his grave.

Chris had already contributed his own independent fortune to the C O V Fund and convinced himself that the senior Lucey was reconciled to his only son's vow of poverty with full awareness that whatever benefit his scion was to derive from his will and testament—certainly of far greater value than what had already been donated by the Junior—would likewise be conveyed to the Trustees—unless (as he may have secretly hoped) his one pride and joy disavowed the Order, a plausible possibility only after Father Duncannon's death, should that occur before his own. Thus Chris had set himself the most delicate task of his life as a son.

A cajolery of hints having failed, at last he succeeded—indelicately—by means of a suicidal tantrum. But with proviso. Almost as absolutely as King Lear, Mr Lucey would divest himself of nearly all his net wealth, mortgaging his very mansion, selling the rest of his real and personal property, and relinquishing all hope to leave his ghostly presence attached to the property he had himself inherited in beloved Nashdom, if—if his brilliantly erratic son was proven correct in the belief that Professor Capstick, sovereign of Incroesus Bank and spider of Financial Usufruct, had all along participated personally in Darien, Caduceus, or Thule (if not indeed more intimately in Python, Icarus, or Dedaelus)—*and* if Chris was able, in anticipation, to get Capstick's practicable agreement to sell the Trustees most or all of his remaining interest in Halymboyd's tubers at a fair price—all in the unlikely event that it wasn't already too late to do so in the extremely complex process of fission within the self-reorganizing empire.

For a dozen legal, financial, psychological, and otherwise unfathomable reasons the odds were a million to one against Chris's success in meeting these provisos, even granting that no one else would have been so likely to cut through the manners and mores of Graveyard Street to take advantage of the divorce by preempting the inside fortune-hunters.

And of course even if the Trustees were able to purchase the private securities of which Zane Capstick was divesting himself, it might turn out that he'd never been an innermost member of Arthur Halymboyd's personal investment circle, and that therefore they might get little more than dividends from a portion neither well enough placed to infiltrate Parity management by securing Chris a seat on its main or subsidiary boards nor liquid enough to raise cash for other investments (such as Paraclete) by hypothecation.

Still, without any well defined course or objective, and with no prudent alternative in mind for the retention of his freedom as the Order's financial manager, the Father Economist hoped to commit the Trustees to a stable yet interesting situation untainted by either the appearance of speculation or the odor of classical usury, relying on enlarged income to pacify all but the most medieval of holy hounds.

To this vague end, without informing Arthur Halymboyd or consulting that financier's erstwhile colleague Jason Anacoluther (who remained a substantial stockholder of Parity)—or Father Duncannon, Caleb, or anyone else—Chris had made an appointment once again to visit Hamilton DeCamp, Jr at the Smart Avenue headquarters in Ur. DeCamp was still Executive Vice-President of Parity and officer or director of practically every company in both moieties of the dyadic web, though presumed to be on the verge of overtly taking Capstick's side in the opening rupture. Chris had guessed that DeCamp, though temporarily remaining Halymboyd's first mate, had long been Capstick's man at heart, without having lost his nominal chief's estimation as an honorable fiduciary of past confidences, and more of an expert than anyone else in imperial administration.

The explorer's initial aim was to obtain from DeCamp a word of introduction to the former professor of dentistry and Brigadier General pro tem in the Army Medical Corps, so that he might continue south to Washington and beard the Byzantine lion in his den at Incroesus Bank. Chris believed that this his uncharacteristic rudeness—nay, his apparent insolence in a diplomatic blunder of the first magnitude, in omitting to seek the permission and advice of the very magnate he proposed to join as a gratuitous ally—was necessary not only in order to precipitate a deal before it was too late to be possible but also to take advantage of perhaps his final liberty to seek out any financiers; and that anyhow the innocence of his cloth would soon excuse him in the eyes of worldly men. Without daring to examine his expectations with a critical eye, he trusted theatrical ingenuousness to put things right with his intended liege (the present enemy of his intended vendor) after an agreement was readied for that surviving lord's approval, which would naturally be demanded by common decency even after the falling out of friends, if not by regulation litigation or covenant.

*

Of course Halymboyd had at once been informed by the honorable and prudent DeCamp of his appointment with the Reverend Lucey for an expatiating midtown lunch. It was not their first drink together, but this time Chris's invitation had pointedly omitted any reference to the President, with whom he'd conferred a couple of times in New Uruk and become cordially acquainted at the Dogtown dinner with Father Duncannon in his simple role as an exceptionally interested investor in Parity's common stock.

At that point neither Halymboyd nor DeCamp knew what the gallant priest was aiming at, but they speculated from his previous questions and allusions that it wasn't likely to be nothing in particular. Many a significant stockholder deserved the Vice President's two-hour lunchtime, however vague or casual the ostensible motive—in this case no more than the friendly urge to take advantage of a fortuitous business trip to Graveyard Street for the provincial branch of his brokerage house by returning DeCamp's earlier entertainment in midtown Ur. But they both knew that Father Lucey was urbanely sensitive to the possibility of abusing his welcome at 103 Smart, and they believed that in his unconventional way, on behalf of "the Church", he calculated every move.

Preoccupied though Arthur Halymboyd was with the unconsciously half-welcome harassments of the Security and Exchange Commission lawyers—who were forcing him to break up his vexatious collaboration with Zane Capstick for the perfectly good reason that their lines of business were at odds with each other (contrary to the rules under which Parity was registered), with the intricate problems of getting at least fair value in cash and securities for the webbed divestitures that would spare him prosecution, and with the counterbalancing investments by which he meant to broaden Parity's holdings in its chosen fields of manufacturing—semisubconsciously he had been waiting for just such an accidental opportunity to visit Father Duncannon in Dogtown when the Father Economist wasn't there. His own absence from Smart Street was easily explained, since at the moment there happened to be a lull in his business engagements (owing to Mrs Grundy's usual scattering of graduations, seasonal weddings, and other Society events) and a brief "vacation" for his short temper would please both himself and his office staff. He was frankly aware that he'd been growing testier than usual with the boredom and fatigue of unconstructive details that could well be delegated or deferred for a few days.

Until Halymboyd could satisfy himself as to the authorization dependability resources and motives of the bizarrely intriguing but potentially troublesome junior religious he thought it best to affect a C E O 's concern for the goodwill of any considerable stockholder: pretext for a jaunt which was actually conceived in a genuine craving for restful change of venue and borne by the tide of an apolaustic nisus that like the grace of God encouraged and harmonized the prevailing velleities of his haggard spirit:: a recently remagnetized nostalgia for Dogtown. He did not pretend to himself that his rationalization for interrupting a productive routine was half as cogent as the Hydra-voiced demand for continuous attention to his chrematistic responsibilities as a bold and devious leader in the cooperative fission of a double-spun web.

He told no one in New Uruk where he was going to take his "day or two off", or why, though he promised to call in once or twice if he happened to be near a telephone. In fact he didn't even phone Father Duncannon until he reached Botolph by parlor car, like a prince escaping to a foreign city incognito. From there to Dogtown he traveled on the local train as a commoner, entirely divested of the trappings of power but unmindful of his well tailored clothes and aristocratic valise which (apart from rugose face, circumference of waist, and height of forehead) distinguished him from the merely ambitious young pilgrim who'd ridden this line under steam power more than twenty five years earlier when he had been scarcely able to imagine the burdens that ability and experience would lead him to bear in each working hour of no greater length than the one he was now wasting in precious idle reverie—at that time too moonstruck to sympathize deeply with the Weltschmerz of his European clients.

Could I have been so unsure of her just because I was neither tall nor handsome? He thought he remembered the facts of his desire and elation, disappointment and jealousy, but he found it now impossible to recall what it *felt* like to be intimidated by reckless love. Those must have been the days of my inner self. I remember that Spinoza saw cupiditas as man's principal emotion, and I think he meant longing of all kinds. Am I now really a Captain of Industry, or merely what Veblen called a Captain of Solvency collecting other people's trophies—the arch-usurer that those priests' Christians are so leery of? They long for immortality.

Immediate exclusive consciousness entirely omitted his later few years in Dogtown as a rich sojourner with a different woman for wife, and children too, maintaining the dowered house not for aestivation only—and spared the ineluctable consequences of having had his improvident longing fulfilled in commitment to a life of erotic turmoil without so much as the comfort of money.

In harmony with his uncertain mood a time-suspending rain gently caressed the train until it reached the weather's edge along the north shore of Vinland Bight. At the Dogtown station he chose to be ensconced downtown, and was taken to the shabby Van in an IXAT cab. After finding himself assigned to the Poet's Corner by Edie Schlossberg (who judged the man by his clothes), he walked for an hour, all the way to the Laboratory. Much of the route had once been almost as familiar as his own body. On his recent flying visit to the Fathers, a swift trip on pure business, he had been sequestered both ways between the airport and his destination in a sealed limousine.

*

The misty light green-smelling moisture on virginal blossoms of white and pink had given way before the brilliant blues of brine-mirrored sky, and Caleb had gone home for the day with his caleb, when Father Duncannon went to sit alone in his sun porch, facing the western hills across the outer harbor from his ledges of pine, to await the visitor and wonder whether he should help himself to his customary sherry before he was fetched for dining at the Windmill.

But thanks to habits of self-discipline—as he sighed in moderate satisfaction with an early start at writing and editing an allocution, two hours of dictating letters to Gretta Doloroso, a lunchtime conference with Caleb about tiresome petty plans, and an afternoon of pondering agendas (in long-distance consultation with Father Davy)—he almost forgot the preprandial habit of his palate. In the motionless repose of a wicker armchair, listening to contented birds and gazing vacantly at whorled gulls in aimless sky-play, his thoughts sank to a private level, like water disappearing from plowed furrows after the rain, almost as if he too, under the telepathic influence of Arthur Halymboyd, was questioning his career; but in truth he was weary of his organization's affairs only at this end of a hard day.

Without caring to disturb his comparatively ataractic state any sooner than necessary by guessing at the reason for Mr Halymboyd's second visit to the Laboratory, he looked forward to the refreshment of unfamiliar liberty. For the moment—a transitory pause toward the end of his life's expectations—he nearly regretted his renunciation of totally free Creative Mind: free of responsible analysis, decision, and supervision; free of others' psychic distress, free of society's sufferings, free of Christian sensitivity to the suffering world. He assumed without thinking that Mr Halymboyd was seeking pragmatic discussion, in easily quantified terms of value, and (as he'd said on the phone) thought it a pity that Father Lucey happened to be absent for this unexpected occasion to hear more from the highest authority about his present main object of profane attention.

Mechanically picking up his latest copy of the *New Uruk Review of Books*, he soon threw it back onto the coffee table with an expression of disgust that he never permitted himself in the presence of others, having immediately encountered with inveterate dismay a solecism of prose discourse which nowadays was permeating even the best of writing and about which only he and Caleb would commiserate in repugnance: the barbarous practice of inserting a full declarative sentence (without proper initial and terminal markings) into the midst of another simply by the slipshod means of parentheses, in careless disdain of the effort and skill to organize interpolations with syntactical logic as good as algebra's. Like many other corruptions of English—for instance the use of a demonstrative adjective without its reference (as in such isolated locutions as "the book wasn't all that long")—this evasive abuse of parentheses by educated writers exemplified for him the countless degradations of "living, breathing language" that were being hastened by contemporary arbiters of lexicography and grammar, all under the sloppy persuasions of broadcasting.

No doubt I'm pissing against the tide, he thought—with a sudden atavistic chuckle. The phrase suddenly presented itself from a life long past, when he was still called Lance and was still roaming in the ironies of science. In those days entropy was fashionable cause for despair, offset only by art. Didn't Kierkegaard say that poetry is "victory over the world"—that it "softens and mitigates that deep pain which would darken and obscure all things"? But then he also said that only the religious "is capable of effecting the true reconciliation" between real and ideal—instead of simply abandoning actuality. I'm glad that Caleb too is at least not simply an ironist.

Now, as often of late, Lancelot Duncannon's philosophical meditation gravitated to what he thought of as "the final problem", to which he was led by all the questions relating to information and free will. Though he'd worked out the connection between liturgy and the social gospel for which sacramental theologians and liberal preachers were perennially groping, and explained that through the Grace of sacrament in a corporate church we have means to overcome entropy in society, even in a world ever populating with anger and pain, he was beginning to wonder if Christ's counter-entropy could prevail in the human mesocosm without increasing disorder somewhere else in the cosmic system. All other formations of organized energy, including those swirls of intensity which according to statistical thermodynamics temporarily occurred in nature without the assistance of an angelic Demon and could be found locally with what Poincaré called "a little patience", and not excluding (he was convinced) all the structures of willful life or art—in fact, all forms of order—, were achieved at the entropic expense of their environment, or of parallel systems, generally degrading the earth air and water that sustained mankind. Was God's grace positively antiscientific after all? Could we have as miracle the Kingdom of God along with the Peaceable Kingdom of nature and a perpetually ordered universe?

But God could be understood to override the Second Law only by considering as a whole the one truly closed system at the metacosmic limit of an infinitely regressive succession of metasystems, the idea of which was suggested by rational analogy to Anselm's Proof and by his old friend Scott Dunne's theory of the "serial universe" as a series of time dimensions in which God's infinity was the limit.

Otherwise I've been demented in the hope I teach! What if I've failed not merely by propagating the liturgical gospel in anachronistic terms but also by mistaking the idea itself? Have I wasted my life and disappointed God in specious kerygma, making a fool of myself with mere metaphors, antagonizing the few open-minded theologians to no purpose, and confusing the good people who follow me to no avail—especially the one who loves me more than his own father?

Even within the finite system, is God's grace limited by a corollary to the First Law that governs the conservation of quality? Does one man's qualification make for another man's disqualification? one good government, the corruption of others? Order only exiles disorder, not canceling but displacing or dispersing it. Can we educate here without advertising there? Can society begin to regenerate only with compensatory degradation in unnoticed parts or at the edges? Or can our species be saved only at the expense of our ecological world?

Perhaps I have been disinforming my church all along by riding scientific tropes, like a sophomore of the Enlightenment, despite my acknowledgement that science is altogether a raft built of Gedankenexperiments and my vivid memory of fallible complacency at the time when I and all the mossback professors thought there was no need for Quantum Mechanics in that floating platform! Other illogics will follow, and perhaps exclude from our empiric platform even my advanced reasoning. Certainly the raft will never grow large enough to rescue human life in the flood of death. Nor can the system ever know the metasystem, any more than an ion can know the mind of a body it joins.

It may be that my infinitely Christian opponent the Rev Mr Kierkegaard did not understand the social origin of his own religion, but he might justly have attacked me for confusing the outward with the inward. Who am I to correct Saint Paul and two thousand years of the church? I'm neither a theologian nor a philosopher, and I'm totally disqualified as either mystic or simple believer by my addiction to reason (which I can never cure without extinguishing my existence), if not by that great sin against chastity that I am unable to repent as Anselm did his own, whom Kierkegaard could never have justly attacked.

That Petrine intellectual and statesman uniquely deserved his sainthood. He was able through prayer to recover permanent counterentropic innocence from what Poincaré called the irreversibility of "real experience". Kierkegaard too, the purest Pauline, for whom good works were only the natural fruits of faith, suffered infinitely better than I the essentials of personal Christianity—which does indeed come first! Is my raft of reason too trussed and stiff ever to succumb to the fearful Grace of "Religiousness B"? Have I been construing our Mass *merely* as the technology of sacrifice? Have I been trapped in my own "Religiousness A" all these years?

But how can I warn the people at Chapter to doubt my own abstractions without enervating the corporate hope that's unmistakably essential? Must I desist, as only half a Christian? Should I recant my work before I die?

Just when Father Duncannon was about to yield to weakness with a thimbleful of sherry, Arthur Halymboyd, utterly refreshed by pedestrian nostalgia, made his appearance amidst the greenery of the driveway, smiling like Pan in search of a Christian dinner companion, whose self-surprising descent into a rare personal melancholy he unwittingly headed off with the sheer buoyancy of his own recovery from introspection, having reflected that he was lucky to have lost his heart's desire in 1934 without having never loved at all. "The scene of suffering is a scene of joy when the suffering is past;" even the young Redburn had said, "and the silent reminiscence of hardship departed is sweeter than the presence of delight."

*

Father Duncannon was somewhat fussy in his driving but he did nothing to alarm his visitor as they drove downtown in the little Autotod. Halymboyd was amused to find himself riding in the front seat of such a Lumpenvolk car, after fifteen years of getting used to deluxe tonneaus. A sense of freedom imparted by the intimacy of demotic transportation close to the pavement of irregular small-scale streets almost obliterated the memory of what he had purportedly come to discuss, but the priest showed no inclination to find out what in particular had precipitated the occasion.

What the busy June-time waitress saw, besides the categorical difference in their clothes, was an obviously younger and more powerful stranger whose mercurial face looked older than the other, which she'd seen more than once before. The softspoken senior, grayhaired and frail, with sparely wired eyeglasses and the refined features of wellborn sensibility [which she recognized by instinct], was somewhat the taller and more deliberate in manner; the junior, broad in mouth and shoulder, dark of brow, had been born less reserved, with greatly superior strength and vigor, alternately motionless and quick in feral movement, perhaps farouche—his deeper voice almost aggressively self-assured; but if she'd been a common reader in the last century she would have guessed that the elder was a king interviewing his deferential prime minister whose respect for everyone else was ironical.

    The dinner went as if they had tacitly agreed to postpone until next morning a topic too confidential to be broached even tête-à-tête in the muted bustle of a large public room. The virile financier known on Graveyard Street as a shark had been moved to come here for an unscheduled holiday by a tender urge to warn the touchingly tranquil priest, who seemed innocent of his adjutant's attempts (whether disingenuous or demented) to storm the Parity citadel for some unknown reason, and perhaps to meddle in its divorce proceedings. Halymboyd was loathe to distress his calmly integrated dinner guest more abruptly than necessary with a personnel problem now primarily secular; but more to the point, by waiting till tomorrow he hoped to have the benefit of communication with DeCamp later tonight, which should at least reveal the import of Lucey's effrontery in attempting to penetrate by guile the inner circle at Smart Avenue. He already suspected some sort of annoying overture to Capstick's camp.

    The priest for his part was willing enough to postpone for one more evening any naked consideration of the difficulties Christopher Lucey had brought upon the Order. Meanwhile he'd study Mr Halymboyd's character.

    So that evening, as most of the other diners dispersed, until the harbor's mirror grew starry and the navigation lights emerged, the two unlike veterans of dissimilar Dogtown experience, scarcely noticing the food or their self-effacing observer, talked about Dogtown itself, as they had had no reason to do so at their first meeting when the third party Southerner was present. One of them spoke with the broad and time-collapsing perspective of a native, without the enthusiasm of a pilgrim or sojourner. But in this polite conversation the man of power, who'd long since relinquished his sometime denizenship, seemed almost as unsophisticated about the town as an ordinary quondam aestivator, since all the work that had involved him in this place so long ago—even reality deals for his clients and his wife—had been abstractly fungible, undifferentiated by the self-made island's idiosyncrasies and essentially unaffected by the personalities or foibles of its living citizens. As a merely fortuitous mise en scene for both profession and passion this particular locale had at first seemed nothing more remarkable than a settlement curiously more improbable than others, which happened to have been noticed by people he'd heard of but was not in itself worthy of aesthetic transports. As a bit of cultivated space it had not struck him as publicly extraordinary. The banausic purposes of those for whom he'd acted might have been executed at scores of more apolaustic seaside resorts in New Armorica alone, and with less disorderly populations. It was for purely personal memories that he envied Father Duncannon the place of his childhood.

No less instinctively than the urbane Ur-islander, however, Lance Duncannon guarded the private reasons for which he cherished the microtopopolis as ekistically unequaled—and therefore in a certain thermodynamic sense counterentropic—in its *dis*order! In some ways he was more of a mysterious outsider than Halymboyd. His mother had taught him to regard himself as an aborigine not by character but merely by birth. And as a mesocosmic cleric repatriated to his hometown he had continued to find it even more unaware of his edifications than of the walled rich's. They at least were named in the Domesday Book as taxpayers of the largest estates, spared the justice of sans-culotte assessment only by the abatements of uneducated personal-property appraisers.

At last interrupting their gradually less reserved conversation about the tempers and mores of local institutions, with an interest that appeared to be genuine the profane tycoon asked his sacred dinner guest to define the forthcoming function known as "Chapter".

Father Duncannon explained the conference of C O V members as succinctly and openly as possible to an inquirer whose religious and literary background seemed likely to be devoid of Petrine culture. "But everyone speaks freely." he concluded. "Especially this time. It happens to be scheduled in the week of an extremely late Pentecost."

"The Feast of Weeks? If I remember, reading the Book of Ruth, David's great-grandmother: the proselyte who accepted the *Torah*. It happens that about that time, all too soon on my calendar, Professor Capstick's nephew is having a wedding up here."

"During Dogtown's festival time: this year especially, weddings will be comparatively unnoticed. After Whitsun and Trinity comes the immovable octave of Gloucestermas proper, from the Midsummer solstice to the feast of Saints Peter and Paul, followed by the Fourth of July! We're promised the greatest fireworks and water music since 1934, the last conjunction of all these solar and lunar celebrations."

Halymboyd did not immediately reply as he considered the risks of allowing himself freedom of speech, all but yielding to semi-trust in the semi-secrecy of semi-Christian semi-confession. Then he said "I was here that year, but I went away before it was over." For the first time in a quarter of a century he permitted himself to open at least gradually and in small measure the sea-cocks of his vessel and speak of its history semi-frankly. It didn't seem to be necessary—in fact it seemed both humiliating to himself and insulting to this honorable Christian—to ask in advance, gratuitously, for the privilege of absolute privacy that he did not earn as a confessing Christian.

"The year before A Year of the Dog, I was told!" he went on. "But June 30 was the Night of the Long Knives in Germany. It seems to have been Hitler's master stroke in proving himself irresistibly indispensable, coopting the Junkers and the Aryan capitalists by exterminating the socialist mob in his own National Socialist Workers Party. It confirmed old Jacob Arnheim's wisdom in having anticipated the success of Nazi dynocracy on the whole Continent. He'd already hired me secretly to prepare the way for transferring assets to this country and to make contingent plans for family expatriations from all over Europe. It was my first professional job, and I never needed another one. Some of my bonuses were worthless paper until after the war when reparations were settled, and others, such as Eastern European bonds, will have very little speculative value as long as the Soviet hegemony lasts, but altogether they made a poor Jew rich enough to accumulate his own money.

"Arnheim didn't realize I was Jewish until his Christianized granddaughter mentioned it when we were ready to get married. He was annoyed because he thought I'd deceived him. It turned out that one of the reason he'd decided on me as his North Atlantean lawyer—when I knew nothing of him as my real employer and thought I was being chosen by the president of a bank in Charter Oak for ordinary international legal services—was the assumption that I was untainted by birth or association. Though a naturalized citizen of the

U S , you see, I'd emigrated from Saint James's in the very British colony of Terra Nova as a baptized graduate of Tudor schools and done my undergraduate stint in the States at Hawthorne College. If the banker had asked for my genealogy I would have been rejected. The Halymboyds were assimilated Ashkenazim for a hundred years, and my mother was descended from a Marrano survivor of the Spanish Armada who came ashore with a sea-chest on the island of Thule in the Shetlands. Meanwhile the Sephardic tributary of the Arnheim line arrived in Amsterdam by way of the Venice Ghetto from a family of Lusitanian New Christians!"

"I've never doubted that the index of a culture is its alloy of Jews. But neither has Ezra Sterling, I'm afraid, our malignant mad poet, for his own opposite polyhistorical reasons. He seems to blame them for all usury."

"Anyway, the Arnheim people were looking for a proxy above such suspicion, but unknown on the Street and otherwise unobtrusive, as well as young enough to outlast their own generation and the Third Reich too, if it ended in less than a thousand years. I was just finishing up at the Norumbega B-School, already had my Law degree, and was a member of the Bar; but more important, I'd worked my way with all sorts of jobs at bookkeeping levels. Exactly what they wanted—if I could keep my mouth shut and my eyes open, and appreciate deferred compensation as a primary incentive. Mainly they needed reliable judgment on financial affiliations in this country. Cape Gloucester happened to be the off-season refuge of some able investors. And I found that even among natives there has always been a lot of quiet old money that didn't seem to come from either fish or granite."

Father Duncannon sounded a faint tone of unlinked wry indignation, responsibly historical. "It started with what they officially called "Commerce"—what the people here spoke of as 'whaling', or sometimes as 'sugaring'. Until just before the Civil War, even though they were said to be 'premature Abolitionists' (thanks to the moral agitations of their womenfolk), some of Dogtown's ships were still stealing off to Africa, on the way to Guyana, while Bethsalem's and Botolph's were legitimately trading with China. Our branch of the railroad and the annexation of Seamark were personally financed by the residual beneficiaries of whaling. Some of the whaling fortunes had married fishing fortunes and gone on to multiply in Botolph and New Uruk. Mingling with plutocrats, they drew attention to the Cape's summertime attractions. Mr Anacoluther says J P Morganatic's two-hundred-foot steam yacht was anchored right out there"—Father Duncannon indicated the outer harbor with a turn of his face—"when he came ashore to visit old mistresses and cobble together North Atlantean Steel with the world's richest mining engineer."

"Jason should know. It must have been because of the old money you mention that his father-in-law owned a banana republic, and was probably the one who had originally suggested Dogtown as a port of call for the *Picaroon*. It's not surprising that when she was taken over by the government for the Hispanic-Atlantean War the Navy re-christened her the *U S S Cape Gloucester*; but, oddly enough, to my childish mind, it was in *Saint James* Bay, namesake of my own launching port, that she sank two enemy destroyers! I used to pretend that was a good omen for my career as a provincial interloper!

"But before I knew anything about Dogtown, or even suspected whom I was really working for, they kept me on short rations, partly because old Jacob insisted on managing every detail himself from behind the Atlantic Ocean; for even in the thirties Arnheim Electrical Industries got along without his daily attendance, leaving him time to worry about his family and all other Jews. He was naturally parsimonious, as well as ignorant—existentially speaking—of Atlantean living standards at the contemporary rate of exchange. During the Depression he could take advantage of the fact that it was hard for a penniless young outsider to get any job all.

"But it was mainly for the instinctive reasons of a black operator that for a long time he kept me working alone and half starved, in fact short of supplies and travel allowances. Like the Rothschilds and the Sassoons he was a born manager of clandestine intelligence. My discretion was still untested, and he wanted to make sure I had no leeway for ostentation that might attract the slightest attention at any level of society. The banker himself didn't know what I was being hired for. The degree of secrecy in his precautions may seem ridiculous in retrospect, but he was acutely aware of the ingrained antisemitism over here, even though I never reported the rental signs in Dogtown that said 'No dogs, no Jews'. He knew enough to fear antiprematureantifascist control of Washington if the Catholicrats ever lost power. Even so, he believed that the U S A was the safest country in the world for his people!

"At first I had only a shabby box of an office in Charter Oak, and no secretary at all. Luckily, though sinister by birth, I was also righthanded by training; that made me pretty good at picking up rhythmically ambidextrous skills on things like pianos and office machines. In order to handle alone the paperwork of the various so-called 'trading companies' and 'factors' I was setting up, I worked like a one-man band with six different letterheads set up in six typewriters, one for each separate phone line and set of books. (Later, when we were rescuing Jews, I had clerical help and a dozen or more business entities, but my methods were similar.) The chart you showed me when I was here before shows that some of those obscure entities are still used—for the mutual private convenience of Arnheim Electrical and Parity subsidiaries in minor collaborations. I've never forgotten how to minimize administrative costs!"

"I think you would find Caleb Karcist interesting for more than the chart he made."

"So I was of considerable service to the Arnheims before I went into the S I S , where I made the most of my business experience; and thereafter I made the most of that wartime experience in helping the family recover damages in Europe. They in turn helped me get started on my own. Jacob is gone now, but one of the sons that no one ever hears of even on the Street has made them the biggest industrial on the Continent; and of course they have companies over here, as you may have noticed on the chart. My comparatively obscure little outfit still has interlocking directorates with them. As for my wife, she'd be far richer than I am if she didn't fund foundations faster than dividends are declared. Yet I've never had anything but a wedding present as an outright gift from the Arnheims. They treated me like a Christian who was once their faithful servant. But they are honorable people and sometimes seem to believe the invidious rumors about me.

"I suppose you've heard that I have a reputation for finding hidden or undervalued assets, tangible or intangible, in stagnant or self-effacing existing enterprises. I never overlook the small nominally worthless assets that come with our acquisitions—like defaulted Polish or Amazon Railroad bonds, or Messpot irrigation debentures, or stock in the Tropical Belt Coal Company on Black Diamond Bay of Samburan Island—which occasionally have ways of becoming valuable through the turn of political events or the unforeseen discovery of commercial or military use for worn-out properties, if only for the mineral possibilities of the land they lie on, or its indigenous herbs.

"I also dive deeper into organizational details than boardroom dignity allows. Furthermore, when I hire young men I'm notorious for slighting management degrees awarded by the Laurel Amphyctyony to relatives and protégés of my acquaintances. (Aside from accounting and finance, there's all but nothing that can be taught about management and all but everything for the teachers to learn. Competence comes mainly from practical intelligence, general education, and bottom-up experience.) I'm regarded with suspicion also because I keep a controlling interest in my companies according to perfectly accepted capitalistic principles while selling certain amounts of stock when it's occasionally overvalued and buying it back when it's underestimated, especially if I can do both within the same quarter without tax problems."

"Parity stock seems to fluctuate in a sinusoidal wave." Father Duncannon smiled. "It would be interesting to see a Fourier analysis."

"The S E C lawyers might welcome some electrical engineering to pin me down. They've tried everything else. Yet the Street itself considers me somehow a spy for the Crat liberals in Washington! Once when I was young I worried enough about my feelings of isolation to consult Auto Drang, because he was the best educated of all the psychiatrists, here or over there, and I thought he could be trusted with a deliberately deviant Jewish psyche. He said my European work was too important for me to be wasting time on self-examination, and after one visit sent me home with a bill of health. Now my mature work is simply at the other end of the spectrum. I think I'm not wicked but I'm afraid I'm neither glad nor sorry that I seldom stop to question myself."

Halymboyd paused but his guest listened for more: "Be that as it may, for various reasons I'm no longer close enough or sufficiently important to this second generation of Arnheims to ask or even wish their cooperation in the current restructuring of my interests, which is required by the mutual spin-offs of Parity and Financial Usufruct that your Economist has made some pretty good guesses about."

But Father Duncannon still seemed not fully to appreciate the unique privilege of hearing this confession. The priest dwelt on the earlier thought that had surprised Halymboyd by its apparent irrelevance, who suddenly feared that he'd overestimated the confessor's intelligent interest in real-life affairs. "Perhaps you'd be willing to help our young man, if he were willing to leave Dogtown with his dog. He's an admirer of your corporate seal with the double axe, which he takes to be a symbol of your labyrinth."

Halymboyd smiled widely for the first time. "Well I've sometimes thought of it that way too, but Capstick and I originally intended it to denote *parity*. But I knew that the word meant fecundity as well as equalization of advantage, if not equity, I suppose with other etymological connotations. Hammy DeCamp jokes that after he and Capstick finish their decamping I should re-register the company as *Dis*parity. One doesn't expect that sort of wit from a Vice-President of such unimaginative objectivity."

"We can't keep Caleb Karcist much longer, I'm sorry to say. Many of our members wish us to get out of the market entirely. I'm afraid we've been drifting a little too far from our social economic principles."

"Oh yes, the fellow who made the chart? It makes Parity look more like the brainchild of a city planner than of a Graveyard Street lawyer! But often amateurs are more perceptive than professionals. I'm glad he isn't working for the S E C . I may mention Karcist to one of our managers, if he decides where he'd like to fit into his own picture. I never take anyone onto my own staff until he's had some line experience in one of our companies."

Father Duncannon pursued his concern. "I think he'd go anywhere—with his Viking Shepherd—if he were given a chance to work with his Synectic Method of Diagnostic Correlation, especially on C R F and OHM machines!" Even this his dry smile struck the new acquaintance as unwonted. "If you don't mind I'll have him to lunch with us tomorrow."

Halymboyd would have preferred not to waste time in good works but he could scarcely gainsay a gentle host. "I once knew a Viking Shepherd." he mumbled. But he was groping for Father Duncannon's working principles, about which he grew ever more curious than when he'd impulsively committed himself to this extraordinary hiatus in productive time. Now it seemed as if ethical discussion was the underlying purpose of his confusingly justified excursion to the place he'd used to call The Little Rock (as distinguished from his native island, a small continent, which was still called *the* Rock by its remaining colonists).

"Will your people still regard me as a usurer?"

"Still? Do you mean members of the Order or Tudor Petrines in general?"

"After we've sold off all our holdings in financial institutions."

"As long as money is not being sold merely for the sake of interest—making *tokos* from treasure alone, as Aristotle put it—in my view both increase and decrease through time should be allowed for, as well as inflation and the minimum cost of administration. For Aristotelians the natural function of money was to facilitate the exchange of goods, later extended quite reasonably to their manufacture. Muslims got around the usury stumbling block by pretending the banker was a partner sharing profit with his clients. Medieval Christian financiers also claimed they were sharing the risks of argosies and adventurers. Indeed I'm not sure it's usury to make a profit by sharing the risk, or by reversing some local entropy for a little while with brains and muscles organized at your expense. It all depends on what you think is valuable. That's the real issue—not borrowing or lending, which we can no longer avoid in any case, at least indirectly. The more people there are in the world the more we need capital for public works, whoever may own it.

"But urging consumers to borrow in order to buy what they might have saved up for, or do not need—surely that's a latterday sin. Especially when the lender has borrowed from someone else at a lower rate of interest solely for that purpose! Our economy is becoming dependent upon that sort of business, and the roots of useful production will wither if we don't check the tendency. That's why I don't dispute our members who take up the Biblical cry against usury, whatever the word may mean nowadays.

"It seems to me that the value of money at any given point can be defined in its proper fourth dimensional perspective by a reasoned rate of interest. But interest on capital remains a question with us, one way or another. For the borrower it's like friction in mechanics—a steady entropic loss; it may be necessary, like dissipated heat, to fabricate required artifacts; but if too much, cascading negatively from level to level in the economic chain from the supplier of raw material to the consumer, it eventually chokes off useful production like tares in every planting of a seed-corn acre.

"But I must say that by negative feedback, to use Norbert Weimar's term," Father Duncannon continued dryly, "the usury of lenders at least eventually limits the popular illusion of perpetual motion in our cumulative raising of the national debt to avoid fair taxation.

"But the world is already too much with us, and we can't deny our historical standpoint in the Relativity of economics. In one view the growth of money is as natural as the growth of population. Interest these days is the compounded acceleration that may simply compensate for losses by the inflation to which it so much contributes! I'm sorry to say that we're obliged to accept the general belief that our economy must grow in order not to fail, basically because there are always more people. If Aristotle held that usury—meaning interest—is a sin against nature he must have agreed with Plato that history is a sin against geometry.

"Even Crusaders were financed by Hanseatic and Tuscan merchants with letters of credit from hometown magnates who certainly took discounts for the service. The Church didn't call that usury. But usury was hard to deny when by law London pawnbrokers, whatever social function they may have served, were allowed to charge the poor twenty percent. Yet Ezra Sterling, for one, could never see that money *is* perishable if it isn't used, like all buried talents. Of course my personal opinion on the line between fairness and usury calls for much conditional argument, but it may reduce to applying Aristotle's normative proposition that the acquisition of wealth is justified only by its contingency upon the management of what nature provides, insofar as management—economy—requires the fungibility of money to achieve the good life; the virtuous manager subordinates moneymaking just as he delegates the supervision of his herds. The trouble is that we have it backwards: modern management is not the end but the means of wealth, or at best merely the defense of it.

"So I think the fundamental moral problem is not usury but ownership."

"I think I could relinquish ownership to the public—if I were granted the management of it!" Halymboyd laughed. "And then of course, as a component of projected Return on Investment, interest would still be needed to apply public money in the perspective you speak of. Meanwhile, whatever may be said of my past, I'm no more guilty of usury in the narrow meaning of the term than I am of fraud in the limited sense it's come to have in law. Still, I admit feeling *somewhat* purified by the spin-offs, split-offs, split-ups, and other divestitures of Parity's most usurious investments and investors!"

"I suppose the pragmatic question we would have, as stockholders, is what you will acquire with the proceeds of those sales. The Classic Order of the Vine would be far more concerned about profits from armaments and poisons than profits from money. I expect that our debate at Chapter will end in that direction."

"I'm afraid that complicates my defense."

"And Father Lucey's." Father Duncannon's tone saddened in acknowledgment. "But he hopes we could influence your investment policy. In the use of capital and labor."

Halymboyd responded soberly, staring at the candlelit tablecloth, one hand twirling his glass. "I may be a Catholicrat, but I'm still a businessman who supports the nation's benign self-confidence."

"Benignity too is hard to draw the line of."

"Perhaps tomorrow I can try, with some details."

Between bites, with nods of arms-length fellowship, they raised their glasses in small gestures of understanding and sipped the wine of mutual respect.

"But ruling out the possibility of my conversion, what can I do for you? I am told that your Order makes a religious connection between the soul and society. How can I personally, if not officially, contribute to that cause?"

Father Duncannon smiled once more. "I'm grateful for your kindness, but we hardly need *more* money!"

"There may be some other way."

The older man paused, staring out over the darkling harbor. "Why, come to think of it, I believe there is. But I'm a little too tired to bring it up tonight."

*

Father Duncannon wanted to pray about it first. That night, in pajamas which according to vow he did not own, wearing as always the pectoral cross that was his sole remaining possession, he was on his knees like a storybook child at the Tuscan faldstool near his bed. After the Lord's Prayer and others, ordinary and variable, said in English or Latin all the world over, as his divine office, and after his particular prayers of intercession—for each of the Order's members and their families, including Father Davy as his designated successor; for certain of the world's sick or imprisoned; for the providence of politicians and scientists; for Caleb's future livelihood and for the Brotherhood of the Peaceable Kingdom; for Mrs Cibber and other local friends of the Laboratory; and most especially for Christopher Lucey—he asked for wisdom and strength to overcome his shortcomings as a confessor and leader who had never acted for his God with Apostolic courage or suffering (or even with pastoral responsibility); who indeed had never done enough as a Christian to trouble the Bishop; who like Thomas Jefferson had looked down on storms from his mountain top; who had never assumed the burdens and anxieties of vulgar life; and whose unsuccessful struggle to love singly every unwashed or vicious person in his ken—without [as Kierkegaard put it] the "intoxicating predilection" of shared distinctions or complementary differences—was his broadest failing, no matter how devoutly he might teach the church its primitive social essence, for his fault lay not in a dualism of matter and spirit but in that of *eros* and *agape*.

Thus once more his nightly prayers became a supplication for intercession with the Holy Spirit by all-too-human Peter and the loving Blessed Mary in his striving, as always, for the alien ability to tolerate, understand, and relieve the disordered feelings of the human being closest under his cure, the one neighbor he found most difficult to love without falsifying the religious work to which he had been called as the sole acquittal for his privileged life. He implored God's grace for the strength and skill to govern the wayward body and discontinuous mind in his charge, when pious or sinful, when brilliant or reckless.

For the meeting of Trustees only a few days hence he asked firmness of will, practical foresight, and the recovery of at least his monastic thought-regime's formal integrity.

As for the morrow, he prayed not to be disarmed by his liking for Arthur Halymboyd.

Crossing himself, he rose stiffly and moved slowly to his bed, thankful in spite of himself for the respite of a vacancy in the other one—the bed of his devoted nurse whose shoulders more than once had borne him across a torrent but whose night-watch sometimes seemed less tolerable than the fear of another heart attack. This solitude fortified his will to live to the end with all his wits. With a flux of amusement he tried to remember what an agile tennis-player he had been, what a tireless walker of fells in Wales and the Lake Country.

So his reverie in awaiting sleep was as random as any old brain's. As usual, these moments of night were less terrifying than the sudden clarifications of failure that sometimes awoke him at dawn, yet their elements were those of dread. It seemed an easy test of faith to doubt the Second Law either for the mesocosm as a whole or for Melchizedec alone, whose life was perpetuated by scripture; but for one born into an age of prodigal and promiscuous communication, whose work—rejected by publishers receptive to everything else the human brain could imagine—hung by a thread on the intellectual sympathy of a few scattered mortals overwhelmed by their own burdens of creation or responsibility, none of them known to the world at large. . . .

He reminded himself that he would not be the only old man to have spent a lifetime (at the entropic expense of somebody, or of society, or of mother earth, or of the mesocosm, or at least of the cosmos) informing himself only to form ideas—acquiring, integrating, reflecting, creating—developing a uniquely dedicated self—only to die and leave the entire creature in which his neurons participated to suffer dissolution and absolute intellectual (if not spiritual) oblivion, thereby utterly wasting all the experience and thought that would not have been communicated or at least recorded in writing made available to other brains for possible preservation. . . .

But soon his mind drifted back to the mooring buoy of an ugly fact that he knew he had been intentionally missing in the merciful fog ever since he'd first overrun it—the new report and inference that were impossible to discredit and would be all too easily verified—which had been disturbing his spiritual somnolence ever since the first shock of its revelation. For days his heart had been gravitating to it at every moment of indisciplined and undiverted consciousness. At last Christopher's third vow was broken unequivocally and unmistakably.

Long ago the Father Economist had been directed never to use his unlimited power of attorney, as plenipotentiary for the Father Superior and Trustees, to trade or sell or encumber any real property of the Laboratory. Economic mischief was hardly the worst of sins; but to Anselm disobedience would not have been the least of a spoiled monk's three greatest transgressions. Christopher Lucey had been disobedient before, and likewise casuistically deceitful, but until now his disobedience had not stricken the personal vitals of his Superior, whose religious renunciation as he founded the Order implicitly trusted to the irrevocable transfer of his real estate, which had been bequeathed him with an unregistered covenant forbidding its sale.

He still believed that the Father Economist had no intention of actually selling the gift that inevitably embodied the Father Founder's personal history, but now (thanks to the excruciatingly delicate good offices of Raphael Opsimath) there was no doubt that the professed monk had jeopardized its security with instruments of hypothecation. Nor was there any doubt that the deceptively insubstantial disobedience comprised one or more calculated act of desperation, for the purpose of establishing his position as a prospective insider at Parity's roots, upon the accomplishment of which he expected to have the Trustees too enmeshed in financial relationships for the other two of them to entertain any serious objection about a mortgage or two that might be noticed by someone in a parcel of beloved innocents who didn't understand what was good for their Order.

Thank God for the pedantic competence of Mortimer Ockam, whose loyalty as a passionate charter Member was not to the arriveste Father Economist who supervised his accounting but to the Founder himself. The Trustees at least could be assured of a truthful financial statement (due the day before their meeting), which would probably show a normal growth of net worth—the only figure that the Superior usually paid attention to (loathe as he was to confront banausic demands upon his remaining time in life)—subject to the fluctuating market value of the portfolio. Any extraordinary increase in assets would not be remarkable for a trader operating on margin if it was offset by blandly lumped liabilities.

The demeaning question that should have presented itself before now to a Chairman of Trustees, he now realized with freshly humiliating anguish, was how the Fund was able to get so much credit beyond the legal limit of borrowing against securities from brokers and/or banks (who might be delinquent in insisting upon physical possession of a trusted client's certificates for the stocks he hypothecated). Lancelot Duncannon blamed himself for not having stooped to require classified schedules of all the credits that had been granted, distinguishing long-term from short-term debts and periodically itemizing the pledges against them. How he regretted his lifelong distaste for accounting—a mathematics he had refused to read at his leisure!

His was the authority to order immediate liquidation of the portfolio in order to pay off outstanding obligations before any legally serious irregularities might be exposed—God forbid, when a well-meaning mind is unhinged!—such as fraudulently duplicated pledges of assets. Contracting and consolidating, paying cancellation penalties, and withdrawing from the market entirely would probably obviate any further legal anxiety, and it would certainly remove the moral reservations of Members.

But he was burdened with the understanding that a radical correction would bring down the religious house that served as present and future nucleus of the Order by precipitating the catastrophe of a passionate soul. The Laboratory of Melchizedec and the Mesocosm could not function with one sick old man alone, ridiculously living out his vanity as a Father Superior to phantoms—abandoned by the world in his fantasy of poverty chastity and obedience! But far more terrible than devastation of his communal dream was the nearly certain sin—greater than any climactic abrogation of vows—the one sin that would absolutely destroy the possibility of felicity for an insane soul in its final struggle to atone for the defeat it had brought upon its spiritual father by virtue of its very devotion.

In any case, how could a Superior allow the life of a religious to be openly examined before even a confidential lawyer like Endicott Krebs at the Trustees' meeting? As Chairman he himself could probably forfend any unusual attention to balance-sheet details—but only if he found a way to resolve the predicament as an intramural problem of the monastery's; and that was by far the more difficult way to confront the agonizing dilemma, all by himself: a weak curer of souls, a childless orphan, a lonely failure whose signal contribution to a world religion was shamefully linked to the world-line of one unreliable and unbalanced follower.

Yet even in the dismal illumination of his situation he was grateful for the tactful hint of Mr Opsimath that had opened his eyes to the ominous new stormcloud during a neighborly afternoon visit (as if he simply happened to be driving by) to ask if there was anything he could do to help the Fathers prepare for their retreat, which would be up against Dogtown's Dionysia.

As if in offhand approval of the Father Superior's practical wisdom, the affable entrepreneur had remarked, with a sympathetic smile for the irony of a Father Superior's position in both worlds, "I've decided to keep my Parity stock, if the dividends offset the interest costs for carrying it on margin, with the hope that it will appreciate enough to keep our new business going during the first few years of uncertainty, in case I have to borrow more. Father Lucey fortunately doesn't have a capitalization problem like mine, but I suppose any fund has liabilities that have to be continually reviewed for the relative significance of whatever they entail—securities, personal property, real estate, or what not."

The conversation had immediately passed on to other topics, but the Chairman of the COV Trustees hadn't failed to notice the unemphasized change of subject in Opsimath's last sentence, and in retrospect the sense of enthymeme had prompted deeper reflection. It had then occurred to him that it would be prudent to call up Mr Anacoluther's bank at least in order to refresh his memory with a review of the Trustees' accounts. Two days ago, in the Father Economist's absence, he'd found the opportunity and courage to do so. Without betraying surprise or dismay he'd discovered that the Cape Gloucester Security Trust now held a three hundred thousand dollar mortgage loan comfortably secured by the Laboratory property (well known to the bank for its far greater real value)—not only the residence but also the great adjacent tract of open land entitled Duncannon's Farm in the city's archival cadastre (and in vernacular contraction still called "Duncan's Farm").

Sleep receded before his hours like a sea-horizon unaware of an approaching sailor. He thought of getting up again to pray. In his self-accusing mind the fundamental moral transgression was involuntarily concatenated not only to the practical question of whether or not Christopher Lucey's negotiating hopes were plausible—whatever they might be—but also to the fear that his evident haste for financial reorganization could be explained only by the imminence of society's retribution for past misjudgments or misdeeds.

How could Arthur Halymboyd help the Order, even if he were made privy to the internal problem of the Laboratory, without locking the actor out of the theater and bringing him to a spike of desperation? The guilt of a good man's destruction would fall upon the soul that had led him into the temptations of power in return for misdirectedly human loyalty as unquestionable as the North Star. Of course these affairs were none of Halymboyd's business; but by the same token the Father Superior's nuncio had no business prying into Halymboyd's private corporations, which was exactly what he seemed to be doing. Under the circumstances an apology to the sensitive industrial baron tomorrow might not be considered either religiously improper or personally disloyal to the culprit.

Yet even now in meditative solitude Father Duncannon hardly dared cease to suspend his response to the private shock of outrage and betrayal, for fear that he would lose control of its expression and produce by its exposure the same effect that he dreaded from any abrupt failure of Christopher's highly wrought intentions in opposition to the profession of a true monk. For Mr Opsimath had also contrived to mention a little later that his friend the City Planner had met Father Lucey when he visited Ibicity Hall to make supererogatory inquiry about the possible requirement of a special "variance" to permit the accommodation of more than a certain number of transients at the Laboratory during Chapter. No invidious hint seemed intended in Opsimath's remark, yet it required no worldly and suspicious manager to see that the roving priest's pedantic errand may have been a last-ditch effort to frustrate the Order's convention minute by throwing up a legalistic roadblock. But the most unconscionable wound, too painful to analyze subjectively, was inflicted on the Superior by his own inference from the visitor's information that Christopher's far-fetched excuse for visiting Mr Keith's office might have been instead a diversionary pretext for starting an ordinary civil conversation with officials in which, without tipping his hand, he could intersperse casual prompts and queries to sound the zoning and subdivision regulations that applied to the moorland that was once the Duncannon farm!

The integrity of that tract, a reservation of ledges, ravines, and scrub vegetation—undulating rocky upland that resembled the landscape of Purdeyville commons—was more precious to Lancelot Duncannon than the possession of it. Although the Trustees owned that eleemosynary monument of his family and paid the land-taxes on it, few Dogtowners had any idea that it was private land dedicated to perpetual conservation, for public use by unarmed pedestrians. In one corner of a former pasture, by custom amounting to covenant, the city's D P W had always been expected to maintain a pair of donated tennis courts, a rectangle of berms for ice-skating, and a grassy sandlot baseball diamond; but most of the Duncan's Farm acreage, extending northward nearly to the rockbound golf course of the country club, was preserved for the natural recovery of flora and fauna that had been extirpated for the sake of saltwater cows and horses more than a century before the Duncannons arrived in Dogtown. Its present market value would be multiplied a thousandfold if made saleable to building speculators. It would guarantee a vastly larger line of credit at any Cape Gloucester bank.

Lancelot Duncannon couldn't help defending himself, to himself, against his own accusation that he was nothing but an aesthetic miser cherishing a patrician view of restored wilderness all the way to Ocean's rocks from his Monticello (where slave quarters had always been out of sight). He remembered the time when he had declined to liquidate his patrimony even in order to help intellectuals and artists escape from the Continent, some of whom he warmly liked in person.

*

Meanwhile Arthur Halymboyd was somewhat satisfied by having revealed at least a little of his history to one whom he could trust for motives of the kind that he missed in the society of Paumanok or Duke and Vesper counties in Nether Land. The spiritual relaxation (which he accepted as temporary absolution) loosened his limbs and lowered his guard. On this peculiar island, with which nearly thirty years earlier he'd been disenchanted before it could enthrall him, he felt as far from the island of Ur as from the bleak Rock of Terra Nova.

After telephoning Hamilton DeCamp from the pseudonymous safety of Shelly Schlossberg's underclass hotel—for he had registered under the name Max Phillips (coded for only two or three of his closest associates)—he took off his tie and strolled into the Main-Top Bar, vaguely amorous, wryly hoping to recall the innocence of a young predator, if not to find an aleatory companionship of the gregarious kind to which an element in his nature had always responded, especially when he used to shoot craps in wartime chambers far shabbier than this one on both sides of the Atlantic.

But the bartender didn't look as interesting as either of his parents, and there wasn't a woman in sight. He found at once that he could not tolerate the loudmouthed disconversation dominating sights and sounds from the devilvision receiver, which oriented everyone without being heeded and stole the thunder of the aged jukebox. Besides, he was no longer insensitive to cheap smoke, spilled beer, and the shouts of an otiosely repetitious vocabulary that passed for friendly curses or independent social criticism. The wickedness of these gypsies lumpers and fishermen was nothing but noise.

He turned back before he'd even reached the bar-stools—as perhaps many a guest of the Van had done before him. Instead, smoking a cigar, he sauntered down to the waterfront to look at the fishing boats and see how things had changed since 1934, the year he remembered last attempting to get at the heart of Dogtown. Then there had been more chugging and tooting in the harbor; fully rigged schooners had lined most of the piers like hedge rows more or less hiding the tide that raised and lowered them, and even the trawlers had still borne masts for sail. A slight whiff of salt cod from vestigial drying racks under the shadow of Mercator-Steelyard's modern redbrick plant reminded him that then the stench had been ubiquitous—powerful enough to drive pilgrims further along the Cape, as far as possible from this working slum on the inner harbor strand. The ruins of a beehive gas-works were now gone, and many of the old lofts and sheds were likewise cleared away in anticipation of Civic Instauration, exposing ramshackle wharves and isolated pilings left in the mud like skeleton spines from a forest fire. He had been told that everything would be cleaned up in a few years, and that the frozen-fish industry's rapidly developing system of distribution would create a national demand for "seafood" without fishiness, so he found himself wondering if Parity should really get rid of its minor accidental interest in Stockton-Van Nuys Foods, which had recently bought a tuna-packing plant on the West Coast.

Shaking off that quotidian question, he fell into a pensive state unrelated to what he was staring at, for the scene had changed too much to bind him to its associations with the personal past. Hamilton DeCamp had never been given any more operational discretion than such minor decisions as getting into the cannery business, but he'd be sorely missed when he went over lock-stock-and-barrel to Professor Capstick the sly semiantisemitic war-scavenging general, because none of the younger men were patient enough, or experienced, to anticipate financial details so well, or had his skills for conducting public relations while appearing uninterested in public relations. Poor guy, solid but not agile, decent as a Can can be, and brought up with a self-confidence that could never be acquired by mere ambition—the only one on the payroll who never hesitated to "Hal" and "Cap" the two of us. Like Jason, born rich, but much less obviously "preserved by alcohol, embalmed alive"; yet unlike Jason he'd never have been mistaken for a dithering idiot if he traded clothes with a villager. I can do nothing about the fact that he knows too much about me; I must trust to his sense of honor.

Hammy will be indispensable right up until the last minute. His old-boy Princedom and old-money Bull-Moose connections have warded off a lot of trouble and spared me countless garden parties. But I suppose I must bring Judy up here for Capstick's judicious Mooncusser-Leary wedding. She wouldn't let me find any excuse. Women have succeeded in persuading all classes that weddings wash away the social sins of those who attend, not just those of the four parents and the two principals. Men can sometimes dodge ceremonies of baptism, circumcision, birthday, anniversary, confirmation, Bar-Mitzvah, engagement, graduation, promotion, inauguration, or death, as well as Sabbaths, Sundays, Easters, Pentecosts, and all the other religious holidays, but never the solemn trappings that seal the bargain of formal defloration.

The war between men and women is not for domination; it's for peace. Still, before I met Judith Arnheim I'd learned my lesson never again to fall hard enough to lose my wits.

I sometimes wonder if Moira secretly wanted an altar marriage. She would have been too proud to say so. She thought a civil marriage was profane, but making love without it no more sacrilegious than a meal of bread and wine at the kitchen table! Yet she was the one who raised the question of sacrament, and she often wore on her left hand the gold ring I gave her. She told me about advances made to her by my rivals and other men (whom she attracted by merely walking or speaking), but she would never tell me anything about the "minister" she declared herself in love with—as if his cloth rendered her disloyalty pardonable as I lay peacefully between her legs, at a time when I still think we hadn't yet stopped eating bread and drinking wine exclusively together.

After Gloucestermas, when I came back, she was gone, leaving the message that I didn't really love her—maybe in disappointment about my intentions, maybe to spare herself confession, or maybe to spare me a life of tormented responsibility, which was threatening me after two years of tremendously lovely passion despite circumstances, vocational preoccupations, and moods of gender that would have been impossible for me to suffer in marriage. The aftermath would have dragged me under. I am not unselfish, I am not spiritual, I am not patient, and I was never sympathetic with the temperamental ravings of an artist—except when they were erotic. She treated me like an all-sustaining longsuffering mother who would never die or abandon her. I can hardly believe how diffident and compliant I was with her in those tumultuous days! Yet all along I was doing my job for Arnheim, and the experience eventually casehardened my skin.

I don't like to lie or cheat—but I usually have no regrets afterwards. I can rationalize everything I do. I'm not against religion: I just don't understand the spiritual part of it. Eternity is simply what happens to everything but me after death. But am I too callous to remember that I once would have taken more pains to learn what this wonderful priest has given up nature and success to get at? Something primitive and social, it seems, like a pagan version of Jewish Christianity!

Yes, it's too late for "theodynamics" when you're irrevocably entangled with wealth. Not indeed with the ownership, but with the power. He'll leave something original behind him when he dies, whereas my kind of assets, except for what gets merged into the Hawthorne Development Fund, will only be transferred back to the sort of ownership they began with—to spoiled brats and millionaires—or to some foundation of my wife's that I've never been interested in; and my little empire will soon look like any other agglomeration of black boxes, or else dissolve like the molecules of a German corpse under a French wheat field.

But at the same time an unanchored wisp in Arthur Halymboyd's head prompted him to recall, unsought, a sermon's sentence that he'd unaccountably retained from his Christian school—the only doctrinal point that had ever penetrated his engrossment with profane desires during church services: "When one is lonely and desperate he should remember that someone is praying for him—as an unknown person, loved not only by God but by others, by the Church."

Even me—even now? he wondered with the Pyrrhonic amusement of a vigorous middle age crowded with further possibilities and laden with no remorse.

*

Next morning Halymboyd took one more long walk, retracing yesterday's route from the Van's midpoint of Front Street, along East Front from beginning to end and on up the steep byway to the Laboratory for his business conference with Father Duncannon. The sun had the sky to itself, the air was dry, and until the final ascent no noticeable breeze would have been necessary to cool the brisk walker without his briefcase, who was reviewing still-lifes of the past instead of preparing his thoughts for a meeting that was set for something more important than the pleasure of uncommon conversation.

He was interested in knowing both the effect and the affect of Domino's appointment with Capstick in Washington, but its immediate success or failure would be all one to the eventual outcome, for at the outset long ago he had provided for his veto of any corporate associate in his limited consortiums of subterranean power. (That presumptuous priest is said to have a "feminine intuition" for the market, and I admire his hermaphroditic élan, but any woman who condescended to enter into our foolish money games would have foreseen my response to his tactics.) Let Cappy sweat a while to find investors that King Arthur would agree to, even if it means persuading such knights as J Anacoluther or O Leary to rejoin the cabinet.

He was puffing a little when he reached the crest of Moor Rock Road, to turn off further upward on the Laboratory's drive, and noticed a weathered tennis ball lodged at the corner of a gutter whither it had evidently rolled from the grounds above. Ignoring the years by which his dignity outdistanced the acquisitive habits of a colonial boy, he stooped to pick it up with the simple reflexive intuition that it had been lost by a puzzled dog; and as he paused to catch his breath the dog itself appeared at poise between the borders of shrubbery with its ears cocked in the suspended action of interrogation. But the guardian did not bark, and for ten seconds they both stood still.

To the man this majestic Viking Shepherd was an "immortal model"—a reincarnation perpetuated by the apparently unchanging reproduction of others, like a goddess produced by ritual—yet mortal indeed for her individual presence! The apparition lanced his heart with memories of an otherwise unique beauty: a beauty linked im Augenblick to a continuum of beauties in vision, act, and grief.

Then without further hesitation, as if he'd never ceased his service to this dog, he threw the ball high enough for her to estimate its trajectory, and far enough beyond her station to make a merry chase. But as he slowly followed his instant friend he saw that the goddess was a god, not a ghost at all, and, if memory served, even larger than the archetype magnified in memory, though perhaps not as refined in visage. And as the game proceeded by reiteration and variation of azimuth he found that despite instructions that were varied in tone and diction this male avatar was less intelligent than the female spectre about encouraging the prolongation of his own delight, for he failed to fetch the ball to hand after its retrieval. He was as good as the New Uruk Nimrods centerfielder in leaping and catching, but instead of returning the ball to home plate he would proudly wag and worry it in his mouth as he gamboled toward the thrower like a dribbling basketball player. After much laughable experiment in commands and suggestion the dog could be persuaded to drop the ball only somewhere within the stranger's range of stooping and reaching. "Puppy, are you making fun of me?" Halymboyd asked at last. "You need a technical education!"

It was the man-tiring end of this rather boring pastime that Caleb spied from his upper-floor office window, having been informed that the mysterious Arthur Halymboyd was expected; and he watched as the visitor apologized to Ibi for discontinuing the game when Father Duncannon appeared at the front door. The young dog was left with his tail wanly wagging in saddened gratitude for the pleasure that his master was rarely patient enough to serve up at such length.

Ibi-Roi would rather play ball than eat copulate or hunt, but the perfect recreation of capturing a live ball vanished almost as soon as it ceased to resist his jaws unless there was someone to contend for its possession and start the chase all over again. It was almost unprecedented to encounter a stranger kind enough to use his God-given paw for that purpose even once or twice. Now with a certain amusement he noticed for the first time that his master's throwing was weak and feminine by comparison.

Halymboyd's demonstration of symbiotic friendliness pleased Caleb very much; but he knew that he was expected not to show his own face and meet the great man until lunchtime. Only then was he going to confirm his surprise at the formidable magnate's unimpressive stature, homely phiz, and unrefined manner.

*

Until then Halymboyd and Father Duncannon were closeted in the study, which Caleb had never been invited to enter, at the far end of the library on the main floor.

HAL: When I was here during the Depression I knew a dog that looked like that. She died in a fire. But for the life of me I can't remember her name! I think it was Classical, or Shakespearean.

DUN: Sycorax perhaps?

HAL: Yes, by God! It's strange that I could forget that one. How did you know?

DUN: I never saw the dog but I heard about her. Very few Viking Shepherds are seen in public. It used to be said that J P Morganatic originally came here to raid the breeding kennels and corner the most exclusive market in the Cynic trade. But the indigenes were too much for him, and later Tybbott was too much for every other pirate. This one's name is Ibi-Roy, spelled R O I.

HAL: Return on Investment: just the name for whatever Morganatic coveted, though that term came in after his time! I understood that Vikings were supernormal, bred from an even smaller population than Jewish Shepherds, which are closest to a standard Canis familiaris, nearest the ancestor wolf. We once had a fine white Shepherd out in Vesper County, but he couldn't match Sycorax or this king for size, and he wasn't so crazy about tennis balls.

DUN: Poincaré divided mathematicians according to whether their intuitions were visual or auditory, but the categories of dogs aren't so limited. Although Jewish Shepherds do balance all the senses better than any other race, they seem to specialize in the olfactory; but I think Ibi excels in sequential abstraction, which seems to be an auditory talent, like Jasper von Neumann's. Yet he's very affectionate, and analogical like Norbert Weimar, who visualizes his abstractions: at least so he once told me.

HAL: Both shepherds of the intellect! Well dog-shepherds are the best sentries because ears and noses are always awake. Does Weimar sleep any sounder than von Neumann did?

DUN: He's probably still an unbeliever but I think he has a clearer conscience. After the war against Hitler he stopped doing military work, though he'd not been as guilty as I was during the first war when I did poison-gas research in the Army. To his great credit, too, he would never join the Universe Club in Washington, as I also did. But Von Neumann, who died in the bosom of the Offense Department, possibly a victim of radiation, was a deathbed convert to Scholasticism, like his political comrade Prosper Ozone, Dogtown's late antisemitic radio engineer!

HAL: It seems that no more than one out of two smart Jews ever converts. But how can one help two Christians without drawing them into the labyrinth that's swallowed many a lamb? I must tell you that one of the two is beginning to disturb my honorably confidential plans with his charismatic appearances. He hasn't the slightest chance of helping himself or your Order thereby.

DUN: I'm afraid he's determined not to understand that.

HAL: At this very minute he may be sitting with my old confederate in the hope of gaining favor for an extremely intimate business relationship with me. Who knows how such an exceptional personality will affect an innocent banker and investor like Capstick who's never before negotiated with a complicatedly selfless agent of the Lord's business? Yet your Father Economist himself seems too pure in heart to suspect us of estimating that even if your Trust's collaboration were acceptable to me he would need to increase his buying power by a hundredfold to interest Capstick in the proposition. I wonder why he didn't come to me first. I would have told him so, and spared you some loss of his time and expense.

DUN: I should suppose he mistook the seller's willingness as the more likely obstacle to an association with you, intending not to trouble you until he knew that it wasn't too late to broach the possibility of an offer to Professor Capstick. Father Lucey is sometimes too subtle in his service to the Lord. But without sparing your own time and expense you have already helped us by so thoughtfully broaching the subject of our indiscretion before it goes too far. I know that some time ago you might easily have put a stop to our inappropriate overtures if you hadn't excused Father Lucey's ingenuousness and considered the feelings of our Order. I think your very presence here shows a disinterested sensitivity to the fact that our wellbeing depends more on the spiritual condition of our members—and especially of the one Member Regular besides myself—than on the temporal condition of our portfolio. Still, I do accept your offer of further help, if it is possible, in gently undoing—you might almost say absolving—the nuisance we have been to you.

HAL: I'm disinterested only in the financial sense. Otherwise I'm as partial to your cause as an agnostic can be. And it's not a nuisance but I hope an opportunity—I might say a pleasure—to defend your work. I'd like to separate this adventure from my less innocent life. But how can I rebuff your monk without hurting his feelings?

DUN: I'm afraid I'm too poor a statesman to suggest a diplomatic course.

HAL: In the financial world it's often foolish to be frank, but maybe I can serve you best by letting you know that I may lose control over Parity's future. In anticipation of which I may break up the corporation to my personal advantage. It would be exhilarating to embark on something entirely new, or even to retire from business. My course will depend largely upon Capstick's success in finding me a large ally to take his place. In any event it's unlikely that your chart will continue to resemble Parity's relationships, either above or below the nuclear circle. In fact it's already much out of date as far as proportions of ownership are concerned. Behind my back the Professor has been acquiring private stock from neutral parties which won't have to be reported in the 10Ks until after the fate is accompli. He cares nothing about industrial integration, let alone social responsibility.

DUN: I thank you for the information. Of course I'll keep it to myself. Any hint of it for Father Lucey I should think must come from you in person, if you would take my word that he can be trusted with a declared secret. But in this connection you might be willing to see him one last time. If you could somehow find reasons for turning him down that don't seem to reflect upon his competence or his value in either your esteem or mine it would certainly simplify our internal difficulty. —But of course [*with a wan smile*] it's too much to ask a privately responsible businessman to trust an enthusiastic monk in business matters. Nonetheless, in any case, your warning of disintegration will strengthen my intention to approve the majority's most likely request in our Chapter discussions of financial policy. We have a whole afternoon reserved for that debate.

[*Pause, a trace of hesitation, followed by the lower tones of yet more confidential uncertainty*:]

Still there remains my embarrassment, my dilemma, as the one privately responsible for this emotional religious under the vow of obedience: really a calamitous—a psychological problem!

HAL: Yes. I would like not to precipitate a premature solution.

DUN: As far as that's concerned, probably no one but the Holy Ghost can help.

HAL: Maybe I could take the initiative by diverting his secular talents. Would he be permitted to accept a directorship or financial consultantcy with one of the Arnheim charities?

DUN: I'd consider such a proposal, with provision of course for religious constraints of time and place. We construe our Rule to allow social work. But knowing that it's not in his nature to sit on a committee or to advise without free rein, I doubt that he'd devote himself to it. No, whatever's in the future, I think he's gone so far in showing himself unsuited to the investment side of a Trustee's function that I must ask him to confine his remaining chrematistic efforts to the recovery of our original conservative and comparatively invulnerable position, free of debt in any form. I must hope that he'll begin to take to heart the job of conserving and administering wealth in accordance with our purpose, especially if the regular life is not perpetuated after I die. He no more loves money for its own sake than any of the other members.

HAL: I never took him for a worldly clergyman!

DUN: As you can see, I'm only begging my own question about how to save from himself a wonderful and precious priest. One can only keep praying for sufficient wisdom.

*

Without great success Caleb had tried to suppress his jealousy and resentment at not having been made privy to so much as the reason for that closeted visit, which obviously concerned a subject in which he continued to invest much thought and emotion as a de facto confidential servant of the highest order. Until now he had not been invited even to meet the Daedalus upon whose work he conferred glamour by having made himself its scholar. But a friendly lunch (gladly served by Gretta, who was always volunteering to extend her temporary engagement beyond secretarial bounds) went far to mollify his stiff neck and expel the grievance from his heart.

The meal lasted longer than anyone had expected: in fact the two principals dawdled like inveterate idlers. Listening to both of them Caleb was for a time charmed into harmonically complementary admirations.

On such an occasion he was not encouraged to talk business or ask questions that might betray curiosity about the reason for Mr Halymboyd's sudden appearance at the Lab in Chris's absence. The conversation on Halymboyd's part was largely political, who knew many of the people clustering around President Kennedy in Washington, and equally interesting on Father Duncannon's, the names of whose distinguished acquaintances had never been known to most Atlantean journalists. Even so, Dogtown was the alpha and omega of the gossip looping out in space and time. At times the acolyte was quite content to find his self-effacing presence practically forgotten. Once or twice he suavely assisted Gretta in removing dishes.

Father Duncannon, as a peculiar son of Dogtown—"in it but not of it", in accordance with his mother's shibboleth—was trying to recover, as much for himself as for his audience, a diachronic spectrum of memories that he as a scientific child (condescendingly fastidious father of the present man), reminding himself how uneducated his fellows were, hadn't dreamed of cherishing when they were being formed and fixed. 1934, at the end of his prolonged inexperience in youth, was the terminus ante quem of these impressions, which he was rarely inclined to fetch up and articulate. Suddenly, it seemed, his loosened ruminations led him pastward, not by reversal of the city's cinematic graduations through threescore years (most of which as an almost continuous expatriate he had scarcely witnessed), nor even by the linkages between affections or disaffections of actual incident, but by delimiting the history that he had missed—as he nearly confessed in his comments to the two unalike strangers whose experiences and memories, however enviable in certain human respects, were as yet short of other particulars by decades of living.

Halymboyd, on the other hand, whenever nothing of what was now recalled had remained in his own Dogtown times, such as the marine semaphore tower, referred the priest's memories to his own recollection of other times or places.

But Caleb assimilated all he heard to the romantic world-line wherein his birthplace was both extended and consolidated in almost unpeopled images of successively obsolete artifacts. The Cape's streetcars, unseen by his own eyes, had followed livery stables into a history no more appreciated by his contemporaries than poetry; schooners, the harbor ferry; steam, wind machines; dairy farms, lumbering; anchor-forging, shipbuilding; quarry rails, granite sloops; coal, firewood; telegraph, signal flags; and soon Mr Duncannon's dynamo would be no more verifiable than the gas works: all superseded by bitumen, nets hauled by infernal consumption, milking machines, wireless intelligence, and imported high tension power, leaving gaps in the hills and landfill in the coves.

*

Ibi, who as a familiar of the Laboratory demesne four or five days a week had naturally assumed a picket's responsibility, was very excited when the IXAT cab arrived to take Mr Halymboyd back to the Van and thence to the airport because he remembered Sam Craigie its driver as his first and immediate friend outside the messuage of Chateau Noir. If he hadn't stopped to take thought he might fain have hopped once again into the front seat in anticipation of the joyful life his one previous taxi ride had introduced him to.

But his loud announcement of recognition brought Halymboyd to the door escorted by the host and he was presented with a dilemma as confounding as if two cats were fleeing equally in opposite directions. At first he oscillated back and forth between cab and house, up the steps and down, as he demonstrated his double-directed welcome, looking both ways like a happily confused Janus. But presently his love of the ball prevailed; fetching it from under a rose bush, he dropped it at the visitor's feet as he reached the driveway.

Alas, though the two cats joined each other to wheel away, he must needs be doubly disappointed, and the silencing pathos of departure seemed mutual for all parties as he reproachfully wagged farewell for a few steps before glancing back at Caleb for anchorage—at whose side the emotional flurry would have instantly lost its sound without aftermath if duty and pleasure hadn't at the same moment impelled him down the drive again to greet Mrs Teddi Cibber with an inexplicably intimate crooning.

She climbed the hill in denim overalls, wheeling her bicycle with its basket full. Although Ibi had never been introduced to her he had sometimes met her on the street not far from his friend Phisto whose affiliation was plainly enough confirmed by the scent about her ankles. He was sorry the phlegmatic black Cabotlander hadn't followed her here, but he knew that at this time of day Phisto usually hung around Wat's shop down on the Neck, or was even out to sea (if fine weather came in conjunction with the prospect of break-even prices for fish).

Father Duncannon had expected her later in the afternoon. She came for respite from her cheerful housewifery. The visit was a civilized recreation from mothering and domestic charring, but she had brought her favorite garden trowel (as well as two different supplies of cookies) in order to work for an hour or two on the Laboratory flower beds (to which the off-duty municipal firefighter who kept the grounds deigned not to truckle) before she stayed for tea. Mrs Cibber was always eager to do things "for the Fathers", whom she otherwise saw only now and then in their ecclesiastical function at a weekday morning "Communion".

"I think we have the only two dogs in Dogtown that never earn rebuke!" she said to Caleb. "Mephisto and Ibi-Roi are both perfect gentlemen, and I've been so glad to notice that they're such good friends! I just hope that your beautiful creature has as much respect for this garden as we demand of our heavy-footed black devil! —Oh, by the way, I was delighted to get a letter from your mother in South Atlantis the other day: the first I've heard from her in many years. I was very very happy to learn that she's found a peaceful life down there! Like all mothers, she asked me to chide you for not writing her."

Caleb quaked, suddenly shorn of all illusion about his anonymity. —Could the cat have been out of the bag all along? Had Teddi Cibber identified him right from the beginning? The dread of her enlightenment having been nearly forgotten of late, the shock of this communication came too quickly for him to feel the penetration of his defenses, but the exposure of his vulnerability left him trembling. Whether or not she'd been surprised by the connection between Mary Tremont and Caleb Karcist, her knowledge of it was at once absorbed by his practical intelligence simply as a new fact for induction that altered the whole picture of his situation. At once he began to prepare himself for the painful possibilities.

How much else was told in the letter, or alluded to, or demanded in reply? Was an epistolary revival of dangerous friendship in the making, after a long lapse presumably self-imposed by the shame of a scarlet ewe? He was confident of Mrs Cibber's tolerance and goodwill, but how much could he rely on the sensitivity of her discretion?

Yet he managed to pass off the message lightly, as if from any ordinary mother to a normal sailor-boy. To the son's great relief no more was said about his kinship.

Afterwards, when he came down from the office to join Father Duncannon, Gretta, and Mrs Cibber, resting from their respective labors on the sun porch with tea and pastries, at his apotropaic request the guest recited from memory in the soft sweet enunciation of an excellent student the lyric of Goethe's that he'd been told was often evoked in the Superior's summertime musings, as in his own, by the Laboratory's pine grove when there was no sea-breeze on the hilltop:

> Über allen Gipfeln
> Ist Ruh,
> In allen Wipfeln
> Spürest du
> Kaum einen Hauch . . .

After tea, when Gretta had washed things up and gone home, and Caleb had returned to the office, Mrs Cibber and Father Duncannon stood out in front of the house as she prepared with both hands to step onto her bike. "That man I saw leaving in the taxi:" she said, staring thoughtfully down at the gravel, "I've been trying to think where I've seen him before, long ago but often, here in East Harbor! If you care to tell me his name it might satisfy my idle effort to remember what I can't get out of my foolish mind!"

"Arthur Halymboyd."

"—Of course! It was on the tip of my tongue! For a few years after the war he and his family lived out near Crow Hill in the summer; but long before that, when he was around our part of East Harbor, I think Caleb's mother knew him."

"Yes, I believe she did. If her name was Mary Tremont."

"It had crossed my mind that he might be her Caleb." She lingered, bemused. "Today I noticed the scar on his forehead and wrinkled skin on the back of his right hand. I'd forgotten the little boy's last name."

In the stillness of hill-top pines Caleb happened to hear this much through his open office window.

9
EXISLE

*C*hilde Caleb's long-sought impression of King Arthur was therefore dimmed by an uneasily intensifying preoccupation with the matter of Mary his own mother, which sometimes disturbed even his efforts to organize thought and will for a second Gilgamesh play. (His interest in the unfinished design never flagged but an impulse to start laying bricks for the play itself was long in coming.) Having finally forced himself to begin a methodical perusal of her composite "Autobiography", the congeries of motley manuscripts, he'd discovered that he was reading segments of narrative (both proleptic and retrospective) beginning in reverse chronological sequence but soon and often reversing time's arrow in an associative concatenation of descriptions, reflections, prayers, representative events, and circulating themes. His search for a particular place in time was so obfuscated by the formidable medium of long crowded paragraphs in faded ink on tattered and sporadically numbered paper, bound and unbound, that the whole of the living matter had successfully defied all initial attempts to serve his purpose by sampling, skimming, and skipping.

The extended exordium, treating the most recent experience of Mary Tremont's life (some of which he'd already read), was composed from the vantage of her present situation in the Vernalia community of the Brotherhood of the Peaceable Kingdom. But despite the fact that in the living perspective of any life the foreground is largest in scale, the B P K spiritual aura did not mistify the confessional content of her reminiscences, even in censoring (as the content itself suggested) some of the "shameful" episodes.

Though that community of confessors was meant to be a fellowship speaking with tongues, her urge of expression and exhibition was too powerful to be contained by prayer or tolerable speech. Her elations and sympathies were worn on her sleeve, and she had to be warned by one of the "democratic" leaders that she must not speak too much in meetings. "I know that—and *tried hard* to hold back the flood of words that came to me. For *in silence is truth*!"

Yet Caleb hoped that the rather formal tone with which she introduced her self-history (compared to the torrential screeds of earlier years) would subsequently evaporate and disclose more of the inconsistent but inexpugnable allusions than he'd ever cared to submit himself to by admitting an interest in.

*

"Consider both the kindness and the severity of God."
I am now fifty-five years old. Thank you, God, for a wonderful life! If I should die in the next hour, I could not reproach my Creator for withholding from me anything inherent in His gift of life! I've had everything: robust health; a sunny, abundant childhood; an intelligent mother and a kind *de jure* father; a loving sister; many loyal friends; the delight and disillusionment of many kinds of love; inklings of marriage; a child of my own as satisfying as two sons and a daughter—God's *very most precious gift!*—; and a broad life-experience of exhilarating joy, sorrows a-plenty, hardships galore, with such profoundly illuminating self-revelation and humiliation that, at my age, I should be far wiser than I am. It has been a good life, a *full* life!

I ask you, God, to hear my prayer for a quick death, when death comes. Grant that I do not become a burden to my child, the cause of his protracted worry and service. Send your angel to call and take me away *express*, so that my departure may be speedily complete.

Thank you for everything! Sophisticates and intellectuals poohpooh a personal God who listens to the prayers of individual human beings and "saves their souls". But you, God, my dear all-wise Creator, have attended to my prayers and answered them in infinite wisdom. I know you from my own experience in this the life you gave me. What greater assurance have I than that you have given me "every good and perfect gift" for which I asked in life? —and as a wise and compassionate father have disciplined me personally even while your omniscience and omnipotence have been engaged with the conduct of great affairs in all worlds simultaneously?

... At last it began! It had taken all but a whole year to earn enough money for a *round*-trip (as the Vernalia Community always requires of its invited postulants)—working first as a camp counsellor for rich Jewish children, where I was very fairly treated, and then as a cook in the guest house of the Tudor-Apostolic Convent of Saint Agatha, where I saw the tawdry shallowness of "world religion", where I was more deeply than ever convinced that the observances of worship, assiduously carried on, are in themselves of no avail to hearts that "have not love" (though I will always be grateful to the good Sisters for giving me the job that made this journey to Orellana an actuality).

I finally embarked at Brotherly, on Benjamin Franklin's windswept, coal-stained South River—as a *passenger* in the *M\S Grundtvig*!—for Belém on the muggy mudstained Rio Orellana ("King of Waters" to the aboriginals); and thence on a series of chugging single-decked boats, and finally in a covered wagon—into the hinterland and OUT OF THE WORLD. I could not possibly have made this exit from my former way of self-defensive exhibitionist life without the loyal, loving, prayerful support of the U S branch of the Brotherhood of the Peaceable Kingdom on the North River of Nether Land—the community in which I was prepared for the greatest adventure of my life, down here at the Equator.

If, at the depth of my despair, when even the hopes of a general New Deal "recovery" from the Great Depression left me faced with the prospect of my son's imminent *starvation*, so that I "threatened" suicide, and (when asked about the child) said "Why of course I will take him with me!" (because I could never leave him in a world so cruel, hungry and alone, with no one to properly love him)—IF I *had* had the actual courage of my conviction that Death is better than life—would Christ's forgiveness of our sins have included forgiveness of taking my life and my son's? (Luckily, anyway, I never *did* have that "courage"!)

[*It was beyond a mere "threat", that first time with me—at least if it depended on anybody but me to halt the action. I understood well enough what she was telling me, though I remember little else of our circumstances at that house, which now I sometimes think I recognize in Tinkersdale, and nothing of what immediately followed. She made me huddle with her in front of the open oven. Now and then the smell of that coal-gas comes back to me, always for some reason associated with the words* ether *and* ozone. *It must have been I who opened the door and cried aloud for help. Sometime later I was staying with strangers who kept terrifying turkeys. Later I found myself in the convent of walls and oak trees, having no idea that it was out on the Foreside, though I knew well enough that I was being protected from urban miseries as well as from the ocean, which was gently audible, as if from inside the hull of a prison-ship, and often visible from windows at what seemed a great distance. It never occurred to me that the outer harbor I saw had any connection with the beach we were taken to once a week in the summer, at Dilemma Cove (as I now believe it to have been), where I was a passionate architect of sand, wishing I could have thereto the oak twigs I used for the construction of wigwam and log-cabin compounds on hard dirt inside the walls.*]

But Arnold Eberhard, the German founder of B P K , has in his book a passage so descriptive of my hysteria at that time that I must copy it out here, in shame, never to let it be forgotten amid all my moments of weakness and confusion: "We all know the diseased, nervous condition in which we have sought, by making the most extraordinary remarks, to make our neighbors take an interest in us. When that did not seem likely to succeed, we tried to draw attention to ourselves by means of jokes and fun; and when that, also, did not work, we drove people by our insolent behavior to give us their attention, if only out of irritation. Should that in turn fail to achieve our purpose, the hysterics of Self reach their peak when, through shivering, weeping, or fainting, or even through genuine (or half-genuine) attempts at suicide, they finally succeed in making those around us, however unwillingly, devote themselves to the diseased individual ego."

I ask myself: Was it mere "hysterics" at that time; or was I really capable of a philosophic rationalization of the ideal of Death as preferable to Life in such an evil world? I only know that I am indeed thankful, as the doctor told me then that I would be, for the SHOCK that brought me up short and cured me—the shock of being taken for crazy and committed to a mental hospital "for observation"! I am *very* thankful too for the surgery I got there, in addition, which was such a boon. It restored the well-being I had lost after my terrible ordeal in childbirth. But now—now that I'm about to become a member of the Brotherhood—I am not so sure that I wasn't guilty of pre-empting God's powers when I asked for *sterilization* and burdened poor little Caliban-Dog with the responsibility of fulfilling my life-long, unwavering, bed-rock vow to rear *three* children, male and female, of distinctly different markings! How MUCH I have to regret—*truly* repentant, and hence to be forgiven—yet cannot re-live my years to make amends.

For I wasn't really "cured" in that hospital. I often think back, especially, to those bleak dark times many years later, after the War—when Caleb had abandoned me and was leading a secret life of his own, and before I had met P M (who helped restore my soul) in the *M/V Olav Trygvason*. I would sit for hours at a time arguing with myself that I should—if only I were brave enough—*get off the earth* by killing myself. I argued that since there was no place in the world for me (irrevocably cut off from the beloved Dogtown in which my life was formed); since it "cost money" to keep me alive; since I was told everywhere that I was too old (at 45, et seq) to earn a living; since I could no longer be useful to anyone, and was "wanted" by no one—there was a vast amount of evidence that I *ought* to die. I used to climb up on a stool, twist a strap over a rafter, fasten the other end about my neck, and *pull*, till I could feel my eyes begin to bulge. But I never could *do* it! I would fill a bathtub with water, get into it, and try to summon the courage to *really* cut the veins in my wrists. (All I ever did was scratch them.) I *couldn't* do it! I would turn on all the outlets of the stove and breathe in gas till I got groggy ; but I always ended up turning them off and opening the windows again. I *couldn't* do it! *Couldn't* jump off the top of Court Tower in Yerba Buena! *Couldn't* fling myself into the Bay from the deck of the Babylon Oaks ferry! COULDN'T have what I almost believed was the "common decency" to remove my nuisance from the face of the earth! [*In the old Unabridge years I would pretend to ignore the grimacing pantomimes and gurgles of a rope tightening around her neck, or calmly turn off the kitchen gas as soon as she turned it on.*] I did all these things in breathless secrecy, afraid that someone, seeing me, would send me (again) to a terrible madhouse. I *knew* I wasn't insane; I thought I was "philosophical". What I really was was SELFISH, self-centered, *guilty*, and proud. *Too proud to live* unless I could live as I thought some special quality entitled me to live—in dignity, in happiness—in the peace which my own self-love would not allow! But now I am killing my SELF, in order that I may live *quietly*, without show, *at the bottom*. This is a *good* "suicide"! Thanks, God!

. . . When I was 4, I promised Mama to die when she died, and to be buried with her. But two years ago I was at sea, off the west coast of South Atlantis, unaware of her illness, death, and burial until it was all over! My relationship with her was troubled and turbulent, after I was 15; but I loved her, and she loved me, and perhaps now that she has gone on, somewhere closer to God, she and I will be at peace—for always. She was such a timid person—fearful of perils both real and imaginary—that I almost feel I *should* have gone with her to give such protection as I could! —But that, of course, is the sort of feeling I must not indulge, for (as the Brotherhood is teaching me, slowly) I am nothing, nobody—only a "poor thing" in God's sight who can do nothing myself, for anyone at all, unless I am "used" by God for His purposes. Therefore, I must keep my spirit clear against the clogs and obstructions of conceited self-importance, & be an open "channel" for the Spirit that directs thought, deed, & word for the Brotherhood. —For now, having made my decision to forsake all the world, *& leave even my child behind, in it*—until God calls him too!—the Brotherhood is my family: my Father, Mother, Sister, Brother, and Child. How very little I *deserve* the goodness of God in leading me to this Life! "The last of life, for which the first was made."

It is so beautifully *quiet* here in Vernalia—! that is, so free of *man-made* noises! Yes, the diesel engine generating electricity, the sawmill whine & grind, the machines in the laundry—&, rarely, the sound of our truck or our tractor—but no traffic noises! No screeching of brakes, no factory whistles, no blasts from a railroad, no cross-sounding voices, no human quarreling or shouting! We hear Nature's noises, aplenty! The birds sing, the cattle low, the horses neigh, the donkeys bray, the cocks crow, the hens cluck, the bullfrogs keep up a nightly chorus, and before rain certain treefrogs "miaow" like cats with exasperating continuity, and on some nights there are hideous sounds of howling monkeys across the savannah in the plantation beyond the power plant. But all of these are God's creatures making "a joyful noise unto the Lord". No roar of Elevated trains drowns their hymn.

Here I am slowly learning—the hard way—to do the Will of God on earth, as it is done in Heaven, that I may do my minuscule part to prepare for His Kingdom! And this is what all my life I prayed for an opportunity to do: to WORK FOR GOD! To do work well & humbly, with punctuality and goodwill, was of *no avail* "out in the world" (which is so thankfully left behind forever!)—for I was working *competitively*, for a "boss", for a pay-check. In that routine I could not survive.

I am glad, and thankful, and humble in my heart for the privilege of being sent here. Surely, as everyone in the Community has said, *God* directed me here. It is very late in my life to dedicate my years to Him, of which not many are left. I could have heard His call long ago, doubtless, had I not been making so much noise myself—"showing-off" to make myself the center of attention because I wished to hide from myself, my family, my fellow-men, and even God Himself that I was guilty of the sins that crucified His son, my Savior.

*

... Another setback! I am having a new taste of the "pain" that my friends here predicted for me. IT IS NOT EASY to surrender "self". And *all* our "selves" are miserable, crippled, devilish monsters of two-faced lying, deceptive smugness! We have *all* "fallen short" indeed! I am now coming up from under a *bad* time!

I had forgotten to collect my weekly-stores basket at the warehouse yesterday. After brewing my maté, making my toast, and collecting my daily egg, I went down to get my supply—in a very black mood (blaming someone else for my own oversight)—and *how wonderful* it was that I went, and saw the sun rising in the east over the wooded hill, and mist lifting off the level vastnesses. "It restoreth my soul" to see God's beauty all around me. I should be even *more* grateful to be here—and I want to continue with being "withdrawn" and QUIET—yet awhile!

... In a way I've kept my childhood word to Mama, to die when she died; for I have *left the world*, as she has. I have left behind all the old ways—the "freedom" that was slavery for the slavery that is freedom; left the pressure of competition in work, in social life, in Art; the vanities of dress and personality; and, *very* slowly, the glib-tongued persiflage by which I deceived others and myself, too, into thinking I was the cleverest "life of the party" wherever I found myself—&, also even *more* slowly, the constant noise & chatter I used to make. (I am growing ever more *silent—I!* Yes, *I!* I shall continue on this course till I become one whose "Yeah" & "Nay" are all that others need to hear from me.)

This is a period of "training". I am now learning to ACT "like a Brother". The irritability that has persisted here, since I came away from the world, is also decreasing. I am learning how true it is that here, as I've been taught, "we do not live together because we love each other but because *God called us out of the world to live in the sharing of work, 'wealth', and worship.*" I am *slowly* learning to tolerate more; to resent less; to give a softer answer every time.

*

... I BELONG here! In many phases of my life I have definitely NOT belonged. I remember my bewilderment in Brummagen, when I had my first commercial-art job, on the *Brummagen Post*. I lived in a clean newly furnished room in a downtown Swedish hotel, "eating out". I didn't "belong" to the place at all. And when I went walking, exploring that miserable city, I was lost and lonely. Then at work I met the unconscionable madcap Polly Kindred, who was anxious to "take up" with me; & she and I & Bunny Estabrook, and someone I vaguely remember as Reggie, a sulky-boy son of an ice-cream manufacturer, used to "go out" together in kilroys, and to "speakeasies". But I wasn't happy. I never belonged to that life, those people (though I *did* belong with Monica & Dallas Grahame in Brummagen, and I used to *belong* in Dogtown and Unabridge, and at home with my family, & in the hearts and homes of my friends).

I remember also my sensation of dismay in my first experiences with "Bohemia" on the western slopes of Governor's Hill in Botolph. I didn't understand all I saw, and I was *mis*understood by practically every "long-haired man and short-haired woman" who lived there. My only excuse or reason for gravitating to such a place was that I was "bereaved" for the first time—by a combination of things: my first lover's desertion, my sister Susan's engagement, Mama's withdrawal of interest in me, and my own frustrated striving for a "career" in art. My job then, as a fashion-illustrator for the *Botolph Trumpet*, made me happy at work; but the paper was fusty and out-of-date, and the pay was ridiculous.

So—to New Uruk City! How DAZED I was at first! How terrified by Mama's dire forewarnings of the certain fate awaiting young women alone in the great city! My first three days—because I was still shaken by the awful quarrel with Daddy (my putative sire) that precipitated my leaving home—I barricaded myself into the hotel room, afraid even of going down to the lobby or the café. I had heard of "Room Service", and how by lifting the phone I could have food brought up. So, not knowing the scope of the menu, I lived on chocolate ice cream—shivering and lonely, & longing for a good square meal. On the 4th day I ventured out for breakfast on Monroe Avenue. It was 7:00 AM, and the whole city was asleep!

It didn't take me long to re-gather my (egotistic) "forces", once I dared find my way around. Bruce Gaskell, the great advertising executive of the Twenties, was gracious enough to see me, when (brazenly) I sent in a message by his highly amused secretary that "Miss Trevisa from Vinland" was here to see him. (Trevisa was still my dishonestly legal name.) Bruce looked at my country-fresh face, "health" shoes, tweed coat, knitted cap—heard my "Botolph accent", patted my (unmanicured) hand, & said: "Go home to Cape Gloucester! Find a husband and bring up a family!"

But I had lost hope (and "innocence") when my *un*true love, Todd Elton, with whom I had spent a lovely dalliant summer planning domestic bliss—even *naming* our three children—and the house in which we would live (with a great stone fireplace at one end of the living room and a built-in organ at the other, one wall lined with our best books, the other looking out over the landscape above the sea that we would have roamed and camped in all through our incredible romantic idyll). Todd had gone his way when I wrote about him:

> My love and I would wedded be,
> A family we would beget.
> My love he sailed away from me:
> My love, he could forget!
> Our children are but shadow-souls;
> Their little hearts will know no sin
> Because they'll never see this world
> They might have bided in!
> Yet they are mine! And every night
> I make the rounds of all their beds
> To kiss their lovely cheeks, and ask
> God's blessing on their unborn heads!

And "To My Children":

> Now my youth is passing lightly,
> All day long my heart is singing.
> But in dreams my fancies nightly
> With thy future laughter ringing
> Shows this youth, its joys and graces

> Shining on *thy* lovéd faces.
> All my youthful heart is yearning
> For that promiséd hereafter
> When life's ways I shall be learning,
> Sweetened by thy merry laughter.

I had still not got a job when Nelson Houghton, my family's insurance agent, came to the rescue, Daddy's ambassador of forgiveness and goodwill (financed, I'm sure, by my real father, who could easily afford it!), with a purse full of contrition-money, to buy me smart New Uruk clothes, "show me around" the island of Ur, and teach me cosmopolitan ways. (Nellie thoroughly enjoyed spending that money, more of it on himself, I fancy, for "Travel & Expenses" in a *good* hotel, than on me. I didn't inquire how he divided it.) When I had been properly outfitted at decent shops, & had (I well remember) a *beautiful* soft black cloth coat with a *real* leopard collar (I am now ashamed to say), and a pretty hat with real *chic*, & some practical business dresses, a suit, many pairs of silk stockings, and "smart" shoes, I *did* gather confidence. Nellie made a great fanfaron installing me at a "girls' Residence Club", under hawk-eyed chaperonage by the management. But it was on my *own* that I got a fine illustrating job and really began to be a "career girl".

I'm afraid my confidence grew TOO fast. I had no long wait for a gay social life. I looked up Ramon Arratia, the Chilean professor of Romance Languages living at the Ur University International House, who spent his summers in Taraville. His shiny red roadster made me "the envy of other poor girls", parked outside the Club on 30th St (east of Concord Avenue), with his handsome brother and *his* fiancée, he himself (even handsomer) at the wheel, waiting to take me for a springtime drive on Sundays, out to Vesper County. The association with Esther & Bill Hodgman, and their Smart Avenue in-laws, also "set me up" in the eyes of Club membership. And Odette Mathis, when she first arrived from Lonestar, "took me up" (till I unmasked her perversions for the horrified old-maid Directors). And when I met the Limeway musical-comedy crowd through Earl Williams, & began going to movie- and radio-studio parties on Estuary Drive, & Smart Ave, & the Mellon Hall studios on 57th St, I was "gayer" than I ever bargained for.

I remember one champagne-flowing party of film star Douglas Blackstream's, when I met the two scions of the Nether Land branch of the House of Vanderlyn (N U "Society Boys"), and Andrew singled me out. I had never had champagne before! It made me dance like an angel! We FLOATED about a golden-waxed floor, in an enchantment. When the room got over-heated we ran, holding hands, down a long corridor to where an open window admitted a draft of air from the right. We groped into that room, looking for a light, & smelled ROSES—beautiful roses! They were long-stemmed Atlantean Beauties, standing in inch-deep water, in a *huge* bathtub.

"Oh," said I (*drunk* for the first time in my life), "*a bed of roses!*" And I climbed into the tub, & Andrew after me, despite the water at the bottom (which saturated my blue velvet dress with its band of fur at the hem!)—& and we lay down like kittens & slept coolly through the hot summer night, amid petals and thorns. It was daylight when we got home. "Gorgon McMahon", the Director, saw from her window how draggled & wrung-out I was when I alighted in light of day before the front door of the Girls' Community Club & *dared* to let myself in with my key!

Ah, that was the beginning of the end of my high standing at the Club! I, the "Vinland girl of good family", with such careful parents, etc , etc .

But all the gold & glitter & flim-flam didn't do anything to stop the internal weeping for my unborn children! And all the smart New Uruk clothes, & the worship of my little Jewess assistant at the office (who considered me a "genius" and a "glamour-girl") didn't help my aching empty heart. I longed for Mama & Daddy & my sister & my little dog & the Harbor & Tinkersdam & Troika Pit & Taraville & the chaste Liberty of Seamark & North Village—the *honest* & *natural* life with dew in the morning & sweet smells from the honeysuckle vines at supper on the porch! (It's a *sad* thing when a young person starts out to conquer the world; for there is a danger that she may instead *be conquered* by the world!)

Thank God for preserving my inmost integrity & faith in Him through all sorts of brash ventures into the "realistic", materialistic life of Babylon! Thank God for my early life with the beauty of rock & sea & sun & wind & sky of Cape Gloucester, where Beauty and Nature taught me to love God innocently. —But never, never let me forget the "rattle-grind" sound of the little granite-laden "dolly" cars that I heard after the shrill 7 o'clock morning whistle at Hollow Point quarry, which symbolized the wicked slavery of those brutally treated workers in the granite industry. *God help Man!*

*

... The Brotherhood is preparing for the Lord's Supper—a solemnity here that's new to me—to achieve deeper unity in the Holy Spirit before Easter. After Easter our Novice group will be prepared for Baptism. How I long for that!

As an infant I was baptized by the Rector of St Paul's Tudor Apostolic Church (before the ugly little pseudo-Gothic edifice had been given beautiful stained-glass windows of fishing and fishermen). Many years later, when my study of the Bible made me understand, at last, what God requires of man, and I had begun to see the futile errors of humanistic, Bohemian "realism", which (like the credulous fool I used to be!) I had tried all my life to adjust to my *real, enduring* Faith in God—and never could, of course! —I wanted so much to become a Christian in the fellowship of other simple, faithful souls that I went back to the little town of Heraldville in Cornucopia to ask for proper Baptism there, in the plain little Christian Church. Ethel and Albert Gale, that devout, sincere old couple who had rented me a room in their house for 6 weeks when I was selling Bibles, were very glad. A tall gangling former tree-surgeon, Bryan Foy, who had become their pastor, baptized me there in a tank of water. If only the fussiness of wearing the great white robe, & the distractions of the people & the place had not actually taken my mind off the *real meaning* of what I was doing, it might have been an adequate Baptism; but I fear it was not. I long to be baptized here, among my Brothers & Sisters, in token of a *far greater* understanding of *true repentance* (that will not admit ever again of Temptation by the Evil One) and a re-birth now that will be far more thoroughgoing!

In reading Joseph Boehme's odd revelations of his religious experience, I feel that my whole life has been illumined by similar flashes of Understanding of God, beginning with very young days when I sat in Mama's bedroom window-seat and stared out at the sunset over the West Marsh hills, absolutely LOSING myself for hours at a time. The greatest experience of my young maturity was the "ether dream" I had on the 21st of March, 1935, when Caleb was born. Then I *ascended* height upon height from earthly reality to the dazzling light of God, passing the whirling, gyrating *sun* (which smiled at me, winking and saying: *Woops, Bang! Bang!*), and went on & on upward into the silence & glory, infinitely *higher* than the sun and stars, & felt rapt and translated by God's great light. I remember His promise then, to tell me the secret of his Heart, & the meaning of life! (He has kept the promise! —That realization comes over me, again & again, here in Vernalia.) Fay Morgan (that most wonderful nurse, anthropologist, and truest friend!) said that when, struggling out of anesthesia, hours later, I tried to explain what God had said to me, I must have been recalling something very near death; for that delivery of my beloved little only-born baby, whose survival was even more miraculous than my own, was indeed very nearly an end to my life on earth.

How I floundered, & floundered, & wallowed in error, *even after that*! How *could* I have continued to be a smart-alecky Bohemian mother, when I got "back to normal" & resumed daily life in the "intellectual circle" I wanted to cultivate in Unabridge? How *could* I have ever lost (fleeting) sight of that promise? —For *I* have never considered that experience as "only an ether-dream"! I *know* it was a *real* religious experience!

And then, four years later, I attained to another inexpressible afflatus, at the time of my life's greatest dilemma, when I had been railroaded into the "madhouse", led through ward after horrible ward full of wailing, howling, possessed women, & had door after steel door locked behind me by an attendant.

I was put to bed in the "Suicidal Ward". They gave me a sedative. But for a long time before it took effect I was still quite clear in my mind & memory. There was a frightfully unhappy woman in the next bed to mine—a dark-haired hatchet-faced middle-aged woman sitting up, wringing her hands, & wailing: "Oh, how *could* I! —How *could* I burn up *all my children*!"

That afternoon I had left *my* child with a Sunday-school teacher in Middlesex Farms and hitch-hiked to Auburn Fells to try to arrange for a free bed and operation at the hospital there. They had locked me into an examination room, and kept me until after dark. A parade of doctors, nurses, & interns kept coming in to "check-up" on me. One contemptible little Jewish smart-alec intern came again & again, & subjected me repeatedly to (*quite unnecessary*) "pelvic examination", till I fought him off, slapping his face, and telling him he was just a "horrid little ball of wool". (He was thick-lipped, freckled, & kinky-haired—and *utterly odious*!) After that they'd let me alone for a while; but then they came & told me "someone" was waiting for me downstairs. I got dressed—I still remember the powder-blue crepe dress I wore that awful night!—& they took me down.

The Dogtown Chief of Police (called all the way over there from Cape Gloucester!), 2 deputies, & a smelly old woman like a gypsy grabbed me, hustled me out of the lobby, & thrust me into the tonneau of a big black sedan driven by another policeman. The

Chief (a beefy Irish ignoramus) sat next to me, keeping his gun in my ribs.

"Where are we going?" I demanded. "I have to get back to my child!" They wouldn't answer; just told me to shut up, & "*Come along quietly*"! I kept asking *where* we were going—because *I HAD to get back to Caleb*! And the brainless Chief only butted his gun deeper into my side, and said "Where people like you belong!" It couldn't be *jail*, I knew, being innocent of crime. I kept on telling them I couldn't go *anywhere! I had to get back to my son!* And then they told me that the smelly old hag beside me (who was a "special" police matron!) was going to care for my child till I came back! My heart sank, but I kept trying to tell her what he should be fed, and about baths, naps, & bed-time. (They wouldn't say *how long* I must be gone!) I was frantic! —And then, from conversation over the back of the front seat, I realized we had lost our way. The driver had missed a turn. —It was late, by now. There was a full moon shining. Whenever I spoke they roughly told me to "shut up" and things would go better for me!

At last we'd turned in at a high iron-grille gate, and soon a great lighted building loomed up before us at the top of a hill like a castle of evil. *Shrieks* reverberating from the angles of its walls told me what it was: a MAD HOUSE! Well, now I knew! Now I could not expect to be home to my child before *morning*! I made no more resistance. The foolish Chief of Police was the "mad" one!

I followed docilely, and we waited while two or three other patients were admitted. When it came to my turn I was quite self-possessed—but *exhausted* with anger, fear, and worry—and I answered all their questions quietly & calmly. The admitting doctor was a small Jewish Viennese with red hair. She looked at me narrowly and said: "Isn't this a mistake—for *you* to be here?" "Yes, it is," I replied gratefully. "I'm afraid the minimum for observation is 9 days," she said, implying that she would look out for my interests. She made a little face of disgust behind the Chief's back. "You need a good *rest*, child!" she added.

They then undressed and washed me, took away all my clothing, purse, & so on, & led me away behind 50 locked doors—to "rest", while that smelly old woman was to "care for" my poor child!

The whole of that experience—which revealed, among other things, the Pharisaical "love" and despicable treachery of my own mother, sister, uncle, & aunt, who *allowed* that devastating humiliation of me (myself a mother!)—is too bitter to record. Suffice it to say that, after the 9-day observation, when I was taken to a "full staff conference" and harried by a hundred cross-questions to test my sanity, I was given by bléssed Dr Goldstein (the senior physician) "a clean bill of health", and leave to go at once, if I chose—"unless," he said, "there is something you would like us to do for you."

So I asked the staff for the much-needed, long-postponed operation I had been trying to get at the Auburn Fells Hospital. They told me that if I wanted surgery I must *commit myself* to 24 more days in that awful asylum, and be content to convalesce in their Infirmary (full of violent "dementia cases"). I needed the job done. Having gone through so much already, I assented. They gave me *a $1000 operation absolutely free*, treated me with the utmost kindness—and I was grateful, grateful, grateful!

The smelly old woman fed my child on canned beans, and stole his clothes for her own grandchildren, before he was rescued and (by the merciful will of God!) sent to Saint Martha's convent in Dogtown. I never saw her again.

But the thing that had seen me through that 9+24-day ordeal—to say nothing of the post-operative shock after 5 hours' surgery!—was what happened in the first bed I laid myself down upon in that suicide ward of the North Bethsalem State Hospital. The sedative had not had time to take effect when, right before me, on the soft-green wall, a great white light was shining, & God's voice spoke to me, and said "Be calm! I will be with you, and get you out of here!" It was the only thing I had to live by.

(Oh, how could I have been so slow to come to the Brotherhood, when He has been calling, calling me, & so patiently leading me, & forgiving me for so many, many years!)

"You must not waste your energy on hating that Chief of Police for abusing his 'commitment authority' and trying to 'put you away' for political opposition to his administration," Dr Goldstein said to me. "You must not dwell on the fact that your own family refused to come to visit you or help you in any way. And one thing I must tell you: Forget Captain Ozone! Write him quite off your books! He is a cad. He is a beast. You need not regret your decision to denounce him, but you must never destroy your family by making public what you know about him, nor appeal to him ever again in private." He told me how Captain Ozone had gone to the Commissioner of Mental Diseases at the State House in Botolph and tried to have me "committed for life". "It is just these awful abuses that our Department stands to oppose," he said.

God bless Dr Goldstein! And the surgeon who patched up my wrenched insides and made me over. (I never saw him. He arrived at the Hospital after I was "prepared", & I was under ether before he entered the operating room.) That operation was long overdue. I had needed it ever since my baby's birth, but my family "could never afford" such things for *me*.

Sometimes, trying to get to sleep at night (when I am not admitted to Meeting, &/or the electricity goes out early, so I can't read), flashes of the past come to my mind. Always they make me marvel at the unfailing protection God has given me through so much poverty, loneliness, & even dangers too! People—beginning with Mama— have always said: "Moira has a good heart!" Is it for that reason that God has preserved not only my life, my health, & my "sense of humor" but also my SPIRIT, despite its ignorant and thoughtless trafficking with Satan's temptations (to "Bohemianism")?

That brutal Chief of Police! His grudge against me was *hereditary*! It began before he was Chief when Daddy caught him coming (legs-first) out of the window of the Cheevers' summer-home, after the resort-season ended, when they had gone back to Middlesex Farms and Daddy had gone over to board up the cottage windows of Sam Henderson, his Unabridge friend (and a "silent partner" in his fishing schooners). My father (unarmed) confronted the scoundrel, but "let him go". Chief McCarthy never forgave poor Daddy for knowing he was a house-breaker. And then, when the Chief's own bad boy, Bobby, was growing up, and started committing the same sort of crimes, the Chief (to save Bobby) "railroaded" other young boys, unprotected and undefended—not one, but *several*, over a period of years—into Reform Schools. And when Bobby, always able to "get away with it", went on from "pranks" to real crimes, & *I* was one of his victims, the Chief was "taking it out" on my father's daughter!

I was living alone in North Village, after Daddy's death, in the summer of 1926, broken-hearted over the treachery of Todd (to whom I was "engaged" until his mother returned from Europe and put an end to our dreams so ruthlessly!). At first my parents refused to let me take the cottage out there *alone* (though I was almost 21 and had the protection of my good little faithful dog Tuesday, who had "guarded" me all through my "sleeping sickness" when I was 15). But I went, anyway—took my bicycle out of the garage and whistled for Tuesday to follow! (I'm afraid he was utterly exhausted by the trip.) The cottage had been built by Daddy's father for occasional use by the family or its friends. I arrived in April, I think, and it was still boarded up. Mr Bailey, the caretaker for most of the Matthews Point summer houses, gave me the keys. The Point's electricity had not yet been turned on but the house always had kerosene lamps & candles for emergencies. No other residents would arrive at that wooded, sea-blown, sparsely "developed" summer neighborhood at least until June 1st. That first windy wet night in the shuttered house Tuesday and I were too tired to be frightened.

Early the next day we bicycled (or ran) down to the Village for groceries, and to greet my friends there who had known me "from a baby". An out-of-season arrival in that quiet little settlement was a sensation. A 20-yr-old girl with only a dog, who was preparing to *live alone* in an 8-room house on the edge of the sea-rocks with a half-mile stretch of woodland between her house and the caretaker's, made gossip HEADLINES! The news travelled fast!

I had a strong back in those days. I unscrewed all the heavy board shutters on the lower floor, carried them to the barn, & stored them in numerical order in the old horse stalls. I washed the windows, cleaned the house, aired the mattresses, etc . By this time my family missed me—though they were then concentrating on my sister's wedding to a medical man. Daddy was out at sea, so Mama telephoned Police Headquarters & asked Chief McCarthy to send me back home!

How happy he was to have a real opportunity for intimidation! I was the "pioneer" feminist who had *cut her hair off*!—*who rode horseback astride in riding-breeches!*—who wore the first "one-piece" bathing suit seen in those parts!—who *smoked cigarettes!*—and old Mrs Grundy had been "after me" (both among the "summer folks" and among the natives in the Village) for the past three or four summers. Of course the Chief sided with them, & must have memorized the "Blue Laws" in order to read me a "sermon"! But I wasn't afraid of him—nor of anyone! (I was a half-baked "rationalist-realist" in those days.)

When I rode up from the Village on my bicycle with the bag of groceries & a fresh-caught haddock from Hokker's fish shack, I found him in the shed searching my garbage can (which was empty except for a few egg shells from my traveling lunch-box). But Daddy & his "stag party", at their annual house-closing the previous Fall, had left empty bottles on the shelf. The bulbous-nosed Chief held one up to me, shutting one eye under his shaggy brow, and sneered: "We all knowed you was a smoker, but we didn't know you'd started *drinkin'*—!"

I scoffed at him, & told him to drink up the half-teaspoonful of whiskey that might still be in one of the bottles. "My father left that swig for you last October," I taunted.

He demanded that I get into his car so that he could drive me home, portentously quoting my mother (as proxy for my seagoing father's "orders").

"I'm *not* going home," I told him. "You can inspect my rubbish every day. If I ever get any liquor, I'll leave a shot for you in the bottom of the bottle, out here where you can find it." I walked into the house and started cooking my fish.

After a while he drove away.

I continued to live alone. My mother said I "must" come home. A week or two later Mama & Daddy both came over in the car, to TAKE me back; but I refused, talking only to her; Daddy didn't attempt to "reason" with me. He knew I vehemently opposed his longstanding proposal to sell that house, where I had spent much of almost twenty happy summers—the house he had conveyed to Mama as a present when I was born! Now, while Mama was (weakly) urging me to "be a sensible girl", Daddy nailed up a red, white, and black FOR SALE sign on the post of the veranda!

I knew they didn't *really* care for my return to the Harbor, because Susie & Ronnie, the engaged couple, were then the focus of their lives. I wanted no part in that marriage! I had been against it from the beginning! (The premature cancer-death of my dear sister, in 1951, revealed even to Mama that I had been right in my instinctive distrust of the mealy-mouthed Ronald. Too long, too sad a story of my brilliant sister's wasted life as a doctor's docile wife in far-off Lonestar!)

So, having delivered the ultimatum that if I *would* be so "crazy" as to live alone with my dog in a big house on a dark lonely road at the edge of the woods on a wild ocean shore I'd have to pay my own living expenses, they drove off and left me. But Mama had whispered to me that there were 10 mahogany dining-room chairs up in the attic that would be saleable if I could find an antique dealer to take them off my hands.

That was a good tip! Though I sold the Queen Anne chairs for much less than their city market value, I thereby had a nest-egg to start with. And a plan took shape for earning money besides, by running a summer school for "organized play". In those days it was an innovation of my own, nursery & play schools being unheard of! And it worked! I had cards printed, which I mailed to a list of summer residents in the Cape Gloucester Blue Book, and by June 15 I had a daily class of 10 or 12 children for 3 hours every morning. *I* had more fun than any of them, & it paid me very well. Afternoons

& evenings I had for myself—& my circle of friends among the sojourners and aestivators.

But there had been nearly two whole months before my Play School was in its seasonal operation, & for a while I lived a lonely, frugal life from the proceeds of the chairs, on a cash basis at the Village grocery. (I remember that for 5 weeks I adopted a diet of oatmeal, fish, and boiled onions—and *liked* it!)

Until Matthews Point's electrical circuit was turned on—always about May 30—I got along very well with a good supply of oil lamps and candles. Most of the time, except when Spring nightstorms were roaring outside, I felt no alarm. But then, when the North Cape boys had been "alerted" by Chief McCarthy's naughty boy Bobby that I was living all alone down there, far from the protection of any neighbor, they began a series of Saturday-night "raids" from the woods behind the house. The *first* one did "give me a turn", till I realized it was just "kid-stuff". Tuesday and I went upstairs and buried ourselves under bed clothes, I holding his muzzle shut so he'd not bark while the gang of boys whooped out of the dark, clattered the full length of the veranda, & trooped up the trellis over the old cistern to the porch roof, stamping around it, with whistles, catcalls, & dirty jibes, banging the blinds shut, & yelling "Ooooh Mary! Bloody May-ree, where aaaare you?" But I gave no answer. At last they went away.

They repeated their foray the following week, with the same demonstration. But the third week I had a plan. I prepared a big feast for them, & had it all set out buffet-style on the table and sideboard in the dining room. I waited in the house without light, standing just inside the front door with the doorknob in my hand; and when they came, as soon as they ganged up on the veranda, I switched on my flashlight, swung the door wide, & called out: "How nice to see you! Won't you come in?" I lighted the big lamp over the table and invited them all to help themselves! It *really* took the wind out of their sails! At first they huddled sheepishly by the door, hiding their embarrassment & refusing to enter. But the heaps of sandwiches, cookies, doughnuts, & hot cocoa were too great a lure. They all ate, behaving very decently, till everything was gone. Bobby McCarthy already had charming manners for special occasions. We all talked like friends together, with no mention of past events.

The boys never raided my house again.

But years later, before Restoration, when I started a campaign for an amendment to the city charter that would abolish life-tenure for the Chief of Police, the aging law-man was definitely "out to get me"! I had with my own eyes witnessed him supervising the delivery of a huge liquor shipment landing on Cache Cove Beach by speedboats from a ship on "Rum Row" twelve miles off shore, at 3:00 AM one misty August morning. (I was lying in the bayberry bushes at the top of the shore, having been tipped off by a Botolph newspaperman, who knew I wanted to print the *truth* about Dogtown, that a load was coming in at high tide that morning.) The Chief, returning to his police car (to "chaperon" the Livery Garage trucks, stepped on my elbow as he passed me in the dark. He flashed his light in my face, pulled me to my feet, & threatened me in deadly earnest: "Ma'am, if you wasn't the daughter of a respectable lady I'd shoot you now! Get up & go home, and leave town within a week!"

But *I didn't leave town*, and three or four years after that I instigated a jam-packed meeting in Ibicity Hall—a hearing on the proposed "Plan E City Management Charter"—and he was really worried. When I was called to the platform to introduce the speaker we'd invited up from the Vinland Civic League, the Chief was alone where no one could see him up in the dark balcony ("condemned" for public use by the Building Code), and he kept his service revolver pointed at me while I spoke—warning me to say nothing about the rum-running episode, I suppose. Of course I knew better than to do that anyway, for I was schooled in practical politics and libel-law restrictions! But at last I was terribly *scared*—for my baby's sake as much as for myself.

So I finally did leave Dogtown forever, and moved to Unabridge (a city I thought was large enough for Caleb & me to be "anonymous")—exiled, in great relief, for this as well as other reasons, where I hoped I could make a living, feed my child, and write poems in safety.

But long thereafter, following his success in getting me "committed for observation", the Chief was still by no means through with me. When a long-deferred lawsuit I had against the owner of a department store in Botolph came up for trial, there was a "stacked" jury & a "bought" judge; and the defense lawyer had been instructed to ask 2 insulting questions: (1) "Were you ever ordered to leave the city of Dogtown by its Chief of Police?", and (2) "Have you ever been committed to a mental hospital in Vinland?" They *had* to be answered either by "Yes" or "No". Of course I replied truthfully. The Judge rapped with his gavel: *"Plaintiff unreliable! Case dismissed!"*

The old Chief is dead now, but his son Bobby, having avoided official suspicion for 2 "unsolved" murders (of which I am sure he was guilty), is still at large—serving in the State Police!

*

... My "poetical works"—my truth-telling "stories-in-verse"— how I labored and prayed for their publication! Frustration and "near-success" crowned my efforts. Caleb said they were "too good" for Atlantean commerce. Editors said: "above the level of current prose fiction". And I said, "Then, dear God in Heaven, WHY did you give me my 'gift' for writing—and turn me from the sinful vanity of an "ART"-studio life of IMAGE-making with the truthless lines and colors of real-life's mere *appearance*, for which my talent was by turns facile and unequal to my true vision, but at least potentially successful in the eyes of the world, even though I couldn't afford the paints and materials, not to mention the space and time for working at it?" There has been no answer, so far.

But even now it is not too late for a career of TRUTH! Life is just beginning for me now—"the last of life for which the first was made". After reading the Bible carefully, and studying it over & over, I have finally learned that everything worth being written is already written there. I have now come to Boehme's "Confessions", which, with David's Psalms, express *exactly* all the innermost aspirations, longings, hopes, & inspirations I've had from childhood.

How greatly CLUTTERED has been my mind (hence also my poetic output!) by the obstructions of *Self*—of bitterness, spite, hate, contempt, sneering, jeering, & scorn!—but, above all, of *PAIN*! I have been too much hurt by the world I have known all too well (and described so vividly in my "lays and ballads")—& too much "identified" (psychologically) with my "imaginary" characters!

Now I am all-but-completely HEALED! I still have my "gift". Oh, God, can *You* USE it? And use *me*! *Whatever* work you give—peeling onions, folding laundry, mending sheets, scouring pots!—*use* my hand, my heart, my mind, my soul, through YOUR HOLY SPIRIT! If I live to "threescore & ten" I shall be given 15 more years to work in this life. —Use it all, take it all, refine & fill it all with your Spirit. If it can't be done with ink & paper, use it to best advantage for the service of my Brothers & Sisters, & thus for serving Thee. *Amen.*

*

... Today I awoke at "false dawn" (when the cocks first crow) with an intense memory of Caleb's little-boy face & trustful eyes looking up into mine as he lay on the operating table at Mount Oliver Hospital Emergency Room in Unabridge with a great gash in his fair white brow (near the scar of the mangling forceps that brought him so painfully into the world), just before Doctor Dudley stitched him up.

{Leading my gang vaingloriously, I had fallen off a shed roof. But I never remembered hitting that ash-can, nor any pain, nor getting taken to the hospital. When I became aware of lying there I had no fear because the event seemed to have no importance. I learned about the stitches only after I was told about them at home. They left no second scar.}

That look of his, *deeply trusting*, I have never forgotten; it came back to me this morning as clearly as ever! And everything became so plain to me that by a flash of understanding I KNOW I shall be baptized by the Holy Spirit, in the coming Group for Preparation! And I KNOW that I shall be *wholly* REBORN in the Spirit—even *virginal* again! *Thank God! Thank God! Thank God!* This will be a fulfillment of the promise God made when Caleb was born.

*

... At 8:30 this morning, with a small ringing of the bell to summon us, we had a Household Meeting with the older children of the Community—the only one for today, except the Midday Meal which we eat in silence. Our Guide made the great point—arresting the attention even of the wriggling boys!—that what happened on the Hill of Golgotha was the most important event the world has ever known—dividing Time itself, & the years of man, "B C " from "A D ". Only the Son of God—obscure, meek, gentle, *quiet*!—could have brought such a fact to bear upon the ages of human life.

As he read the Bible's story of Good Friday, I thought of the crucifix hanging on the wall over my bed at the Saint Agatha's Guest House—where I still was working a year ago today. (SO MUCH HAS HAPPENED to me since then! Thank God! Oh, praise Him!). Though I have a horror of pagan-Scholastic symbols, that cross and its twisting figure of the Agony of God in the throes of human death has never left my memory since those 6 long, laborious months I spent my nights in a comfortable bed beneath it. It was the symbol not only of His sacrifice (*for me!*) but also of my repentance for my share of the sins of the world which he took upon Himself to secure *my* forgiveness by Our Father.

Oh God, Father of us all, & of Thine Only Son, our Lord Jesus Christ, in His name I pray that my child may hear the call I have heard and followed (*so belatedly*) to bring me here. Forgive me everything, and forgive me most of all for not teaching him better! Keep the Evil One away from him at all times! Call him to life in Church Community! Open his ears! Free him from the bonds of worldly cynicism which *I*—his honestly loving mother!—so mistakenly instilled in him, in ignorance, in my years of lustful life. Forgive me, forgive me! *I love him!* Forgive me!

*

... My Advisor has put his finger on the meaning of my old *nightmare-dream*! I've tried to "interpret" it for years:—hurrying from house to house, sneaking in front or back doors, or windows—running over rooftops & through corridors & cellars, & up & down in elevators—always being *driven out*! It was not a looking for house-room, after all, nor for mere "safe haven", nor for shelter of any kind. (Though the chase usually started at a house on Huguenot Ave in Unabridge where Mama's father's people once lived.) It is not even a "homestead" my poor daft spirit was seeking. *It was a SPIRITUAL HOME!* Now I need *never* dream that dream again, for (physically & socially isolated as I may be, even in the Brotherhood itself), I HAVE FOUND my spiritual *home*: the community of a true church!

After the age of 32 I profited by a 4-year "course" in Gnujian psychoanalysis (thanks to the professional and *charitable* interest of Mrs Chauncy, my therapist). It was a great help because it taught me to face up to the evil in myself, throughout a very difficult period of my life. I found that, although I had believed myself a "victim" of my father's "injustice", while my mother stood "protectingly" between us, the fact of the matter was that my mother was my "enemy", Daddy the true friend I would have had if I had only realized it before his sudden death. I also learned that I was *jealous* of my sister!—I who scorned jealousy as the admission of inferiority! I learned that I was capable of spite. I found, in short, that I was as rotten as anyone else! Of course it is hard for an idealist to acknowledge such hideous traits in her own soul, which she has regarded as the citadel of human virtue!

Yes, it did me good to realize that I was not the "misunderstood heroine" of epic or tragedy, but only a nastily conceited female with a peeve. —Life is simpler for the less lofty soul. And that is about as far a psychoanalysis took me. I did learn self-dependence during those years, so that in times of stress I could refrain from running with my newest sorrows to the first available ear. And I learned to see the world for the matter-of-fact, heartless testing ground that it is even for its most pampered citizens—whereas, before, it had looked to my romantic eye like *a world to conquer*! —The world can*not* be conquered by one individual human being. "For here," says Paul, "we wrestle not against flesh & blood, but against principalities, against powers, against rulers of the darkness of this world. . . ."

*

As the autobiographical components thus loosened and lost themselves in a confessional that might have interested Caleb as a common reader or critic with the leisure to explore a soul so foreign to his own, Caleb's rather inured sympathy gave way to impatience. Judging for the most part by the physical characteristics of bound or bundled manuscripts, he began ruthlessly to skip some of the pages that seemed homogenous with what he had been reading and to look for passages written before her B P K conversion that she had evidently intended to incorporate into her present autobiography. He hoped to find that she had not culled or edited any such surviving productions of her earlier life.

He worried about missing the hints and clues he was seeking, which might be buried in digressive sentences or subordinate clauses anywhere in her voluminous private prose; but the failing stamina of his scholarship, as well as the conflicting demands upon his time, obliged him to complete his first pass at research according to superficial probabilities. He was confident of finding nothing personal enough in her extant poetry, much of which had been read to him in his uncomprehending youth, and which he'd been storing for her in an unopened trunk lugged around with him ever since she first went to sea from Babylon Oaks. God only knew how many romantic or religious or bitterly realistic poems were languishing in the hands of editors or correspondents, if not absolutely departed from the earth.

So, rummaging further in his treasure chest, he came upon an old battered broken-spined blank book with a plain dark green hard cover, held together less by its binding than by three rubber bands, one of which, though broken by age and climate, was fixed to half its former circumference like a glued night-crawler. Because of its prehistoric appearance, faded fragile condition, and small six-by-nine size (no more than an inch thick), he had previously ignored it. His prejudice had kept him from discovering that it spanned the era which his mother's unfinished "autobiography" apparently never got to. It now appeared that it had been her occasional diary and commonplace book for many years of trial and vicissitude.

At first he wasn't astonished at anything he read; yet not seldom he found himself fascinated by the picaresque amplification of a life he'd thought himself all too familiar with. There were some sentences of sensory sensuous and sensual experience that he hadn't previously been aware of, as well as evidence, alas, of torn-out pages. But at times he still gave short shrift to religious passages that slowed him down without recounting experience of crucial interest to himself under present circumstances.

CHAPTER 10

*C*aleb had been warned not to send his Lil-Amin playscript to directors or producers—not even with prepaid return postage. Whether or not they promised in advance to read a manuscript, they were notoriously careless and irresponsible, inveterately prejudiced against unknown writers, and usually discourteous; read or unread, they would lose or forget it. Furthermore, a childhood of witness to his mother's disappointments in poetry (with editors willing however to return even her heavyweight matter) had left him all too prepared for cold-turkey failure; he was loathe to waste time and postage in casting his anachronistic bread upon waters of the deluge.

He was too busy at this conjunction of fixed and movable contingencies to insure himself against the danger of loss. His most compelling excuse to demur at the detestable task of offering his thought-comedy for realization—to say nothing of actively soliciting interest (which was almost impossible, in light of his personality, as well as humiliating)—was that he had only one fair copy of the manuscript, having given up the laborious effort of duplicating on the carbon copy his many laborious and meticulous corrections, and that he could hardly trust it to the mails, still less to the careless secretaries or theatrical M B A's who practiced triage for dramaturges besieged by charmingly and perhaps seductively ambitious competitors.

The expense and inconvenience of getting the manuscript photographed was wholly beyond consideration. He could only promise himself to eventually search out in the metropolis some blueprint establishment with a small Browning Chancellor diazo copy machine, knowing well enough that copies of his none-too-black typescript on opaque 20-pound bond would be comparatively hard to read against the mottled gray of an imperfectly bleached background; but even then it would cost too much for the probably unemployed patron of a wolfish Viking.

In any case, he sometimes thought, it would be premature for an untheatrical person to hint at staging until the trilogy was all on paper. *"Do great things; don't dream them all day long!"* his mother had always quoted to him, and one-third of the scheme was naught but a comic dream. The *Tower* alone might adumbrate too much, like Ozymandias, thereupon proving that *"Pride goeth before a fall, and a haughty spirit before destruction."*

*

Before even the Controller foresaw that usury would interbreed with advertising and amusements to disqualify manufacturing as the golden goose of free-enterprise prosperity—when lending money at interest would no longer be justified primarily as a facilitation of production or distribution, and private debt would be universally urged to usurp thrift as a national virtue, with the lure of demotic credit cards that profit not only original gatherers of savings and the financial retailers but also a cascade of middlemen in manifold money-changing and commission-taking—long before the nation was actually possessed by such a self-defeating economy, the Classic Order of the Vine (as well as the Petrine Workers and a few Scholastic theologians) was attempting to define in terms of Christian doctrine the sin of usury as empowering the vandalism of mass consumption.

"Usury", a word representing the usufruct of capitalism and all Return on Investment in the religious vocabulary of certain "primitive Christian" Members, would be the hottest topic of discussion—a matter of outright debate—as Father Duncannon and Caleb were both keenly aware in their circumspect construction of the Chapter agenda. It was understood that the Father Economist had been excused from most of the administrative preparations in order to gird himself for the spiritual onslaught upon his avocation.

After much deliberation the Father Superior had agreed to the expediency of holding the "business meeting" in the first session of the week (instead of the last), so that there would be time for wounds to heal, for brotherhood to be restored, before the final *Missa est*, especially during the liturgical prayers and absolutions uttered by various celebrants representing both critics and defenders of Father Lucy's contribution to the corporate Offertory, and during his own principal Allocution, which was always a Chapter's sermon par excellence, the summum bonum of Members' attention—usually indeed a major incentive for attendance by distant and foreign comrades. A number of liturgical philosophical political historical pastoral eleemosynary ecological spiritual ethical or new mesocosmological suggestions would also bear upon the painful subject of moneymaking as talks or papers were delivered for edification or mooting in other sessions, not to mention divers short homilies before the morning Offertories. It would be well if the usury controversy had been previously vented and put to corporate (if not private) rest, for the nonce at least. Chapter was intended to serve as council seminar caucus and senate, not as a court of Agape to prefer impeachment.

Besides the two Laboratory residents, and Caleb (who was welcome at liturgies meals and social forgatherings but was not generally invited to the closed sessions, despite the privileges he'd enjoyed as a mercenary confidant), there were only eighteen more or less representative Members to appreciate and comment upon the written communications of unwillingly absent Members (some of whom, owing to the Order's internationally scattered habitations, were unacquainted with each other personally), as well as to pray confess listen speak deliberate and participate in the theodynamic Mass called the *Anamnesis*. Many of them came to Chapter at considerable inconvenience or personal expense, a few for the first time, perhaps after years of hoping for an experience very dear to all followers of Father Duncannon—and in fact urged upon them, in certain cases with the offer of travel stipends from the Trustees' funds. Except for tenured academicians, few of the Order's Members at any one time could escape the necessities of parish, family, shop, office, school, or factory in making travel plans. Some came with their non-Member spouses or children, billeted elsewhere according to Caleb's arrangements, who spent the days of Chapter as vacation, wandering about Gloucestermas affairs downtown or otherwise sightseeing. All things considered, therefore, this muster was remarkable—for a tiny antithetical "society of the Offertory" that rejected all "purely spiritual and non-sacramental idealism, both metaphysical and subjective, as the most subtle and deadly enemy of the sacramental religion of God's Incarnation".

*

Little did Chapter, seen ensemble, call to mind a devout "retreat". It was a small congress of uncommonly critical persons, distinguished in common (at their several levels and sectors of education) by an intelligent recognition of what Caleb believed was an epochal protest against spiritual persuasions that their "Little Red Book" called "extrication religion"—which "got individual souls into heaven by extricating or 'fishing them out' *from* the evil world". They disavowed "a Christianity with little to recommend it over Buddhism or Islam" and, thus, "the individualistic pietism of many Paulines, typical Scholastic papalism, ivory-tower Tudor-Classicism, sentimental and non-liturgical or obscurantist rituals pandering to subjective emotionalism, legalistic views of reward for goodness and punishment for sin, indifference to the character of society's political and economic life, and withdrawal or aloofness from the natural world regarded as a hindrance to salvation rather than as potentially the substantial foundation necessary to it". Their solidarity was anything but esoteric in intention.

Though still keeping his evasive distance from faith, Caleb was enthusiastic with hope. He was excited by the easy company of likeminded priests and laymen whom he'd previously had no occasion to meet. Male or female, pious or raffish, radical or progressive, Atlantean or foreign, manual or cerebral, working or reflecting—they were doers or thinkers of private or public distinction. He took great pleasure in sherry-drinking conversations with certain of the personages whose formal presentations at one of the conferences it would be his happy duty to transcribe and edit from magnetic tape recordings (so that Gretta Doloroso could re-type and mimeograph them for the official Proceedings). Often so absorbed was he in good feeling that he lost sight of the fact that some weeks hence he would have no job at all.

He was especially pleased to make the acquaintance of a few oddly loyal Members who were more disposed to confide informal remarks tête-à-tête to the mercenary Swiss Guard, between sessions, than to express opinions in an assembly of sensitive fellows. Of these, some seemed purer than the body as a whole, others less pure and more inclined toward dialectic with a foreigner. But almost all of them relished the fun in their corporate thing. Caleb heard many a joke, ecclesiastical and political—often affectionately mocking the language of their shared profession as Father Duncannon's disciples unarmed on a sea of disordered powers. One class of their familiar jests alluded to the Father Founder's "Ninety-five Antitheses".

The friendly critic he liked best (except for a genial woman anthropologist from Cistern College to whom he never had a chance to speak of Fay Morgan's works) was baldheaded Julian Bender, a short roundfaced somewhat swarthy man of about fifty whose continuously moving eyes were intensely black and round. He had little to say when more than two or three were gathered before or after a meal, but was known not to have been famous in several dioceses for diffidence reticence or chastity. He'd started in the church as an acclaimed tenor chorister, and for other qualities also had easily attracted scholarships first to college in Botolph and then to the High Church divinity school at Refuge Harbor. He immediately became a fearlessly sociable and eloquent preacher, much favored by bishops for missionary work where Apostolics were poor or sparse, especially where it was useful to get along well with local Scholastic priests. But working in the Rockies of Tahosa he'd seduced a bishop's daughter with whom he was romantically in love, who soon abandoned him, driving him worse to drink without destroying his charms for others, several of whom he subsequently married. He was now divorced for probably the last time, a priest spoiled by the barleycorn he was now inconstantly struggling to swear off, earning his solitary living (sometimes shabby, often prodigal) as a commission salesman of radio and devilvision time for "spot advertising" in New Armorica and Nether Land.

Like a midshipman listening to the stories of a retired seadog the Lab's acolyte attentively took in tantalizing accounts of unvarnished ecclesiastical life after hours or below stairs in other settings, cathedral or parochial. But Julian, "a priest forever, after the order of Melchizedec", now made religious confessions to Father Duncannon, when he made them at all, and he still wryly loved the

Tudor Apostolic Church by which he'd been cosseted before he was justly expelled and to which the Order belonged uneasily.

Caleb greatly admired Julian's powers of speech—acerbic, flagellant, ironically boastful, humble, funny, and tenderly satirical—often mellifluous withal—fairly Irish in charm; and listened avidly to bizarre anecdotes that mourned and proclaimed an exceptionally unsuccessful history. For instance, one midnight when drunk on a bonanza of fuliginous earnings from telephone sales for a radio station, instead of paying off debts Julian had one by one tossed to the wind his wad of hundred-dollar bills from the middle of an upstate bridge over the North River in triumphing disgust. On another occasion his romantic joy had been reembittered by a lovely appealing girl he'd fed in a restaurant who at the moment of tender consummation displayed PAY AS YOU ENTER in a tattoo across her groin.

Several times he and Caleb lingered together after dinner, when everyone else had dispersed to cell or family quarters. (The autonomic mind of the acolyte could not but compare the whisky priest's ambivalent perseverance in the faith, obliquely revealed, with Mary his mother's uninhibited expressions of reclamation. Both those sufferers of experience had weathered many trials of despair, yet even in this case the woman's were superior in multiplicity and courage, more painful than any man's.) Julian knew he was in no better position to join the hitherto muted protest against Chris Lucey's abuse of the Regular life than Caleb Karcist the assistant who'd egged him on.

In less personal ways Caleb's intellectual interests were engaged by other attending Members—lay and professional, most of whom appeared to be more rational than emotional (though all were united with Julian in loyalty to the gentle Father Founder's vision of a Church commonwealth that integrated "the Evangelical social gospel with the full Petrine theology"). He was especially grateful for the stimulating privilege of conversation with Members who found interesting ideas in the printed word. Even in the inner realm of thought, learning gained solely from experience is no more reliable than the observations of your own sole senses, whereas learning extended if only from a few books has the benefit of many minds, since each book grows from many books. Nevertheless his position as an uninitiated servant was too extraneous—he was too busy with his strictly auxiliary duties (and they with their collegial greetings, meetings, prayers, and confessions)—to afford opportunity for more than brief conversations with a few of these mainly cheerful and friendly new acquaintances, whom he would have delighted to attend like a respectful student, albeit full of his own contributions.

Thanks largely to the thoughtful courtesy of both Members Regular, who introduced him to Members as a close friend of the Laboratory, he was relieved of an alien's anxiety by the general understanding that neither his piety nor his approval need be any more counted on than the inner thoughts of an altar boy. But especially at Mass, which he was eager to join in the back row of the tiny chapel whenever possible, paying a penny for his bread, the consistent sense of solidarity—though for him less spiritual than social—called to mind his mother's joy in the Brotherhood of the Peaceable Kingdom.

Such easiness with a group of strangers he had never known before. He felt no guilt about anybody's untested presumption of credal unison. Though there would not be enough time to gratify his appetite for exchange of views on political or cultural matters that were of special concern to himself but only peripherally related or relatable to the theodynamics that had brought them all together, as far as sheer conviviality was concerned he wished that Ibi and Lilian could have been allowed to share his satisfaction. But the former was posted as an outdoor Swiss, and the latter was seen only once or twice a day in the kitchen, where she silently dodged his kisses even when he could catch her alone for two seconds.

*

The first hundred pages and more of Mary Tremont's journal showed that it had begun as a day-book of fair-copied, dated, titled, and subsequently indexed poems written by Mary Trevisa from her sophomore year of high school to the age of nineteen. Besides the few leaves that had been torn out, some of those remaining had been annotated with names unknown to Caleb, or with initials meaningful only to herself. Many bore ironic or cross-referenced comments entered at much later dates—as the woman's view of the girl, the mother's of the virgin, the experienced's of the innocent, the disillusioned's of the romantic, Mary Tremont's of Mary Trevisa, postwar's of between-war folly. The poems themselves ceased at the year before she left Dogtown for the first time; the diary resumed, as prose entries, only after Caleb was well established as her one and only fatherless three children.

Caleb thus expected no clues to 1934 from the poetry, but for the sake of her retrospective marginalia he didn't skip it. And behold, he found it interesting! He found his mother's life interesting, in itself, long before the year before the Year of Cubie-Dog! Her talent, her imagination, her bravery—even before the really hard times—put him to shame; he was astonished at her school-girl facility with the rhymed-lyric forms she had been taught, especially the short ballad. The very first, in two long stanzas, was about the Cathedral of "Father Brig in sable robes" slowly sinking into the sea like Lyonesse off Land's End in Cornwall; in refrain, Avalon's "bells beneath the deep" can still be heard.

Many of the rest were personal lyrics of four seasons, osprey among angels, sunrise over sea, sunset over hills, rocks and surf in ocean storm, or tranquility at dawn. Early poems had such titles as "The Ballad of Sir Barber Bright and his Lady, Kitty Gale", "Bunny Bright-Eyes", "A Year Ago Tonight", "Starlight, My Love-Child", "The May Queen", "Time", "Death", "Nepenthe", "To a Bit of Sea-foam", "Dirge", "To a Baby Son". "The Hills" was imagery, apparently inspired by a visit to western Vinland, in which the "unfriendly hills . . . narrow my sweet thoughts with shadowed walls" and

>   . . . my sad soul calls
> For one deep draught of fragrant ocean air . . .
>   . . . Farewell, ye hills.
> I love your beauty, but ye selfishly
> Shut out my freedom, and with darkening frowns
> Forbid my love. I leave ye for the sea!

[*But before her son was a sophomore in another kind of high school she had come to love also the inland mountains of Montvert that curtailed the sun, East and West, which in between sometimes warmed the little house in Allenton.*]

Caleb found himself engrossed in the effort to identify or guess the allusions to that minority of her life as he had heard it told over his own years, and to place in nursery history the incidentals or circumstances that appeared in title, salutation, or margin. One of the earliest imaginations was titled "Who?"—and annotated in later pencil "S A E . Damn him!"

>   There's a body I think o' each night in my dreams.
>   Who's tha' body, who?
>   My heart thinks tha' tha'at the body I love,
>   And, sure, I think so, too!

> We're alway' together , tha' body and I.
> Who's tha' body, who?
> I'm thinkin' tha' body is lovin' me much,
> And, sure, I hope it's you!

Several intimate or idolized swains seemed to have existed whom he did not remember ever hearing of, or whose names in his childhood lore he had innocently taken as those of casual schoolmates or summertime chums.

There were also romantic addresses to loved or admired girls, real or imaginary, uttered by a male persona. Toward the end Caleb came to a franker "Passion":

> I have oft vanquished passion
> In many a hard-fought hour.
> Now, in this flaming fashion
> Passion defies my power!
> This time I fail! My love shall know
> A red kiss on her breast of snow!

—and its commentary, written seven or eight years later: "Homosexual as hell, wasn't I? Still feel the same when I let myself go. Narcissism more likely."

But amid maidenhood songs there was one he thought typical of all her meditations on loneliness:

> Were I to wander whither fancy calls
> I'd pass, untempted, Fame's white marble halls,
> Spurning the highroad, seeking everyday
> Windblown places on the rocky way
> I'd take my memories of my love with me
> And sing the hours until I reached the sea!

—footnoted in blacker ink by Mary Tremont while living in Unabridge with her child: "The ocean is absolutely a necessity. Makes me happy. Why? Would the Pacific, too?" Again and again, often in the form of prayers to God, there were poems of longing for the sea, to which she believed her Todd had fled.

The last note to the poems, vertically marginal, in red ink: "This much I *do* know: a woman has no business trying to make a profession of a man. That is a perversion. A woman is, a man is, mutually interdependent. But neither can 'live for' the other."

*

By virtue of Caleb's theoretical appreciation of Theodynamics, and of his supererogatory service as the Lab's acolyte in default of local Members, Father Duncannon invited him to attend as observer a day of papers and talks about matters that deserved the open world's attention. Some Members may have wondered why Caleb had not professed himself at least as a Postulant, but they had all seen his lovingly choreographed chart of the low-mass Anamnesis, as he had learned it in detail, and there was no objection to his presence on this occasion. Besides, it was advantageous to have on hand to tend a tricky tape recorder the editor who would see that the presentations of the "philosophy session" were suitably published for the whole membership, if not for broader dissemination of its most significant papers. Having assisted in construction of the agenda for two or three months, the dedicated employee had been anticipating this colloquium at least as keenly as the principals themselves.

The all-important business meeting had concluded with no communication of its outcome to Caleb, who had taken some pains to execute several enlarged sheets of figures (in conventional format) and even as the congregation was entering the Great Hall had like a staff officer carried them in on an easel for the Father Economist to display and explain. He couldn't help resenting that his own pointed exclusion from that crucial meeting only confirmed that its fundamental subject was more general than the financial reports yet especially personal and painful for his vulnerable protector and of course fatal to his own position in the Laboratory.

Mortimer Ockham too was a salaried retainer, the Trustees' taciturn accountant, but as also one of the oldest Members, he quite rightly sat as one of the peers, naturally trusted in full fellowship. Besides, even a discalced community could hardly dispense with a bookkeeper's attestation. Mort ordinarily preferred not to express an opinion on anything at all but a point of dispute among the Church Fathers, let alone a matter related to his own interests. For all his reticence he was something of a pedant in matters of canon law, and Caleb suspected that even his studious devotion to Father Duncannon's vision of Christianity had not cooled his passion for medieval theology. It was to be hoped that he would not vouchsafe anecdotes or judgments of Father Lucey's practices at the brokerage office, nor point out the mootability of certain fine points with which the operating Trustee was always prepared to defend the "non-profit charitable organization" against zealots either of S E C and Internal Revenue regulation or of the Order's own rule.

After the prorogation, at lunchtime, it seemed to Caleb's dog-alert ears that no one was even mentioning the words *money, investment*, or *usury*, as though chrematistic issues had amazingly been either ignored or thoroughly resolved and dismissed from everyone's mind in eagerness for the week's really important agendas. More than any butler or waitress at a cabinet lunch, he was as conscious as a sitting ghost of inhibiting certain topics of conversation. He almost wished he'd been expected to eat in the kitchen.

Indifferent to cardinal numbers, and indeed to dollars themselves, had Members merely questioned the moral principle of Chris's occupation, ignoring both his success and his payroll—proceeding straight to the theological significance of speculative capitalism without marveling at the extraordinary increase of their Trustees' unburied talents? He knew that all their major internal divisions concerned the political economics of a just society; regarding all other applications of principle—of faith hope charity and works—those who remained in the Order (unlike a number of backsliding former enthusiasts who were seldom mentioned in the presence of outsiders like himself) appeared always to be in substantial unity, however open they might be to debate about particular problems of organization, outreach, and survival. At lunch Father Lucey himself, with soft voice and bent head, humbly self-effacing among his confreres, seemed as cheerful as ever, a courteous ostrich attending to the speech of swans.

Caleb was therefore on pins and needles about the deliberations of this Chapter most important to himself—waiting until he could get Chris alone, his only likely full informant, to hear the consensus and how it was reached. But both the Members Regular had so many official and informal demands on their time from the seldom-gathered Seculars that he feared it wouldn't be until after the final adjournment of Chapter several days later that he could have Chris to himself.

Of course there was no question of reversing the Regulars' previous determination to give up Caleb's services; nor did he wish to have that decision rescinded. Much as he loved Father Duncannon and relished the extraordinary experience of working for Chris Lucey, he no longer liked his service to the one in its major-domo aspect or wished to continue in support of the other's equivocal commerce.

His increasing intimacy with Father Duncannon had revealed petty vanities, outdated aestheticisms, and a certain psychic infirmity that seemed unworthy of a mind infinitely more independent than a connoisseur's. Not a whit did these foibles tarnish his admiration of Theodynamic anthropology, but familiarity did contribute to a slight disappointment in his master's guts as a private person.

For quite apart from the boundless veneration of Father Duncannon's religious work whereby Caleb joined all those who had been radically enlightened by Theodynamics, his express devotion in both domestic and intellectual details (far exceeding the call of salaried service)—concomitant as it was with Chris's increasingly pronounced frustration of the monastic discipline and scholarly peace—seemed to have induced or revived in Lancelot Duncannon certain effeminate locutions and mannerisms of testy inconsideration in small matters of taste or preference, hitherto recessive or suppressed, which in an ordinary case would suggest a snobbish mother's inculcation of preciosity and dependence in her brilliant only-child. Fastidious crotchets and trifling self-indulgences, however refined, required passive response too humiliating for a waiter of Caleb's mettle. He would rather be Father Duncannon's unemployed and unbeholden friend, all but equal in everything except age learning and piety.

But most disquieting, notwithstanding Caleb's own pleasure in the priceless experience by which he had benefitted from Chris's freewheeling notion of service to God, was the Father Superior's hierarchical and moral failure to curb the disobedience of his cenobitic subordinate. This weakness in determination was beginning to infect Caleb's esteem for Father Duncannon as more than merely solecistic. Indeed it seemed very unlikely that the flaw was lost upon Father Davy, Endicott Krebs, Arthur Halymboyd, or anyone else who'd had more than a glimpse of the Laboratory's actual symbiosis.

As to Caleb's cooling regard for Chris Lucey, it likewise neither attenuated his affection nor diluted his gratitude and loyalty; but it resulted less from graduated familiarity than from the same revelation that had shocked Father Duncannon. For one brief moment, betraying as though to his only kith the frailty of an elderly kinless orphan, almost recklessly risking his dignity as a savant—he might as well have torn off his collar and dashed it to the floor—Lancelot Duncannon had been unable to refrain from opening to Caleb (extemporaneously accepted as the only human being in whose company he could at least once utter a few unguarded words) the expostulatory aftermath of his discovery that Christopher Lucey had violated the most personal as well as sacred trust and truth by mortgaging the Laboratory and (what was worse) the whole of

Dun's Farm. Yet that heinous transgression, which must be kept painfully secret until it was either rectified or made public in scandal, would have justified an anger far more bitter—far less qualified by conflicting love—than the dismay that Father Duncannon fully confided.

For his part, Caleb was no more aggrieved by Chris's betrayal of Father Duncannon than by his disingenuousness in concealing the act from himself, the presumptive private secretary for business affairs. He was too chagrined at his own culpable ignorance to be righteously angry; too embarrassed to find himself such a feckless amateur by failing to notice from any of Mort Ockham's worksheets a sudden expansion of the Trustees' cash, if indeed it was not still too soon for the loans to show up on an interim report.

But if the proceeds of the mortgage loan had already been issued by Jason Anacoluther's bank and routinely recorded, was the painfully honest Mort, a dogged scrivener of numbers, sufficiently interested in the purpose of accounting to have wondered about the significance of his figures and detected this abuse of fiduciary power? Perhaps, like most bookkeepers, Mort had simply never thought of assaying greatly enlarged terms in his accounting equation since, as a matter of form, they seemed nothing but neatly equipoised numbers that would continue to meet the perfunctory test of his trial balances.

On the other hand, Mort's passive intelligence was always as reserved as his undemonstrative loyalty to Father Duncannon—his indubitable faithfulness to the ideals of the Order. The possibility of a scandalously embarrassing question or disclosure during the closed session by this putative internal auditor occupied a larger place in Caleb's worry about Chapter than Chris's possible deposition or his own certain loss of an extremely interesting vantage.

But there was nothing to worry about in looking forward to "philosophy day".

He had often heard Father Duncannon speak of Paul Potterfield, who was to deliver a paper on Kierkegaard's irony as epitomizing the genuine Pauline contribution to contemporary Christianity. This scholar had joined the Order in Unabridge while writing his dissertation on Whitehead and was now a professor at the Hume School of Religion and regarded as a Young Turk in the history of ideas. His sympathetic interest in the Danish arch-Pauline (who ironically seemed utterly uninterested in liturgy) had been disturbing some of the academic Members as a symptom of incipient apostasy.

Caleb had also seen an advance precís of Professor Heartborne's paper, an Old Turk of Medieval literature at Chicago, an apologist for the orthodoxy of "antithetical" Theodynamics in light of Anselm's "ontological problem" as understood in terms of modern logic and applied to the inevitably metaphysical questions of science. But while criticizing some of Anselm's arguments—even as he corrected centuries of oversimplification by both partisans and standard critics of the Saint by defending the essential Proof with an unusually precise reading of the Latin text—his delivered text emphasized the enduring importance of "the problem of existential contingency and necessity" not for what it proved but for what it illustrated as a paradigm of metalogical reasoning. After all, the axioms and enthymemes implied in "the Proof" were no less indisputable than those of empirical philosophies.

Yet as if declaring the passion that motivated his own critical scholarship Dick Heartborne warned his present comrades to heed the contextual Augustinian idea in all Anselm's works that experience is required to understand the secular sciences as much as faith is required to understand Christian reason: "We strive to understand because we believe . . .". And the distinctions he drew in refuting Anselm's logical opponents were very welcome to Caleb (despite his liking for Gilgamesh's doublebitted axe) because they ignored the strictures of "dichotomous thinking", both medieval and modern, and—like so much else in experience—suggested to him the schematic symbol of Gilgamesh's isorectotetrahedron!

Then too everybody had looked forward to the offering of Jim Savage, a vibrant Professor of Philosophy at Norumbega, who talked about his new book *The Political Modes of Contemporary Gnosticism.* Jane Swift (from the French Department of Pequod University) also spoke, from notes, on the new Phenomenolgy in theodynamic terms, with special reference to Montaigne's religious mentality as a mediator in the wars between Christians.

And in fact the colloquium proved so stimulating to the silent auditor sitting against the back wall of the great hall that his intellectual passion was exceedingly evident to anyone he afterwards conversed with. For a time he forgot his playwriting, his bloodline research, his wanderlust, even his personal pursuits of experience and pleasure. Although Caleb's comprehension of Heartborne's metaphysics was vague, intuitive, and vexatiously elusive, he was quite willing to think of God as the limiting exception to otherwise valid generalizations about infinite regression in ontology as well as logic; but his real interest, he told himself, lay in the consilience, integration, or antinomy of definitely mesocosmic ideas.

More than ever before he was overtaken by the urge to talk study and write to the main purpose of propagating a general theory of everything interesting that would reconcile Theodynamics with the Pauline "social gospel", yet also with Kierkegaard's distinction between religion and politics; with premature antifascism; with the Resistance; with Anselm's "unsurpassability" Proof, Kierkegaard's statement that "the secret in all comprehension is that comprehending is itself higher than every position which it posits", Dunne's concept of time's infinitely regressive metasystem, and Gödel's Theorem; with the primitive idea of sacrifice and the romantic idea of tragedy; with Whitehead's organic metaphysics; with Fayaway Morgan's anthropological critique of causality; and above all with Doc Charlemagne's General Theory of Dromenology as modified and subsumed by his own comprehension! The intuition of this inchoate vision—as emotional as any religious afflatus—took possession of his body and soul, pervading like the Spring air a sense of noetic power unhindered by the reasoning it operated. It seemed quite capable of extending this unification not only to disparate systems of quantity (by the Synectic Method of Diagnostic Correlation) but also to qualitative vectors and their negatives, fusing asymmetrical evolutionary and relativistic process with the dichotomous and trichotomous dialectic of IRTH's complex numbers!

Even after Caleb's joyful fever subsided to the level of his quotidian zest for practicable tasks and planning it didn't occur to him that this esemplastic but nebulous ambition would necessarily be thwarted, no matter how long he lived, by the absolute limitation of his counterentropic energy, by the preponderant determination of mass circumstances, and by the antithetical demands of both art and love, as well as by his own insuperable deficiencies of learning memory and intelligence. But among the inextinguishable embers of his Chapter blaze he thought one heterodox coal remained steadily aglow as a net gain in idiosight: Except at a single point in history, and subsequently in one particular only, the mesocosmic world has always been *wholly* natural; what became and remains at least theoretically supernatural is the primitive sacramental option for liturgical communication with the infinite or indefinite metasystem: the means of counterentropic grace within sublunar disorder.

*

After a single excised page, a hiatus of more than six years preceding and spanning Caleb's conception birth and infancy, the day-book resumed as a prose journal; but the frustration of his quest by this essential gap was tinged with cowardly relief at the disappointment of anagnorisis. Like Ion the nameless acolyte at Delphi, he wished to know nothing of an ignoble origin; and he regarded a father as Cuchulain had regarded a son before his discovery of one:

> I think myself most lucky that I leave
> No pallid ghost or mockery of a man
> To drift and mutter in the corridors
> Where I have laughed and sung. . . .
> For I would need a weightier argument
> Than one that marred me in the copying,
> As I have the clean hawk out of the air
> That, as men say, begot this body of mine
> Upon a mortal woman.

He persevered, however, looking for echoes or reminiscences that might allude to the missing period, during which she had bitterly changed her surname to that of her mother's maidenhood, lost Sycorax and all her art-work in a fire, and herself become a sorely experienced unmarried mother. Marginal entries now overlay each other in increasingly pathetic strata of irregularly alternating hard and soft hindsights; but shamefully ripped-out sheets were also damnably more frequent. Gradually he was led into years that he remembered as a more or less innocent witness, yet little that he read was subject to trial by significant facts within the memory of a self-absorbing childhood almost entirely as indifferent to paternity as to the natural history of flowers and bees, at least before the age at which he had grown either too proud or too gun-shy to probe.

Latterly he had thought he knew all he wanted to know about what was going on during those remembered years of his life with her (which she called the A D Era of her life—"After the Dog", denoted not by the acquisition or death of Tuesday or Sycorax, but by the *birth* of her own whelp "Cubie-Dog"), yet he was now surprised by the number of faceless individuals referred to as transitory lovers during his own intelligent residence at home, even though he'd been all too well informed of her boldly unrequited love for the nobly excruciated Rector of St George's Apostolic Church in Unabridge (where he himself was a very active member of the Sunday

School, the Pup Scouts, and the Sir Galahad Society), of her temporary friendships with two or three "suitors", and of her grand passion for Dogtown's Tony Porter in both Unabridge and Allenton.

But as to the B D Era which more vitally interested him, and not solely because of its etiological significance for his anticipated difficulty in identifying himself in a passport application: his reading of the desultory log was concentrated like the flow of a tundish by the intimate acknowledgment he had repeatedly heard from as far back as he could remember anything of the kind that at the time of his conception she had had "seven admirers, including three lovers". Indeed he remembered verbatim that during one of Tony's "desertions", when the dumb child was mentally old enough to be the confessor of "a fallen woman" in defiant repentance of her sins, she had appended to her stormy words an apologetically droll remark: "I was never a virgin, but I want you never to forget that I had many more admirers than lovers."

On a certain cold Montvert afternoon in January, at the age of twelve, he had consented to lie for the last time as a child in her arms on the sofa, his cardboard suitcase at the door, awaiting the driver sent from Dutchkill School to fetch him away from home for a whole Term. In previous years, on the charity of the Apostolic Church or of private philanthropists, he had lived at summer camps for a week or two at a time, but now she was honestly sacrificing all the remaining semesters of her little boy's education—all three of her children's schooling—for sake of the superior education she insisted that he deserved, and in order to "cut the mother-bond" that might hobble his masculine independence, seeing that he had no father to teach him. College was to follow, and a cosmopolitan career; he would probably never again stay for long at home—until he should have one of his own, with her grandchildren, she was thinking as she sang the "family cradle songs" and praised her little oak tree for being her stalwart Honor Boy, her pride and joy who'd earned the scholarship she'd begged for him among rich kids who paid for culture.

At first, curled on the sofa sadly facing the door together, his back to her hugs, almost weeping with her in trembling desolation, as if about to be spirited [seven years younger than Redburn] along the frozen Gansevoort valley over to the North River all the way down to heartless Ur and into a brutal fo'csle for ordeal and terror at sea, he listened to her as he had never listened before, though for all he was feeling he never answered her love in words, quietly accepting the end of his childhood as a bullock on the Acropolis accepted its fate at the altar.

But the offering was hers, hers the dedication of Samuel. And she persisted in her early release of the child to whose life thereafter her life was still to be devoted only in accordance with the degree to which his resistance to her love relented, launching the man-child's unended adventure in separation though it happened to take place just when she was suffering what would have been one of her most desperate times even if he had remained at home in the public school of Allenton.

Tony, who had at last followed her from Unabridge to become her "boarder" in the little first-floor bedroom, had left her again— this time, she was sure, for her hateful enemy on the East side of town, a "sly, grasping hill-woman" by the name of Dolly, undoubtedly for the sake of her property. All of Mary Tremont's letters to Tony care of General Delivery were ignored, if not "returned to sender". Her unequalled love for the handsome Lusitanian seacook, cab driver, and handyman was betrayed for the last time.

The state of the nation, a magnifying mirror, seemed reason enough for her despair: F D R was dead; the War was over, but the E-Bomb had wrought excessive victory, and the unleashed Cans of vengeance were certain to bring down his successor. Her hope for the expansion of God's stunted Kingdom was sorely discouraged by the strife and suffering that continued all across the world like the inextinguishable fire ever smoldering and flaring underground in a Labelle coal field. She had no job; her most hopeful manuscript of verse had been rejected (reportedly at the last round of decision) by the most promising editor.

The sole prospect of survival lay in giving up the precious little house to creditors, the only claim to a possession that she'd ever foolishly deceived herself into making (with capital help from an admiring benefactor on the strength of her irrepressible hopes for "success"), and retreating to the proletarian dependencies of city life. She told Cubie it was unlikely that he'd ever again see the inside of their bottomland refuge from slums where for more than a year he'd taken his baths in a washtub on the kitchen floor and where she'd watched him respond undaunted to the roughshod and joyous experiences of wholly new life in a railroad village surrounded by mountainous woods and streams. At his first vacation from boarding school he would very likely go home to the kind of tenement they had occupied one after another before escaping to the riverside fringe of this beautiful Can-ruled township inhabited by less than fifteen hundred souls.

His next "permanent" address, she said, might be in New Uruk (that exciting concentration of tolerance and intellect, and of publishing too!)—where, failing a decent job worthy of her intelligence, she might qualify for the dole and continue her writing in greater poverty than ever. Meanwhile she would expunge Tony Porter from all her imagery of the pleasures granted human beings by the God who made our bodies, and never again trust a male for more than transitory relief of pain.

Thus she had reviewed for him their prospects, cuddling his final infancy as she prepared herself for the liberation of his manhood while they awaited the stroke of brave alienation that she had striven to precipitate for the benefit of her three-in-one pride and joy but much to her own sorrow. Yet early or late it was never to be regretted either by the fledgling son aloft or by the dismated osprey remaining in her lonely nests of desolation. The shrouded sun above the bleak gray ceiling of clouds was westering behind their beloved Batten Mountain, already half darkened, looming with frigid intimacy just beyond the tree-lined Gansevoort River, which now sheltered its trout in pools all down the valley's invert under a wadi of snow-covered ice. The Dutchkill School driver was delayed, they would hear, because the roads of recently glazed dirt were not sanded beyond the turn-offs, even on the hills, on the way between spurs of the nearest range to Dutchkill Falls at the dead-end, and he had stopped to bend chains onto the torus of each rear wheel with benumbed fingers. Spindrifts of stale snow blustered across trackless meadows frozen white without the moisture to hold their cover.

When the harsh world's knock after all at last surprised mother and son he'd been dozing with his back enfolded in the warm amplitude of her purring breast, never imagining that it brought to an end his last hour of uncritical mother-love. Only many years later did he understand that the ghost of the umbilical cord which she always said had almost strangled him at birth was finally being severed.

But what else had he heard her mourn and celebrate in that final communion, nearly unheeded then but since recollected at such times as her words presented themselves to his broadening consciousness of desire, frustration, conflict, and common experience? Crooning and chuckling, thus she'd praised him: "Go seek your fortune, my God-given Cubie-dog, brave light of my life, the head of the family, the only man I can trust! You have been tested by tobacco smoke in the womb, the wrench of forceps on your cranium, strangulation, burns, rickets, and bloody tumbles; you have weathered all the sins of heedless motherhood with which I have requited God's greatest gift—the gift I longed for all my life! Like the Virgin Mary I now give back to God my undeserved gift— to go at the age of twelve and reason among wisemen in their Temple! Father Pole's little southpaw Samuel at the convent altar! Honor Boy of St George's parish! Chief of Pup Scouts! Sir Galahad! Leader of the Class! Admiral of the Bathtub! General Housework! The miraculous Runt of my litter!"

But her tone soon dropped to what at the time seemed a more complex and less comprehensible level. "My miracle of Long Rocks at Gloucestermas in 1934 is a scandal to reason, no more plausible than the conception announced on Lady Day—and even I, who can't keep my mouth shut about anything else, could never attempt to tell it, not even to you from whom no other secrets are kept and no desires are hidden. So when the other boys ask you questions about your father just keep telling them your mother has been divorced since your first year on earth, and that's why you can't account for the husband. There's enough shame and mortification in such a white lie for any hero who must suffer the Philistines until they are silenced by his jawbone!" Again low laughter reverberated in her overweight body and set off tremors in the sofa.

"You are sent out into the world an only child," she cooed: "and your mother spayed; Mary Tremont can have no others! But never forget, amid all your pursuits and conquests: Women are the better people!"

And that was the tenderly spontaneous origin of her taunting motto, not to be forgotten by any male or female she ever smote with her triumphantly ostentatious repetition of it: *Women are the better people!*"

*

Caleb was never informed that before Chapter when Chris Lucey had returned from the trip to visit his father in Cherokee there was hell to pay in the privacy of the monastery. Sam Craigie (the poet), driving his best customer and clandestine friend back from Guy Winthrop International in the front seat of his IXAT cab, had mentioned a visit to the Lab by a generous Mr Phillips whom he delivered to the same airport, though Caleb's summons to the dispatcher had been on behalf of a Mr Halymboyd. Having questioned the unknown name with surprise, and guessed that

Caleb had called for the cab in innocence of a pseudonym, Chris had then readily extracted much of the truth from his Superior. Father Duncannon had been uneasy about his tacit dismissal of the disguise as an unimportant detail of his unexpected conference with an uninvited visitor who obviously was concerned about affairs in which Christopher had the greatest interest but who plainly hoped that his second appearance at the Lab would escape the Father Economist's attention.

Repercussions of the ensuing tantrum nearly forced cancellation of the Chapter. Father Duncannon had weathered that threat by cross-confronting Father Lucey with the far more appalling "treachery" (and fiduciary guilt) by which the mortgage on the Lab and the Farm had been negotiated; and this exceptionally violent storm was at last silenced by a not-unfamiliar repentance.

But Caleb wished to know nothing about the blazing quarrel for unequal causes or the Superior's pragmatism that must have ended it equivocally. What should have been a cataclysmic breach had been inconclusively suspended for the Vine's sake.

Thus perhaps contrition and penance, as well as ambition for the membership's vote of confidence, intensified Father Lucey's courtly behavior toward everyone in attendance or service, including Caleb—maybe Caleb especially, who had been as deceived by omission as Father Duncannon about the bank negotiation but whose presence during Halymboyd's visit seemed evidence of participation in a conspiracy against Chris himself, his more immediate boss and all-too-intimate friend. The comparatively slight estrangement of Caleb and his sometime champion was noticeable to no one except themselves; but the serious estrangement of the two Regulars was sensed by the Seculars who had known them together in the past.

Because Caleb so feared that he would never regain the full privilege of Chris's indiscreet confidences he was extremely alert for any opportunity to get intelligence of at least the less delicate proceedings of the meeting that had been devoted to moral evaluation of the trade in investments which he himself had assiduously abetted. His chance came on the first day of the Midsummer's Night octave, when he was almost too preoccupied with seizing it to heed the Beltane Hill bonfire which this year marked the end of Pentecost and the normal beginning of Gloucestermas, whereas in past years that public symbol had shaken his modicum of self-assurance with the reminder of anniversary disgrace that always overshadowed his birthday nine months later.

[The city's initial Glo'mas celebration at the solstice was an echo of the former Ma'eve fires on the same high place (when it was known as Beacon Hill). Owing to the flagrant fire hazard in such a congested and windblown neighborhood, the modern event, translated from the Celtic to the Julian mentality, was annually staged by the Fire Department on a much reduced scale, engines standing by with hoses connected to hydrants. The original custom had lasted throughout the early times of piracy and French raiders, before the colonists felt safe enough to abandon marginal agriculture and timbering for more prosperous trades on the margin of the tide at such time as the local seas were no longer disputed. The ensuing festivities had long since established themselves down below the hill on the waterfront and nowadays were spread throughout the Harbor: parades and processions, carnival glee, music, dancing, masques, blessings, exhibitions, High Mass, and nautical fireworks—in general dedicated religiously and commercially to SS Peter and Paul, but also in particular, by the Tuscans at least, to St John the Baptist.]

From the obscured vantage of Apostles Dock the conflagration was detectable only by flickerings of unelectric light reflected upon the light-polluted poliscape by clouds and water. Up on the rock summit of the small park in Caleb's former neighborhood, though often to the windward of the large frame house close by, which occupied the site of a Napoleonic era semaphore telegraph pylon, it was nervously under official control. For Caleb on previous occasions much of its incandescence had been screened from his Cod Street valley, too far under the lee of that hill, but now in his imagination it lighted up his old attic window even more flamboyantly than the Barebones fire. And this year, in intervals of immediate unexclusive consciousness before he went to sleep, liminal awareness of the distant blaze drew his speculative mind once again to the far less vividly imagined Dionysia of the last Great Year, then as now seamlessly enclosed between lunar Pentecost and solar Independence Day, before the first of his own cells was formed. The obtrusion, always vague, kept him too long awake wondering if he could casually ask Wat Cibber where the Long Rocks were. He'd been unable to find such a listing in the index of any local map or history book in his possession. Should he make bold to ask the Reference Librarian?

Yet again, an immediate consciousness, exclusive or not, can repeatedly displace another, whether or not at a different depth. After dinner on the eve of Chapter's final Mass, when some of the

Members had already been obliged to depart, and while the two monks were busy in a series of individual conferences with several of those remaining who had had only this evening's opportunity for confession, spiritual advice, or doctrinal counsel, Caleb was glad to join his companionable new friend Julian sipping luse on the sun porch. They watched the day's lord trail his glory down behind the hills across the outer harbor, redirecting his incidental rays from sea to sky—until, in the opposite sky he'd swept, the moon relieved twilight of failure by showing herself already aloft with a plenitude but three days past fulfillment. In the deferment or forfeiture of a confidential report from Chris, Julian was Caleb's best possible informant about the financial debate, and possibly also its most objective witness, since he held no brief for or against the moral issue of usury but was mildly cynical about its practical bearing on the nation's ineluctable economic system and undoubtedly sensitive to profane motive in sacred argument.

After dinner, as on any other day of Chapter, most Members not in conference with a Regular were in secluded meditation or strolling contemplatively along one of the nearby beaches, or wandering over at the Harbor with wives or children to enjoy some of the Glo'mas festivities that filled the calendar between the solstice and St Peter's blessing of the fishing vessels (with St Paul's cooperation as an archaic sailmaker), which always fell on the last day of the fiscal year; but from time to time one or two would join Julian on the sunporch for a thimbleful.

It was soon apparent to Caleb (who anyway considered himself practically invisible when in the presence of two or more strangers) that Julian and his associates kept forgetting the restricted status of the Lab's factotum as a profane non-Member unauthorized to participate in sacred affairs. They went so far as to speak openly of fear for the health of their revered leader, whom some of the old Members were familiar enough to call Father Dun, even to his face.

Caleb learned that the Founder himself had advised the Members that questions of procedure for choosing his successor would be resolved at the next Chapter, playfully assuring them that he had no intention of abdicating before his death even if he had to be involuntarily replaced as Superior for reasons of petrification. Father Davy, though somewhat embarrassed as the heir presumptive, was assigned to draft an amendment to the Little Red Book, guided only as much as practicable by the traditions of monastic rule; for it went without saying and was left unsaid that Father Duncannon's most fervent vision—a perpetuated nucleus of religious for a durably antithetical order in the secular mesocosm—had hardly proved successful even during his lifetime. Now for the first time Father Duncannon seemed about to acknowledge that his concept of sustaining the monastic tradition like old wine in a new bottle was doomed by times that were changing in every other profession. Apparently his melancholy undertone was tempering the usual optimism of this tiny apostolic fellowship, as if the Pentecost just past had recognized history's latest disappointment in mankind's acceptance of the Holy Spirit.

Each evening Julian was the last to retire from these casual gatherings. Some withdrew down the hill to commercial lodgings; like others, he retreated upstairs. But until then he smoked cigarettes, and as soon as the postprandial bottle was empty he fidgeted again as he had fidgeted before the meal. As he listened or found words his ebony eyes darted in thought, at floor or wall or ceiling, away from any point of rest, never at anyone else's.

On this last evening as Caleb watched Julian's prodigious memory at work he was aware that Lilian, having as usual helped her kitchen crew remove all traces of the dinner and delivered to Ibi on the flagstones outdoors a Levitical remnant of meat from the sin-offering, had quietly evaded his vigilance and driven away before he could intercept her for a light word or even a distant twist of the lips.

In his uppermost consciousness he caught no reference to the Father Economist's morning in the dock until he and Julian found themselves with Father Jeffrey Collier, the worker-priest from the Isle of Dogs in the slums around the war-devastated docks of East London, his Atlantean wife Alice, and Father Stephen Dwight (like Chris, like Hamilton DeCamp of Parity and Financial Usufruct, a graduate of Princedom), the High Church diocesan priest of the low Bishop Derwent's most effective mission church, among blacks browns and whites in Botolph's South End. Steve shared the daily pain of each sheep in his flock, and except in adherence to the Order's general doctrine on social justice took scarcely any interest in systems of human government, though doggedly persistent with the means at his disposal in dealing with the civil authorities who affected the poverty within his purview, and of course no more Marxian than Protestican. (His exhausted wife was at comparative leisure for the first time in a year; she had gone to the Arts Festival at the High School with their children.) But Jeff and Alice were zealots against capitalism, the united voice most resentful of money in any form, which for them was personified within the Order by a monk Economist who did not labor with his own hands.

Taking in the three of them, as well as Julian the lucre-polluted incast from the outer Church, Caleb believed that no four Members could have served as better Christian jurors in the case. Yet he could hardly expect them to do more than justice to the lovable man by whom he'd been so generously introduced to a fascinating kind of work that he never else would have dreamed of.

Alice Collier almost at once mooted that sense of equivocal morality that to one degree or another had troubled all Members ever since Chris had assumed the function previously relegated to the perfunctory supervision of an old-time conservative professional advisor no more sympathetic than a respectable bank. Save for Father Duncannon, who in some small measure had overseen his personal fortune before he endowed it as the Fund of the Trustees, all of the Members were at least normally innocent of financial experience. For a long time none of them had wondered much about the Lab's ways and means, but Alice and Jeff were among the first.

Not that they had untactfully requested anything like an audit of the Fund, which they knew was legally independent of the Order on whose behalf it had been created; but it was they who had conscientiously put the Regulars' heels to the fire by encouraging Members Secular to take a practical interest in modern usury from the Theodynamic point of view set forth in Father Duncannon's writings—who now in providing the question a definite space on the agenda, Caleb surmised, was actually glad to have the issue objectively bruited, almost as if the Colliers were coming to his rescue.

"Do you think Father Dun will take our advice?" Alice asked at large. As a lean intense layman, younger and newer than most of the Members but with the authority of an educated mother who impartially worked herself to the bone in an unjust society for the welfare of all children, she was a gadfly to compromising priests and professors in the uprising against Chris; but she still respected the disciplines and courtesies of the traditional Tudor Petrine church insofar as they were observed by the "antithetical" and "democratic" Order to which she and her husband had dedicated themselves. More than other Members, in fact, she submitted to religious authority and its ceremony as if in penance for reserving a shred of private life from her fervid contributions of faith and good works to the revolutionary struggle against oppression of class and sex by a "disordered establishment" in Britain and Atlantis.

"After all," she conceded, "none of us but Father Lucey himself has taken Religious vows. It's only the Lab that lives off the Trustees, not us the Seculars. Least of all in England, maybe, have we any right to criticize its means of support."

Her attempt at sincere moderation brought a jesting diversion from Julian. "Dun's Farm is running to brambles, and no monks around to plow and reap! But I'm sure Father Lucey would take up mattock and hoe if Father asked him to."

"Alice," Jeff began to say, "I'm afraid we can never expect an aristocrat like Father Dun to understand—".

"Then why are we Members?" she demanded, nearly abandoning the effort of self-control. "What greater violation of the Kingdom of God than unearned wealth? It seems antithetical to our liturgical antithesis! How do we square it with a communal Offertory?"

"I reckon it's one of Christianity's paradoxes." Julian remarked.

"One of its sadly necessary scandals, perhaps." Stephen put in ironically. "Did you read that last Newsletter message from Sten Lindgren?" He was referring to one of the original Members who was now an economist high in the secretariat of the World Health Organization at Geneva. "He's certainly a socialist, if any of us are, but he advocates 'private investment' to overcome poverty and disease in the long run. Isn't that usury according to your definition when you challenged Chris? Investment in that birth-control company seems to me a rather favorable example of capitalism. None of its profits come from armaments, and overpopulation is nature's self-defeating problem in a disordered world."

"Think of all the sewage!" Julian chuckled half aside. "—But if the pill is going to stimulate copulation it may be too much of a good thing."

"It's not necessary for the rich to get richer on the good thing" Jeff retorted "—especially if governments must buy it in order to give it away free."

"It's hard enough to get our taxpayers to provide childrens' vaccinations." said Stephen. "Even for too much of a good thing I can't imagine them voting to spend public funds on ten years of herbal research expeditions down in the Atlindu rain forests."

But Jeff was not to be distracted. "Ten years of piracy and fraud! Lucey was trying to throw dust in our eyes by turning our argument against investments into an argument merely against Parity. He was too subtle by half in trying to divert our attention from the basic principle with hints of a symbolical alternative. What name could seem more auspicious to us than Paraclete?"

"It's sacrilege anyway!" Alice complained.

"That's what Abelard named his oratory hut, after his calamity." said Julian. "But Parity is favorable too, at least for us Seculars! I would have preferred Equity, though: in theodicy it would have been the more general term, and I sometimes can't help respecting conservatives who insist upon a justice that doesn't necessarily entail equality. That's certainly better than parity without equity!"

Caleb's sympathy for Julian broadened, whose play of mind the others paid no attention to.

"Obviously he'd much rather we made him switch from Parity to Paraclete than simply quit trafficking in usury." Jeff went on.

"Usury is any trade in money." Alice declared.

"I don't think this is the same sort of thing as money-changing just because money is necessarily the measure of economic value." Stephen mused. "Even the sparrows sacrificed at the Temple had to be purchased, and so does our Offertory bread. I think Father Dun's test is whether or not, given the present substance of history and our tiny part in it, the Trustees' ownership of Parity's stock contributes more or less to the *whole* world's disorder than their possession of Paraclete's would—"

"Or of a savings account" Alice interrupted "just large enough to keep the Lab!"

"—Yes, I know there's nothing new about any of our sophistries; still, if you believe our actual world is a fallen one you have to take into account the relative good we may be able to do for the Kingdom of Heaven as a vine kept alive by money, not simply our money's part in the general degradation of earth's soil. Not many of us get our daily bread as you do by the sweat of our brow."

"Well, even Jeff has no choice but to take his pay in an envelope," Alice allowed on her husband's behalf, "in order to *buy* what we truly need; and if he's going to help the laboring class right now, he contributes perforce to the shopowners' profit. I agree that our goodwill should take in the powerful as well as the weak, since it's so much harder for them to get through the needle's eye."

"Of course we want the world's good as an entirety, including animals plants rocks and waters." Jeff answered for his own part. "But you have to draw the line about money somewhere even if you're not a fundamentalist."

"I'm sure Father Dun assents to that." Julian put in. "But he asks our advice about exactly where. At least Chris Lucey will no longer be wheeling so freely. He'll have more time for prayer and housework." Here he winked at Caleb, who had remained silent lest he call attention to his anomalous presence, anxiously waiting to find himself alone with Julian.

It was hard for Chris's lay collaborator to contain himself as he listened to this discussion about what he was in a much better position than innocent moralists to understand the complexities and ramifications of. Caleb would have liked to comment that even though at first blush Kierkegaard's "religious inwardness" seemed contrary to the Theodynamic insistence on the social basis of Christianity, his view that religion is prior to politics did not deny the importance of evolutionary economic praxis in the Church's approach to the Kingdom of God on earth.

At last the married couple and the married priest left for their bedtime prayers and personal comforts. Caleb was on the point of asking Julian (as if casually) about the emotional tone of the business meeting. He hoped that a private conversation opening with an estimate of collegiate feelings would yield an account of the agon itself, and especially the objective outcome for Chris its protagonist. It was clear that Julian's attitude toward the Order, as if still a Postulant's cautious as a cat about plenary vows, was less solemn, or at least more liberal, than others' at Chapter. At the opposite end of the spectrum, for example, Father Davy, the probable successor to Father Dun as leader of the Order, a celibate secular priest with a thrivingly active parish in Markland, the model for any Member not called to a thoroughgoing religious life, seemed by contrast as devoutly circumspect as a Loyolan Cephasite.

But before Caleb could say anything to expose his curiosity Julian surprised him with a passionate dive into deeper conversation, as if divining that he had the ear of one bred to understand all kinds of thinking. Though he overestimated Caleb's spiritual sensitivity he was not wrong about his inexperienced listener's interest in extraordinary experience.

"In Carolingian times many prayers were said to the saints because they couldn't well be directed to the B V M, since she did not in the least share with any suppliant the experience of sin. But St Peter especially did, the one who'd once lost his faith and who'd thrice denied his apostleship. To him who had for this very reason been granted the power they prayed 'loose me from all the bonds of my iniquities, and intercede for me, that the Lord, your Master, may look on me, as he looked on you; and may save me from the deep waters of wickedness, who saved you from the waters of Galilee; and that he may drive out of me all that he hates, and give me all that pleases him for ever.' I've had good reason to memorize that prayer.

"And Anselm, in his anguish as a monk about to be thrust unwillingly into international power, added his own classic prayer: '. . . behold, I the poorest and basest of homunculi, stand in miserable need of the help of thy kindly power. . . . Again and again I try to stir up my dull mind and hold it back from the vanities that destroy it; but even when my mind has summoned up all its strength, it cannot break through the darkness of the torpor which the stains of sin have brought upon it. It cannot even continue long in its intention. Who will help the wretched being who can neither express tribulation in his words nor find sorrow in his mind?'

"We believe that sin is willed contribution to disorder, and that merely in living we can't help increasing the entropy of the world unless we receive the grace of God; but Jeff and Alice don't seem to understand the *historical* problem of sin: as Father Dun calls it, the perpetually compounding disorder that always offsets—by diffusion, you might say—the convergence and selection of cultural evolution. I have a hunch that he fears his emphasis on the social nature of sacrifice has made some Members mistake the Gospel's social message for the sacramental religion itself. What he tried to make us see in his homily this morning is that the present state of the world, and thus of each inhabitant, is the result of long intersecting and interacting cascades of sin to which further disorder is continually contributed not merely by chance and causality but primarily by the conscious will of human individuals."

However much Caleb differed with the Colliers about economic mechanisms, he wondered if he too had been interpreting Father Duncannon too much out of the traditional Christian context, finding only what he wanted to find in Theodynamics.

"He even quoted Kierkegaard on what's essential in Christianity: 'The particular is higher than the universal.'" Julian went on, his eyes shifting faster than he chose his words. "The cause of the Vine is not only to set right the web of worldliness that has produced our disorder on earth but also—as the Church has always preached—to stop ourselves from personally increasing it. Unlike souls whose religion extricates them from the world as well as from the self, individual Christians (as well as Christianity itself) are disturbed by history, which all too often tempts a turn to the extricationism of personal salvation (or else to the heresy of pessimism). But some members of this Coven seem in danger of erring the other way—by losing themselves in wholly profane politics or economics, which are only contingent and topical means to catholic ends.

"Isn't it ironic that Kierkegaard—the arch-preacher of subjective personality—found it necessary to inveigh against the 'disastrous confounding of politics and Christianity' even in Pauline Daneland? The Consecration we identify with the mactation of Christ may be the 'Moment' he speaks of, when the mode of eternity penetrates into inferior time. That may be a medieval orthodox way of expressing what modernists would rather think of in Relativistic terms; but you must agree—unless you're here simply as a spy—when he says that '*essentially*' Christianity is inwardness of the subjective personality. 'Just as it is the human's advantage over the animal to be able to live in every climate, so it is the Christian's excellence, precisely because of this inwardness, to be able according to his individual strength to live under even the most imperfect forms. Politics is this external being, this tantalizing busyness with changing the externals.'"

"Sounds like Yeats!" Caleb responded. But maybe I *am* here under false colors, he thought. Is Christianity for me merely a primitive social religion extended from the one local cult that was successful in inventing the means of grace?

Julian was exploring his own ideas about Father Duncannon's, as if still developing them in the pulpit without a text. "The liturgical function of the Offertory is retroactive. A particular dogmatic alternative to today's polity may seem obvious to reason, but as Hegel says 'the owl of Minerva flies only at dusk', meaning that the only outcomes that can be known are dead and past—as with the stock market. Entropy is evil but counterentropy is commonly abused. Even with the insight of revelation and the grace of sacrament the antitheses to disorder are countless and ephemeral. In actual human affairs a singleminded doctrine only makes things worse. To rectify history in eternity, revolution would have to be supernatural."

But even Caleb's liking for Julian (whose shifting black eyes, incessantly darting askance at every word of his own while he smoked and resisted one cigarette after another, seemed to scan a rainbow of guilt), his attraction to the man's febrile multifariousness, and the urge to reply with his own ideas hardly slackened his determination not to miss this fleeting opportunity for plain intelligence of what had been decided about Chris's career, upon which had depended his own illusion of practical reason's counterentropic power. "Literally, how did the argument about usury get started? That word doesn't appear on the agenda."

"Jeff questioned the word *investment* and asked Chris to reconcile it with the Little Red Book, where it says (in words surely written by the Superior himself) that the Order 'disavows a Church which can live corporately and organizationally at peace with an evil world, accepting money and power on that world's terms, providing only she herself is left undisturbed to fish out individual souls and to get them into heaven when individual bodies die.' That quote set up a murmur, I can tell you—partly perhaps in support of Jeff's honesty but mostly crying foul for his pointed embarrassment of Father Dun."

"Did Chris find a way to bring up his new-found defense that he's in 'double condition', according to monastic tradition, as a religious Member Regular but also as steward in the outer world, charged to safeguard corporate possessions against inflation and 'to distribute the same for purposes of common fraternal charity'? He's more sensitive about the delicate issue of personal poverty than he is about usury or capitalism."

"He never got the chance. In Father Dun's presence nobody dared confront him head-on with the vows of Members Regular. But I'm sure most of us would have considered it Cephasitical if Chris had denied his enjoyment of something equivalent to personal possessions beyond mere 'food and raiment'. Dick Heartborne, although he doesn't accept Jeff's broad definition of usury, mentioned that the Council of Nicea did prohibit the clergy from exacting it.

"But it's funny to hear people like Jeff and Alice calling on Aquinas and Dante for justification. There was a lot of talk about the Seventh Circle—violence against nature and all that—as if its special significance in this case was taken for granted. And poor Chris, despite his argument that usury (if it's used as a label for any profit on money) is merely an art of increase in a really natural evolution of culture, almost found, himself drawn into an apology for the unnatural that would have been dangerously suggestive to anyone who remembers Dante's taxonomic associations; but Father Dun protected the innocence of our innocent Members by calling the discussion back to its menu."

"But did they talk about Chris's job at the brokerage?"

"Oh yes, that's what seems to have been sticking in almost everyone's craw. I wouldn't be surprised if Father Dun was glad to have the almost unanimous vote against it. Mr Bartleby of course abstained. I was against Jeff's resolution because I like the idea of worker-priests!"

"So he's got to quit his job—and sell all the securities too?"

"Advisory referenda are subject to Father Dun's veto, but he recognizes the will of the majority."

"I'm sure Chris wasn't surprised. But how did he seem to take it?"

"With an upper lip that I much admire he cheerfully explained that, if the Father Superior wished him to comply, it would take a little time to honorably extricate himself from the Weatherglass outfit, and especially to dispose of the securities without dumping them on the market for an unnecessary loss. They were all willing to indulge his proviso by assuming or pretending to assume that the business was laid to rest."

Julian hesitated, puffed, glanced out at the dark ocean, eyed corners of the ceiling, scanned lights here and there in the outer harbor. "But at lunchtime I blundered upon him alone in the chapel, kneeling behind one of the chairs in the back. He was weeping—in fact sobbing with his head down. Of course I retreated up the stairs on tiptoe—much as I would have liked to hug the poor guy. Yet afterwards you'd never have known he was suffering a blow; there hasn't been a trace of resentment or sulkiness. That's the kind of guts I've never had."

Julian said nothing about the financial report itself, which apparently had impressed the Members only by the sum shown for total assets. Caleb was greatly relieved to infer from what he heard that nothing had been said about a mortgage on the Lab or any other debt. The presentation of numbers seemed to have been regarded simply as a technical formality in accordance with the form of a "democratic" Order.

After all, the reported figures were only for the latest quarter, already almost three months old. Both assets and liabilities might have excited far more interest and required much more explanation if the balance sheet had been constructed, say, for the previous Saturday, the end of the antepenultimate week of the calendar year's midpoint. In any case, despite Members' moral sensitivity to the Father Economist's function, considering their legal status as merely indirect and practically nuncupative beneficiaries of the Fund, none was likely to be so sophisticated and indiscreet as to question the composition of the Fund's liabilities.

But seeing that the nefarious mortgage was too recent to be disclosed by any conventional report, Caleb hoped that Chris, however else he might react, had at least the will and the time to undo that most grievous hypothecation before the end of June.

But Julian was thinking about the antinomy with which the man Lancelot Duncannon now wrestled. "Lloyd Davy, Mort Ockham, and I are probably the only ones here who know how Chris Lucey kept Father Dun alive during those years of stress in Unabridge—literally saving his life during two or three heart attacks, and tending him afterwards like a professional nurse working three shifts. And even before he was the one Member ever to follow him into the religious life Chris used up most of his own money to support the house there, and its dependents, so that the founding trust fund could be kept intact. He quietly subsidized several of Father's early protégés while they were students, as well as many a convivial open-house reception. After Divinity School and a social-welfare degree, he worked like hell wherever he was needed in parishes and slums while running things for Father Dun. Remembering all this, it's very distressing—for all three of us, I'm sure—to know the agony Father Dun must be suffering. It's shocking to see how tired he looks now. A year ago he still had the face of his youth.

"The first time I saw him, which happened to be in Dogtown, was in 1934. I was still a college student and he hadn't yet stopped doing science to study for holy orders. I was earning my way through B U by singing or playing the organ at churches I could commute to, especially during vacations. I came up here to St George's on the train just at this season—as a matter of fact, it was during Gloucestermas twenty-seven years ago. Lance Duncannon was a parishioner just back from a long sojourn in Europe, and he knew a lot about music. I looked up to him as a squire would have looked up to Sir Galahad—purity of intellect and gentleness of spirit shining in his face. I was a scholarship-boy longing for the favor of an aristocratic mentor.

"But I'd still spoken to him scarcely half a dozen times, and only once did I see him outside the church. I was invited to a private Midsummer's Night costume party given by the son of a rich vestryman at a big house halfway down the face of Beltane Hill, where you could see the whole harbor by looking down and the bonfire by looking almost straight up over your left shoulder. Those were hard times, but you'd never have known it from the fun going on all over the city, especially around Sacrum Square, which was all lighted up like a huge carousel. You could hear the music and the shouting down there—the Knights of the Turntable for St Paul, the fishermen for St Peter, and the Tuscan Jews for John the Baptist! Even the schooners moored along the waterfront, many of them, were decorated and noisy. In the outer harbor there were some Navy ships at anchor, dressed with strings of flags and lighted up after dark. They must have been celebrating St Franklin's fleet-building budget.

"All kinds of impressive people came to the party up there, including two or three clean-cut Navy officers in uniform, strangers invited at the drop of their anchor. Most of the other men wore conventional masks. The women were more or less disguised, and I recognized Lance Duncannon, among others, in rapt attendance on one of them. But there was never a moment to present myself to him because he was always in conversation with her crowd, and of course I was busy with my own dance, concealing my youth as well as I could and soon forgetting all other pursuits."

Julian described the scene: the flickering bonfire overhead and the sweeping searchlights of the ships below were paled by the steadily sailing moon that had stared into all their faces. In the champagne whirl everybody was coming or going from other parties, or simply disappearing and reappearing. It was a big frame house with a captain's tower, a widow's walk on the roof, multiple staircases, and plenty of rooms on divers intriguing levels. "I bet it's still there."

Caleb recognized the great white Victorian pile, its clapboards now rather shabby. It lay on one of his former running routes, the only property on the segment of Hailing Street that ran along a shoulder of the peak's southern escarpment, the granite ledges of which, screened from ordinary notice by tangles of steeply clinging vegetation, separated it from jumbled neighborhoods forty or fifty feet above and below. Its porches and windows looked out over thickly populous roofs and treetops to all the waters within and beyond both spread arms of the harbor, as if from the very bosom of Lady Gloucester. It was said to have been the matrilinear residence of Richard Tybbot, Duke of Dogtown, until he let it go in favor of a stone mansion when he made his millions selling short before the Crash of '29.

"You know, I never mentioned to Father Dun that I saw him there that night." Julian ruminated. "Somehow I've always suspected it would be embarrassing. Not that I was making a fool of myself, or that he was anything but naturally distinguished in his token eye-mask. In those days he was a local tennis champion and he didn't need spectacles. I had a feeling he was more attractive to women than any brute there—maybe just because all the others seemed a drunken throng—

"Fishing up idle memories, instead of going down to celebrate Gloucestermas right now, must augur my pious old age.

"—I believe the owners called their house 'Long Rocks', because in the old days that great ledge was used by pilots as a broad landmark."